Great Detectives

Great Detectives

A Century of the Best
Mysteries from England
and America

Edited by

David Willis McCullough

PANTHEON BOOKS · NEW YORK

Owing to limitations of space, all acknowledgments of permission to reprint
material will be found at the end of the book.

The characters in this book are imaginary and bear
no relation to any person living or dead.

Library of Congress Cataloging in Publication Data
Main entry under title:

Great detectives.

1. Detective and mystery stories, American.
2. Detective and mystery stories, English.
I. McCullough, David W.
PS648.D4G68 1984   813'.0872'08   84-42707
ISBN 0-394-54065-4

For the Davies girls and Elizabeth Fischer,
And for Mary and Margaret, too.

Contents

The Elegant Art of Detection

THE PLACE is a quirky but suitably stately English country house, well stocked with servants, champagne, and eccentric weekend guests. It is the night of Sir Charles and Lady Deverill's Christmas costume party, and the hostess has asked everyone to come dressed as a game. Most are rigged out as playing cards or chess pieces, but one imaginative sort is disguised as a miniature billiards table and Nina Hartford has had the audacity to turn up in a bathing suit and claim she represents water polo.

It is well past midnight and the vicar is leading the local carolers in a chorus of "Good King Wenceslas" when someone dressed as the white king bursts into the ballroom and shouts, "Charmian . . . in the tapestry room . . . dead . . . strangled." Within hours Superintendent Jones is systematically questioning guests in the library, while Lord Peter, one of the guests himself and the Dowager Duchess of Denver's younger son, a chap known to be quite clever at this sort of thing, has begun to make certain inquiries of his own.

We are of course in the world of detective fiction. These events are from a story Dorothy L. Sayers wrote back in what has been called the Golden Age of detective literature, the late twenties and thirties. It is a rarefied, elegant, and always comforting world. There may be a corpse in the tapestry room (and therefore a murderer in the ballroom) and the solution may be devilishly intricate, but rules are observed, clues are served up in proper order (allowing naturally for an acceptable number of red herrings) and in time the debonair amateur detective (the superintendent and his men being hopelessly dense when it comes to actually solving crimes) announces the name of the villain.

For all their grit, grime, and street-wise world-weariness, the supposedly more realistic detectives who began to flourish a decade later in the United States dwell in a world no less romantic—or fanciful—than Lord Peter's. The difference is basically one of style and perspective. As Ellery Queen once wrote of Dashiell Hammett's work: "The stories are flamboyant extravaganzas, but the characters in those stories are authentic human beings who talk, think and act like real people." Sayers's Lord Peter and Hammett's Sam Spade and all their brother and sister detectives with or without badges are more alike than not.

Raymond Chandler once called murder a "simple art." Maybe so, but detection is a decidedly elegant one, elegant in the way a mathematician calls a tidy solution to a particularly knotty problem elegant. Sherlock Holmes used logic, Father Brown an ability to put himself in the murderer's skin, Lord Peter a knack for intuitive bursts of inspiration, Sam Spade an instinct to distrust his suspects only so far, Lew Archer a belief that more crime can be explained by Freud than Blackstone. But more central than the methods and mannerisms of the great detectives is the fact that they cut through confusion and chaos, solve puzzles, and set things right to make the world seem quite a logical place after all. They restore order. As for those methods and mannerisms—there, for the readers of detective stories, is where the fun lies.

It all began with Edgar Allan Poe. Back before there was a Scotland Yard, Poe created the first fictional detective (although the word "detective" was never used), the Chevalier C. Auguste Dupin, and sent him, in 1841, to investigate some murders in the rue Morgue. Other "tales of ratiocination," as Poe called them, followed—"The Gold-Bug," "The Purloined Letter." In "The Mystery of Marie Roget" he took the mysterious death of an actual New York tobacconist named Mary Rogers and Gallicized all the names and locations so his Parisian detective could try his hand at solving the case.

Poe's claim as father of the detective story does not, of course, go unchallenged. Germans like to give that honor to E. T. A. Hoffmann, who in 1818 published "Das Fräulein von Scuderi," a mysterious tale about a series of murders and jewel thefts in the Paris of Louis XIV. It became the basis of a Hindemith opera (many of Hoffmann's other tales having already been appropriated by Offenbach), but Mademoiselle de Scuderi, a romantic novelist with good connections in the royal court, is not so much a detective as a sympathetic listener to convenient confessions.

Since all these early stories seem to be set in France, it is fitting that the French themselves have a candidate for the founding father, François-Eugène Vidocq. Vidocq was a criminal, a retired criminal who organized his own Sûreté, and in 1828 published the first of a series of books about his most spectacular cases. Since Vidocq's agents were former associates from the underworld he was accused of engineering crimes that he could solve with a flourish, and more than a few of the exploits in his *Mémoires* are suspected of being more fiction than fact. But with all his skill at disguises and his forensic theories (an unusually high percentage of criminals, he noted, are bowlegged) Vidocq seems more a subject for detective fiction than a writer. Indeed, his friend Balzac used him—under the name Vautrin—in several novels, and the memoir-writing former detective in Israel Zangwill's *The Big Bow Mystery* owes more than a little to the French Chef de la Sûreté.

In 1878, thirty-seven years after the first appearance of Poe's Dupin and seven years before Sherlock Holmes arrived on the scene, Anna Katharine Green of

Brooklyn, daughter of a fashionable criminal lawyer, published *The Leavenworth Case*. The British mystery writer Julian Symons believes it to be the first detective novel written by a woman. In any case, according to the critic Michele Slung, it was the first mystery novel to attract "the interest of the respectable classes." The novel was an astonishing best seller, and both Woodrow Wilson and British prime minister Stanley Baldwin later listed it among their favorite novels. Miss Green's detective, whom she used in ten more mysteries, was Ebenezer Gryce, and if his euphonious name is no longer a household word, he said something that has echoed through detective fiction ever since. Asked, soon after taking charge of the Leavenworth murder, whom he suspected, Gryce answered: "Everyone and nobody. It is not for me to suspect, but to detect."

By the time Holmes had established himself, first with A *Study in Scarlet* (1887) and then with dozens of other adventures, the detective story was recognized as fit reading material for just about everyone. W. H. Auden has written that the form flourishes in predominantly Protestant countries (but then he believed that the average mystery reader to be one like himself, "who suffers from a sense of sin"), while Dorothy Sayers thought they do best in societies—like England—where respect for law and fair play is stronger than admiration for criminal cunning. One point, however, is clear—that whether guilt-ridden or legalistic, the society most hospitable to the detective is an urban one.

G. K. Chesterton, the creator of Father Brown, noted that the detective story was the first form of popular literature that "expressed some sense of the poetry of modern life," by which he meant city life. The early fictional detectives were all city men. Holmes might have gone off for the odd country visit—to the Baskervilles, for instance—but he kept his Baker Street apartment and he had a city man's knack for being able to catch a cab when he needed one. During the so-called Golden Age the detective story took a long English weekend in the country, with Agatha Christie, Josephine Tey, Dorothy Sayers, and others finding all sorts of mayhem hidden away in vicarages, manor houses, boarding schools, and the like, but with the flowering of the American crime story, detectives got back to the cities, where they belong.

The tough new American writers did not look to their English country cousins with undue reverence. "The English may not always be the best writers in the world," Raymond Chandler, the creator of Philip Marlowe, observed, "but they are incomparably the best dull writers." For Chandler it was his and Dashiell Hammett's and the other realists' job "to get murder away from the upper classes, the weekend house party and the vicar's rose-garden and back to the people who are really good at it."

Hammett himself was probably more critical of American writers who tried to mimic British airs, the most offensive to him being S. S. Van Dine, whose dandified detective Philo Vance he once described as having the conversational manner of a "high-school girl who has been studying the foreign words and phrases in the back of her dictionary." When Hammett created his own debonair detective in *The Thin Man*, he introduced a witty, caustic, hard-drinking realist who, with his wife, Nora, and their dog, Asta, was cannily beating the society swells at their own game. His engraved calling cards may have read Nick Charles, but his real name was Charalambides.

Typically, Hammett was offended as much by the way Philo Vance talked as he was by his author's ignorance of actual police methods. Setting the right conversational tone was just as important to him as using realistic procedures of detection. Today the deadpan but slightly florid Hammett "sound" still reverberates through the contemporary American detective story. "The cheaper the crook," as Sam Spade says in *The Maltese Falcon*, "the gaudier the patter."

Ernest Wilhelm Julius Borneman, a German who in 1935 wrote an English detective novel, *The Face on the Cutting Room Floor*, under the pseudonym Cameron McCabe, was an admirer of the American tough-guy persona, but he included in his novel a character who wasn't. And that character nicely sums up the American style: "How funny, those modern he-mannerisms: telling important things in a trifling way and trifles with an important air, saying things you don't think and thinking things you don't say."

The Face on the Cutting Room Floor, a rather pale Nabokovian send-up of a number of mystery genres, offended some critics and titillated others by the cavalier way it treated the all-but-sacred rules of detective writing. There are no doubt more rules to writing a proper sestina than to writing a detective story, but there is probably no other prose form that at least pretends to be governed by so many notions of what a writer can or cannot do. Luckily, like the British constitution, the rules have never been written down in one place, so they are always changing. And they are always being broken.

The narrator can't be the killer; key facts cannot be withheld from the reader; the killer can't be introduced in the last few pages; there are to be no rare poisons that can't be detected; the murderer cannot turn out to be an animal; the butler (or detective) can't do it unless it is someone pretending to be a butler (or detective). In every case a seasoned reader can name a well-established writer who has broken each of those rules.

Other strictures are more specialized. W. H. Auden demands that "if there is more than one murder, the subsequent victims be more innocent than the initial victim, i.e., the murderer should start with a real grievance and, as a consequence of righting it by an illegitimate means, be forced to murder against his will where he has no grievances but his own guilt." S. S. Van Dine ruled, "There must be no love interest," but there must always be a corpse ("No lesser crime than murder will suffice"), and the murderer must never be a servant, since "the culprit must be a decidedly worth-while person—one who wouldn't normally come under suspicion." * Monsignor Ronald A. Knox declared, perhaps just short of *ex cathedra*, that "not more than one secret room or passage is allowable," that the intelligence of the detective's friend, the Watson character, be "slightly, but very slightly, below that of the average reader," and that identical twins always be handled with exceptional care.

R. Austin Freeman, creator of the "scientific" detective Dr. Thorndyke and a popular writer of the twenties, served up what may be the detective writer's ace in the hole: "The reader can always be trusted to mislead himself, no matter how plainly the data are given. . . . This failure of the reader to perceive the evidential value of the facts is the foundation on which detective fiction is built."

Yet all this worry over rules and fair play, while not always serious even on the part of the law-givers, is indicative of how fragile the world of the detective story actually is. In *The Great Cat Massacre* Robert Darnton retells an old French folk tale in which a hunchback comes upon a band of witches dancing about and singing the words "Monday, Tuesday, Wednesday" over and over. Inspired, he jumps up and sings, "Monday, Tuesday, Wednesday, Thursday." The witches are so delighted with this improvement that they remove his deformity. Another hunchback, seeing what happened, jumps up and sings, "Monday, Tuesday, Wednesday, Thursday, Friday." The witches are horrified. One of them says, "That doesn't go." Another adds, "Not at all," and they punish him by giving him the hump they removed from the first man. Now doubly deformed, the second man is tormented to death by his fellow villagers.

That is the sort of perverse irrationality that could never be tolerated in the tidy and—no matter how violent—basically just world of detective fiction. We all know that in the real world, crimes go unsolved and that chance and paid informants often have more to do with criminal justice than does old-fashioned detection. But when a detective novel breaks the rules and accepts the inelegant irrationality of the witches—and the real world—it can be profoundly disturbing. Chester Himes's often comic *Blind Man with a Pistol* is just such a book. It deals with a series of crimes and murders in Harlem, and just as Himes's black detectives, Coffin Ed Johnson and Grave Digger Jones, seem to be closing in on a solution, a bizarre riot sparked by a blind man randomly shooting up a subway train spills out of the 125th Street station. None of the loose ends connect or can be tied up, and the novel ends—in one of the most jarring conclusions in detective fiction—

---

* This sort of blasé snobbery and genteel racism was common during the Golden Age. In Josephine Tey's first novel, *The Man in the Queue* (1929), the victim is quietly stabbed to death while waiting in a theater line, and the much-admired detective immediately observes that the murderer cannot be an Englishman. Englishmen don't stab. "The very femininity of it proclaimed the dago," he declares and chooses as his chief suspect a poor soul with the bad luck of having an Italian grandmother. When the novel was reissued decades later the word *dago* was replaced with *Levantine*.

with a policeman saying, "That don't make any sense," and Coffin Ed replying, "Sure don't."

Dorothy Sayers compares the detective to Sir Roland and Lancelot. To the critic Leslie Fiedler he is "the cowboy adapted to life on the city streets, the embodiment of innocence moving untouched through universal guilt." Ross Macdonald has rejected such notions as "sentimental romance," but the detective remains a figure readers cannot accept as being powerless amid chaos.

All this talk of the detective as knight-errant, cowboy, and redeemer can become pretentious. Edmund Wilson, in his essay "Who Cares Who Killed Roger Ackroyd?" dismissed the reading of detective stories as "a kind of vice that, for silliness and minor harmfulness, ranks somewhere between smoking and crossword puzzles." It was an essay that brought a record number of irate letters to the *New Yorker*, as readers proclaimed their favorite vice to be something more than that.

But it is curious the way mystery fans talk of their love for detective stories. They tend to speak of it as a vice or an addiction or a habit that perhaps should be broken (but not today). Cyril Connolly has written about his "recurrent habit" almost in terms an alcoholic would use reminiscing about vaguely remembered binges: "For months, sometimes for years, one does not read them all; then an illness or a visit or a trip abroad sends one back to them, and it seems for a time inconceivable that one would want to read anything else." A favorite line of compulsive mystery readers, said almost as though it might excuse the whole problem, is that they never remember a story once it is finished and that they can reread almost an entire novel without realizing it, until some phrase or clue reminds them. Since Agatha Christie's paperback publishers regularly produce new cover designs for her novels, thousands of fans no doubt find themselves going down paths in Miss Marple's village of St. Mary Mead with a curious sense of *déjà vu*.

The simple fact, of course, is that detective stories are fun. Puzzles are fun. The detectives' eccentricities are fun. Knowing a culprit is not going to get away with something the reader dared not try himself is satisfying. And at a time when serious fiction is not as strong on plot as it once was, the very form of a detective story makes a reader ask, "What happens next?" That, too, is fun.

The victim, of course, isn't part of this fun. Ellery Queen once quoted the literary agent Carl Brandt comparing the victim in a murder mystery to a rock thrown into a fishpond: "The reader doesn't want to know what happened to the rock—the reader wants to know what happened to the fish." Leslie Charteris's Simon Templar, the Saint, seems to feel the rock is being slighted. In a short story published in the late forties we learn that "one of Simon Templar's stock criticisms of the classic type of detective story is that the victim of the murderer, the reluctant spark plug of all the entertaining mystery and strife, is usually a mere nonentity who wanders vaguely through the first few pages with the sole purpose of becoming a convenient body in the library by the end of Chapter One."

In its trend toward increased realism in speech, setting, and characterization

the detective story has in recent years updated the role of that once merely convenient corpse. As the influence of Ross Macdonald spreads it may be said that the
body on the library floor is no longer a nonentity but bears a weight in the story
that is as important and as mysterious as the killer's.

The detective story has been around now for over a hundred years, and even
with all its rules and traditions shows no sign of atrophying. Bodies still turn up in
inconvenient places. New detectives continue to search for clues in ways that range
from the mundane to the bizarre, and if asked whom they suspect they will answer
along the lines of "Everyone and nobody"—a very elegant answer indeed.

The stories in this anthology of great—and perhaps not so great as beguiling—
detectives are arranged in vaguely chronological order, although no attempt has
been made to be doggedly systematic about this. It begins not with the usual
appearances by Poe and Conan Doyle, since their stories are easily available from
many other sources, but by a more obscure and perhaps more entertaining nineteenth-century novella; it continues with detectives—official, unofficial, and accidental—from England and America.

DAVID WILLIS McCULLOUGH
April 1, 1984

Israel Zangwill

THE BIG BOW MYSTERY

The Big Bow Mystery, *which first appeared as a serial in the London* Star *in 1891, was written—so the author later claimed—"during the silly season [when] the editor of a popular London evening paper, anxious to let the sea-serpent have a year off, asked me to provide him with a more original piece of fiction."*

Israel Zangwill (1864–1926) would later make a name for himself as a novelist (Children of the Ghetto, King of the Schnorrers) *and playwright* (The Melting Pot) *who dealt with life in the London ghetto, as an advocate of woman's suffrage and as a leader of the Zionist movement. But in 1891 he was a struggling newspaper reporter, and the setting for his mystery—his only attempt at detective fiction—was not a ghetto but a workingman's neighborhood complete with union organizers and a slumming do-gooder.*

When the novella first appeared in book form, Zangwill wrote, "The Big Bow Mystery *seems to me an excellent murder story, as murder stories go, for while as sensational as the most of them, it contains more humor and character creation than the best. Indeed, the humor is too abundant. Mysteries should be sedate and sober. . . . But I was a realist in those days, and in real life mysteries occur to real persons with their individual humors, and mysterious circumstances are apt to be complicated by the comic. The indispensable condition of a good mystery is that it should be able and unable to be solved by the reader, and that the writer's solution should satisfy."*

There were earlier "locked-room" mysteries (Poe's "Murders in the Rue Morgue," for instance), but this was the first time the problem of a murder committed in an apparently sealed room was treated at length. Zangwill once boasted, "The only person who ever solved The Big Bow Mystery *was myself." See if he's right.*

The Big Bow Mystery

O N A MEMORABLE morning of early December London opened its eyes on a frigid gray mist. There are mornings when King Fog masses his molecules of carbon in serried squadrons in the city, while he scatters them tenuously in the suburbs; so that your morning train may bear you from twilight to darkness. But today the enemy's maneuvering was more monotonous. From Bow even unto Hammersmith there draggled a dull, wretched vapor, like the wraith of an impecunious suicide come into a fortune immediately after the fatal deed. The barometers and thermometers had sympathetically shared its depression, and their spirits (when they had any) were low. The cold cut like a many-bladed knife.

Mrs. Drabdump, of 11 Glover Street, Bow, was one of the few persons in London whom fog did not depress. She went about her work quite as cheerlessly as usual. She had been among the earliest to be aware of the enemy's advent, picking out the strands of fog from the coils of darkness the moment she rolled up her bedroom blind and unveiled the somber picture of the winter morning. She knew that the fog had come to stay for the day at least, and that the gas-bill for the quarter was going to beat the record in high-jumping. She also knew that this was because she had allowed her new gentleman lodger, Mr. Arthur Constant, to pay a fixed sum of a shilling a week for gas, instead of charging him a proportion of the actual account for the whole house. The meteorologists might have saved the credit of their science if they had reckoned with Mrs. Drabdump's next gas-bill when they predicted the weather and made "Snow" the favorite, and said that "Fog" would be nowhere. Fog was everywhere, yet Mrs. Drabdump took no credit to herself for her prescience. Mrs. Drabdump indeed took no credit for anything, paying her way along doggedly, and struggling through life like a wearied swimmer trying to touch the horizon. That things always went as badly as she had foreseen did not exhilarate her in the least.

Mrs. Drabdump was a widow. Widows are not born but made, else you might have fancied Mrs. Drabdump had always been a widow. Nature had given her that tall, spare form, and that pale, thin-lipped, elongated, hard-eyed visage, and that painfully precise hair, which are always associated with widowhood in low life. It is only in higher circles that women can lose their husbands and yet remain bewitching. The late Mr. Drabdump had scratched the base of his thumb with a rusty nail, and Mrs. Drabdump's foreboding that he would die of lockjaw had not prevented her wrestling day and night with the shadow of Death, as she had wrestled with it vainly twice before, when Katie died of diphtheria and little Johnny of scarlet fever. Perhaps it is from overwork among the poor that Death has been reduced to a shadow.

Mrs. Drabdump was lighting the kitchen fire. She did it very scientifically, as knowing the contrariety of coal and the anxiety of flaming sticks to end in smoke unless rigidly kept up to the mark. Science was a success as usual; and Mrs. Drabdump rose from her knees content, like a Parsee priestess who had duly paid her morning devotions to her deity. Then she started violently, and nearly lost her balance. Her eye had caught the hands of the clock on the mantel. They pointed to fifteen minutes to seven. Mrs. Drabdump's devotion to the kitchen fire invariably terminated at fifteen minutes past six. What was the matter with the clock?

Mrs. Drabdump had an immediate vision of Snoppet, the neighboring horologist, keeping the clock in hand for weeks and then returning it only superficially repaired and secretly injured more vitally "for the good of the trade." The evil vision vanished as quickly as it came, exorcized by the deep boom of St. Dunstan's bells chiming the three-quarters. In its place a greater horror surged. Instinct had failed; Mrs. Drabdump had risen at half-past six instead of six. Now she understood why she had been feeling so dazed and strange and sleepy. She had overslept herself.

Chagrined and puzzled, she hastily set the kettle over the crackling coal, discovering a second later that she had overslept herself because Mr. Constant wished to be woke three-quarters of an hour earlier than usual, and to have his breakfast at seven, having to speak at an early meeting of discontented tram-men. She ran at once, candle in hand, to his bedroom. It was upstairs. All "upstairs" was Arthur Constant's domain, for it consisted of but two mutually independent rooms. Mrs. Drabdump knocked viciously at the door of the one he used for a bedroom, crying, "Seven o'clock, sir. You'll be late, sir. You must get up at once." The usual slumberous "All right" was not forthcoming; but, as she herself had varied her morning salute, her ear was less expectant of the echo. She went downstairs, with no foreboding save that the kettle would come off second best in the race between its boiling and her lodger's dressing.

For she knew there was no fear of Arthur Constant's lying deaf to the call of Duty—temporarily represented by Mrs. Drabdump. He was a light sleeper, and the tram conductors' bells were probably ringing in his ears, summoning him to the meeting. Why Arthur Constant, B.A.—white-handed and white-shirted, and gentleman to the very purse of him—should concern himself with tram-men, when fortune had confined his necessary relations with drivers to cabmen at the least, Mrs. Drabdump could not quite make out. He probably aspired to represent Bow in Parliament; but then it would surely have been wiser to lodge with a landlady who possessed a vote by having a husband alive. Nor was there much practical wisdom in his wish to black his own boots (an occupation in which he shone but little), and to live in every way like a Bow working man. Bow working men were not so lavish in their patronage of water, whether existing in drinking glasses, morning tubs, or laundress's establishments. Nor did they eat the delicacies with which Mrs. Drabdump supplied him, with the assurance that they were the artisan's appanage. She could not bear to see him eat things unbefitting his station. Arthur Constant opened his mouth and ate what his landlady gave him, not first deliberately shutting his eyes according to the formula, but rather pluming himself on keeping them very wide open. But it is difficult for saints to see through their own halos; and in practice an aureole about the head is often indistinguishable from a mist.

The tea to be scalded in Mr. Constant's pot, when that cantankerous kettle should boil, was not the coarse mixture of black and green sacred to herself and Mr. Mortlake, of whom the thoughts of breakfast now reminded her. Poor Mr. Mortlake, gone off without any to Devonport, somewhere about four in the fog-thickened darkness of a winter night! Well, she hoped his journey would be duly rewarded, that his perks would be heavy, and that he would make as good a thing out of the "traveling expenses" as rival labor leaders roundly accused him of to other people's faces. She did not grudge him his gains, nor was it her business if, as they alleged, in introducing Mr. Constant to her vacant rooms, his idea was not merely to benefit his landlady. He had done her an uncommon good turn, queer as was the lodger thus introduced. His own apostleship to the sons of toil gave Mrs. Drabdump no twinges of perplexity. Tom Mortlake had been a compositor; and apostleship was obviously a profession better paid and of a higher social status. Tom Mortlake—the hero of a hundred strikes—set up in print on a poster, was unmistakably superior to Tom Mortlake setting up other men's names at a case. Still, the work was not all beer and skittles, and Mrs. Drabdump felt that Tom's latest job was not enviable.

She shook his door as she passed it on her way back to the kitchen, but there was no response. The street door was only a few feet off down the passage, and a glance at it dispelled the last hope that Tom had abandoned the journey. The door was unbolted and unchained, and the only security was the latchkey lock. Mrs. Drabdump felt a whit uneasy, though, to give her her due, she never suffered as much as most good housewives do from criminals who never come. Not quite opposite, but still only a few doors off, on the other side of the street, lived the celebrated ex-detective Grodman, and, illogically enough, his presence in the street gave Mrs. Drabdump a curious sense of security, as of a believer living under the shadow of the fane. That any human being of ill-odor should consciously come within a mile of the scent of so famous a sleuth-hound seemed to her highly improbable. Grodman had retired (with a competence) and was only a sleeping dog now; still, even criminals would have sense enough to let him lie.

So Mrs. Drabdump did not really feel that there had been any danger, especially as a second glance at the street door showed that Mortlake had been thoughtful enough to slip the loop that held back the bolt of the big lock. She allowed herself another throb of sympathy for the labor leader whirling on his dreary way towards Devonport Dockyard. Not that he had told her anything of his journey, beyond the town; but she knew Devonport had a Dockyard because Jessie Dymond —Tom's sweetheart—once mentioned that her aunt lived near there, and it lay on the surface that Tom had gone to help the dockers, who were imitating their London brethren. Mrs. Drabdump did not need to be told things to be aware of them. She went back to prepare Mr. Constant's superfine tea, vaguely wondering why people were so discontented nowadays. But when she brought up the tea and the toast and the eggs to Mr. Constant's sitting-room (which adjoined his bedroom, though without communicating with it), Mr. Constant was not sitting in it. She lit the gas, and laid the cloth; then she returned to the landing and beat at the bedroom door with an imperative palm. Silence alone answered her. She called him by name and told him the hour, but hers was the only voice she heard, and it sounded strangely to her in the shadows of the staircase. Then, muttering, "Poor gentleman, he had the toothache last night; and p'r'haps he's only just got a wink o' sleep. Pity to disturb him for the sake of them grizzling conductors. I'll let him sleep his usual time," she bore the tea-pot downstairs with a mournful, almost poetic, consciousness that soft boiled eggs (like love) must grow cold.

Half-past seven came—and she knocked again. But Constant slept on.

His letters, always a strange assortment, arrived at eight, and a telegram came soon after. Mrs. Drabdump rattled his door, shouted, and at last put the wire under it. Her heart was beating fast enough now, though there seemed to be a cold, clammy snake curling round it. She went downstairs again and turned the handle of Mortlake's room, and went in without knowing why. The coverlet of the bed showed that the occupant had only laid down in his clothes, as if fearing to miss the early train. She had not for a moment expected to find him in the room; yet somehow the consciousness that she was alone in the house with the sleeping Constant seemed to flash for the first time upon her, and the clammy snake tightened its folds round her heart.

She opened the street door, and her eye wandered nervously up and down. It was half-past eight. The little street stretched cold and still in the gray mist, blinking bleary eyes at either end, where the street lamps smoldered on. No one was visible for the moment, though smoke was rising from many of the chimneys to greet its sister mist. At the house of the detective across the way the blinds were still down and the shutters up. Yet the familiar, prosaic aspect of the street calmed her. The bleak air set her coughing; she slammed the door to, and returned to the kitchen to make fresh tea for Constant, who could only be in a deep sleep. But the canister trembled in her grasp. She did not know whether she dropped it or threw it down, but there was nothing in the hand that battered again a moment later at the bedroom door. No sound within answered the clamor without. She rained blow upon blow in a sort of spasm of frenzy, scarce remembering that her object was merely to wake her lodger, and almost staving in the lower panels with her kicks.

Then she turned the handle and tried to open the door, but it was locked. The resistance recalled her to herself—she had a moment of shocked decency at the thought that she had been about to enter Constant's bedroom. Then the terror came over her afresh. She felt that she was alone in the house with a corpse. She sank to the floor, cowering, with difficulty stifling a desire to scream. Then she rose with a jerk and raced down the stairs without looking behind her, and threw open the door and ran out into the street, only pulling up with her left hand violently agitating Grodman's door-knocker. In a moment the first-floor window was raised—the little house was of the same pattern as her own—and Grodman's full fleshy face loomed through the fog in sleepy irritation from under a nightcap. Despite its scowl the ex-detective's face dawned upon her like the sun upon an occupant of the haunted chamber.

"What in the devil's the matter?" he growled. Grodman was not an early bird, now that he had no worms to catch. He could afford to despise proverbs now, for the house in which he lived was his, and he lived in it because several other houses in the street were also his, and it is well for the landlord to be about his own estate in Bow, where poachers often shoot the moon. Perhaps the desire to enjoy his greatness among his early cronies counted for something, too, for he had been born and bred at Bow, receiving when a youth his first engagement from the local police quarters, whence he had drawn a few shillings a week as an amateur detective in his leisure hours.

Grodman was still a bachelor. In the celestial matrimonial bureau a partner might have been selected for him, but he had never been able to discover her. It was his one failure as a detective. He was a self-sufficing person, who preferred a gas stove to a domestic; but in deference to Glover Street opinion he admitted a female factotum between ten a.m. and ten p.m., and equally in deference to Glover Street opinion, excluded her between ten p.m. and ten a.m.

"I want you to come across at once," Mrs. Drabdump gasped, "something has happened to Mr. Constant."

"What! Not bludgeoned by the police at the meeting this morning, I hope?"

"No, no! He didn't go. He is dead."

"Dead?" Grodman's face grew very serious now.

"Yes. Murdered!"

"What?" almost shouted the ex-detective. "How? When? Where? Who?"

"I don't know. I can't get to him. I have beaten at his door. He does not answer."

Grodman's face lit up with relief.

"You silly woman! Is that all? I shall have a cold in my head. Bitter weather. He's dog-tired after yesterday—processions, three speeches, kindergarten, lecture on 'the moon,' article on cooperation. That's his style." It was also Grodman's style. He never wasted words.

"No," Mrs. Drabdump breathed up at him solemnly, "he's dead."

"All right; go back. Don't alarm the neighborhood unnecessarily. Wait for me. Down in five minutes." Grodman did not take this Cassandra of the kitchen too seriously. Probably he knew his woman. His small, bead-like eyes glittered with an almost amused smile as he withdrew them from Mrs. Drabdump's ken, and shut down the sash with a bang. The poor woman ran back across the road and through her door, which she would not close behind her. It seemed to shut her in with the dead. She waited in the passage. After an age—seven minutes by any honest clock —Grodman made his appearance, looking as dressed as usual, but with unkempt hair and with disconsolate side-whisker. He was not quite used to that side-whisker yet, for it had only recently come within the margin of cultivation. In active service Grodman had been clean-shaven, like all members of *the* profession—for surely your detective is the most versatile of actors. Mrs. Drabdump closed the street-door quietly, and pointed to the stairs, fear operating like a polite desire to give him precedence. Grodman ascended, amusement still glimmering in his eyes. Arrived on the landing he knocked peremptorily at the door, crying, "Nine o'clock, Mr. Constant; nine o'clock?" When he ceased there was no other sound or movement. His face grew more serious. He waited, then knocked, and cried louder. He turned the handle, but the door was fast. He tried to peer through the keyhole, but it was blocked. He shook the upper panels, but the door seemed bolted as well as locked. He stood still, his face set and rigid, for he liked and esteemed the man.

"Ay, knock your loudest," whispered the pale-faced woman. "You'll not wake him now."

The gray mist had followed them through the street-door, and hovered about the staircase, charging the air with a moist sepulchral odor.

"Locked and bolted," muttered Grodman, shaking the door afresh.

"Burst it open," breathed the woman, trembling violently all over, and holding her hands before her as if to ward off the dreadful vision. Without another word, Grodman applied his shoulder to the door, and made a violent muscular effort. He had been an athlete in his time, and the sap was yet in him. The door creaked, little by little it began to give, the woodwork enclosing the bolt of the lock splintered, the panels bent inwards, the large upper bolt tore off its iron staple, the door flew back with a crash. Grodman rushed in.

"My God!" he cried. The woman shrieked. The sight was too terrible.

Within a few hours the jubilant newsboys were shrieking "Horrible Suicide in Bow," and *The Moon* poster added, for the satisfaction of those too poor to purchase: "A Philanthropist Cuts His Throat."

2

But the newspapers were premature. Scotland Yard refused to prejudice the case despite the penny-a-liners. Several arrests were made, so that later editions were compelled to soften "Suicide" into "Mystery." The people arrested were a nondescript collection of tramps. Most of them had committed other offences for which the police had not arrested them. One bewildered-looking gentleman gave himself up (as if he were a riddle), but the police would have none of him, and restored him forthwith to his friends and keepers. The number of candidates for each new opening in Newgate is astonishing.

The full significance of this tragedy of a noble young life cut short had hardly time to filter into the public mind when a fresh sensation absorbed it. Tom Mortlake had been arrested the same day at Liverpool on suspicion of being concerned in the death of his fellow-lodger. The news fell like a bombshell upon a land in which Tom Mortlake's name was a household word. That the gifted artisan orator, who had never shrunk upon occasion from launching red rhetoric at society, should actually have shed blood seemed too startling, especially as the blood shed was not blue, but the property of a lovable young middle-class idealist, who had now literally given his life to the Cause. But this supplementary sensation did not grow to a head, and everybody (save a few labor leaders) was relieved to hear that Tom had been released almost immediately, being merely subpoenaed to appear at the inquest. In an interview which he accorded to the representative of a Liverpool paper the same afternoon, he stated that he put his arrest down entirely to the enmity and rancor entertained towards him by the police throughout the country. He had come to Liverpool to trace the movements of a friend about whom he was very uneasy, and he was making anxious inquiries at the docks to discover at what times steamers left for America when the detectives stationed there had, in accordance with instructions from headquarters, arrested him as a suspicious-looking character. "Though," said Tom, "they must very well have known my phiz, as I have been sketched and caricatured all over the shop. When I told them who I was they had the decency to let me go. They thought they'd scored off me enough, I reckon. Yes, it certainly *is* a strange coincidence that I might actually have had something to do with the poor fellow's death, which has cut me up as much as anybody; though if they had known I had just come from the 'scene of the crime,' and actually lived in the house, they would probably have—let me alone." He laughed sarcastically. "They are a queer lot of muddleheads are the police. Their motto is, 'First catch your man, then cook the evidence.' If you're on the spot you're guilty because you're there, and if you're elsewhere you're guilty because you have gone away. Oh, I know them! If they could have seen their way to clap me in quod, they'd ha' done it. Luckily I know the number of the cabman who took me to Euston before five this morning."

"If they clapped you in quod," the interviewer reported himself as facetiously observing, "the prisoners would be on strike in a week."

"Yes, but there would be so many blacklegs ready to take their places," Mortlake flashed back, "that I'm afraid it 'ould be no go. But do excuse me. I am so upset about my friend. I'm afraid he has left England, and I have to make inquiries; and now there's poor Constant gone—horrible! horrible! and I'm due in London at the inquest. I must really run away. Good-bye. Tell your readers it's all a policy grudge."

"One last word, Mr. Mortlake, if you please. Is it true that you were billed to preside at a great meeting of clerks at St. James's Hall between one and two to-day to protest against the German invasion?"

"Whew! so I was. But the beggars arrested me just before one, when I was going to wire, and then the news of poor Constant's end drove it out of my head. What a nuisance! Lord, how troubles do come together! Well, good-bye, send me a copy of the paper."

Tom Mortlake's evidence at the inquest added little beyond this to the public knowledge of his movements on the morning of the Mystery. The cabman who drove him to Euston had written indignantly to the papers to say that he picked up his celebrated fare at Bow Railway Station at about half-past four a.m., and the arrest was a deliberate insult to democracy, and he offered to make an affidavit to that effect, leaving it dubious to which effect. But Scotland Yard betrayed no itch for the affidavit in question, and No. 2138 subsided again into the obscurity of his rank. Mortlake—whose face was very pale below the black mane brushed back from his fine forehead—gave his evidence in low, sympathetic tones. He had known the deceased for over a year, coming constantly across him in their common political and social work, and had found the furnished rooms for him in Glover Street at his own request, they just being to let when Constant resolved to leave his rooms at Oxford House in Bethnal Green, and to share the actual life of the people. The locality suited the deceased, as being near the People's Palace. He respected and admired the deceased, whose genuine goodness had won all hearts. The deceased was an untiring worker; never grumbled, was always in fair spirits, regarded his life and wealth as a sacred trust to be used for the benefit of humanity. He had last seen him at a quarter past nine p.m., on the day preceding his death. He (witness) had received a letter by the last post which made him uneasy about a friend. He went up to consult deceased about it. Deceased was evidently suffering from toothache, and was fixing a piece of cotton-wool in a hollow tooth, but he did not complain. Deceased seemed rather upset by the news he brought, and they both discussed it rather excitedly.

BY A JURYMAN: Did the news concern him?

MORTLAKE: Only impersonally. He knew my friend, and was keenly sympathetic when one was in trouble.

CORONER: Could you show the jury the letter you received?

MORTLAKE: I have mislaid it, and cannot make out where it has got to. If you think it relevant or essential, I will state what the trouble was.

CORONER: Was the toothache very violent?

MORTLAKE: I cannot tell. I think not, though he told me it had disturbed his rest the night before.

CORONER: What time did you leave him?

MORTLAKE: About twenty to ten.

CORONER: And what did you do then?

MORTLAKE: I went out for an hour or so to make some inquiries. Then I returned, and told my landlady I should be leaving by an early train for—for the country.

CORONER: And that was the last you saw of the deceased?

MORTLAKE (with emotion): The last.

CORONER: How was he when you left him?

MORTLAKE: Mainly concerned about my trouble.

CORONER: Otherwise you saw nothing unusual about him?

MORTLAKE: Nothing.

CORONER: What time did you leave the house on Tuesday morning?

MORTLAKE: At about five-and-twenty minutes past four.

CORONER: Are you sure that you shut the street door?

MORTLAKE: Quite sure. Knowing my landlady was rather a timid person, I even slipped the bolt of the big lock, which was usually tied back. It was impossible for anyone to get in, even with a latchkey.

Mrs. Drabdump's evidence (which, of course, preceded his) was more important, and occupied a considerable time, unduly eked out by Drabdumpian padding. Thus she not only deposed that Mr. Constant had the toothache, but that it was going to last about a week; in tragi-comic indifference to the radical cure that had been effected. Her account of the last hours of the deceased tallied with Mortlake's, only that she feared Mortlake was quarreling with him over something in a letter that came by the nine o'clock post. Deceased had left the house a little after Mortlake, but had returned before him, and had gone straight to his bedroom. She had not actually seen him come in, having been in the kitchen, but she heard his latchkey, followed by his light step up the stairs.

A JURYMAN: How do you know it was not somebody else? (Sensation, of which the juryman tries to look unconscious.)

WITNESS: He called down to me over the banisters, and says in his sweetest voice, "Be hextra sure to wake me at a quarter to seven, Mrs. Drabdump, or else I shan't get to my tram meeting."

(Juryman collapses.)

CORONER: And did you wake him?

MRS. DRABDUMP (breaking down): Oh, my lud, how can you ask?

CORONER: There, there, compose yourself. I mean did you try to wake him?

MRS. DRABDUMP: I have taken in and done for lodgers this seventeen years, my lud, and have always gave satisfaction; and Mr. Mortlake, he wouldn't ha' recommended me otherwise, though I wish to Heaven the poor gentleman had never—

CORONER: Yes, yes, of course. You tried to rouse him?

But it was some time before Mrs. Drabdump was sufficiently calm to explain that, though she had overslept herself, and though it would have been all the same anyhow, she *had* come up to time. Bit by bit the tragic story was forced from her lips—a tragedy that even her telling could not make tawdry. She told with superfluous detail how—when Mr. Grodman broke in the door—she saw her unhappy gentleman-lodger lying on his back in bed, stone dead, with a gaping red wound in his throat; how her stronger-minded companion calmed her a little by spreading a handkerchief over the distorted face; how they then looked vainly about and under the bed for any instrument by which the deed could have been done, the veteran detective carefully making a rapid inventory of the contents of the room, and taking notes of the precise position and condition of the body before anything was disturbed by the arrival of gapers or bunglers; how she had pointed out to him that both the windows were firmly bolted to keep out the cold night air; how, having noted this down with a puzzled pitying shake of the head, he had opened the window to summon the police, and espied in the fog one Denzil Cantercot, whom he called, and told to run to the nearest police-station and ask them to send on an inspector and a surgeon. How they both remained in the room till the police arrived, Grodman pondering deeply the while and making notes every now and again, as fresh points occurred to him, and asking her questions about the poor, weak-headed young man. Pressed as to what she meant by calling the deceased "weak-headed," she replied that some of her neighbors wrote him begging letters, though, Heaven knew, they were better off than herself, who had to scrape her fingers to the bone for every penny she earned. Under further pressure from Mr. Talbot, who was watching the inquiry on behalf of Arthur Constant's family, Mrs. Drabdump admitted that the deceased had behaved like a human being, nor was there anything externally eccentric or queer in his conduct. He was always cheerful and pleasant spoken, though certainly soft—God rest his soul. No; he never shaved, but wore all the hair that Heaven had given him.

She thought deceased was in the habit of locking his door when he went to bed. Of course, she couldn't say for certain. (Laughter.) There was no need to bolt the door as well. The bolt slid upwards, and was at the top of the door. When she first let lodgings, her reasons for which she seemed anxious to publish, there had only been a bolt, but a suspicious lodger, she would not call him a gentleman, had complained that he could not fasten his door behind him, and so she had been put to the expense of having a lock made. The complaining lodger went off soon after without paying his rent. (Laughter.) She had always known he would.

THE CORONER: Was deceased at all nervous?

WITNESS: No, he was a very nice gentleman. (A laugh.)

CORONER: I mean did he seem afraid of being robbed?

WITNESS: No, he was always goin' to demonstrations. (Laughter.) I told him to be careful. I told him I lost a purse with 3s. 2d. myself on Jubilee Day.

MRS. DRABDUMP resumed her seat, weeping vaguely.

THE CORONER: Gentlemen, we shall have an opportunity of viewing the room shortly.

The story of the discovery of the body was retold, though more scientifically, by Mr. George Grodman, whose unexpected resurgence into the realm of his early exploits excited as keen a curiosity as the reappearance "for this occasion only" of a retired prima donna. His book, *Criminals I Have Caught*, passed from the twenty-third to the twenty-fourth edition merely on the strength of it. Mr. Grodman stated that the body was still warm when he found it. He thought that death was quite recent. The door he had had to burst was bolted as well as locked. He confirmed Mrs. Drabdump's statement about the windows; the chimney was very narrow. The cut looked as if done by a razor. There was no instrument lying about the room. He had known the deceased about a month. He seemed a very earnest, simple-minded young fellow, who spoke a great deal about the brotherhood of man. (The hardened old man-hunter's voice was not free from a tremor as he spoke jerkily of the dead man's enthusiasms.) He should have thought the deceased the last man in the world to commit suicide.

Mr. Denzil Cantercot was next called: He was a poet. (Laughter.) He was on his way to Mr. Grodman's house to tell him he had been unable to do some writing for him because he was suffering from writer's cramp, when Mr. Grodman called to him from the window of No. 11 and asked him to run for the police. No, he did not run; he was a philosopher. (Laughter.) He returned with them to the door, but did not go up. He had no stomach for crude sensations. (Laughter.) The gray fog was sufficiently unbeautiful for him for one morning. (Laughter.)

Inspector Howlett said: About 9:45 on the morning of Tuesday, 4th December, from information received, he went to 11 Glover Street, Bow, and there found the dead body of a young man, lying on his back with his throat cut. The door of the room had been smashed in, and the lock and the bolt evidently forced. The room was tidy. There were no marks of blood on the floor. A purse full of gold was on the dressing-table beside a big book. A hip-bath, with cold water, stood beside the bed, over which was a hanging bookcase. There was a large wardrobe against the wall next to the door. The chimney was very narrow. There were two windows, one bolted. It was about eighteen feet to the pavement. There was no way of climbing up. No one could possibly have got out of the room, and then bolted the doors and windows behind him; and he had searched all parts of the room in which anyone might have been concealed. He had been unable to find any instrument in the room in spite of exhaustive search, there being not even a penknife in the pockets of the clothes of the deceased, which lay on a chair. The house and the backyard, and the adjacent pavement, had also been fruitlessly searched.

Sergeant Runnymede made an identical statement, saving only that *he* had gone with Dr. Robinson and Inspector Howlett.

DR. ROBINSON, divisional surgeon, said: The deceased was lying on his back, with his throat cut. The body was not yet cold, the abdominal region being quite warm. Rigor mortis had set in in the lower jaw, neck, and upper extremities. The muscles contracted when beaten. I inferred that life had been extinct some two or three hours, probably not longer, it might have been less. The bed-clothes would keep the lower part warm for some time. The wound, which was a deep one, was five and a half inches right to left across the throat to a point under the left ear. The upper portion of the windpipe was severed, and likewise the jugular vein. The muscular coating of the carotid artery was divided. There was a slight cut, as if in continuation of the wound, on the thumb of the left hand. The hands were clasped underneath the head. There was no blood on the right hand. The wound could not have been self-inflicted. A sharp instrument had been used, such as a razor. The cut might have been made by a left-handed person. No doubt death was practically instantaneous. I saw no signs of a struggle about the body or the room. I noticed a purse on the dressing-table, lying next to Madame Blavatsky's big book on Theosophy. Sergeant Runnymede drew my attention to the fact that the door had evidently been locked and bolted from within.

I do not say the cuts could not have been made by a right-handed person. I can offer no suggestion as to how the inflictor of the wound got in or out. Extremely improbable that the cut was self-inflicted. There was little trace of the outside fog in the room.

Police-constable Williams said he was on duty in the early hours of the morning of the 4th inst. Glover Street lay within his beat. He saw or heard nothing suspicious. The fog was never very dense, though nasty to the throat. He had passed through Glover Street about half-past four. He had not seen Mr. Mortlake or anybody else leave the house.

The Court here adjourned, the Coroner and the jury repairing in a body to 11 Glover Street, to view the house and the bedroom of the deceased. And the evening posters announced "The Bow Mystery Thickens."

3

Before the inquiry was resumed, all the poor wretches in custody had been released on suspicion that they were innocent; there was not a single case even for a magistrate. Clues, which at such seasons are gathered by the police like blackberries off the hedges, were scanty and unripe. Inferior specimens were offered them by bushels, but there was not a good one among the lot. The police could not even manufacture a clue.

Arthur Constant's death was already the theme of every hearth, railway-carriage and public-house. The dead idealist had points of contact with so many spheres. The East-end and the West-end alike were moved and excited, the Democratic Leagues and the Churches, the Doss-houses and the Universities. The pity of it! And then the impenetrable mystery of it!

The evidence given in the concluding portion of the investigation was necessarily less sensational. There were no more witnesses to bring the scent of blood over the coroner's table; those who had yet to be heard were merely relatives and friends of the deceased, who spoke of him as he had been in life. His parents were dead, perhaps happily for them; his relatives had seen little of him, and had scarce heard as much about him as the outside world. No man is a prophet in his own country, and, even if he migrates, it is advisable for him to leave his family at home. His friends were a motley crew; friends of the same friend are not necessarily friends of one another. But their diversity only made the congruity of the tale they had to tell more striking. It was a tale of a man who had never made an enemy even by benefitting him, nor lost a friend even by refusing his favors; the tale of a man whose heart overflowed with peace and goodwill to all men all the year round; of a man to whom Christmas came not once, but three hundred and sixty-five times a year; it was the tale of a brilliant intellect, who gave up to mankind what was meant for himself, and worked as a laborer in the vineyard of humanity, never crying that the grapes were sour; of a man uniformly cheerful and of good courage, living in that forgetfulness of self which is the truest antidote to despair. And yet there was not quite wanting the note of pain to jar the harmony and make it human. Richard Elton, his chum from boyhood, and vicar of Somerton, in Midlandshire, handed to the coroner a letter received from the deceased about ten days before his death, containing some passages which the coroner read aloud:—"Do you know anything of Schopenhauer? I mean anything beyond the current misconceptions? I have been making his acquaintance lately. He is an agreeable rattle of a pessimist; his essay on 'The Misery of Mankind' is quite lively reading. At first his assimilation of Christianity and Pessimism (it occurs in his essay on 'Suicide') dazzled me as an audacious paradox. But there is truth in it. Verily the whole creation groaneth and travaileth, and man is a degraded monster, and sin is over all. Ah, my friend, I have shed many of my illusions since I came to this seething

hive of misery and wrongdoing. What shall one man's life—a million men's lives
—avail against the corruption, the vulgarity, and the squalor of civilization? Sometimes I feel like a farthing rushlight in the Hall of Eblis. Selfishness is so long and
life so short. And the worst of it is that everybody is so beastly contented. The poor
no more desire comfort than the rich culture. The woman, to whom a penny
school fee for her child represents an appreciable slice off her income, is satisfied
that the rich we shall always have with us.

"The real old Tories are the paupers in the Workhouse. The Radical working
men are jealous of their own leaders, and the leaders are jealous of one another.
Schopenhauer must have organized a Labor Party in his salad days. And yet one
can't help feeling that he committed suicide as a philosopher by not committing it
as a man. He claims kinship with Buddha, too; though Esoteric Buddhism at least
seems spheres removed from the philosophy of 'the Will and the Idea.' What a
wonderful woman Madame Blavatsky must be! I can't say I follow her, for she is
up in the clouds nearly all the time, and I haven't as yet developed an astral body.
Shall I send you on her book? It is fascinating. . . . I am becoming quite a fluent
orator. One soon gets into the way of it. The horrible thing is that you catch
yourself saying things to lead up to 'Cheers' instead of sticking to the plain realities
of the business. Lucy is still doing the galleries in Italy. It used to pain me sometimes to think of my darling's happiness when I came across a flat-chested factory-
girl. Now I feel her happiness is as important as a factory-girl's."

Lucy, the witness explained, was Lucy Brent, the betrothed of the deceased.
The poor girl had been telegraphed for, and had started for England. The witness
stated that the outburst of despondency in this letter was almost a solitary one, most
of the letters in his possession being bright, buoyant, and hopeful. Even this letter
ended with a humorous statement of the writer's manifold plans and projects for
the New Year. The deceased was a good Churchman.

CORONER: Was there any private trouble in his own life to account for the temporary
    despondency?
WITNESS: Not so far as I am aware. His financial position was exceptionally favor-
    able.
CORONER: There had been no quarrel with Miss Brent?
WITNESS: I have the best authority for saying that no shadow of difference had ever
    come between them.
CORONER: Was the deceased left-handed?
WITNESS: Certainly not. He was not even ambidexter.
A JURYMAN: Isn't Shoppinhour one of the infidel writers, published by the Free-
    thought Publication Society?
WITNESS: I do not know who publishes his books.
THE JURYMAN (a small grocer and big raw-boned Scotchman, rejoicing in the name

of Sandy Sanderson and the dignities of deaconry and membership of the committee of the Bow Conservative Association): No equeevocation, sir. Is he not a secularist, who has lectured at the Hall of Science?

WITNESS: No, he is a foreign writer—(Mr. Sanderson was heard to thank Heaven for this small mercy)—who believes that life is not worth living.

THE JURYMAN: Were you not shocked to find the friend of a meenister reading such impure leeterature?

WITNESS: The deceased read everything. Schopenhauer is the author of a system of philosophy, and not what you seem to imagine. Perhaps you would like to inspect the book? (Laughter.)

THE JURYMAN: I would na' touch it with a pitchfork. Such books should be burnt. And this Madame Blavatsky's book—what is that? Is that also pheelosophy?

WITNESS: No. It is Theosophy.(Laughter.)

Mr. Allan Smith, secretary of the Tram-men's Union, stated that he had had an interview with the deceased on the day before his death, when he (the deceased) spoke hopefully of the prospects of the movement, and wrote him out a check for ten guineas for his Union. Deceased promised to speak at a meeting called for a quarter past seven a.m. the next day.

Mr. Edward Wimp, of the Scotland Yard Detective Department, said that the letters and papers of the deceased threw no light upon the manner of his death, and they would be handed back to the family. His Department had not formed any theory on the subject.

The Coroner proceeded to sum up the evidence. "We have to deal, gentlemen," he said, "with a most incomprehensible and mysterious case, the details of which are yet astonishingly simple. On the morning of Tuesday, the 4th inst., Mrs. Drabdump, a worthy hard-working widow, who lets lodgings at 11 Glover Street, Bow, was unable to arouse the deceased, who occupied the entire upper floor of the house. Becoming alarmed, she went across to fetch Mr. George Grodman, a gentleman known to us all by reputation, and to whose clear and scientific evidence we are much indebted, and got him to batter in the door. They found the deceased lying back in bed with a deep wound in his throat. Life had only recently become extinct. There was no trace of any instrument by which the cut could have been effected; there was no trace of any person who could have effected the cut. No person could apparently have got in or out. The medical evidence goes to show that the deceased could not have inflicted the wound himself. And yet, gentlemen, there are, in the nature of things, two—only two—alternative explanations of his death. Either the wound was inflicted by his own hand, or it was inflicted by another's. I shall take each of these possibilities separately. First, did the deceased commit suicide? The medical evidence says deceased was lying with his hands clasped behind his head. Now the wound was made from right to left, and terminated by a cut on the left thumb. If the deceased had made it he would have had to do it with his right hand, while his left hand remained under his head—a most peculiar and unnatural position to assume. Moreover, in making a cut with the right hand, one would naturally move the hand from left to right. It is unlikely that the deceased would move his right hand so awkwardly and unnaturally, unless, of course, his object was to baffle suspicion. Another point is that on this hypothesis, the deceased would have had to replace his right hand beneath his head. But Dr. Robinson believes that death was instantaneous. If so, deceased could have had no time to pose so neatly. It is just possible the cut was made with the left hand, but then the deceased was right-handed. The absence of any signs of a possible weapon undoubtedly goes to corroborate the medical evidence. The police have made an exhaustive search in all places where the razor or other weapon or instrument might by any possibility have been concealed, including the bedclothes, the mattress, the pillow, and the street into which it might have been dropped. But all theories involving the willful concealment of the fatal instrument have to reckon with the fact or probability that death was instantaneous, also with the fact that there was no blood about the floor. Finally, the instrument used was in all likelihood a razor, and the deceased did not shave, and was never known to be in possession of any such instrument. If, then, we were to confine ourselves to the medical and police evidence, there would, I think, be little hesitation in dismissing the idea of suicide. Nevertheless, it is well to forget the physical aspect of the case for a moment and to apply our minds to an unprejudiced inquiry into the mental aspect of it. Was there any reason why the deceased should wish to take his own life? He was young, wealthy, and popular, loving and loved; life stretched fair before him. He had no vices. Plain living, high thinking, and noble doing were the three guiding stars of his life. If he had had ambition, an illustrious public career was within his reach. He was an orator of no mean power, a brilliant and industrious man. His outlook was always on the future—he was always sketching out ways in which he could be useful to his fellow-men. His purse and his time were ever at the command of whosoever could show fair claim upon them. If such a man were likely to end his own life, the science of human nature would be at an end. Still, some of the shadows of the picture have been presented to us. The man had his moments of despondency—as which of us has not? But they seem to have been few and passing. Anyhow, he was cheerful enough on the day before his death. He was suffering, too, from toothache. But it does not seem to have been violent, nor did he complain. Possibly, of course, the pain became very acute in the night. Nor must we forget that he may have overworked himself, and got his nerves into a morbid state. He worked very hard, never rising later than half-past seven, and doing far more than the professional 'labor leader.' He taught, and wrote, as well as spoke and organized. But on the other hand all witnesses agreed that he was looking forward eagerly to the meeting of the tram-men on the morning of the 4th inst. His whole heart was in the movement. Is it likely that this was the night he would choose for quitting the scene of his usefulness? Is it likely that if he had chosen it, he would not have left letters and a statement behind, or made a last will and testament? Mr. Wimp has found no possible clue to such conduct in his papers. Or is it likely he would have concealed the instrument? The only positive sign of intention is the bolting of his door in addition to the usual locking of it, but one cannot lay much stress on that. Regarding the mental aspects alone, the balance is largely against suicide; looking at the physical aspects, suicide is well-nigh impossible. Putting the two together, the case against suicide is all but mathematically complete. The answer, then, to our first question, Did the deceased commit suicide? is, that he did not."

The Coroner paused, and everybody drew a long breath. The lucid exposition had been followed with admiration. If the Coroner had stopped now, the jury would have unhesitatingly returned a verdict of "murder." But the Coroner swallowed a mouthful of water and went on:

"We now come to the second alternative—was the deceased the victim of homicide? In order to answer that question in the affirmative it is essential that we should be able to form some conception of the *modus operandi*. It is all very well for Dr. Robinson to say the cut was made by another hand; but in the absence of any theory as to how the cut could possibly have been made by that other hand, we should be driven back to the theory of self-infliction, however improbable it may seem to medical gentlemen. Now, what are the facts? When Mrs. Drabdump and Mr. Grodman found the body it was yet warm, and Mr. Grodman, a witness fortunately qualified by special experience, states that death had been quite recent. This tallies closely enough with the view of Dr. Robinson, who, examining the body about an hour later, put the time of death at two or three hours before, say seven o'clock. Mrs. Drabdump had attempted to wake the deceased at a quarter to seven, which would put back the act to a little earlier. As I understand from Dr. Robinson, that it is impossible to fix the time very precisely, death may have very well taken place several hours before Mrs. Drabdump's first attempt to wake deceased. Of course, it may have taken place between the first and second calls, as he may merely have been sound asleep at first; it may also not impossibly have taken place considerably earlier than the first call, for all the physical data seem to prove. Nevertheless, on the whole, I think we shall be least likely to err if we assume the time of death to be half-past six. Gentlemen, let us picture to ourselves No. 11 Glover Street, at half-past six. We have seen the house; we know exactly how it is constructed. On the ground floor a front room tenanted by Mr. Mortlake, with two windows giving on the street, both securely bolted; a back room occupied by the landlady; and the kitchen. Mrs. Drabdump did not leave her bedroom till half-past six, so that we may be sure all the various doors and windows have not yet been unfastened; while the season of the year is a guarantee that nothing had been left open. The front door, through which Mr. Mortlake has gone out before half-past four, is guarded by the latchkey and the big lock. On the upper floor are two rooms—a front room used by deceased for a bedroom, and a back room which he used as a sitting-room. The back room has been left open, with the key inside, but the window is fastened. The door of the front room is not only locked, but bolted. We have seen the splintered mortice and the staple of the upper bolt violently forced from the woodwork and resting on the pin. The windows are bolted, the fasteners being firmly fixed in the catches. The chimney is too narrow to admit of the passage of even a child. This room, in fact, is as firmly barred in as if besieged. It has no communication with any other part of the house. It is as absolutely self-centered and isolated as if it were a fort in the sea or a log-hut in the forest. Even if any strange person is in the house, nay, in the very sitting-room of the deceased, he cannot get into the bedroom, for the house is one built for the poor, with no communication between the different rooms, so that separate families, if need be, may inhabit each. Now, however, let us grant that some person has achieved the miracle of getting into the front room, first floor, 18 feet from the ground. At half-past six, or thereabouts, he cuts the throat of the sleeping occupant. How is he then to get out without attracting the attention of the now roused landlady? But let us concede him that miracle, too. How is he to go away and yet leave the doors and windows locked and bolted from within? This is a degree of miracle at which my credulity must draw the line. No, the room had been closed all night—there is scarce a trace of fog in it. No one could get in or out. Finally, murders do not take place without motive. Robbery and revenge are the only conceivable motives. The deceased had not an enemy in the world; his money and valuables were left untouched. Everything was in order. There were no signs of a struggle. The answer, then, to our second inquiry—was the deceased killed by another person?—is that he was not.

"Gentlemen, I am aware that this sounds impossible and contradictory. But it is the facts that contradict themselves. It seems clear that the deceased did not commit suicide. It seems equally clear that the deceased was not murdered. There is nothing for it therefore, gentlemen, but to return a verdict tantamount to an acknowledgment of our incompetence to come to any adequately grounded conviction whatever as to the means or the manner by which the deceased met his death. It is the most inexplicable mystery in all my experience." (Sensation.)

The Foreman (after a colloquy with Mr. Sandy Sanderson) said: "We are not agreed, sir. One of the jurors insists on a verdict of 'Death from visitation by the act of God.'"

4

But Sandy Sanderson's burning solicitude to fix the crime flickered out in the face of opposition, and in the end he bowed his head to the inevitable "open verdict." Then the floodgates of inkland were opened, and the deluge pattered for nine days on the deaf coffin where the poor idealist moldered. The tongues of the Press were loosened, and the leader-writers reveled in recapitulating the circumstances of "The Big Bow Mystery," though they could contribute nothing but adjectives to the solution. The papers teemed with letters—it was a kind of Indian summer of the silly season. But the editors could not keep them out, nor cared to. The mystery was the one topic of conversation everywhere—it was on the carpet and the bare boards alike, in the kitchen and the drawing-room. It was discussed with science or stupidity, with aspirates or without. It came up for breakfast with the rolls, and was swept off the supper-table with the last crumbs.

No. 11 Glover Street, Bow, remained for days a shrine of pilgrimage. The once sleepy little street buzzed from morning till night. From all parts of the town people came to stare up at the bedroom window and wonder with a foolish face of horror. The pavement was often blocked for hours together, and itinerant vendors of refreshment made it a new market center, while vocalists hastened thither to sing the delectable ditty of the deed without having any voice in the matter. It was a pity the Government did not erect a toll-gate at either end of the street. But Chancellors of the Exchequer rarely avail themselves of the more obvious expedients for paying off the National Debt.

Finally, familiarity bred contempt, and the wits grew facetious at the expense of the Mystery. Jokes on the subject appeared even in the comic papers.

To the proverb, "You must not say Bo to a goose," one added: "or else she will explain you the Mystery." The name of the gentleman who asked whether the Bow Mystery was not 'arrowing shall not be divulged. There was more point in "Dagonet's" remark that, if he had been one of the unhappy jurymen, he would have been driven to "suicide." A professional paradox-monger pointed triumphantly to the somewhat similar situation in "The Murder in the Rue Morgue," and said that Nature had been plagiarizing again—like the monkey she was—and he recommended Poe's publishers to apply for an injunction. More seriously, Poe's solution was re-suggested by "Constant Reader" as an original idea. He thought that a small organ-grinder's monkey might have got down the chimney with its master's razor, and, after attempting to shave the occupant of the bed, had returned the way it came. This idea created considerable sensation, but a correspondent with a long train of letters draggling after his name pointed out that a monkey small enough to get down so narrow a flue would not be strong enough to inflict so deep a wound. This was disputed by a third writer, and the contest raged so keenly about the power of monkey's muscles that it was almost taken for granted that a monkey was the guilty party. The bubble was pricked by the pen of "Common Sense," who laconically remarked that no traces of soot or blood had been discovered on the floor, or on the nightshirt, or the counterpane. The *Lancet's* leader on the Mystery was awaited with interest. It said: "We cannot join in the praises that have been showered upon the coroner's summing up. It shows again the evils resulting from having coroners who are not medical men. He seems to have appreciated but inadequately the significance of the medical evidence. He should certainly have directed the jury to return a verdict of murder on that. What was it to do with him that he could see no way by which the wound could have been inflicted by an outside agency? It was for the police to find how that was done. Enough that it was impossible for the unhappy young man to have inflicted such a wound, and then to have had strength and will power enough to hide the instrument and to remove perfectly every trace of his having left the bed for the purpose." It is impossible to enumerate all the theories propounded by the amateur detectives, while Scotland Yard religiously held its tongue. Ultimately the interest on the subject became confined to a few papers which had received the best letters. Those papers that couldn't get interesting letters stopped the correspondence and sneered at the "sensationalism" of those that could. Among the mass of fantasy there were not a few notable solutions, which failed brilliantly, like rockets posing as fixed stars. One was that in the obscurity of the fog the murderer had ascended to the window of the bedroom by means of a ladder from the pavement. He had then with a diamond cut one of the panes away, and effected an entry through the aperture. On leaving he fixed in the pane of glass again (or another which he had brought with him) and thus the room remained with its bolts and locks untouched. On its being pointed out that the panes were too small, a third correspondent showed that that didn't matter, as it was only necessary to insert the hand and undo the fastening, when the entire window could be opened, the process being reversed by the murderer on leaving. This pretty edifice of glass was smashed by a glazier, who wrote to say that a pane could hardly be fixed in from only one side of a window frame, that it would fall out when touched, and that in any case the wet putty could not have escaped detection. A door panel sliced out and replaced was also put forward, and as many trap-doors and secret passages were ascribed to No. 11 Glover Street as if it were a medieval castle. Another of these clever theories was that the murderer was in the room the whole time the police were there—hidden in the wardrobe. Or he had got behind the door when Grodman broke it open, so that he was not noticed in the excitement of the discovery, and escaped with his weapon at the moment when Grodman and Mrs. Drabdump were examining the window fastenings.

Scientific explanations also were to hand to explain how the assassin locked and bolted the door behind him. Powerful magnets outside the door had been used to turn the key and push the bolt within. Murderers armed with magnets loomed on the popular imagination like a new microbe. There was only one defect in this ingenious theory—the thing could not be done. A physiologist recalled the conjurors who swallow swords—by an anatomical peculiarity of the throat—and said that the deceased might have swallowed the weapon after cutting his own throat. This was too much for the public to swallow. As for the idea that the suicide had been effected with a penknife or its blade, or a bit of steel, which had then got buried in the wound, not even the quotation of Shelley's line:

Makes such a wound, the knife is lost in it.

could secure it a moment's acceptance. The same reception was accorded to the idea that the cut had been made with a candle-stick (or other harmless necessary bedroom article) constructed like a swordstick. Theories of this sort caused a humorist to explain that the deceased had hidden the razor in his hollow tooth! Some kind friend of Messrs. Maskelyne and Cook suggested that they were the only persons who could have done the deed, as no one else could get out of a locked cabinet. But perhaps the most brilliant of these flashes of false fire was the facetious, yet probably half seriously meant letter that appeared in the *Pell Mell Press* under the heading of

THE BIG BOW MYSTERY SOLVED.

Sir,—You will remember that when the Whitechapel murders were agitating the universe, I suggested that the district coroner was the assassin. My suggestion has been disregarded. The coroner is still at large. So is the Whitechapel murderer. Perhaps this suggestive coincidence will incline the authorities to pay more attention to me this time. The problem seems to be this. The deceased could not have cut his own throat. The deceased could not have had his throat cut for him. As one of the two must have happened, this is obvious nonsense. As this is obvious nonsense I am justified in disbelieving it. As this obvious nonsense was primarily put in circulation by Mrs. Drabdump and Mr. Grodman, I am justified in disbelieving *them*. In short, sir, what guarantee have we that the whole tale is not a cock-and-bull story, invented by the two persons who first found the body? What proof is there that the deed was not done by these persons themselves, who then went to work to smash the door and break the locks and the bolts, and fasten up all windows before they called the police in?—I enclose my card, and am, sir, yours truly,

ONE WHO LOOKS THROUGH
HIS OWN SPECTACLES.

[Our correspondent's theory is not so audaciously original as he seems to imagine. Has he not looked through the spectacles of the people who persistently suggested that the Whitechapel murderer was invariably the policeman who found the body? *Somebody* must find the body, if it is to be found at all.—ED. *P.M.P.*]

The editor had reason to be pleased that he inserted this letter, for it drew the following interesting communication from the great detective himself:

THE BIG BOW MYSTERY SOLVED.

Sir,—I do not agree with you that your correspondent's theory lacks originality. On the contrary, I think it is delightfully original. In fact it has given me an idea. What that idea is I do not yet propose to say, but if "One Who Looks Through His Own Spectacles" will favor me with his name and address I shall be happy to inform him a little before the rest of the world whether his germ has borne any fruit. I feel he is a kindred spirit, and take this opportunity of saying publicly that I was extremely disappointed at the unsatisfactory verdict. The thing was a palpable assassination; an open verdict has a tendency to relax the exertions of Scotland Yard. I hope I shall not be accused of immodesty, or of making personal reflections, when I say that the Department has had several notorious failures of late. It is not what it used to be. Crime is becoming impertinent. It no longer knows its place, so to speak. It throws down the gauntlet where once it used to cower in its fastnesses. I repeat, I make these remarks solely in the interest of law and order. I do not for one moment believe that Arthur Constant killed himself, and if Scotland Yard satisfies itself with that explanation, and turns on its other side and goes to sleep again, then, sir, one of the foulest and most horrible crimes of the century will for ever go unpunished. My acquaintance with the unhappy victim was but recent; still, I saw and knew enough of the man to be certain (and I hope I have seen and known enough of other men to judge) that he was a man constitutionally incapable of committing an act of violence, whether against himself or anybody else. He would not hurt a fly, as the saying goes. And a man of that gentle stamp always lacks the active energy to lay hands on himself. He was a man to be esteemed in no common degree, and I feel proud to be able to say that he considered me a friend. I am hardly at the time of life at which a man cares to put on his harness again; but, sir, it is impossible that I should ever know a day's rest till the perpetrator of this foul deed is discovered. I have already put myself in communication with the family of the victim, who, I am pleased to say, have every confidence in me, and look to me to clear the name of their unhappy relative from the semi-imputation of suicide. I shall be pleased if anyone who shares my distrust of the authorities, and who has any clue whatever to this terrible mystery or any plausible suggestion to offer, if, in brief, any "One who looks through his own spectacles" will communicate with me. If I were asked to indicate the direction in which new clues might be most usefully sought, I should say, in the first instance, anything is valuable that helps us to piece together a complete picture of the manifold activities of the man in the East-end. He entered one way or another into the lives of a good many people; is it true that he nowhere made enemies? With the best intentions a man may wound or offend; his interference may be resented; he may even excite jealousy. A young man like the late Mr. Constant could not have had as much practical sagacity as he had goodness. Whose corns did he tread on? The more we know of the last few months of his life the more we shall know of the manner of death.

Thanking you by anticipation for the insertion of this letter in your valuable columns, I am, sir, yours truly,

GEORGE GRODMAN.

46 Glover Street, Bow.

P.S.—Since writing the above lines, I have, by the kindness of Miss Brent, been placed in possession of a most valuable letter, probably the last letter written by the unhappy gentleman. It is dated Monday, 3 December, the very eve of the murder, and was addressed to her at Florence, and has now, after some delay, followed her back to London where the sad news unexpectedly brought her. It is a letter couched, on the whole, in the most hopeful spirit, and speaks in detail of his schemes. Of course there are things in it not meant for the ears of the public, but there can be no harm in transcribing an important passage:

"You seem to have imbibed the idea that the East-end is a kind of Golgotha, and this despite that the books out of which you probably got it are carefully labeled 'Fiction.' Lamb says somewhere that we think of the 'Dark Ages' as literally without sunlight, and so I fancy people like you, dear, think of the 'East-end' as a mixture of mire, misery, and murder. How's that for alliteration? Why, within five minutes' walk of me there are the loveliest houses, with gardens back and front, inhabited by very fine people and furniture. Many of my university friends' mouths would water if they knew the income of some of the shopkeepers in the High Road.

"The rich people about here may not be so fashionable as those in Kensington and Bayswater, but they are every bit as stupid and materialistic. I don't deny, Lucy, I *do* have my black moments, and I do sometimes pine to get away from all this to the lands of sun and lotus-eating. But, on the whole, I am too busy even to dream of dreaming. My real black moments are when I doubt if I am really doing any good. But yet on the whole my conscience or my self-conceit tells me that I am. If one cannot do much with the mass, there is at least the consolation of doing good to the individual. And, after all, is it not enough to have been an influence for good over one or two human souls? There are quite fine characters hereabout— especially in the women—natures capable not only of self-sacrifice, but of delicacy of sentiment. To have learnt to know of such, to have been of services to one or two of such—is not this ample return? I could not get to St. James's Hall to hear your friend's symphony at the Henschel concert. I have been reading Mme. Blavatsky's latest book, and getting quite interested in occult philosophy. Unfortunately I have to do all my reading in bed; and I don't find the book as soothing a soporific as most new books. For keeping one awake I find Theosophy as bad as a toothache . . ."

THE BIG BOW MYSTERY SOLVED.

Sir,—I wonder if any one besides myself has been struck by the incredible bad taste of Mr. Grodman's letter in your last issue. That he, a former servant of the Department, should publicly insult and run it down can only be charitably explained by the supposition that his judgment is failing him in his old age. In view of this letter, are the relatives of the deceased justified in entrusting him with any private documents? It is, no doubt, very good of him to undertake to avenge one whom he seems snobbishly anxious to claim as a friend; but, all things considered, should not his letter have been headed, "The Big Bow Mystery Shelved?"—I enclose my card, and am, sir, your obedient servant,

SCOTLAND YARD.

George Grodman read this letter with annoyance, and crumpling up the paper, murmured scornfully, "Edward Wimp!"

5

"Yes, but what will become of the Beautiful?" said Denzil Cantercot.

"Hang the Beautiful!" said Peter Crowl, as if he were on the committee of the Academy. "Give me the True."

Denzil did nothing of the sort. He didn't happen to have it about him.

Denzil Cantercot stood smoking a cigarette in his landlord's shop, and imparting an air of distinction and an agreeable aroma to the close leathery atmosphere. Crowl cobbled away, talking to his tenant without raising his eyes. He was a small, big-headed, sallow, sad-eyed man, with a greasy apron. Denzil was wearing a heavy overcoat with a fur collar. He was never seen without it in public during the winter. In private he removed it and sat in his shirt sleeves. Crowl was a thinker, or thought he was—which seems to involve original thinking anyway. His hair was thinning rapidly at the top, as if his brain were struggling to get as near as possible to the realities of things. He prided himself on having no fads. Few men are without some foible or hobby; Crowl felt almost lonely at times in his superiority. He was a Vegetarian, a Secularist, a Blue Ribbonite, a Republican, and an Anti-tobacconist. Meat was a fad. Drink was a fad. Religion was a fad. Monarchy was a fad. Tobacco was a fad. "A plain man like me," Crowl used to say, "can live without fads." "A plain man" was Crowl's catchword. When of a Sunday morning he stood on Mile End Waste, which was opposite his shop—and held forth to the crowd on the evils of kings, priests, and mutton chops, the "plain man" turned up at intervals like the "theme" of a symphonic movement. "I am only a plain man and I want to know." It was a phrase that sabered the spider-webs of logical refinement, and held

them up scornfully on the point. When Crowl went for a little recreation in
Victoria Park on Sunday afternoons, it was with this phrase that he invariably
routed the supernaturalists. Crowl knew his Bible better than most ministers, and
always carried a minutely-printed copy in his pocket, dog-eared to mark contradictions in the text. The second chapter of Jeremiah says one thing; the first chapter
of Corinthians says another. Two contradictory statements *may* both be true, but
"I am only a plain man, and I want to know." Crowl spent a large part of his time
in setting "the word against the word." Cock-fighting affords its votaries no acuter
pleasure than Crowl derived from setting two texts by the ears. Crowl had a metaphysical genius which sent his Sunday morning disciples frantic with admiration,
and struck the enemy dumb with dismay. He had discovered, for instance, that the
Deity could not *move*, owing to already filling all space. He was also the first to
invent, for the confusion of the clerical, the crucial case of a saint dying at the
Antipodes contemporaneously with another in London. Both went skyward to
Heaven, yet the two traveled in directly opposite directions. In all eternity they
would never meet. Which, then, got to Heaven? Or was there no such place? "I
am only a plain man, and I want to know."

Preserve us our open spaces; they exist to testify to the incurable interest of
humanity in the Unknown and the Misunderstood. Even 'Arry is capable of five
minutes' attention to speculative theology, if 'Arriet isn't in a 'urry.

Peter Crowl was not sorry to have a lodger like Denzil Cantercot, who, though
a man of parts and thus worth powder and shot, was so hopelessly wrong on all
subjects under the sun. In only one point did Peter Crowl agree with Denzil
Cantercot—he admired Denzil Cantercot secretly. When he asked him for the
True—which was about twice a day on the average—he didn't really expect to get
it from him. He knew that Denzil was a poet.

"The Beautiful," he went on, "is a thing that only appeals to men like you.
The True is for all men. The majority have the first claim. Till then you poets
must stand aside. The True and the Useful—that's what we want. The Good of
Society is the only test of things. Everything stands or falls by the Good of Society."

"The Good of Society!" echoed Denzil scornfully. "What's the good of Society?
The Individual is before all. The mass must be sacrificed to the Great Man.
Otherwise the Great Man will be sacrificed to the mass. Without great men there
would be no art. Without art life would be a blank."

"Ah, but we should fill it up with bread and butter," said Peter Crowl.

"Yes, it is bread and butter that kills the Beautiful," said Denzil Cantercot
bitterly. "Many of us start by following the butterfly through the verdant meadows,
but we turn aside—"

"To get the grub," chuckled Peter, cobbling away.

"Peter, if you make a jest of everything, I'll not waste my time on you."

Denzil's wild eyes flashed angrily. He shook his long hair. Life was very serious
to him. He never wrote comic verse intentionally.

There are three reasons why men of genius have long hair. One is, that they forget it is growing. The second is, that they like it. The third is, that it comes cheaper; they wear it long for the same reason that they wear their hats long.

Owing to this pecularity of genius, you may get quite a reputation for lack of twopence. The economic reason did not apply to Denzil, who could always get credit with the profession on the strength of his appearance. Therefore, when street arabs vocally commanded him to get his hair cut, they were doing no service to barbers. Why does all the world watch over barbers and conspire to promote their interests? Denzil would have told you it was not to serve the barbers, but to gratify the crowd's instinctive resentment of originality. In his palmy days Denzil had been an editor, but he no more thought of turning his scissors against himself than of swallowing his paste. The efficacy of hair has changed since the days of Samson, otherwise Denzil would have been a Hercules instead of a long, thin, nervous man, looking too brittle and delicate to be used even for a pipe-cleaner. The narrow oval of his face sloped to a pointed, untrimmed beard. His linen was reproachable, his dingy boots were down at heel, and his cocked hat was drab with dust. Such are the effects of a love for the Beautiful.

Peter Crowl was impressed with Denzil's condemnation of flippancy, and he hastened to turn off the joke.

"I'm quite serious," he said. "Butterflies are no good to nothing or nobody; caterpillars at least save the birds from starving."

"Just like your view of things, Peter," said Denzil. "Good morning, madam." This to Mrs. Crowl, to whom he removed his hat with elaborate courtesy. Mrs. Crowl grunted and looked at her husband with a note of interrogation in each eye. For some seconds Crowl stuck to his last, endeavoring not to see the question. He shifted uneasily on his stool. His wife coughed grimly. He looked up, saw her towering over him, and helplessly shook his head in a horizontal direction. It was wonderful how Mrs. Crowl towered over Mr. Crowl, even when he stood up in his shoes. She measured half an inch less. It was quite an optical illusion.

"Mr. Crowl," said Mrs. Crowl, "then I'll tell him."

"No, no, my dear, not yet," faltered Peter, helplessly; "leave it to me."

"I've left it to you long enough. You'll never do nothing. If it was a question of provin' to a lot of chuckleheads that Jollygee and Genesis, or some other dead and gone Scripture folk that don't consarn no mortal soul, used to contradict each other, your tongue 'ud run thirteen to the dozen. But when it's a matter of takin' the bread out o' the mouths o' your own children, you ain't got no more to say for yourself than a lamppost. Here's a man stayin' with you for weeks and weeks— eatin' and drinkin' the flesh off your bones—without payin' a far—"

"Hush, hush, mother; it's all right," said poor Crowl, red as fire.

Denzil looked at her dreamily. "It is possible you are alluding to me, Mrs. Crowl?" he said.

"Who then should I be alludin' to, Mr. Cantercot? Here's seven weeks come and gone, and not a blessed 'aypenny have I—"

"My dear Mrs. Crowl," said Denzil, removing his cigarette from his mouth with a pained air, "why reproach *me* for *your* neglect?"

"*My* neglect! I like that!"

"I don't," said Denzil more sharply. "If you had sent me in the bill you would have had the money long ago. How do you expect me to think of these details?"

"We ain't so grand down here. People pays their way—they don't get no *bills*," said Mrs. Crowl, accentuating the word with infinite scorn.

Peter hammered away at a nail, as though to drown his spouse's voice.

"It's three pounds fourteen and eightpence, if you're so anxious to know," Mrs. Crowl resumed. "And there ain't a woman in the Mile End Road as 'ud a-done it cheaper, with bread at fourpence three-farden a quartern and landlords clamorin' for rent every Monday morning almost afore the sun's up and folks draggin' and slidderin' on till their shoes is only fit to throw after brides and Christmas comin' and sevenpence a week for schoolin'!"

Peter winced under the last item. He had felt it coming—like Christmas. His wife and he parted company on the question of Free Education. Peter felt that having brought nine children into the world, it was only fair he should pay a penny a week for each of those old enough to bear educating. His better half argued that, having so many children, they ought in reason to be exempted. Only people who had few children could spare the penny. But the one point on which the cobbler-skeptic of the Mile End Road got his way was this of the fees. It was a question of conscience, and Mrs. Crowl had never made application for their remission, though she often slapped her children in vexation instead. They were used to slapping, and when nobody else slapped them they slapped one another. They were bright, ill-mannered brats, who pestered their parents and worried their teachers, and were as happy as the Road was long.

"Bother the school fees!" Peter retorted, vexed. "Mr. Cantercot's not responsible for your children."

"I should hope not, indeed, Mr. Crowl," Mrs. Crowl said sternly. "I'm ashamed of you." And with that she flounced out of the shop into the back parlor.

"It's all right," Peter called after her soothingly. "The money'll be all right, mother."

In lower circles it is customary to call your wife your mother; in somewhat superior circles it is the fashion to speak of her as "the wife," as you speak of "the Stock Exchange," or "the Thames," without claiming any peculiar property. Instinctively men are ashamed of being moral and domesticated.

Denzil puffed his cigarette, unembarrassed. Peter bent attentively over his work, making nervous stabs with his awl. There was a long silence. An organ-grinder played a waltz outside, unregarded; and, failing to annoy anybody, moved on. Denzil lit another cigarette. The dirty-faced clock on the wall chimed twelve.

"What do you think," said Crowl, "of Republics?"

"They are low," Denzil replied. "Without a Monarch there is no visible incarnation of Authority."

"What! do you call Queen Victoria visible?"

"Peter, do you want to drive me from the house? Leave frivolousness to women, whose minds are only large enough for domestic difficulties. Republics are low. Plato mercifully kept the poets out of his. Republics are not congenial soil for poetry."

"What nonsense! If England dropped its fad of Monarchy and became a Republic to-morrow, do you mean to say that—?"

"I mean to say there would be no Poet Laureate to begin with."

"Who's fribbling now, you or me, Cantercot? But I don't care a button-hook about poets, present company always excepted. I'm only a plain man, and I want to know where's the sense of givin' any one person authority over everybody else?"

"Ah, that's what Tom Mortlake used to say. Wait till you're in power, Peter, with trade-union money to control, and working men bursting to give you flying angels and to carry you aloft, like a banner, huzzahing."

"Ah, that's because he's head and shoulders above 'em already," said Crowl, with a flash in his sad grey eyes. "Still, it don't prove that I'd talk any different. And I think you're quite wrong about his being spoilt. Tom's a fine fellow—a man every inch of him, and that's a good many. I don't deny he has his weaknesses, and there was a time when he stood in this very shop and denounced that poor dead Constant. 'Crowl,' said he, 'that man'll do mischief. I don't like these kid-glove philanthropists mixing themselves up in practical labor disputes they don't understand.' "

Denzil whistled involuntarily. It was a piece of news.

"I dare say," continued Crowl, "he's a bit jealous of anybody's interference with his influence. But in this case the jealousy did wear off, you see, for the poor fellow and he got quite pals, as everybody knows. Tom's not the man to hug a prejudice. However, all that don't prove nothing against Republics. Look at the Czar and the Jews. I'm only a plain man, but I wouldn't live in Russia for—not for all the leather in it! An Englishman, taxed as he is to keep up his Fad of Monarchy, is at least king in his own castle, whoever bosses it at Windsor. Excuse me a minute, the missus is callin'."

"Excuse *me* a minute. I'm going, and I want to say before I go—I feel it only right you should know at once—that after what has passed to-day I can never be on the same footing here as in the—shall I say pleasant?—days of yore."

"Oh, no, Cantercot. Don't say that; don't say that!" pleaded the little cobbler.

"Well, shall I say unpleasant, then?"

"No, no, Cantercot. Don't misunderstand me. Mother has been very much put to it lately to rub along. You see she has such a growing family. It grows—daily. But never mind her. You pay whenever you've got the money."

Denzil shook his head. "It cannot be. You know when I came here first I rented your top room and boarded myself. Then I learnt to know you. We talked together. Of the Beautiful. And the Useful. I found you had no soul. But you were honest, and I liked you. I went so far as to take my meals with your family. I made myself at home in your back parlor. But the vase has been shattered (I do not refer to that on the mantelpiece), and though the scent of the roses may cling to it still, it can be pieced together—nevermore." He shook his hair sadly and shambled out of the shop. Crowl would have gone after him, but Mrs. Crowl was still calling, and ladies must have the precedence in all polite societies.

Cantercot went straight—or as straight as his loose gait permitted—to 46 Glover Street, and knocked at the door. Grodman's factotum opened it. She was a pock-marked person, with a brickdust complexion and a coquettish manner.

"Oh! here we are again!" she said vivaciously.

"Don't talk like a clown," Cantercot snapped. "Is Mr. Grodman in?"

"No, you've put him out," growled the gentleman himself, suddenly appearing in his slippers. "Come in. What the devil have you been doing with yourself since the inquest? Drinking again?"

"I've sworn off. Haven't touched a drop since—"

"The murder?"

"Eh?" said Denzil Cantercot, startled. "What do you mean?"

"What I say. Since December 4. I reckon everything from that murder, now, as they reckon longitude from Greenwich."

"Oh," said Denzil Cantercot.

"Let me see. Nearly a fortnight. What a long time to keep away from Drink—and Me."

"I don't know which is worse," said Denzil, irritated. "You both steal away my brains."

"Indeed?" said Grodman, with an amused smile. "Well, it's only petty pilfering, after all. What's put salt on your wounds?"

"The twenty-fourth edition of my book."

"*Whose* book?"

"Well, *your* book. You must be making piles of money out of *Criminals I Have Caught*."

" 'Criminals *I* Have Caught,' " corrected Grodman. "My dear Denzil, how often am I to point out that *I* went through the experiences that make the backbone of my book, not *you?* In each case *I* cooked the criminal's goose. Any journalist could have supplied the dressing."

"The contrary. The journeymen of journalism would have left the truth naked. You yourself could have done that—for there is no man to beat you at cold, lucid, scientific statement. But I idealized the bare facts and lifted them into the realm of poetry and literature. The twenty-fourth edition of the book attests my success."

"Rot! The twenty-fourth edition was all owing to the murder. Did you do that?"

"You take one up so sharply, Mr. Grodman," said Denzil, changing his tone.

"No—I've retired," laughed Grodman.

Denzil did not reprove the ex-detective's flippancy. He even laughed a little.

"Well, give me another fiver, and I'll cry 'quits.' I'm in debt."

"Not a penny. Why haven't you been to see me since the murder? I had to write that letter to the *Pell Mell Press* myself. You might have earned a crown."

"I've had writer's cramp, and couldn't do your last job. I was coming to tell you so on the morning of the—"

"Murder. So you said at the inquest."

"It's true."

"Of course. Weren't you on your oath? It was very zealous of you to get up so early to tell me. In which hand did you have the cramp?"

"Why, in the right, of course."

"And you couldn't write with your left?"

"I don't think I could even hold a pen."

"Or any other instrument, mayhap. What had you been doing to bring it on?"

"Writing too much. That is the only possible cause."

"Oh! I didn't know. Writing what?"

Denzil hesitated. "An epic poem."

"No wonder you're in debt. Will a sovereign get you out of it?"

"No; it wouldn't be in the least use to me."

"Here it is, then."

Denzil took the coin and his hat.

"Aren't you going to earn it, you beggar? Sit down and write something for me."

Denzil got pen and paper, and took his place.

"What do you want me to write?"

"Your Epic Poem."

Denzil started and flushed. But he set to work. Grodman leaned back in his arm-chair and laughed, studying the poet's grave face.

Denzil wrote three lines and paused.

"Can't remember any more? Well, read me the start."

Denzil read:

> Of man's first disobedience and the fruit
> Of that forbidden tree whose mortal taste
> Brought death into the world—

"Hold on!" cried Grodman. "What morbid subjects you choose, to be sure."

"Morbid! Why, Milton chose the same subject!"

"Blow Milton. Take yourself off—you and your Epics."

Denzil went. The pock-marked person opened the street door for him.

"When am I to have that new dress, dear?" she whispered coquettishly.

"I have no money, Jane," he said shortly.

"You have a sovereign."

Denzil gave her the sovereign, and slammed the door viciously. Grodman overheard their whispers, and laughed silently. His hearing was acute. Jane had first introduced Denzil to his acquaintance about two years ago, when he spoke of getting an amanuensis, and the poet had been doing odd jobs for him ever since. Grodman argued that Jane had her reasons. Without knowing them, he got a hold over both. There was no one, he felt, he could not get a hold over. All men—and women—have something to conceal, and you have only to pretend to know what it is. Thus Grodman, who was nothing if not scientific.

Denzil Cantercot shambled home thoughtfully, and abstractedly took his place at the Crowl dinner-table.

6

Mrs. Crowl surveyed Denzil Cantercot so stonily and cut him his beef so savagely that he said grace when the dinner was over. Peter fed his metaphysical genius on tomatoes. He was tolerant enough to allow his family to follow their Fads; but no savory smells ever tempted him to be false to his vegetable loves. Besides, meat might have reminded him too much of his work. There is nothing like leather, but Bow beefsteaks occasionally come very near it.

After dinner Denzil usually indulged in poetic reverie. But to-day he did not take his nap. He went out at once to "raise the wind." But there was a dead calm everywhere. In vain he asked for an advance at the office of the *Mile End Mirror*, to which he contributed scathing leaderettes about vestrymen. In vain he trudged to the City and offered to write the *Ham and Eggs Gazette* an essay on the modern methods of bacon-curing. Denzil knew a great deal about the breeding and slaughtering of pigs, smoke-lofts and drying processes, having for years dictated the policy of the *New Pork Herald* in these momentous matters. Denzil also knew a great deal about many other esoteric matters, including weaving machines, the manufacture of cabbage leaves and snuff, and the inner economy of drain-pipes. He had written for the trade papers since boyhood. But there is great competition on these papers. So many men of literary gifts know all about the intricate technicalities of manufactures and markets, and are eager to set the trade right. Grodman perhaps hardly allowed sufficiently for the step backwards that Denzil made when he devoted his whole time for months to *Criminals I Have Caught*. It was as damaging as a debauch. For when your rivals are pushing forwards, to stand still is to go back.

In despair Denzil shambled toilsomely to Bethnal Green. He paused before a window of a little tobacconist's shop, wherein was displayed a placard announcing

PLOTS FOR SALE

The announcement went on to state that a large stock of plots was to be obtained on the premises—embracing sensational plots, humorous plots, love plots, religious plots, and poetic plots; also complete manuscripts, original novels, poems, and tales. Apply within.

It was a very dirty-looking shop, with begrimed bricks and blackened woodwork. The window contained some musty old books, an assortment of pipes and tobacco, and a large number of the vilest daubs unhung, painted in oil on Academy boards, and unframed. These were intended for landscapes, as you could tell from the titles. The most expensive was "Chingford Church," and it was marked 1s. 9d. The others ran from 6d. to 1s. 3d., and were mostly representations of Scottish scenery—a loch with mountains in the background, with solid reflections in the water and a tree in the foreground. Sometimes the tree would be in the background. Then the loch would be in the foreground. Sky and water were intensely blue in all. The name of the collection was "Original oil-paintings done by hand." Dust lay thick upon everything, as if carefully shoveled on; and the proprietor looked as if he slept in his shop-window at night without taking his clothes off. He was a gaunt man with a red nose, long but scanty black locks covered by a smoking cap, and a luxuriant black mustache. He smoked a long clay pipe, and had the air of a broken-down operatic villain.

"Ah, good afternoon, Mr. Cantercot," he said, rubbing his hands, half from cold, half from usage; "what have you brought me?"

"Nothing," said Denzil, "but if you will lend me a sovereign I'll do you a stunner."

The operatic villain shook his locks, his eyes full of pawky cunning. "If you did it after that, it *would* be a stunner."

What the operatic villain did with these plots, and who bought them, Cantercot never knew nor cared to know. Brains are cheap to-day, and Denzil was glad enough to find a customer.

"Surely you've known me long enough to trust me," he cried.

"Trust is dead," said the operatic villain, puffing away.

"So is Queen Anne," cried the irritated poet. His eyes took a dangerous hunted look. Money he must have. But the operatic villain was inflexible. No plot, no supper.

Poor Denzil went out flaming. He knew not where to turn. Temporarily he turned on his heel again and stared despairingly at the shop-window. Again he read the legend

PLOTS FOR SALE.

He stared so long at this that it lost its meaning. When the sense of the words suddenly flashed upon him again, they bore a new significance. He went in meekly, and borrowed fourpence of the operatic villain. Then he took the 'bus for

Scotland Yard. There was a not ill-looking servant girl in the 'bus. The rhythm of the vehicle shaped itself into rhymes in his brain. He forgot all about his situation and his object. He had never really written an epic—except "Paradise Lost"—but he composed lyrics about wine and women and often wept to think how miserable he was. But nobody ever bought anything of him, except articles on bacon-curing or attacks on vestrymen. He was a strange, wild creature, and the wench felt quite pretty under his ardent gaze. It almost hypnotized her, though, and she looked down at her new French kid boots to escape it.

At Scotland Yard Denzil asked for Edward Wimp. Edward Wimp was not on view. Like kings and editors, detectives are difficult of approach—unless you are a criminal, when you cannot see anything of them at all. Denzil knew of Edward Wimp, principally because of Grodman's contempt for his successor. Wimp was a man of taste and culture. Grodman's interests were entirely concentrated on the problems of logic and evidence. Books about these formed his sole reading; for *belles lettres* he cared not a straw. Wimp, with his flexible intellect, had a great contempt for Grodman and his slow, laborious, ponderous, almost Teutonic methods. Worse, he almost threatened to eclipse the radiant tradition of Grodman by some wonderfully ingenious bits of workmanship. Wimp was at his greatest in collecting circumstantial evidence; in putting two and two together to make five. He would collect together a number of dark and disconnected data and flash across them the electric light of some unifying hypothesis in a way which would have done credit to a Darwin or a Faraday. An intellect which might have served to unveil the secret workings of nature was subverted to the protection of a capitalistic civilization.

By the assistance of a friendly policeman, whom the poet magnetized into the belief that his business was a matter of life and death, Denzil obtained the great detective's private address. It was near King's Cross. By a miracle Wimp was at home in the afternoon. He was writing when Denzil was ushered up three pairs of stairs into his presence, but he got up and flashed the bull's-eye of his glance upon the visitor.

"Mr. Denzil Cantercot, I believe," said Wimp.

Denzil started. He had not sent up his name, merely describing himself as a gentleman.

"That is my name," he murmured.

"You were one of the witnesses at the inquest on the body of the late Arthur Constant. I have your evidence there." He pointed to a file. "Why have you come to give fresh evidence?"

Again Denzil started, flushing in addition this time. "I want money," he said, almost involuntarily.

"Sit down." Denzil sat. Wimp stood.

Wimp was young and fresh-colored. He had a Roman nose, and was smartly dressed. He had beaten Grodman by discovering the wife Heaven meant for him.

He had a bouncing boy, who stole jam out of the pantry without anyone being the wiser. Wimp did what work he could do at home in a secluded study at the top of the house. Outside his chamber of horrors he was the ordinary husband of commerce. He adored his wife, who thought poorly of his intellect but highly of his heart. In domestic difficulties Wimp was helpless. He could not tell even whether the servant's "character" was forged or genuine. Probably he could not level himself to such petty problems. He was like the senior wrangler who has forgotten how to do quadratics, and has to solve equations of the second degree by the calculus.

"How much money do you want?" he asked.

"I do not make bargains," Denzil replied, his calm come back by this time. "I came here to tender you a suggestion. It struck me that you might offer me a fiver for my trouble. Should you do so, I shall not refuse it."

"You shall not refuse it—if you deserve it."

"Good. I will come to the point at once. My suggestion concerns—Tom Mortlake."

Denzil threw out the name as if it were a torpedo. Wimp did not move.

"Tom Mortlake," went on Denzil, looking disappointed, "had a sweetheart." He paused impressively.

Wimp said, "Yes?"

"Where is that sweetheart now?"

"Where, indeed?"

"You know about her disappearance?"

"You have just informed me of it."

"Yes, she is gone—without a trace. She went about a fortnight before Mr. Constant's murder."

"Murder? How do you know it was murder?"

"Mr. Grodman says so," said Denzil, startled again.

"H'm! Isn't that rather a proof that it was suicide? Well, go on."

"About a fortnight before the suicide, Jessie Dymond disappeared. So they tell me in Stepney Green, where she lodged and worked."

"What was she?"

"She was a dressmaker. She had a wonderful talent. Quite fashionable ladies got to know of it. One of her dresses was presented at Court. I think the lady forgot to pay for it; so Jessie's landlady said."

"Did she live alone?"

"She had no parents, but the house was respectable."

"Good-looking, I suppose?"

"As a poet's dream."

"As yours, for instance?"

"I am a poet; I dream."

"You dream you are a poet. Well, well! She was engaged to Mortlake?"

"Oh yes! They made no secret of it. The engagement was an old one. When he was earning 36s. a week as a compositor, they were saving up to buy a home. He worked at Railton and Hockes' who print the *New Pork Herald*. I used to take my 'copy' into the comps' room, and one day the Father of the Chapel told me all about 'Mortlake and his young woman.' Ye gods! How times are changed! Two years ago Mortlake had to struggle with my calligraphy—now he is in with all the nobs, and goes to the 'At Homes' of the aristocracy."

"Radical M.P.'s," murmured Wimp, smiling.

"While I am still barred from the dazzling drawing-rooms, where beauty and intellect forgather. A mere artisan! A manual laborer!" Denzil's eyes flashed angrily. He rose with excitement. "They say he always *was* a jabberer in the composing room, and he has jabbered himself right out of it and into a pretty good thing. He didn't have much to say about the crimes of capital when he was set up to second the toast of 'Railton and Hockes' at the beanfest."

"Toast and butter, toast and butter," said Wimp genially. "I shouldn't blame a man for serving the two together, Mr. Cantercot."

Denzil forced a laugh. "Yes; but consistency's *my* motto. I like to see the royal soul immaculate. unchanging, immovable by fortune. Anyhow, when better times came for Mortlake the engagement still dragged on. He did not visit her so much. This last autumn he saw very little of her."

"How do you know?"

"I—I was often in Stepney Green. My business took me past the house of an evening. Sometimes there was no light in her room. That meant she was downstairs gossiping with the landlady."

"She might have been out with Tom?"

"No, sir; I knew Tom was on the platform somewhere or other. He was working up to all hours organizing the eight hours working movement."

"A very good reason for relaxing his sweethearting."

"It was. He never went to Stepney Green on a week night."

"But you always did."

"No—not every night."

"You didn't go in?"

"Never. She wouldn't permit my visits. She was a girl of strong character. She always reminded me of Flora Macdonald."

"Another lady of your acquaintance?"

"A lady I know better than the shadows who surround me, who is more real to me than the women who pester me for the price of apartments. Jessie Dymond, too, was of the race of heroines. Her eyes were clear blue, two wells with Truth at the bottom of each. When I looked into those eyes my own were dazzled. They were the only eyes I could never make dreamy." He waved his hand as if making a pass with it. "It was she who had the influence over me."

"You knew her, then?"

"Oh, yes. I knew Tom from the old *New Pork Herald* days, and when I first met him with Jessie hanging on his arm he was quite proud to introduce her to a poet. When he got on he tried to shake me off."

"You should have repaid him what you borrowed."

"It—it—was only a trifle," stammered Denzil.

"Yes, but the world turns on trifles," said the wise Wimp.

"The world is itself a trifle," said the pensive poet. "The Beautiful alone is deserving of our regard."

"And when the Beautiful was not gossiping with her landlady, did she gossip with you as you passed the door?"

"Alas, no! She sat in her room reading, and cast a shadow—"

"On your life?"

"No; on the blind."

"Always one shadow?"

"No, sir. Once or twice, two."

"Ah, you had been drinking."

"On my life, not. I have sworn off the treacherous wine-cup."

"That's right. Beer is bad for poets. It makes their feet shaky. Whose was the second shadow?"

"A man's."

"Naturally. Mortlake's, perhaps."

"Impossible. He was still striking eight hours."

"You found out whose shadow? You didn't leave a shadow of doubt?"

"No; I waited till the substance came out."

"It was Arthur Constant."

"You are a magician! You—you terrify me. Yes, it was he."

"Only once or twice, you say?"

"I didn't keep watch over them."

"No, no, of course not. You only passed casually, I understand you thoroughly."

Denzil did not feel comfortable at the assertion.

"What did he go there for?" Wimp went on.

"I don't know. I'd stake my soul on Jessie's honor."

"You might double your stake without risk."

"Yes, I might! I would! You see her with my eyes."

"For the moment they are the only ones available. When was the last time you saw the two together?"

"About the middle of November."

"Mortlake knew nothing of the meetings?"

"I don't know. Perhaps he did. Mr. Constant had probably enlisted her in his social mission work. I knew she was one of the attendants at the big children's tea in the Great Assembly Hall early in November. He treated her quite like a lady. She was the only attendant who worked with her hands."

"The others carried the cups on their feet, I suppose."

"No; how could that be? My meaning is that all the other attendants were real ladies, and Jessie was only an amateur, so to speak. There was no novelty for her in handing kids cups of tea. I daresay she had helped her landlady often enough at that—there's quite a bushel of brats below stairs. It's almost as bad as at friend Crowl's. Jessie was a real brick. But perhaps Tom didn't know her value. Perhaps he didn't like Constant to call on her, and it led to a quarrel. Anyhow, she's disappeared, like the snowfall on the river. There's not a trace. The landlady, who was such a friend of hers that Jessie used to make up her stuff into dresses for nothing, tells me that she's dreadfully annoyed at not having been left the slightest clue to her late tenant's whereabouts."

"You have been making inquiries on your own account apparently?"

"Only of the landlady. Jessie never even gave her the week's notice, but paid her in lieu of it, and left immediately. The landlady told me I could have knocked her down with a feather. Unfortunately, I wasn't there to do it, or I should certainly have knocked her down for not keeping her eyes open better. She says if she had only had the least suspicion beforehand that the minx (she dared to call Jessie a minx) was going, she'd have known where, or her name would have been somebody else's. And yet she admits that Jessie was looking ill and worried. Stupid old hag!"

"A woman of character," murmured the detective.

"Didn't I tell you so?" cried Denzil eagerly. "Another girl would have let it out that she was going. But no, not a word. She plumped down the money and walked out. The landlady ran upstairs. None of Jessie's things were there. She must have quietly sold them off, or transferred them to the new place. I never in my life met a girl who so thoroughly knew her own mind or had a mind so worth knowing. She always reminded me of the Maid of Saragossa."

"Indeed! And when did she leave?"

"On the 19th of November."

"Mortlake of course knows where she is?"

"I can't say. Last time I was at the house to inquire—it was at the end of November—he hadn't been seen there for six weeks. He wrote to her, of course, sometimes—the landlady knew his writing."

Wimp looked Denzil straight in the eyes, and said, "You mean, of course, to accuse Mortlake of the murder of Mr. Constant?"

"N-n-no, not at all," stammered Denzil, "only you know what Mr. Grodman wrote to the *Pell Mell*. The more we know about Mr. Constant's life the more we shall know about the manner of his death. I thought my information would be valuable to you, and I brought it."

"And why didn't you take it to Mr. Grodman?"

"Because I thought it wouldn't be valuable to *me*."

"You wrote *Criminals I Have Caught*?"

"How—how do you know that?" Wimp was startling him today with a vengeance.

"Your style, my dear Mr. Cantercot. The unique noble style."

"Yes, I was afraid it would betray me," said Denzil. "And since you know, I may tell you that Grodman's a mean curmudgeon. What does he want with all that money and those houses—a man with no sense of the Beautiful? He'd have taken my information, and given me more kicks than ha'pence for it, so to speak."

"Yes, he is a shrewd man after all. I don't see anything valuable in your evidence against Mortlake."

"No!" said Denzil in a disappointed tone, and fearing he was going to be robbed. "Not when Mortlake was already jealous of Mr. Constant, who was a sort of rival organizer, unpaid! A kind of blackleg doing the work cheaper—nay, for nothing."

"Did Mortlake tell you he was jealous?" said Wimp, a shade of sarcastic contempt piercing through his tones.

"Oh, yes! He said to me, 'That man will work mischief. I don't like your kid-glove philanthropists meddling in matters they don't understand.' "

"Those were his very words?"

"His *ipsissima verba*."

"Very well. I have your address in my files. Here is a sovereign for you."

"Only one sovereign! It's not the least use to me."

"Very well. It's of great use to me. I have a wife to keep."

"I haven't," said Denzil with a sickly smile, "so perhaps I can manage on it after all." He took his hat and the sovereign.

Outside the door he met a rather pretty servant just bringing in some tea to her master. He nearly upset her tray at sight of her. She seemed more amused at the *rencontre* than he.

"Good afternoon, dear," she said coquettishly. "You might let me have that sovereign. I do so want a new Sunday bonnet."

Denzil gave her the sovereign, and slammed the hall-door viciously when he got to the bottom of the stairs. He seemed to be walking arm-in-arm with the long arm of coincidence. Wimp did not hear the duologue. He was already busy on his evening's report to headquarters. The next day Denzil had a body-guard wherever he went. It might have gratified his vanity had he known it. But to-night he was yet unattended, so no one noted that he went to 46 Glover Street, after the early Crowl supper. He could not help going. He wanted to get another sovereign. He also itched to taunt Grodman. Not succeeding in the former object, he felt the road open for the second.

"Do you still hope to discover the Bow murderer?" he asked the old blood-hound.

"I can lay my hand on him now," Grodman announced curtly.

Denzil hitched his chair back involuntarily. He found conversation with detectives as lively as playing at skittles with bombshells. They got on his nerves terribly, these undemonstrative gentlemen with no sense of the Beautiful.

"But why don't you give him up to justice?" he murmured.

"Ah—it has to be proved yet. But it is only a matter of time."

"Oh!" said Denzil, "and shall I write the story for you?"

"No. You will not live long enough."

Denzil turned white. "Nonsense! I am years younger than you," he gasped.

"Yes," said Grodman, "but you drink so much."

7

When Wimp invited Grodman to eat his Christmas plum-pudding at King's Cross, Grodman was only a little surprised. The two men were always overwhelmingly cordial when they met, in order to disguise their mutual detestation. When people really like each other, they make no concealment of their mutual contempt. In his letter to Grodman, Wimp said that he thought it might be nicer for him to keep Christmas in company than in solitary state. There seems to be a general prejudice in favor of Christmas numbers, and Grodman yielded to it. Besides, he thought that a peep at the Wimp domestic interior would be as good as a pantomime. He quite enjoyed the fun that was coming, for he knew that Wimp had not invited him out of mere "peace and goodwill."

There was only one other guest at the festive board. This was Wimp's wife's mother's mother, a lady of sweet seventy. Only a minority of mankind can obtain a grandmother-in-law by marrying, but Wimp was not unduly conceited. The old lady suffered from delusions. One of them was that she was a centenarian. She dressed for the part. It is extraordinary what pains ladies will take to conceal their age. Another of Wimp's grandmother-in-law's delusions was that Wimp had married to get her into the family. Not to frustrate his design, she always gave him her company on high-days and holidays. Wilfred Wimp—the little boy who stole the jam—was in great form at the Christmas dinner. The only drawback to his enjoyment was that its sweets needed no stealing. His mother presided over the platters, and thought how much cleverer Grodman was than her husband. When the pretty servant who waited on them was momentarily out of the room, Grodman had remarked that she seemed very inquisitive. This coincided with Mrs. Wimp's own convictions, though Mr. Wimp could never be brought to see anything unsatisfactory or suspicious about the girl, not even though there were faults in spelling in the "character" with which her last mistress had supplied her.

It was true that the puss had pricked up her ears when Denzil Cantercot's name was mentioned. Grodman saw it, and watched her, and fooled Wimp to the top of his bent. It was, of course, Wimp who introduced the poet's name, and he did it so casually that Grodman perceived at once that he wished to pump him. The idea that the rival bloodhound should come to him for confirmation of suspicions against his pet jackal was too funny. It was almost as funny to Grodman that evidence of some sort should be obviously lying to hand in the bosom of Wimp's hand-maiden; so obviously that Wimp could not see it. Grodman enjoyed his Christmas dinner, secure that he not found a successor after all. Wimp, for his part, contemptuously wondered at the way Grodman's thought hovered about Denzil without grazing the truth. A man constantly about him, too!

"Denzil is a man of genius," said Grodman. "And as such comes under the heading of Suspicious Characters. He has written an Epic Poem and read it to me. It is morbid from start to finish. There is 'death' in the third line. I daresay you know he polished up my book?" Grodman's artlessness was perfect.

"No. You surprise me," Wimp replied. "I'm sure he couldn't have done much to it. Look at your letter in the *Pell Mell*. Who wants more polish and refinement than that showed?"

"Ah, I didn't know you did me the honor of reading that."

"Oh, yes; we both read it," put in Mrs. Wimp. "I told Mr. Wimp it was very clever and cogent. After that quotation from the letter to the poor fellow's *fiancée* there could be no more doubt but that it was murder. Mr. Wimp was convinced by it too, weren't you, Edward?"

Edward coughed uneasily. It was a true statement, and therefore an indiscreet. Grodman would plume himself terribly. At this moment Wimp felt that Grodman had been right in remaining a bachelor. Grodman perceived the humor of the situation, and wore a curious, sub-mocking smile.

"On the day I was born," said Wimp's grandmother-in-law, "over a hundred years ago, there was a babe murdered"—Wimp found himself wishing it had been she. He was anxious to get back to Cantercot. "Don't let us talk shop on Christmas Day," he said, smiling at Grodman. "Besides, murder isn't a very appropriate subject."

"No, it ain't," said Grodman. "How did we get on to it? Oh, yes—Denzil Cantercot. Ha! ha! ha! That's curious, for since Denzil revised *Criminals I Have Caught*, his mind's running on nothing but murders. A poet's brain is easily turned."

Wimp's eye glittered with excitement and contempt for Grodman's blindness. In Grodman's eye there danced an amused scorn of Wimp; to the outsider his amusement appeared at the expense of the poet.

Having wrought his rival up to the highest pitch, Grodman slyly and suddenly unstrung him.

"How lucky for Denzil!" he said, still in the same naïve, facetious Christmasy tone, "that he can prove an alibi in this Constant affair."

"An alibi!" gasped Wimp. "Really?"

"Oh, yes. He was with his wife, you know. She's my woman of all work, Jane. She happened to mention his being with her."

Jane had done nothing of the kind. After the colloquy he had overheard, Grodman had set himself to find out the relation between his two employees. By casually referring to Denzil as "your husband," he so startled the poor woman that she did not attempt to deny the bond. Only once did he use the two words, but he was satisfied. As to the alibi, he had not yet troubled her; but to take its existence for granted would upset and discomfort Wimp. For the moment that was triumph enough for Wimp's guest.

"Par," said Wilfred Wimp, "what's a alleybi? A marble?"

"No, my lad," said Grodman, "it means being somewhere else when you're supposed to be somewhere."

"Ah, playing truant," said Wilfred self-consciously; his school-master had often proved an alibi against him. "Then Denzil will be hanged."

Was it a prophecy? Wimp accepted it as such; as an oracle from the gods bidding him mistrust Grodman. Out of the mouths of little children issueth wisdom; sometimes even when they are not saying their lessons.

"When I was in my cradle, a century ago," said Wimp's grandmother-in-law, "men were hanged for stealing horses."

They silenced her with snapdragon performances.

Wimp was busy thinking how to get at Grodman's factotum.

Grodman was busy thinking how to get at Wimp's domestic.

Neither received any of the usual messages from the Christmas Bells.

The next day was sloppy and uncertain. A thin rain drizzled languidly. One can stand that sort of thing on a summer Bank Holiday; one expects it. But to have a bad December Bank Holiday is too much of a bad thing. Some steps should surely be taken to confuse the weather clerk's chronology. Once let him know that Bank Holiday is coming, and he writes to the company for more water. To-day his stock seemed low, and he was dribbling it out; at times the wintry sun would shine in a feeble, diluted way, and though the holiday-makers would have preferred to take their sunshine neat, they swarmed forth in their myriads whenever there was a ray of hope. But it was only dodging the raindrops; up went the umbrellas again, and the streets became meadows of ambulating mushrooms.

Denzil Cantercot sat in his fur overcoat at the open window, looking at the landscape in water-colors. He smoked an after-dinner cigarette, and spoke of the Beautiful. Crowl was with him. They were in the first-floor front, Crowl's bedroom, which, from its view of the Mile End Road, was livelier than the parlor with its outlook on the backyard. Mrs. Crowl was an anti-tobacconist as regards the best bedroom; but Peter did not like to put the poet or his cigarette out. He felt there was something in common between smoke and poetry, over and above their being both Fads. Besides, Mrs. Crowl was sulking in the kitchen. She had been arranging for an excursion with Peter and the children to Victoria Park. (She had dreamed of the Crystal Palace, but Santa Claus had put no gifts in the cobbler's shoes.) Now she could not risk spoiling the feather in her bonnet. The nine brats expressed their disappointment by slapping one another on the staircases. Peter felt that Mrs. Crowl connected him in some way with the rainfall, and was unhappy. Was it not enough that he had been deprived of the pleasure of pointing out to the superstitious majority the mutual contradictions of Leviticus and the Song of Solomon? It was not often that Crowl could count on such an audience.

"And you still call Nature Beautiful?" he said to Denzil, pointing to the ragged sky and the dripping eaves. "Ugly old scarecrow!"

"Ugly she seems to-day," admitted Denzil. "But what is Ugliness but a higher form of Beauty? You have to look deeper into it to see it; such vision is the priceless gift of the few. To me this wan desolation of sighing rain is lovely as the sea-washed ruins of cities."

"Ah, but you wouldn't like to go out into it," said Peter Crowl. As he spoke the drizzle suddenly thickened into a torrent.

"We do not always kiss the woman we love."

"Speak for yourself, Denzil. I'm only a plain man, and I want to know if Nature isn't a Fad. Hallo, there goes Mortlake! Lord, a minute of this will soak him to the skin."

The labor leader was walking along with bowed head. He did not seem to mind the shower. It was some seconds before he even heard Crowl's invitation to him to take shelter. When he did hear it he shook his head.

"I know I can't offer you a drawing-room with duchesses stuck about it," said Peter, vexed.

Tom turned the handle of the shop door and went in. There was nothing in the world which now galled him more than the suspicion that he was stuck-up and wished to cut old friends. He picked his way through the nine brats who clung affectionately to his wet knees, dispersing them finally by a jet of coppers to scramble for. Peter met him on the stairs and shook his hand lovingly and admiringly, and took him into Mrs. Crowl's bedroom.

"Don't mind what I say, Tom. I'm only a plain man, and my tongue will say what comes uppermost! But it ain't from the soul, Tom, it ain't from the soul," said Peter, punning feebly, and letting a mirthless smile play over his sallow features. "You know Mr. Cantercot, I suppose? The poet."

"Oh, yes; how do you do, Tom?" cried the Poet. "Seen the New Pork Herald lately? Not bad, those old times, eh?"

"No," said Tom, "I wish I was back in them."

"Nonsense, nonsense," said Peter, in much concern. "Look at the good you are doing to the working man. Look how you are sweeping away the Fads. Ah, it's a grand thing to be gifted, Tom. The idea of your chuckin' yourself away on a composin' room! Manual labor is all very well for plain men like me, with no gift but just enough brains to see into the realities of things—to understand that we've got no soul and no immortality, and all that—and too selfish to look after anybody's comfort but my own and mother's and the kids'. But men like you and Cantercot —it ain't right that you should be peggin' away at low material things. Not that I think Cantercot's gospel any value to the masses. The Beautiful is all very well for folks who've got nothing else to think of, but give me the True. You're the man for my money, Mortlake. No reference to the funds, Tom, to which I contribute little enough, Heaven knows; though how a *place* can know anything, Heaven alone knows. *You* give us the Useful, Tom; that's what the world wants more than the Beautiful."

"Socrates said that the Useful *is* the Beautiful," said Denzil.

"That may be," said Peter, "but the Beautiful ain't the Useful."

"Nonsense!" said Denzil. "What about Jessie—I mean Miss Dymond? There's a combination for you. She always reminds me of Grace Darling. How *is* she, Tom?"

"She's dead!" snapped Tom.

"What?" Denzil turned as white as a Christmas ghost.

"It was in the papers," said Tom; "all about her and the lifeboat."

"Oh, you mean Grace Darling," said Denzil, visibly relieved. "I meant Miss Dymond."

"You needn't be so interested in her," said Tom surlily. "She don't appreciate it. Ah, the shower is over. I must be going."

"No, stay a little longer, Tom," pleaded Peter. "I see a lot about you in the papers, but very little of your dear old phiz now. I can't spare the time to go and hear you. But I really must give myself a treat. When's your next show?"

"Oh, I am always giving shows," said Tom, smiling a little. "But my next big performance is on the twenty-first of January, when that picture of poor Mr. Constant is to be unveiled at the Bow Break o' Day Club. They have written to Gladstone and other big pots to come down. I do hope the old man accepts. A non-political gathering like this is the only occasion we could both speak at, and I have never been on the same platform with Gladstone."

He forgot his depression and ill-temper in the prospect, and spoke with more animation.

"No, I should hope not, Tom," said Peter. "What with his Fads about the Bible being a Rock, and Monarchy being the right thing, he is a most dangerous man to lead the Radicals. He never lays his ax to the root of anything—except oak trees."

"Mr. Cantercot!" It was Mrs. Crowl's voice that broke in upon the tirade. "There's a *gentleman* to see you." The astonishment Mrs. Crowl put into the "gentleman" was delightful. It was almost as good as a week's rent to her to give vent to her feelings. The controversial couple had moved away from the window when Tom entered, and had not noticed the immediate advent of another visitor who had spent his time profitably in listening to Mrs. Crowl before asking to see the presumable object of his visit.

"Ask him up if it's a friend of yours, Cantercot," said Peter. It was Wimp. Denzil was rather dubious as to the friendship, but he preferred to take Wimp diluted. "Mortlake's upstairs," he said; "will you come up and see him?"

Wimp had intended a duologue, but he made no objection, so he, too, stumbled through the nine brats to Mrs. Crowl's bedroom. It was a queer quartette. Wimp had hardly expected to find anybody at the house on Boxing Day, but he did not care to waste a day. Was not Grodman, too, on the track? How lucky it was that Denzil had made the first overtures, so that he could approach him without exciting his suspicion.

Mortlake scowled when he saw the detective. He objected to the police—on principle. But Crowl had no idea who the visitor was, even when told his name. He was rather pleased to meet one of Denzil's high-class friends, and welcomed him warmly. Probably he was some famous editor, which would account for his name stirring vague recollections. He summoned the eldest brat and sent him for beer (people would have their Fads), and not without trepidation called down to "Mother" for glasses. "Mother" observed at night (in the same apartment) that the beer money might have paid the week's school fees for half the family.

"We were just talking of poor Mr. Constant's portrait, Mr. Wimp," said the unconscious Crowl; "they're going to unveil it, Mortlake tells me, on the twenty-first of next month at the Bow Break o' Day Club."

"Ah," said Wimp, elated at being spared the trouble of maneuvering the conversation. "Mysterious affair that, Mr. Crowl."

"No; it's the right thing," said Peter. "There ought to be some memorial of the man in the district where he worked and where he died, poor chap." The cobbler brushed away a tear.

"Yes, it's only right," echoed Mortlake a whit eagerly. "He was a noble fellow, a true philanthropist. The only thoroughly unselfish worker I've ever met."

"He was that," said Peter: "and it's a rare pattern in unselfishness. Poor fellow, poor fellow. He preached the Useful, too. I've never met his like. Ah, I wish there was a Heaven for him to go to!" He blew his nose violently with a red pocket-handkerchief.

"Well, he's there, if there *is*," said Tom.

"I hope he is," added Wimp fervently; "but I shouldn't like to go there the way he did."

"You were the last person to see him, Tom, weren't you?" said Denzil.

"Oh, no," answered Tom quickly. "You remember he went out after me; at least, so Mrs. Drabdump said at the inquest."

"That last conversation he had with you, Tom," said Denzil. "He didn't say anything to you that would lead you to suppose—"

"No, of course not!" interrupted Mortlake impatiently.

"Do you really think he was murdered, Tom?" said Denzil.

"Mr. Wimp's opinion on that point is more valuable than mine," replied Tom testily. "It may have been suicide. Men often get sick of life—especially if they are bored," he added meaningly.

"Ah, but you were the last person known to be with him," said Denzil.

Crowl laughed. "Had you there, Tom."

But they did not have Tom there much longer, for he departed, looking even worse-tempered than when he came. Wimp went soon after, and Crowl and Denzil were left to their interminable argumentation concerning the Useful and the Beautiful.

Wimp went West. He had several strings (or cords) to his bow, and he ultimately found himself at Kensal Green Cemetery. Being there, he went down the avenues of the dead to a grave to note down the exact date of a death. It was a day on which the dead seemed enviable. The dull, sodden sky, the dripping, leafless trees, the wet spongy soil, the reeking grass—everything combined to make one long to be in a warm, comfortable grave away from the leaden *ennuis* of life. Suddenly the detective's keen eye caught sight of a figure that made his heart throb with sudden excitement. It was that of a woman in a gray shawl and a brown bonnet standing before a railed-in grave. She had no umbrella. The rain plashed mournfully upon her, but left no trace on her soaking garments. Wimp crept up behind her, but she paid no heed to him. Her eyes were lowered to the grave, which seemed to be drawing them towards it by some strange morbid fascination. His eyes followed hers. The simple headstone bore the name: "Arthur Constant."

Wimp tapped her suddenly on the shoulder.

"How do you do, Mrs. Drabdump?"

Mrs. Drabdump went deadly white. She turned round, staring at Wimp without any recognition.

"You remember me, surely," he said, "I've been down once or twice to your place about that poor gentleman's papers." His eye indicated the grave.

"Lor! I remember you now," said Mrs. Drabdump.

"Won't you come under my umbrella? You must be drenched to the skin."

"It don't matter, sir. I can't take no hurt. I've had the rheumatics this twenty year."

Mrs. Drabdump shrank from accepting Wimp's attentions, not so much perhaps because he was a man as because he was a gentleman. Mrs. Drabdump liked to see the fine folks keep their place, and not contaminate their skirts by contact with the lower castes. "It's set wet, it'll rain right into the new year," she announced. "And they say a bad beginnin' makes a worse endin'." Mrs. Drabdump was one of those persons who give you the idea that they just missed being born barometers.

"But what are you doing in this miserable spot, so far from home?" queried the detective.

"It's Bank Holiday," Mrs. Drabdump reminded him in tones of acute surprise. "I always make a hexcursion on Bank Holiday."

8

The New Year brought Mrs. Drabdump a new lodger. He was an old gentleman with a long gray beard. He rented the rooms of the late Mr. Constant, and lived a very retired life. Haunted rooms or rooms that ought to be haunted if the ghosts of those murdered in them had any self-respect—are supposed to fetch a lower rent in the market. The whole Irish problem might be solved if the spirits of "Mr. Balfour's victims" would only depreciate the value of property to a point consistent with the support of an agricultural population. But Mrs. Drabdump's new lodger paid so much for his rooms that he laid himself open to a suspicion of a special interest in ghosts. Perhaps he was a member of the Psychical Society. The neighborhood imagined him another mad philanthropist, but as he did not appear to be doing any good to anybody it relented and conceded his sanity. Mortlake, who occasionally stumbled across him in the passage, did not trouble himself to think about him at all. He was too full of other troubles and cares. Though he worked harder than ever, the spirit seemed to have gone out of him. Sometimes he forgot himself in a fine rapture of eloquence—lashing himself up into a divine resentment of injustice or a passion of sympathy with the sufferings of his brethren—but mostly he plodded on in dull, mechanical fashion. He still made brief provincial tours, starring a day here and a day there, and everywhere his admirers remarked how jaded and overworked he looked. There was talk of starting a subscription to give him a holiday on the Continent—a luxury obviously unobtainable on the few pounds allowed him per week. The new lodger would doubtless have been pleased to subscribe, for he seemed quite to like occupying Mortlake's chamber the nights he was absent, though he was thoughtful enough not to disturb that hard-working landlady in the adjoining room by unseemly noise. Wimp was always a quiet man.

Meantime the 21st of the month approached, and the East End was in excitement. Mr. Gladstone had consented to be present at the ceremony of unveiling the portrait of Arthur Constant, presented by an unknown donor to the Bow Break o' Day Club, and it was to be a great function. The whole affair was outside the lines of party politics, so that even Conservatives and Socialists considered themselves justified in pestering the committee for tickets. To say nothing of ladies. As the committee decided to be present, nine-tenths of the applications for admission had to be refused, as is usual on these occasions. The committee agreed among themselves to exclude the fair sex altogether as the only way of disposing of their

womankind, who were making speeches as long as Mr. Gladstone's. Each committeeman told his sisters, female cousins, and aunts that the other committeemen
had insisted on divesting the function of all grace; and what could a man do when
he was in a minority of one?

Crowl, who was not a member of the Break o' Day Club, was particularly
anxious to hear the great orator whom he despised; fortunately Mortlake remembered the cobbler's anxiety to hear himself, and on the eve of the ceremony sent
him a ticket. Crowl was in the first flush of possession when Denzil Cantercot
returned, after a sudden and unannounced absence of three days. His clothes were
muddy and tattered, his cocked hat was deformed, his cavalier beard was matted,
and his eyes were bloodshot. The cobbler nearly dropped the ticket at the sight of
him. "Hullo, Cantercot!" he gasped. "Why, where have you been all these days?"

"Terribly busy!" said Denzil. "Here, give me a glass of water. I'm dry as the
Sahara."

Crowl ran inside and got the water, trying hard not to inform Mrs. Crowl of
their lodger's return. "Mother" had expressed herself freely on the subject of the
poet during his absence, and not in terms which would have commended themselves to the poet's fastidious literary sense. Indeed, she did not hesitate to call him
a sponger and a low swindler, who had run away to avoid paying the piper. Her
fool of a husband might be quite sure he would never set eyes on the scoundrel
again. However, Mrs. Crowl was wrong. Here was Denzil back again. And yet Mr.
Crowl felt no sense of victory. He had no desire to crow over his partner and to
utter that "See! didn't I tell you so?" which is a greater consolation than religion in
most of the misfortunes of life. Unfortunately, to get the water, Crowl had to go to
the kitchen; and as he was usually such a temperate man, this desire for drink in
the middle of the day attracted the attention of the lady in possession. Crowl had
to explain the situation. Mrs. Crowl ran into the shop to improve it. Mr. Crowl
followed in dismay, leaving a trail of spilt water in his wake.

"You good-for-nothing, disreputable scarecrow, where have—"

"Hush, mother. Let him drink. Mr. Cantercot is thirsty."

"Does he care if my children are hungry?"

Denzil tossed the water greedily down his throat almost at a gulp, as if it were
brandy.

"Madam," he said, smacking his lips, "I do care. I care intensely. Few things
in life would grieve me more deeply than to hear that a child, a dear little child—
the Beautiful in a nutshell—had suffered hunger. You wrong me." His voice was
tremulous with the sense of injury. Tears stood in his eyes.

"Wrong you? I've no wish to *wrong* you," said Mrs. Crowl. "I should like to
hang you."

"Don't talk of such ugly things," said Denzil, touching his throat nervously.

"Well, what have you been doin' all this time?"

"Why, what should I be doing?"

"How should I know what became of you? I thought it was another murder."

"What!" Denzil's glass dashed to fragments on the floor. "What do you mean?"

But Mrs. Crowl was glaring too viciously at Mr. Crowl to reply. He understood the message as if it were printed. It ran: "You have broken one of my best glasses. You have annihilated threepence, or a week's school fees for half the family." Peter wished she would turn the lightning upon Denzil, a conductor down whom it would run innocuously. He stooped down and picked up the pieces as carefully as if they were cuttings from the Koh-i-noor. Thus the lightning passed harmlessly over his head and flew towards Cantercot.

"What do I mean?" Mrs. Crowl echoed, as if there had been no interval. "I mean that it would be a good thing if you *had* been murdered."

"What beautiful ideas you have, to be sure!" murmured Denzil.

"Yes; but they'd be useful," said Mrs. Crowl, who had not lived with Peter all these years for nothing. "And if you haven't been murdered what *have* you been doing?"

"My dear, my dear," put in Crowl, deprecatingly, looking up from his quadrupedal position like a sad dog, "you are not Cantercot's keeper."

"Oh, ain't I?" flashed his spouse. "Who else keeps him, I should like to know?"

Peter went on picking up the pieces of the Koh-i-noor.

"I have no secrets from Mrs. Crowl," Denzil explained courteously. "I have been working day and night bringing out a new paper. Haven't had a wink of sleep for three nights."

Peter looked up at his bloodshot eyes with respectful interest.

"The capitalist met me in the street—an old friend of mine—I was overjoyed at the *rencontre* and told him the idea I'd been brooding over for months, and he promised to stand all the racket."

"What sort of a paper?" said Peter.

"Can you ask? To what do you think I've been devoting my days and nights but to the cultivation of the Beautiful?"

"Is that what the paper will be devoted to?"

"Yes. To the Beautiful."

"I know," snorted Mrs. Crowl, "with portraits of actresses."

"Portraits? Oh, no!" said Denzil. "That would be the True. Not the Beautiful."

"And what's the name of the paper?" asked Crowl.

"Ah, that's a secret, Peter. Like Scott, I prefer to remain anonymous."

"Just like your Fads. I'm only a plain man, and I want to know where the fun of anonymity comes in? If I had any gifts, I should like to get the credit. It's a right and natural feeling, to my thinking."

"Unnatural, Peter; unnatural. We're all born anonymous, and I'm for sticking close to Nature. Enough for me that I disseminate the Beautiful. Any letters come during my absence, Mrs. Crowl?"

"No," she snapped. "But a gent named Grodman called. He said you hadn't been to see him for some time, and looked annoyed to hear you'd disappeared. How much have you let *him* in for?"

"The man's in *my* debt," said Denzil, annoyed. "I wrote a book for him and he's taken all the credit for it, the rogue! My name doesn't appear even in the Preface. What's that ticket you're looking so lovingly at, Peter?"

"That's for to-night—the unveiling of Constant's portrait. Gladstone speaks. Awful demand for places."

"Gladstone!" sneered Denzil. "Who wants to hear Gladstone! A man who's devoted his life to pulling down the pillars of Church and State."

"A man who's devoted his whole life to propping up the crumbling Fads of Religion and Monarchy. But, for all that, the man has his gifts, and I'm burnin' to hear him."

"I wouldn't go out of my way an inch to hear him," said Denzil; and went up to his room, and when Mrs. Crowl sent him up a cup of nice strong tea at tea-time, the brat who bore it found him lying dressed on the bed, snoring unbeautifully.

The evening wore on. It was fine frosty weather. The Whitechapel Road swarmed with noisy life, as though it were a Saturday night. The stars flared in the sky like the lights of celestial costermongers. Everybody was on the alert for the advent of Mr. Gladstone. He must surely come through the Road on his journey from the West Bow-wards. But nobody saw him or his carriage, except those about the Hall. Probably he went by tram most of the way. He would have caught cold in an open carriage, or bobbing his head out of the window of a closed.

"If he had only been a German prince, or a cannibal king," said Crowl bitterly, as he plodded towards the Club, "we should have disguised Mile End in bunting and blue fire. But perhaps it's a compliment. He knows his London, and it's no use trying to hide the facts from him. They must have queer notions of cities, those monarchs. They must fancy everybody lives in a flutter of flags and walks about under triumphal arches, like as if I were to stitch shoes in my Sunday clothes." By a defiance of chronology Crowl had them on to-day, and they seemed to accentuate the simile.

"And why shouldn't life be fuller of the Beautiful?" said Denzil. The poet had brushed the reluctant mud off his garments to the extent it was willing to go, and had washed his face, but his eyes were still bloodshot from the cultivation of the Beautiful. Denzil was accompanying Crowl to the door of the Club out of good fellowship. Denzil was himself accompanied by Grodman, though less obtrusively. Least obtrusively was he accompanied by his usual Scotland Yard shadows, Wimp's agents. There was a surging nondescript crowd about the Club, so that the police, and the doorkeeper, and the stewards could with difficulty keep out the tide of the ticketless, through which the current of the privileged had equal difficulty in permeating. The streets all around were thronged with people longing for a glimpse of Gladstone. Mortlake drove up in a hansom (his head a self-conscious pendulum of popularity, swaying and bowing to right and left) and received all the pent-up enthusiasm.

"Well, goodbye, Cantercot," said Crowl.

"No, I'll see you to the door, Peter."

They fought their way shoulder to shoulder.

Now that Grodman had found Denzil he was not going to lose him again. He had only found him by accident, for he was himself bound to the unveiling ceremony, to which he had been invited in view of his known devotion to the task of unveiling the Mystery. He spoke to one of the policemen about, who said, "Ay, ay, sir," and he was prepared to follow Denzil, if necessary, and to give up the pleasure of hearing Gladstone for an acuter thrill. The arrest must be delayed no longer.

But Denzil seemed as if he were going in on the heels of Crowl. This would suit Grodman better. He could then have the two pleasures. But Denzil was stopped half-way through the door.

"Ticket, sir!"

Denzil drew himself up to his full height.

"Press," he said majestically. All the glories and grandeurs of the Fourth Estate were concentrated in that haughty monosyllable. Heaven itself is full of journalists who have overawed St. Peter. But the doorkeeper was a veritable dragon.

"What paper, sir?"

"*New Pork Herald*," said Denzil sharply. He did not relish his word being distrusted.

"*New York Herald*," said one of the bystanding stewards, scarce catching the sounds. "Pass him in."

And in the twinkling of an eye Denzil had eagerly slipped inside.

But during the brief altercation Wimp had come up. Even he could not make his face quite impassive, and there was a suppressed intensity in the eyes and a quiver about the mouth. He went in on Denzil's heels, blocking up the doorway with Grodman. The two men were so full of their coming *coups* that they struggled for some seconds, side by side, before they recognized each other. Then they shook hands heartily.

"That was Cantercot just went in, wasn't it, Grodman?" said Wimp.

"I didn't notice," said Grodman, in tones of utter indifference.

At bottom Wimp was terribly excited. He felt that his *coup* was going to be executed under very sensational circumstances. Everything would combine to turn the eyes of the country upon him—nay, of the world, for had not the Big Bow Mystery been discussed in every language under the sun? In these electric times the criminal receives a cosmopolitan reputation. It is a privilege he shares with few other artists. This time Wimp would be one of them. And, he felt, deservedly so. If the criminal had been cunning to the point of genius in planning the murder, he had been acute to the point of divination in detecting it. Never before had he pieced together so broken a chain. He could not resist the unique opportunity of setting a sensational scheme in a sensational framework. The dramatic instinct was strong in him; he felt like a playwright who has constructed a strong melodramatic plot, and has the Drury Lane stage suddenly offered him to present it on. It would be folly to deny himself the luxury, though the presence of Mr. Gladstone and the nature of the ceremony should perhaps have given him pause. Yet, on the other hand, these were the very factors of the temptation. Wimp went in and took a seat behind Denzil. All the seats were numbered, so that everybody might have the satisfaction of occupying somebody else's. Denzil was in the special reserved places in the front row just by the central gangway; Crowl was squeezed into a corner behind a pillar near the back of the hall. Grodman had been honored with a seat on the platform, which was accessible by steps on the right and left, but he kept his eye on Denzil. The picture of the poor idealist hung on the wall behind Grodman's head, covered by its curtain of brown holland. There was a subdued buzz of excitement about the hall, which swelled into cheers every now and again as some gentleman known to fame or Bow took his place upon the platform. It was occupied by several local M.P.'s of varying politics, a number of other Parliamentary satellites of the great man, three or four labor leaders, a peer or two of philanthropic pretensions, a sprinkling of Toynbee and Oxford Hall men, the president and other honorary officials, some of the family and friends of the deceased, together with the inevitable percentage of persons who had no claim to be there save cheek. Gladstone was late—later than Mortlake, who was cheered to the echo when he arrived, someone starting, "For He's a Jolly Good Fellow," as if it were a political meeting. Gladstone came in just in time to acknowledge the compliment. The noise of the song, trolled out from iron lungs, had drowned the huzzahs heralding the old man's advent. The convivial chorus went to Mortlake's head, as if champagne had really preceded it. His eyes grew moist and dim. He saw himself swimming to the Millennium on waves of enthusiasm. Ah, how his brother toilers should be rewarded for their trust in him!

With his usual courtesy and consideration, Mr. Gladstone had refused to perform the actual unveiling of Arthur Constant's portrait. "That," he said in his postcard, "will fall most appropriately to Mr. Mortlake, a gentleman who has, I am given to understand, enjoyed the personal friendship of the late Mr. Constant, and has co-operated with him in various schemes for the organization of skilled and unskilled classes of labor, as well as for the diffusion of better ideals—ideals of self-culture and self-restraint—among the working men of Bow, who have been fortunate, so far as I can perceive, in the possession (if in one case unhappily only temporary possession) of two such men of undoubted ability and honesty to direct their divided counsels and to lead them along a road, which, though I cannot pledge myself to appprove of it in all its turnings and windings, is yet not unfitted to bring them somewhat nearer to goals to which there are few of us but would extend some measure of hope that the working-classes of this great Empire may in due course, yet with no unnecessary delay, be enabled to arrive."

Mr. Gladstone's speech was an expansion of his postcard, punctuated by cheers. The only new thing in it was the graceful and touching way in which he revealed what had been a secret up till then—that the portrait had been painted and presented to the Bow Break o' Day Club, by Lucy Brent, who in the fullness of time would have been Arthur Constant's wife. It was a painting for which he had sat to her while alive, and she had stifled yet pampered her grief by working hard at it since his death. The fact added the last touch of pathos to the occasion. Crowl's face was hidden behind his red handkerchief; even the fire of excitement in Wimp's eye was quenched for a moment by a tear-drop, as he thought of Mrs. Wimp and Wilfred. As for Grodman, there was almost a lump in his throat. Denzil Cantercot was the only unmoved man in the room. He thought the episode quite too Beautiful, and was already weaving it into rhyme.

At the conclusion of his speech Mr. Gladstone called upon Tom Mortlake to unveil the portrait. Tom rose, pale and excited. His hand faltered as he touched the cord. He seemed overcome with emotion. Was it the mention of Lucy Brent that had moved him to his depths?

The brown holland fell away—the dead stood revealed as he had been in life. Every feature, painted by the hand of Love, was instinct with vitality: the fine, earnest face, the sad kindly eyes, the noble brow seeming still a-throb with the thought of Humanity. A thrill ran through the room—there was a low, undefinable murmur. Oh, the pathos and the tragedy of it! Every eye was fixed, misty with emotion, upon the dead man in the picture and the living man who stood, pale and agitated, and visibly unable to commence his speech, at the side of the canvas. Suddenly a hand was laid upon the labor leader's shoulder, and there rang through the hall in Wimp's clear decisive tones the words—"Tom Mortlake, I arrest you for the murder of Arthur Constant!"

9

For a moment there was an acute, terrible silence. Mortlake's face was that of a corpse; the face of the dead man at his side was flushed with the hues of life. To the overstrung nerves of the onlookers, the brooding eyes of the picture seemed sad and stern with menace, and charged with the lightnings of doom.

It was a horrible contrast. For Wimp, alone, the painted face had fuller, more tragical meanings. The audience seemed turned to stone. They sat or stood—in every variety of attitude—frozen, rigid. Arthur Constant's picture dominated the scene, the only living thing in a hall of the dead.

But only for a moment. Mortlake shook off the detective's hand.

"Boys!" he cried, in accents of infinite indignation, "this is a police conspiracy."

His words relaxed the tension. The stony figures were agitated. A dull excited hubbub answered him. The little cobbler darted from behind his pillar, and leaped up on a bench. The cords of his brow were swollen with excitement. He seemed a giant overshadowing the hall.

"Boys!" he roared, in his best Victoria Park voice, "listen to me. This charge is a foul and damnable lie."

"Bravo!" "Hear, hear!" "Horray!" "It is!" was roared back at him from all parts of the room. Everybody rose and stood in tentative attitudes, excited to the last degree.

"Boys!" Peter roared on, "you all know me. I'm a plain man, and I want to know if it's likely a man would murder his best friend."

"No," in a mighty volume of sound.

Wimp had scarcely calculated upon Mortlake's popularity. He stood on the platform, as pale and anxious as his prisoner.

"And if he did, why didn't they prove it the first time?"

"HEAR, HEAR!"

"And if they want to arrest him, why couldn't they leave it till the ceremony was over? Tom Mortlake's not the man to run away."

"Tom Mortlake! Tom Mortlake! Three cheers for Tom Mortlake! Hip, hip, hip, hooray!"

"Three groans for the police!" "Hoo! Oo! Oo!"

Wimp's melodrama was not going well. He felt like the author to whose ears is borne the ominous sibilance of the pit. He almost wished he had not followed the curtain-raiser with his own stronger drama. Unconsciously the police, scattered about the hall, drew together. The people on the platform knew not what to do. They had all risen and stood in a densely-packed mass. Even Mr. Gladstone's speech failed him in circumstances so novel. The groans died away; the cheers for Mortlake rose and swelled and fell and rose again. Sticks and umbrellas were banged and rattled, handkerchiefs were waved, the thunder deepened. The motley crowd still surging about the hall took up the cheers, and for hundreds of yards around people were going black in the face out of mere irresponsible enthusiasm. At last Tom waved his hand—the thunder dwindled, died. The prisoner was master of the situation.

Grodman stood on the platform, grasping the back of his chair, a curious mocking Mephistophelian glitter about his eyes, his lips wreathed into a half smile. There was no hurry for him to get Denzil Cantercot arrested now. Wimp had made an egregious, a colossal blunder. In Grodman's heart there was a great glad calm as of a man who has strained his sinews to win in a famous match, and has heard the judge's word. He felt almost kindly to Denzil now.

Tom Mortlake spoke. His face was set and stony. His tall figure was drawn up haughtily to its full height. He pushed the black mane back from his forehead with a characteristic gesture. The fevered audience hung upon his lips—the men at the back leaned eagerly forward—the reporters were breathless with fear lest they should miss a word. What would the great labor leader have to say at this supreme moment?

"Mr. Chairman and gentlemen—It is to me a melancholy pleasure to have been honored with the task of unveiling to-night this portrait of a great benefactor to Bow and a true friend to the laboring classes. Except that he honored me with his friendship while living, and that the aspirations of my life have, in my small and restricted way, been identical with his, there is little reason why this honorable duty should have fallen upon me. Gentlemen, I trust that we shall all find an inspiring influence in the daily vision of the dead, who yet liveth in our hearts and in this noble work of art—wrought, as Mr. Gladstone has told us, by the hand of one who loved him." The speaker paused a moment, his low vibrant tones faltering into silence. "If we humble working men of Bow can never hope to exert individ-ually a tithe of the beneficial influence wielded by Arthur Constant, it is yet possible for each of us to walk in the light he has kindled in our midst—a perpetual lamp of self-sacrifice and brotherhood."

That was all. The room rang with cheers. Tom Mortlake resumed his seat. To Wimp the man's audacity verged on the Sublime; to Denzil on the Beautiful. Again there was a breathless hush. Mr. Gladstone's mobile face was working with excitement. No such extraordinary scene had occurred in the whole of his extraor-dinary experience. He seemed about to rise. The cheering subsided to a painful stillness. Wimp cut the situation by laying his hand again upon Tom's shoulder.

"Come quietly with me," he said. The words were almost a whisper, but in the supreme silence they traveled to the ends of the hall.

"Don't you go, Tom!" The trumpet tones were Peter's. The call thrilled an answering chord of defiance in every breast, and a low ominous murmur swept through the hall.

Tom rose, and there was silence again. "Boys," he said, "let me go. Don't make any noise about it. I shall be with you again to-morrow."

But the blood of the Break o' Day boys was at fever heat. A hurtling mass of men struggled confusedly from their seats. In a moment all was chaos. Tom did not move. Half a dozen men, headed by Peter, scaled the platform. Wimp was thrown to one side, and the invaders formed a ring round Tom's chair. The platform people scampered like mice from the center. Some huddled together in the corners, others slipped out at the rear. The committee congratulated themselves on having had the self-denial to exclude ladies. Mr. Gladstone's satellites hurried the old man off and into his carriage, though the fight promised to become Ho-meric. Grodman stood at the side of the platform secretly more amused then ever, concerning himself no more with Denzil Cantercot, who was already strengthening his nerves at the bar upstairs. The police about the hall blew their whistles, and policemen came rushing in from outside and the neighborhood. An Irish M.P. on the platform was waving his gingham like a shillelagh in sheer excitement, forgetting his new-found respectability and dreaming himself back at Donnybrook Fair. Him a conscientious constable floored with a truncheon. But a shower of fists fell on the zealot's face, and he tottered back bleeding. Then the storm broke in all its fury. The upper air was black with staves, sticks, and umbrellas, mingled with the pallid hailstones of knobby fists. Yells, and groans, and hoots, and battle-cries blended in grotesque chorus, like one of Dvořák's weird diabolical movements. Mortlake stood impassive, with arms folded, making no further effort, and the battle raged round him as the water swirls round some steadfast rock. A posse of police from the back fought their way steadily towards him, and charged up the heights of the platform steps, only to be sent tumbling backwards, as their leader was hurled at them like a battering-ram. Upon the top of the heap he fell, surmounting the strata of policemen. But others clambered upon them, escalading the platform. A moment more and Mortlake would have been taken. Then the miracle happened.

As when of old a reputable goddess *ex machina* saw her favorite hero in dire peril, straightway she drew down a cloud from the celestial stores of Jupiter and enveloped her fondling in kindly night, so that his adversary strove with the darkness, so did Crowl, the cunning cobbler, the much-daring, essay to ensure his friend's safety. He turned off the gas at the meter.

An Arctic night—unpreceded by twilight—fell, and there dawned the sabbath of the witches. The darkness could be felt—and it left blood and bruises behind it. When the lights were turned on again, Mortlake was gone. But several of the rioters were arrested, triumphantly.

And through all, and over all, the face of the dead man who had sought to bring peace on earth brooded.

Crowl sat meekly eating his supper of bread and cheese, with his head bandaged, while Denzil Cantercot told him the story of how he had rescued Tom Mortlake. He had been among the first to scale the height, and had never budged from Tom's side or from the forefront of the battle till he had seen him safely outside and into a by-street.

"I am so glad you saw that he got away safely," said Crowl, "I wasn't quite sure he would."

"Yes; but I wish some cowardly fool hadn't turned off the gas. I like men to *see* they are beaten."

"But it seemed—easier," faltered Crowl.

"Easier!" echoed Denzil, taking a deep draught of bitter. "Really, Peter, I'm sorry to find you always will take such low views. It may be easier, but it's shabby. It shocks one's sense of the Beautiful."

Crowl ate his bread and cheese shamefacedly.

"But what was the use of breaking your head to save him?" said Mrs. Crowl with an unconscious pun. "He must be caught."

"Ah, I don't see how the Useful *does* come in, now," said Peter, thoughtfully. "But I didn't think of that at the time."

He swallowed his water quickly, and it went the wrong way and added to his confusion. It also began to dawn upon him that he might be called to account. Let it be said that he wasn't. He had taken too prominent a part.

Meantime, Mrs. Wimp was bathing Mr. Wimp's eye, and rubbing him generally with arnica. Wimp's melodrama had been, indeed, a sight for the gods. Only, virtue was vanquished and vice triumphant. The villain had escaped, and without striking a blow.

10

There was matter and to spare for the papers the next day. The striking ceremony —Mr. Gladstone's speech—the sensational arrest—these would of themselves have made excellent themes for reports and leaders. But the personality of the man arrested, and the Big Bow Mystery Battle—as it came to be called—gave additional piquancy to the paragraphs and the posters. The behavior of Mortlake put the last touch to the picturesqueness of the position. He left the hall when the lights went out, and walked unnoticed and unmolested through pleiads of policemen to the nearest police station, where the superintendent was almost too excited to take any notice of his demand to be arrested. But to do him justice, the official yielded as soon as he understood the situation. It seems inconceivable that he did not violate some red-tape regulation in so doing. To some this self-surrender was limpid proof of innocence; to others it was the damning token of despairing guilt.

The morning papers were pleasant reading for Grodman, who chuckled as continuously over his morning egg as if he had laid it. Jane was alarmed for the sanity of her saturnine master. As her husband would have said, Grodman's grins were not Beautiful. But he made no effort to suppress them. Not only had Wimp perpetrated a grotesque blunder, but the journalists to a man were down on his great sensation tableau, though their denunciations did not appear in the dramatic columns. The Liberal papers said that he had endangered Mr. Gladstone's life; the Conservative that he had unloosed the raging elements of Bow blackguardism, and set in motion forces which might have easily swelled to a riot, involving severe destruction of property. But "Tom Mortlake" was, after all, the thought swamping every other. It was, in a sense, a triumph for the man.

But Wimp's turn came when Mortlake, who reserved his defense, was brought up before a magistrate, and by force of the new evidence, fully committed for trial on the charge of murdering Arthur Constant. Then men's thoughts centered again on the Mystery, and the solution of the inexplicable problem agitated mankind from China to Peru.

In the middle of February, the great trial befell. It was another of the opportunities which the Chancellor of the Exchequer neglects. So stirring a drama might have easily cleared its expenses—despite the length of the cast, the salaries of the stars, and the rent of the house—in mere advance booking. For it was a drama which (by the rights of Magna Charta) could never be repeated; a drama which ladies of fashion would have given their earrings to witness, even with the central figure not a woman. And there *was* a woman in it anyhow, to judge by the little that had transpired at the magisterial examination, and the fact that the country was placarded with bills offering a reward for information concerning a Miss Jessie Dymond. Mortlake was defended by Sir Charles Brown-Harland, Q.C., retained at the expense of the Mortlake Defense Fund (subscriptions to which came also from Australia and the Continent), and set on his mettle by the fact that he was the accepted labor candidate for an East-end constituency. Their Majesties, Victoria and the Law, were represented by Mr. Robert Spigot, Q.C.

Mr. Spigot, Q.C., in presenting his case, said: "I propose to show that the prisoner murdered his friend and fellow-lodger, Mr. Arthur Constant, in cold blood, and with the most careful premeditation; premeditation so studied as to leave the circumstances of the death an impenetrable mystery for weeks to all the world, though, fortunately, without altogether baffling the almost superhuman ingenuity of Mr. Edward Wimp, of the Scotland Yard Detective Department. I propose to show that the motives of the prisoner were jealousy and revenge; jealousy, not only of his friend's superior influence over the working men he himself aspired to lead, but the more commonplace animosity engendered by the disturbing element of a woman having relations to both. If, before my case is complete, it will be my painful duty to show that the murdered man was not the saint the world had agreed to paint him, I shall not shrink from unveiling the truer picture, in the interests of justice, which cannot say *nil nisi bonum* even of the dead. I propose to show that the murder was committed by the prisoner shortly before half-past six on the morning of December 4th, and that the prisoner having, with the remarkable ingenuity which he has shown throughout, attempted to prepare an alibi by feigning to leave London by the *first* train to Liverpool, returned home, got in with his latchkey through the street-door, which he had left on the latch, unlocked his victim's bedroom with a key which he possessed, cut the sleeping man's throat, pocketed the razor, locked the door again, and gave it the appearance of being bolted, went downstairs, unslipped the bolt of the big lock, closed the door behind him, and got to Euston in time for the *second* train to Liverpool. The fog helped his proceedings throughout." Such was in sum the theory of the prosecution. The pale, defiant figure in the dock winced perceptibly under parts of it.

Mrs. Drabdump was the first witness called for the prosecution. She was quite used to legal inquisitiveness by this time, but did not appear in good spirits.

"On the night of December 3rd, you gave the prisoner a letter?"

"Yes, your ludship."

"How did he behave when he read it?"

"He turned very pale and excited. He went up to the poor gentleman's room, and I'm afraid he quarreled with him. He might have left his last hours peaceful." (Amusement.)

"What happened then?"

"Mr. Mortlake went out in a passion, and came in again in about an hour."

"He told you he was going away to Liverpool very early the next morning?"

"No, your ludship, he said he was going to Devonport." (Sensation.)

"What time did you get up the next morning?"

"Half-past six."

"That is not your usual time?"

"No, I always get up at six."

"How do you account for the extra sleepiness?"

"Misfortunes will happen."

"It wasn't the dull, foggy weather?"

"No, my lud, else I should never get up early." (Laughter.)

"You drink something before going to bed?"

"I like my cup o' tea. I take it strong, without sugar. It always steadies my nerves."

"Quite so. Where were you when the prisoner told you he was going to Devonport?"

"Drinkin' my tea in the kitchen."

"What should you say if prisoner dropped something in it to make you sleep late?"

Witness (startled): "He ought to be shot."

"He might have done it without your noticing it, I suppose?"

"If he was clever enough to murder the poor gentleman, he was clever enough to try and poison me."

The Judge: "The witness in her replies must confine herself to the evidence."

Mr. Spigot, Q.C.: "I must submit to your lordship that it is a very logical answer, and exactly illustrates the interdependence of the probabilities. Now, Mrs. Drabdump, let us know what happened when you awoke at half-past six the next morning."

Thereupon Mrs. Drabdump recapitulated the evidence (with new redundancies, but slight variations) given by her at the inquest. How she became alarmed—how she found the street-door locked by the big lock—how she roused Grodman, and got him to burst open the door—how they found the body—all this with which the public was already familiar *ad nauseam* was extorted from her afresh.

"Look at this key (key passed to witness). Do you recognize it?"

"Yes; how did you get it? It's the key of my first-floor front. I am sure I left it sticking in the door."

"Did you know a Miss Dymond?"

"Yes, Mr. Mortlake's sweetheart. But I knew he would never marry her, poor thing." (Sensation.)

"Why not?"

"He was getting too grand for her." (Amusement.)

"You don't mean anything more than that?"

"I don't know; she only came to my place once or twice. The last time I set eyes on her must have been in October."

"How did she appear?"

"She was very miserable, but she wouldn't let you see it." (Laughter.)

"How has the prisoner behaved since the murder?"

"He always seemed very glum and sorry for it."

Cross-examined: "Did not the prisoner once occupy the bedroom of Mr. Constant, and give it up to him, so that Mr. Constant might have the two rooms on the same floor?"

"Yes, but he didn't pay as much."

"And, while occupying this front bedroom, did not the prisoner once lose his key and have another made?"

"He did; he was very careless."

"Do you know what the prisoner and Mr. Constant spoke about on the night of December 3rd?"

"No; I couldn't hear."

"Then how did you know they were quarreling?"

"They were talkin' so loud."

Sir Charles Brown-Harland, Q.C. (sharply): "But I'm talking loudly to you now. Should you say I was quarreling?"

"It takes two to make a quarrel." (Laughter.)

"Was prisoner the sort of man who, in your opinion, would commit a murder?"

"No, I never should ha' guessed it was him."

"He always struck you as a thorough gentleman?"

"No, my lud. I knew he was only a comp."

"You say the prisoner has seemed depressed since the murder. Might not that have been due to the disappearance of his sweetheart?"

"No, he'd more likely be glad to get rid of her."

"Then he wouldn't be jealous if Mr. Constant took her off his hands?" (Sensation.)

"Men are dog-in-the-mangers."

"Never mind about men, Mrs. Drabdump. Had the prisoner ceased to care for Miss Dymond?"

"He didn't seem to think of her, my lud. When he got a letter in her handwriting among his heap he used to throw it aside till he'd torn open the others."

BROWN-HARLAND, Q.C. (with a triumphant ring in his voice): Thank you, Mrs. Drabdump. You may sit down.

SPIGOT, Q.C.: One moment, Mrs. Drabdump. You say the prisoner had ceased to care for Miss Dymond. Might not this have been on consequence of his suspecting for some time that she had relations with Mr. Constant?

THE JUDGE: That is not a fair question.

SPIGOT, Q.C.: That will do, thank you, Mrs. Drabdump.

BROWN-HARLAND, Q.C.: No, one question more, Mrs. Drabdump. Did you ever see anything—say, when Miss Dymond came to your house—to make you suspect anything between Mr. Constant and the prisoner's sweetheart?

"She did meet him once when Mr. Mortlake was out." (Sensation.)

"Where did she meet him?"

"In the passage. He was going out when she knocked and he opened the door." (Amusement.)

"You didn't hear what they said?"

"I ain't a eavesdropper. They spoke friendly and went away together."

Mr. George Grodman was called, and repeated his evidence at the inquest. Cross-examined, he testified to the warm friendship between Mr. Constant and the prisoner. He knew very little about Miss Dymond, having scarcely seen her. Prisoner had never spoken to him much about her. He should not think she was much in prisoner's thoughts. Naturally the prisoner had been depressed by the death of his friend. Besides, he was overworked. Witness thought highly of Mortlake's character. It was incredible that Constant had had improper relations of any kind with his friend's promised wife. Grodman's evidence made a very favorable impression on the jury, the prisoner looked his gratitude, and the prosecution felt sorry it had been necessary to call this witness.

Inspector Howlett and Sergeant Runnymede had also to repeat their evidence. Dr. Robinson, police surgeon, likewise re-tendered his evidence as to the nature of the wound, and the approximate hour of death. But this time he was much more severely examined. He would not bind himself down to state the time within an hour or two. He thought life had been extinct two or three hours when he arrived, so that the deed had been committed between seven and eight. Under gentle pressure from the prosecuting counsel, he admitted that it might possibly have been between six and seven. Cross-examined, he reiterated his impression in favor of the later hour.

Supplementary evidence from medical experts proved as dubious and uncertain as if the court had confined itself to the original witness. It seemed to be generally agreed that the data for determining the time of death of any body were too complex and variable to admit of very precise inference; rigor mortis and other symptoms setting in within very wide limits and differing largely in different persons. All agreed that death from such a cut must have been practically instantaneous, and the theory of suicide was rejected by all. As a whole the medical evidence tended to fix the time of death, with a high degree of probability, between the hours of six and half-past eight. The efforts of the prosecution were bent upon throwing back the time of death to as early as possible after about half-past five. The defense spent all its strength upon pinning the experts to the conclusion that death could not have been earlier than seven. Evidently the prosecution was going to fight hard for the hypothesis that Mortlake had committed the crime in the interval between the first and second trains for Liverpool, while the defense was concentrating itself on an alibi, showing that the prisoner had traveled by the second train, which left Euston Station at a quarter-past seven, so that there could have been no possible time for the passage between Bow and Euston. It was an exciting struggle. As yet the contending forces seemed equally matched. The evidence had gone as much for as against the prisoner. But everybody knew that worse lay behind.

"Call Edward Wimp."

The story Edward Wimp had to tell began tamely enough with thrice-threshed-out facts. But at last the new facts came.

"In consequence of suspicions that had formed in your mind you took up your quarters, disguised, in the late Mr. Constant's rooms?"

"I did, at the commencement of the year. My suspicions had gradually gathered against the occupants of No. 11 Glover Street, and I resolved to quash or confirm these suspicions once for all."

"Will you tell the jury what followed?"

"Whenever the prisoner was away for the night I searched his room. I found the key of Mr. Constant's bedroom buried deeply in the side of prisoner's leather sofa. I found what I imagine to be the letter he received on December 3rd, in the pages of a 'Bradshaw' lying under the same sofa. There were two razors about."

Mr. Spigot, Q.C., said: "The key has already been identified by Mrs. Drabdump. The letter I now propose to read."

It was undated, and ran as follows:

DEAR TOM,

This is to bid you farewell. It is best for us all. I am going a long way, dearest. Do not seek to find me, for it will be useless. Think of me as one swallowed up by the waters, and be assured that it is only to spare you shame and humiliation in the future that I tear myself from you and all the sweetness of life. Darling, there is no other way. I feel you could never marry me now. I have felt it for months. Dear Tom, you will understand what I mean. We must look facts in the face. I hope you will always be friends with Mr. Constant. Goodbye, dear. God bless you! May you always be happy, and find a worthier wife than I. Perhaps when you are great, and rich, and famous, as you deserve, you will sometimes think not unkindly of one who, however faulty and unworthy of you, will at least love you till the end.—Yours, till death,

JESSIE.

By the time this letter was finished numerous old gentlemen, with wigs or without, were observed to be polishing their glasses. Mr. Wimp's examination was resumed.

"After making these discoveries what did you do?"

"I made inquiries about Miss Dymond, and found Mr. Constant had visited her once or twice in the evening. I imagined there would be some traces of a pecuniary connection. I was allowed by the family to inspect Mr. Constant's cheque-book, and found a paid cheque made out for £25 in the name of Miss Dymond. By inquiry at the Bank, I found it had been cashed on November 12th of last year. I then applied for a warrant against the prisoner."

Cross-examined: "Do you suggest that the prisoner opened Mr. Constant's bedroom with the key you found?"

"Certainly."

Brown-Harland, Q.C. (sarcastically): "And locked the door from within with it on leaving?"

"Certainly."

"Will you have the goodness to explain how the trick was done?"

"It wasn't done. (Laughter.) The prisoner probably locked the door from the outside. Those who broke it open naturally imagined it had been locked from the inside when they found the key inside. The key would, on this theory, be on the floor, as the outside locking could not have been effected if it had been in the lock. The first persons to enter the room would naturally believe it had been thrown down in the bursting of the door. Or it might have been left sticking very loosely inside the lock so as not to interfere with the turning of the outside key, in which case it would also probably have been thrown to the ground."

"Indeed. Very ingenious. And can you also explain how the prisoner could have bolted the door within from the outside?"

"I can. (Renewed sensation.) There is only one way in which it was possible— and that was, of course, a mere conjuror's illusion. To cause a locked door to appear bolted in addition, it would only be necessary for the person on the inside of the door to wrest the staple containing the bolt from the woodwork. The bolt in Mr. Constant's bedroom worked perpendicularly. When the staple was torn off, it would simply remain at rest on the pin of the bolt instead of supporting it or keeping it fixed. A person bursting open the door and finding the staple resting on the pin and torn away from the lintel of the door, would, of course, imagine he

had torn it away, never dreaming the wresting off had been done beforehand."
(Applause in court, which was instantly checked by the ushers.) The counsel for
the defense felt he had been entrapped in attempting to be sarcastic with the
redoubtable detective. Grodman seemed green with envy. It was the one thing he
had not thought of.

Mrs. Drabdump, Grodman, Inspector Howlett, and Sergeant Runnymede were
recalled and re-examined by the embarrassed Sir Charles Brown-Harland as to the
exact condition of the lock and the bolt and the position of the key. It turned out
as Wimp had suggested; so prepossessed were the witnesses with the conviction that
the door was locked and bolted from the inside when it was burst open that they
were a little hazy about the exact details. The damage had been repaired, so that it
was all a question of precise past observation. The inspector and the sergeant
testified that the key was in the lock when they saw it, though both the mortise and
the bolt were broken. They were not prepared to say that Wimp's theory was
impossible; they would even admit it was quite possible that the staple of the bolt
had been torn off beforehand. Mrs. Drabdump could give no clear account of such
petty facts in view of her immediate engrossing interest in the horrible sight of the
corpse. Grodman alone was positive that the key was in the door when he burst it
open. No, he did not remember picking it up from the floor and putting it in. And
he was certain that the staple of the bolt was *not* broken, from the resistance he
experienced in trying to shake the upper panels of the door.

By the Prosecution: "Don't you think, from the comparative ease with which
the door yielded to your onslaught, that it is highly probable that the pin of the
bolt was not in a firmly fixed staple, but in one already detached from the woodwork
of the lintel?"

"The door did not yield so easily."

"But you must be a Hercules."

"Not quite; the bolt was old, and the woodwork crumbling; the lock was new
and shoddy. But I have always been a strong man."

"Very well, Mr. Grodman. I hope you will never appear at the music-halls."
(Laughter.)

Jessie Dymond's landlady was the next witness for the prosecution. She corroborated Wimp's statements as to Constant's occasional visits, and narrated how the
girl had been enlisted by the dead philanthropist as a collaborator in some of his
enterprises. But the most telling portion of her evidence was the story of how, late
at night, on December 3rd, the prisoner called upon her and inquired wildly about
the whereabouts of his sweetheart. He said he had just received a mysterious letter
from Miss Dymond saying she was gone. She (the landlady) replied that she could
have told him that weeks ago, as her ungrateful lodger was gone now some three
weeks without leaving a hint behind her. In answer to his most ungentlemanly
raging and raving, she told him it served him right, as he should have looked after
her better, and not kept away for so long. She reminded him that there were as

good fish in the sea as ever came out, and a girl of Jessie's attractions need not pine away (as she had seemed to be pining away) for lack of appreciation. He then called her a liar and left her, and she hoped never to see his face again, though she was not surprised to see it in the dock.

Mr. Fitzjames Montgomery, a bank clerk, remembered cashing the cheque produced. He particularly remembered it because he paid the money to a very pretty girl. She took the entire amount in gold. At this point the case was adjourned.

Denzil Cantercot was the first witness called for the prosecution on the resumption of the trial. Pressed as to whether he had not told Mr. Wimp that he had overheard the prisoner denouncing Mr. Constant, he could not say. He had not actually heard the prisoner's denunciations; he might have given Mr. Wimp a false impression, but then Mr. Wimp was so prosaically literal. (Laughter.) Mr. Crowl had told him something of the kind. Cross-examined, he said Jessie Dymond was a rare spirit and she always reminded him of Joan of Arc.

Mr. Crowl, being called, was extremely agitated. He refused to take the oath, and informed the court that the Bible was a Fad. He could not swear by anything so self-contradictory. He would affirm. He could not deny—though he looked like wishing to—that the prisoner had at first been rather mistrustful of Mr. Constant, but he was certain that the feeling had quickly worn off. Yes, he was a great friend of the prisoner, but he didn't see why that should invalidate his testimony especially as he had not taken an oath. Certainly the prisoner seemed rather depressed when he saw him on Bank Holiday, but it was overwork on behalf of the people and for the demolition of the Fads.

Several other familiars of the prisoner gave more or less reluctant testimony as to his sometimes prejudice against the amateur rival labor leader. His expressions of dislike had been strong and bitter. The prosecution also produced a poster announcing that the prisoner would preside at a great meeting of clerks on December 4th. He had not turned up at this meeting nor sent any explanation. Finally, there was the evidence of the detectives who originally arrested him at Liverpool Docks in view of his suspicious demeanor. This completed the case for the prosecution.

Sir Charles Brown-Harland, Q.C., rose with a swagger and a rustle of his silk gown, and proceeded to set forth the theory of the defense. He said he did not purpose to call many witnesses. The hypothesis of the prosecution was so inherently childish and inconsequential, and so dependent upon a bundle of interdependent probabilities that it crumbled away at the merest touch. The prisoner's character was of unblemished integrity, his last public appearance had been made on the same platform with Mr. Gladstone, and his honesty and highmindedness had been vouched for by statesmen of the highest standing. His movements could be accounted for from hour to hour—and those with which the prosecution credited him rested on no tangible evidence whatever. He was also credited with superhu-

man ingenuity and diabolical cunning of which he had shown no previous symp-
tom. Hypothesis was piled on hypothesis, as in the old Oriental legend, where the
world rested on the elephant and the elephant on the tortoise. It might be worth
while, however, to point out that it was at least quite likely that the death of Mr.
Constant had not taken place before seven, and as the prisoner left Euston Station
at 7:15 a.m. for Liverpool, he could certainly not have got there from Bow in the
time; also that it was hardly possible for the prisoner, who could prove being at
Euston Station at 5:25 a.m., to travel backwards and forwards to Glover Street and
commit the crime all within less than two hours. "The real facts," said Sir Charles
impressively, "are most simple. The prisoner, partly from pressure of work, partly
(he had no wish to conceal) from worldly ambition, had begun to neglect Miss
Dymond, to whom he was engaged to be married. The man was but human, and
his head was a little turned by his growing importance. Nevertheless, at heart he
was still deeply attached to Miss Dymond. She, however, appears to have jumped
to the conclusion that he had ceased to love her, that she was unworthy of him,
unfitted by education to take her place side by side with him in the new spheres to
which he was mounting—that, in short, she was a drag on his career. Being, by
all accounts, a girl of remarkable force of character, she resolved to cut the Gordian
knot by leaving London, and, fearing lest her affianced husband's conscientiousness
should induce him to sacrifice himself to her; dreading also, perhaps, her own
weakness, she made the parting absolute, and the place of her refuge a mystery. A
theory has been suggested which drags an honored name in the mire—a theory so
superfluous that I shall only allude to it. That Arthur Constant could have seduced,
or had any improper relations with, his friend's betrothed, is a hypothesis to which
the lives of both give the lie. Before leaving London—or England—Miss Dymond
wrote to her aunt in Devonport—her only living relative in this country—asking
her as a great favor to forward an addressed letter to the prisoner, a fortnight after
receipt. The aunt obeyed implicitly. This was the letter which fell like a thunder-
bolt on the prisoner on the night of December 3rd. All his old love returned—he
was full of self-reproach and pity for the poor girl. The letter read ominously.
Perhaps she was going to put an end to herself. His first thought was to rush up to
his friend, Constant, to seek his advice. Perhaps Constant knew something of the
affair. The prisoner knew the two were in not infrequent communication. It is
possible—my lord and gentlemen of the jury, I do not wish to follow the methods
of the prosecution and confuse theory with fact, so I say it is possible—that Mr.
Constant had supplied her with the £25 to leave the country. He was like a brother
to her, perhaps even acted imprudently in calling upon her, though neither
dreamed of evil. It is possible that he may have encouraged her in her abnegation
and in her altruistic aspirations, perhaps even without knowing their exact drift, for
does he not speak in his very last letter of the fine female characters he was meeting,
and the influence for good he had over individual human souls? Still, this we can
now never know, unless the dead speak or the absent return. It is also not impossible

that Miss Dymond was entrusted with the £25 for charitable purposes. But to come back to certainties. The prisoner consulted Mr. Constant about the letter. He then ran to Miss Dymond's lodgings in Stepney Green, knowing beforehand his trouble would be futile. The letter bore the postmark of Devonport. He knew the girl had an aunt there; possibly she might have gone to her. He could not telegraph, for he was ignorant of the address. He consulted his 'Bradshaw,' and resolved to leave by the 5:30 a.m. from Paddington, and told his landlady so. He left the letter in the 'Bradshaw,' which ultimately got thrust among a pile of papers under the sofa, so that he had to get another. He was careless and disorderly, and the key found by Mr. Wimp in his sofa, which he was absurdly supposed to have hidden there after the murder, must have lain there for some years, having been lost there in the days when he occupied the bedroom afterwards rented by Mr. Constant. For it was his own sofa, removed from that room, and the suction of sofas was well known. Afraid to miss his train, he did not undress on that distressful night. Meantime the thought occurred to him that Jessie was too clever a girl to leave so easy a trail, and he jumped to the conclusion that she would be going to her married brother in America, and had gone to Devonport merely to bid her aunt farewell. He determined therefore to get to Liverpool, without wasting time at Devonport, to institute inquiries. Not suspecting the delay in the transit of the letter, he thought he might yet stop her, even at the landing-stage or on the tender. Unfortunately his cab went slowly in the fog, he missed the first train, and wandered about brooding disconsolately in the mist till the second. At Liverpool his suspicious, excited demeanor procured his momentary arrest. Since then the thought of the lost girl has haunted and broken him. That is the whole, the plain, and the sufficing story."

The effective witnesses for the defense were, indeed, few. It is so hard to prove a negative. There was Jessie's aunt, who bore out the statement of the counsel for the defense. There were the porters who saw him leave Euston by the 7:15 train for Liverpool, and arrive just too late for the 5:15; there was the cabman (2138), who drove him to Euston just in time, he (witness) thought, to catch the 5:15 a.m. Under cross-examination, the cabman got a little confused; he was asked whether, if he really picked up the prisoner at Bow Railway Station at about 4:30, he ought not to have caught the first train at Euston. He said the fog made him drive rather slowly, but admitted the mist was transparent enough to warrant full speed. He also admitted being a strong trade unionist, Spigot, Q.C. artfully extorting the admission as if it were of the utmost significance. Finally, there were numerous witnesses—of all sorts and conditions—to the prisoner's high character, as well as to Arthur Constant's blameless and moral life.

In his closing speech on the third day of the trial, Sir Charles pointed out with great exhaustiveness and cogency the flimsiness of the case for the prosecution, the number of hypotheses it involved, and their mutual interdependence. Mrs. Drabdump was a witness whose evidence must be accepted with extreme caution. The jury must remember that she was unable to dissociate her observations from her inferences, and thought that the prisoner and Mr. Constant were quarreling merely because they were agitated. He dissected her evidence, and showed that it entirely bore out the story of the defense. He asked the jury to bear in mind that no positive evidence (whether of cabmen or others) had been given of the various and complicated movements attributed to the prisoner on the morning of December 4th, between the hours of 5:25 and 7:15 a.m., and that the most important witness on the theory of the prosecution—he meant, of course, Miss Dymond—had not been produced. Even if she were dead, and her body were found, no countenance would be given to the theory of the prosecution, for the mere conviction that her lover had deserted her would be a sufficient explanation of her suicide. Beyond the ambiguous letter, no tittle of evidence of her dishonor—on which the bulk of the case against the prisoner rested—had been adduced. As for the motive of political jealousy, that had been a mere passing cloud. The two men had become fast friends. As to the circumstances of the alleged crime, the medical evidence was on the whole in favor of the time of death being late; and the prisoner had left London at a quarter-past seven. The drugging theory was absurd, and as for the too clever bolt and lock theories, Mr. Grodman, a trained scientific observer, had poohpoohed them. He would solemnly exhort the jury to remember that if they condemned the prisoner they would not only send an innocent man to an ignominious death on the flimsiest circumstantial evidence, but they would deprive the working men of this country of one of their truest friends and their ablest leader.

The conclusion of Sir Charles's vigorous speech was greeted with irrepressible applause.

Mr. Spigot, Q.C., in closing the case for the prosecution, asked the jury to return a verdict against the prisoner for as malicious and premeditated a crime as ever disgraced the annals of any civilized country. His cleverness and education had only been utilized for the devil's ends, while his reputation had been used as a cloak. Everything pointed strongly to the prisoner's guilt. On receiving Miss Dymond's letter announcing her shame, and (probably) her intention to commit suicide, he had hastened upstairs to denounce Constant. He had then rushed to the girl's lodgings, and, finding his worst fears confirmed, planned at once his diabolically ingenious scheme of revenge. He told his landlady he was going to Devonport, so that if he bungled, the police would be put temporarily off his track. His real destination was Liverpool, for he intended to leave the country. Lest, however, his plan should break down here, too, he arranged an ingenious alibi by being driven to Euston for the 5:15 train to Liverpool. The cabman would not know he did not intend to go by it, but meant to return to 11 Glover Street, there to perpetrate this foul crime, interruption to which he had possibly barred by drugging his landlady. His presence at Liverpool (whither he really went by the second train) would corroborate the cabman's story. That night he had not undressed nor gone to bed; he had plotted out his devilish scheme till it was perfect; the fog came as an unexpected ally to cover his movements. Jealousy, outraged affection, the desire for revenge, the lust for political power—these were human. They might pity the criminal; they could not find him innocent of the crime.

Mr. Justice Crogie, summing up, began dead against the prisoner. Reviewing the evidence, he pointed out that plausible hypotheses neatly dovetailed did not necessarily weaken one another, the fitting so well together of the whole rather making for the truth of the parts. Besides, the case for the prosecution was as far from being all hypothesis as the case for the defense was from excluding hypotheses. The key, the letter, the reluctance to produce the letter, the heated interview with Constant, the mis-statement about the prisoner's destination, the flight to Liverpool, the false tale about searching for a "him," the denunciations of Constant, all these were facts. On the other hand, there were various lacunæ and hypotheses in the case for the defense. Even conceding the somewhat dubious alibi afforded by the prisoner's presence at Euston at 5:25 a.m., there was no attempt to account for his movements between that and 7:15 a.m. It was as possible that he returned to Bow as that he lingered about Euston. There was nothing in the medical evidence to make his guilt impossible. Nor was there anything inherently impossible in Constant's yielding to the sudden temptation of a beautiful girl, nor in a working girl deeming herself deserted, temporarily succumbing to the fascinations of a gentleman and regretting it bitterly afterwards. What had become of the girl was a mystery. Hers might have been one of those nameless corpses which the tide swirls up on slimy river banks. The jury must remember, too, that the relation might not have actually passed into dishonor; it might have been just grave enough to smite the girl's conscience, and to induce her to behave as she had done. It was enough that her letter should have excited the jealousy of the prisoner. There was one other point which he would like to impress on the jury, and which the counsel for the prosecution had not sufficiently insisted upon. This was that the prisoner's guiltiness was the only plausible solution that had ever been advanced of the Bow Mystery. The medical evidence agreed that Mr. Constant did not die by his own hand. Someone must therefore have murdered him. The number of people who could have had any possible reason or opportunity to murder him was extremely small. The prisoner had both reason and opportunity. By what logicians called the method of exclusion, suspicion would attach to him on even slight evidence. The actual evidence was strong and plausible, and now that Mr. Wimp's ingenious theory had enabled them to understand how the door could have been apparently locked and bolted from within, the last difficulty and the last argument for suicide had been removed. The prisoner's guilt was as clear as circumstantial evidence could make it. If they let him go free, the Bow Mystery might henceforward be placed among the archives of unavenged assassinations. Having thus well-nigh hung the prisoner, the judge wound up by insisting on the high probability of the story for the defense, though that, too, was dependent in important details upon the prisoner's mere private statements to his counsel. The jury, being by this time sufficiently muddled by his impartiality, was dismissed, with the exhortation to allow due weight to every fact and probability in determining their righteous verdict.

The minutes ran into hours, but the jury did not return. The shadows of night fell across the reeking fevered court before they announced their verdict—

"Guilty."

The judge put on his black cap.

The great reception arranged outside was a fiasco; the evening banquet was indefinitely postponed. Wimp had won; Grodman felt like a whipped cur.

11

"So you were right," Denzil could not help saying as he greeted Grodman a week afterwards. "I shall *not* live to tell the story of how you discovered the Bow murderer."

"Sit down," growled Grodman; "perhaps you will, after all." There was a dangerous gleam in his eyes. Denzil was sorry he had spoken.

"I sent for you," Grodman said, "to tell you that on the night Wimp arrested Mortlake I had made preparations for your arrest."

Denzil gasped, "What for?"

"My dear Denzil, there is a little law in this country invented for the confusion of the poetic. The greatest exponent of the Beautiful is only allowed the same number of wives as the greengrocer. I do not blame you for not being satisfied with Jane—she is a good servant but a bad mistress—but it was cruel to Kitty not to inform her that Jane had a prior right to you, and unjust to Jane to let her know of the contract with Kitty."

"They both know it now well enough, curse 'em," said the poet.

"Yes; your secrets are like your situations—you can't keep 'em long. My poor poet, I pity you—betwixt the devil and the deep sea."

"They're a pair of harpies, each holding over me the Damocles sword of an arrest for bigamy. Neither loves men."

"I should think they would come in very useful to you. You plant one in my house to tell my secrets to Wimp, and you plant one in Wimp's house to tell Wimp's secrets to me, I suppose. Out with some, then."

"Upon my honor you wrong me. Jane brought *me* here, not I Jane. As for Kitty, I never had such a shock in my life as at finding her installed in Wimp's house."

"She thought it safer to have the law handy for your arrest. Besides, she probably desired to occupy a parallel position to Jane's. She must do something for a living; *you* wouldn't do anything for hers. And so you couldn't go anywhere without meeting a wife! Ha! ha! ha! Serves you right, my polygamous poet."

"But why should *you* arrest me?"

"Revenge, Denzil. I have been the best friend you ever had in this cold, prosaic world. You have eaten my bread, drunk my claret, written my book, smoked my cigars, and pocketed my money. And yet, when you have an important piece of information bearing on a mystery about which I am thinking day and night, you calmly go and sell it to Wimp."

"I did-didn't," stammered Denzil.

"Liar! Do you think Kitty has any secrets from me? As soon as I discovered your two marriages I determined to have you arrested for—your treachery. But when I found you had, as I thought, put Wimp on the wrong scent, when I felt sure that by arresting Mortlake he was going to make a greater ass of himself than even nature had been able to do, then I forgave you. I let you walk about the earth— and drink—freely. Now it is Wimp who crows—everybody pats him on the back —they call him the mystery man of the Scotland Yard tribe. Poor Tom Mortlake will be hanged, and all through your telling Wimp about Jessie Dymond!"

"It was you yourself," said Denzil sullenly. "Everybody was giving it up. But you said 'Let us find out all that Arthur Constant did in the last few months of his life.' Wimp couldn't miss stumbling on Jessie sooner or later. I'd have throttled Constant if I had known he'd touched her," he wound up with irrelevant indignation.

Grodman winced at the idea that he himself had worked *ad majorem gloriam* of Wimp. And yet, had not Mrs. Wimp let out as much at the Christmas dinner?

"What's past is past," he said gruffly. "But if Tom Mortlake hangs, you go to Portland."

"How can I help Tom hanging?"

"Help the agitation as much as you can. Write letters under all sorts of names to all the papers. Get everybody you know to sign the great petition. Find out where Jessie Dymond is—the girl who holds the proof of Mortlake's innocence."

"You really believe him innocent?"

"Don't be satirical, Denzil. Haven't I taken the chair at all the meetings? Am I not the most copious correspondent of the Press?"

"I thought it was only to spite Wimp."

"Rubbish. It's to save poor Tom. He no more murdered Arthur Constant than —you did!" He laughed an unpleasant laugh.

Denzil bade him farewell, frigid with fear.

Grodman was up to his ears in letters and telegrams. Somehow he had become the leader of the rescue party—suggestions, subscriptions came from all sides. The suggestions were burned, the subscriptions acknowledged in the papers and used for hunting up the missing girl. Lucy Brent headed the list with a hundred pounds. It was a fine testimony to her faith in her dead lover's honor.

The release of the Jury had unloosed "The Greater Jury," which always now sits upon the smaller. Every means was taken to nullify the value of the "palladium of British liberty." The foreman and the jurors were interviewed, the judge was judged, and by those who were no judges. The Home Secretary (who had done nothing beyond accepting office under the Crown) was vituperated, and sundry provincial persons wrote confidentially to the Queen. Arthur Constant's backsliding cheered many by convincing them that others were as bad as themselves; and well-to-do tradesmen saw in Mortlake's wickedness the pernicious effects of Socialism. A dozen new theories were afloat. Constant had committed suicide by Esoteric Buddhism, as witness his devotion to Madame Blavatsky, or he had been murdered by his Mahatma or victimized by Hypnotism, Mesmerism, Somnambulism, and other weird abstractions. Grodman's great point was—Jessie Dymond must be produced, dead or alive. The electric current scoured the civilized world in search of her. What wonder if the shrewder sort divined that the indomitable detective had fixed his last hope on the girl's guilt? If Jessie had wrongs why should she not have avenged them herself? Did she not always remind the poet of Joan of Arc?

Another week passed; the shadow of the gallows crept over the days; on, on, remorselessly drawing nearer, as the last ray of hope sank below the horizon. The Home Secretary remained inflexible; the great petitions discharged their signatures at him in vain. He was a Conservative, sternly conscientious; and the mere insinuation that his obstinacy was due to the politics of the condemned only hardened him against the temptation of a cheap reputation for magnanimity. He would not even grant a respite, to increase the chances of the discovery of Jessie Dymond. In the last of the three weeks there was a final monster meeting of protest. Grodman again took the chair, and several distinguished faddists were present, as well as numerous respectable members of society. The Home Secretary acknowledged the receipt of their resolutions. The Trade Unions were divided in their allegiance; some whispered of faith and hope, others of financial defalcations. The former essayed to organize a procession and an indignation meeting on the Sunday preceding the Tuesday fixed for the execution, but it fell through on a rumor of confession. The Monday papers contained a last masterly letter from Grodman exposing the weakness of the evidence, but they knew nothing of a confession. The prisoner was mute and disdainful, professing little regard for a life empty of love and burdened with self-reproach. He refused to see clergymen. He was accorded an interview with Miss Brent in the presence of a gaoler, and solemnly asseverated his respect for her dead lover's memory. Monday buzzed with rumors; the evening papers chronicled them hour by hour. A poignant anxiety was abroad. The girl would be found. Some miracle would happen. A reprieve would arrive. The sentence would be commuted. But the short day darkened into night even as Mortlake's short day was darkening. And the shadow of the gallows crept on and on, and seemed to mingle with the twilight.

Crowl stood at the door of his shop, unable to work. His big gray eyes were heavy with unshed tears. The dingy wintry road seemed one vast cemetery; the street lamps twinkled like corpse-lights. The confused sounds of the street-life reached his ear as from another world. He did not see the people who flitted to and fro amid the gathering shadows of the cold, dreary night. One ghastly vision flashed and faded and flashed upon the background of the duskiness.

Denzil stood beside him, smoking in silence. A cold fear was at his heart. That terrible Grodman! As the hangman's cord was tightening round Mortlake, he felt the convict's chains tightening round himself. And yet there was one gleam of hope, feeble as the yellow flicker of the gas-lamp across the way. Grodman had obtained an interview with the condemned late that afternoon, and the parting had been painful, but the evening paper, that in its turn had obtained an interview with the ex-detective, announced on its placard

GRODMAN STILL CONFIDENT,

and the thousands who yet pinned their faith on this extraordinary man refused to extinguish the last sparks of hope. Denzil had bought the paper and scanned it eagerly, but there was nothing save the vague assurance that the indefatigable Grodman was still almost pathetically expectant of the miracle. Denzil did not share the expectation; he meditated flight.

"Peter," he said at last, "I'm afraid it's all over."

Crowl nodded, heart-broken. "All over!" he repeated, "and to think that he dies—and it is—all over!"

He looked despairingly at the blank wintry sky, where leaden clouds shut out the stars. "Poor, poor, young fellow! To-night alive and thinking. To-morrow night a clod, with no more sense or motion than a bit of leather! No compensation nowhere for being cut off innocent in the pride of youth and strength! A man who has always preached the Useful day and night, and toiled and suffered for his fellows. Where's the justice of it, where's the justice of it?" he demanded fiercely. Again his wet eyes wandered upwards towards Heaven, that Heaven away from which the soul of a dead saint at the Antipodes was speeding into infinite space.

"Well, where was the justice for Arthur Constant if he, too, was innocent?" said Denzil. "Really, Peter, I don't see why you should take it for granted that Tom is so dreadfully injured. Your horny-handed labor leaders are, after all, men of no aesthetic refinement, with no sense of the Beautiful; you cannot expect them to be exempt from the coarser forms of crime. Humanity must look for other leaders— to the seers and the poets!"

"Cantercot, if you say Tom's guilty I'll knock you down." The little cobbler turned upon his tall friend like a roused lion. Then he added, "I beg your pardon, Cantercot, I don't mean that. After all, I've no grounds. The judge is an honest man, and with gifts I can't lay claim to. But I believe in Tom with all my heart. And if Tom is guilty I believe in the Cause of the People with all my heart all the same. The Fads are doomed to death; they may be reprieved, but they must die at last."

He drew a deep sigh, and looked along the dreary Road. It was quite dark now, but by the light of the lamps and the gas in the shop windows the dull, monotonous Road lay revealed in all its sordid, familiar outlines; with its long stretches of chill pavement, its unlovely architecture, and its endless stream of prosaic pedestrians.

A sudden consciousness of the futility of his existence pierced the little cobbler like an icy wind. He saw his own life, and a hundred million lives like his, swelling and breaking like bubbles on a dark ocean, unheeded, uncared for.

A newsboy passed along, clamoring "The Bow murderer, preparations for the hexecution!"

A terrible shudder shook the cobbler's frame. His eyes ranged sightlessly after the boy; the merciful tears filled them at last.

"The Cause of the People," he murmured, brokenly, "I believe in the Cause of the People. There is nothing else."

"Peter, come in to tea, you'll catch cold," said Mrs. Crowl.

Denzil went in to tea and Peter followed.

Meantime, round the house of the Home Secretary, who was in town, an ever-augmenting crowd was gathered, eager to catch the first whisper of a reprieve.

The house was guarded by a cordon of police, for there was no inconsiderable danger of a popular riot. At times a section of the crowd groaned and hooted. Once a volley of stones was discharged at the windows. The newsboys were busy vending their special editions, and the reporters struggled through the crowd, clutching descriptive pencils, and ready to rush off to telegraph offices should anything "extra special" occur. Telegraph boys were coming up every now and again with threats, messages, petitions, and exhortations from all parts of the country to the unfortunate Home Secretary, who was striving to keep his aching head cool as he went through the voluminous evidence for the last time and pondered over the more important letters which "The Greater Jury" had contributed to the obscuration of the problem. Grodman's letters in that morning's paper shook him most; under his scientific analysis the circumstantial chain seemed forged of painted cardboard. Then the poor man read the judge's summing up, and the chain became tempered steel. The noise of the crowd outside broke upon his ear in his study like the roar of a distant ocean. The more the rabble hooted him, the more he essayed to hold scrupulously the scales of life and death. And the crowd grew and grew, as men came away from their work. There were many that loved the man who lay in the jaws of death, and a spirit of mad revolt surged in their breasts. And the sky was gray, and the bleak night deepened, and the shadow of the gallows crept on.

Suddenly a strange inarticulate murmur spread through the crowd, a vague whisper of no one knew what. Something had happened. Somebody was coming. A second later and one of the outskirts of the throng was agitated, and a convulsive cheer went up from it, and was taken up infectiously all along the street. The crowd parted—a hansom dashed through the center. "Grodman! Grodman!" shouted those who recognized the occupant. "Grodman! Hurrah!" Grodman was outwardly calm and pale, but his eyes glittered; he waved his hand encouragingly as the hansom dashed up to the door, cleaving the turbulent crowd as a canoe cleaves the waters. Grodman sprang out, the constables at the portal made way for him respectfully. He knocked imperatively, the door was opened cautiously; a boy rushed up and delivered a telegram; Grodman forced his way in, gave his name, and insisted on seeing the Home Secretary on a matter of life and death. Those near the door heard his words and cheered, and the crowd divined the good omen, and the air throbbed with canonades of joyous sound. The cheers rang in Grodman's ears as the door slammed behind him. The reporters struggled to the front. An excited knot of working men pressed round the arrested hansom; they took the horse out. A dozen enthusiasts struggled for the honor of placing themselves between the shafts. And the crowd awaited Grodman.

12

Grodman was ushered into the conscientious Minister's study. The doughty chief of the agitation was, perhaps, the one man who could not be denied. As he entered, the Home Secretary's face seemed lit up with relief. At a sign from his master, the amanuensis who had brought in the last telegram took it back with him into the outer room where he worked. Needless to say, not a tithe of the Minister's correspondence ever came under his own eyes.

"You have a valid reason for troubling me, I suppose, Mr. Grodman?" said the Home Secretary, almost cheerfully. "Of course it is about Mortlake?"

"It is; and I have the best of all reasons."

"Take a seat. Proceed."

"Pray do not consider me impertinent, but have you ever given any attention to the science of evidence?"

"How do you mean?" asked the Home Secretary, rather puzzled, adding, with a melancholy smile, "I have had to do so, lately. Of course, I've never been a criminal lawyer, like some of my predecessors. But I should hardly speak of it as a science; I look upon it as a question of common-sense."

"Pardon me, sir. It is the most subtle and difficult of all the sciences. It is, indeed, rather the science of the sciences. What is the whole of Inductive Logic, as laid down, say, by Bacon and Mill, but an attempt to appraise the value of evidence, the said evidence being the trails left by the Creator, so to speak? The Creator has—I say it in all reverence—drawn a myriad red herrings across the track, but the true scientist refuses to be baffled by superficial appearances in detecting the secrets of Nature. The vulgar herd catches at the gross apparent fact, but the man of insight knows that what lies on the surface does lie."

"Very interesting, Mr. Grodman, but really—"

"Bear with me, sir. The science of evidence being thus so extremely subtle, and demanding the most acute and trained observation of facts, the most comprehensive understanding of human psychology, is naturally given over to professors who have not the remotest idea that 'things are not what they seem,' and that everything is other than it appears; to professors, most of whom by their year-long devotion to the shop-counter or the desk, have acquired an intimate acquaintance with all the infinite shades and complexities of things and human nature. When twelve of these professors are put in a box, it is called a jury. When one of these professors is put in a box by himself, he is called a witness. The retailing of evidence —the observation of facts—is given over to people who go through their lives without eyes; the appreciation of evidence—the judging of these facts—is surrendered to people who may possibly be adept in weighing out pounds of sugar. Apart from their sheer inability to fulfill either function—to observe, or to judge—their observation and their judgment alike are vitiated by all sorts of irrelevant prejudices."

"You are attacking trial by jury."

"Not necessarily. I am prepared to accept that scientifically, on the ground that, as there are, as a rule, only two alternatives, the balance of probability is slightly in favor of the true decision being come to. Then, in cases where experts like myself have got up the evidence, the jury can be made to see through trained eyes."

The Home Secretary tapped impatiently with his foot.

"I can't listen to abstract theorizing," he said. "Have you any fresh concrete evidence?"

"Sir, everything depends on our getting down to the root of the matter. What percentage of average evidence should you think is thorough, plain, simple, unvarnished fact, 'the truth, the whole truth, and nothing but the truth'?"

"Fifty?" said the Minister, humoring him a little.

"Not five. I say nothing of lapses of memory, of inborn defects of observational power—though the suspiciously precise recollection of dates and events possessed by ordinary witnesses in important trials taking place years after the occurrences involved, is one of the most amazing things in the curiosities of modern jurisprudence. I defy you, sir, to tell me what you had for dinner last Monday, or what exactly you were saying and doing at five o'clock last Tuesday afternoon. Nobody whose life does not run in mechanical grooves can do anything of the sort; unless, of course, the facts have been very impressive. But this by the way. The great obstacle to veracious observation is the element of prepossession in all vision. Has it ever struck you, sir, that we never *see* anyone more than once, if that? The first time we meet a man we may possibly see him as he is; the second time our vision is colored and modified by the memory of the first. Do our friends appear to us as they appear to strangers? Do our rooms, our furniture, our pipes strike our eye as they would strike the eye of an outsider, looking on them for the first time? Can a mother see her babe's ugliness, or a lover his mistress's shortcomings, though they stare everybody else in the face? Can we see ourselves as others see us? No; habit, prepossession changes all. The mind is a large factor of every so-called external fact. The eye sees, sometimes, what it wishes to see, more often what it expects to see. You follow me, sir?"

The Home Secretary nodded his head less impatiently. He was beginning to be interested. The hubbub from without broke faintly upon their ears.

"To give you a definite example. Mr. Wimp says that when I burst open the door of Mr. Constant's room on the morning of December 4th, and saw that the staple of the bolt had been wrested by the pin from the lintel, I jumped at once to the conclusion that I had broken the bolt. Now I admit that this was so; only in things like this you do not seem to *conclude*, you jump so fast that you *see*, or seem to see. On the other hand, when you *see* a *standing* ring of fire produced by whirling a burning stick, you do *not* believe in its continuous existence. It is the same when witnessing a legerdemain performance. Seeing is not always believing, despite the proverb; but believing is often seeing. It is not to the point that in that little matter of the door Wimp was as hopelessly and incurably wrong as he has been in everything all along. The door *was* securely bolted. Still, I confess that I should have seen that I had broken the bolt in forcing the door, even if it had been broken beforehand. Never once since December 4th did this possibility occur to me till Wimp with perverted ingenuity suggested it. If this is the case with a trained observer, one moreover fully conscious of this ineradicable tendency of the human mind, how must it be with an untrained observer?"

"Come to the point, come to the point," said the Home Secretary, putting out his hand as if it itched to touch the bell on the writing-table.

"Such as," went on Grodman imperturbably, "such as—Mrs. Drabdump. That worthy person is unable, by repeated violent knocking, to arouse her lodger who yet desires to be aroused; she becomes alarmed, she rushes across to get my assistance; I burst open the door—what do you think the good lady expected to see?"

"Mr. Constant murdered, I suppose," murmured the Home Secretary wonderingly.

"Exactly. And so she saw it. And what should you think was the condition of Arthur Constant when the door yielded to my violent exertions and flew open?"

"Why, was he not dead?" gasped the Home Secretary, his heart fluttering violently.

"Dead? A young, healthy fellow like that! When the door flew open, Arthur Constant was sleeping the sleep of the just. It was a deep, a very deep sleep, of course, else the blows at his door would long since have awakened him. But all the while Mrs. Drabdump's fancy was picturing her lodger cold and stark, the poor young fellow was lying in bed in a nice warm sleep."

"You mean to say you found Arthur Constant alive?"

"As you were last night."

The Minister was silent, striving confusedly to take in the situation. Outside the crowd was cheering again. It was probably to pass the time.

"Then, when was he murdered?"

"Immediately afterwards."

"By whom?"

"Well, that is, if you will pardon me, not a very intelligent question. Science and common-sense are in accord for once. Try the method of exhaustion. It must have been either by Mrs. Drabdump or myself."

"You mean to say that Mrs. Drabdump—!"

"Poor dear Mrs. Drabdump, you don't deserve this of your Home Secretary! The idea of that good lady!"

"It was *you!*"

"Calm yourself, my dear Home Secretary. There is nothing to be alarmed at. It was a solitary experiment, and I intend it to remain so." The noise without grew louder. "Three cheers for Grodman! Hip, hip, hip, hooray," fell faintly on their ears.

But the Minister, pallid and deeply moved, touched the bell. The Home Secretary's home secretary appeared. He looked at the great man's agitated face with suppressed surprise.

"Thank you for calling in your amanuensis," said Grodman. "I intended to ask you to lend me his services. I suppose he can write shorthand."

The Minister nodded, speechless.

"That is well. I intend this statement to form the basis of an appendix to the twenty-fifth edition—sort of silver wedding—of my book, *Criminals I Have Caught*. Mr. Denzil Cantercot, who, by the will I have made to-day, is appointed my literary executor, will have the task of working it up with literary and dramatic touches after the model of the other chapters of my book. I have every confidence he will be able to do me as much justice, from a literary point of view, as you, sir, no doubt will from a legal. I feel certain he will succeed in catching the style of the other chapters to perfection."

"Templeton," whispered the Home Secretary, "this man may be a lunatic. The effort to solve the Big Bow Mystery may have addled his brain. Still," he added aloud, "it will be as well for you to take down his statement in shorthand."

"Thank you, sir," said Grodman, heartily. "Ready, Mr. Templeton? Here goes. My career till I left the Scotland Yard Detective Department is known to all the world. Is that too fast for you, Mr. Templeton? A little? Well, I'll go slower; but pull me up if I forget to keep the brake on. When I retired, I discovered that I was a bachelor. But it was too late to marry. Time hung heavy on my hands. The preparation of my book, *Criminals I Have Caught*, kept me occupied for some months. When it was published, I had nothing more to do but think. I had plenty of money, and it was safely invested; there was no call for speculation. The future was meaningless to me; I regretted I had not elected to die in harness. As idle old men must, I lived in the past. I went over and over again my ancient exploits; I re-read my book. And as I thought and thought, away from the excitement of the actual hunt, and seeing the facts in a truer perspective, so it grew daily clearer to me that criminals were more fools than rogues. Every crime I had traced, however cleverly perpetrated, was from the point of view of penetrability a weak failure. Traces and trails were left on all sides—ragged edges, rough-hewn corners; in short, the job was botched, artistic completeness unattained. To the vulgar, my feats might seem marvelous—the average man is mystified to grasp how you detect the letter 'e' in a simple cryptogram—to myself they were as commonplace as the crimes they unveiled. To me now, with my lifelong study of the science of evidence, it seemed possible to commit not merely one but a thousand crimes that should be absolutely undiscoverable. And yet criminals would go on sinning, and giving themselves away, in the same old grooves—no originality, no dash, no individual insight, no fresh conception! One would imagine there were an Academy of crime with forty thousand armchairs. And gradually, as I pondered and brooded over the thought, there came upon me the desire to commit a crime that should baffle detection. I could invent hundreds of such crimes, and please myself by imagining them done; but would they really work out in practice? Evidently the sole performer of my experiment must be myself; the subject—whom or what? Accident should determine. I itched to commence with murder—to tackle the stiffest problems first, and I burned to startle and baffle the world—especially the world of which I had ceased to be. Outwardly I was calm, and spoke to the people about me as usual. Inwardly I was on fire with a consuming scientific passion. I sported with my pet theories, and fitted them mentally on everyone I met. Every friend or acquaintance I sat and gossiped with, I was plotting how to murder without leaving a clue. There is not one of my friends or acquaintances I have not done away with in thought. There is no public man—have no fear, my dear Home Secretary—I have not planned to assassinate secretly, mysteriously, unintelligibly, undiscoverably. Ah, how I could give the stock criminals points—with their second-hand motives, their conventional conceptions, their commonplace details, their lack of artistic feeling and restraint."

The crowd had again started cheering. Impatient as the watchers were, they felt that no news was good news. The longer the interview accorded by the Home Secretary to the chairman of the Defense Committee, the greater the hope his obduracy was melting. The idol of the people would be saved, and "Grodman" and "Tom Mortlake" were mingled in the exultant plaudits.

"The late Arthur Constant," continued the great criminologist, "came to live nearly opposite me. I cultivated his acquaintance—he was a lovable young fellow, an excellent subject for experiment. I do not know when I have ever taken to a man more. From the moment I first set eyes on him, there was a peculiar sympathy between us. We were drawn to each other. I felt instinctively he would be the man. I loved to hear him speak enthusiastically of the Brotherhood of Man—I, who knew the brotherhood of man was to the ape, the serpent, and the tiger—and he seemed to find a pleasure in stealing a moment's chat with me from his engrossing self-appointed duties. It is a pity humanity should have been robbed of so valuable a life. But it had to be. At a quarter to ten on the night of December 3rd he came to me. Naturally I said nothing about this visit at the inquest or the trial. His object was to consult me mysteriously about some girl. He said he had privately lent her money—which she was to repay at her convenience. What the money was for he did not know, except that it was somehow connected with an act of abnegation in which he had vaguely encouraged her. The girl had since disappeared, and he was in distress about her. He would not tell me who it was—of course now, sir, you know as well as I it was Jessie Dymond—but asked for advice as to how to set about finding her. He mentioned that Mortlake was leaving for Devonport by the first train on the next day. Of old I should have connected these two facts and sought the thread: now, as he spoke, all my thoughts were dyed red. He was suffering perceptibly from toothache, and in answer to my sympathetic inquiries told me it had been allowing him very little sleep. Everything combined to invite the trial of one of my favorite theories. I spoke to him in a fatherly way, and when I had tendered some vague advice about the girl, I made him promise to secure a night's rest (before he faced the arduous tram-men's meeting in the morning) by taking a sleeping draught. I gave him a quantity of sulphonal in a phial. It is a new drug, which produces protracted sleep without disturbing digestion, and which I use myself. He promised faithfully to take the draught; and I also exhorted him earnestly to bolt and bar and lock himself in, so as to stop up every chink or aperture by which the cold air of the winter's night might creep into the room. I remonstrated with him on the careless manner he treated his body, and he laughed in his good-humored, gentle way, and promised to obey me in all things. And he did. That Mrs. Drabdump, failing to rouse him, would cry 'Murder!' I took for certain. She is built that way. As even Sir Charles Brown-Harland remarked, she habitually takes her prepossessions for facts, her inferences for observations. She forecasts the future in gray. Most women of Mrs. Drabdump's class would have behaved as she did. She happened to be a peculiarly favorable specimen for working on by 'suggestion,' but I would have undertaken to produce the same effect on almost any woman. The Key to the Big Bow Mystery is feminine psychology. The only uncertain link in the chain was, Would Mrs. Drabdump rush across to get *me* to break open the door? Women always rush for a man. I was well-nigh the nearest, and certainly the most authoritative man in the street, and I took it for granted she would."

"But suppose she hadn't?" the Home Secretary could not help asking.

"Then the murder wouldn't have happened, that's all. In due course Arthur Constant would have awoke, or somebody else breaking open the door would have found him sleeping; no harm done, nobody any the wiser. I could hardly sleep myself that night. The thought of the extraordinary crime I was about to commit —a burning curiosity to know whether Wimp would detect the *modus operandi*— the prospect of sharing the feeling of murderers with whom I had been in contact all my life without being in touch with the terrible joys of their inner life—the fear lest I should be too fast asleep to hear Mrs. Drabdump's knock—these things agitated me and disturbed my rest. I lay tossing on my bed, planning every detail of poor Constant's end. The hours dragged slowly and wretchedly on towards the misty dawn. I was racked with suspense. Was I to be disappointed after all? At last the welcome sound came—the rat-tat-tat of murder. The echoes of that knock are yet in my ears. 'Come over and kill him!' I put my nightcapped head out of the window and told her to wait for me. I dressed hurriedly, took my razor, and went across to 11 Glover Street. As I broke open the door of the bedroom in which Arthur Constant lay sleeping, his head resting on his hands, I cried, 'My God!' as if I saw some awful vision. A mist as of blood swam before Mrs. Drabdump's eyes. She cowered back; for an instant (I divined rather than saw the action) she shut off the dreaded sight with her hands. In that instant I had made my cut—precisely, scientifically—made so deep a cut and drawn out the weapon so sharply that there was scarce a drop of blood on it; then there came from the throat a jet of blood which Mrs. Drabdump, conscious only of the horrid gash, saw but vaguely. I covered up the face quickly with a handkerchief to hide any convulsive distortion. But as the medical evidence (in this detail accurate) testified, death was instantaneous. I pocketed the razor and the empty sulphonal phial. With a woman like Mrs. Drabdump to watch me, I could do anything I pleased. I got her to draw my attention to the fact that both the windows were fastened. Some fool, by the by, thought there was a discrepancy in the evidence because the police found only one window fastened, forgetting that, in my innocence, I took care not to refasten the window I had opened to call for aid. Naturally I did not call for aid before a considerable time had elapsed. There was Mrs. Drabdump to quiet, and the excuse of making notes—as an old hand. My object was to gain time. I wanted the body to be fairly cold and stiff before being discovered, though there was not much danger here; for, as you saw by the medical evidence, there is no telling the time of death to an hour or two. The frank way in which I said the death was very recent disarmed all suspicion, and even Dr. Robinson was unconsciously worked upon, in adjudging the time of death, by the knowledge (query here, Mr. Templeton) that it had preceded my advent on the scene.

"Before leaving Mrs. Drabdump, there is just one point I should like to say a word about. You have listened so patiently, sir, to my lectures on the science of sciences that you will not refuse to hear the last. A good deal of importance has been attached to Mrs. Drabdump's oversleeping herself by half an hour. It happens that this (like the innocent fog which has also been made responsible for much) is a purely accidental and irrelevant circumstance. In all works on inductive logic it is thoroughly recognized that only some of the circumstances of a phenomenon are of its essence and casually interconnected; there is always a certain proportion of heterogeneous accompaniments which have no intimate relation whatever with the phenomenon. Yet, so crude is as yet the comprehension of the science of evidence, that *every* feature of the phenomenon under investigation is made equally important, and sought to be linked with the chain of evidence. To attempt to explain everything is always the mark of the tiro. The fog and Mrs. Drabdump's oversleeping herself were mere accidents. There are always these irrelevant accompaniments, and the true scientist allows for this element of (so to speak) chemically unrelated detail. Even I never counted on the unfortunate series of accidental phenomena which have led to Mortlake's implication in a net-work of suspicion. On the other hand, the fact that my servant, Jane, who usually goes about ten, left a few minutes earlier on the night of December 3rd, so that she didn't know of Constant's visit, was a relevant accident. In fact, just as the art of the artist or the editor consists largely in knowing what to leave out, so does the art of the scientific detector or crime consist in knowing what details to ignore. In short, to explain everything is to explain too much. And too much is worse than too little.

"To return to my experiment. My success exceeded my wildest dreams. None had an inkling of the truth. The insolubility of the Big Bow Mystery teased the acutest minds in Europe and the civilized world. That a man could have been murdered in a thoroughly inaccessible room savored the ages of magic. The redoubtable Wimp, who had been blazoned as my successor, fell back on the theory of suicide. The mystery would have slept till my death, but—I fear—for my own ingenuity. I tried to stand outside myself, and to look at the crime with the eyes of another, or of my old self. I found the work of art so perfect as to leave only one sublimely simple solution. The very terms of the problem were so inconceivable that, had I not been the murderer, I should have suspected myself, in conjunction, of course, with Mrs. Drabdump. The first persons to enter the room would have seemed to me guilty. I wrote at once (in a disguised hand and over the signature of 'One Who Looks Through His Own Spectacles') to the *Pell Mell Press* to suggest this. By associating myself thus with Mrs. Drabdump I made it difficult for people to dissociate the two who entered the room together. To dash a half-truth in the world's eyes is the surest way of blinding it altogether. This pseudonymous letter of mine I contradicted (in my own name) the next day, and in the course of the long letter which I was tempted to write, I adduced fresh evidence against the theory of suicide. I was disgusted with the open verdict, and wanted men to be up and doing and trying to find me out. I enjoyed the hunt more.

"Unfortunately, Wimp, set on the chase again by my own letter, by dint of persistent blundering, blundered into a track which—by a devilish tissue of coincidences I had neither foreseen nor dreamed of—seemed to the world the true.

Mortlake was arrested and condemned. Wimp had apparently crowned his reputation. This was too much. I had taken all this trouble merely to put a feather in Wimp's cap, whereas I had expected to shake his reputation by it. It was bad enough that an innocent man should suffer; but that Wimp should achieve a reputation he did not deserve, and overshadow all his predecessors by dint of a colossal mistake, this seemed to me intolerable. I have moved Heaven and earth to get the verdict set aside, and to save the prisoner; I have exposed the weakness of the evidence; I have had the world searched for the missing girl; I have petitioned and agitated. In vain. I have failed. Now I play my last card. As the overweening Wimp could not be allowed to go down to posterity as the solver of this terrible mystery. I decided that the condemned man might just as well profit by his exposure. That is the reason I make the exposure to-night, before it is too late to save Mortlake."

"So that is the reason?" said the Home Secretary with a suspicion of mockery in his tones.

"The sole reason."

Even as he spoke, a deeper roar than ever penetrated the study. "A Reprieve! Hooray! Hooray!" The whole street seemed to rock with earthquake, and the names of Grodman and Mortlake to be thrown up in a fiery jet. "A Reprieve! A Reprieve!" The very windows rattled. And even above the roar rose the shrill voices of the newsboys: "Reprieve of Mortlake! Mortlake reprieved!"

Grodman looked wonderingly towards the street. "How do they know?" he murmured.

"Those evening papers are amazing," said the Minister drily. "But I suppose they had everything ready in type for the contingency." He turned to his secretary. "Templeton, have you got down every word of Mr. Grodman's confession?"

"Every word, sir."

"Then bring in the cable you received just as Mr. Grodman entered the house."

Templeton went back into the outer room and brought back the cablegram that had been lying on the Minister's writing-table when Grodman came in. The Home Secretary silently handed it to his visitor. It was from the Chief of Police of Melbourne, announcing that Jessie Dymond had just arrived in that city in a sailing vessel, ignorant of all that had occurred, and had been immediately dispatched back to England, having made a statement entirely corroborating the theory of the defense.

"Pending further inquiries into this," said the Home Secretary, not without appreciation of the grim humor of the situation as he glanced at Grodman's ashen cheeks, "I had already reprieved the prisoner. Mr. Templeton went out to dispatch the messenger to the governor of Newgate as you entered this room. Mr. Wimp's card-castle would have tumbled to pieces without your assistance. Your still undiscoverable crime would have shaken his reputation as you intended."

A sudden explosion shook the room and blended with the cheers of the populace. Grodman had shot himself—very scientifically—in the heart. He fell at the Home Secretary's feet, stone dead.

Some of the working men who had been standing waiting by the shafts of the hansom helped to bear the stretcher.

Dorothy L. Sayers

THE QUEEN'S SQUARE

Peter Death Bredon Wimsey: clearly a name to conjure with.

The younger son of the fifteenth Duke of Denver made his first appearance as an amateur detective in 1923 when his mother asked him to find some explanation for why a nude corpse turned up in a friend's bathtub. Lord Peter was on his way to a rare-book auction at the time and sent his faithful butler, Bunter, on to do his bidding for him. Over the years Wimsey appeared in eleven detective novels and several collections of short stories and often seemed to get involved in cases because his relatives were suspects: his brother, the current duke; his sister; the woman —mystery writer Harriet Vane—he would marry; even one of his sons.

Dorothy L. Sayers (1893–1957) has been a favorite of people who claim they don't really read mystery stories. She always made it clear that her true interests—religion, medieval literature—were more lofty than detection, and in 1947, after announcing that she would write no more detective stories, was quoted as saying, "I wrote the Peter Wimsey books when I was very young and had no money. I made some money, and then stopped writing novels and began to write what I had always wanted to write." She spent the last ten years of her life translating, and writing about, Dante.

She also put together one of the first major mystery anthologies, the twelve-hundred-page Omnibus of Crime *(which sold for $3 in August 1929, when it was a Book-of-the-Month Club selection). It began with an introductory history of the genre which, Christopher Morley wrote, would be "a comfort to any serious reader who doubts whether detective stories are sufficiently dignified."*

The introduction ends with Miss Sayers predicting that as the reading public became more aware of the detective writer's limited bag of tricks, mysteries would become more linked to "the novel of manners" than to the adventure novel, but "the crime thriller" would continue to exist as long as crime exists. "It is, as always," she concluded, "the higher type that is threatened with extinction."

The Queen's Square

"Y OU JACK O' DI'MONDS, you Jack o'Di'monds," said Mark Sambourne, shaking
a reproachful head, "I know you of old." He rummaged beneath the white
satin of his costume, paneled with gigantic oblongs and spotted to represent a set
of dominoes. "Hang this fancy rig! Where the blazes has the fellow put my pockets?
You rob my pocket, yes, you rob-a my pocket, you rob my pocket of silver and go-
ho-hold. How much do you make it?" He extracted a fountain-pen and a check-
book.

"Five-seventeen-six," said Lord Peter Wimsey. "That's right, isn't it, partner?"
His huge blue-and-scarlet sleeves rustled as he turned to Lady Hermione Cree-
thorpe, who, in her Queen of Clubs costume, looked a very redoubtable virgin, as,
indeed, she was.

"Quite right," said the old lady, "and I consider that very cheap."

"We haven't been playing long," said Wimsey apologetically.

"It would have been more, Auntie," observed Mrs. Wrayburn, "if you hadn't
been greedy. You shouldn't have doubled those four spades of mine."

Lady Hermione snorted, and Wimsey hastily cut in:

"It's a pity we've got to stop, but Deverill will never forgive us if we're not there
to dance Sir Roger. He feels strongly about it. What's the time? Twenty past one.
Sir Roger is timed to start sharp at half past. I suppose we'd better tootle back to the
ballroom."

"I suppose we had," agreed Mrs. Wrayburn. She stood up, displaying her dress,
boldly patterned with the red and black points of a backgammon board. "It's very
good of you," she added, as Lady Hermione's voluminous skirts swept through the
hall ahead of them, "to chuck your dancing to give Auntie her bridge. She does so
hate to miss it."

"Not at all," replied Wimsey. "It's a pleasure. And in any case I was jolly glad
of a rest. These costumes are dashed hot for dancing in."

"You make a splendid Jack of Diamonds, though. Such a good idea of Lady
Deverill's, to make everybody come as a game. It cuts out all those wearisome
pierrots and columbines." They skirted the south-west angle of the ballroom and
emerged into the south corridor, lit by a great hanging lantern in four lurid colors.
Under the arcading they paused and stood watching the floor, where Sir Charles
Deverill's guests were fox-trotting to a lively tune discoursed by the band in the
musicians' gallery at the far end. "Hullo, Giles!" added Mrs. Wrayburn, "you look
hot."

"I am hot," said Giles Pomfret. "I wish to goodness I hadn't been so clever
about this infernal costume. It's a beautiful billiard-table, but I can't sit down in
it." He mopped his heated brow, crowned with an elegant green lamp-shade. "The

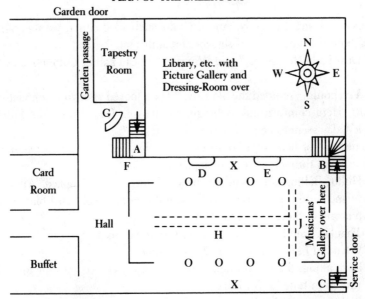

A, Stair to Dressing-room and Gallery; B, Stair to Gallery; C, Stair to Musicians' Gallery only; D, Settee where Joan Carstairs sat; E, Settee where Jim Playfair sat; F, Where Waits stood; G, Where Ephraim Dodd sat; H, Guests' "Sir Roger"; J, Servants' "Sir Roger"; XX, Hanging Lanterns; O O O O, Arcading.

only rest I can get is to hitch my behind on a radiator, and as they're all in full blast, it's not very cooling. Thank goodness, I can always make these damned sandwich boards an excuse to get out of dancing." He propped himself against the nearest column looking martyred.

"Nina Hartford comes off best," said Mrs. Wrayburn. "Water-polo—so sensible—just a bathing-dress and a ball; though I must say it would look better on a less *Restoration* figure. You playing cards are much the prettiest, and I think the chess-pieces run you close. There goes Gerda Bellingham, dancing with her husband—isn't she *too* marvelous in that red wig? And the bustle and everything—my dear, so attractive. I'm glad they didn't make themselves too Lewis Carroll; Charmian Grayle is the sweetest White Queen—where is she, by the way?"

"I don't like that young woman," said Lady Hermione, "she's fast."

"Dear lady!"

"I've no doubt you think me old-fashioned. Well, I'm glad I am. I say she's fast, and, what's more, heartless. I was watching her before supper, and I'm sorry for Tony Lee. She's been flirting as hard as she can go with Harry Vibart—not to give it a worse name—and she's got Jim Playfair on a string, too. She can't even leave Frank Bellingham alone, though she's staying in his house."

"Oh, I say, Lady H!" protested Sambourne, "you're a bit hard on Miss Grayle. I mean, she's an awfully sporting kid and all that."

"I detest that word 'sporting,' " snapped Lady Hermione. "Nowadays it merely means drunk and disorderly. And she's not such a kid either, young man. In three years' time she'll be a hag, if she goes on at this rate."

"Dear Lady Hermione," said Wimsey, "we can't all be untouched by time, like you."

"You could," retorted the old lady, "if you looked after your stomachs and your morals. Here comes Frank Bellingham—looking for a drink, no doubt. Young people today seem to be positively pickled in gin."

The fox-trot had come to an end, and the Red King was threading his ways towards them through a group of applauding couples.

"Hullo, Bellingham!" said Wimsey. "Your crown's crooked. Allow me." He set wig and head-dress to rights with skillful fingers. "Not that I blame you. What crown is safe in these Bolshevik days?"

"Thanks," said Bellingham. "I say, I want a drink."

"What did I tell you?" said Lady Hermione.

"Buzz along, then, old man," said Wimsey. "You've got four minutes. Mind you turn up in time for Sir Roger."

"Right you are. Oh, I'm dancing it with Gerda, by the way. If you see her, you might tell her where I've gone to."

"We will. Lady Hermione, you're honoring me, of course?"

"Nonsense! You're not expecting me to dance at my age? The Old Maid ought to be a wallflower."

"Nothing of the sort. If only I'd had the luck to be born earlier, you and I should have appeared side by side, as Matrimony. Of course you're going to dance it with me—unless you mean to throw me over for one of these youngsters."

"I've no use for youngsters," said Lady Hermione. "No guts. Spindle-shanks." She darted a swift glance at Wimsey's scarlet hose. "You at least have some suggestion of calves. I can stand up with you without blushing for you."

Wimsey bowed his scarlet cap and curled wig in deep reverence over the gnarled knuckles extended to him.

"You make me the happiest of men. We'll show them all how to do it. Right hand, left hand, both hands across, back to back, round you go and up the middle. There's Deverill going down to tell the band to begin. Punctual old bird, isn't he? Just two minutes to go . . . What's the matter, Miss Carstairs? Lost your partner?"

"Yes—have you seen Tony Lee anywhere?"

"The White King? Not a sign. Nor the White Queen either. I expect they're together somewhere."

"Probably. Poor old Jimmie Playfair is sitting patiently in the north corridor, looking like Casabianca."

"You'd better go along and console him," said Wimsey, laughing.

Joan Carstairs made a face and disappeared in the direction of the buffet, just as Sir Charles Deverill, giver of the party, bustled up to Wimsey and his companions, resplendent in a Chinese costume patterned with red and green dragons, bamboos, circles, and characters, and carrying on his shoulder a stuffed bird with an enormous tail.

"Now, now," he exclaimed, "come along, come along, come along! All ready for Sir Roger. Got your partner, Wimsey? Ah, yes, Lady Hermione—splendid. You must come and stand next to your dear mother and me, Wimsey. Don't be late, don't be late. We want to dance it right through. The waits will begin at two o'clock—I hope they will arrive in good time. Dear me, dear me! Why aren't the servants in yet? I told Watson—I must go and speak to him."

He darted away, and Wimsey, laughing, led his partner up to the top of the room, where his mother, the Dowager Duchess of Denver, stood waiting, magnificent as the Queen of Spades.

"Ah! here you are," said the Duchess placidly. "Dear Sir Charles—he was getting quite flustered. Such a man for punctuality—he ought to have been a Royalty. A delightful party, Hermione, isn't it? Sir Roger and the waits—quite medieval—and a Yule-log in the hall, with the steam radiators and everything— so oppressive!"

"Tumty, tumty, tiddledy, tumty, tumty, tiddledy," sang Lord Peter, as the band broke into the old tune. "I do adore this music. Foot it featly here and there —oh! there's Gerda Bellingham. Just a moment! Mrs. Bellingham—hi! your royal spouse awaits your Red Majesty's pleasure in the buffet. Do hurry him up. He's only got half a minute."

The Red Queen smiled at him, her pale face and black eyes startlingly brilliant beneath her scarlet wig and crown.

"I'll bring him up to scratch all right," she said, and passed on, laughing.

"So she will," said the Dowager. "You'll see that young man in the Cabinet before very long. Such a handsome couple on a public platform, and very sound, I'm told, about pigs, and that's so important, the British breakfast-table being what it is."

Sir Charles Deverill, looking a trifle heated, came hurrying back and took his place at the head of the double line of guests, which now extended three-quarters of the way down the ball-room. At the lower end, just in front of the Musicians' Gallery, the staff had filed in, to form a second Sir Roger, at right angles to the main set. The clock chimed the half-hour. Sir Charles, craning an anxious neck, counted the dancers.

"Eighteen couples. We're two couples short. How vexatious! Who are missing?"

"The Bellinghams?" said Wimsey. "No, they're here. It's the White King and Queen, Badminton and Diabolo."

"There's Badminton!" cried Mrs. Wrayburn, signaling frantically across the room. "Jim! Jim! Bother! He's gone back again. He's waiting for Charmian Grayle."

"Well, we can't wait any longer," said Sir Charles peevishly. "Duchess, will you lead off?"

The Dowager obediently threw her black velvet train over her arm and skipped away down the center, displaying an uncommonly neat pair of scarlet ankles. The two lines of dancers, breaking into the hop-and-skip step of the country dance, jigged sympathetically. Below them, the cross lines of black and white and livery coats followed their example with respect. Sir Charles Deverill, dancing solemnly down after the Duchess, joined hands with Nina Hartford from the far end of the line. Tumty, tumty, tiddledy, tumty, tumty, tiddledy . . . the first couple turned outward and led the dancers down. Wimsey, catching the hand of Lady Hermione, stooped with her beneath the arch and came triumphantly up to the top of the room, in a magnificent rustle of silk and satin. "My love," sighed Wimsey, "was clad in the black velvet, and I myself in cramoisie." The old lady, well pleased, rapped him over the knuckles with her gilt scepter. Hands clapped merrily.

"Down we go again," said Wimsey, and the Queen of Clubs and Emperor of the great Mahjongg dynasty twirled and capered in the center. The Queen of Spades danced up to meet her Jack of Diamonds. "Bézique," said Wimsey; "double Bézique," as he gave both his hands to the Dowager. Tumty, tumty, tiddledy. He again gave his hand to the Queen of Clubs and led her down. Under their lifted arms the other seventeen couples passed. Then Lady Deverill and her partner followed them down—then five more couples.

"We're working nicely to time," said Sir Charles, with his eye on the clock. "I worked it out at two minutes per couple. Ah! here's one of the missing pairs." He waved an agitated arm. "Come into the center—come along—in here."

A man whose head was decorated with a huge shuttlecock, and Joan Carstairs, dressed as a Diabolo, had emerged from the north corridor. Sir Charles, like a fussy rooster with two frightened hens, guided and pushed them into place between two couples who had not yet done their "hands across," and heaved a sigh of relief. It would have worried him to see them miss their turn. The clock chimed a quarter to two.

"I say, Playfair, have you seen Charmian Grayle or Tony Lee anywhere about?" asked Giles Pomfret of the Badminton costume. "Sir Charles is quite upset because we aren't complete."

"Not a sign of 'em. I was supposed to be dancing this with Charmian, but she vanished upstairs and hasn't come down again. Then Joan came barging along looking for Tony, and we thought we'd better see it through together."

"Here are the waits coming in," broke in Joan Carstairs. "Aren't they sweet? Too-too-truly-rural!"

Between the columns on the north side of the ballroom the waits could be seen filing into place in the corridor, under the command of the Vicar. Sir Roger jigged on his exhausting way. Hands across. Down the center and up again. Giles Pomfret, groaning, scrambled in his sandwich boards beneath the lengthening arch of hands for the fifteenth time. Tumty, tiddledy. The nineteenth couple wove their way through the dance. Once again, Sir Charles and the Dowager Duchess, both as fresh as paint, stood at the top of the room. The clapping was loudly renewed; the orchestra fell silent; the guests broke up into groups; the servants arranged themselves in a neat line at the lower end of the room; the clock struck two; and the Vicar, receiving a signal from Sir Charles, held his tuning-fork to his ear and gave forth a sonorous A. The waits burst shrilly into the opening bars of "Good King Wenceslas."

It was just as the night was growing darker and the wind blowing stronger that a figure came thrusting its way through the ranks of the singers, and hurried across to where Sir Charles stood; Tony Lee, with his face as white as his costume.

"Charmian . . . in the tapestry room . . . dead . . . strangled."

Superintendent Johnson sat in the library, taking down the evidence of the haggard revelers, who were ushered in upon him one by one. First, Tony Lee, his haunted eyes like dark hollows in a mask of gray paper.

"Miss Grayle had promised to dance with me the last dance before Sir Roger; it was a fox-trot. I waited for her in the passage under the Musicians' Gallery. She never came. I did not search for her. I did not see her dancing with anyone else. When the dance was nearly over, I went out into the garden, by way of the service door under the musicians' stair. I stayed in the garden till Sir Roger de Coverley was over—"

"Was anybody with you, sir?"

"No, nobody."

"You stayed alone in the garden from—yes, from 1:20 past 2 o'clock. Rather disagreeable, was it not, sir, with the snow on the ground?" The Superintendent glanced keenly from Tony's stained and sodden white shoes to his strained face.

"I didn't notice. The room was hot—I wanted air. I saw the waits arrive at about 1:40—I daresay they saw me. I came in a little after 2 o'clock—"

"By the service door again, sir?"

"No; by the garden door on the other side of the house, at the end of the passage which runs along beside the tapestry room. I heard singing going on in the ballroom and saw two men sitting in the little recess at the foot of the staircase on the left-hand side of the passage. I think one of them was the gardener. I went into the tapestry room—"

"With any particular purpose in mind, sir?"

"No—except that I wasn't keen on rejoining the party. I wanted to be quiet." He paused; the Superintendent said nothing. "Then I went into the tapestry room. The light was out. I switched it on and saw—Miss Grayle. She was lying close against the radiator. I thought she had fainted. I went over to her and found she was—dead. I only waited long enough to be sure, and then I went into the ballroom and gave the alarm."

"Thank you, sir. Now, may I ask, what were your relations with Miss Grayle?"

"I—I admired her very much."

"Engaged to her, sir?"

"No, not exactly."

"No quarrel—misunderstanding—anything of that sort?"

"Oh, no!"

Superintendent Johnson looked at him again, and again said nothing, but his experienced mind informed him:

"He's lying."

Aloud he only thanked and dismissed Tony. The White King stumbled drearily out, and the Red King took his place.

"Miss Grayle," said Frank Bellingham, "is a friend of my wife and myself; she was staying at our house. Mr. Lee is also our guest. We all came in one party. I believe there was some kind of understanding between Miss Grayle and Mr. Lee —no actual engagement. She was a very bright, lively, popular girl. I have known her for about six years, and my wife has known her since our marriage. I know of no one who could have borne a grudge against Miss Grayle. I danced with her the last dance but two—it was a waltz. After that came a fox-trot and then Sir Roger. She left me at the end of the waltz; I think she said she was going upstairs to tidy. I think she went out by the door at the upper end of the ballroom. I never saw her again. The ladies' dressing-room is on the second floor, next door to the picture-gallery. You reach it by the staircase that goes up from the garden-passage. You have to pass the door of the tapestry room to get there. The only other way to the dressing-room is by the stair at the east end of the ballroom, which goes up to the picture-gallery. You would then have to pass through the picture-gallery to get to the dressing-room. I know the house well; my wife and I have often stayed here."

Next came Lady Hermione, whose evidence, delivered at great length, amounted to this:

"Charmian Grayle was a minx and no loss to anybody. I am not surprised that someone has strangled her. Women like that ought to be strangled. I would cheerfully have strangled her myself. She has been making Tony Lee's life a burden to him for the last six weeks. I saw her flirting with Mr. Vibart tonight on purpose to make Mr. Lee jealous. She made eyes at Mr. Bellingham and Mr. Playfair. She made eyes at everybody. I should think at least half a dozen people had very good reason to wish her dead."

Mr. Vibart, who arrived dressed in a gaudy Polo costume, and still ludicrously clutching a hobby-horse, said that he had danced several times that evening with Miss Grayle. She was a damn sportin' girl, rattlin' good fun. Well, a bit hot, perhaps, but, dash it all, the poor kid was dead. He might have kissed her once or twice, perhaps, but no harm in that. Well, perhaps poor old Lee did take it a bit hard. Miss Grayle liked pulling Tony's leg. He himself had liked Miss Grayle and was dashed cut-up about the whole beastly business.

Mrs. Bellingham confirmed her husband's evidence. Miss Grayle had been their guest, and they were all on the very best of terms. She felt sure that Mr. Lee and Miss Grayle had been very fond of one another. She had not seen Miss Grayle during the last three dances, but had attached no importance to that. If she had thought about it at all, she would have supposed Miss Grayle was sitting out with somebody. She herself had not been up to the dressing-room since about midnight, and had not seen Miss Grayle go upstairs. She had first missed Miss Grayle when they all stood up for Sir Roger.

Mrs. Wrayburn mentioned that she had seen Miss Carstairs in the ballroom looking for Mr. Lee, just as Sir Charles Deverill went down to speak to the band. Miss Carstairs had then mentioned that Mr. Playfair was in the north corridor, waiting for Miss Grayle. She could say for certain that the time was then 1:28. She had seen Mr. Playfair himself at 1:30. He had looked in from the corridor and gone out again. The whole party had then been standing up together, except Miss Grayle, Miss Carstairs, Mr. Lee, and Mr. Playfair. She knew that, because Sir Charles had counted the couples.

Then came Jim Playfair, with a most valuable piece of evidence.

"Miss Grayle was engaged to me for Sir Roger de Coverley. I went to wait for her in the north corridor as soon as the previous dance was over. That was at 1:25. I sat on the settee in the eastern half of the corridor. I saw Sir Charles go down to speak to the band. Almost immediately afterwards, I saw Miss Grayle come out of the passage, under the Musicians' Gallery and go up the stairs at the end of the corridor. I called out: 'Hurry up! they're just going to begin.' I do not think she heard me; she did not reply. I am quite sure I saw her. The staircase has open banisters. There is no light in that corner except from the swinging lantern in the corridor, but that is very powerful. I could not be mistaken in the costume. I waited for Miss Grayle till the dance was half over; then I gave it up and joined forces with Miss Carstairs, who had also mislaid her partner."

The maid in attendance on the dressing-room was next examined. She and the gardener were the only two servants who had not danced Sir Roger. She had not quitted the dressing-room at any time since supper, except that she might have gone as far as the door. Miss Grayle had certainly not entered the dressing-room during the last hour of the dance.

The Vicar, much worried and distressed, said that his party had arrived by the garden door at 1:40. He had noticed a man in a white costume smoking a cigarette in the garden. The waits had removed their outer clothing in the garden passage and then gone out to take up their position in the north corridor. Nobody had passed them till Mr. Lee had come in with his sad news.

Mr. Ephraim Dodd, the sexton, made an important addition to this evidence.

This aged gentleman was, as he confessed, no singer, but was accustomed to go round with the waits to carry the lantern and collecting box. He had taken a seat in the garden passage "to rest me pore feet." He had seen the gentleman come in from the garden "all in white with a crown on 'is 'ead." The choir were then singing "Bring me flesh and bring me wine." The gentleman had looked about a bit, "made a face, like," and gone into the room at the foot of the stairs. He hadn't been absent "more nor a minute," when he "come out faster than he gone in," and had rushed immediately into the ballroom.

In addition to all this, there was, of course, the evidence of Dr. Pattison. He was a guest at the dance, and had hastened to view the body of Miss Grayle as soon as the alarm was given. He was of opinion that she had been brutally strangled by someone standing in front of her. She was a tall, strong girl, and he thought it would have needed a man's strength to overpower her. When he saw her at five minutes past two he concluded that she must have been killed within the last hour, but not within the last five minutes or so. The body was still quite warm, but, since it had fallen close to the hot radiator, they could not rely very much upon that indication.

Superintendent Johnson rubbed a thoughtful ear and turned to Lord Peter Wimsey, who had been able to confirm much of the previous evidence and, in particular, the exact times at which various incidents had occurred. The Superintendent knew Wimsey well, and made no bones about taking him into his confidence.

"You see how it stands, my lord. If the poor young lady was killed when Dr. Pattison says, it narrows it down a good bit. She was last seen dancing with Mr. Bellingham at—call it 1:20. At 2 o'clock she was dead. That gives us forty minutes. But if we're to believe Mr. Playfair, it narrows it down still further. He says he saw her alive just after Sir Charles went down to speak to the band, which you put at 1:28. That means that there's only five people who could possibly have done it, because all the rest were in the ballroom after that, dancing Sir Roger. There's the maid in the dressing-room; between you and me, sir, I think we can leave her out. She's a little slip of a thing, and it's not clear what motive she could have had. Besides, I've known her from a child, and she isn't the sort to do it. Then there's the gardener; I haven't seen him yet, but there again, he's a man I know well, and I'd as soon suspect myself. Well now, there's this Mr. Tony Lee, Miss Carstairs, and Mr. Playfair himself. The girl's the least probable, for physical reasons, and besides, strangling isn't a woman's crime—not as a rule. But Mr. Lee—that's a queer story, if you like. What was he doing all that time out in the garden by himself?"

"It sounds to me," said Wimsey, "as if Miss Grayle had given him the push and he had gone into the garden to eat worms."

"Exactly, my lord; and that's where his motive might come in."

"So it might," said Wimsey, "but look here. There's a couple of inches of snow on the ground. If you can confirm the time at which he went out, you ought to be able to see, from his tracks, whether he came in again before Ephraim Dodd saw him. Also, where he went in the interval and whether he was alone."

"That's a good idea, my lord. I'll send my sergeant to make inquiries."

"Then there's Mr. Bellingham. Suppose he killed her after the end of his waltz with her. Did anyone see him in the interval between that and the fox-trot?"

"Quite, my lord. I've thought of that. But you see where *that* leads. It means that Mr. Playfair must have been in a conspiracy with him to do it. And from all we hear, that doesn't seem likely."

"No more it does. In fact, I happen to know that Mr. Bellingham and Mr. Playfair were not on the best of terms. You can wash that out."

"I think so, my lord. And that brings us to Mr. Playfair. It's him we're relying on for the time. We haven't found anyone who saw Miss Grayle during the dance before his—that was the fox-trot. What was to prevent him doing it then? Wait a bit. What does he say himself? Says he danced the fox-trot with the Duchess of Denver." The Superintendent's face fell, and he hunted through his notes again. "She confirms that. Says she was with him during the interval and danced the whole dance with him. Well, my lord, I suppose we can take Her Grace's word for it."

"I think you can," said Wimsey, smiling. "I've known my mother practically since my birth, and have always found her very reliable."

"Yes, my lord. Well, that brings us to the end of the fox-trot. After that, Miss Carstairs saw Mr. Playfair waiting in the north corridor. She says she noticed him several times during the interval and spoke to him. And Mrs. Wrayburn saw him there at 1:30 or thereabouts. Then at 1:45 he and Miss Carstairs came and joined the company. Now, is there anyone who can check all these points? That's the next thing we've got to see to."

Within a very few minutes, abundant confirmation was forthcoming. Mervyn Bunter, Lord Peter's personal man, said that he had been helping to take refreshments along to the buffet. Throughout the interval between the waltz and the fox-trot, Mr. Lee had been standing by the service door beneath the musicians' stair, and half-way through the fox-trot he had been seen to go out into the garden by way of the servants' hall. The police-sergeant had examined the tracks in the snow and found that Mr. Lee had not been joined by any other person, and that there was only the one set of his footprints, leaving the house by the servants' hall and returning by the garden door near the tapestry room. Several persons were also found who had seen Mr. Bellingham in the interval between the waltz and the fox-trot, and who were able to say that he had danced the fox-trot through with Mrs. Bellingham. Joan Carstairs had also been seen continuously throughout the waltz and the fox-trot, and during the following interval and the beginning of Sir Roger. Moreover, the servants who had danced at the lower end of the room were positive that from 1:29 to 1:45 Mr. Playfair had sat continuously on the settee in the north corridor, except for the few seconds during which he had glanced into the ball-room. They were also certain that during that time no one had gone up the staircase at the lower end of the corridor, while Mr. Dodd was equally positive that, after 1:40, nobody except Mr. Lee had entered the garden passage or the tapestry room.

Finally, the circle was closed by William Hoggarty, the gardener. He asserted with the most obvious sincerity that from 1:30 to 1:40 he had been stationed in the garden passage to receive the waits and marshal them to their places. During that time, no one had come down the stair from the picture-gallery or entered the tapestry room. From 1:40 onwards, he had sat beside Mr. Dodd in the passage and nobody had passed him except Mr. Lee.

These points being settled, there was no further reason to doubt Jim Playfair's evidence, since his partners were able to prove his whereabouts during the waltz, the fox-trot, and the intervening interval. At 1:28 or just after, he had seen Char-mian Grayle alive. At 2:02 she had been found dead in the tapestry room. During that interval, no one had been seen to enter the room, and every person had been accounted for.

At 6 o'clock, the exhausted guests had been allowed to go to their rooms, accom-modation being provided in the house for those who, like the Bellinghams, had come from a distance, since the Superintendent had announced his intention of interrogating them all afresh later in the day.

This new inquiry produced no result. Lord Peter Wimsey did not take part in it. He and Bunter (who was an expert photographer) occupied themselves in photo-graphing the ballroom and adjacent rooms and corridors from every imaginable point of view, for, as Lord Peter said, "You never know what may turn out to be relevant." Late in the afternoon they retired together to the cellar, where with dishes, chemicals, and safelight hastily procured from the local chemist, they proceeded to develop the plates.

"That's the lot, my lord," observed Bunter at length, sloshing the final plate in the water and tipping it into the hypo. "You can switch the light on now, my lord."

Wimsey did so, blinking in the sudden white glare.

"A very hefty bit of work," said he. "Hullo! What's that plateful of blood you've got there?"

"That's the red backing they put on these plates, my lord, to obviate halation. You may have observed me washing it off before inserting the plate in the devel-oping-dish. Halation, my lord, is a phenomenon—"

Wimsey was not attending.

"But why didn't I notice it before?" he demanded. "That stuff looked to me exactly like clear water."

"So it would, my lord, in the red safe-light. The appearance of whiteness is produced," added Bunter sententiously, "by the reflection of *all* the available light. When all the available light is red, red and white are, naturally, indistinguishable. Similarly, in a green light—"

"Good God!" said Wimsey. "Wait a moment, Bunter, I must think this out . . . Here! damn those plates—let them be. I want you upstairs."

He led the way at a canter to the ballroom, dark now, with the windows in the south corridor already curtained and only the dimness of the December evening filtering through the high windows of the clerestory above the arcading. He first turned on the three great chandeliers in the ballroom itself. Owing to the heavy oak paneling that rose to the roof at both ends and all four angles of the room, these threw no light at all upon the staircase at the lower end of the north corridor. Next, he turned on the light in the four-sided hanging lantern, which hung in the north corridor above and between the two settees. A vivid shaft of green light immediately flooded the lower half of the corridor and the staircase; the upper half was bathed in strong amber, while the remaining sides of the lantern showed red towards the ballroom and blue towards the corridor wall.

Wimsey shook his head.

"Not much room for error there. Unless—I know! Run, Bunter, and ask Miss Carstairs and Mr. Playfair to come here a moment."

While Bunter was gone, Wimsey borrowed a step-ladder from the kitchen and carefully examined the fixing of the lantern. It was a temporary affair, the lantern being supported by a hook screwed into a beam and lit by means of a flex run from the socket of a permanent fixture at a little distance.

"Now, you two," said Wimsey, when the two guests arrived, "I want to make a little experiment. Will you sit down on this settee, Playfair, as you did last night. And you, Miss Carstairs—I picked you out to help because you're wearing a white dress. Will you go up the stairs at the end of the corridor as Miss Grayle did last night. I want to know whether it looks the same to Playfair as it did then—bar all the other people, of course."

He watched them as they carried out this maneuver. Playfair looked puzzled.

"It doesn't seem quite the same, somehow. I don't know what the difference is, but there is a difference."

Joan, returning, agreed with him.

"I was sitting on that other settee part of the time," she said, "and it looks different to me. I think it's darker."

"Lighter," said Jim.

"Good!" said Wimsey. "That's what I wanted you to say. Now, Bunter, swing that lantern through a quarter-turn to the left."

The moment this was done, Joan gave a little cry.

"That's it! That's it! The blue light! I remember thinking how frosty-faced those poor waits looked as they came in."

"And you, Playfair?"

"That's right," said Jim, satisfied. "The light was red last night. *I* remember thinking how warm and cosy it looked."

Wimsey laughed.

"We're on to it, Bunter. What's the chessboard rule? *The Queen stands on a square of her own color.* Find the maid who looked after the dressing-room, and ask her whether Mrs. Bellingham was there last night between the fox-trot and Sir Roger."

In five minutes Bunter was back with his report.

"The maid says, my lord, that Mrs. Bellingham did not come into the dressing-room at that time. But she saw her come out of the picture-gallery and run downstairs towards the tapestry room just as the band struck up Sir Roger."

"And that," said Wimsey, "was at 1:29."

"Mrs. Bellingham?" said Jim. "But you said you saw her yourself in the ball-room before 1:30. She couldn't have had time to commit the murder."

"No, she couldn't," said Wimsey. "But Charmian Grayle was dead long before that. It was the Red Queen, not the White, you saw upon the staircase. Find out why Mrs. Bellingham lied about her movements, and then we shall know the truth."

"A very sad affair, my lord," said Superintendent Johnson, some hours later. "Mr. Bellingham came across with it like a gentleman as soon as we told him we had evidence against his wife. It appears that Miss Grayle knew certain facts about him which would have been very damaging to his political career. She'd been getting money out of him for years. Earlier in the evening she surprised him by making fresh demands. During the last waltz they had together, they went into the tapestry room and a quarrel took place. He lost his temper and laid hands on her. He says he never meant to hurt her seriously. but she started to scream and he took hold of her throat to silence her and—sort of accidentally—throttled her. When he found what he'd done, he left her there and came away, feeling, as he says, all of a daze. He had the next dance with his wife. He told her what had happened, and then discovered that he'd left the little scepter affair he was carrying in the room with the body. Mrs. Bellingham—she's a brave woman—undertook to fetch it back. She slipped through the dark passage under the Musicians' Gallery—which was empty—and up the stair to the picture-gallery. She did not hear Mr. Playfair speak to her. She ran through the gallery and down the other stair, secured the scepter, and hid it under her own dress. Later, she heard from Mr. Playfair about what he saw, and realized that in the red light he had mistaken her for the White Queen. In the early hours of this morning, she slipped downstairs and managed to get the lantern shifted round. Of course, she's an accessory after the fact, but she's the kind of wife a man would like to have. I hope they let her off light."

"Amen!" said Lord Peter Wimsey.

G. K. Chesterton

THE INVISIBLE MAN

In one story he is identified as "the Reverend J. Brown, who is attached to St. Francis Xavier Church, Camberwell." In another, he is called "Paul." But whatever his first name, and despite the fact that his methods of deduction are hardly orthodox, Father Brown is one of the world's memorable detectives.

He once explained his method this way: "I wait till I know I am inside a murderer, thinking his thoughts, wrestling with his passions; till I have bent myself into the posture of his hunched and peering hatred; till I see the world with his bloodshot and squinting eyes, looking between the blinkers of his half-witted concentration; looking up the short and sharp perspective of a straight road to a pool of blood. Till I am really a murderer. And when I am quite sure that I feel exactly like the murderer myself, of course, I know who he is."

Father Brown stories usually end not with an arrest but with the guilty party having a quiet talk with the good father, for, as W. H. Auden has pointed out, "His prime motive is compassion, of which the guilty are in greater need than the innocent, and he investigates murders, not for his own sake, nor even for the sake of the innocent, but for the sake of the murderer who can save his soul if he will confess and repent."

Between 1911 and 1934, G. K. Chesterton (1874–1936) wrote fifty-one Father Brown stories as a playful sideline to his more serious literary output of novels, plays, criticism, poems, and literary biography. And an experienced reader will soon discover two general rules: the culprit is rarely Catholic, and any character who comes out against strong drink usually deserves at least a second suspicious look.

The Invisible Man

IN THE COOL BLUE TWILIGHT of two steep streets in Camden Town, the shop at the corner, a confectioner's, glowed like the butt of a cigar. One should rather say, perhaps, like the butt of a firework, for the light was of many colors and some complexity, broken up by many mirrors and dancing on many gilt and gaily-colored cakes and sweetmeats. Against this one fiery glass were glued the noses of many gutter-snipes, for the chocolates were all wrapped in those red and gold and green metallic colors which are almost better than chocolate itself; and the huge white wedding-cake in the window was somehow at once remote and satisfying, just as if the whole North Pole were good to eat. Such rainbow provocations could naturally collect the youth of the neighborhood up to the ages of ten or twelve. But this corner was also attractive to youth at a later stage; and a young man, not less than twenty-four, was staring into the same shop window. To him, also, the shop was of fiery charm, but this attraction was not wholly to be explained by chocolates, which, however, he was far from despising.

He was a tall, burly, red-haired young man, with a resolute face but a listless manner. He carried under his arm a flat, gray portfolio of black-and-white sketches, which he had sold with more or less success to publishers ever since his uncle (who was an admiral) had disinherited him for Socialism, because of a lecture which he had delivered against that economic theory. He name was John Turnbull Angus.

Entering at last, he walked through the confectioner's shop to the back room, which was a sort of pastry-cook restaurant, merely raising his hat to the young lady who was serving there. She was a dark, elegant, alert girl in black, with a high color and very quick, dark eyes; and after the ordinary interval she followed him into the inner room to take his order.

His order was evidently a usual one. "I want, please," he said with precision, "one halfpenny bun and a small cup of black coffee." An instant before the girl could turn away he added, "Also, I want you to marry me."

The young lady of the shop stiffened suddenly and said, "Those are jokes I don't allow."

The red-haired young man lifted gray eyes of an unexpected gravity.

"Really and truly," he said, "it's as serious—as serious as the halfpenny bun. It is expensive, like the bun; one pays for it. It is indigestible, like the bun. It hurts."

The dark young lady had never taken her dark eyes off him, but seemed to be studying him with almost tragic exactitude. At the end of her scrutiny she had something like the shadow of a smile, and she sat down in a chair.

"Don't you think," observed Angus, absently, "that it's rather cruel to eat these halfpenny buns? They might grow up into penny buns. I shall give up these brutal sports when we are married."

The dark young lady rose from her chair and walked to the window, evidently in a state of strong but not unsympathetic cogitation. When at last she swung round again with an air of resolution she was bewildered to observe that the young man was carefully laying out on the table various objects from the shop-window. They included a pyramid of highly colored sweets, several plates of sandwiches, and the two decanters containing that mysterious port and sherry which are peculiar to pastry-cooks. In the middle of this neat arrangement he had carefully let down the enormous load of white sugared cake which had been the huge ornament of the window.

"What on earth are you doing?" she asked.

"Duty, my dear Laura," he began.

"Oh, for the Lord's sake, stop a minute," she cried, "and don't talk to me in that way. I mean, what is all that?"

"A ceremonial meal, Miss Hope."

"And what is *that?*" she asked impatiently, pointing to the mountain of sugar.

"The wedding-cake, Mrs. Angus," he said.

The girl marched to that article, removed it with some clatter, and put it back in the shop window; she then returned, and, putting her elegant elbows on the table, regarded the young man not unfavorably but with considerable exasperation.

"You don't give me any time to think," she said.

"I'm not such a fool," he answered; "that's my Christian humility."

She was still looking at him; but she had grown considerably graver behind the smile.

"Mr. Angus," she said steadily, "before there is a minute more of this nonsense I must tell you something about myself as shortly as I can."

"Delighted," replied Angus gravely. "You might tell me something about myself, too, while you are about it."

"Oh, do hold your tongue and listen," she said. "It's nothing that I'm ashamed of, and it isn't even anything that I'm specially sorry about. But what would you say if there were something that is no business of mine and yet is my nightmare?"

"In that case," said the man seriously, "I should suggest that you bring back the cake."

"Well, you must listen to the story first," said Laura, persistently. "To begin with, I must tell you that my father owned the inn called the 'Red Fish' at Ludbury, and I used to serve people in the bar."

"I have often wondered," he said, "why there was a kind of a Christian air about this one confectioner's shop."

"Ludbury is a sleepy, grassy little hole in the Eastern Counties, and the only kind of people who ever came to the 'Red Fish' were occasional commercial travelers, and for the rest, the most awful people you can see, only you've never seen them. I mean little, loungy men, who had just enough to live on and had nothing to do but lean about in bar-rooms and bet on horses, in bad clothes that were just too good for them. Even these wretched young rotters were not very common at our house; but there were two of them that were a lot too common—common in every sort of way. They both lived on money of their own, and were wearisomely idle and over-dressed. But yet I was a bit sorry for them, because I half believe they slunk into our little empty bar because each of them had a slight deformity, the sort of thing that some yokels laugh at. It wasn't exactly a deformity either; it was more an oddity. One of them was a surprisingly small man, something like a dwarf, or at least like a jockey. He was not at all jockeyish to look at, though; he had a round black head and a well-trimmed black beard, bright eyes like a bird's; he jingled money in his pockets; he jangled a great gold watch chain; and he never turned up except dressed just too much like a gentleman to be one. He was no fool though, though a futile idler; he was curiously clever at all kinds of things that couldn't be the slightest use—a sort of impromptu conjuring; making fifteen matches set fire to each other like a regular firework; or cutting a banana or some such thing into a dancing doll. His name was Isidore Smythe; and I can see him still, with his little dark face, just coming up to the counter, making a jumping kangaroo out of five cigars.

"The other fellow was more silent and more ordinary; but somehow he alarmed me much more than poor little Smythe. He was very tall and slight, and light-haired; his nose had a high bridge, and he might almost have been handsome in a spectral sort of way; but he had one of the most appalling squints I have ever seen or heard of. When he looked straight at you, you didn't know where you were yourself, let alone what he was looking at. I fancy this sort of disfigurement embittered the poor chap a little; for while Smythe was ready to show off his monkey tricks anywhere, James Welkin (that was the squinting man's name) never did anything except soak in our bar parlor, and go for great walks by himself in the flat, gray country all round. All the same, I think Smythe, too, was a little sensitive about being so small, though he carried it off more smartly. And so it was that I was really puzzled, as well as startled, and very sorry, when they both offered to marry me in the same week.

"Well, I did what I've since thought was perhaps a silly thing. But, after all, these freaks were my friends in a way; and I had a horror of their thinking I refused them for the real reason, which was that they were so impossibly ugly. So I made up some gas of another sort, about never meaning to marry anyone who hadn't carved his way in the world. I said it was a point of principle with me not to live on money that was just inherited like theirs. Two days after I had talked in this well-meaning sort of way, the whole trouble began. The first thing I heard was that both of them had gone off to seek their fortunes, as if they were in some silly fairy tale.

"Well, I've never seen either of them from that day to this. But I've had two letters from the little man called Smythe, and really they were rather exciting."

"Ever heard of the other man?" asked Angus.

"No, he never wrote," said the girl, after an instant's hesitation. "Smythe's first letter was simply to say that he had started out walking with Welkin to London; but Welkin was such a good walker that the little man dropped out of it, and took a rest by the roadside. He happened to be picked up by some traveling show, and, partly because he was nearly a dwarf, and partly because he was really a clever little wretch, he got on quite well in the show business, and was soon sent up to the Aquarium, to do some tricks that I forget. That was his first letter. His second was much more of a startler, and I only got it last week."

The man called Angus emptied his coffee-cup and regarded her with mild and patient eyes. Her own mouth took a slight twist of laughter as she resumed, "I suppose you've seen on the hoardings all about this 'Smythe's Silent Service'? Or you must be the only person that hasn't. Oh, I don't know much about it; it's some clockwork invention for doing all the housework by machinery. You know the sort of thing: 'Press a Button—A Butler who Never Drinks.' 'Turn a Handle—Ten Housemaids who Never Flirt.' You must have seen the advertisements. Well, whatever these machines are, they are making pots of money; and they are making it all for that little imp whom I knew down in Ludbury. I can't help feeling pleased the poor little chap has fallen on his feet; but the plain fact is, I'm in terror of his turning up any minute and telling me he's carved his way in the world—as he certainly has."

"And the other man?" repeated Angus with a sort of obstinate quietude.

Laura Hope got to her feet suddenly. "My friend," she said, "I think you are a witch. Yes, you are quite right. I have not seen a line of the other man's writing; and I have no more notion than the dead of what or where he is. But it is of him that I am frightened. It is he who is all about my path. It is he who has half driven me mad. Indeed, I think he has driven me mad; for I have felt him where he could not have been, and I have heard his voice when he could not have spoken."

"Well, my dear," said the young man, cheerfully, "if he were Satan himself, he is done for now you have told somebody. One goes mad all alone, old girl. But when was it you fancied you felt and heard our squinting friend?"

"I heard James Welkin laugh as plainly as I hear you speak," said the girl, steadily. "There was nobody there, for I stood just outside the shop at the corner, and could see down both streets at once. I had forgotten how he laughed, though his laugh was as odd as his squint. I had not thought of him for nearly a year. But it's a solemn truth that a few seconds later the first letter came from his rival."

"Did you ever make the specter speak or squeak, or anything?" asked Angus, with some interest.

Laura suddenly shuddered, and then said, with an unshaken voice, "Yes. Just when I had finished reading the second letter from Isidore Smythe announcing his success, just then, I heard Welkin say, 'he shan't have you, though.' It was quite plain, as if he were in the room. It is awful, I think I must be mad."

"If you really were mad," said the young man, "you would think you must be sane. But certainly there seems to me to be something a little rum about this unseen gentleman. Two heads are better than one—I spare you allusions to any other organs—and really, if you would allow me, as a sturdy, practical man, to bring back the wedding-cake out of the window—"

Even as he spoke, there was a sort of steely shriek in the street outside, and a small motor, driven at devilish speed, shot up to the door of the shop and stuck there. In the same flash of time a small man in a shiny top hat stood stamping in the outer room.

Angus, who had hitherto maintained hilarious ease from motives of mental hygiene, revealed the strain of his soul by striding abruptly out of the inner room and confronting the new-comer. A glance at him was quite sufficient to confirm the savage guess-work of a man in love. This very dapper but dwarfish figure, with the spike of black beard carried insolently forward, the clever unrestful eyes, the neat but very nervous fingers, could be none other than the man just described to him: Isidore Smythe, who made dolls out of banana skins and match-boxes; Isidore Smythe, who made millions out of undrinking butlers and unflirting housemaids of metal. For a moment the two men, instinctively understanding each other's air of possession, looked at each other with that curious cold generosity which is the soul of rivalry.

Mr. Smythe, however, made no allusion to the ultimate ground of their antagonism, but said simply and explosively, "Has Miss Hope seen that thing on the window?"

"On the window?" repeated the staring Angus.

"There's no time to explain other things," said the small millionaire shortly. "There's some tomfoolery going on here that has to be investigated."

He pointed his polished walking-stick at the window, recently depleted by the bridal preparations of Mr. Angus; and that gentleman was astonished to see along the front of the glass a long strip of paper pasted, which had certainly not been on the window when he looked through it some time before. Following the energetic Smythe outside into the street, he found that some yard and a half of stamp paper had been carefully gummed along the glass outside, and on this was written in straggly characters, "If you marry Smythe, he will die."

"Laura," said Angus, putting his big red head into the shop, "you're not mad."

"It's the writing of that fellow Welkin," said Smythe gruffly. "I haven't seen him for years, but he's always bothering me. Five times in the last fortnight he's had threatening letters left at my flat, and I can't even find out who leaves them, let alone if it is Welkin himself. The porter of the flats swears that no suspicious characters have been seen, and here he has pasted up a sort of dado on a public shop window, while the people in the shop—"

"Quite so," said Angus modestly, "while the people in the shop were having tea. Well, sir, I can assure you I appreciate your common sense in dealing so directly with the matter. We can talk about other things afterwards. The fellow cannot be very far off yet, for I swear there was no paper there when I went last to the window, ten or fifteen minutes ago. On the other hand, he's too far off to be chased, as we don't even know the direction. If you'll take my advice, Mr. Smythe, you'll put this at once in the hands of some energetic inquiry man, private rather than public. I know an extremely clever fellow, who has set up in business five minutes from here in your car. His name's Flambeau, and though his youth was a bit stormy, he's a strictly honest man now, and his brains are worth money. He lives in Lucknow Mansions, Hampstead."

"That is odd," said the little man, arching his black eyebrows. "I live, myself, in Himylaya Mansions, round the corner. Perhaps you might care to come with me; I can go to my rooms and sort out these queer Welkin documents, while you run round and get your friend the detective."

"You are very good," said Angus politely. "Well, the sooner we act the better."

Both men, with a queer kind of impromptu fairness, took the same sort of formal farewell of the lady, and both jumped into the brisk little car. As Smythe took the handles and they turned the great corner of the street, Angus was amused to see a gigantesque poster of "Smythe's Silent Service," with a picture of a huge headless iron doll, carrying a saucepan with the legend, "A Cook Who is Never Cross."

"I use them in my own flat," said the little black-bearded man, laughing, "partly for advertisements, and partly for real convenience. Honestly, and all above board, those big clockwork dolls of mine do bring your coals or claret or a timetable quicker than any live servants I've ever known, if you know which knob to press. But I'll never deny, between ourselves, that such servants have their disadvantages, too."

"Indeed?" said Angus; "is there something they can't do?"

"Yes," replied Smythe coolly; "they can't tell me who left those threatening letters at my flat."

The man's motor was small and swift like himself; in fact, like his domestic service, it was of his own invention. If he was an advertising quack, he was one who believed in his own wares. The sense of something tiny and flying was accentuated as they swept up long white curves of road in the dead but open daylight of evening. Soon the white curves came sharper and dizzier; they were upon ascending spirals, as they say in the modern religions. For, indeed, they were cresting a corner of London which is almost as precipitous as Edinburgh, if not quite so picturesque. Terrace rose above terrace, and the special tower of flats they sought, rose above them all to almost Egyptian height, gilded by the level sunset. The change, as they turned the corner and entered the crescent known as Himylaya Mansions, was as abrupt as the opening of a window; for they found that pile of flats sitting above London as above a green sea of slate. Opposite to the mansions, on the other side of the gravel crescent, was a bushy enclosure more like a steep hedge or dyke than a garden, and some way below that ran a strip of artificial water, a sort of canal, like the moat of that embowered fortress. As the car swept round the crescent it passed, at one corner, the stray stall of a man selling chestnuts; and right away at the other end of the curve, Angus could see a dim blue policeman walking slowly. These were the only human shapes in that high suburban solitude; but he had an irrational sense that they expressed the speechless poetry of London. He felt as if they were figures in a story.

The little car shot up to the right house like a bullet, and shot out its owner like a bomb shell. He was immediately inquiring of a tall commissionaire in shining braid, and a short porter in shirt sleeves, whether anybody or anything had been seeking his apartments. He was assured that nobody and nothing had passed these officials since his last inquiries; whereupon he and the slightly bewildered Angus were shot up in the lift like a rocket, till they reached the top floor.

"Just come in for a minute," said the breathless Smythe. "I want to show you those Welkin letters. Then you might run round the corner and fetch your friend." He pressed a button concealed in the wall, and the door opened of itself.

It opened on a long, commodious ante-room, of which the only arresting features, ordinarily speaking, were the rows of tall half-human mechanical figures that stood up on both sides like tailors' dummies. Like tailors' dummies they were headless; and like tailors' dummies they had a handsome unnecessary humpiness in the shoulders, and a pigeon-breasted protuberance of chest; but barring this, they were not much more like a human figure than any automatic machine at a station that is about the human height. They had two great hooks like arms, for carrying trays; and they were painted pea-green, or vermilion, or black for convenience of distinction; in every other way they were only automatic machines and nobody would have looked twice at them. On this occasion, at least, nobody did. For between the rows of these domestic dummies lay something more interesting than most of the mechanics of the world. It was a white, tattered scrap of paper scrawled with red ink; and the agile inventor had snatched it up almost as soon as the door flew open. He handed it to Angus without a word. The red ink on it actually was not dry, and the message ran, "If you have been to see her today, I shall kill you."

There was a short silence, and then Isidore Smythe said quietly, "Would you like a little whiskey? I rather feel as if I should."

"Thank you; I should like a little Flambeau," said Angus, gloomily. "This business seems to me to be getting rather grave. I'm going round at once to fetch him."

"Right you are," said the other, with admirable cheerfulness. "Bring him round here as quick as you can."

But as Angus closed the front door behind him he saw Smythe push back a button, and one of the clockwork images glided from its place and slid along a groove in the floor carrying a tray with syphon and decanter. There did seem something a trifle weird about leaving the little man alone among those dead servants, who were coming to life as the door closed.

Six steps down from Smythe's landing the man in shirt sleeves was doing something with a pail. Angus stopped to extract a promise, fortified with a prospective bribe, that he would remain in that place until the return with the detective, and would keep count of any kind of stranger coming up those stairs. Dashing down to the front hall he then laid similar charges of vigilance on the commissionaire at the front door, from whom he learned the simplifying circumstances that there was no back door. Not content with this, he captured the floating policeman and induced him to stand opposite the entrance and watch it; and finally paused an instant for a pennyworth of chestnuts, and an inquiry as to the probable length of the merchant's stay in the neighborhood.

The chestnut seller, turning up the collar of his coat, told him he should probably be moving shortly, as he thought it was going to snow. Indeed, the evening was growing gray and bitter, but Angus, with all his eloquence, proceeded to nail the chestnut man to his post.

"Keep yourself warm on your own chestnuts," he said earnestly. "Eat up your whole stock; I'll make it worth your while. I'll give you a sovereign if you'll wait here till I come back, and then tell me whether any man, woman, or child has gone into that house where the commissionaire is standing."

He then walked away smartly, with a last look at the besieged tower.

"I've made a ring round that room, anyhow," he said. "They can't all four of them be Mr. Welkin's accomplices."

Lucknow Mansions were, so to speak, on a lower platform of that hill of houses of which Himylaya Mansions might be called the peak. Mr. Flambeau's semi-official flat was on the ground floor, and presented in every way a marked contrast to the American machinery and cold hotel-like luxury of the flat of the Silent Service. Flambeau, who was a friend of Angus, received him in a rococo artistic den behind his office, of which the ornaments were sabers, harquebuses, Eastern curiosities, flasks of Italian wine, savage cooking-pots, a plumy Persian cat, and a small dusty-looking Roman Catholic priest, who looked particularly out of place.

"This is my friend Father Brown," said Flambeau. "I've often wanted you to meet him. Splendid weather, this; a little cold for Southerners like me."

"Yes, I think it will keep clear," said Angus, sitting down on a violet-striped Eastern ottoman.

"No," said the priest quietly, "it has begun to snow."

And, indeed, as he spoke, the first few flakes, foreseen by the man of chestnuts, began to drift across the darkening windowpane.

"Well," said Angus heavily. "I'm afraid I've come on business, and rather jumpy business at that. The fact is, Flambeau, within a stone's throw of your house is a fellow who badly wants your help; he's perpetually being haunted and threatened by an invisible enemy—a scoundrel whom nobody has even seen." As Angus proceeded to tell the whole tale of Smythe and Welkin, beginning with Laura's story, and going on with his own, the supernatural laugh at the corner of two empty streets, the strange distinct words spoken in an empty room, Flambeau grew more and more vividly concerned, and the little priest seemed to be left out of it, like a piece of furniture. When it came to the scribbled stamp-paper pasted on the window, Flambeau rose, seeming to fill the room with his huge shoulders.

"If you don't mind," he said, "I think you had better tell me the rest on the nearest road to this man's house. It strikes me, somehow, that there is no time to be lost."

"Delighted," said Angus, rising also, "though he's safe enough for the present, for I've set four men to watch the only hole to his burrow."

They turned out into the street, the small priest trundling after them with the docility of a small dog. He merely said, in a cheerful way like one making conversation, "How quick the snow gets thick on the ground."

As they threaded the steep side streets already powdered with silver, Angus finished his story; and by the time they reached the crescent with the towering flats, he had leisure to turn his attention to the four sentinels. The chestnut seller, both before and after receiving a sovereign, swore stubbornly that he had watched the door and seen no visitor enter. The policeman was even more emphatic. He said he had had experience of crooks of all kinds, in top hats and in rags; he wasn't so green as to expect suspicious characters to look suspicious; he looked out for anybody, and, so help him, there had been nobody. And when all three men gathered round the gilded commissionaire, who still stood smiling astride of the porch, the verdict was more final still.

"I've got a right to ask any man, duke or dustman, what he wants in these flats," said the genial and gold-laced giant, "and I'll swear there's been nobody to ask since this gentleman went away."

The unimportant Father Brown, who stood back, looking modestly at the pavement, here ventured to say meekly, "Has nobody been up and down stairs, then, since the snow began to fall? It began while we were all round at Flambeau's."

"Nobody's been in here, sir, you can take it from me," said the official, with beaming authority.

"Then I wonder what that is?" said the priest, and stared at the ground blankly like a fish.

The others all looked down also; and Flambeau used a fierce exclamation and a French gesture. For it was unquestionably true that down the middle of the entrance guarded by the man in gold lace, actually between the arrogant, stretched legs of that colossus, ran a stringy pattern of gray footprints stamped upon the white snow.

"God!" cried Angus involuntarily, "the Invisible Man!"

Without another word he turned and dashed up the stairs, with Flambeau following; but Father Brown still stood looking about him in the snow-clad street as if he had lost interest in his query.

Flambeau was plainly in a mood to break down the door with his big shoulders; but the Scotchman, with more reason, if less intuition, fumbled about on the frame of the door till he found the invisible button; and the door swung slowly open.

It showed substantially the same serried interior; the hall had grown darker, though it was still struck here and there with the last crimson shafts of sunset, and one or two of the headless machines had been moved from their places for this or that purpose, and stood here and there about the twilit place. The green and red of their coats were all darkened in the dusk; and their likeness to human shapes slightly increased by their very shapelessness. But in the middle of them all, exactly where the paper with the red ink had lain, there lay something that looked like red ink spilled out of its bottle. But it was not red ink.

With a French combination of reason and violence Flambeau simply said "Murder!" and, plunging into the flat, had explored every corner and cupboard of it in five minutes. But if he expected to find a corpse he found none. Isidore Smythe was not in the place, either dead or alive. After the most tearing search the two men met each other in the outer hall, with streaming faces and staring eyes. "My friend," said Flambeau, talking French in his excitement, "not only is your murderer invisible, but he makes invisible also the murdered man."

Angus looked round at the dim room full of dummies, and in some Celtic corner of his Scotch soul a shudder started. One of the life-size dolls stood immediately overshadowing the blood stain, summoned, perhaps, by the slain man an instant before he fell. One of the high-shouldered hooks that served the thing for arms was a little lifted, and Angus had suddenly the horrid fancy that poor Smythe's own iron child had struck him down. Matter had rebelled, and these machines had killed their master. But even so, what had they done with him?

"Eaten him?" said the nightmare at his ear; and he sickened for an instant at the idea of rent, human remains absorbed and crushed into all that acephalous clockwork.

He recovered his mental health by an emphatic effort, and said to Flambeau, "Well, there it is. The poor fellow has evaporated like a cloud and left a red streak on the floor. The tale does not belong to this world."

"There is only one thing to be done," said Flambeau, "whether it belongs to this world or the other. I must go down and talk to my friend."

They descended, passing the man with the pail, who again asseverated that he had let no intruder pass, down to the commissionaire and the hovering chestnut man, who rigidly reasserted their own watchfulness. But when Angus looked round for his fourth confirmation he could not see it, and called out with some nervousness, "Where is the policeman?"

"I beg your pardon," said Father Brown; "that is my fault. I just sent him down the road to investigate something—that I just thought worth investigating."

"Well, we want him back pretty soon," said Angus abruptly, "for the wretched man upstairs has not only been murdered, but wiped out."

"How?" asked the priest.

"Father," said Flambeau, after a pause, "upon my soul I believe it is more in your department than mine. No friend or foe has entered the house, but Smythe is gone, as if stolen by the fairies. If that is not supernatural, I—"

As he spoke they were all checked by an unusual sight; the big blue policeman came round the corner of the crescent, running. He came straight up to Brown.

"You're right, sir," he panted, "they've just found poor Mr. Smythe's body in the canal down below."

Angus put his hand wildly to his head. "Did he run down and drown himself?" he asked.

"He never came down, I'll swear," said the constable, "and he wasn't drowned either, for he died of a great stab over the heart."

"And yet you saw no one enter?" said Flambeau in a grave voice.

"Let us walk down the road a little," said the priest.

As they reached the other end of the crescent he observed abruptly, "Stupid of me! I forgot to ask the policeman something. I wonder if they found a light brown sack."

"Why a light brown sack?" asked Angus, astonished.

"Because if it was any other colored sack, the case must begin over again," said Father Brown; "but if it was a light brown sack, why, the case is finished."

"I am pleased to hear it," said Angus with hearty irony. "It hasn't begun, so far as I am concerned."

"You must tell us all about it," said Flambeau with a strange heavy simplicity, like a child.

Unconsciously they were walking with quickening steps down the long sweep of road on the other side of the high crescent, Father Brown leading briskly, though in silence. At last he said with an almost touching vagueness, "Well, I'm afraid you'll think it so prosy. We always begin at the abstract end of things, and you can't begin this story anywhere else.

"Have you ever noticed this—that people never answer what you say? They answer what you mean—or what they think you mean. Suppose one lady says to another in a country house, 'Is anybody staying with you?' the lady doesn't answer 'Yes; the butler, the three footmen, the parlormaid, and so on,' though the parlormaid may be in the room, or the butler behind her chair. She says 'There is *nobody* staying with us,' meaning nobody of the sort you mean. But suppose a doctor inquiring into an epidemic asks, 'Who is staying in the house?' then the lady will remember the butler, the parlormaid, and the rest. All language is used like that;

you never get a question answered literally, even when you get it answered truly. When those four quite honest men said that no man had gone into the Mansions, they did not really mean that *no man* had gone into them. They meant no man whom they could suspect of being your man. A man did go into the house, and did come out of it, but they never noticed him."

"An invisible man?" inquired Angus, raising his red eyebrows.

"A mentally invisible man," said Father Brown.

A minute or two after he resumed in the same unassuming voice, like a man thinking his way. "Of course you can't think of such a man, until you do think of him. That's where his cleverness comes in. But I came to think of him through two or three little things in the tale Mr. Angus told us. First, there was the fact that this Welkin went for long walks. And then there was the vast lot of stamp paper on the window. And then, most of all, there were the two things the young lady said —things that couldn't be true. Don't get annoyed," he added hastily, noting a sudden movement of the Scotchman's head; "she thought they were true. A person *can't* be quite alone in a street a second before she receives a letter. She can't be quite alone in a street when she starts reading a letter just received. There must be somebody pretty near her; he must be mentally invisible."

"Why must there be somebody near her?" asked Angus.

"Because," said Father Brown, "barring carrier-pigeons, somebody must have brought her the letter."

"Do you really mean to say," asked Flambeau, with energy, "that Welkin carried his rival's letters to his lady?"

"Yes," said the priest. "Welkin carried his rival's letters to his lady. You see, he had to."

"Oh, I can't stand much more of this," exploded Flambeau. "Who is this fellow? What does he look like? What is the usual get-up of a mentally invisible man?"

"He is dressed rather handsomely in red, blue and gold," replied the priest promptly with precision, "and in this striking, and even showy, costume he entered Himylaya Mansions under eight human eyes; he killed Smythe in cold blood, and came down into the street again carrying the dead body in his arms—"

"Reverend sir," cried Angus, standing still, "are you raving mad, or am I?"

"You are not mad," said Brown, "only a little unobservant. You have not noticed such a man as this, for example."

He took three quick strides forward, and put his hand on the shoulder of an ordinary passing postman who had bustled by them unnoticed under the shade of the trees.

"Nobody ever notices postmen somehow," he said thoughtfully; "yet they have passions like other men, and even carry large bags where a small corpse can be stowed quite easily."

The postman, instead of turning naturally, had ducked and tumbled against the garden fence. He was a lean fair-bearded man of very ordinary appearance, but as he turned an alarmed face over his shoulder, all three men were fixed with an almost fiendish squint.

Flambeau went back to his sabers, purple rugs and Persian cat, having many things to attend to. John Turnbull Angus went back to the lady at the shop, with whom that imprudent young man contrives to be extremely comfortable. But Father Brown walked those snow-covered hills under the stars for many hours with a murderer, and what they said to each other will never be known.

Agatha Christie

THE GIRL IN
THE TRAIN

Agatha Christie (1890–1976) created two of this century's most popular detectives: Hercule Poirot, who appeared in her first novel, The Mysterious Affair at Styles, *published in 1920, and Miss Jane Marple, whose first case, published ten years later, was* Murder at the Vicarage. *The two of them, he with his famous "little gray cells" and she with her knack of catching the darker subtleties in what passes for everyday gossip, have appeared in more than fifty novels and short-story collections.*

The mystery writer Marjorie Allingham has said that Dame Agatha (as she became in 1971 when named a Dame Commander of the Order of the British Empire) entertained "more people for more hours at a time than almost any other writer of her generation." Yet she maintained a certain playfulness about her craft. In one collection of short stories, featuring a husband-and-wife detective team, the Beresfords, she parodies a number of famous detectives, including Holmes, Father Brown, and her own Hercule Poirot. When she turned Appointment With Death *into a play, not only did she leave out the detective (Poirot in the novel) but also came up with an entirely different murderer. In fact a puckish sense of humor underlies the ornate puzzles in many of her novels, including the notorious* Who Killed Roger Ackroyd? *where she plays fast and loose with one of the most honored "rules" of detective fiction.*

Representing Agatha Christie in this collection is not one of her great detectives (Poirot and Miss Marple are never at their best in short stories) but an accommodating gentleman named George Rowland, who quits his job in search of adventure and is soon delighted to find himself, as he puts it, "mixed up in a real mystery." He is perhaps an unlikely detective, but Dame Agatha is having fun, again, with her readers.

The Girl in the Train

A<small>ND THAT'S THAT!</small>" observed George Rowland ruefully, as he gazed up at the imposing smoke-grimed façade of the building he had just quitted.

It might be said to represent very aptly the power of Money—and Money, in the person of William Rowland, uncle to the aforementioned George, had just spoken its mind very freely. In the course of a brief ten minutes, from being the apple of his uncle's eye, the heir to his wealth, and a young man with a promising business career in front of him, George had suddenly become one of the vast army of the unemployed.

"And in these clothes they won't even give me the dole," reflected Mr. Rowland gloomily, "and as for writing poems and selling them at the door at twopence (or 'what you care to give, lydy') I simply haven't got the brains."

It was true that George embodied a veritable triumph of the tailor's art. He was exquisitely and beautifully arrayed. Solomon and the lilies of the field were simply not in it with George. But man cannot live by clothes alone—unless he has had some considerable training in the art—and Mr. Rowland was painfully aware of the fact.

"And all because of that rotten show last night," he reflected sadly.

The rotten show last night had been a Covent Garden Ball. Mr. Rowland had returned from it at a somewhat late—or rather early—hour; as a matter of fact, he could not strictly say that he remembered returning at all. Rogers, his uncle's butler, was a helpful fellow, and could doubtless give more details on the matter. A splitting head, a cup of strong tea, and an arrival at the office at five minutes to twelve instead of half-past nine had precipitated the catastrophe. Mr. Rowland, senior, who for twenty-four years had condoned and paid up as a tactful relative should, had suddenly abandoned these tactics and revealed himself in a totally new light. The inconsequence of George's replies (the young man's head was still opening and shutting like some medieval instrument of the Inquisition) had displeased him still further. William Rowland was nothing if not thorough. He cast his nephew adrift upon the world in a few short succinct words, and then settled down to his interrupted survey of some oil fields in Peru.

George Rowland shook the dust of his uncle's office from off his feet, and stepped out into the City of London. George was a practical fellow. A good lunch, he considered, was essential to a review of the situation. He had it. Then he retraced his steps to the family mansion. Rogers opened the door. His well-trained face expressed no surprise at seeing George at this unusual hour.

"Good afternoon, Rogers. Just pack up my things for me, will you? I'm leaving here."

"Yes, sir. Just for a short visit, sir?"

"For good, Rogers. I am going to the colonies this afternoon."

"Indeed, sir?"

"Yes. That is, if there is a suitable boat. Do you know anything about the boats, Rogers?"

"Which colony were you thinking of visiting, sir?"

"I'm not particular. Any of 'em will do. Let's say Australia. What do you think of the idea, Rogers?"

Rogers coughed discreetly.

"Well, sir, I've certainly heard it said that there's room out there for anyone who really wants to work."

Mr. Rowland gazed at him with interest and admiration.

"Very neatly put, Rogers. Just what I was thinking myself. I shan't go to Australia—not today, at any rate. Fetch me an *ABC*, will you? We will select something nearer at hand."

Rogers brought the required volume. George opened it at random and turned the pages with a rapid hand.

"Perth—too far away—Putney Bridge—too near at hand. Ramsgate? I think not. Reigate also leaves me cold. Why—what an extraordinary thing! There's actually a place called Rowland's Castle. Ever heard of it, Rogers?"

"I fancy, sir, that you go there from Waterloo."

"What an extraordinary fellow you are, Rogers. You know everything. Well, well, Rowland's Castle! I wonder what sort of a place it is."

"Not much of a place, I should say, sir."

"All the better; there'll be less competition. These quiet little country hamlets have a lot of the old feudal spirit knocking about. The last of the original Rowlands ought to meet with instant appreciation. I shouldn't wonder if they elected me mayor in a week."

He shut up the *ABC* with a bang.

"The die is cast. Pack me a small suitcase, will you, Rogers? Also my compliments to the cook, and will she oblige me with a loan of the cat. Dick Whittington, you know. When you set out to become a Lord Mayor, a cat is essential."

"I'm sorry, sir, but the cat is not available at the present moment."

"How is that?"

"A family of eight, sir. Arrived this morning."

"You don't say so. I thought its name was Peter."

"So it is, sir. A great surprise to all of us."

"A case of careless christening and the deceitful sex, eh? Well, well, I shall have to go catless. Pack up those things at once, will you?"

"Very good, sir."

Rogers withdrew, to reappear ten minutes later.

"Shall I call a taxi, sir?"

"Yes, please."

Rogers hesitated, then advanced a little farther into the room.

"You'll excuse the liberty, sir, but if I was you, I shouldn't take too much notice of anything Mr. Rowland said this morning. He was at one of those city dinners last night and—"

"Say no more," said George. "I understand."

"And being inclined to gout—"

"I know, I know. Rather a strenuous evening for you, Rogers, with two of us, eh? But I've set my heart on distinguishing myself at Rowland's Castle—the cradle of my historic race—that would go well in a speech, wouldn't it? A wire to me there, or a discreet advertisement in the morning papers, will recall me at any time if a fricassee of veal is in preparation. And now—to Waterloo!—as Wellington said on the eve of the historic battle."

Waterloo Station was not at its brightest and best that afternoon. Mr. Rowland eventually discovered a train that would take him to his destination, but it was an undistinguished train, an unimposing train—a train that nobody seemed anxious to travel by. Mr. Rowland had a first-class carriage to himself, up in the front of the train. A fog was descending in an indeterminate way over the metropolis, now it lifted, now it descended. The platform was deserted, and only the asthmatic breathing of the engine broke the silence.

And then, all of a sudden, things began to happen with bewildering rapidity.

A girl happened first. She wrenched open the door and jumped in, rousing Mr. Rowland from something perilously near a nap, exclaiming as she did so: "Oh! Hide me—oh! Please hide me."

George was essentially a man of action—his not to reason why, his but to do and die, etc. There is only one place to hide in a railway carriage—under the seat. In seven seconds the girl was bestowed there, and George's suitcase, negligently standing on end, covered her retreat. None too soon. An infuriated face appeared at the carriage window.

"My niece! You have her here. I want my niece."

George, a little breathless, was reclining in the corner, deep in the sporting column of the evening paper, one-thirty edition. He laid it aside with the air of a man recalling himself from far away.

"I beg your pardon, sir?" he said politely.

"My niece—what have you done with her?"

Acting on the policy that attack is always better than defense, George leaped into action.

"What the devil do you mean?" he cried, with a very creditable imitation of his own uncle's manner.

The other paused a minute, taken aback by this sudden fierceness. He was a fat man, still panting a little as though he had run some way. His hair was cut *en brosse*, and he had a mustache of the Hohenzollern persuasion. His accents were decidedly guttural, and the stiffness of his carriage denoted that he was more at home in uniform than out of it. George had the trueborn Briton's prejudice against foreigners—and an especial distaste for German-looking foreigners.

"What the devil do you mean, sir?" he repeated angrily.

"She came in here," said the other. "I saw her. What have you done with her?"

George flung aside the paper and thrust his head and shoulders through the window.

"So that's it, is it?" he roared. "Blackmail. But you've tried it on the wrong person. I read all about you in the *Daily Mail* this morning. Here, guard, guard!"

Already attracted from afar by the altercation, that functionary came hurrying up.

"Here, guard," said Mr. Rowland, with that air of authority which the lower classes so adore. "This fellow is annoying me. I'll give him in charge for attempted blackmail if necessary. Pretends I've got his niece hidden in here. There's a regular gang of these foreigners trying this sort of thing on. It ought to be stopped. Take him away, will you? Here's my card if you want it."

The guard looked from one to the other. His mind was soon made up. His training led him to despise foreigners and to respect and admire well-dressed gentlemen who traveled first-class.

He laid his hand on the shoulder of the intruder.

"Here," he said, "you come out of this."

At this crisis the stranger's English failed him, and he plunged into passionate profanity in his native tongue.

"That's enough of that," said the guard. "Stand away, will you? She's due out."

Flags were waved and whistles were blown. With an unwilling jerk the train drew out of the station.

George remained at his observation post until they were clear of the platform. Then he drew in his head, and picking up the suitcase tossed it into the rack.

"It's quite all right. You can come out," he said reassuringly.

The girl crawled out.

"Oh!" she gasped. "How can I thank you?"

"That's quite all right. It's been a pleasure, I assure you," returned George nonchalantly.

He smiled at her reassuringly. There was a slightly puzzled look in her eyes. She seemed to be missing something to which she was accustomed. At that moment, she caught sight of herself in the narrow glass opposite, and gave a heartfelt gasp.

Whether the carriage cleaners do, or do not, sweep under the seats every day is doubtful. Appearances were against their doing so, but it may be that every particle of dirt and smoke finds its way there like a homing bird. George had hardly had time to take in the girl's appearance, so sudden had been her arrival, and so brief the space of time before she crawled into hiding, but it was certainly a trim and well-dressed young woman who had disappeared under the seat. Now her little red hat was crushed and dented, and her face was disfigured with long streaks of dirt.

"Oh!" said the girl.

She fumbled for her bag. George, with the tact of a true gentleman, looked fixedly out of the window and admired the streets of London south of the Thames.

"How can I thank you?" said the girl again.

Taking this as a hint that conversation might now be resumed, George withdrew his gaze and made another polite disclaimer, but this time with a good deal of added warmth in his manner.

The girl was absolutely lovely! Never before, George told himself, had he seen such a lovely girl. The *empressement* of his manner became even more marked.

"I think it was simply splendid of you," said the girl with enthusiasm.

"Not at all. Easiest thing in the world. Only too pleased been of use," mumbled George.

"Splendid," she reiterated emphatically.

It is undoubtedly pleasant to have the loveliest girl you have ever seen gazing into your eyes and telling you how splendid you are. George enjoyed it as much as anyone would.

Then there came a rather difficult silence. It seemed to dawn upon the girl that further explanation might be expected. She flushed a little.

"The awkward part of it is," she said nervously, "that I'm afraid I can't explain."

She looked at him with a piteous air of uncertainty.

"You can't explain?"

"No."

"How perfectly splendid!" said Mr. Rowland with enthusiasm.

"I beg your pardon?"

"I said, 'How perfectly splendid.' Just like one of those books that keep you up all night. The heroine always says, 'I can't explain' in the first chapter. She explains in the last, of course, and there's never any real reason why she shouldn't have done so in the beginning—except that it would spoil the story. I can't tell you how pleased I am to be mixed up in a real mystery—I didn't know there were such things. I hope it's got something to do with secret documents of immense importance, and the Balkan express. I dote upon the Balkan express."

The girl stared at him with wide, suspicious eyes.

"What makes you say the Balkan express?" she asked sharply.

"I hope I haven't been indiscreet," George hastened to put in. "Your uncle traveled by it, perhaps."

"My uncle—" She paused, then began again, "My uncle—"

"Quite so," said George sympathetically. "I've got an uncle myself. Nobody should be held responsible for their uncles. Nature's little throwbacks—that's how I look at it."

The girl began to laugh suddenly. When she spoke, George was aware of the slight foreign inflection in her voice. At first he had taken her to be English.

"What a refreshing and unusual person you are, Mr.—"

"Rowland. George to my friends."

"My name is Elizabeth—"

She stopped abruptly.

"I like the name of Elizabeth," said George, to cover her momentary confusion. "They don't call you Bessie or anything horrible like that, I hope?"

She shook her head.

"Well," said George, "now that we know each other, we'd better get down to business. If you'll stand up, Elizabeth, I'll brush down the back of your coat."

She stood up obediently, and George was as good as his word.

"Thank you, Mr. Rowland."

"George. George to my friends, remember. And you can't come into my nice empty carriage, roll under the seat, induce me to tell lies to your uncle, and then refuse to be friends, can you?"

"Thank you, George."

"That's better."

"Do I look quite all right now?" asked Elizabeth, trying to see over her left shoulder.

"You look—oh! you look—you look all right," said George, curbing himself sternly.

"It was all so sudden, you see," explained the girl.

"It must have been."

"He saw us in the taxi, and then at the station I just bolted in here knowing he was close behind me. Where is this train going to, by the way?"

"Rowland's Castle," said George firmly.

The girl looked puzzled.

"Rowland's Castle?"

"Not at once, of course. Only after a good deal of stopping and slow going. But I confidently expect to be there before midnight. The old South-Western was a very reliable line—slow but sure—and I'm sure the Southern Railway is keeping up the old traditions."

"I don't know that I want to go to Rowland's Castle," said Elizabeth doubtfully.

"You hurt me. It's a delightful spot."

"Have you ever been there?"

"Not exactly. But there are lots of other places you can go to, if you don't fancy Rowland's Castle. There's Woking, and Weybridge, and Wimbledon. The train is sure to stop at one or other of them."

"I see," said the girl. "Yes, I can get out there, and perhaps motor back to London. That would be the best plan, I think."

Even as she spoke, the train began to slow up. Mr. Rowland gazed at her with appealing eyes.

"If I can do anything—"

"No, indeed. You've done a lot already."

There was a pause, then the girl broke out suddenly:

"I—I wish I could explain. I—"

"For heaven's sake, don't do that! It would spoil everything. But look here, isn't there anything that I could do? Carry the secret papers to Vienna—or something of that kind? There always are secret papers. Do give me a chance."

The train had stopped. Elizabeth jumped quickly out onto the platform. She turned and spoke to him through the window.

"Are you in earnest? Would you really do something for us—for me?"

"I'd do anything in the world for you, Elizabeth."

"Even if I could give you no reasons?"

"Rotten things, reasons!"

"Even if it were—dangerous?"

"The more danger, the better."

She hesitated a minute, then seemed to make up her mind.

"Lean out of the window. Look down the platform as though you weren't really looking." Mr. Rowland endeavored to comply with this somewhat difficult recommendation. "Do you see that man getting in—with a small dark beard—light overcoat? Follow him, see what he does and where he goes."

"Is that all?" asked Mr. Rowland. "What do I—"

She interrupted him.

"Further instructions will be sent to you. Watch him—and guard this." She thrust a small sealed packet into his hand. "Guard it with your life. It's the key to everything."

The train went on. Mr. Rowland remained staring out the window, watching Elizabeth's tall, graceful figure threading its way down the platform. In his hand he clutched the small sealed packet.

The rest of his journey was both monotonous and uneventful. The train was a slow one. It stopped everywhere. At every station, George's head shot out of the window, in case his quarry should alight. Occasionally he strolled up and down the platform when the wait promised to be a long one, and reassured himself that the man was still there.

The eventual destination of the train was Portsmouth, and it was there that the black-bearded traveler alighted. He made his way to a small second-class hotel where he booked a room. Mr. Rowland also booked a room.

The rooms were in the same corridor, two doors from each other. The arrangement seemed satisfactory to George. He was a complete novice in the art of shadowing, but was anxious to acquit himself well, and justify Elizabeth's trust in him.

At dinner George was given a table not far from that of his quarry. The room was not full, and the majority of the diners George put down as commercial travelers, quiet respectable men who ate their food with appetite. Only one man attracted his special notice, a small man with ginger hair and mustache and a suggestion of horsiness in his apparel. He seemed to be interested in George also, and suggested a drink and a game of billiards when the meal had come to a close. But George had just espied the black-bearded man putting on his hat and overcoat, and declined politely. In another minute he was out in the street, gaining fresh insight into the difficult art of shadowing. The chase was a long and a weary one —and in the end it seemed to lead nowhere. After twisting and turning through the streets of Portsmouth for about four miles, the man returned to the hotel, George hard upon his heels. A faint doubt assailed the latter. Was it possible that the man was aware of his presence? As he debated this point, standing in the hall, the outer door was pushed open, and the little ginger man entered. Evidently he, too, had been out for a stroll.

George was suddenly aware that the beauteous damsel in the office was addressing him.

"Mr. Rowland, isn't it? Two gentlemen have called to see you. Two foreign gentlemen. They are in the little room at the end of the passage."

Somewhat astonished, George sought the room in question. Two men who were sitting there rose to their feet and bowed punctiliously.

"Mr. Rowland? I have no doubt, sir, that you can guess our identity."

George gazed from one to the other of them. The spokesman was the elder of the two, a gray-haired, pompous gentleman who spoke excellent English. The other was a tall, somewhat pimply young man, with a blond Teutonic cast of countenance which was not rendered more attractive by the fierce scowl which he wore at the present moment.

Somewhat relieved to find that neither of his visitors was the old gentleman he had encountered at Waterloo, George assumed his most debonair manner.

"Pray sit down, gentlemen. I'm delighted to make your acquaintance. How about a drink?"

The elder man held up a protesting hand.

"Thank you, Lord Rowland—not for us. We have but a few brief moments— just time for you to answer one question."

"It's very kind of you to elect me to the peerage," said George. "I'm sorry you won't have a drink. And what is this momentous question?"

"Lord Rowland, you left London in company with a certain lady. You arrived here alone. Where is the lady?"

George rose to his feet.

"I fail to understand the question," he said coldly, speaking as much like the hero of a novel as he could. "I have the honor to wish you good evening, gentlemen."

"But you do understand it. You understand it perfectly," cried the younger man, breaking out suddenly. "What have you done with Alexa?"

"Be calm, sir," murmured the other. "I beg of you to be calm."

"I can assure you," said George, "that I know no lady of that name. There is some mistake."

The older man was eyeing him keenly.

"That can hardly be," he said dryly. "I took the liberty of examining the hotel register. You entered yourself as Mr. G. Rowland of Rowland's Castle."

George was forced to blush.

"A—a little joke of mine," he explained feebly.

"A somewhat poor subterfuge. Come, let us not beat about the bush. Where is Her Highness?"

"If you mean Elizabeth—"

With a howl of rage the young man flung himself forward again.

"Insolent pig-dog! To speak of her thus."

"I am referring," said the other slowly, "as you very well know, to the Grand Duchess Anastasia Sophia Alexandra Marie Helena Olga Elizabeth of Catonia."

"Oh!" said Mr. Rowland helplessly.

He tried to recall all that he had ever known of Catonia. It was, as far as he remembered, a small Balkan kingdom, and he seemed to remember something about a revolution having occurred there. He rallied himself with an effort.

"Evidently we mean the same person," he said cheerfully, "only I call her Elizabeth."

"You will give me satisfaction for that," snarled the younger man. "We will fight."

"Fight?"

"A duel."

"I never fight duels," said Mr. Rowland firmly.

"Why not?" demanded the other unpleasantly.

"I'm too afraid of getting hurt."

"Aha! Is that so? Then I will at least pull your nose for you."

The young man advanced fiercely. Exactly what happened was difficult to see, but he described a sudden semicircle in the air and fell to the ground with a heavy thud. He picked himself up in a dazed manner. Mr. Rowland was smiling pleasantly.

"As I was saying," he remarked. "I'm always afraid of getting hurt. That's why I thought it well to learn jujitsu."

There was a pause. The two foreigners looked doubtfully at this amiable-looking young man, as though they suddenly realized that some dangerous quality lurked behind the pleasant nonchalance of his manner. The young Teuton was white with passion.

"You will repent this," he hissed.

The older man retained his dignity.

"That is your last word, Lord Rowland? You refuse to tell us Her Highness's whereabouts?"

"I am unaware of them myself."

"You can hardly expect me to believe that."

"I am afraid you are of an unbelieving nature, sir."

The other merely shook his head, and murmuring: "This is not the end; you will hear from us again," the two men took their leave.

George passed his hand over his brow. Events were proceeding at a bewildering rate. He was evidently mixed up in a first-class European scandal.

"It might even mean another war," said George hopefully, as he hunted round to see what had become of the man with the black beard.

To his great relief, he discovered him sitting in a corner of the commercial room. George sat down in another corner. In about three minutes the black-bearded man got up and went up to bed. George followed and saw him go into his room and close the door. George heaved a sigh of relief.

"I need a night's rest," he murmured. "Need it badly."

Then a dire thought struck him. Supposing the black-bearded man had realized that George was on his trail? Supposing that he should slip away during the night while George himself was sleeping the sleep of the just? A few minutes' reflection suggested to Mr. Rowland a way of dealing with this difficulty. He unraveled one of his socks till he got a good length of neutral-colored wool, then creeping quietly out of his room, he pasted one end of the wool to the farther side of the stranger's door with stamp paper, carrying the wool across it and along to his own room. There he hung the end with a small silver bell—a relic of last night's entertainment. He surveyed these arrangements with a good deal of satisfaction. Should the black-bearded man attempt to leave his room, George would be instantly warned by the ringing of the bell.

This matter disposed of, George lost no time in seeking his couch. The small packet he placed carefully under his pillow. As he did so, he fell into a momentary brown study. His thoughts could have been translated thus:

"Anastasia Sophia Marie Alexandra Olga Elizabeth. Hang it all, I've missed out one. I wonder now—"

He was unable to go to sleep immediately, being tantalized with his failure to grasp the situation. What was it all about? What was the connection between the escaping Grand Duchess, the sealed packet and the black-bearded man? What was the Grand Duchess escaping from? Were the two foreigners aware that the sealed packet was in his possession? What was it likely to contain?

Pondering these matters, with an irritated sense that he was no nearer their solution, Mr. Rowland fell asleep.

He was awakened by the faint jangle of a bell. Not one of those men who awake to instant action, it took him just a minute and a half to realize the situation. Then he jumped up, thrust on some slippers, and, opening the door with the utmost caution, slipped out into the corridor. A faint moving patch of shadow at the far end of the passage showed him the direction taken by his quarry. Moving as noiselessly as possible, Mr. Rowland followed the trail. He was just in time to see the black-bearded man disappear into a bathroom. That was puzzling, particularly so as there was a bathroom just opposite his own room. Moving up close to the door, which was ajar, George peered through the crack. The man was on his knees by the side of the bath, doing something to the skirting board immediately behind it. He remained there for about five minutes, then he rose to his feet, and George beat a prudent retreat. Safe in the shadow of his own door, he watched the other pass and regain his own room.

"Good," said George to himself. "The mystery of the bathroom will be investigated tomorrow morning."

He got into bed and slipped his hand under the pillow to assure himself that the precious packet was still there. In another minute, he was scattering the bedclothes in a panic. The packet was gone!

It was a sadly chastened George who sat consuming eggs and bacon the following morning. He had failed Elizabeth. He had allowed the precious packet she had entrusted to his charge to be taken from him, and the "Mystery of the Bathroom" was miserably inadequate. Yes, undoubtedly George had made a mutt of himself.

After breakfast he strolled upstairs again. A chambermaid was standing in the passage looking perplexed.

"Anything wrong, my dear?" said George kindly.

"It's the gentleman here, sir. He asked to be called at half-past eight, and I can't get any answer and the door's locked."

"You don't say so," said George.

An uneasy feeling arose in his own breast. He hurried into his room. Whatever plans he was forming were instantly brushed aside by a most unexpected sight. There on the dressing table was the little packet which had been stolen from him the night before!

George picked it up and examined it. Yes, it was undoubtedly the same. But the seals had been broken. After a minute's hesitation, he unwrapped it. If other people had seen its contents, there was no reason why he should not see them also. Besides, it was possible that the contents had been abstracted. The unwound paper revealed a small cardboard box, such as jewelers use. George opened it. Inside, nestling on a bed of cotton wool, was a plain gold wedding ring.

He picked it up and examined it. There was no inscription inside—nothing whatever to mark it out from any other wedding ring. George dropped his head into his hands with a groan.

"Lunacy," he murmured. "That's what it is. Stark, staring lunacy. There's no sense anywhere."

Suddenly he remembered the chambermaid's statement, and at the same time he observed that there was a broad parapet outside the window. It was not a feat he would ordinarily have attempted, but he was so aflame with curiosity and anger that he was in the mood to make light of difficulties. He sprang upon the window sill. A few seconds later he was peering in at the window of the room occupied by the black-bearded man. The window was open and the room was empty. A little farther along was a fire escape. It was clear how the quarry had taken his departure.

George jumped in through the window. The missing man's effects were still scattered about. There might be some clue among them to shed light on George's perplexities. He began to hunt about, starting with the contents of a battered kit bag.

It was a sound that arrested his search—a very slight sound, but a sound indubitably in the room. George's glance leapt to the big wardrobe. He sprang up and wrenched open the door. As he did so, a man jumped out from it and went rolling over the floor locked in George's embrace. He was no mean antagonist. All George's special tricks availed very little. They fell apart at length in sheer exhaustion, and for the first time George saw who his adversary was. It was the little man with the ginger mustache!

"Who the devil are you?" demanded George.

For answer the other drew out a card and handed it to him. George read it aloud.

"Detective-Inspector Jarrold, Scotland Yard."

"That's right, sir. And you'd do well to tell me all you know about this business."

"I would, would I?" said George thoughtfully. "Do you know, inspector, I believe you're right. Shall we adjourn to a more cheerful spot?"

In a quiet corner of the bar George unfolded his soul. Inspector Jarrold listened sympathetically.

"Very puzzling, as you say, sir," he remarked when George had finished. "There's a lot as I can't make head or tail of myself, but there's one or two points I can clear up for you. I was here after Mardenberg (your black-bearded friend) and your turning up and watching him the way you did made me suspicious. I couldn't place you. I slipped into your room last night when you were out of it, and it was I who sneaked the little packet from under your pillow. When I opened it and found it wasn't what I was after, I took the first opportunity of returning it to your room."

"That makes things a little clearer certainly," said George thoughtfully. "I seem to have made rather an ass of myself all through."

"I wouldn't say that, sir. You did uncommon well for a beginner. You say you visited the bathroom this morning and took away what was concealed behind the skirting board?"

"Yes. But it's only a rotten love letter," said George gloomily. "Dash it all, I didn't mean to go nosing out the poor fellow's private life."

"Would you mind letting me see it, sir?"

George took a folded letter from his pocket and passed it to the inspector. The latter unfolded it.

"As you say, sir. But I rather fancy that if you drew lines from one dotted *i* to another, you'd get a different result. Why, bless you, sir, this is a plan of the Portsmouth harbor defenses."

"What?"

"Yes. We've had our eye on the gentleman for some time. But he was too sharp for us. Got a woman to do most of the dirty work."

"A woman?" said George in a faint voice. "What was her name?"

"She goes by a good many, sir. Most usually known as Betty Brighteyes. A remarkably good-looking young woman she is."

"Betty—Brighteyes," said George. "Thank you, inspector."

"Excuse me, sir, but you're not looking well."

"I'm not well. I'm very ill. In fact, I think I'd better take the first train back to town."

The inspector looked at his watch.

"That will be a slow train, I'm afraid, sir. Better wait for the express."

"It doesn't matter," said George gloomily. "No train could be slower than the one I came down by yesterday."

Seated once more in a first-class carriage, George leisurely perused the day's news. Suddenly he sat bolt upright and stared at the sheet in front of him.

"A romantic wedding took place yesterday in London when Lord Roland Gaigh, second son of the Marquis of Axminster, was married to the Grand Duchess Anastasia of Catonia. The ceremony was kept a profound secret. The Grand Duchess has been living in Paris with her uncle since the upheaval in Catonia. She met Lord Roland when he was secretary to the British Embassy in Catonia and their attachment dates from that time."

"Well, I'm—"

Mr. Rowland could not think of anything strong enough to express his feelings. He continued to stare into space. The train stopped at a small station and a lady got in. She sat down opposite him.

"Good morning, George," she said sweetly.

"Good heavens!" cried George. "Elizabeth!"

She smiled at him. She was, if possible, lovelier than ever.

"Look here," cried George, clutching his head. "For God's sake tell me. Are you the Grand Duchess Anastasia, or are you Betty Brighteyes?"

She stared at him.

"I'm not either. I'm Elizabeth Gaigh. I can tell you all about it now. And I've got to apologize too. You see, Roland (that's my brother) has always been in love with Alexa—"

"Meaning the Grand Duchess?"

"Yes, that's what the family call her. Well, as I say, Roland was always in love with her, and she with him. And then the revolution came, and Alexa was in Paris, and they were just going to fix it up when old Stürm, the chancellor, came along and insisted on carrying off Alexa and forcing her to marry Prince Karl, her cousin, a horrid pimply person—"

"I fancy I've met him," said George.

"Whom she simply hates. And old Prince Osric, her uncle, forbade her to see Roland again. So she ran away to England, and I came up to town and met her, and we wired to Roland, who was in Scotland. And just at the very last minute, when we were driving to the Registry Office in a taxi, whom should we meet in another taxi face to face, but old Prince Osric. Of course he followed us, and we were at our wits' end what to do because he'd have made the most fearful scene, and, anyway, he is her guardian. Then I had the brilliant idea of changing places. You can practically see nothing of a girl nowadays but the tip of her nose. I put on Alexa's red hat and brown wrap coat, and she put on my gray. Then we told the taxi to go to Waterloo, and I skipped out there and hurried into the station. Old Osric followed the red hat all right, without a thought for the other occupant of the taxi sitting huddled up inside, but of course it wouldn't do for him to see my face. So I just bolted into your carriage and threw myself on your mercy."

"I've got that all right," said George. "It's the rest of it."

"I know. That's what I've got to apologize about. I hope you won't be awfully cross. You see, you looked so keen on its being a real mystery—like in books, that I really couldn't resist the temptation. I picked out a rather sinister-looking man on the platform and told you to follow him. And then I thrust the parcel on you."

"Containing a wedding ring."

"Yes. Alexa and I bought that, because Roland wasn't due to arrive from Scotland until just before the wedding. And of course I knew that by the time I got to London, they wouldn't want it—they would have had to use a curtain ring or something."

"I see," said George. "It's like all these things—so simple when you know! Allow me, Elizabeth."

He stripped off her left glove and uttered a sigh of relief at the sight of the bare third finger.

"That's all right," he remarked. "That ring won't be wasted after all."

"Oh!" cried Elizabeth. "But I don't know anything about you."

"You know how nice I am," said George. "By the way, it has just occurred to me, you are the Lady Elizabeth Gaigh, of course."

"Oh! George, are you a snob?"

"As a matter of fact, I am, rather. My best dream was one where King George borrowed half a crown from me to see him over the weekend. But I was thinking of my uncle—the one from whom I am estranged. He's a frightful snob. When he knows I'm going to marry you, and that we'll have a title in the family, he'll make me a partner at once!"

"Oh! George, is he very rich?"

"Elizabeth, are you mercenary?"

"Very. I adore spending money. But I was thinking of Father. Five daughters, full of beauty and blue blood. He's just yearning for a rich son-in-law."

"H'm," said George. "It will be one of those marriages made in heaven and approved on earth. Shall we live at Rowland's Castle? They'd be sure to make me Lord Mayor with you for a wife. Oh! Elizabeth, darling, it's probably contravening the company's bylaws, but I simply must kiss you!"

Robert van Gulik

THE MURDER ON THE LOTUS POND

"Judge Dee was a historical person," Robert van Gulik wrote in 1967, while serving as the Dutch ambassador to Japan. "His full name was Dee Jen-djieh and he lived from a.d. 630 to 700. In the latter half of his career he became Minister of State, and through his wise counsels executed a beneficial influence on the internal and external affairs of the T'ang empire. However, it is chiefly because of his reputation as a detector of crimes, acquired while serving as district magistrate, that his name lives among the Chinese people. Today the Chinese still consider him their master detective, and his name is as popular with them as that of Sherlock Holmes with us."

Robert Hans van Gulik (1910–1967) was a Dutch diplomat and orientalist who spent most of his life in the Far East. In 1940 he came upon a copy of Dee Goong An (The Criminal Cases of Judge Dee), *a seventeenth- or early-eighteenth-century account, and translated it into English. Later, he reworked these historical cases featuring the judge into mystery novels and still later—as in the case of this story, "The Murder on the Lotus Pond"—wrote original cases set in historically accurate settings.*

In his dozen or so Judge Dee books, van Gulik preserves the Chinese tradition of presenting two or three interrelated mysteries for the judge to solve, but his skill as a western mystery writer overcame his scholarly instincts when it came to another tradition: unlike the originals, his versions do not reveal the identity of the culprit from the beginning.

Selecting something by an ambassador of Holland for an anthology of detective stories "from England and America" may seem a bit arbitrary. And it is. But van Gulik wrote his Judge Dee stories in English and published them first outside Holland. That—and the fact that they are so downright entertaining—is reason enough to include one.

The Murder on
the Lotus Pond

This case occurred in the year A.D. 667 in Han-yuan, an ancient little town built on the shore of a lake near the capital. There Judge Dee has to solve the murder of an elderly poet, who lived in retirement on his modest property behind the Willow Quarter, the abode of the courtesans and singing-girls. The poet was murdered while peacefully contemplating the moon in his garden pavilion, set in the center of a lotus pond. There were no witnesses—or so it seemed.

FROM THE SMALL PAVILION in the center of the lotus pond he could survey the entire garden, bathed in moonlight. He listened intently. Everything remained quiet. With a satisfied smile he looked down at the dead man in the bamboo chair, at the hilt of the knife sticking up from his breast. Only a few drops of blood trickled down the gray cloth of his robe. The man took up one of the two porcelain cups that stood by the pewter wine jar on the round table. He emptied it at one draft, then muttered to the corpse, "Rest in peace! If you had been only a fool, I would probably have spared you. But since you were an interfering fool . . ."

He shrugged his shoulders. All had gone well. It was past midnight; no one would come to this lonely country house on the outskirts of the city. And in the dark house at the other end of the garden nothing stirred. He examined his hands —there was no trace of blood. Then he stooped and scrutinized the floor of the pavilion, and the chair he had been sitting on opposite the dead man. No, he hadn't left any clue. He could leave now, all was safe.

Suddenly, he heard a plopping sound behind him. He swung round, startled. Then he sighed with relief; it was only a large, green frog. It had jumped up out of the pond on to the marble steps of the pavilion. Now it sat there looking up at him solemnly with its blinking, protruding eyes.

"You can't talk, bastard!" the man sneered. "But I'll make double-sure!" So speaking, he gave the frog a vicious kick that smashed it against the table leg. The animal's long hindlegs twitched, then it lay still. The man picked up the second wine cup, the one his victim had been drinking from. He examined it, then he put it in his wide sleeve. Now he was ready. As he turned to go, his eye fell on the dead frog.

"Join your comrades!" he said with contempt and kicked it into the water. It fell with a splash among the lotus plants. At once the croaking of hundreds of frightened frogs tore the quiet night.

The man cursed violently. He quickly crossed the curved bridge that led over the pond to the garden gate. After he had slipped outside and pulled the gate shut, the frogs grew quiet again.

A few hours later three horsemen were riding along the lake road, back to the city. The red glow of dawn shone on their brown hunting-robes and black caps. A cool morning breeze rippled the surface of the lake, but soon it would grow hot, for it was mid-summer.

The broad-shouldered, bearded man said with a smile to his thin, elderly companion, "Our duck-hunt suggested a good method for catching wily criminals! You set up a decoy, then stay in hiding with your clap-net ready. When your bird shows up, you net him!"

Four peasants walking in the opposite direction quickly set down the loads of vegetables they were carrying and knelt down by the roadside. They had recognized the bearded man: It was Judge Dee, the magistrate of the lake-district of Han-yuan.

"We did a powerful lot of clapping among the reeds, sir," the stalwart man who was riding behind them remarked wryly. "But all we got was a few water-plants!"

"Anyway it was good exercise, Ma Joong!" Judge Dee said over his shoulder to his lieutenant. Then he went on to the thin man riding by his side: "If we did this every morning, Mr. Yuan, we'd never need your pills and powders!"

The thin man smiled bleakly. His name was Yuan Kai, and he was the wealthy owner of the largest pharmacy in Judge Dee's district. Duck-hunting was his favorite sport.

Judge Dee drove his horse on, and soon they entered the city of Han-yuan, built against the mountain slope. At the market place, in front of the Temple of Confucius, the three men dismounted; then they climbed the stone steps leading up to the street where the tribunal stood, overlooking the city and the lake.

Ma Joong pointed at the squat man standing in front of the monumental gate of the tribunal. "Heavens!" he growled, "I have never seen our good headman up so early. I fear he must be gravely ill!"

The headman of the constables came running towards them. He made a bow, then said excitedly to the judge, "The poet Meng Lan has been murdered, Your Honor! Half an hour ago his servant came rushing here and reported that he had found his master's dead body in the garden pavilion."

"Meng Lan? A poet?" Judge Dee said with a frown. "In the year I have been here in Han-yuan I have never even heard the name."

"He lives in an old country house, near the marsh to the east of the city, sir," the pharmacist said. "He is not very well known here; he rarely comes to the city. But I heard that in the capital his poetry is praised highly by connoisseurs."

"We'd better go there at once," the judge said. "Have Sergeant Hoong and my two other lieutenants come back yet, Headman?"

"No sir, they are still in the village near the west boundary of our district. Just after Your Honor left this morning, a man came with a note from Sergeant Hoong. It said that they hadn't yet found a single clue to the men who robbed the treasury messenger."

Judge Dee tugged at his long beard. "That robbery is a vexing case!" he said testily. "The messenger was carrying a dozen gold bars. And now we have a murder on our hands too! Well, we'll manage, Ma Joong. Do you know the way to the dead poet's country place?"

"I know a short-cut through the east quarter, sir," Yuan Kai said. "If you'll allow me . . ."

"By all means! You come along too, Headman. You sent a couple of constables back with Meng's servant to see that nothing is disturbed, I trust?"

"I certainly did, sir!" the headman said importantly.

"You are making progress," Judge Dee observed. Seeing the headman's smug smile, he added dryly, "A pity that the progress is so slow. Get four horses from the stables!"

The pharmacist rode ahead and led them along several narrow alleys, zigzagging down to the bank of the lake. Soon they were riding through a lane lined with willow trees. These had given their name to the Willow Quarter, the abode of the dancing-girls and courtesans that lay to the east of the city.

"Tell me about Meng Lan," the judge said to the pharmacist.

"I didn't know him too well, sir. I visited him only three or four times, but he seemed a nice, modest kind of person. He settled down here two years ago, in an old country house behind the Willow Quarter. It has only three rooms or so, but there is a beautiful large garden, with a lotus pond."

"Has he got a large family?"

"No sir, he was a widower when he came here; his two grownup sons live in the capital. Last year he met a courtesan from the Willow Quarter. He bought her out, and married her. She didn't have much to commend herself besides her looks —she can't read or write, sing or dance. Meng Lan was able to buy her cheaply, therefore, but it took all his savings. He was living on a small annuity an admirer in the capital was sending him. I am told it was a happy marriage, although Meng was of course much older than she."

"One would have thought," Judge Dee remarked, "that a poet would choose an educated girl who could share his literary interests."

"She is a quiet, soft-spoken woman, sir," the pharmacist said with a shrug. "And she looked after him well."

"Meng Lan was a smart customer, even though he wrote poetry," Ma Joong muttered. "A nice, quiet girl that looks after you well—a man can hardly do better than that!"

The willow lane had narrowed to a pathway. It led through the high oak trees and thick undergrowth that marked the vicinity of the marsh behind the Willow Quarter.

The four men dismounted in front of a rustic bamboo gate. The two constables standing guard there saluted, then pushed the gate open. Before entering, Judge Dee surveyed the large garden. It was not very well kept. The flowering shrubs and bushes round the lotus pond were running wild, but they gave the place a kind of savage beauty. Some butterflies were fluttering lazily over the large lotus leaves that covered the pond's surface.

"Meng Lan was very fond of this garden," Yuan Kai remarked.

The judge nodded. He looked at the red-lacquered wooden bridge that led over the water to a hexagonal pavilion, open on all sides. Slender pillars supported the pointed roof, decked with green tiles. Beyond the pond, at the back of the garden, he saw a low, rambling wooden building. Its thatched roof was half covered by the low foliage of the tall oak trees that stood behind the house.

It was getting very hot. Judge Dee wiped the perspiration from his brow and crossed the narrow bridge, the three others following behind him. The small pavilion offered hardly enough space for the four men. Judge Dee stood looking for a while at the thin figure, clad in a simple house-robe of gray cloth, lying back in the bamboo armchair. Then he felt the shoulders, and the limp arms. Righting himself, he said, "The body is just getting stiff. In this hot, humid weather it's hard to fix the time of death. In any case after midnight, I would say." He carefully pulled the knife out of the dead man's breast. He examined the long, thin blade and the plain ivory hilt. Ma Joong pursed his lips and said, "Won't help us much, sir. Every ironmonger in town keeps these cheap knives in stock."

Judge Dee silently handed the knife to him. Ma Joong wrapped it up in a sheet of paper he had taken from his sleeve. The judge studied the thin face of the dead man. It was frozen in an eery, lopsided grin. The poet had a long, ragged mustache and a wispy gray goatee; the judge put his age at about sixty. He took the large wine jar from the table and shook it. Only a little wine was left. Then he picked up the wine cup standing next to it, and examined it. With a puzzled look he put it in his sleeve. Turning to the headman he said:

"Tell the constables to make a stretcher of some branches, and convey the body to the tribunal, for the autopsy." And to Yuan Kai: "You might sit on that stone bench over there near the fence for a while, Mr. Yuan. I won't be long." He motioned Ma Joong to follow him.

They crossed the bridge again. The thin planks creaked under the weight of the two heavy men. They walked round the lotus pond and on to the house. With relief Judge Dee inhaled the cool air in the shadow under the porch. Ma Joong knocked.

A rather handsome but surly-looking youngster opened. Ma Joong told him that the magistrate wanted to see Mrs. Meng. As the boy went hurriedly inside,

Judge Dee sat down at the rickety bamboo table in the center of the sparsely furnished room. Ma Joong stood with folded arms behind his chair. The judge took in the old, worn furniture, and the cracked plaster walls. He said, "Robbery can't have been the motive, evidently."

"There—the motive is coming, sir!" Ma Joong whispered. "Old husband, pretty young wife—we know the rest!"

Judge Dee looked round and saw that a slender woman of about twenty-five had appeared in the door opening. Her face was not made up and her cheeks showed the traces of tears. But her large, liquid eyes, gracefully curved eyebrows, full red lips and smooth complexion made her a very attractive woman. The robe she wore was of faded blue cloth, but it did not conceal her splendid figure. After one frightened look at the judge she made an obeisance, then remained standing there with downcast eyes, waiting respectfully till he would address her.

"I am distressed, madam," Judge Dee said in a gentle voice, "that I have to bother you so soon after the tragedy. I trust that you'll understand, however, that I must take swift action to bring the vile murderer to justice." As she nodded he went on: "When did you see your husband last?"

"We had our evening rice here in this room," Mrs. Meng replied in a soft, melodious voice. "Thereafter, when I had cleared the table, my husband read here for a few hours, and then said that since there was a beautiful moon he would go to the garden pavilion and have a few cups of wine there."

"Did he often do that?"

"Oh yes, he would go out there nearly every other night, enjoying the cool evening breeze, and humming songs."

"Did he often receive visitors there?"

"Never, Your Honor. He liked to be left alone, and did not encourage visitors. The few people who came to see him he always received in the afternoon, and here in the hall, for a cup of tea. I loved this peaceful life, my husband was so considerate, he . . ."

Her eyes became moist and her mouth twitched. But soon she took hold of herself and went on, "I prepared a large jar of warm wine, and brought it out to the pavilion. My husband said that I need not wait up for him, since he planned to be sitting there till a late hour. Thus I went to bed. Early this morning the servant knocked frantically on the door of our bedroom. I then saw that my husband wasn't there. The boy told me that he had found him in the pavilion . . ."

"Does this boy live here in the house?" Judge Dee asked.

"No, Your Honor, he stays with his father, the gardener of the largest house in the Willow Quarter. The boy only comes for the day; he leaves after I have prepared the evening rice."

"Did you hear anything unusual during the night?"

Mrs. Meng frowned, then answered, "I woke up once, it must have been shortly after midnight. The frogs in the pond were making a terrible noise. During the daytime one never hears them, they stay under water. Even when I wade into the pond to gather lotus flowers they remain quiet. But at night they come out, and they are easily startled. Therefore I thought that my husband was coming inside, and had dropped a stone or so into the pond. Then I dozed off again."

"I see," Judge Dee said. He thought for a while, caressing his long sidewhiskers. "Your husband's face didn't show any signs of terror or astonishment; he must have been stabbed quite unexpectedly. He was dead before he knew what was happening. That proves your husband knew his murderer well; they must have been sitting there drinking wine together. The large jar was nearly empty, but there was only one cup. I suppose that it would be difficult to check whether a wine cup is missing?"

"It's not difficult at all," Mrs. Meng replied with a thin smile. "We have only seven cups, a set of six, of green porcelain, and one larger cup of white porcelain, which my husband always used."

The judge raised his eyebrows. The cup he had found was of green porcelain. He resumed: "Did your husband have any enemies?"

"None, Your Honor!" she exclaimed. "I can't understand who . . ."

"Do *you* have enemies?" Judge Dee interrupted.

She grew red in the face, and bit her lip. Then she said contritely, "Of course Your Honor knows that until a year ago I worked in the quarter over there. Occasionally I refused a person who sought my favors, but I am certain that none of them would ever . . . And after all that time . . ." Her voice trailed off.

The judge rose. He thanked Mrs. Meng, expressed his sympathy, and took his leave.

When the two men were walking down the garden path Ma Joong said, "You ought to have asked her also about her friends, sir!"

"I depend on you for that information, Ma Joong. Have you kept in contact with that girl from the quarter—Apple Blossom is her name, I think."

"Peach Blossom, sir. Certainly I have!"

"Good. You'll go to the quarter right now, and get her to tell you everything she knows about Mrs. Meng at the time she was still working there. Especially about the men she used to associate with."

"It's very early in the day, sir," Ma Joong said doubtfully. "She'll still be asleep."

"Then you wake her up! Get going!"

Ma Joong looked dejected, but he hurried to the gate. Judge Dee reflected idly that if he sent his amorous lieutenant often enough to interview his lady-friends before breakfast, he might yet cure him of his weakness. As a rule such women don't look their best in the early morning after a late night.

Yuan Kai was standing by the lotus pond talking earnestly with a newcomer, a tall, neatly dressed man with a heavy-jowled, rather solemn face. The pharmacist introduced him as Mr. Wen Shou-fang, newly elected master of the tea-merchants' guild. The guildmaster made a low bow, then began an elaborate apology for not having called on the judge yet. Judge Dee cut him short, asking, "What brings you here so early in the morning, Mr. Wen?"

Wen seemed taken aback by this sudden question. He stammered, "I . . . I wanted to express my sympathy to Mrs. Meng, and . . . to ask her whether I could help her in any way. . . ."

"So you knew the Mengs well?" Judge Dee asked.

"I was just talking this matter over with my friend Wen, sir," Yuan Kai interposed hurriedly. "We decided to report to Your Honor here and now that both Wen and I myself sought Mrs. Meng's favors when she was still a courtesan, and that neither of us was successful. Both of us want to state that we perfectly understood that a courtesan is free to grant or withhold her favors, and that neither of us bore her any malice. Also that we had a high regard for Meng Lan, and were very glad that their marriage proved to turn out so well. Therefore . . ."

"Just to get the record straight," the judge interrupted, "I suppose that both of you can prove that you weren't in this vicinity last night?"

The pharmacist gave his friend an embarrassed look. Wen Shou-fang replied diffidently, "As a matter of fact, Your Honor, both of us took part in a banquet, held in the largest house in the Willow Quarter last night. Later we ah . . . retired upstairs with ah . . . company. We went home a few hours after midnight."

"I had a brief nap at home," Yuan Kai added, "then changed into hunting-dress and went to the tribunal to fetch Your Honor for our duck-hunt."

"I see," Judge Dee said. "I am glad you told me, it saves me unnecessary work."

"This lotus pond is really very attractive," Wen said, looking relieved. While they were conducting the judge to the gate, he added: "Unfortunately such ponds are usually infested with frogs."

"They make an infernal noise at times," Yuan Kai remarked as he opened the gate for Judge Dee.

The judge mounted his horse, and rode back to the tribunal.

The headman came to meet him in the courtyard and reported that in the side hall everything was ready for the autopsy. Judge Dee went first to his private office. While the clerk was pouring him a cup of hot tea the judge wrote a brief note to Ma Joong, instructing him to question the two courtesans Yuan Kai and Wen Shou-fang had slept with the night before. He thought a moment, then added: "Verify also whether the servant of the Mengs passed last night in his father's house." He sealed the note and ordered the clerk to have it delivered to Ma Joong immediately. Then Judge Dee quickly munched a few dry cakes, and went to the side hall where the coroner and his two assistants were waiting for him.

The autopsy brought to light nothing new: the poet had been in good health; death had been caused by a dagger thrust that had penetrated the heart. The judge ordered the headman to have the body placed in a temporary coffin, pending final instructions as to the time and place of burial. He returned to his private office and set to work on the official papers that had come in, assisted by the senior clerk of the tribunal.

It was nearly noon when Ma Joong came back. After the judge had sent the clerk away, Ma Joong seated himself opposite Judge Dee's desk, twirled his short mustache and began with a smug smile, "Peach Blossom was already up and about, sir! She was just making her toilet when I knocked. Last night had been her evening off, so she had gone to bed early. She was looking more charming than ever, I . . ."

"Yes, yes, come to your point!" the judge cut him short peevishly. Part of his stratagem had apparently miscarried. "She must have told you quite a lot," he continued, "since you were gone nearly all morning."

Ma Joong gave him a reproachful look. He said earnestly, "One has to handle those girls carefully, sir. We had breakfast together, and I gradually brought her round to the subject of Mrs. Meng. Her professional name was Agate, her real name Shih Mei-lan; she's a farmer's daughter from up north. Three years ago, when the big drought had caused famine and the people were dying like rats, her father sold her to a procurer, and he in turn sold her to the house where Peach Blossom is working. She was a pleasant, cheerful girl. The owner of the house confirmed that Yuan Kai had sought Agate's favors, and that she had refused. He thinks she did so only in order to raise her price, for she seemed rather sorry when the pharmacist didn't insist but found himself another playmate. With Wen Shou-fang it was a little different. Wen is a rather shy fellow; when Agate didn't respond to his first overtures, he didn't try again but confined himself to worshipping her from a distance. Then Meng Lan met her, and bought her then and there. But Peach Blossom thinks that Wen is still very fond of Agate; he often talks about her with the other girls and recently said again that Agate had deserved a better husband than that grumpy old poetaster. I also found out that Agate had a younger brother, called Shih Ming, and that he is a really bag egg. He is a drinker and gambler, who followed his sister out here and used to live off her earnings. He disappeared about a year ago, just before Meng Lan married her. But last week he suddenly turned up in the quarter and asked after his sister. When the owner told him that Meng Lan had bought and married her, Shih Ming went at once to their country house. Later Meng's servant told people that Shih Ming had quarreled with the poet; he hadn't understood what it was all about, but it had something to do with money. Mrs. Meng cried bitterly, and Shih Ming left in a rage. He hasn't been seen since."

Ma Joong paused, but Judge Dee made no comment. He slowly sipped his tea, his bushy eyebrows knitted in a deep frown. Suddenly he asked: "Did Meng's servant go out last night?"

"No, sir. I questioned his father, the old gardener and also their neighbors. The youngster came home directly after dinner, fell down on the bed he shares with two brothers, and lay snoring there till daybreak. And that reminds me of your second point, sir. I found that Yuan Kai stayed last night with Peony, a friend of Peach Blossom. They went up to her room at midnight, and Yuan left the house two hours later, on foot—in order to enjoy the moonlight, he said. Wen Shoufang stayed with a girl called Carnation, a comely wench, though she was in a bit of a sullen mood this morning. It seems that Wen had drunk too much during the banquet, and when he was up in Carnation's room he laid himself down on the bed and passed out. Carnation tried to rouse him in vain, went over to the girls in the next room for a card game and forgot all about him. He came to life three hours later, but to Carnation's disappointment he had such a hangover that he went straight home, also on foot. He preferred walking to sitting in a sedan chair, because he hoped the fresh air would clear his brain—so he said. That's all, sir. I think that Shih Ming is our man. By marrying his sister, Meng Lan took Shih Ming's rice-bowl away from him, so to speak. Shall I tell the headman to institute a search for Shih Ming? I have a good description of him."

"Do that," Judge Dee said. "You can go now and have your noon rice, I won't need you until tonight."

"Then I'll have a little nap," Ma Joong said with satisfaction. "I had quite a strenuous morning. What with the duck-hunt and everything."

"I don't doubt it!" the judge said dryly.

When Ma Joong had taken his leave Judge Dee went upstairs to the marble terrace that overlooked the lake. He sat down in a large armchair, and had his noon rice served there. He didn't feel like going to his private residence at the back of the tribunal; preoccupied as he was with the murder case, he wouldn't be pleasant company for his family. When he had finished his meal he pulled the armchair into a shadowy corner on the terrace. But just as he was preparing himself for a brief nap, a messenger came up and handed him a long report from Sergeant Hoong. The sergeant wrote that the investigation in the western part of the district revealed that the attack on the treasury messenger had been perpetrated by a band of six ruffians. After they had beaten the man unconscious and taken the package with the gold bars, they coolly proceeded to an inn near the district boundary, and there they had a good meal. Then a stranger arrived; he kept his neckcloth over his nose and mouth, and the people of the inn had never seen him before. The leader of the robbers handed him a package, and then they all left in the direction of the forests of the neighboring district. Later the body of the stranger had been found in a ditch, not far from the inn. He was recognized by his dress; his face had been beaten to pulp. The local coroner was an experienced man; he examined the contents of the dead man's stomach, and discovered traces of a strong drug. The package with the gold bars had, of course, disappeared. "Thus the attack on the treasury messenger was carefully planned," the sergeant wrote in conclusion, "and by someone who has remained behind the scenes. He had his accomplice hire the ruffians to do the rough work, then sent that same accomplice to the inn to collect the booty. He himself followed the accomplice, drugged him and beat him to death, either because he wanted to eliminate a possible witness against him, or because he didn't want to pay him his share. In order to trace the criminal behind this affair we'll have to ask for the co-operation of Your Honor's colleague in the neighboring district. I respectfully request Your Honor to proceed here so as to conduct the investigation personally.

Judge Dee slowly rolled up the report. The sergeant was right, he ought to go there at once. But the poet's murder needed his attention too. Both Yuan Kai and Wen Shou-fang had had the opportunity, but neither of them seemed to have a motive. Mrs. Meng's brother did indeed have a motive, but if he had done the deed he would doubtless have fled to some distant place by now. With a sigh he leaned back in his chair, pensively stroking his beard. Before he knew it he was sound asleep.

When he woke up he noticed to his annoyance that he had slept too long; dusk was already falling. Ma Joong and the headman were standing by the balustrade. The latter reported that the hue and cry was out for Shih Ming, but that as yet no trace of him had been found.

Judge Dee gave Ma Joong the sergeant's report, saying, "You'd better read this carefully. Then you can make the necessary preparations for traveling to the west boundary of our district, for we shall go there early tomorrow morning. Among the incoming mail was a letter from the Treasury in the capital, ordering me to report without delay on the robbery. A missing string of coppers causes them sleepless nights, let alone a dozen good gold bars!"

The judge went downstairs and drafted in his private office a preliminary report to the Treasury. Then he had his evening meal served on his desk. He hardly tasted what he ate, his thoughts were elsewhere. Laying down his chopsticks, he reflected with a sigh that it was most unfortunate that the two crimes should have occurred at approximately the same time. Suddenly he set down his tea cup. He got up and started to pace the floor. He thought he had found the explanation of the missing wine cup. He would have to verify this at once. He stepped up to the window and looked at the courtyard outside. When he saw that there was no one about, he quickly crossed over to the side gate and left the tribunal unnoticed.

In the street he pulled his neckcloth up over the lower half of his face, and on the corner rented a small sedan chair. He paid the bearers off in front of the largest house in the Willow Quarter. Confused sounds of singing and laughter came from the brilliantly lit windows; apparently a gay banquet was already in progress there. Judge Dee quickly walked on and started along the path leading to Meng Lan's country house.

When he was approaching the garden gate he noticed that it was very quiet here; the trees cut off the noise from the Willow Quarter. He softly pushed the gate open and studied the garden. The moonlight shone on the lotus pond, the house at the back of the garden was completely dark. Judge Dee walked around the pond, then stooped and picked up a stone. He threw it into the pond. Immediately the frogs started to croak in chorus. With a satisfied smile Judge Dee went on to the door, again pulling his neckcloth up over his mouth and nose. Standing in the shadow of the porch, he knocked.

A light appeared behind the window. Then the door opened and he heard Mrs. Meng's voice whispering, "Come inside, quick!"

She was standing in the doorway, her torso naked. She only wore a thin loin-cloth, and her hair was hanging loose. When the judge let the neckcloth drop from his face she uttered a smothered cry.

"I am not the one you were expecting," he said coldly, "but I'll come in anyway." He stepped inside, shut the door behind him and continued sternly to the cowering woman, "Who were you waiting for?"

Her lips moved but no sound came forth.

"Speak up!" Judge Dee barked.

Clutching the loin-cloth round her waist she stammered, "I wasn't waiting for anyone. I was awakened by the noise of the frogs, and feared there was an intruder. So I came to have a look and . . ."

"And asked the intruder to come inside quickly! If you must lie, you'd better be more clever about it! Show me your bedroom where you were waiting for your lover!"

Silently she took the candle from the table, and led the judge to a small side room. It only contained a narrow plank-bed, covered by a thin reed mat. The judge quickly stepped up to the bed and felt the mat. It was still warm from her body. Righting himself, he asked sharply: "Do you always sleep here?"

"No, Your Honor, this is the servant's room, the boy uses it for his afternoon nap. My bedroom is over on the other side of the hall we passed just now."

"Take me there!"

When she had crossed the hall and shown the judge into the large bedroom he took the candle from her and quickly looked the room over. There was a dressing-table with a bamboo chair, four clothes-boxes, and a large bedstead. Judge Dee pulled the bedcurtains aside. He saw that the thick bedmat of soft reed had been rolled up, and that the pillows had been stored away in the recess in the back wall. He turned round to her and said angrily, "I don't care where you were going to sleep with your lover, I only want to know his name. Speak up!"

She didn't answer, she only gave him a sidelong glance. Then her loin-cloth slipped down to the floor and she stood there stark naked. Covering herself with her hands, she looked coyly at him.

Judge Dee turned away. "Those silly tricks bore me," he said coldly. "Get dressed at once, you'll come with me to the tribunal and pass the night in jail. Tomorrow I shall interrogate you in court, if necessary under torture."

She silently opened a clothes-box and started to dress. The judge went to the hall and sat down there. He reflected that she was prepared to go a long way to shield her lover. Then he shrugged. Since she was a former courtesan, it wasn't really such a very long way. When she came in, fully dressed, he motioned her to follow him.

They met the night watch at the entrance of the Willow Quarter. The judge told their leader to take Mrs. Meng in a sedan chair to the tribunal, and hand her to the warden of the jail. He was also to send four of his men to the dead poet's house; they were to hide in the hall and arrest anyone who knocked. Then Judge Dee walked back at a leisurely pace, deep in thought.

Passing the gatehouse of the tribunal, he saw Ma Joong sitting in the guardroom talking with the soldiers. He took his lieutenant to his private office. When he had told him what had happened in the country house, Ma Joong shook his head sadly and said, "So she had a secret lover, and it was he who killed her husband. Well, that means that the case is practically solved. With some further persuasion, she'll come across with the fellow's name."

Judge Dee took a sip from his tea, then said slowly, "There are a few points that worry me, though. There's a definite connection between Meng's murder and the attack on the treasury messenger, but I haven't the faintest idea what it means. However, I want your opinion on two other points. First, how could Mrs. Meng conduct a secret love affair? She and her husband practically never went out, and the few guests they received came during the day. Second, I verified that she was sleeping tonight in the servant's room, on a narrow plank-bed. Why didn't she prepare to receive her lover in the bedroom, where there is a large and comfortable bedstead? Deference to her dead husband couldn't have prevented her from that, if she had been merrily deceiving him behind his back! I know, of course, that lovers don't care much about comfort, but even so, that hard, narrow plank-bed . . ."

"Well," Ma Joong said with a grin, "as regards the first point, if a woman is determined on having her little games, you can be dead sure that she'll somehow manage to find ways and means. Perhaps it was that servant of theirs she was playing around with, and then her private pleasures had nothing to do with the murder. As to the second point, I have often enough slept on a plank-bed, but I confess I never thought of sharing it. I'll gladly go to the Willow Quarter, though, and make inquiries about its special advantages if any." He looked hopefully at the judge.

Judge Dee was staring at him, but his thoughts seemed to be elsewhere. Slowly tugging at his mustache, he remained silent for some time. Suddenly the judge smiled. "Yes," he said, "we might try that." Ma Joong looked pleased. But his face fell as Judge Dee continued briskly, "Go at once to the Inn of the Red Carp, behind the fishmarket. Tell the head of the beggars there to get you half a dozen beggars who frequent the vicinity of the Willow Quarter, and bring those fellows here. Tell the head of the guild that I want to interrogate them about important new facts that have come to light regarding the murder of the poet Meng Lan. Make no secret of it. On the contrary, see to it that everybody knows I am summoning these beggars, and for what purpose. Get going!"

As Ma Joong remained sitting there, looking dumbfounded at the judge, he added, "If my scheme succeeds, I'll have solved both Meng's murder and the robbery of the gold bars. Do your best!"

Ma Joong got up and hurried outside.

When Ma Joong came back to Judge Dee's private office herding four ragged beggars he saw on the side table large platters with cakes and sweetmeats, and a few jugs of wine.

Judge Dee put the frightened men at their ease with some friendly words of greeting, then told them to taste the food and have a cup of wine. As the astonished beggars shuffled up to the table looking hungrily at the repast, Judge Dee took Ma Joong apart and said in a low voice:

"Go to the guardroom and select three good men from among the constables. You wait with them at the gate. In an hour or so I'll send the four beggars away. Each of them must be secretly followed. Arrest any person who accosts any one of them and bring him here, together with the beggar he addressed!"

Then he turned to the beggars and encouraged them to partake freely of the food and wine. The perplexed vagabonds hesitated long before they fell to, but then the platters and cups were empty in an amazingly brief time. Their leader, a one-eyed scoundrel, wiped his hands on his greasy beard, then muttered resignedly to his companions, "Now he'll have our heads chopped off. But I must say that it was a generous last meal."

To their amazement, however, Judge Dee made them sit down on tabourets in front of his desk. He questioned each of them about the place he came from, his age, his family and many other innocent details. When the beggars found that he didn't touch upon any awkward subjects, they began to talk more freely, and soon an hour had passed.

Judge Dee rose, thanked them for their co-operation and told them they could go. Then he began to pace the floor, his hands clasped behind his back.

Sooner than he had expected there was a knock. Ma Joong came in, dragging the one-eyed beggar along.

"He gave me the silver piece before I knew what was happening, Excellency!" the old man whined. "I swear I didn't pick his pocket!"

"I know you didn't," Judge Dee said. "Don't worry, you can keep that silver piece. Just tell me what he said to you."

"He comes up to me when I am rounding the street corner, Excellency, and presses that silver piece into my hand. He says: 'Come with me, you'll get another one if you tell me what that judge asked you and your friends.' I swear that's the truth, Excellency!"

"Good! You can go. Don't spend the money on wine and gambling!" As the beggar scurried away the judge said to Ma Joong: "Bring the prisoner!"

The pharmacist Yuan Kai started to protest loudly as soon as he was inside. "A prominent citizen arrested like a common criminal! I demand to know . . ."

"And I demand to know," Judge Dee interrupted him coldly, "why you were lying in wait for that beggar, and why you questioned him."

"Of course I am deeply interested in the progress of the investigation, Your Honor! I was eager to know whether . . ."

"Whether I had found a clue leading to you which you had overlooked," the judge completed the sentence for him. "Yuan Kai, you murdered the poet Meng Lan, and also Shih Ming, whom you used to contact the ruffians that robbed the treasury messenger. Confess your crimes!"

Yuan Kai's face had turned pale. But he had his voice well under control when he asked sharply: "I suppose Your Honor has good grounds for proffering such grave accusations?"

"I have. Mrs. Meng stated that they never received visitors at night. She also stated that the frogs in the lotus pond never croak during the day. Yet you remarked on the noise they make—sometimes. That suggested that you had been there at night. Further, Meng had been drinking wine with his murderer, who left his own cup on the table, but took away Meng's special cup. That, together with Meng's calm face, told me that he had been drugged before he was killed, and that the murderer had taken his victim's cup away with him because he feared that it would still smell after the drug, even if he washed it there in the pond. Now the accomplice of the criminal who organized the attack on the treasury messenger was also drugged before he was killed. This suggested that both crimes were committed by one and the same person. It made me suspect you, because as a pharmacist you know all about drugs, and because you had the opportunity to kill Meng Lan after you had left the Willow Quarter. I also remembered that we hadn't done too well on our duck-hunt this morning—we caught nothing. Although an expert hunter like you led our party. You were in bad form, because you had quite a strenuous night behind you. But by teaching me the method of duck-hunting with a decoy, you suggested to me a simple means for verifying my suspicions. Tonight I used the beggars as a decoy, and I caught you."

"And my motive?" Yuan Kai asked slowly.

"Some facts that are no concern of yours made me discover that Mrs. Meng had been expecting her brother Shih Ming to visit her secretly at night, and that proved that she knew that he had committed some crime. When Shih Ming visited his sister and his brother-in-law last week, and when they refused to give him money, he became angry and boasted that you had enlisted his help in an affair that would bring in a lot of money. Meng and his wife knew that Shih Ming was no good, so when they heard about the attack on the treasury messenger, and when Shih Ming didn't show up, they concluded it must be the affair Shih Ming had alluded to. Meng Lan was an honest man, and he taxed you with the robbery— there was your motive. Mrs. Meng wanted to shield her brother, but when presently she learns that it was you who murdered her husband, and also her brother, she'll speak, and her testimony will conclude the case against you, Yuan Kai."

The pharmacist looked down; he was breathing heavily. Judge Dee went on, "I shall apologize to Mrs. Meng. The unfortunate profession she exercised hasn't affected her staunch character. She was genuinely fond of her husband, and although she knew that her brother was a good-for-nothing, she was prepared to be flogged in the tribunal for contempt of court, rather than give him away. Well, she'll soon be a rich woman, for half of your property shall be assigned to her, as blood-money for her husband's murder. And doubtless Wen Shou-fang will in due time ask her to marry him, for he is still deeply in love with her. As to you, Yuan Kai, you are a foul murderer, and your head will fall on the execution ground."

Suddenly Yuan looked up. He said in a toneless voice, "It was that accursed frog that did for me! I killed the creature, and kicked it into the pond. That set the other frogs going." Then he added bitterly: "And, fool that I was, I said frogs can't talk!"

"They can," Judge Dee said soberly. "And they did."

William Faulkner

HAND UPON THE WATERS

Edmund Wilson's disdain for detective stories was made clear in his essay "Who Cares Who Killed Roger Ackroyd?" But when William Faulkner (1897–1962) published Knight's Gambit, *a collection of "six masterly whodunits" (that's how* The New York Times *described it) featuring the Yoknapatawpha County attorney Gavin Stevens, Wilson struck a surprisingly mellow attitude. Though the collection did not, he felt, show the genius of the author of such works as* The Sound and the Fury *and* Absalom, Absalom! *at its best, "none of these stories, however farfetched, fails to awaken that anxious suspense as to what is going to be revealed, to summon that troubled emotion in the presence of human anomaly, which make the strength of his finer fiction."*

Gavin Stevens, with his Phi Beta Kappa key from Harvard and his Ph.D. from Heidelberg, appears in more novels and short stories than any other character in Faulkner's vast dramatis personae (at least four novels and eight stories). He is a member of one of the county's oldest white families, and if he has a weakness for young girls, he is also one of Faulkner's most logical and rational creations. One scholar, however, warns: "Faulkner clearly admires him and is inclined to be perhaps too uncritical of him."

"Hand Upon the Waters," the third story in Knight's Gambit, *first appeared in* The Saturday Evening Post *(which paid the author $1,000 for it) and was included in* The Best Short Stories of 1940. *It is one of the rare detective stories to "cross over" into that annual compendium of orthodoxy. No doubt having been written by William Faulkner helped.*

Hand Upon the Waters

THE TWO MEN followed the path where it ran between the river and the dense wall of cypress and cane and gum and brier. One of them carried a gunny sack which had been washed and looked as if it had been ironed too. The other was a youth, less than twenty, by his face. The river was low, at mid-July level.

"He ought to been catching fish in this water," the youth said.

"If he happened to feel like fishing," the one with the sack said. "Him and Joe run that line when Lonnie feels like it, not when the fish are biting."

"They'll be on the line, anyway," the youth said. "I don't reckon Lonnie cares who takes them off for him."

Presently the ground rose to a cleared point almost like a headland. Upon it sat a conical hut with a pointed roof, built partly of mildewed canvas and odd-shaped boards and partly of oil tins hammered out flat. A rusted stove pipe projected crazily above it, there was a meager woodpile and an ax, and a bunch of cane poles leaned against it. Then they saw, on the earth before the open door, a dozen or so short lengths of cord just cut from a spool near by, and a rusted can half full of heavy fishhooks, some of which had already been bent onto the cords. But there was nobody there.

"The boat's gone," the man with the sack said. "So he ain't gone to the store." Then he discovered that the youth had gone on, and he drew in his breath and was just about to shout when suddenly a man rushed out of the undergrowth and stopped, facing him and making an urgent whimpering sound—a man not large, but with tremendous arms and shoulders; an adult, yet with something childlike about him, about the way he moved, barefoot, in battered overalls and with the urgent eyes of the deaf and dumb.

"Hi, Joe," the man with the sack said, raising his voice as people will with those who they know cannot understand them. "Where's Lonnie?" He held up the sack. "Got some fish?"

But the other only stared at him, making that rapid whimpering. Then he turned and scuttled on up the path where the youth had disappeared, who, at that moment, shouted: "Just look at this line!"

The older one followed. The youth was leaning eagerly out over the water beside a tree from which a light cotton rope slanted tautly downward into the water. The deaf-and-dumb man stood just behind him, still whimpering and lifting his feet rapidly in turn, though before the older man reached him he turned and scuttled back past him, toward the hut. At this stage of the river the line should have been clear of the water, stretching from bank to bank, between the two trees, with only the hooks on the dependent cords submerged. But now it slanted into the water from either end, with a heavy downstream sag, and even the older man could feel movement on it. "It's big as a man!" the youth cried.

"Yonder's his boat," the older man said. The youth saw it, too—across the stream and below them, floated into a willow clump inside a point. "Cross and get it, and we'll see how big this fish is."

The youth stepped out of his shoes and overalls and removed his shirt and waded out and began to swim, holding straight across to let the current carry him down to the skiff and got the skiff and paddled back, standing erect in it and staring eagerly upstream toward the heavy sag of the line, near the center of which the water, from time to time roiled heavily with submerged movement. He brought the skiff in below the older man, who, at that moment, discovered the deaf-and-dumb man just behind him again, still making the rapid and urgent sound and trying to enter the skiff.

"Get back!" the older man said, pushing the other back with his arm. "Get back, Joe!"

"Hurry up!" the youth said, staring eagerly toward the submerged line, where, as he watched, something rolled sluggishly to the surface, then sank again. There's something on there, or there ain't a hog in Georgia. It's big as a man too!"

The older one stepped into the skiff. He still held the rope, and he drew the skiff, hand over hand, along the line itself.

Suddenly, from the bank of the river behind them, the deaf-and-dumb man began to make an actual sound. It was quite loud.

2

"Inquest?" Stevens said.

"Lonnie Grinnup." The coroner was an old country doctor. "Two fellows found him drowned on his own trotline this morning."

"No!" Stevens said. "Poor damned feeb. I'll come out." As county attorney he had no business there, even if it had not been an accident. He knew it. He was going to look at the dead man's face for a sentimental reason. What was now Yoknapatawpha County had been founded not by one pioneer but by three simultaneous ones. They came together on horseback, through the Cumberland Gap from the Carolinas, when Jefferson was still a Chickasaw Agency post, and bought land in the Indian patent and established families and flourished and vanished, so that now, a hundred years afterward, there was in all the county they helped to found but one representative of the three names.

This was Stevens, because the last of the Holston family had died before the end of the last century, and the Louis Grenier, whose dead face Stevens was driving eight miles in the heat of a July afternoon to look at, had never even known he was

Louis Grenier. He could not even spell the Lonnie Grinnup he called himself—
an orphan, too, like Stevens, a man a little under the medium size and somewhere
in his middle thirties, whom the whole county knew—the face which was almost
delicate when you looked at it again, equable, constant, always cheerful, with an
invariable fuzz of soft golden beard which had never known a razor, and light-
colored peaceful eyes—"touched," they said, but whatever it was, had touched
him lightly, taking not very much away that need be missed—living, year in and
year out, in the hovel he had built himself of an old tent and a few mismatched
boards and flattened oil tins, with the deaf-and-dumb orphan he had taken into his
hut ten years ago and clothed and fed and raised, and who had not even grown
mentally as far as he himself had.

Actually his hut and trotline and fish trap were in almost the exact center
of the thousand and more acres his ancestors had once owned. But he never
knew it.

Stevens believed he would not have cared, would have declined to accept the
idea that any one man could or should own that much of the earth which belongs
to all, to every man for his use and pleasure—in his own case, that thirty or forty
square feet where his hut sat and the span of river across which his trotline stretched
where anyone was welcome at any time, whether he was there or not, to use his
gear and eat his food as long as there was food.

And at times he would wedge his door shut against prowling animals and with
his deaf-and-dumb companion he would appear without warning or invitation at
houses or cabins ten and fifteen miles away, where he would remain for weeks,
pleasant, equable, demanding nothing and without servility, sleeping wherever it
was convenient for his hosts to have him sleep—in the hay of lofts, or in beds in
family or company rooms, while the deaf-and-dumb youth lay on the porch or the
ground just outside, where he could hear him who was brother and father both,
breathing. It was his one sound out of all the voiceless earth. He was infallibly
aware of it.

It was early afternoon. The distances were blue with heat. Then, across the
long flat where the highway began to parallel the river bottom, Stevens saw
the store. By ordinary it would have been deserted, but now he could already
see clotted about it the topless and battered cars, the saddled horses and mules
and the wagons, the riders and drivers of which he knew by name. Better still,
they knew him, voting for him year after year and calling him by his given name
even though they did not quite understand him, just as they did not understand
the Harvard Phi Beta Kappa key on his watch chain. He drew in beside the
coroner's car.

Apparently it was not to be in the store, but in the grist mill beside it, before
the open door of which the clean Saturday overalls and shirts and the bared heads
and the sunburned necks striped with the white razor lines of Saturday neck shaves

were densest and quietest. They made way for him to enter. There was a table and three chairs where the coroner and two witnesses sat.

Stevens noticed a man of about forty holding a clean gunny sack, folded and refolded until it resembled a book, and a youth whose face wore an expression of weary yet indomitable amazement. The body lay under a quilt on the low platform to which the silent mill was bolted. He crossed to it and raised the corner of the quilt and looked at the face and lowered the quilt and turned, already on his way back to town, and then he did not go back to town. He moved over among the men who stood along the wall, their hats in their hands, and listened to the two witnesses—it was the youth telling it in his amazed, spent, incredulous voice—finish describing the finding of the body. He watched the coroner sign the certificate and return the pen to his pocket, and he knew he was not going back to town.

"I reckon that's all," the coroner said. He glanced toward the door. "All right, Ike," he said. "You can take him now."

Stevens moved aside with the others and watched the four men cross toward the quilt. "You going to take him, Ike?" he said.

The eldest of the four glanced back at him for a moment. "Yes. He had his burying money with Mitchell at the store."

"You, and Pose, and Matthew, and Jim Blake," Stevens said.

This time the other glanced back at him almost with surprise, almost impatiently.

"We can make up the difference," he said.

"I'll help," Stevens said.

"I thank you," the other said. "We got enough."

Then the coroner was among them, speaking testily: "All right, boys. Give them room."

With the others, Stevens moved out into the air, the afternoon again. There was a wagon backed up to the door now which had not been there before. Its tail gate was open, the bed was filled with straw, and with the others Stevens stood bareheaded and watched the four men emerge from the shed, carrying the quilt-wrapped bundle, and approach the wagon. Three or four others moved forward to help, and Stevens moved, too, and touched the youth's shoulder, seeing again that expression of spent and incredulous wild amazement.

"You went and got the boat before you knew anything was wrong," he said.

"That's right," the youth said. He spoke quietly enough at first. "I swum over and got the boat and rowed back. I knowed something was on the line. I could see it swagged—

"You mean you swam the boat back," Stevens said.

"—down into the—Sir?"

"You swam the boat back. You swam over and got it and swam it back."

"No, sir! I rowed the boat back. I rowed it straight back across! I never suspected nothing! I could see them fish—"

"What with?" Stevens said. The youth glared at him. "What did you row it back with?"

"With the oar! I picked up the oar and rowed it right back, and all the time I could see them flopping around in the water. They didn't want to let go! They held on to him even after we hauled him up, still eating him! Fish were! I knowed turtles would, but these were fish! Eating him! Of course it was fish we thought was there! It was! I won't never eat another one! Never!"

It had not seemed long, yet the afternoon had gone somewhere, taking some of the heat with it. Again in his car, his hand on the switch, Stevens sat looking at the wagon, now about to depart. *And it's not right,* he thought. *It don't add. Something more that I missed, didn't see. Or something that hasn't happened yet.*

The wagon was now moving, crossing the dusty banquette toward the highroad, with two men on the seat and the other two on saddled mules beside it. Stevens' hand turned the switch; the car was already in gear. It passed the wagon, already going fast.

A mile down the road he turned into a dirt lane, back toward the hills. It began to rise, the sun intermittent now, for in places among the ridges sunset had already come. Presently the road forked. In the V of the fork stood a church, white-painted and steepleless, beside an unfenced straggle of cheap marble headstones and other graves outlined only by rows of inverted glass jars and crockery and broken brick.

He did not hesitate. He drove up beside the church and turned and stopped the car facing the fork and the road over which he had just come where it curved away and vanished. Because of the curve, he could hear the wagon for some time before he saw it, then he heard the truck. It was coming down out of the hills behind him, fast, sweeping into sight, already slowing—a cab, a shallow bed with a tarpaulin spread over it.

It drew out of the road at the fork and stopped; then he could hear the wagon again, and then he saw it and the two riders come around the curve in the dusk, and there was a man standing in the road beside the truck now, and Stevens recognized him: Tyler Ballenbaugh—a farmer, married and with a family and a reputation for self-sufficiency and violence, who had been born in the county and went out West and returned, bringing with him, like an effluvium, rumors of sums he had won gambling, who had married and bought land and no longer gambled at cards, but on certain years would mortgage his own crop and buy or sell cotton futures with the money—standing in the road beside the wagon, tall in the dusk, talking to the men in the wagon without raising his voice or making any gesture. Then there was another man beside him, in a white shirt, whom Stevens did not recognize or look at again.

His hand dropped to the switch; again the car was in motion with the sound of the engine. He turned the headlights on and dropped rapidly down out of the churchyard and into the road and up behind the wagon as the man in the white shirt leaped onto the running board, shouting at him, and Stevens recognized him too: A younger brother of Ballenbaugh's, who had gone to Memphis years ago, where it was understood he had been a hired armed guard during a textile strike, but who, for the last two or three years, had been at his brother's, hiding, it was said, not from the police but from some of his Memphis friends or later business associates. From time to time his name made one in reported brawls and fights at country dances and picnics. He was subdued and thrown into jail once by two officers in Jefferson, where, on Saturdays, drunk, he would brag about his past exploits or curse his present luck and the older brother who made him work about the farm.

"Who in hell you spying on?" he shouted.

"Boyd," the other Ballenbaugh said. He did not even raise his voice. "Get back in the truck." He had not moved—a big somber-faced man who stared at Stevens out of pale, cold, absolutely expressionless eyes. "Howdy, Gavin," he said.

"Howdy, Tyler," Stevens said. "You going to take Lonnie?"

"Does anybody here object?"

"I don't," Stevens said, getting out of the car. "I'll help you swamp him."

Then he got back into the car. The wagon moved on. The truck backed and turned, already gaining speed; the two faces fled past—the one which Stevens saw now was not truculent, but frightened; the other, in which there was nothing at all save the still, cold, pale eyes. The cracked tail lamp vanished over the hill. *That was an Okatoba County license number*, he thought.

Lonnie Grinnup was buried the next afternoon, from Tyler Ballenbaugh's house.

Stevens was not there. "Joe wasn't there, either, I suppose," he said. "Lonnie's dummy."

"No. He wasn't there, either. The folks that went in to Lonnie's camp on Sunday morning to look at that trotline said that he was still there, hunting for Lonnie. But he wasn't at the burying. When he finds Lonnie this time, he can lie down by him, but he won't hear him breathing."

3

"No," Stevens said.

He was in Mottstown, the seat of Okatoba County, on that afternoon. And although it was Sunday, and although he would not know until he found it just what he was looking for, he found it before dark—the agent for the company which, eleven years ago, had issued to Lonnie Grinnup a five-thousand-dollar policy, with double indemnity for accidental death, on his life, with Tyler Ballenbaugh as beneficiary.

It was quite correct. The examining doctor had never seen Lonnie Grinnup before, but he had known Tyler Ballenbaugh for years, and Lonnie had made his mark on the application and Ballenbaugh had paid the first premium and kept them up ever since.

There had been no particular secrecy about it other than transacting the business in another town, and Stevens realized that even that was not unduly strange.

Okatoba County was just across the river, three miles from where Ballenbaugh lived, and Stevens knew of more men than Ballenbaugh who owned land in one county and bought their cars and trucks and banked their money in another, obeying the country-bred man's inherent, possibly atavistic, faint distrust, perhaps, not of men in white collars but of paving and electricity.

"Then I'm not to notify the company yet?" the agent asked.

"No. I want you to accept the claim when he comes in to file it, explain to him it will take a week or so to settle it, wait three days and send him word to come in to your office to see you at nine o'clock or ten o'clock the next morning; don't tell him why, what for. Then telephone me at Jefferson when you know he has got the message."

Early the next morning, about daybreak, the heat wave broke. He lay in bed watching and listening to the crash and glare of lightning and the rain's loud fury, thinking of the drumming of it and the fierce channeling of clay-colored water across Lonnie Grinnup's raw and kinless grave in the barren hill beside the steepleless church, and of the sound it would make, above the turmoil of the rising river, on the tin-and-canvas hut where the deaf-and-dumb youth probably still waited for him to come home, knowing that something had happened, but not how, not why. *Not how*, Stevens thought. *They fooled him someway. They didn't even bother to tie him up. They just fooled him.*

On Wednesday night he received a telephone message from the Mottstown agent that Tyler Ballenbaugh had filed his claim.

"All right," Stevens said. "Send him the message Monday, to come in Tuesday. And let me know when you know he has gotten it." He put the phone down. *I am playing stud poker with a man who has proved himself a gambler, which I have not*, he thought. *But at least I have forced him to draw a card. And he knows who is in the pot with him.*

So when the second message came, on the following Monday afternoon, he knew only what he himself was going to do. He had thought once of asking the sheriff for a deputy, or of taking some friend with him. *But even a friend would not believe that what I have is a hold card*, he told himself, *even though I do: That one man, even an amateur at murder, might be satisfied that he had cleaned up after*

*himself. But when there are two of them, neither one is going to be satisfied that the
other has left no ravelings.*

So he went alone. He owned a pistol. He looked at it and put it back into its
drawer. *At least nobody is going to shoot me with that,* he told himself. He left
town just after dusk.

This time he passed the store, dark at the roadside. When he reached the lane
into which he had turned nine days ago, this time he turned to the right and drove
on for a quarter of a mile and turned into a littered yard, his headlights full upon
a dark cabin. He did not turn them off. He walked full in the yellow beam, toward
the cabin, shouting: "Nate! Nate!"

After a moment a Negro voice answered, though no light showed.

"I'm going in to Mr. Lonnie Grinnup's camp. If I'm not back by daylight, you
better go up to the store and tell them."

There was no answer. Then a woman's voice said: "You come on away from
that door!" The man's voice murmured something.

"I can't help it!" the woman cried. "You come away and let them white folks
alone!"

So there are others besides me, Stevens thought, thinking how quite often,
almost always, there is in Negroes an instinct not for evil but to recognize evil at
once when it exists. He went back to the car and snapped off the lights and took
his flashlight from the seat.

He found the truck. In the close-held beam of the light he read again the
license number which he had watched nine days ago flee over the hill. He snapped
off the light and put it into his pocket.

Twenty minutes later he realized he need not have worried about the light. He
was in the path, between the black wall of jungle and the river, he saw the faint
glow inside the canvas wall of the hut and he could already hear the two voices—
the one cold, level and steady, the other harsh and high. He stumbled over the
woodpile and then over something else and found the door and flung it back and
entered the devastation of the dead man's house—the shuck mattresses dragged out
of the wooden bunks, the overturned stove and scattered cooking vessels—where
Tyler Ballenbaugh stood facing him with a pistol and the younger one stood half-
crouched above an overturned box.

"Stand back, Gavin," Ballenbaugh said.

"Stand back yourself, Tyler," Stevens said. "You're too late."

The younger one stood up. Stevens saw recognition come into his face. "Well,
by—" he said.

"Is it all up, Gavin?" Ballenbaugh said. "Don't lie to me."

"I reckon it is," Stevens said. "Put your pistol down."

"Who else is with you?"

"Enough," Stevens said. "Put your pistol down, Tyler."

"Hell," the younger one said. He began to move; Stevens saw his eyes go swiftly from him to the door behind him. "He's lying. There ain't anybody with him. He's just spying around like he was the other day, putting his nose into business he's going to wish he had kept it out of. Because this time it's going to get bit off."

He was moving towards Stevens, stooping a little, his arms held slightly away from his sides.

"Boyd!" Tyler said. The other continued to approach Stevens, not smiling, but with a queer light, a glitter, in his face. "Boyd!" Tyler said. Then he moved, too, with astonishing speed, and overtook the younger and with one sweep of his arm hurled him back into the bunk. They faced each other—the one cold, still, expressionless, the pistol held before him aimed at nothing, the other half-crouched, snarling.

"What the hell you going to do? Let him take us back to town like two damn sheep?"

"That's for me to decide," Tyler said. He looked at Stevens. "I never intended this, Gavin. I insured his life, kept the premiums paid—yes. But it was good business: If he had outlived me, I wouldn't have had any use for the money, and if I had outlived him, I would have collected on my judgment. There was no secret about it. It was done in open daylight. Anybody could have found out about it. Maybe he told about it. I never told him not to. And who's to say against it anyway? I always fed him when he came to my house, he always stayed as long as he wanted to, come when he wanted to. But I never intended this."

Suddenly the younger one began to laugh, half-crouched against the bunk where the other had flung him. "So that's the tune," he said. "That's the way it's going." Then it was not laughter any more, though the transition was so slight or perhaps so swift as to be imperceptible. He was standing now, leaning forward a little, facing his brother. "I never insured him for five thousand dollars! I wasn't going to get—"

"Hush," Tyler said.

"—five thousand dollars when they found him dead on that—"

Tyler walked steadily to the other and slapped him in two motions, palm and back, of the same hand, the pistol still held before him in the other.

"I said, hush, Boyd," he said. He looked at Stevens again. "I never intended this. I don't want that money now, even if they were going to pay it, because this is not the way I aimed for it to be. Not the way I bet. What are you going to do?"

"Do you need to ask that? I want an indictment for murder."

"And then prove it!" the younger one snarled. "Try and prove it! I never insured his life for—"

"Hush," Tyler said. He spoke almost gently, looking at Stevens with the pale eyes in which there was absolutely nothing. "You can't do that. It's a good name.

Has been. Maybe nobody's done much for it yet, but nobody's hurt it bad yet, up to now. I have owed no man, I have taken nothing that was not mine. You musn't do that, Gavin."

"I mustn't do anything else, Tyler."

The other looked at him. Stevens heard him draw a long breath and expel it. But his face did not change at all. "You want your eye for an eye and tooth for a tooth."

"Justice wants it. Maybe Lonnie Grinnup wants it. Wouldn't you?"

For a moment longer the other looked at him. Then Ballenbaugh turned and made a quiet gesture at his brother and another toward Stevens, quiet and peremptory.

Then they were out of the hut, standing in the light from the door; a breeze came up from somewhere and rustled in the leaves overhead and died away, ceased.

At first Stevens did not know what Ballenbaugh was about. He watched in mounting surprise as Ballenbaugh turned to face his brother, his hand extended, speaking in a voice which was actually harsh now: "This is the end of the row. I was afraid from that night when you came home and told me. I should have raised you better, but I didn't. Here. Stand up and finish it."

"Look out, Tyler!" Stevens said. "Don't do that!"

"Keep out of this, Gavin. If it's meat for meat you want, you will get it." He still faced his brother, he did not even glance at Stevens. "Here," he said. "Take it and stand up."

Then it was too late. Stevens saw the younger one spring back. He saw Tyler take a step forward and he seemed to hear in the other's voice the surprise, the disbelief, then the realization of the mistake. "Drop the pistol, Boyd," he said. "Drop it."

"So you want it back, do you?" the younger said. "I come to you that night and told you you were worth five thousand dollars as soon as somebody happened to look on that trotline, and asked you to give me ten dollars, and you turned me down. Ten dollars, and you wouldn't. Sure you can have it. Take it." It flashed, low against his side; the orange fire lanced downward again as the other fell.

Now it's my turn, Stevens thought. They faced each other; he heard again that brief wind come from somewhere and shake the leaves overhead and fall still.

"Run while you can, Boyd," he said. "You've done enough. Run, now."

"Sure I'll run. You do all your worrying about me now, because in a minute you won't have any worries. I'll run all right, after I've said a word to smart guys that come sticking their noses where they'll wish to hell they hadn't—"

Now he's going to shoot, Stevens thought, and he sprang. For an instant he had the illusion of watching himself springing, reflected somehow by the faint light from the river, that luminousness which water gives back to the dark, in the air above Boyd Ballenbaugh's head. Then he knew it was not himself he saw, it had not been wind he heard, as the creature, the shape which had no tongue and needed none, which had been waiting nine days now for Lonnie Grinnup to come home, dropped toward the murderer's back with its hands already extended and its body curved and rigid with silent and deadly purpose.

He was in the tree, Stevens thought. The pistol glared. He saw the flash, but he heard no sound.

4

He was sitting on the veranda with his neat surgeon's bandage after supper when the sheriff of the county came up the walk—a big man, too, pleasant, affable, with eyes even paler and colder and more expressionless than Tyler Ballenbaugh's. "It won't take but a minute," he said, "or I wouldn't have bothered you."

"How bothered me?" Stevens said.

The sheriff lowered one thigh to the veranda rail. "Head feel all right?"

"Feels all right," Stevens said.

"That's good, I reckon you heard where we found Boyd."

Stevens looked back at him just as blankly. "I may have," he said pleasantly. "Haven't remembered much today but a headache."

"You told us where to look. You were conscious when I got there. You were trying to give Tyler water. You told us to look on that trotline."

"Did I? Well, well, what won't a man say, drunk or out of his head? Sometimes he's right too."

"You were. We looked on the line, and there was Boyd hung on one of the hooks, dead, just like Lonnie Grinnup was. And Tyler Ballenbaugh with a broken leg and another bullet in his shoulder, and you with a crease in your skull you could hide a cigar in. How did he get on that trotline, Gavin?"

"I don't know," Stevens said.

"All right. I'm not sheriff now. How did Boyd get on that trotline?"

"I don't know."

The sheriff looked at him; they looked at each other. "Is that what you answer any friend that asks?"

"Yes. Because I was shot, you see. I don't know."

The sheriff took a cigar from his pocket and looked at it for a time. "Joe—that deaf-and-dumb boy Lonnie raised—seems to have gone away at last. He was still around there last Sunday, but nobody has seen him since. He could have stayed. Nobody would have bothered him."

"Maybe he missed Lonnie too much to stay," Stevens said.

"Maybe he missed Lonnie." The sheriff rose. He bit the end from the cigar and lit it. "Did that bullet cause you to forget this too? Just what made you suspect something was wrong? What was it the rest of us seem to have missed?"

"It was that paddle," Stevens said.

"Paddle?"

"Didn't you ever run a trotline, a trotline right at your camp? You don't paddle, you pull the boat hand over hand along the line itself from one hook to the next. Lonnie never did use his paddle; he even kept the skiff tied to the same tree his trotline was fastened to, and the paddle stayed in his house. If you had ever been there, you would have seen it. But the paddle was in the skiff when that boy found it."

Dashiell Hammett

THE *SAM SPADE* STORIES

Dashiell Hammett (1894–1961) wrote only four adventures of Sam Spade—The Maltese Falcon *and three short stories, "A Man Called Spade," "They Can Only Hang You Once," and "Too Many Have Lived." When the stories were collected for the first—and until now only—time in a 1944 paperback,* A Man Called Spade, *Ellery Queen wrote an introduction full of wartime, All-American fervor.*

"That we owe a great debt to Hammett no honest writer, reader or reviewer of detective fiction can deny," Queen wrote. "He broke away—violently—from the overpowering influence of the polished English writers; he divorced us from effete, nambypamby classicism; he gave us the first 100 percent American, the first truly native, detective story. He is our most important originator. He didn't invent a new kind of detective story—he invented a new way of telling it."

Hammett, a former Pinkerton detective and San Francisco advertising writer, first made himself known to readers of a hardhitting pulp magazine called Black Mask *with a nameless private detective—or operative—known as the Continental Op. The Op appeared in two novels,* Red Harvest *and* The Dain Curse; *later came Sam Spade,* The Glass Key, *and* The Thin Man, *which introduced Nick and Nora Charles.*

Proud of having been a real private eye in a world of competitors who had no authentic experience to fall back on, Hammett once published a list of twenty-eight numbered items called "From the Memoirs of a Private Detective" in Smart Set *magazine. They included such observations as "House burglary is probably the poorest paid trade in the world; I have never known anyone to make a living at it" and "Pocket-picking is the easiest to master of all the criminal trades. Anyone who is not crippled can become adept in a day." But item number twenty-seven bears special attention before beginning the adventures of Sam Spade: "The chief difference between the exceptionally knotty problem confronting the detective in fiction and that facing the real detective is that in the former there is usually a paucity of clues, and in the latter altogether too many."*

A Man Called Spade

S AMUEL SPADE PUT his telephone aside and looked at his watch. It was not quite four o'clock. He called, "Yoo-hoo!"

Effie Perine came in from the outer office. She was eating a piece of chocolate cake.

"Tell Sid Wise I won't be able to keep that date this afternoon," he said.

She put the last of the cake into her mouth and licked the tips of forefinger and thumb.

"That's the third time this week."

When he smiled, the v's of his chin, mouth, and brows grew longer.

"I know, but I've got to go out and save a life." He nodded at the telephone. "Somebody's scaring Max Bliss."

She laughed. "Probably somebody named John D. Conscience."

He looked up at her from the cigarette he had begun to make. "Know anything I ought to know about him?"

"Nothing you don't know. I was just thinking about the time he let his brother go to San Quentin."

Spade shrugged. "That's not the worst thing he's done." He lit his cigarette, stood up, and reached for his hat. "But he's all right now. All Samuel Spade clients are honest, God-fearing folk. If I'm not back at closing time just run along."

He went to a tall apartment building on Nob Hill, pressed a button set in the frame of a door marked 10K. The door was opened immediately by a burly dark man in wrinkled dark clothes. He was nearly bald and carried a gray hat in one hand.

The burly man said, "Hello, Sam." He smiled, but his small eyes lost none of their shrewdness. "What are you doing here?"

Spade said, "Hello, Tom." His face was wooden, his voice expressionless. "Bliss in?"

"Is he!" Tom pulled down the corners of his thick-lipped mouth. "You don't have to worry about that."

Spade's brows came together. "Well?"

A man appeared in the vestibule behind Tom. He was smaller than either Spade or Tom, but compactly built. He had a ruddy, square face and a close-trimmed, grizzled mustache. His clothes were neat. He wore a black bowler perched on the back of his head.

Spade addressed this man over Tom's shoulder:

"Hello, Dundy."

Dundy nodded briefly and came to the door. His blue eyes were hard and prying.

"What is it?" he asked Tom.

"B-l-i-s-s, M-a-x," Spade spelled patiently. "I want to see him. He wants to see me. Catch on?"

Tom laughed. Dundy did not.

Tom said, "Only one of you gets your wish." Then he glanced sidewise at Dundy and abruptly stopped laughing. He seemed uncomfortable.

Spade scowled. "All right," he demanded irritably; "is he dead or has he killed somebody?"

Dundy thrust his square face up at Spade and seemed to push his words out with his lower lip:

"What makes you think either?"

Spade said, "Oh, sure! I come calling on Mr. Bliss and I'm stopped at the door by a couple of men from the police Homicide Detail, and I'm supposed to think I'm just interrupting a game of rummy."

"Aw, stop it, Sam," Tom grumbled, looking at neither Spade nor Dundy. "He's dead."

"Killed?"

Tom wagged his head slowly up and down. He looked at Spade now. "What've you got on it?"

Spade replied in a deliberate monotone, "He called me up this afternoon—say at five minutes to four—I looked at my watch after he hung up and there was still a minute or so to go—and said somebody was after his scalp. He wanted me to come over. It seemed real enough to him—it was up in his neck all right." He made a small gesture with one hand. "Well, here I am."

"Didn't say who or how?" Dundy asked.

Spade shook his head. "No. Just somebody had offered to kill him and he believed them, and would I come over right away."

"Didn't he?" Dundy began quickly.

"He didn't say anything else," Spade said. "Don't you people tell me any-thing?"

Dundy said curtly, "Come in and take a look at him."

Tom said, "It's a sight."

They went across the vestibule and through a door into a green and rose living-room.

A man near the door stopped sprinkling white powder on the end of a glass-covered small table to say, "Hello, Sam."

Spade nodded, said, "How are you, Phels?" and then nodded at the two men who stood talking by a window.

The dead man lay with his mouth open. Some of his clothes had been taken off. His throat was puffy and dark. The end of his tongue showing in a corner of his mouth was bluish, swollen. On his bare chest, over the heart, a five-pointed star had been outlined in black ink and in the center of it a T.

Spade looked down at the dead man and stood for a moment silently studying him.

Then he asked, "He was found like that?"

"About," Tom said. "We moved him around a little." He jerked a thumb at the shirt, undershirt, vest, and coat lying on a table. "They were spread over the floor."

Spade rubbed his chin. His yellow-gray eyes were dreamy.

"When?"

Tom said, "We got it at four-twenty. His daughter gave it to us." He moved his head to indicate a closed door. "You'll see her."

"Know anything?"

"Heaven knows," Tom said wearily. "She's been kind of hard to get along with so far." He turned to Dundy. "Want to try her again now?"

Dundy nodded, then spoke to one of the men at the window. "Start sifting his papers, Mack. He's supposed to've been threatened."

Mack said, "Right." He pulled his hat down over his eyes and walked toward a green secrétaire in the far end of the room.

A man came in from the corridor, a heavy man of fifty with a deeply lined, grayish face under a broad-brimmed black hat.

He said, "Hello, Sam," and then told Dundy, "He had company around half past two, stayed just about an hour. A big blond man in brown, maybe forty or forty-five. Didn't send his name up. I got it from the Filipino in the elevator that rode him both ways."

"Sure it was only an hour?" Dundy asked.

The gray-faced man shook his head. "But he's sure it wasn't more than half past three when he left. He says the afternoon papers came in then, and this man had ridden down with him before they came."

He pushed his hat back to scratch his head, then pointed a thick finger at the design inked on the dead man's breast and asked somewhat plaintively, "What the deuce do you suppose that thing is?"

Nobody replied.

Dundy asked, "Can the elevator boy identify him?"

"He says he could, but that ain't always the same thing. Says he never saw him before." He stopped looking at the dead man. "The girl's getting me a list of his phone calls. How you been, Sam?"

Spade said he had been all right. Then he said slowly, "His brother's big and blond and maybe forty or forty-five."

Dundy's blue eyes were hard and bright.

"So what?" he asked.

"You remember the Graystone Loan swindle. They were both in it, but Max eased the load over on Theodore and it turned out to be one to fourteen years in San Quentin."

Dundy was slowly wagging his head up and down. "I remember now. Where is he?"

Spade shrugged and began to make a cigarette.

Dundy nudged Tom with an elbow. "Find out."

Tom said, "Sure, but if he was out of here at half past three and this fellow was still alive at five to four—"

"And he broke his leg so he couldn't duck back in," the gray-faced man said jovially.

"Find out," Dundy repeated.

Tom said, "Sure, sure," and went to the telephone.

Dundy addressed the gray-faced man:

"Check up on the newspapers; see what time they were actually delivered this afternoon."

The gray-faced man nodded and left the room.

The man who had been searching the secrétaire said, "Uh-huh," and turned around holding an envelope in one hand, a sheet of paper in the other.

Dundy held out his hand. "Something?"

The man said, "Uh-huh," again and gave Dundy the sheet of paper.

Spade was looking over Dundy's shoulder.

It was a small sheet of common white paper bearing a penciled message in neat, undistinguished handwriting:

When this reaches you I will be too close for you to escape—this time.
We will balance our accounts—for good.

The signature was a five-pointed star enclosing a T, the design on the dead man's left breast.

Dundy held out his hand again and was given the envelope. Its stamp was French. The address was typewritten:

Max Bliss, Esq.
Amsterdam Apartments
San Francisco, Calif., U.S.A.

"Postmarked Paris," he said, "the second of the month." He counted swiftly on his fingers. "That would get it here today, all right."

He folded the message slowly, put it in the envelope, put the envelope in his coat pocket.

"Keep digging," he told the man who had found the message.

The man nodded and returned to the secrétaire.

Dundy looked at Spade. "What do you think of it?"

Spade's brown cigarette wagged up and down with his words: "I don't like it. I don't like any of it."

Tom put down the telephone.

"He got out the fifteenth of last month," he said. "I got them trying to locate him."

Spade went to the telephone, called a number, and asked for Mr. Darrell. Then:

"Hello, Harry, this is Sam Spade . . . Fine. How's Lil? . . . Yes . . . Listen, Harry, what does a five-pointed star with a capital T in the middle mean? . . . What? How do you spell it? . . . Yes, I see . . . And if you found it on a body? . . . Neither do I . . . Yes, and thanks. I'll tell you about it when I see you . . . Yes, give me a ring . . . Thanks . . . 'Bye."

Dundy and Tom were watching him closely when he turned from the telephone.

He said, "That's a fellow who knows things sometimes. He says it's a pentagram with a Greek tau—t-a-u—in the middle; a sign magicians used to use. Maybe Rosicrucians still do."

"What's a Rosicrucian?" Tom asked.

"It could be Theodore's first initial, too," Dundy said.

Spade moved his shoulders, said carelessly, "Yes, but if he wanted to autograph the job it'd been just as easy for him to sign his name."

He then went on more thoughtfully, "There are Rosicrucians at both San Jose and Point Loma. I don't go much for this, but maybe we ought to look them up."

Dundy nodded.

Spade looked at the dead man's clothes on the table. "Anything in his pockets?"

"Only what you'd expect to find," Dundy replied. "It's on the table there."

Spade went to the table and looked down at the little pile of watch and chain, keys, wallet, address book, money, gold pencil, handkerchief, and spectacle case beside the clothing. He did not touch them, but slowly picked up, one at a time, the dead man's shirt, undershirt, vest, and coat. A blue necktie lay on the table beneath them. He scowled irritably at it.

"It hasn't been worn," he complained.

Dundy, Tom, and the coroner's deputy, who had stood silent all this while by the window—he was a small man with a slim, dark, intelligent face—came together to stare down at the unwrinkled blue silk.

Tom groaned miserably.

Dundy cursed under his breath.

Spade lifted the necktie to look at its back. The label was a London haberdasher's.

Spade said cheerfully, "Swell. San Francisco, Point Loma, San Jose, Paris, London."

Dundy glowered at him.

The gray-faced man came in.

"The papers got here at three-thirty, all right," he said. His eyes widened a little. "What's up?" As he crossed the room toward them he said, "I can't find anybody that saw Blondy sneak back in here again."

He looked uncomprehendingly at the necktie until Tom growled, "It's brand-new"; then he whistled softly.

Dundy turned to Spade.

"The deuce with all this," he said bitterly. "He's got a brother with reasons for not liking him. The brother just got out of stir. Somebody who looks like his brother left here at half past three. Twenty-five minutes later he phoned you he'd been threatened. Less than half an hour after that his daughter came in and found him dead—strangled." He poked a finger at the small, dark-faced man's chest. "Right?"

"Strangled," the dark-faced man said precisely, "by a man. The hands were large."

"O.K." Dundy turned to Spade again. "We find a threatening letter. Maybe that's what he was telling you about, maybe it was something his brother said to him. Don't let's guess. Let's stick to what we know. We know he—"

The man at the secrétaire turned around and said, "Got another one." His mien was somewhat smug.

The eyes with which the five men at the table looked at him were identically cold, unsympathetic.

He, nowise disturbed by their hostility, read aloud:

"Dear Bliss: I am writing this to tell you for the last time that I want my money back, and I want it back by the first of the month, all of it. If I don't get it I am going to do something about it, and you ought to be able to guess what I mean. And don't think I am kidding. Yours truly, Daniel Talbot."

He grinned. "That's another T for you." He picked up an envelope. "Post-marked San Diego, the twenty-fifth of last month." He grinned again. "And that's another city for you."

Spade shook his head. "Point Loma's down that way," he said.

He went over with Dundy to look at the letter. It was written in blue ink on white stationery of good quality, as was the address on the envelope, in a cramped, angular handwriting that seemed to have nothing in common with that of the penciled letter.

Spade said ironically, "Now we're getting somewhere."

Dundy made an impatient gesture. "Let's stick to what we know," he growled.

"Sure," Spade agreed. "What is it?"

There was no reply.

Spade took tobacco and cigarette papers from his pocket.

"Didn't somebody say something about talking to a daughter?" he asked.

"We'll talk to her." Dundy turned on his heel, then suddenly frowned at the dead man on the floor. He jerked a thumb at the small, dark-faced man. "Through with it?"

"I'm through."

Dundy addressed Tom curtly: "Get rid of it." He addressed the gray-faced man: "I want to see both elevator boys when I'm finished with the girl."

He went to the closed door Tom had pointed out to Spade and knocked on it.

A slightly harsh female voice within asked, "What is it?"

"Lieutenant Dundy. I want to talk to Miss Bliss."

There was a pause; then the voice said, "Come in."

Dundy opened the door and Spade followed him into a black, gray, and silver room, where a big-boned and ugly middle-aged woman in black dress and white apron sat beside a bed on which a girl lay.

The girl lay, elbow on pillow, cheek on hand, facing the big-boned, ugly woman. She was apparently about eighteen years old. She wore a gray suit. Her hair was blond and short, her face firm-featured and remarkably symmetrical. She did not look at the two men coming into the room.

Dundy spoke to the big-boned woman, while Spade was lighting his cigarette:

"We want to ask you a couple of questions, too, Mrs. Hooper. You're Bliss's housekeeper, aren't you?"

The woman said, "I am."

Her slightly harsh voice, the level gaze of her deep-set gray eyes, the stillness and size of her hands lying in her lap, all contributed to the impression she gave of resting strength.

"What do you know about this?"

"I don't know anything about it. I was let off this morning to go over to Oakland to my nephew's funeral, and when I got back you and the other gentlemen were here and—and this had happened."

Dundy nodded, asked, "What do you think about it?"

"I don't know what to think," she replied simply.

"Didn't you know he expected it to happen?"

Now the girl suddenly stopped watching Mrs. Hooper. She sat up in bed, turning wide, excited eyes on Dundy, and asked, "What do you mean?"

"I mean what I said. He'd been threatened. He called up Mr. Spade"—he indicated Spade with a nod—"and told him so just a few minutes before he was killed."

"But who—?" she began.

"That's what we're asking you," Dundy said. "Who had that much against him?"

She stared at him in astonishment. "Nobody would."

This time Spade interrupted her, speaking with a softness that made his words seem less brutal than they were:

"Somebody did." When she turned her stare on him he asked, "You don't know of any threats?"

She shook her head from side to side with emphasis.

He looked at Mrs. Hooper. "You?"

"No, sir," she said.

He returned his attention to the girl. "Do you know Daniel Talbot?"

"Why, yes," she said. "He was here for dinner last night."

"Who is he?"

"I don't know, except that he lives in San Diego, and he and father had some sort of business together. I'd never met him before."

"What sort of terms were they on?"

She frowned a little, said slowly, "Friendly."

Dundy spoke: "What business was your father in?"

"He was a financier."

"You mean a promoter?"

"Yes, I suppose you could call it that."

"Where is Talbot staying, or has he gone back to San Diego?"

"I don't know."

"What does he look like?"

She frowned again, thoughtfully. "He's kind of large, with a red face and white hair and a white mustache."

"Old?"

"I guess he must be sixty; fifty-five at least."

Dundy looked at Spade, who put the stub of his cigarette in a tray on the dressing table and took up the questioning:

"How long since you've seen your uncle?"

Her face flushed. "You mean Uncle Ted?"

He nodded.

"Not since," she began, and bit her lip. Then she said, "Of course, you know. Not since he first got out of prison."

"He came here?"

"Yes."

"To see your father?"

"Of course."

"What sort of terms were they on?"

She opened her eyes wide.

"Neither of them is very demonstrative," she said, "but they are brothers, and father was giving him money to set him up in business again."

"Then they were on good terms?"

"Yes," she replied in the tone of one answering an unnecessary question.

"Where does he live?"

"On Post Street," she said, and gave a number.

"And you haven't seen him since?"

"No. He was shy, you know, about having been in prison—" She finished the sentence with a gesture of one hand.

Spade addressed Mrs. Hooper: "You've seen him since?"

"No, sir."

He pursed his lips, asked slowly, "Either of you know he was here this afternoon?"

They said, "No," together.

"Where did—?"

Someone knocked on the door.

Dundy said, "Come in."

Tom opened the door far enough to stick his head in.

"His brother's here," he said.

The girl, leaning forward, called, "Oh, Uncle Ted!"

A big blond man in brown appeared behind Tom. He was sunburned to an extent that made his teeth seem whiter, his clear eyes bluer, than they were.

He asked, "What's the matter, Miriam?"

"Father's dead," she said, and began to cry.

Dundy nodded at Tom, who stepped out of Theodore Bliss's way and let him come into the room.

A woman came in behind him, slowly, hesitantly. She was a tall woman in her late twenties, blond, not quite plump. Her features were generous, her face pleasant and intelligent. She wore a small brown hat and a mink coat.

Bliss put an arm around his niece, kissed her forehead, sat on the bed beside her. "There, there," he said awkwardly.

She saw the blond woman, stared through her tears at her for a moment, then said, "Oh, how do you do, Miss Barrow."

The blond woman said, "I'm awfully sorry to—"

Bliss cleared his throat, and said, "She's Mrs. Bliss now. We were married this afternoon."

Dundy looked angrily at Spade. Spade, making a cigarette, seemed about to laugh.

Miriam Bliss, after a moment's surprised silence, said, "Oh, I do wish you all the happiness in the world." She turned to her uncle while his wife was murmuring, "Thank you," and said, "And you too, Uncle Ted."

He patted her shoulder and squeezed her to him. He was looking questioningly at Spade and Dundy.

"Your brother died this afternoon," Dundy said. "He was murdered."

Mrs. Bliss caught her breath. Bliss's arm tightened around his niece with a little jerk, but there was not yet any change in his face.

"Murdered?" he repeated uncomprehendingly.

"Yes." Dundy put his hands in his coat pockets. "You were here this after-noon."

Theodore Bliss paled a little under his sunburn, but said, "I was," steadily enough.

"How long?"

"About an hour. I got here about half past two and—" He turned to his wife. "It was almost half past three when I phoned you, wasn't it?"

She said, "Yes."

"Well, I left right after that."

"Did you have a date with him?" Dundy asked.

"No. I phoned his office"—he nodded at his wife—"and was told he'd left for home, so I came on up. I wanted to see him before Elise and I left, of course, and I wanted him to come to the wedding, but he couldn't. He said he was expecting somebody. We sat here and talked longer than I had intended, so I had to phone Elise to meet me at the Municipal Building."

After a thoughtful pause, Dundy asked, "What time?"

"That we met there?" Bliss looked inquiringly at his wife, who said:

"It was just quarter to four." She laughed a little. "I got there first and I kept looking at my watch."

Bliss said very deliberately, "It was a few minutes after four when we were married. We had to wait for Judge Whitefield—about ten minutes, and it was a few more before we got started—to get through with the case he was hearing. You can check it up—Superior Court, Part Two, I think."

Spade whirled around and pointed at Tom. "Maybe you'd better check it up."

Tom said, "Oke," and went away from the door.

"If that's so, you're all right, Mr. Bliss," Dundy said, "but I have to ask these things. Now, did your brother say who he was expecting?"

"No."

"Did he say anything about having been threatened?"

"No. He never talked much about his affairs to anybody, not even to me. Had he been threatened?"

Dundy's lips tightened a little. "Were you and he on intimate terms?"

"Friendly, if that's what you mean."

"Are you sure?" Dundy asked. "Are you sure neither of you held any grudge against the other?"

Theodore Bliss took his arm free from around his niece. Increasing pallor made his sunburned face yellowish.

He said, "Everybody here knows about my having been in San Quentin. You can speak out, if that's what you're getting at."

"It is," Dundy said, and then, after a pause, "Well?"

Bliss stood up.

"Well, what?" he asked impatiently. "Did I hold a grudge against him for that? No. Why should I? We were both in it. He could get out, I couldn't. I was sure of being convicted whether he was or not. Having him sent over with me wasn't going to make it any better for me. We talked it over and decided I'd go it alone, leaving him outside to pull things together. And he did. If you look up his bank account you'll see he gave me a check for twenty-five thousand dollars two days after I was discharged from San Quentin, and the registrar of the National Steel Corporation can tell you a thousand shares of stock have been transferred from his name to mine since then."

He smiled apologetically and sat down on the bed again. "I'm sorry. I know you have to ask things."

Dundy ignored the apology.

"Do you know Daniel Talbot?" he asked.

Bliss said, "No."

His wife said, "I do; that is, I've seen him. He was in the office yesterday."

Dundy looked her up and down carefully before asking, "What office?"

"I am—I was Mr. Bliss's secretary, and—"

"Max Bliss's?"

"Yes, and a Daniel Talbot came in to see him yesterday afternoon, if it's the same one."

"What happened?"

She looked at her husband, who said, "If you know anything, for heaven's sake tell them."

She said, "But nothing really happened. I thought they were angry with each other at first, but when they left together they were laughing and talking, and before they went Mr. Bliss rang for me and told me to have Trapper—he's the bookkeeper —make out a check to Mr. Talbot's order."

"Did he?"

"Oh, yes. I took it in to him. It was for seventy-five hundred and some dollars."

"What was it for?"

She shook her head. "I don't know."

"If you were Bliss's secretary," Dundy insisted, "you must have some idea of what his business with Talbot was."

"But I haven't," she said. "I'd never even heard of him before."

Dundy looked at Spade. Spade's face was wooden. Dundy glowered at him, then put a question to the man on the bed:

"What kind of necktie was your brother wearing when you saw him last?"

Bliss blinked, then stared distantly past Dundy, and finally shut his eyes. When he opened them he said, "It was green with—I'd know it if I saw it. Why?"

Mrs. Bliss said, "Narrow diagonal stripes of different shades of green. That's the one he had on at the office this morning."

"Where does he keep his neckties?" Dundy asked the housekeeper.

She rose, saying, "In a closet in his bedroom. I'll show you."

Dundy and the newly married Blisses followed her out.

Spade put his hat on the dressing table and asked Miriam Bliss:

"What time did you go out?" He sat on the foot of her bed.

"Today? About one o'clock. I had a luncheon engagement for one and I was a little late, and then I went shopping, and then—" She broke off with a shudder.

"And then you came home at what time?" His voice was friendly, matter-of-fact.

"Some time after four, I guess."

"And what happened?"

"I f-found father lying there and I phoned—I don't know whether I phoned downstairs or the police, and then I don't know what I did. I fainted or had hysterics or something, and the first thing I remember is coming to and finding those men here and Mrs. Hooper." She looked him full in the face now.

"You didn't phone a doctor?"

She lowered her eyes again. "No, I don't think so."

"Of course you wouldn't, if you knew he was dead," he said casually.

She was silent.

"You knew he was dead?" he asked.

She raised her eyes and looked blankly at him.

"But he was dead," she said.

He smiled. "Of course; but what I'm getting at is, did you make sure before you phoned?"

She put a hand to her throat.

"I don't remember what I did," she said earnestly. "I think I just knew he was dead."

He nodded understandingly. "And if you phoned the police it was because you knew he had been murdered."

She worked her hands together and looked at them and said, "I suppose so. It was awful. I don't know what I thought or did."

Spade leaned forward and made his voice low and persuasive. "I'm not a police detective, Miss Bliss. I was engaged by your father—a few minutes too late to save him. I am, in a way, working for you now, so if there is anything I can do—maybe something the police wouldn't—" He broke off as Dundy, followed by the Blisses and the housekeeper, returned to the room. "What luck?"

Dundy said, "The green tie's not there." His suspicious gaze darted from Spade to the girl. "Mrs. Hooper says the blue tie we found is one of half a dozen he just got from England."

Bliss asked, "What's the importance of the tie?"

Dundy scowled at him. "He was partly undressed when we found him. The tie with his clothes had never been worn."

"Couldn't he have been changing clothes when whoever killed him came, and was killed before he had finished dressing?"

Dundy's scowl deepened. "Yes, but what did he do with the green tie? Eat it?"

Spade said, "He wasn't changing clothes. If you'll look at the shirt collar you'll see he must've had it on when he was choked."

Tom came to the door.

"Checks all right," he told Dundy. "The judge and a bailiff named Kittredge say they were there from about a quarter to four till five or ten minutes after. I told Kittredge to come over and take a look at them to make sure they're the same ones."

Dundy said, "Right," without turning his head and took the penciled threat signed with the T in a star from his pocket. He folded it so only the signature was visible.

Then he asked, "Anybody know what this is?"

Miriam Bliss left the bed to join the others in looking at it. From it they looked at one another blankly.

"Anybody know anything about it?" Dundy asked.

Mrs. Hooper said, "It's like what was on poor Mr. Bliss's chest, but—"

The others said, "No."

"Anybody ever seen anything like it before?"

They said they had not.

Dundy said, "All right. Wait here. Maybe I'll have something else to ask you after a while."

Spade said, "Just a minute. Mr. Bliss, how long have you known Mrs. Bliss?"

Bliss looked curiously at Spade.

"Since I got out of prison," he replied somewhat cautiously. "Why?"

"Just since last month," Spade said as if to himself. "Meet her through your brother?"

"Of course—in his office. Why?"

"And at the Municipal Building this afternoon, were you together all the time?"

"Yes, certainly." Bliss spoke sharply. "What are you getting at?"

Spade smiled at him, a friendly smile.

"I have to ask things," he said.

Bliss smiled too. "It's all right." His smile broadened. "As a matter of fact, I'm a liar. We weren't actually together all the time. I went out into the corridor to smoke a cigarette, but I assure you every time I looked through the glass of the door I could see her still sitting in the courtroom where I had left her."

Spade's smile was as light as Bliss's.

Nevertheless, he asked, "And when you weren't looking through the glass you were in sight of the door? She couldn't've left the courtroom without your seeing her?"

Bliss's smile went away.

"Of course she couldn't," he said, "and I wasn't out there more than five minutes."

Spade said, "Thanks," and followed Dundy into the living-room, shutting the door behind him.

Dundy looked sidewise at Spade. "Anything to it?"

Spade shrugged.

Max Bliss's body had been removed. Besides the man at the secrétaire and the gray-faced man, two Filipino boys in plum-colored uniforms were in the room. They sat close together on the sofa.

Dundy said, "Mack, I want to find a green necktie. I want this house taken apart, this block taken apart, and the whole neighborhood taken apart till you find it. Get what men you need."

The man at the secrétaire rose, said, "Right," pulled his hat down over his eyes, and went out.

Dundy scowled at the Filipinos. "Which of you saw the man in brown?"

The smaller stood up. "Me, sir."

Dundy opened the bedroom door and said, "Bliss."

Bliss came to the door.

The Filipino's face lighted up. "Yes, sir, him."

Dundy shut the door in Bliss's face. "Sit down."

The boy sat down hastily.

Dundy stared gloomily at the boys until they began to fidget. Then, "Who else did you bring up to this apartment this afternoon?"

They shook their heads in unison from side to side.

"Nobody else, sir," the smaller one said. A desperately ingratiating smile stretched his mouth wide across his face.

Dundy took a threatening step toward them.

"Nuts!" he snarled. "You brought up Miss Bliss."

The larger boy's head bobbed up and down. "Yes, sir. Yes, sir. I bring them up. I think you mean other people." He too tried a smile.

Dundy was glaring at him. "Never mind what you think I mean. Tell me what I ask. Now, what do you mean by 'them'?"

The boy's smile died under the glare. He looked at the floor between his feet and said, "Miss Bliss and the gentleman."

"What gentleman? The gentleman in there?" He jerked his head toward the door he had shut on Bliss.

"No, sir. Another gentleman, not an American gentleman." He had raised his head again and now brightness came back into his face. "I think he is Armenian."

"Why?"

"Because he not like us Americans, not talk like us."

Spade laughed, asked, "Ever seen an Armenian?"

"No, sir. That is why I think he—" He shut his mouth with a click as Dundy made a growling noise in his throat.

"What'd he look like?" Dundy asked.

The boy lifted his shoulders, spread his hands. "He tall, like this gentleman." He indicated Spade. "Got dark hair, dark mustache. Very"—he frowned earnestly —"very nice clothes. Very nice-looking man. Cane, gloves, spats, even, and—"

"Young?" Dundy asked.

The head went up and down again. "Young. Yes, sir."

"When did he leave?"

"Five minutes," the boy replied.

Dundy made a chewing motion with his jaws, then asked, "What time did they come in?"

The boy spread his hands, lifted his shoulders again. "Four o'clock—maybe ten minutes after."

"Did you bring anybody else up before we got here?"

The Filipinos shook their heads in unison once more.

Dundy spoke out the side of his mouth to Spade:

"Get her."

Spade opened the bedroom door, bowed slightly, said, "Will you come out a moment, Miss Bliss?"

"What is it?" she asked warily.

"Just for a moment," he said, holding the door open. Then he suddenly added, "And you'd better come along too, Mr. Bliss."

Miriam Bliss came slowly into the living-room followed by her uncle, and Spade shut the door behind them.

Miss Bliss's lower lip twitched a little when she saw the elevator boys. She looked apprehensively at Dundy.

He asked, "What's this fiddlededee about the man that came in with you?"

Her lower lip twitched again. "Wh-what?" She tried to put bewilderment on her face.

Theodore Bliss hastily crossed the room, stood for a moment before her as if he intended to say something, and then, apparently changing his mind, took up a position behind her, his arms crossed over the back of a chair.

"The man who came in with you," Dundy said harshly, rapidly. "Who is he? Where is he? Why'd he leave? Why didn't you say anything about him?"

The girl put her hands over her face and began to cry.

"He didn't have anything to do with it," she blubbered through her hands. "He didn't, and it would just make trouble for him."

"Nice boy," Dundy said. "So, to keep his name out of the newspapers, he runs off and leaves you alone with your murdered father."

She took her hands away from her face.

"Oh, but he had to," she cried. "His wife is so jealous, and if she knew he had been with me again she'd certainly divorce him, and he hasn't a cent in the world of his own."

Dundy looked at Spade. Spade looked at the goggling Filipinos and jerked a thumb at the outer door.

"Scram," he said.

They went out quickly.

"And who is this gem?" Dundy asked the girl.

"But he didn't have any—"

"Who is he?"

Her shoulders drooped a little and she lowered her eyes.

"His name is Boris Smekalov," she said wearily.

"Spell it."

She spelled it.

"Where does he live?"

"At the St. Mark Hotel."

"Does he do anything for a living except marry money?"

Anger came into her face as she raised it, but went away as quickly.

"He doesn't do anything," she said.

Dundy wheeled to address the gray-faced man:

"Get him."

The gray-faced man grunted and went out.

Dundy faced the girl again. "You and this Smekalov in love with each other?"

Her face became scornful. She looked at him with scornful eyes and said nothing.

He said, "Now your father's dead, will you have enough money for him to marry if his wife divorces him?"

She covered her face with her hands.

He said, "Now your father's dead, will—?"

Spade, leaning far over, caught her as she fell. He lifted her easily and carried her into the bedroom. When he came back he shut the door behind him and leaned against it.

"Whatever the rest of it was," he said, "the faint's a phony."

"Everything's a phony," Dundy growled.

Spade grinned mockingly. "There ought to be a law making criminals give themselves up."

Mr. Bliss smiled and sat down at his brother's desk by the window.

Dundy's voice was disagreeable.

"You got nothing to worry about," he said to Spade. "Even your client's dead and can't complain. But if I don't come across I've got to stand for riding from the captain, the chief, the newspapers, and heaven knows who all."

"Stay with it," Spade said soothingly; "you'll catch a murderer sooner or later yet." His face became serious except for the lights in his yellow-gray eyes. "I don't want to run this job up any more alleys than we have to, but don't you think we ought to check up on the funeral the housekeeper said she went to? There's something funny about that woman."

After looking suspiciously at Spade for a moment, Dundy nodded, and said, "Tom'll do it."

Spade turned about and, shaking his finger at Tom, said, "It's a ten-to-one bet there wasn't any funeral. Check on it—don't miss a trick."

Then he opened the bedroom door and called Mrs. Hooper.

"Sergeant Polhaus wants some information from you," he told her.

While Tom was writing down names and addresses that the woman gave him, Spade sat on the sofa and made and smoked a cigarette, and Dundy walked the floor slowly, scowling at the rug. With Spade's approval, Theodore Bliss rose and rejoined his wife in the bedroom.

Presently Tom put his notebook in his pocket, said, "Thank you," to the housekeeper, "Be seeing you," to Spade and Dundy, and left the apartment.

The housekeeper stood where he had left her, ugly, strong, serene, patient.

Spade twisted himself around on the sofa until he was looking into her deep-set, steady eyes.

"Don't worry about that," he said, flirting a hand toward the door Tom had gone through. "Just routine." He pursed his lips, asked, "What do you honestly think of this thing, Mrs. Hooper?"

She replied calmly, in her strong, somewhat harsh voice, "I think it's the judgment of God."

Dundy stopped pacing the floor.

Spade said, "What?"

There was certainty and no excitement in her voice: "The wages of sin is death."

Dundy began to advance toward Mrs. Hooper in the manner of one stalking game.

Spade waved him back with a hand which the sofa hid from the woman. His face and voice showed interest, but were now as composed as the woman's.

"Sin?" he asked.

She said, " 'Whosoever shall offend one of these little ones that believe in me, it were better for him that a millstone were hanged around his neck, and he were cast into the sea.' " She spoke, not as if quoting, but as if saying something she believed.

Dundy barked a question at her: "What little one?"

She turned her grave gray eyes on him, then looked past him at the bedroom door.

"Her," she said; "Miriam."

Dundy frowned at her. "His daughter?"

The woman said, "Yes, his own adopted daughter."

Angry blood mottled Dundy's square face.

"What the heck is this?" he demanded. He shook his head as if to free it from some clinging thing. "She's not really his daughter?"

The woman's serenity was in no way disturbed by his anger. "No. His wife was an invalid most of her life. They didn't have any children."

Dundy moved his jaws as if chewing for a moment and when he spoke again his voice was cooler:

"What did he do to her?"

"I don't know," she said, "but I truly believe that when the truth's found out you'll see that the money her father—I mean her real father—left her has been—"

Spade interrupted her, taking pains to speak very clearly, moving one hand in small circles with his words:

"You mean you don't actually know he's been gypping her? You just suspect it?"

She put a hand over her heart.

"I know it here," she replied calmly.

Dundy looked at Spade, Spade at Dundy, and Spade's eyes were shiny with not altogether pleasant merriment.

Dundy cleared his throat and addressed the woman again: "And you think this" —he waved a hand at the floor where the dead man had lain—"was the judgment of God, huh?"

"I do."

He kept all but the barest trace of craftiness out of his eyes. "Then whoever did it was just acting as the hand of God?"

"It's not for me to say," she replied.

Red began to mottle his face again.

"That'll be all right now," he said in a choking voice, but by the time she had reached the bedroom door his eyes became alert again and he called, "Wait a minute." And when they were facing each other: "Listen, do you happen to be a Rosicrucian?"

"I wish to be nothing but a Christian."

He growled, "All right, all right," and turned his back on her. She went into the bedroom and shut the door. He wiped his forehead with the palm of his right hand and complained wearily, "Great Scott, what a family!"

Spade shrugged. "Try investigating your own some time."

Dundy's face whitened. His lips, almost colorless, came back tight over his teeth. He balled his fists and lunged toward Spade.

"What do you—?"

The pleasantly surprised look on Spade's face stopped him. He averted his eyes, wet his lips with the tip of his tongue, looked at Spade again and away, essayed an embarrassed smile, and mumbled:

"You mean any family. Uh-huh, I guess so." He turned hastily toward the corridor door as the doorbell rang.

The amusement twitching Spade's face accentuated his likeness to a blond satan.

An amiable, drawling voice came in through the corridor door:

"I'm Jim Kittredge, Superior Court. I was told to come over here."

Dundy's voice: "Yes, come in."

Kittredge was a roly-poly ruddy man in too-tight clothes with the shine of age on them. He nodded at Spade and said:

"I remember you, Mr. Spade, from the Burke–Harris suit."

Spade said, "Sure," and stood up to shake hands with him.

Dundy had gone to the bedroom door to call Theodore Bliss and his wife.

Kittredge looked at them, smiled at them amiably, said, "How do you do?" and turned to Dundy. "That's them, all right." He looked around as if for a place to spit, found none, and said, "It was just about ten minutes to four that the gentleman there came in the courtroom and asked me how long His Honor would be, and I told him about ten minutes, and they waited there; and right after court adjourned at four o'clock we married them."

Dundy said, "Thanks." He sent Kittredge away, the Blisses back to the bedroom, scowled with dissatisfaction at Spade, and said:

"So what?"

Spade, sitting down again, replied, "So you couldn't get from here to the Municipal Building in less than fifteen minutes on a bet, so he couldn't've ducked back here while he was waiting for the judge, and he couldn't have hustled over here to do it after the wedding and before Miriam arrived."

The dissatisfaction in Dundy's face increased. He opened his mouth, but shut it in silence when the gray-faced man came in with a tall, slender, pale young man who fitted the description the Filipino had given of Miriam Bliss's companion.

The gray-faced man said, "Lieutenant Dundy, Mr. Spade, Mr. Boris—uh—Smekalov."

Dundy nodded curtly.

Smekalov began to speak immediately. His accent was not heavy enough to trouble his hearers much, though his r's sounded more like w's.

"Lieutenant, I must beg of you that you keep this confidential. If it should get out it will ruin me, Lieutenant, ruin me completely and most unjustly. I am most innocent, sir. I assure you, in heart, spirit, and deed, not only innocent, but in no way whatever connected with any part of the whole horrible matter. There is no—"

"Wait a minute." Dundy prodded Smekalov's chest with a blunt finger. "Nobody's said anything about you being mixed up in anything—but it'd looked better if you'd stuck around."

The young man spread his arms, his palms forward, in an expansive gesture.

"But what can I do? I have a wife who—" He shook his head violently. "It is impossible. I cannot do it."

The gray-faced man said to Spade in an inadequately subdued voice, "Goofy, these Russians."

Dundy screwed up his eyes at Smekalov and made his voice judicial.

"You've probably," he said, "put yourself in a pretty tough spot."

Smekalov seemed about to cry.

"But only put yourself in my place," he begged. "And you—"

"Wouldn't want to." Dundy seemed, in his callous way, sorry for the young man. "Murder's nothing to play with in this country."

"Murder! But I tell you, Lieutenant, I happen to enter into this situation by the merest mischance only. I am not—"

"You mean you came in here with Miss Bliss by accident?"

The young man looked as if he would like to say, *Yes*. He said, "No," slowly, then went on with increasing rapidity: "But that was nothing, sir, nothing at all. We had been to lunch. I escorted her home and she said, 'Will you come in for a cocktail?' and I would. That is all, I give you my word." He held out his hands, palms up. "Could it not have happened so to you?" He moved his hands in Spade's direction. "To you?"

Spade said, "A lot of things happen to me. Did Bliss know you were running around with his daughter?"

"He knew we were friends, yes."

"Did he know you had a wife?"

Smekalov said cautiously, "I do not think so."

Dundy said, "You know he didn't."

Smekalov moistened his lips and did not contradict the lieutenant.

Dundy asked, "What do you think he'd've done if he found out?"

"I do not know, sir."

Dundy stepped close to the young man and spoke through his teeth in a harsh, deliberate voice:

"What *did* he do when he found out?"

The young man retreated a step, his face white and frightened.

The bedroom door opened and Miriam Bliss came into the room.

"Why don't you leave him alone?" she asked indignantly. "I told you he had nothing to do with it. I told you he didn't know anything about it." She was beside Smekalov now and had one of his hands in hers. "You're simply making trouble for him without doing a bit of good. I'm awfully sorry, Boris, I tried to keep them from bothering you."

The young man mumbled unintelligibly.

"You tried, all right," Dundy agreed. He addressed Spade: "Could it've been like this, Sam? Bliss found out about the wife, knew they had the lunch date, came home early to meet them when they came in, threatened to tell the wife, and was choked to stop him." He looked sidewise at the girl. "Now, if you want to fake another faint, hop to it."

The young man screamed and flung himself at Dundy, clawing with both hands.

Dundy grunted—"Uh!"—and struck him in the face with a heavy fist.

The young man went backward across the room until he collided with a chair. He and the chair went down on the floor together.

Dundy said to the gray-faced man, "Take him down to the Hall—material witness."

The gray-faced man said, "Oke," picked up Smekalov's hat, and went over to help pick him up.

Theodore Bliss, his wife, and the housekeeper had come to the door Miriam Bliss had left open.

Miriam Bliss was crying, stamping her foot, threatening Dundy:

"I'll report you, you coward. You had no right to—" and so on.

Nobody paid much attention to her; they watched the gray-faced man help Smekalov to his feet, take him away. Smekalov's nose and mouth were red smears.

Then Dundy said, "Hush," negligently to Miriam Bliss and took a slip of paper from his pocket. "I got a list of the calls from here today. Sing out when you recognize them."

He read a telephone number.

Mrs. Hooper said, "That is the butcher. I phoned him before I left this morning." She said the next number Dundy read was the grocer's.

He read another.

"That's the St. Mark," Miriam Bliss said. "I called up Boris." She identified two more numbers as those of friends she had called.

The sixth number, Bliss said, was his brother's office. "Probably my call to Elise to ask her to meet me."

Spade said, "Mine," to the seventh number, and Dundy said:

"That last one's police emergency." He put the slip back in his pocket.

Spade said cheerfully, "And that gets us a lot of places."

The doorbell rang.

Dundy went to the door. He and another man could be heard talking in voices too low for their words to be recognized in the living-room.

The telephone rang. Spade answered it:

"Hello . . . No, this is Spade. Wait a min—All right." He listened. "Right, I'll tell him . . . I don't know. I'll have him call you . . . Right."

When he turned from the telephone Dundy was standing, hands behind him, in the vestibule doorway.

Spade said, "O'Gar says your Russian went completely nuts on the way to the Hall. They had to shove him into a straight-jacket."

"He ought to been there long ago," Dundy growled. "Come here."

Spade followed Dundy into the vestibule. A uniformed policeman stood in the outer doorway.

Dundy brought his hands from behind him. In one was a necktie with narrow diagonal stripes in varying shades of green, in the other was a platinum scarfpin in the shape of a crescent set with small diamonds.

Spade bent over to look at three small, irregular spots on the tie.

"Blood?"

"Or dirt," Dundy said. "He found them crumpled up in a newspaper in the rubbish can on the corner."

"Yes, sir," the uniformed man said proudly; "there I found them, all wadded up in—" He stopped because nobody was paying any attention to him.

"Blood's better," Spade was saying. "It gives a reason for taking the tie away. Let's go in and talk to people."

Dundy stuffed the tie in one pocket, thrust his hand holding the pin into another. "Right—and we'll call it blood."

They went into the living-room.

Dundy looked from Bliss to Bliss's wife, to Bliss's niece, to the housekeeper, as if he did not like any of them. He took his fist from his pocket, thrust it straight out in front of him, and opened it to show the crescent pin lying in his hand.

"What's that?" he demanded.

Miriam Bliss was the first to speak.

"Why, it's father's pin," she said.

"So it is?" he said disagreeably. "And did he have it on today?"

"He always wore it." She turned to the others for confirmation.

Mrs. Bliss said, "Yes," while the others nodded.

"Where did you find it?" the girl asked.

Dundy was surveying them one by one again, as if he liked them less than ever. His face was red.

"He always wore it," he said angrily, "but there wasn't one of you could say, 'Father always wore a pin. Where is it?' No, we got to wait till it turns up before we can get a word out of you about it."

Bliss said, "Be fair. How were we to know—?"

"Never mind what you were to know," Dundy said. "It's coming around to the point where I'm going to do some talking about what I know." He took the green necktie from his pocket. "This is his tie?"

Mrs. Hooper said, "Yes, sir."

Dundy said, "Well, it's got blood on it, and it's not his blood, because he didn't have a scratch on him that we could see." He looked narrow-eyed from one to another of them. "Now, suppose you were trying to choke a man that wore a scarfpin and he was wrestling with you, and—"

He broke off to look at Spade.

Spade had crossed to where Mrs. Hooper was standing. Her big hands were clasped in front of her. He took her right hand, turned it over, took the wadded handkerchief from her palm, and there was a two-inch-long fresh scratch in the flesh.

She had passively allowed him to examine her hand. Her mien lost none of its tranquillity now. She said nothing.

"Well?" he asked.

"I scratched it on Miss Miriam's pin fixing her on the bed when she fainted," the housekeeper said calmly.

Dundy's laugh was brief, bitter.

"It'll hang you just the same," he said.

There was no change in the woman's face.

"The Lord's will be done," she replied.

Spade made a peculiar noise in his throat as he dropped her hand.

"Well, let's see how we stand." He grinned at Dundy. "You don't like that star-T, do you?"

Dundy said, "Not by a long shot."

"Neither do I," Spade said. "The Talbot threat was probably on the level, but that debt seems to have been squared. Now—Wait a minute." He went to the telephone and called his office. "The tie thing looked pretty funny, too, for a while," he said while he waited, "but I guess the blood takes care of that."

He spoke into the telephone:

"Hello, Effie. Listen: Within half an hour or so of the time Bliss called me, did you get any call that maybe wasn't on the level? Anything that could have been a stall? . . . Yes, before . . . Think now."

He put his hand over the mouthpiece and said to Dundy, "There's a lot of deviltry going on in this world."

He spoke into the telephone again:

"Yes? . . . Yes . . . Kruger? . . . Yes. Man or woman? . . . Thanks . . . No, I'll be through in half an hour. Wait for me and I'll buy your dinner. 'Bye."

He turned away from the telephone. "About half an hour before Bliss phoned, a man called my office and asked for Mr. Kruger."

Dundy frowned. "So what?"

"Kruger wasn't there."

Dundy's frown deepened. "Who's Kruger?"

"I don't know," Spade said blandly. "I never heard of him." He took tobacco and cigarette papers from his pockets. "All right, Bliss, where's your scratch?"

Theodore Bliss said, "What?" while the others stared blankly at Spade.

"Your scratch," Spade repeated in a consciously patient tone. His attention was on the cigarette he was making. "The place where your brother's pin gouged you when you were choking him."

"Are you crazy?" Bliss demanded. "I was—"

"Uh-huh, you were being married when he was killed. You were not."

Spade moistened the edge of his cigarette paper and smoothed it with his forefingers.

Mrs. Bliss spoke now, stammering a little: "But he—but Max Bliss called—"

"Who says Max Bliss called me?" Spade asked. "I don't know that. I wouldn't know his voice. All I know is a man called me and said he was Max Bliss. Anybody could say that."

"But the telephone records here show the call came from here," she protested.

He shook his head and smiled. "They show I had a call from here, and I did, but not that one. I told you somebody called up half an hour or so before the supposed Max Bliss call and asked for Mr. Kruger." He nodded at Theodore Bliss. "He was smart enough to get a call from this apartment to my office on the record before he left to meet you."

She stared from Spade to her husband with dumbfounded blue eyes.

Her husband said lightly, "It's nonsense, my dear. You know—"

Spade did not let him finish that sentence. "You know he went out to smoke a cigarette in the corridor while waiting for the judge, and he knew there were telephone booths in the corridor. A minute would be all he needed." He lit his cigarette and returned his lighter to his pocket.

Bliss said, "Nonsense!" more sharply. "Why should I want to kill Max?" He smiled reassuringly to his wife's horrified eyes. "Don't let this disturb you, dear. Police methods are sometimes—"

"All right," Spade said, "let's look you over for scratches."

Bliss wheeled to face him more directly. "Damned if you will!" He put a hand behind him.

Spade, wooden-faced and dreamy-eyed, came forward.

Spade and Effie Perine sat at a small table in Julius's Castle on Telegraph Hill. Through the window beside them ferryboats could be seen carrying lights to and from the cities' lights on the other side of the bay.

"—hadn't gone there to kill him, chances are," Spade was saying; "just to shake him down for some more money; but when the fight started, once he got his hands on his throat, I guess, his grudge was too hot in him for him to let go till Max was dead. Understand, I'm just putting together what the evidence says, and what we got out of his wife, and the not much that we got out of him."

Effie nodded. "She's a nice, loyal wife."

Spade drank coffee, shrugged. "What for? She knows now that he made his play for her only because she was Max's secretary. She knows that when he took out the marriage license a couple of weeks ago it was only to string her along so she'd get him the photostatic copies of the records that tied Max up with the Graystone Loan swindle. She knows—Well, she knows she wasn't just helping an injured innocent to clear his good name."

He took another sip of coffee. "So he calls on his brother this afternoon to hold San Quentin over his head for a price again, and there's a fight, and he kills him, and gets his wrist scratched by the pin while he's choking him. Blood on the tie, a scratch on his wrist—that won't do. He takes the tie off the corpse and hunts up another, because the absence of a tie will set the police to thinking. He gets a bad break there. Max's new ties are on the front of the rack, and he grabs the first one he comes to. All right. Now he's got to put it around the dead man's neck—or wait —he gets a better idea. Pull off some more clothes and puzzle the police. The tie'll be just as inconspicuous off as on, if the shirt's off too. Undressing him, he gets another idea. He'll give the police something else to worry about, so he draws a mystic sign he has seen somewhere on the dead man's chest."

Spade emptied his cup, set it down, and went on:

"By now he's getting to be a regular master-mind at bewildering the police. A threatening letter signed with the thing on Max's chest. The afternoon mail is on the desk. One envelope's as good as another so long as it's typewritten and has no return address, but the one from France adds a touch of the foreign, so out comes the original letter and in goes the threat. He's overdoing it now; see? He's giving us so much that's wrong that we can't help suspecting things that seem all right—the phone call, for instance.

"Well, he's ready for the phone calls now—his alibi. He picks my name out of the private detectives in the phone book and does the Mr. Kruger trick; but that's after he calls the blond Elise and tells her that not only have the obstacles to their marriage been removed, but he's had an offer to go in business in New York and has to leave right away, and will she meet him in fifteen minutes and get married? There's more than just an alibi to that. He wants to make sure *she* is dead sure he didn't kill Max, because she knows he doesn't like Max, and he doesn't want her to think he was just stringing her along to get the dope on Max, because she might be able to put two and two together and get something like the right answer.

"With that taken care of, he's ready to leave. He goes out quite openly, with only one thing to worry about now—the tie and pin in his pocket. He takes the pin along because he's not sure the police mightn't find traces of blood around the setting of the stones, no matter how carefully he wipes it. On his way out he picks up a newspaper—buys one from the newsboy he meets at the street door—wads tie and pin up in a piece of it, and drops it in the rubbish can at the corner. That seems all right. No reason for the police to look for the tie. No reason for the street cleaner who empties the can to investigate a crumpled piece of newspaper, and if something does go wrong—what the deuce!—the murderer dropped it there, but he, Theodore, can't be the murderer, because he's going to have an alibi.

"Then he jumps in his car and drives to the Municipal Building. He knows there are plenty of phones there and he can always say he's got to wash his hands, but it turns out he doesn't have to. While they're waiting for the judge to get through with a case he goes out to smoke a cigarette, and there you are—'Mr. Spade, this is Max Bliss and I've been threatened.' "

Effie Perine nodded, then asked:

"Why do you suppose he picked on a private detective instead of the police?"

"Playing safe. If the body had been found, meanwhile, the police might've heard of it and traced the call. A private detective wouldn't be likely to hear about it till he read it in the papers."

She laughed, then said, "And that was your luck."

"Luck? I don't know." He looked gloomily at the back of his left hand. "I hurt a knuckle stopping him and the job only lasted an afternoon. Chances are whoever's handling the estate'll raise hobs if I send them a bill for any decent amount of money." He raised a hand to attract the waiter's attention. "Oh, well, better luck next time. Want to catch a movie or have you got something else to do?"

They Can Only
Hang You Once

S AMUEL SPADE said, "My name is Ronald Ames. I want to see Mr. Binnett—
Mr. Timothy Binnett."

"Mr. Binnett is resting now, sir," the butler replied hesitantly.

"Will you find out when I can see him? It's important." Spade cleared his throat. "I'm—uh—just back from Australia, and it's about some of his properties there."

The butler turned on his heel while saying, "I'll see, sir," and was going up the front stairs before he had finished speaking.

Spade made and lit a cigarette.

The butler came downstairs again.

"I'm sorry, he can't be disturbed now, but Mr. Wallace Binnett—Mr. Timothy's nephew—will see you."

Spade said, "Thanks," and followed the butler upstairs.

Wallace Binnett was a slender, handsome, dark man of about Spade's age—thirty-eight—who rose smiling from a brocaded chair, said, "How do you do, Mr. Ames?" waved his hand at another chair, and sat down again. "You're from Australia?"

"Got in this morning."

"You're a business associate of Uncle Tim's?"

Spade smiled and shook his head. "Hardly that, but I've some information I think he ought to have—quick."

Wallace Binnett looked thoughtfully at the floor, then up at Spade.

"I'll do my best to persuade him to see you, Mr. Ames, but, frankly, I don't know."

Spade seemed mildly surprised. "Why?"

Binnett shrugged. "He's peculiar sometimes. Understand, his mind seems perfectly all right, but he has the testiness and eccentricity of an old man in ill health and—well—at times he can be difficult."

Spade asked slowly, "He's already refused to see me?"

"Yes."

Spade rose from his chair. His blond satan's face was expressionless.

Binnett raised a hand quickly.

"Wait, wait," he said. "I'll do what I can to make him change his mind. Perhaps if—" His dark eyes suddenly became wary. "You're not simply trying to sell him something, are you?"

"No."

The wary gleam went out of Binnett's eyes. "Well, then, I think I can—"

A young woman came in crying angrily, "Wally, that old fool has—"

She broke off with a hand to her breast when she saw Spade.

Spade and Binnett had risen together.

Binnett said suavely, "Joyce, this is Mr. Ames. My sister-in-law, Joyce Court."

Spade bowed.

Joyce Court uttered a short, embarrassed laugh and said, "Please excuse my whirlwind entrance."

She was a tall, blue-eyed, dark woman of twenty-four or -five with good shoulders and a strong, slim body. Her features made up in warmth what they lacked in regularity. She wore wide-legged, blue satin pajamas.

Binnett smiled good-naturedly at her and asked:

"Now what's all the excitement?"

Anger darkened her eyes again and she started to speak. Then she looked at Spade and said:

"But we shouldn't bore Mr. Ames with our stupid domestic affairs. If—" She hesitated.

Spade bowed again. "Sure," he said, "certainly."

"I won't be a minute," Binnett promised, and left the room with her.

Spade went to the open doorway through which they had vanished and, standing just inside, listened. Their footsteps became inaudible. Nothing else could be heard.

Spade was standing there—his yellow-gray eyes dreamy—when he heard the scream. It was a woman's scream, high and shrill with terror. Spade was through the doorway when he heard the shot.

It was a pistol shot, magnified, reverberated by walls and ceilings.

Twenty feet from the doorway Spade found a staircase, and went up it three steps at a time. He turned to the left. Halfway down the hallway a woman lay on her back on the floor.

Wallace Binnett knelt beside her, fondling one of her hands desperately, crying in a low, beseeching voice, "Darling, Molly, darling!"

Joyce Court stood behind him and wrung her hands while tears streaked her cheeks.

The woman on the floor resembled Joyce Court but was older, and her face had a hardness the younger one's had not.

"She's dead, she's been killed," Wallace Binnett said incredulously, raising his white face toward Spade.

When Binnett moved his head Spade could see the round hole in the woman's tan dress over her heart and the dark stain which was rapidly spreading below it.

Spade touched Joyce Court's arm.

"Police, emergency hospital—phone," he said.

As she ran toward the stairs he addressed Wallace Binnett: "Who did—"

A voice groaned feebly behind Spade.

He turned swiftly. Through an open doorway he could see an old man in white pajamas lying sprawled across a rumpled bed. His head, a shoulder, an arm dangled over the edge of the bed. His other hand held his throat tightly. He groaned again and his eyelids twitched, but did not open.

Spade lifted the old man's head and shoulders and put them up on the pillows. The old man groaned again and took his hand from his throat. His throat was red with half a dozen bruises. He was a gaunt man with a seamed face that probably exaggerated his age.

A glass of water was on a table beside the bed. Spade put water on the old man's face and, when the old man's eyes twitched again, leaned down and growled softly: "Who did it?"

The twitching eyelids went up far enough to show a narrow strip of bloodshot gray eyes. The old man spoke painfully, putting a hand to his throat again:

"A man—he—" He coughed.

Spade made an impatient grimace. His lips almost touched the old man's ear. "Where'd he go?" His voice was urgent.

A gaunt hand moved weakly to indicate the rear of the house and fell back on the bed.

The butler and two frightened female servants had joined Wallace Binnett beside the dead woman in the hallway.

"Who did it?" Spade asked them.

They stared at him blankly.

"Somebody look after the old man," he growled and went down the hallway.

At the end of the hallway was a rear staircase. He descended two flights and went through a pantry into the kitchen. He saw nobody. The kitchen door was shut but, when he tried it, not locked. He crossed a narrow back yard to a gate that was shut, not locked. He opened the gate. There was nobody in the narrow alley behind it.

He sighed, shut the gate, and returned to the house.

Spade sat comfortably slack in a deep leather chair in a room that ran across the front second story of Wallace Binnett's house. There were shelves of books and the lights were on. The window showed outer darkness weakly diluted by a distant street lamp.

Facing Spade, Detective Sergeant Polhaus—a big, carelessly shaven, florid man in dark clothes that needed pressing—was sprawled in another leather chair; Lieutenant Dundy—smaller, compactly built, square-faced—stood with legs apart, head thrust a little forward, in the center of the room.

Spade was saying:

"—and the doctor would only let me talk to the old man a couple of minutes. We can try it again when he's rested a little, but it doesn't look like he knows much. He was catching a nap and he woke up with somebody's hands on his throat dragging him around the bed. The best he got was a one-eyed look at the fellow choking him. A big fellow, he says, with a soft hat pulled down over his eyes, dark, needing a shave. Sounds like Tom." Spade nodded at Polhaus.

The detective sergeant chuckled, but Dundy said, "Go on," curtly.

Spade grinned and went on:

"He's pretty far gone when he hears Mrs. Binnett scream at the door. The hands go away from his throat and he hears the shot and just before passing out he gets a flash of the big fellow heading for the rear of the house and Mrs. Binnett tumbling down on the hall floor. He says he never saw the big fellow before."

"What size gun was it?" Dundy asked.

"Thirty-eight. Well, nobody in the house is much more help. Wallace and his sister-in-law, Joyce, were in her room, so they say, and didn't see anything but the dead woman when they ran out, though they think they heard something that could've been somebody running downstairs—the back stairs.

"The butler—his name's Jarboe—was in here when he heard the scream and shot, so he says. Irene Kelly, the maid, was down on the ground floor, so she says. The cook, Margaret Finn, was in her room—third floor back—and didn't even hear anything, so she says. She's deaf as a post, so everybody else says. The back door and gate were unlocked, but are supposed to be kept locked, so everybody says. Nobody says they went in or around the kitchen or yard at the time." Spade spread his hands in a gesture of finality. "That's the crop."

Dundy shook his head. "Not exactly," he said. "How come you were here?"

Spade's face brightened.

"Maybe my client killed her," he said. "He's Wallace's cousin, Ira Binnett. Know him?"

Dundy shook his head. His blue eyes were hard and suspicious.

"He's a San Francisco lawyer," Spade said, "respectable and all that. A couple of days ago he came to me with a story about his uncle Timothy, a miserly old skinflint, lousy with money and pretty well broken up by hard living. He was the black sheep of the family. None of them had heard of him for years. But six or eight months ago he showed up in pretty bad shape every way except financially— he seems to have taken a lot of money out of Australia—wanting to spend his last days with his only living relatives, his nephews Wallace and Ira.

"That was all right with them. 'Only living relatives' meant 'only heirs' in their language. But by and by the nephews began to think it was better to be an heir than to be one of a couple of heirs—twice as good, in fact—and started fiddling for the inside track with the old man. At least, that's what Ira told me about Wallace, and I wouldn't be surprised if Wallace would say the same thing about Ira, though Wallace seems to be the harder up of the two. Anyhow, the nephews fell out, and then Uncle Tim, who had been staying at Ira's, came over here. That was a couple of months ago, and Ira hasn't seen Uncle Tim since, and hasn't been able to get in touch with him by phone or mail.

"That's what he wanted a private detective about. He didn't think Uncle Tim would come to any harm here—oh, no, he went to a lot of trouble to make that clear—but he thought maybe undue pressure was being brought to bear on the old boy, or he was being hornswoggled somehow, and at least being told lies about his loving nephew Ira. He wanted to know what was what. I waited until today, when a boat from Australia docked, and came up here as a Mr. Ames with some important information for Uncle Tim about his properties down there. All I wanted was fifteen minutes alone with him."

Spade frowned thoughtfully. "Well, I didn't get them. Wallace told me the old man refused to see me. I don't know."

Suspicion had deepened in Dundy's cold blue eyes.

"And where is this Ira Binnett now?" he asked.

Spade's yellow-gray eyes were as guileless as his voice. "I wish I knew. I phoned his house and office and left word for him to come right over, but I'm afraid—"

Knuckles knocked sharply twice on the other side of the room's one door.

The three men in the room turned to face the door.

Dundy called, "Come in."

The door was opened by a sunburned blond policeman whose left hand held the right wrist of a plump man of forty or forty-five in well-fitting gray clothes. The policeman pushed the plump man into the room.

"Found him monkeying with the kitchen door," he said.

Spade looked up and said, "Ah!" His tone expressed satisfaction. "Mr. Ira Binnett, Lieutenant Dundy, Sergeant Polhaus."

Ira Binnett said rapidly, "Mr. Spade, will you tell this man that—"

Dundy addressed the policeman: "All right. Good work. You can leave him."

The policeman moved a hand vaguely toward his cap and went away.

Dundy glowered at Ira Binnett and demanded: "Well?"

Binnett looked from Dundy to Spade. "Has something—"

Spade said, "Better tell him why you were at the back door instead of the front."

Ira Binnett suddenly blushed. He cleared his throat in embarrassment.

He said, "I—uh—I should explain. It wasn't my fault, of course, but when Jarboe—he's the butler—phoned me that Uncle Tim wanted to see me he told me he'd leave the kitchen door unlocked, so Wallace wouldn't have to know I'd—"

"What'd he want to see you about?" Dundy asked.

"I don't know. He didn't say. He said it was very important."

"Didn't you get my message?" Spade asked.

Ira Binnett's eyes widened. "No. What was it? Has anything happened? What is—"

Spade was moving toward the door.

"Go ahead," he said to Dundy. "I'll be right back."

He shut the door carefully behind him and went up to the third floor.

The butler Jarboe was on his knees at Timothy Binnett's door with an eye to the keyhole. On the floor beside him was a tray holding an egg in an egg-cup, toast, a pot of coffee, china, silver, and a napkin.

Spade said, "Your toast's going to get cold."

Jarboe, scrambling to his feet, almost upsetting the coffeepot in his haste, his face red and sheepish, stammered:

"I—er—beg your pardon, sir. I wanted to make sure Mr. Timothy was awake before I took this in." He picked up the tray. "I didn't want to disturb his rest if—"

Spade, who had reached the door, said, "Sure, sure," and bent over to put his eye to the keyhole. When he straightened up he said in a mildly complaining tone. "You can't see the bed—only a chair and part of the window."

The butler replied quickly, "Yes, sir, I found that out."

Spade laughed.

The butler coughed, seemed about to say something, but did not. He hesitated, then knocked lightly on the door.

A tired voice said, "Come in."

Spade asked quickly in a low voice, "Where's Miss Court?"

"In her room, I think, sir, the second door on the left," the butler said.

The tired voice inside the room said petulantly, "Well, come on in."

The butler opened the door and went in. Through the door, before the butler shut it, Spade caught a glimpse of Timothy Binnett propped up on pillows in his bed.

Spade went to the second door on the left and knocked. The door was opened almost immediately by Joyce Court. She stood in the doorway, not smiling, not speaking.

He said, "Miss Court, when you came into the room where I was with your brother-in-law you said, 'Wally, that old fool has—' Meaning Timothy?"

She stared at Spade for a moment. Then: "Yes."

"Mind telling me what the rest of the sentence would have been?"

She said slowly, "I don't know who you really are or why you ask, but I don't mind telling you. It would have been 'sent for Ira.' Jarboe had just told me."

"Thanks."

She shut the door before he had turned away.

He returned to Timothy Binnett's door and knocked on it.

"Who is it now?" the old man's voice demanded.

Spade opened the door. The old man was sitting up in bed. Spade said, "This Jarboe was peeping through your keyhole a few minutes ago," and returned to the library.

Ira Binnett, seated in the chair Spade had occupied, was saying to Dundy and

Polhaus, "And Wallace got caught in the crash, like most of us, but he seems to have juggled accounts trying to save himself. He was expelled from the Stock Exchange."

Dundy waved a hand to indicate the room and its furnishings.

"Pretty classy layout for a man that's busted."

"His wife has some money," Ira Binnett said, "and he always lived beyond his means."

Dundy scowled at Binnett. "And you really think he and his missus weren't on good terms?"

"I don't think it," Binnett replied evenly. "I know it."

Dundy nodded. "And you know he's got a yen for the sister-in-law, this Court?"

"I don't know that. But I've heard plenty of gossip to the same effect."

Dundy made a growling noise in his throat, then asked sharply, "How does the old man's will read?"

"I don't know. I don't know whether he's made one." He addressed Spade, now earnestly: "I've told everything I know, every single thing."

Dundy said, "It's not enough." He jerked a thumb at the door. "Show him where to wait, Tom, and let's have the widower in again."

Big Polhaus said, "Right," went out with Ira Binnett, and returned with Wallace Binnett, whose face was hard and pale.

Dundy asked, "Has your uncle made a will?"

"I don't know," Binnett replied.

Spade put the next question, softly: "Did your wife?"

Binnett's mouth tightened in a mirthless smile. He spoke deliberately:

"I'm going to say some things I'd rather not have to say. My wife, properly, had no money. When I got into financial trouble some time ago I made some property over to her, to save it. She turned it into money without my knowing about it till afterward. She paid our bills—our living expenses—out of it, but she refused to return it to me and she assured me that in no event—whether she lived or died or we stayed together or were divorced—would I ever be able to get hold of a penny of it. I believed her, and still do."

"You wanted a divorce?" Dundy asked.

"Yes."

"Why?"

"It wasn't a happy marriage."

"Joyce Court?"

Binnett's face flushed. He said stiffly, "I admire Joyce Court tremendously, but I'd've wanted a divorce anyway."

Spade said, "And you're sure—still absolutely sure—you don't know anybody who fits your uncle's description of the man who choked him?"

"Absolutely sure."

The sound of the doorbell ringing came faintly into the room. Dundy said sourly, "That'll do."

Binnett went out.

Polhaus said, "That guy's as wrong as they make them. And—"

From below came the heavy report of a pistol fired indoors. The lights went out.

In darkness the three detectives collided with one another going through the doorway into the dark hall.

Spade reached the stairs first. There was a clatter of footsteps below him, but nothing could be seen until he reached a bend in the stairs. Then enough light came from the street through the open front door to show the dark figure of a man standing with his back to the open door.

A flashlight clicked in Dundy's hand—he was at Spade's heels—and threw a glaring white beam of light on the man's face.

He was Ira Binnett. He blinked in the light and pointed at something on the floor in front of him.

Dundy turned the beam of his light down on the floor. Jarboe lay there on his face, bleeding from a bullet hole in the back of his head.

Spade grunted softly.

Tom Polhaus came blundering down the stairs, Wallace Binnett close behind him. Joyce Court's frightened voice came from farther up:

"Oh, what's happened? Wally, what's happened?"

"Where's the light switch?" Dundy barked.

"Inside the cellar door, under these stairs," Wallace Binnett said. "What is it?"

Polhaus pushed past Binnett toward the cellar door.

Spade made an inarticulate sound in his throat and pushing Wallace Binnett aside, sprang up the stairs. He brushed past Joyce Court and went on, heedless of her startled scream. He was halfway up the stairs to the third floor when the pistol went off up there.

He ran to Timothy Binnett's door. The door was open. He went in.

Something hard and angular struck him above his right ear, knocking him across the room, bringing him down on one knee. Something thumped and clattered on the floor just outside the door.

The lights came on.

On the floor, in the center of the room, Timothy Binnett lay on his back bleeding from a bullet wound in his left forearm. His pajama jacket was torn. His eyes were shut.

Spade stood up and put a hand to his head. He scowled at the old man on the floor, at the room, at the black automatic pistol lying on the hallway floor.

He said, "Come on, you old cutthroat. Get up and sit on a chair and I'll see if I can stop that bleeding till the doctor gets here."

The man on the floor did not move.

There were footsteps in the hallway and Dundy came in, followed by the two younger Binnetts. Dundy's face was dark and furious.

"Kitchen door wide open," he said in a choked voice. "They run in and out like—"

"Forget it," Spade said. "Uncle Tim is our meat." He paid no attention to Wallace Binnett's gasp, to the incredulous looks on Dundy's and Ira Binnett's faces. "Come on, get up," he said to the old man on the floor, "and tell us what it was the butler saw when he peeped through the keyhole."

The old man did not stir.

"He killed the butler because I told him the butler had peeped," Spade explained to Dundy. "I peeped too, but didn't see anything except that chair and the window, though we'd made enough racket by then to scare him back to bed. Suppose you take the chair apart while I go over the window."

He went to the window and began to examine it carefully. He shook his head, put a hand out behind him, and said, "Give me the flashlight."

Dundy put the flashlight in his hand.

Spade raised the window and leaned out, turning the light on the outside of the building. Presently he grunted and put his other hand out, tugging at a brick a little below the sill. Presently the brick came loose. He put it on the window sill and stuck his hand into the hole its removal had made. Out of the opening, one at a time, he brought an empty black pistol holster, a partially filled box of cartridges, and an unsealed manila envelope.

Holding these things in his hands, he turned to face the others.

Joyce Court came in with a basin of water and a roll of gauze and knelt beside Timothy Binnett.

Spade put the holster and cartridges on a table and opened the manila envelope. Inside were two sheets of paper, covered on both sides with boldly penciled writing. Spade read a paragraph to himself, suddenly laughed, and began at the beginning again, reading aloud:

"I, Timothy Kieran Binnett, being sound of mind and body, do declare this to be my last will and testament. To my dear nephews, Ira Binnett and Wallace Bourke Binnett, in recognition of the loving kindness with which they have received me into their homes and attended my declining years, I give and bequeath, share and share alike, all my worldly possessions of whatever kind, to wit; my carcass and the clothes I stand in.

"I bequeath them, furthermore, the expense of my funeral and these memories: First, the memory of their credulity in believing that the fifteen years I spent in Sing Sing were spent in Australia; second, the memory of their optimism in supposing that those fifteen years had brought me great wealth, and that if I lived on them, borrowed from them, and never spent any of my own money, it was because

I was a miser whose hoard they would inherit; and not because I had no money except what I shook them down for; third, for their hopefulness in thinking that I would leave either of them anything if I had it; and, lastly, because their painful lack of any decent sense of humor will keep them from ever seeing how funny this has all been. Signed and sealed this—"

Spade looked up to say, "There is no date, but it's signed Timothy Kieran Binnett with flourishes."

Ira Binnett was purple with anger.

Wallace's face was ghastly in its pallor and his whole body was trembling.

Joyce Court had stopped working on Timothy Binnett's arm.

The old man sat up and opened his eyes. He looked at his nephews and began to laugh. There was in his laughter neither hysteria nor madness: it was sane, hearty laughter, and subsided slowly.

Spade said, "All right, now you've had your fun. Let's talk about the killings."

"I know nothing more about the first one than I've told you," the old man said, "and this one's not a killing, since I'm only—"

Wallace Binnett, still trembling violently, said painfully through his teeth:

"That's a lie. You killed Molly. Joyce and I came out of her room when we heard Molly scream, and heard the shot and saw her fall out of your room, and nobody came out afterward."

The old man said calmly, "Well, I'll tell you: it was an accident. They told me there was a fellow from Australia here to see me about my properties there. I knew there was something funny about that somewhere"—he grinned—"not ever having been there. I didn't know whether one of my dear nephews was getting suspicious and putting up a game on me or what, but I knew that if Wally wasn't in on it he'd certainly try to pump the gentleman from Australia about me and maybe I'd lose one of my free boarding houses."

He chuckled.

"So I figured I'd get in touch with Ira so I could go back to his house if things worked out bad here, and I'd try to get rid of this Australian. Wally's always thought I'm half-cracked"—he leered at his nephew—"and's afraid they'll lug me off to a madhouse before I could make a will in his favor, or they'll break it if I do. You see, he's got a pretty bad reputation, what with that Stock Exchange trouble and all, and he knows no court would appoint him to handle my affairs if I went screwy —not as long as I've got another nephew"—he turned his leer on Ira—"who's a respectable lawyer. So now I know that rather than have me kick up a row that might wind me up in the madhouse, he'll chase this visitor, and I put on a show for Molly, who happened to be the nearest one to hand. She took it too seriously, though.

"I had a gun and I did a lot of raving about being spied on by my enemies in Australia and that I was going down and shoot this fellow. But she got too excited and tried to take the gun away from me, and the first thing I knew it had gone off, and I had to make these marks on my neck and think up that story about the big dark man."

He looked contemptuously at Wallace.

"I didn't know he was covering me up. Little as I thought of him, I never thought he'd be low enough to cover up his wife's murderer—even if he didn't like her—just for the sake of money."

Spade said, "Never mind that. Now about the butler?"

"I don't know anything about the butler," the old man replied, looking at Spade with steady eyes.

Spade said, "You had to kill him quick, before he had time to do or say anything. So you slip down the back stairs, open the kitchen door to fool people, go to the front door, ring the bell, shut the door, and hide in the shadow of the cellar door under the front steps. When Jarboe answered the doorbell you shot him —the hole was in the back of his head—pulled the light switch, just inside the cellar door, and ducked up the back stairs in the dark and shot yourself carefully in the arm. I got up there too soon for you; so you smacked me with the gun, chucked it through the door, and spread yourself on the floor while I was shaking pinwheels out of my noodle."

The old man sniffed again. "You're just—"

"Stop it," Spade said patiently. "Don't let's argue. The first killing was an accident—all right. The second couldn't be. And it ought to be easy to show that both bullets, and the one in your arm, were fired from the same gun. What difference does it make which killing we can prove first-degree murder on? They can only hang you once." He smiled pleasantly. "And they will."

Too Many Have Lived

THE MAN'S TIE was as orange as a sunset. He was a large man, tall and meaty, without softness. The dark hair parted in the middle, flattened to his scalp, his firm, full cheeks, the clothes that fit him with noticeable snugness, even the small, pink ears flat against the sides of his head—each of these seemed but a differently colored part of one same, smooth surface. His age could have been thirty-five or forty-five.

He sat beside Samuel Spade's desk, leaning forward a little over his Malacca stick, and said:

"No. I want you to find out what happened to him. I hope you never find him." His protuberant green eyes stared solemnly at Spade.

Spade rocked back in his chair. His face—given a not unpleasantly satanic cast by the v's of his bony chin, mouth, nostrils, and thickish brows—was as politely interested as his voice:

"Why?"

The green-eyed man spoke quietly, with assurance:

"I can talk to you, Spade. You've the sort of reputation I want in a private detective. That's why I'm here."

Spade's nod committed him to nothing.

The green-eyed man said, "And any fair price is all right with me."

Spade nodded as before. "And with me," he said, "but I've got to know what you want to buy. You want to find out what's happened to this—uh—Eli Haven, but you don't care what it is?"

The green-eyed man lowered his voice, but there was no other change in his mien:

"In a way I do. For instance, if you found him and fixed it so he stayed away for good, it might be worth more money to me."

"You mean even if he didn't want to stay away?"

The green-eyed man said, "Especially."

Spade smiled and shook his head. "Probably not enough more money—the way you mean it." He took his long, thick-fingered hands from the arms of his chair and turned their palms up. "Well, what's it all about, Colyer?"

Colyer's face reddened a little, but his eyes maintained their unblinking cold stare.

"This man's got a wife. I like her. They had a row last week and he blew. If I can convince her he's gone for good, there's a chance she'll divorce him."

"I'd want to talk to her," Spade said. "Who is this Eli Haven? What does he do?"

"He's a bad egg. He doesn't do anything. Writes poetry or something."

"What can you tell me about him that'll help?"

"Nothing Julia, his wife, can't tell you. You're going to talk to her." Colyer stood up. "I've got connections. Maybe I can get something for you through them later."

A small-boned woman of twenty-five or -six opened the apartment door. Her powder-blue dress was trimmed with silver buttons. She was full-bosomed but slim, with straight shoulders and narrow hips, and she carried herself with a pride that would have been cockiness in one less graceful.

Spade said, "Mrs. Haven?"

She hesitated before saying, "Yes."

"Gene Colyer sent me to see you. My name's Spade. I'm a private detective. He wants me to find your husband."

"And have you found him?"

"I told him I'd have to talk to you first."

Her smile went away. She studied his face gravely, feature by feature.

Then she said, "Certainly," and stepped back, drawing the door back with her.

When they were seated in facing chairs in a cheaply furnished room overlooking a playground where children were noisy, she asked:

"Did Gene tell you why he wanted Eli found?"

"He said if you knew he was gone for good maybe you'd listen to reason."

She said nothing.

"Has he ever gone off like this before?"

"Often."

"What's he like?"

"He's a swell man," she said dispassionately, "when he's sober; and when he's drinking he's all right except with women and money."

"That leaves him a lot of room to be all right on. What does he do for a living?"

"He's a poet," she replied, "but nobody makes a living at that."

"Well?"

"Oh, he pops in with a little money now and then. Poker, races, he says. I don't know."

"How long've you been married?"

"Four years, almost."

He smiled mockingly.

"San Francisco all the time?"

"No, we lived in Seattle the first year and then came here."

"He from Seattle?"

She shook her head. "Some place in Delaware."

"What place?"

"I don't know."

Spade drew his thickish brows together a little.

"Where are you from?"

She said sweetly, "You're not hunting for me."

"You act like it," he grumbled. "Well, who are his friends?"

"Don't ask me!"

He made an impatient grimace.

"You know some of them," he insisted.

"Sure. There's a fellow named Minera and a Louis James and somebody he calls Conny."

"Who are they?"

"I don't know anything about them. They phone or drop by to pick him up, or I see him around town with them. That's all I know."

"What do they do for a living? They can't all write poetry."

She laughed. "They could try. One of them, Louis James, is a—a member of Gene's staff, I think. I honestly don't know any more about them than I've told you."

"Think they'd know where your husband is?"

She shrugged. "They're kidding me if they do. They still call up once in a while to see if he's turned up."

"And these women you mentioned?"

"They're not people I know."

Spade scowled thoughtfully at the floor, asked, "What'd he do before he started not making a living writing poetry?"

"Anything—sold vacuum cleaners, hoboed, went to sea, dealt blackjack, railroaded, canning houses, lumber camps, carnivals, worked on a newspaper—anything."

"Have any money when he left?"

"Three dollars he borrowed from me."

"What'd he say?"

She laughed. "Said if I used whatever influence I had with God while he was gone he'd be back at dinnertime with a surprise for me."

Spade raised his eyebrows. "You were on good terms?"

"Oh, yes. Our last fight had been patched up a couple of days before."

"When did he leave?"

"Thursday afternoon; three o'clock, I guess."

"Got any photographs of him?"

"Yes."

She went to a table by one of the windows, pulled a drawer out, and turned toward Spade again with a photograph in her hand.

Spade looked at the picture of a thin face with deep-set eyes, a sensual mouth, and a heavily lined forehead topped by a disorderly mop of coarse blond hair.

He put Haven's photograph in his pocket and picked up his hat. He turned toward the door, halted.

"What kind of poet is he? Pretty good?"

She shrugged. "That depends on who you ask."

"Any of it around here?"

"No." She smiled. "Think he's hiding between pages?"

"You never can tell what'll lead to what. I'll be back some time. Think things over and see if you can't find some way of loosening up a little more. 'Bye."

He walked down Post Street to Mulford's book store and asked for a volume of Haven's poetry.

"I'm sorry," the girl said. "I sold my last copy last week"—she smiled—"to Mr. Haven himself. I can order it for you."

"You know him?"

"Only through selling his books."

Spade pursed his lips, asked, "What day was it?" He gave her one of his business cards. "Please. It's important."

She went to a desk, turned the pages of a red-bound sales-book, and came back to him with the book open in her hand.

"It was last Wednesday," she said, "and we delivered it to a Mr. Roger Ferris, 1981 Pacific Avenue."

"Thanks a lot," he said.

Outside, he hailed a taxicab and gave the driver Mr. Roger Ferris's address.

The Pacific Avenue house was a four-story, gray-stone one set behind a narrow strip of lawn. The room into which a plump-faced maid ushered Spade was large and high-ceiled.

Spade sat down, but when the maid had gone away he rose and began to walk around the room. He halted at a table where there were three books. One of them had a salmon-colored jacket on which was printed in red an outline drawing of a bolt of lightning striking the ground between a man and a woman, and in black the words:

COLORED LIGHT, BY ELI HAVEN.

Spade picked up the book and went back to his chair.

There was an inscription on the flyleaf—heavy, irregular characters written with blue ink:

TO GOOD OLD BUCK, WHO KNEW HIS COLORED LIGHTS, IN MEMORY OF THEM THERE DAYS.

Eli

Spade turned pages at random and idly read a verse:

Statement

Too many have lived
As we live
For our lives to be
Proof of our living.
Too many have died
As we die
For their deaths to be
Proof of our dying.

He looked up from the book as a man in dinner clothes came into the room. He was not a tall man, but his erectness made him seem tall even when Spade's six feet and a fraction of an inch were standing before him. He had bright blue eyes undimmed by his fifty-some years, a sunburned face in which no muscle sagged, a smooth, broad forehead, and thick, short, nearly white hair. There was dignity in his countenance, and amiability.

He nodded at the book Spade still held. "How do you like it?"

Spade grinned, said, "I guess I'm just a mug," and put the book down. "That's what I came to see you about, though, Mr. Ferris. You know Haven?"

"Yes, certainly. Sit down, Mr. Spade." He sat in a chair not far from Spade's. "I knew him as a kid. He's not in trouble, is he?"

Spade said, "I don't know. I'm trying to find him."

Ferris spoke hesitantly: "Can I ask why?"

"You know Gene Colyer?"

"Yes." Ferris hesitated again, then said, "This is in confidence. I've a chain of picture houses through northern California, you know, and a couple of years ago when I had some labor trouble I was told that Colyer was the man to get in touch with to have it straightened out. That's how I happened to meet him."

"Yes," Spade said dryly. "A lot of people happen to meet Gene that way."

"But what's he got to do with Eli?"

"Wants him found. How long since you've seen him?"

"Last Thursday he was here."

"What time did he leave?"

"Midnight—a little after. He came over in the afternoon around half past three. We hadn't seen each other for years. I persuaded him to stay for dinner—he looked pretty seedy—and lent him some money."

"How much?"

"A hundred and fifty—all I had in the house."

"Say where he was going when he left?"

Ferris shook his head. "He said he'd phone me the next day."

"Did he phone you the next day?"

"No."

"And you've known him all his life?"

"Not exactly, but he worked for me fifteen or sixteen years ago when I had a carnival company—Great Eastern and Western Combined Shows—with a partner for a while and then by myself, and I always liked the kid."

"How long before Thursday since you'd seen him?"

"Lord knows," Ferris replied. "I'd lost track of him for years. Then, Wednesday, out of a clear sky, that book came, with no address or anything, just that stuff written in the front, and the next morning he called me up. I was tickled to death to know he was still alive and doing something with himself. So he came over that afternoon and we put in about nine hours straight talking about old times."

"Tell you much about what he'd been doing since then?"

"Just that he'd been knocking around, doing one thing and another, taking the breaks as they came. He didn't complain much; I had to make him take the hundred and fifty."

Spade stood up.

"Thanks ever so much, Mr. Ferris. I—"

Ferris interrupted him: "Not at all, and if there's anything I can do, call on me."

Spade looked at his watch. "Can I phone my office to see if anything's turned up?"

"Certainly; there's a phone in the next room, to the right."

Spade said, "Thanks," and went out.

When he returned he was rolling a cigarette. His face was wooden.

"Any news?" Ferris asked.

"Yes. Colyer's called the job off. He says Haven's body's been found in some bushes on the other side of San Jose, with three bullets in it." He smiled, adding mildly, "He *told* me he might be able to find out something through his connections."

Morning sunshine, coming through the curtains that screened Spade's office windows, put two fat, yellow rectangles on the floor and gave everything in the room a yellow tint.

He sat at his desk, staring meditatively at a newspaper. He did not look up when Effie Perine came in from the outer office.

She said, "Mrs. Haven is here."

He raised his head then and said, "That's better. Push her in."

Mrs. Haven came in quickly. Her face was white and she was shivering in spite of her fur coat and the warmth of the day.

She came straight to Spade and asked, "Did Gene kill him?"

Spade said, "I don't know."

"I've got to know," she cried.

Spade took her hands.

"Here, sit down." He led her to a chair. He asked, "Colyer tell you he'd called the job off?"

She stared at him in amazement. "He what?"

"He left word here last night that your husband had been found and he wouldn't need me any more."

She hung her head and her words were barely audible:

"Then he did."

Spade shrugged. "Maybe only an innocent man could've afforded to call it off then, or maybe he was guilty, but had brains enough and nerve enough to—"

She was not listening to him. She was leaning toward him, speaking earnestly:

"But, Mr. Spade, you're not going to drop it like that? You're not going to let him stop you?"

While she was speaking his telephone bell rang. He said, "Excuse me," and picked up the receiver.

"Yes? . . . Uh-huh . . . So?" He pursed his lips. "I'll let you know." He pushed the telephone aside slowly and faced Mrs. Haven again. "Colyer's outside."

"Does he know I'm here?" she asked quickly.

"Couldn't say." He stood up, pretending he was not watching her closely. "Do you care?"

She pinched her lower lip between her teeth, said "No" hesitantly.

"Fine. I'll have him in."

She raised a hand as if in protest, then let it drop, and her white face was composed.

"Whatever you want," she said.

Spade opened the door, said, "Hello, Colyer. Come on in. We were just talking about you."

Colyer nodded and came into the office, holding his stick in one hand, his hat in the other.

"How are you this morning, Julia? You ought to've phoned me. I'd've driven you back to town."

"I—I didn't know what I was doing."

Colyer looked at her for a moment longer, then shifted the focus of his expressionless green eyes to Spade's face.

"Well, have you been able to convince her I didn't do it?"

"We hadn't got around to that," Spade said. "I was just trying to find out how much reason there was for suspecting you. Sit down."

Colyer sat down somewhat carefully, asked, "And?"

"And then you arrived."

Colyer nodded gravely.

"All right, Spade," he said; "you're hired again to prove to Mrs. Haven that I didn't have anything to do with it."

"Gene!" she exclaimed in a choked voice and held her hands out toward him appealingly. "I don't think you did—I don't want to think you did—but I'm so afraid."

She put her hands to her face and began to cry.

Colyer went over to the woman.

"Take it easy," he said. "We'll kick it out together."

Spade went into the outer office, shutting the door behind him.

Effie Perine stopped typing a letter.

He grinned at her, said, "Somebody ought to write a book about people sometime—they're peculiar," and went over to the water bottle. "You've got Wally Kellogg's number. Call him up and ask him where I can find Tom Minera."

He returned to the inner office.

Mrs. Haven had stopped crying.

She said, "I'm sorry."

Spade said, "It's all right." He looked sidewise at Colyer. "I still got my job?"

"Yes," Colyer cleared his throat. "But if there's nothing special right now, I'd better take Mrs. Haven home."

"O.K., but there's one thing: According to the *Chronicle*, you identified him. How come you were down there?"

"I went down when I heard they'd found a body," Colyer replied deliberately. "I told you I had connections. I heard about the body through them."

Spade said, "All right; be seeing you," and opened the door for them.

When the corridor door closed behind them, Effie Perine said, "Minera's at the Buxton on Army Street."

Spade said, "Thanks." He went into the inner office to get his hat. On his way out he said, "If I'm not back in a couple of months tell them to look for my body there."

Spade walked down a shabby corridor to a battered green door marked "411." The murmur of voices came through the door, but no words could be distinguished. He stopped listening and knocked.

An obviously disguised male voice asked, "What is it?"

"I want to see Tom. This is Sam Spade."

A pause, then: "Tom ain't here."

Spade put a hand on the knob and shook the frail door.

"Come on, open up," he growled.

Presently the door was opened by a thin, dark man of twenty-five or -six who tried to make his beady dark eyes guileless while saying:

"I didn't think it was your voice at first."

The slackness of his mouth made his chin seem even smaller than it was. His green-striped shirt, open at the neck, was not clean. His gray pants were carefully pressed.

"You've got to be careful these days," Spade said solemnly, and went through the doorway into a room where two men were trying to seem uninterested in his arrival.

One of them leaned against the window sill filing his fingernails. The other was tilted back in a chair with his feet on the edge of a table and a newspaper spread between his hands. They glanced at Spade in unison and went on with their occupations.

Spade said cheerfully, "Always glad to meet any friends of Tom Minera's."

Minera finished shutting the door and said awkwardly:

"Uh—yes—Mr. Spade, meet Mr. Conrad and Mr. James."

Conrad, the man at the window, made a vaguely polite gesture with the nail file in his hand. He was a few years older than Minera, of average height, sturdily built, with a thick-featured, dull-eyed face.

James lowered his paper for an instant to look coolly, appraisingly at Spade and say, "How'r'ye, brother?" Then he returned to his reading. He was as sturdily built as Conrad, but taller, and his face had a shrewdness the other's lacked.

"Ah," Spade said, "and friends of the late Eli Haven."

The man at the window jabbed a finger with his nail file, and cursed it bitterly.

Minera moistened his lips, and then spoke rapidly, with a whining note in his voice:

"But on the level, Spade, we hadn't none of us seen him for a week."

Spade seemed mildly amused by the dark man's manner.

"What do you think he was killed for?"

"All I know is what the paper says: His pockets was all turned inside out and there wasn't as much as a match on him." He drew down the ends of his mouth. "But far as I know he didn't have no dough. He didn't have none Tuesday night."

Spade, speaking softly, said, "I hear he got some Thursday night."

Minera, behind Spade, caught his breath audibly.

James said, "I guess you ought to know. I don't."

"He ever work with you boys?"

James slowly put aside his newspaper and took his feet off the table. His interest in Spade's question seemed great enough, but almost impersonal.

"Now what do you mean by that?"

Spade pretended surprise. "But you boys must work at something?"

Minera came around to Spade's side.

"Aw, listen, Spade," he said. "This guy Haven was just a guy we knew. We didn't have nothing to do with rubbing him out; we don't know nothing about it. You know, we—"

Three deliberate knocks sounded at the door.

Minera and Conrad looked at James, who nodded, but by then Spade, moving swiftly, had reached the door and was opening it.

Roger Ferris was there.

Spade blinked at Ferris, Ferris at Spade.

Then Ferris put out his hand and said, "I *am* glad to see you."

"Come on in," Spade said.

"Look at this, Mr. Spade."

Ferris's hand trembled as he took a slightly soiled envelope from his pocket.

Ferris's name and address were typewritten on the envelope. There was no postage stamp on it. Spade took out the enclosure, a narrow slip of cheap white paper, and unfolded it. On it was typewritten:

> You had better come to Room No 411 Buxton Hotel on Army St at 5 PM this afternoon on account of Thursday night.

There was no signature.

Spade said, "It's a long time before five o'clock."

"It is," Ferris agreed with emphasis. "I came as soon as I got that. It was Thursday night Eli was at my house."

Minera was jostling Spade, asking, "What is all this?"

Spade held the note up for the dark man to read.

He read it and yelled, "Honest, Spade, I don't know nothing about that letter."

"Does anybody?" Spade asked.

Conrad said "No" hastily.

James said, "What letter?"

Spade looked dreamily at Ferris for a moment, then said, as if speaking to himself:

"Of course, Haven was trying to shake you down."

Ferris's face reddened. "What?"

"Shake-down," Spade repeated patiently; "money, blackmail."

"Look here, Spade," Ferris said earnestly, "you don't really believe what you said? What would he have to blackmail me on?"

" 'To good old Buck' "—Spade quoted the dead poet's inscription—" 'who knew his colored lights, in memory of them there days.' " He looked somberly at Ferris from beneath slightly raised brows. "What colored lights? What's the circus and carnival slang term for kicking a guy off a train while it's going? Red-lighting. Sure, that's it—red lights. Who'd you red-light, Ferris, that Haven knew about?"

Minera went over to a chair, sat down, put his elbows on his knees, his head between his hands, and stared blankly at the floor.

Conrad was breathing as if he had been running.

Spade addressed Ferris: "Well?"

Ferris wiped his face with a handkerchief, put the handkerchief in his pocket, and said simply:

"It was a shake-down."

"And you killed him."

Ferris's blue eyes, looking into Spade's yellow-gray ones, were clear and steady, as was his voice.

"I did not," he said. "I swear I did not. Let me tell you what happened. He sent me the book, as I told you, and I knew right away what that joke he wrote in the front meant. So the next day, when he phoned me and said he was coming over to talk over old times and to try to borrow some money for old times' sake, I knew what he meant again, and I went down to the bank and drew out ten thousand dollars. You can check that up. It's the Seamen's National."

"I will," Spade said.

"As it turned out, I didn't need that much. He wasn't very big-time, and I talked him into taking five thousand. I put the other five back in the bank next day. You can check that up."

"I will," Spade said.

"I told him I wasn't going to stand for any more taps, this five thousand was the first and last. I made him sign a paper saying he'd helped in the—in what I'd done —and he signed it. He left sometime around midnight, and that's the last I ever saw of him."

Spade tapped the envelope Ferris had given him.

"And how about this note?"

"A messenger boy brought it at noon, and I came right over. Eli had assured me he hadn't said anything to anybody, but I didn't know. I had to face it, whatever it was."

Spade turned to the others, his face wooden. "Well?"

Minera and Conrad looked at James, who made an impatient grimace and said:

"Oh, sure, we sent him the letter. Why not? We was friends of Eli's, and we hadn't been able to find him since he went to put the squeeze to this baby, and then he turns up dead, so we kind of like to have the gent come over and explain things."

"You knew about the squeeze?"

"Sure. We was all together when he got the idea."

"How'd he happen to get the idea?" Spade asked.

James spread the fingers of his left hand.

"We'd been drinking and talking—you know the way a bunch of guys will, about all they'd seen and done—and he told a yarn about once seeing a guy boot another off a train into a canyon, and he happens to mention the name of the guy that done the booting—Buck Ferris. And somebody says, 'What's this Ferris look like?' Eli tells him what he looked like then, saying he ain't seen him for fifteen years; and whoever it is whistles and says, 'I bet that's the Ferris that owns about half the movie joints in the state. I bet you he'd give something to keep that back trail covered!' "

"Well, the idea kind of hit Eli. You could see that. He thought a little while and then he got cagey. He asked what this movie Ferris's first name is, and when the other guy tells him, 'Roger,' he makes out he's disappointed and says, 'No, it ain't him. His first name was Martin.' We all give him the ha-ha and he finally admits he's thinking of seeing the gent, and when he called me up Thursday around noon and says he's throwing a party at Pogey Hecker's that night, it ain't no trouble to figure out what's what."

"What was the name of the gentleman who was red-lighted?"

"He wouldn't say. He shut up tight. You couldn't blame him."

"Uh-huh," Spade agreed.

"Then nothing. He never showed up at Pogey's. We tried to get him on the phone around two o'clock in the morning, but his wife said he hadn't been home, so we stuck around till four or five and then decided he had given us a run-around, and made Pogey charge the bill to him, and beat it. I ain't seen him since—dead or alive."

Spade said mildly. "Maybe. Sure you didn't find Eli later that morning, take him riding, swap him bullets for Ferris's five thou, dump him in the—?"

A sharp double knock sounded on the door.

Spade's face brightened. He went to the door and opened it.

A young man came in. He was very dapper, and very well proportioned. He wore a light topcoat and his hands were in its pockets. Just inside the door he stepped to the right, and stood with his back to the wall.

By that time another young man was coming in. He stepped to the left.

Though they did not actually look alike, their common dapperness, the similar trimness of their bodies, and their almost identical positions—backs to wall, hands in pockets, cold, bright eyes studying the occupants of the room—gave them, for an instant, the appearance of twins.

Then Gene Colyer came in. He nodded at Spade, but paid no attention to the others in the room, though James said, "Hello, Gene."

"Anything new?" Colyer asked Spade.

Spade nodded. "It seems this gentleman"—he jerked a thumb at Ferris—"was—"

"Any place we can talk?"

"There's a kitchen back here."

Colyer snapped a "Smear anybody that pops" over his shoulder at the two dapper young men and followed Spade into the kitchen. He sat on the one kitchen chair and stared with unblinking green eyes at Spade while Spade told him what he had learned.

When the private detective had finished, the green-eyed man asked:

"Well, what do you make of it?"

Spade looked thoughtfully at the other. "You've picked up something. I'd like to know what it is."

Colyer said, "They found the gun in a stream a quarter of a mile from where they found him. It's James's—got the mark on it where it was shot out of his hand once in Vallejo."

"That's nice," Spade said.

"Listen. A kid named Thurber says James comes to him last Wednesday and gets him to tail Haven. Thurber picks him up Thursday afternoon, puts him in at Ferris's, and phones James. James tells him to take a plant on the place and let him know where Haven goes when he leaves, but some nervous woman in the neighborhood puts in a rumble about the kid hanging around, and the cops chase him along about ten o'clock."

Spade pursed his lips and stared thoughtfully at the ceiling.

Colyer's eyes were expressionless, but sweat made his round face shiny, and his voice was hoarse.

"Spade," he said, "I'm going to turn him in."

Spade switched his gaze from the ceiling to the protuberant green eyes.

"I've never turned in one of my people before," Colyer said, "but this one goes. Julia's *got* to believe I hadn't anything to do with it if it's one of my people and I turn him in, hasn't she?"

Spade nodded slowly. "I think so."

Colyer suddenly averted his eyes and cleared his throat. When he spoke again it was curtly:

"Well, he goes."

Minera, James, and Conrad were seated when Spade and Colyer came out of the kitchen. Ferris was walking the floor. The two dapper young men had not moved.

Colyer went over to James. "Where's your gun, Louis?" he asked.

James moved his right hand a few inches toward his left breast, stopped it, and said:

"Oh, I didn't bring it."

With his gloved hand—open—Colyer struck James on the side of the face, knocking him out of his chair.

James straightened up, mumbling, "I didn't mean nothing." He put a hand to the side of his face. "I know I oughtn't've done it, Chief, but when he called up and said he didn't like to go up against Ferris without something and didn't have any of his own, I said, 'All right,' and sent it over to him."

Colyer said, "And you sent Thurber over to him, too."

"We were just kind of interested in seeing if he did go through with it," James mumbled.

"And you couldn't've gone there yourself, or sent somebody else?"

"After Thurber had stirred up the whole neighborhood?"

Colyer turned to Spade. "Want us to help you take them in, or want to call the wagon?"

"We'll do it regular," Spade said, and went to the wall telephone.

When he turned away from it his face was wooden, his eyes dreamy. He made a cigarette, lit it, and said to Colyer:

"I'm silly enough to think your Louis has got a lot of right answers in that story of his."

James took his hand down from his bruised cheek and stared at Spade with astonished eyes.

Colyer growled, "What's the matter with you?"

"Nothing," Spade said softly, "except I think you're a little too anxious to slam it on him." He blew smoke out. "Why, for instance, should he drop his gun there when it had marks on it that people knew?"

Colyer said, "You think he's got brains."

"If these boys killed him, knew he was dead, why do they wait till the body's found and things are stirred up before they go after Ferris again? What'd they turn his pockets inside out for if they hijacked him? That's a lot of trouble and only done by folks that kill for some other reason and want to make it look like robbery." He shook his head. "You're too anxious to slam it on them. Why should they—?"

"That's not the point right now," Colyer said. "The point is, why do you keep saying I'm too anxious to slam it on him?"

Spade shrugged. "Maybe to clear yourself with Julia as soon as possible and as clear as possible, maybe even to clear yourself with the police, and then you've got clients."

Colyer said, "What?"

Spade made a careless gesture with his cigarette.

"Ferris," he said blandly. "He killed him, of course."

Colyer's eyelids quivered, though he did not actually blink.

Spade said, "First, he's the last person we know of who saw Eli alive, and that's always a good bet. Second, he's the only person I talked to before Eli's body turned up who cared whether I thought they were holding out on me or not. The rest of you just thought I was hunting for a guy who'd gone away. He knew I was hunting for a man he'd killed, so he had to put himself in the clear. He was even afraid to throw that book away, because it had been sent up by the book store and could be traced, and there might be clerks who'd seen the inscription. Third, he was the only one who thought Eli was just a sweet, clean, lovable boy—for the same reasons. Fourth, that story about a blackmailer showing up at three o'clock in the afternoon, making an easy touch for five grand, and then sticking around till midnight is just silly, no matter how good the booze was. Fifth, the story about the paper Eli signed is still worse, though a forged one could be fixed up easy enough. Sixth, he's got the best reason for anybody we know for wanting Eli dead."

Colyer nodded slowly. "Still—"

"Still nothing," Spade said. "Maybe he did the ten-thousand-out-five-thousand-back trick with his bank, but that was easy. Then he got this feeble-minded blackmailer in his house, stalled him along until the servants had gone to bed, took the borrowed gun away from him, shoved him downstairs into his car, took him for a ride—maybe took him already dead, maybe shot him down there by the bushes—frisked him clean to make identification harder and to make it look like robbery, tossed the gun in the water, and came home—"

He broke off to listen to the sound of a siren in the street. He looked then, for the first time since he had begun to talk, at Ferris.

Ferris's face was ghastly white, but he held his eyes steady.

Spade said, "I've got a hunch, Ferris, that we're going to find out about that red-lighting job, too. You told me you had your carnival company with a partner for a while when Eli was working for you, and then by yourself. We oughtn't to have a lot of trouble finding out about your partner—whether he disappeared, or died a natural death, or is still alive."

Ferris had lost some of his erectness. He wet his lips and said:

"I want to see my lawyer. I don't want to talk till I've seen my lawyer."

Spade said, "It's all right with me. You're up against it, but I don't like blackmailers myself. I think Eli wrote a good epitaph for them in that book back there —'Too many have lived.' "

Edmund Crispin

THE HUNCHBACK CAT

Gervase Fen, a fellow of St. Christopher's College, Oxford, is a professor of English language and literature, who has been described by the mystery writer Catherine Aird as "not so much a detective as someone who happens somehow always to be where the action is." He cultivates, although he pretends not to, eccentrics on the order of an organist named Vintner, a poet named Cadogan and—here is a nice switch on tradition—a chief constable who prefers dabbling in literary criticism to pursuing felons.

Although Fen seems a figure with the mannerisms and tics of a Golden Age detective, someone who would get on well during a country-house weekend with Lord Peter Wimsey, his first adventure (The Case of the Gilded Fly) did not appear until 1944. After that, Fen mysteries were published regularly until 1951. A silence followed that lasted until just before he died, in 1978, when The Glimpses of the Moon appeared and the fires of a Fen revival were fanned by old friends who had not forgotten him.

Fen's creator, Robert Bruce Montgomery (1921–1978), a former schoolteacher who wrote under the name Edmund Crispin, was a classical musician who also composed background music for movies (Carry On, Nurse was one of them). During the long silence before the last Fen novel he became known as one of Britain's leading critics of crime fiction.

"The Hunchback Cat" originally ran in the London Evening Standard and is typical of the brief newspaper detective stories that have been more popular in England than in America.

The Hunchback Cat

W E'RE *ALL* SUPERSTITIOUS," said Fen. And from the assembled party, relaxing by the fire, rose loud cries of dissent. "But we are, you know," Fen persisted, "whether we realize it or not. Let me give you a test."

"All right," they said. "Do."

"Let me tell you about the Copping case."

"A crime," they gloated. "Good."

"And if any of you," said Fen, "can solve it unassisted, he (or she, of course) shall be held to be without stain.

"The Copping family was an old one, and like most old families it had its traditions, the most important of these being, unfortunately, parricide.

"This didn't always take the form of actual *murder*. Sometimes it was accident, and sometimes it was neglect, and sometimes Copping parents were driven by the insufferable behavior of their offspring to open a vein in the bath. None the less, there it was. As the toll mounted with the years, the Coppings inevitably became more and more prone to brood.

"By 1948, however, there were only two Coppings in the direct line left alive —Clifford Copping, a widower, and his daughter Isobel. Isobel, moreover, was married, and consequently no longer lived in the family mansion near Wantage. In August of 1948, however, she and her husband went to Wantage for a short visit. And that was when the thing happened.

"As for me, I was making a detour through Wantage, on my way back from Bath to Oxford, so as to be able to have dinner at the White Hart. And it was in the bar of the White Hart, at shortly after six in the evening, that I got into conversation with Isobel's husband, Peter Doyle. He was drinking a fair amount. And by a quarter to eight he had reached the stage of insisting that I return with him to the Copping house for a meal.

"I didn't at all want to do that, but as he already knew that I'd been proposing to dine at the pub, alone, it was difficult to refuse. So in the end I gave in, and we set out to walk to the house by way of the fields.

"It was a beautiful evening: I enjoyed the walk thoroughly. There was a cat, a handsome little high-stepping tortoiseshell cat, which adopted us, following us the whole way. 'She seems to want to come in,' I said when we arrived at the front door. And, 'That's all right,' said Doyle vaguely. 'Isobel and my father-in-law are both fond of cats.' So she did come in, and she and I were introduced to Isobel together.

"I quite liked Isobel. But it was clear from the first that relations between her and her husband were very strained. We all talked commonplaces for a while, and then Doyle suggested that as there was still a little time to use up before dinner, he should take me to meet his father-in-law, who would probably not be joining us for the meal.

" 'He hasn't been too well recently,' Doyle explained. 'You know, broody, a bit . . . But he'd never forgive me if I let you go away without his meeting you.'

"Well, of course I mumbled the usual things about not wanting to be a nuisance and so forth. And I can tell you, I should have been a good deal more emphatic about them if I'd known then what the inquest subsequently brought out: that for a long time now Clifford Copping had been seriously neurotic, with suicidal tendencies . . . However, I didn't know, so I allowed myself to be overruled. Her father was in the top room of the tower, Isobel said. So to the tower, still accompanied by our faithful cat, Doyle and I duly went.

"It stood apart from the rest of the house, fifty feet high or more, with smooth sheer walls and narrow slits for windows; date about 1450, I should think. I expected it to be fairly ruinous inside, but surprisingly, it wasn't. On the top landing Doyle paused in front of a certain door. I was a little way behind him, still negotiating the last flight of stairs.

" 'If you don't mind waiting a moment, I'll just go in and warn him that you're here,' he said—a proposal which didn't seem to me to march very well with his assurance, earlier on, that his father-in-law would never forgive him if I left without being introduced. However, of course, I agreed—whereupon he produced from his pocket a key which I'd seen Isobel give him, and proceeded to unlock (yes, definitely it *was* locked) and to half-open the door. He looked back at me then, saying in a low voice:

" 'I expect you'll think it's odd, but my father-in-law does like to be locked in here from time to time, so long as it's Isobel who keeps the key: he trusts Isobel completely. Being shut in, and having these tremendously thick walls all around him—it gives him a feeling of security. Of course, locking him*self* in is what he'd really like best, but the doctor won't allow that. That's why all the bolts have been taken away.'

" 'Ah,' I said. And something of what I felt must have showed in my face, because Doyle added:

" 'He's all right, you know . . . But naturally, if you—I mean, would you rather we didn't?'

" '*Yes, I'd very much rather,*' would have been the truthful answer to that. But Doyle's question was plainly of a piece with the Latin *Num?*: It expected a negative —and got one. So then we stopped talking, and while I waited nervously on the stair, Doyle entered the room. And found the body.

"Actually, to be just and exact about it, it was the cat which saw the body first. While we'd been talking, the cat had been looking into the room, and not at all liking what was in there. You know how they arch their backs, and the hair stands up all over the spine . . . ? Well, after about a minute and a half, or perhaps as much as two minutes, Doyle came out again, very slow and white and shaken, and sat down on the top stair with his head in his hands. I could have asked him questions, but I didn't. I went past him into the room and saw for myself.

"There was a kitchen knife and a severed throat and an almost inconceivable mess of blood. When I'd satisfied myself that no one was hidden there (and also that not even a child could possibly have escaped through the tiny windows) I felt Copping's skin and looked at the blood and concluded (correctly, as it turned out) that the wretched man had been dead at least an hour (it was then 8:24 exactly). Then I locked the room again and gave the key back to Doyle, and together we returned to the house, where he telephoned the police and a doctor while I went off on my own and—well, you can guess what I did, can't you?

"The rest is easily told. Copping had last been seen alive at 6:15, by Isobel when she locked him into the tower room; also he'd been seen not more than five minutes before that by two of the servants—so if there was any question of murder, at least it was certain that Doyle hadn't done it . . .

"And fortunately there *was* some question of murder—very much so. True, there were no prints except Copping's own on the knife. But low down on one of the panels of the room you could see traces of the blood, as if a splashed skirt-hem, say, had brushed against it . . . That wasn't done by Doyle or myself; there was no blood on either of us, anywhere. And it wasn't done by Copping in his death-agony —for the simple reason that between the body and the panel a considerable area of floor was innocent of blood-spots.

"All of which meant Isobel.

"Isobel who had had the key of that virtually impregnable room. Isobel who would inherit the whole of her father's estate. Isobel in whose wardrobe, hastily hidden away, the police found a stained mackintosh . . .

"That's really a lot. I told the CID my story, just as I've told it to you. And do you know, at the end of it, they were *still* proposing to arrest Isobel . . . Sheer superstition." Fen got to his feet. "Well, it's been a delightful evening, but I think I'd better be getting along now . . ."

The resultant howl nearly deafened him. He shook his head at them mock-mournfully. "No true rationalists? Really none? But unless you happen to be superstitious, it's simple. Doyle's wife was preparing to divorce him, you see, thereby depriving him of his chance of a share in all that lovely inheritance. He hated her bitterly for that, and in his father-in-law's death he saw a chance of revenge. It was he, of course, who planted the stained mackintosh, in the interim before the arrival of the police: I know that much because by then I'd realized what he was up to, and quite simply followed and watched him, without his being aware of it . . ."

"But Gervase, you haven't explained anything," wailed a fair-haired girl plaintively. "What *we* want to know is what made you suspicious of him in the first place."

Fen laughed. "Oh come now. You're none of you superstitious, you've assured me of that. And not being superstitious, you ought to be aware that it's only in melodramas and ghost stories that little tortoiseshell cats react violently to the sight of corpses. In real life I'm afraid it isn't so. For a cat to get into that alarming state there has to be some much livelier stimulus. A dog was one possibility; but a dog would have made itself heard. So how about another cat? The family were fond of cats, I'd heard, so very likely they owned one. And it wouldn't have been difficult for Doyle to stuff the wretched creature through one of the little windows . . . He'd noticed the blood on the panel, you see—which of course had been smeared there by the cat—and worked it out that if the cat were disposed of, that panel could be made the foundation for a murder charge.

"Naturally, he'd have buried the cat, later. But while he was telephoning the police, I was out looking for the poor thing, which eventually I found in the bushes, near the foot of the tower, where it had crawled to die. A white Siamese it was: no blood on its paws, but a big splotch, acquired obviously at the very moment of Copping's death, on its flank."

"So Copping did it himself," said the fair-haired girl who had spoken before. "What a sell . . ." She hesitated, and then suddenly her eyes grew shrewd. "*Or did he?* The fact that this man Doyle tried to incriminate his wife doesn't necessarily mean that she wasn't guilty, does it?"

"Clever girl." Fen smiled at her. "Actually, it wasn't until twelve weeks later that the servant the police had suborned caught Isobel burning the blood-stained frock she'd worn to kill her father . . . But better late than never. And it makes a good ending, don't you think? Nice to know that these old family traditions die so hard."

Raymond Chandler

TROUBLE IS MY BUSINESS

Probably no one worked harder at being the toughest tough-guy writer on the block than Raymond Chandler (1888–1959), but he could never quite forget that he was a failed oil-company executive who wanted to be a poet. He came to writing after his business career collapsed (he was over fifty when his first Philip Marlowe novel, The Big Sleep, *was published) and was delighted to report on a visit to England that "over here I am not regarded as a mystery writer but as an American novelist of some importance."*

In his essay "The Simple Art of Murder" he defined the lone-wolf American private eye: "He must be the best man in his world and a good enough man for any world. I do not care much about his private life; he is neither a eunuch nor a satyr; I think he might seduce a duchess and I am quite sure he would not spoil a virgin; if he is a man of honor in one thing, he is that in all things. He is a relatively poor man, or he would not be a detective at all. . . . He talks as the man of his age talks, that is, with rude wit, a lively sense of the grotesque, a disgust for sham, and a contempt for pettiness."

*Philip Marlowe was created to personify such a man who walks "the mean streets" but is "neither tarnished nor afraid." Between 1939 and 1958 there were seven Marlowe novels (*Farewell, My Lovely, The Little Sister, *and* The Long Goodbye *among them) plus several collections of short stories in which earlier Chandler private eyes were dusted off and renamed Marlowe ("Trouble Is My Business" is one of these).*

Ross Macdonald, reacting to comparisons of his work with Chandler's, once wrote his publisher that as much as he owed Chandler as a writer, he could not accept his vision of good and evil. "It is conventional to the point of occasional old-maidishness, anti-human to the point of frequent sadism (Chandler hates all women and most men, reserving loveable oldsters, boys and Marlowe for his affection)." But as the critic Julian Symons wrote, we read Chandler "first of all for the writing, and afterward for the California background, the jokes, the social observation, the character of Marlowe."

Trouble Is My Business

1

ANNA HALSEY was about two hundred and forty pounds of middle-aged putty-faced woman in a black tailor-made suit. Her eyes were shiny black shoe buttons, her cheeks were as soft as suet and about the same color. She was sitting behind a black glass desk that looked like Napoleon's tomb and she was smoking a cigarette in a black holder that was not quite as long as a rolled umbrella. She said: "I need a man."

I watched her shake ash from the cigarette to the shiny top of the desk where flakes of it curled and crawled in the draft from an open window.

"I need a man good-looking enough to pick up a dame who has a sense of class, but he's got to be tough enough to swap punches with a power shovel. I need a guy who can act like a bar lizard and backchat like Fred Allen, only better, and get hit on the head with a beer truck and think some cutie in the leg-line topped him with a breadstick."

"It's a cinch," I said. "You need the New York Yankees, Robert Donat, and the Yacht Club Boys."

"You might do," Anna said, "cleaned up a little. Twenty bucks a day and ex's. I haven't brokered a job in years, but this one is out of my line. I'm in the smooth angles of the detecting business and I make money without getting my can knocked off. Let's see how Gladys likes you."

She reversed the cigarette holder and tipped a key on a large black-and-chromium annunciator box. "Come in and empty Anna's ash tray, honey."

We waited.

The door opened and a tall blonde dressed better than the Duchess of Windsor strolled in.

She swayed elegantly across the room, emptied Anna's ash tray, patted her fat cheek, gave me a smooth rippling glance and went out again.

"I think she blushed," Anna said when the door closed. "I guess you still have It."

"She blushed—and I have a dinner date with Darryl Zanuck," I said. "Quit horsing around. What's the story?"

"It's to smear a girl. A red-headed number with bedroom eyes. She's shill for a gambler and she's got her hooks into a rich man's pup."

"What do I do to her?"

Anna sighed. "It's kind of a mean job, Philip, I guess. If she's got a record of any sort, you dig it up and toss it in her face. If she hasn't, which is more likely as she comes from good people, it's kind of up to you. You get an idea once in a while, don't you?"

"I can't remember the last one I had. What gambler and what rich man?"

"Marty Estel."

I started to get up from my chair, then remembered that business had been bad for a month and that I needed the money.

I sat down again.

"You might get into trouble, of course," Anna said. "I never heard of Marty bumping anybody off in the public square at high noon, but he don't play with cigar coupons."

"Trouble is my business," I said. "Twenty-five a day and a guarantee of two-fifty, if I pull the job."

"I gotta make a little something for myself," Anna whined.

"Okay. There's plenty of coolie labor around town. Nice to have seen you looking so well. So long, Anna."

I stood up this time. My life wasn't worth much, but it was worth that much. Marty Estel was supposed to be pretty tough people, with the right helpers and the right protection behind him. His place was out in West Hollywood, on the Strip. He wouldn't pull anything crude, but if he pulled at all, something would pop.

"Sit down, it's a deal," Anna sneered. "I'm a poor old broken-down woman trying to run a high-class detective agency on nothing but fat and bad health, so take my last nickel and laugh at me."

"Who's the girl?" I had sat down again.

"Her name is Harriet Huntress—a swell name for the part too. She lives in the El Milano, nineteen-hundred block on North Sycamore, very high-class. Father went broke back in thirty-one and jumped out of his office window. Mother dead. Kid sister in boarding school back in Connecticut. That might make an angle."

"Who dug up all this?"

"The client got a bunch of photostats of notes the pup had given to Marty. Fifty grand worth. The pup—he's an adopted son to the old man—denied the notes, as kids will. So the client had the photostats experted by a guy named Arbogast, who pretends to be good at that sort of thing. He said okay and dug around a bit, but he's too fat to do legwork, like me, and he's off the case now."

"But I could talk to him?"

"I don't know why not." Anna nodded several of her chins.

"This client—does he have a name?"

"Son, you have a treat coming. You can meet him in person—right now." She tipped the key of her call box again. "Have Mr. Jeeter come in, honey."

"That Gladys," I said, "does she have a steady?"

"You lay off Gladys!" Anna almost screamed at me. "She's worth eighteen grand a year in divorce business to me. Any guy that lays a finger on her, Philip Marlowe, is practically cremated."

"She's got to fall some day," I said. "Why couldn't I catch her?"

The opening door stopped that.

I hadn't seen him in the paneled reception room, so he must have been waiting in a private office. He hadn't enjoyed it. He came in quickly, shut the door quickly, and yanked a thin octagonal platinum watch from his vest and glared at it. He was a tall white-blond type in pin-stripe flannel of youthful cut. There was a small pink rosebud in his lapel. He had a keen frozen face, a little pouchy under the eyes, a little thick in the lips. He carried an ebony cane with a silver knob, wore spats and looked a smart sixty, but I gave him close to ten years more. I didn't like him.

"Twenty-six minutes, Miss Halsey," he said icily. "My time happens to be valuable. By regarding it as valuable I have managed to make a great deal of money."

"Well, we're trying to save you some of the money," Anna drawled. She didn't like him either. "Sorry to keep you waiting, Mr. Jeeter, but you wanted to see the operative I selected and I had to send for him."

"He doesn't look the type to me," Mr. Jeeter said, giving me a nasty glance. "I think more of a gentleman—"

"You're not the Jeeter of *Tobacco Road*, are you?" I asked him.

He came slowly towards me and half lifted the stick. His icy eyes tore at me like claws. "So you insult me," he said. "Me—a man in my position."

"Now wait a minute," Anna began.

"Wait a minute nothing," I said. "This party said I was not a gentleman. Maybe that's okay for a man in his position, whatever it is—but a man in my position doesn't take a dirty crack from anybody. He can't afford to. Unless, of course, it wasn't intended."

Mr. Jeeter stiffened and glared at me. He took his watch out again and looked at it. "Twenty-eight minutes," he said. "I apologize, young man. I had no desire to be rude."

"That's swell," I said. "I knew you weren't the Jeeter in *Tobacco Road* all along."

That almost started him again, but he let it go. He wasn't sure how I meant it.

"A question or two while we are together," I said. "Are you willing to give this Huntress girl a little money—for expenses?"

"Not one cent," he barked. "Why should I?"

"It's got to be a sort of custom. Suppose she married him. What would he have?"

"At the moment a thousand dollars a month from a trust fund established by his mother, my late wife." He dipped his head. "When he is twenty-eight years old, far too much money."

"You can't blame the girl for trying," I said. "Not these days. How about Marty Estel? Any settlements there?"

He crumpled his gray gloves with a purple-veined hand. "The debt is uncollectible. It is a gambling debt."

Anna sighed wearily and flicked ash around on her desk.

"Sure," I said. "But gamblers can't afford to let people welsh on them. After all, if your son had won, Marty would have paid *him*."

"I'm not interested in that," the tall thin man said coldly.

"Yeah, but think of Marty sitting there with fifty grand in notes. Not worth a nickel. How will he sleep nights?"

Mr. Jeeter looked thoughtful. "You mean there is danger of violence?" he suggested, almost suavely.

"That's hard to say. He runs an exclusive place, gets a good movie crowd. He has his own reputation to think of. But he's in a racket and he knows people. Things can happen—a long way off from where Marty is. And Marty is no bathmat. He gets up and walks."

Mr. Jeeter looked at his watch again and it annoyed him. He slammed it back into his vest. "All that is your affair," he snapped. "The district attorney is a personal friend of mine. If this matter seems to be beyond your powers—"

"Yeah," I told him. "But you came slumming down our street just the same. Even if the D.A. is in your vest pocket—along with that watch."

He put his hat on, drew on one glove, tapped the edge of his shoe with his stick, walked to the door and opened it.

"I ask results and I pay for them," he said coldly. "I pay promptly. I even pay generously sometimes, although I am not considered a generous man. I think we all understand one another."

He almost winked then and went on out. The door closed softly against the cushion of air in the door-closer. I looked at Anna and grinned.

"Sweet, isn't he?" she said. "I'd like eight of him for my cocktail set."

I gouged twenty dollars out of her—for expenses.

2

The Arbogast I wanted was John D. Arbogast and he had an office on Sunset near Ivar. I called him up from a phone booth. The voice that answered was fat. I wheezed softly, like the voice of a man who had just won a pie-eating contest.

"Mr. John D. Arbogast?"

"Yeah."

"This is Philip Marlowe, a private detective working on a case you did some experting on. Party named Jeeter."

"Yeah?"

"Can I come up and talk to you about it—after I eat lunch?"

"Yeah." He hung up. I decided he was not a talkative man.

I had lunch and drove out there. It was east of Ivar, an old two-story building faced with brick which had been painted recently. The street floor was stores and a restaurant. The building entrance was the foot of a wide straight stairway to the second floor. On the directory at the bottom I read: John D. Arbogast, Suite 212. I went up the stairs and found myself in a wide straight hall that ran parallel with the street. A man in a smock was standing in an open doorway down to my right. He wore a round mirror strapped to his forehead and pushed back, and his face had a puzzled expression. He went back to his office and shut the door.

I went the other way, about half the distance along the hall. A door on the side away from Sunset was lettered:

JOHN D. ARBOGAST,

EXAMINER OF QUESTIONED DOCUMENTS

PRIVATE INVESTIGATOR

ENTER

The door opened without resistance onto a small windowless anteroom with a couple of easy chairs, some magazines, two chromium smoking stands. There were two floor lamps and a ceiling fixture, all lighted. A door on the other side of the cheap but thick and new rug was lettered:

JOHN D. ARBOGAST,

EXAMINER OF QUESTIONED DOCUMENTS

PRIVATE

A buzzer had rung when I opened the outer door and gone on ringing until it closed. Nothing happened. Nobody was in the waiting room. The inner door didn't open. I went over and listened at the panel—no sound of conversation inside. I knocked. That didn't buy me anything either. I tried the knob. It turned, so I opened the door and went in.

This room had two north windows, both curtained at the sides and both shut tight. There was dust on the sills. There was a desk, two filing cases, a carpet which was just a carpet, and walls which were just walls. To the left another door with a glass panel was lettered:

JOHN D. ARBOGAST

LABORATORY

PRIVATE

I had an idea I might be able to remember the name.

The room in which I stood was small. It seemed almost too small even for the pudgy hand that rested on the edge of the desk, motionless, holding a fat pencil like a carpenter's pencil. The hand had a wrist, hairless as a plate. A buttoned shirt cuff, not too clean, came down out of a coat sleeve. The rest of the sleeve dropped over the far edge of the desk out of sight. The desk was less than six feet long, so he couldn't have been a very tall man. The hand and the ends of the sleeves were all I saw of him from where I stood. I went quietly back through the anteroom and fixed its door so that it couldn't be opened from the outside and put out the three lights and went back to the private office. I went around an end of the desk.

He was fat all right, enormously fat, fatter by far than Anna Halsey. His face, what I could see of it, looked about the size of a basketball. It had a pleasant pinkness, even now. He was kneeling on the floor. He had his large head against the sharp inner corner of the kneehole of the desk, and his left hand was flat on the floor with a piece of yellow paper under it. The fingers were outspread as much as such fat fingers could be, and the yellow paper showed between. He looked as if he were pushing hard on the floor, but he wasn't really. What was holding him up was his own fat. His body was folded down against his enormous thighs, and the thickness and fatness of them held him that way, kneeling, poised solid. It would have taken a couple of good blocking backs to knock him over. That wasn't a very nice idea at the moment, but I had it just the same. I took time out and wiped the back of my neck, although it was not a warm day.

His hair was gray and clipped short and his neck had as many folds as a concertina. His feet were small, as the feet of fat men often are, and they were in black shiny shoes which were sideways on the carpet and close together and neat and nasty. He wore a dark suit that needed cleaning. I leaned down and buried my fingers in the bottomless fat of his neck. He had an artery in there somewhere, probably, but I couldn't find it and he didn't need it any more anyway. Between his bloated knees on the carpet a dark stain had spread and spread—

I knelt in another place and lifted the pudgy fingers that were holding down the piece of yellow paper. They were cool, but not cold, and soft and a little sticky. The paper was from a scratch pad. It would have been very nice if it had had a message on it, but it hadn't. There were vague meaningless marks, not words, not even letters. He had tried to write something after he was shot—perhaps even thought he *was* writing something—but all he managed was some hen scratches.

He had slumped down then, still holding the paper, pinned it to the floor with his fat hand, held on to the fat pencil with his other hand, wedged his torso against his huge thighs, and so died. John D. Arbogast, Examiner of Questioned Documents. Private. Very damned private. He had said "yeah" to me three times over the phone.

And here he was.

I wiped doorknobs with my handkerchief, put off the lights in the anteroom, left the outer door so that it was locked from the outside, left the hallway, left the building and left the neighborhood. So far as I could tell nobody saw me go. So far as I could tell.

3

The El Milano was, as Anna had told me, in the 1900 block on North Sycamore. It was most of the block. I parked fairly near the ornamental forecourt and went along to the pale blue neon sign over the entrance to the basement garage. I walked down a railed ramp into a bright space of glistening cars and cold air. A trim light-colored Negro in a spotless coverall suit with blue cuffs came out of a glass office. His black hair was as smooth as a bandleader's.

"Busy?" I asked him.

"Yes and no, sir."

"I've got a car outside that needs a dusting. About five bucks worth of dusting."

It didn't work. He wasn't the type. His chestnut eyes became thoughtful and remote. "That is a good deal of dusting, sir. May I ask if anything else would be included?"

"A little. Is Miss Harriet Huntress' car in?"

He looked. I saw him look along the glistening row at a canary-yellow convertible which was about as inconspicuous as a privy on the front lawn.

"Yes, sir. It is in."

"I'd like her apartment number and a way to get up there without going through the lobby. I'm a private detective." I showed him a buzzer. He looked at the buzzer. It failed to amuse him.

He smiled the faintest smile I ever saw. "Five dollars is nice money, sir, to a working man. It falls a little short of being nice enough to make me risk my position. About from here to Chicago short, sir. I suggest that you save your five dollars, sir, and try the customary mode of entry."

"You're quite a guy," I said. "What are you going to be when you grow up—a five-foot shelf?"

"I am already grown up, sir. I am thirty-four years old, married happily, and have two children. Good afternoon, sir."

He turned on his heel. "Well, goodbye," I said. "And pardon my whiskey breath. I just got in from Butte."

I went back up along the ramp and wandered along the street to where I should have gone in the first place. I might have known that five bucks and a buzzer wouldn't buy me anything in a place like the El Milano.

The Negro was probably telephoning the office right now.

The building was a huge white stucco affair, Moorish in style, with great fretted lanterns in the forecourt and huge date palms. The entrance was at the inside corner of an L, up marble steps, through an arch framed in California or dishpan mosaic.

A doorman opened the door for me and I went in. The lobby was not quite as big as the Yankee Stadium. It was floored with a pale blue carpet with sponge rubber underneath. It was so soft it made me want to lie down and roll. I waded over to the desk and put an elbow on it and was stared at by a pale thin clerk with one of those mustaches that get stuck under your fingernail. He toyed with it and looked past my shoulder at an Ali Baba oil jar big enough to keep a tiger in.

"Miss Huntress in?"

"Who shall I announce?"

"Mr. Marty Estel."

That didn't take any better than my play in the garage. He leaned on something with his left foot. A blue-and-gilt door opened at the end of the desk and a large sandy-haired man with cigar ash on his vest came out and leaned absently on the end of the desk and stared at the Ali Baba oil jar, is if trying to make up his mind whether it was a spittoon.

The clerk raised his voice. "You are Mr. Marty Estel?"

"From him."

"Isn't that a little different? And what is your name, sir, if one may ask?"

"One may ask," I said. "One may not be told. Such are my orders. Sorry to be stubborn and all that rot."

He didn't like my manner. He didn't like anything about me. "I'm afraid I can't announce you," he said coldly. "Mr. Hawkins, might I have your advice on a matter?"

The sandy-haired man took his eyes off the oil jar and slid along the desk until he was within blackjack range of me.

"Yes, Mr. Gregory?" He yawned.

"Nuts to both of you," I said. "And that includes your lady friends."

Hawkins grinned. "Come into my office, bo. We'll kind of see if we can get you straightened out."

I followed him into the doghole he had come out of. It was large enough for a pint-sized desk, two chairs, a knee-high cuspidor, and an open box of cigars. He placed his rear end against the desk and grinned at me sociably.

"Didn't play it very smooth, did you, bo? I'm the house man here. Spill it."

"Some days I feel like playing smooth," I said, "and some days I feel like playing it like a waffle iron." I got my wallet out and showed him the buzzer and the small photostat of my license behind a celluloid window.

"One of the boys, huh?" He nodded. "You ought to of asked for me in the first place."

"Sure. Only I never heard of you. I want to see this Huntress frail. She doesn't know me, but I have business with her, and it's not noisy business."

He made a yard and a half sideways and cocked his cigar in the other corner of his mouth. He looked at my right eyebrow. "What's the gag? Why try to apple polish the dinghe downstairs? You gettin' any expense money?"

"Could be."

"I'm nice people," he said. "But I gotta protect the guests."

"You're almost out of cigars," I said, looking at the ninety or so in the box. I lifted a couple, smelled them, tucked a folded ten-dollar bill below them and put them back.

"That's cute," he said. "You and me could get along. What you want done?"

"Tell her I'm from Marty Estel. She'll see me."

"It's the job if I get a kickback."

"You won't. I've got important people behind me."

I started to reach for my ten, but he pushed my hand away. "I'll take a chance," he said. He reached for his phone and asked for suite 814 and began to hum. His humming sounded like a cow being sick. He leaned forward suddenly and his face became a honeyed smile. His voice dripped.

"Miss Huntress? This is Hawkins, the house man. Hawkins. Yeah . . . Hawkins. Sure, you meet a lot of people, Miss Huntress. Say, there's a gentleman in my office wanting to see you with a message from Mr. Estel. We can't let him up without your say so, because he don't want to give us no name . . . Yeah, Hawkins, the house detective, Miss Huntress. Yeah, he says you don't know him personal, but he looks okay to me . . . Okay. Thanks a lot, Miss Huntress. Serve him right up."

He put the phone down and patted it gently.

"All you needed was some background music," I said.

"You can ride up," he said dreamily. He reached absently into his cigar box and removed the folded bill. "A darb," he said softly. "Every time I think of that dame I have to go out and walk around the block. Let's go."

We went out to the lobby again and Hawkins took me to the elevator and highsigned me in.

As the elevator doors closed I saw him on his way to the entrance, probably for his walk around the block.

The elevator had a carpeted floor and mirrors and indirect lighting. It rose as softly as the mercury in a thermometer. The doors whispered open, I wandered over the moss they used for a hall carpet and came to a door marked 814. I pushed a little button beside it, chimes rang inside and the door opened.

She wore a street dress of pale green wool and a small cockeyed hat that hung on her ear like a butterfly. Her eyes were wide-set and there was thinking room between them. Their color was lapis-lazuli blue and the color of her hair was dusky red, like a fire under control but still dangerous. She was too tall to be cute. She wore plenty of make-up in the right places and the cigarette she was poking at me had a built-on mouthpiece about three inches long. She didn't look hard, but she looked as if she had heard all the answers and remembered the ones she thought she might be able to use sometime.

She looked me over coolly. "Well what's the message, brown eyes?"

"I'd have to come in," I said. "I never could talk on my feet."

She laughed disinterestedly and I slid past the end of her cigarette into a long rather narrow room with plenty of nice furniture, plenty of windows, plenty of drapes, plenty of everything. A fire blazed behind a screen, a big log on top of a gas teaser. There was a silk Oriental rug in front of a nice rose davenport in front of the nice fire, and beside that there was Scotch and swish on a tabouret, ice in a bucket, everything to make a man feel at home.

"You'd better have a drink," she said. "You probably can't talk without a glass in your hand."

I sat down and reached for the Scotch. The girl sat in a deep chair and crossed her knees. I thought of Hawkins walking around the block. I could see a little something in his point of view.

"So you're from Marty Estel," she said, refusing a drink.

"Never met him."

"I had an idea to that effect. What's the racket, bum? Marty will love to hear how you used his name."

"I'm shaking in my shoes. What made you let me up?"

"Curiosity. I've been expecting lads like you any day. I never dodge trouble. Some kind of a dick, aren't you?"

I lit a cigarette and nodded. "Private. I have a little deal to propose."

"Propose it." She yawned.

"How much will you take to lay off young Jeeter?"

She yawned again. "You interest me—so little I could hardly tell you."

"Don't scare me to death. Honest, how much are you asking? Or is that an insult?"

She smiled. She had a nice smile. She had lovely teeth. "I'm a bag girl now," she said. "I don't have to ask. They bring it to me, tied up with ribbon."

"The old man's a little tough. They say he draws a lot of water."

"Water doesn't cost much."

I nodded and drank some more of my drink. It was good Scotch. In fact it was perfect. "His idea is you get nothing. You get smeared. You get put in the middle. I can't see it that way."

"But you're working for him."

"Sounds funny, doesn't it? There's probably a smart way to play this, but I just can't think of it at the moment. How much would you take—or would you?"

"How about fifty grand?"

"Fifty grand for you and another fifty for Marty?"

She laughed. "Now, you ought to know Marty wouldn't like me to mix in his business. I was just thinking of my end."

She crossed her legs the other way. I put another lump of ice in my drink.

"I was thinking of five hundred," I said.

"Five hundred what?" She looked puzzled.

"Dollars—not Rolls-Royces."

She laughed heartily. "You amuse me. I ought to tell you to go to hell, but I like brown eyes. Warm brown eyes with flecks of gold in them."

"You're throwing it away. I don't have a nickel."

She smiled and fitted a fresh cigarette between her lips. I went over to light it for her. Her eyes came up and looked into mine. Hers had sparks in them.

"Maybe I have a nickel already," she said softly.

"Maybe that's why he hired the fat boy—so you couldn't make him dance." I sat down again.

"Who hired what fat boy?"

"Old Jeeter hired a fat boy named Arbogast. He was on the case before me. Didn't you know? He got bumped off this afternoon."

I said it quite casually for the shock effect, but she didn't move. The provocative smile didn't leave the corners of her lips. Her eyes didn't change. She made a dim sound with her breath.

"Does it have to have something to do with me?" she asked quietly.

"I don't know. I don't know who murdered him. It was done in his office, around noon or a little later. It may not have anything to do with the Jeeter case. But it happened pretty pat—just after I had been put on the job and before I got a chance to talk to him."

She nodded. "I see. And you think Marty does things like that. And of course you told the police?"

"Of course I did not."

"You're giving away a little weight there, brother."

"Yeah. But let's get together on a price and it had better be low. Because whatever the cops do to me they'll do plenty to Marty Estel and you when they get the story—if they get it."

"A little spot of blackmail," the girl said coolly. "I think I might call it that. Don't go too far with me, brown eyes. By the way, do I know your name?"

"Philip Marlowe."

"Then listen, Philip. I was in the Social Register once. My family were nice people. Old Man Jeeter ruined my father—all proper and legitimate, the way that kind of heel ruins people—but he ruined him, and my father committed suicide, and my mother died and I've got a kid sister back east in school and perhaps I'm not too damn particular how I get the money to take care of her. And maybe I'm going to take care of old Jeeter one of these days, too—even if I have to marry his son to do it."

"Stepson, adopted son," I said. "No relation at all."

"It'll hurt him just as hard, brother. And the boy will have plenty of the long green in a couple of years. I could do worse—even if he does drink too much."

"You wouldn't say that in front of him, lady."

"No? Take a look behind you, gumshoes. You ought to have the wax taken out of your ears."

I stood up and turned fast. He stood about four feet from me. He had come out of some door and sneaked across the carpet and I had been too busy being clever with nothing on the ball to hear him. He was big, blond, dressed in a rough sporty suit, with a scarf and open-neck shirt. He was red-faced and his eyes glittered and they were not focusing any too well. He was a bit drunk for that early in the day.

"Beat it while you can still walk," he sneered at me. "I heard it. Harry can say anything she likes about me. I like it. Dangle, before I knock your teeth down your throat!"

The girl laughed behind me. I didn't like that. I took a step towards the big blond boy. His eyes blinked. Big as he was, he was a pushover.

"Ruin him, baby," the girl said coldly behind my back. "I love to see these hard numbers bend at the knees."

I looked back at her with a leer. That was a mistake. He was wild, probably, but he could still hit a wall that didn't jump. He hit me while I was looking back over my shoulder. It hurts to be hit that way. He hit me plenty hard, on the back end of the jawbone.

I went over sideways, tried to spread my legs, and slid on the silk rug. I did a nose dive somewhere or other and my head was not as hard as the piece of furniture it smashed into.

For a brief blurred moment I saw his red face sneering down at me in triumph. I think I was a little sorry for him—even then.

Darkness folded down and I went out.

4

When I came to, the light from the windows across the room was hitting me square in the eyes. The back of my head ached. I felt it and it was sticky. I moved around slowly, like a cat in a strange house, got up on my knees and reached for the bottle of Scotch on the tabouret at the end of the davenport. By some miracle I hadn't knocked it over. Falling I had hit my head on the clawlike leg of a chair. That had hurt me a lot more than young Jeeter's haymaker. I could feel the sore place on my jaw all right, but it wasn't important enough to write in my diary.

I got up on my feet, took a swig of the Scotch and looked around. There wasn't anything to see. The room was empty. It was full of silence and the memory of a nice perfume. One of those perfumes you don't notice until they are almost gone, like the last leaf on a tree. I felt my head again, touched the sticky place with my handkerchief, decided it wasn't worth yelling about, and took another drink.

I sat down with the bottle on my knees, listening to traffic noise somewhere, far off. It was a nice room. Miss Harriet Huntress was a nice girl. She knew a few wrong numbers, but who didn't? I should criticize a little thing like that. I took another drink. The level in the bottle was a lot lower now. It was smooth and you hardly noticed it going down. It didn't take half your tonsils with it, like some of the stuff I had to drink. I took some more. My head felt all right now. I felt fine. I felt like singing the Prologue to *Pagliacci*. Yes, she was a nice girl. If she was paying her own rent, she was doing right well. I was for her. She was swell. I used some more of her Scotch.

The bottle was still half full. I shook it gently, stuffed it in my overcoat pocket, put my hat somewhere on my head and left. I made the elevator without hitting the walls on either side of the corridor, floated downstairs, strolled out into the lobby.

Hawkins, the house dick, was leaning on the end of the desk again, staring at the Ali Baba oil jar. The same clerk was nuzzling at the same itsy-bitsy mustache. I smiled at him. He smiled back. Hawkins smiled at me. I smiled back. Everybody was swell.

I made the front door the first time and gave the doorman two bits and floated down the steps and along the walk to the street and my car. The swift California twilight was falling. It was a lovely night. Venus in the west was as bright as a streetlamp, as bright as life, as bright as Miss Huntress' eyes, as bright as a bottle of Scotch. That reminded me. I got the square bottle out and tapped it with discretion, corked it, and tucked it away again. There was still enough to get home on.

I crashed five red lights on the way back but my luck was in and nobody pinched me. I parked more or less in front of my apartment house and more or less near the curb. I rode to my floor in the elevator, had a little trouble opening the doors and helped myself out with my bottle. I got the key into my door and unlocked it and stepped inside and found the light switch. I took a little more of my medicine before exhausting myself any further. Then I started for the kitchen to get some ice and ginger ale for a real drink.

I thought there was a funny smell in the apartment—nothing I could put a name to offhand—a sort of medicinal smell. I hadn't put it there and it hadn't been there when I went out. But I felt too well to argue about it. I started for the kitchen, got about halfway there.

They came out at me, almost side by side, from the dressing room beside the wall bed—two of them—with guns. The tall one was grinning. He had his hat low on his forehead and he had a wedge-shaped face that ended in a point, like the bottom half of the ace of diamonds. He had dark moist eyes and a nose so bloodless that it might have been made of white wax. His gun was a Colt Woodsman with a long barrel and the front sight filed off. That meant he thought he was good.

The other was a little terrierlike punk with bristly reddish hair and no hat and watery blank eyes and bat ears and small feet in dirty white sneakers. He had an automatic that looked too heavy for him to hold up, but he seemed to like holding it. He breathed open-mouthed and noisily and the smell I had noticed came from him in waves—menthol.

"Reach, you bastard," he said.

I put my hands up. There was nothing else to do.

This little one circled around to the side and came at me from the side. "Tell us we can't get away with it," he sneered.

"You can't get away with it," I said.

The tall one kept on grinning loosely and his nose kept on looking as if it was made of white wax. The little one spat on my carpet. "Yah!" He came close to me, leering, and made a pass at my chin with the big gun.

I dodged. Ordinarily that would have been just something which, in the circumstances, I had to take and like. But I was feeling better than ordinary. I was a world-beater. I took them in sets, guns and all. I took the little man around the throat and jerked him hard against my stomach, put a hand over his little gun hand and knocked the gun to the floor. It was easy. Nothing was bad about it but his breath. Blobs of saliva came out on his lips. He spit curses.

The tall man stood and leered and didn't shoot. He didn't move. His eyes looked a little anxious, I thought, but I was too busy to make sure. I went down behind the little punk, still holding him, and got hold of his gun. That was wrong. I ought to have pulled my own.

I threw him away from me and he reeled against a chair and fell down and began to kick the chair savagely. The tall man laughed.

"It ain't got any firing pin in it," he said.

"Listen," I told him earnestly, "I'm half full of good Scotch and ready to go places and get things done. Don't waste much of my time. What do you boys want?"

"It still ain't got any firing pin in it," Waxnose said. "Try and see. I don't never let Frisky carry a loaded rod. He's too impulsive. You got a nice arm action there, pal. I will say that for you."

Frisky sat up on the floor and spat on the carpet again and laughed. I pointed the muzzle of the big automatic at the floor and squeezed the trigger. It clicked dryly, but from the balance it felt as if it had cartridges in it.

"We don't mean no harm," Waxnose said. "Not this trip. Maybe next trip? Who knows? Maybe you're a guy that will take a hint. Lay off the Jeeter kid is the word. See?"

"No."

"You won't do it?"

"No, I don't see. Who's the Jeeter kid?"

Waxnose was not amused. He waved his long .22 gently. "You oughta get your memory fixed, pal, about the same time you get your door fixed. A pushover that was. Frisky just blew it in with his breath."

"I can understand that," I said.

"Gimme my gat," Frisky yelped. He was up off the floor again, but this time he rushed his partner instead of me.

"Lay off, dummy," the tall one said. "We just got a message for a guy. We don't blast him. Not today."

"Says you!" Frisky snarled and tried to grab the .22 out of Waxnose's hand. Waxnose threw him to one side without trouble but the interlude allowed me to switch the big automatic to my left hand and jerk out my Luger. I showed it to Waxnose. He nodded, but did not seem impressed.

"He ain't got no parents," he said sadly. "I just let him run around with me. Don't pay him no attention unless he bites you. We'll be on our way now. You get the idea. Lay off the Jeeter kid."

"You're looking at a Luger," I said. "Who is the Jeeter kid? And maybe we'll have some cops before you leave."

He smiled wearily. "Mister, I pack this small-bore because I can shoot. If you think you can take me, go to it."

"Okay," I said. "Do you know anybody named Arbogast?"

"I meet such a lot of people," he said, with another weary smile. "Maybe yes, maybe no. So long, pal. Be pure."

He strolled over to the door, moving a little sideways, so that he had me covered all the time, and I had him covered, and it was just a case of who shot first and straightest, or whether it was worthwhile to shoot at all, or whether I could hit anything with so much nice warm Scotch in me. I let him go. He didn't look like a killer to me, but I could have been wrong.

The little man rushed me again while I wasn't thinking about him. He clawed his big automatic out of my left hand, skipped over to the door, spat on the carpet again, and slipped out. Waxnose backed after him—long sharp face, white nose, pointed chin, weary expression. I wouldn't forget him.

He closed the door softly and I stood there, foolish, holding my gun. I heard the elevator come up and go down again and stop. I still stood there. Marty Estel wouldn't be very likely to hire a couple of comics like that to throw a scare into anybody. I thought about that, but thinking got me nowhere. I remembered the half-bottle of Scotch I had left and went into executive session with it.

An hour and a half later I felt fine, but I still didn't have any ideas. I just felt sleepy.

The jarring of the telephone bell woke me. I had dozed off in the chair, which was a bad mistake, because I woke up with two flannel blankets in my mouth, a splitting headache, a bruise on the back of my head and another on my jaw, neither of them larger than a Yakima apple, but sore for all that. I felt terrible. I felt like an amputated leg.

I crawled over to the telephone and humped myself in a chair beside it and answered it. The voice dripped icicles.

"Mr. Marlowe? This is Mr. Jeeter. I believe we met this morning. I'm afraid I was a little stiff with you."

"I'm a little stiff myself. Your son poked me in the jaw. I mean your stepson, or your adopted son—or whatever he is."

"He is both my stepson and my adopted son. Indeed?" He sounded interested. "And where did you meet him?"

"In Miss Huntress' apartment."

"Oh I see." There had been a sudden thaw. The icicles had melted. "Very interesting. What did Miss Huntress have to say?"

"She liked it. She liked him poking me in the jaw."

"I see. And why did he do that?"

"She had him hid out. He overheard some of our talk. He didn't like it."

"I see. I have been thinking that perhaps some consideration—not large, of course—should be granted to her for her cooperation. That is, if we can secure it."

"Fifty grand is the price."

"I'm afraid I don't—"

"Don't kid me," I snarled. "Fifty thousand dollars. Fifty grand. I offered her five hundred—just for a gag."

"You seem to treat this whole business in a spirit of considerable levity," he snarled back. "I am not accustomed to that sort of thing and I don't like it."

I yawned. I didn't give a damn if school kept in or not. "Listen, Mr. Jeeter, I'm a great guy to horse around, but I have my mind on the job just the same. And there are some very unusual angles to this case. For instance a couple of gunmen just stuck me up in my apartment here and told me to lay off the Jeeter case. I don't see why it should get so tough."

"Good heavens!" He sounded shocked. "I think you had better come to my house at once and we will discuss matters. I'll send my car for you. Can you come right away?"

"Yeah. But I can drive myself. I—"

"No. I'm sending my car and chauffeur. His name is George; you may rely upon him absolutely. He should be there in about twenty minutes."

"Okay," I said. "That just gives me time to drink my dinner. Have him park around the corner of Kenmore, facing towards Franklin." I hung up.

When I'd had a hot-and-cold shower and put on some clean clothes I felt more respectable. I had a couple of drinks, small ones for a change, and put a light overcoat on and went down to the street.

The car was there already. I could see it half a block down the side street. It looked like a new market opening. It had a couple of head lamps like the one on the front end of a streamliner, two amber foglights hooked to the front fender, and a couple of sidelights as big as ordinary headlights. I came up beside it and stopped and a man stepped out of the shadows, tossing a cigarette over his shoulder with a neat flip of the wrist. He was tall, broad, dark, wore a peaked cap, a Russian tunic with a Sam Browne belt, shiny leggings and breeches that flared like an English staff major's whipcords.

"Mr. Marlowe?" He touched the peak of his cap with a gloved forefinger.

"Yeah," I said. "At ease. Don't tell me that's Old Man Jeeter's car."

"One of them." It was a cool voice that could get fresh.

He opened the rear door and I got in and sank down into the cushions and George slid under the wheel and started the big car. It moved away from the curb and around the corner with as much noise as a bill makes in a wallet. We went west. We seemed to be drifting with the current, but we passed everything. We slid through the heart of Hollywood, the west end of it, down to the Strip and along the glitter of that to the cool quiet of Beverly Hills where the bridle path divides the boulevard.

We gave Beverly Hills the swift and climbed along the foothills, saw the distant lights of the university buildings and swung north into Bel-Air. We began to slide up long narrow streets with high walls and no sidewalks and big gates. Lights on mansions glowed politely through the early night. Nothing stirred. There was no sound but the soft purr of the tires on concrete. We swung left again and I caught a sign which read Calvello Drive. Halfway up this George started to swing the car wide to make a left turn in at a pair of twelve-foot wrought-iron gates. Then something happened.

A pair of lights flared suddenly just beyond the gates and a horn screeched and a motor raced. A car charged at us fast. George straightened out with a flick of the wrist, braked the car and slipped off his right glove, all in one motion.

The car came on, the lights swaying. "Damn drunk," George swore over his shoulder.

It could be. Drunks in cars go all kinds of places to drink. It could be. I slid down onto the floor of the car and yanked the Luger from under my arm and reached up to open the catch. I opened the door a little and held it that way, looking over the sill. The headlights hit me in the face and I ducked, then came up again as the beam passed.

The other car jammed to a stop. Its door slammed open and a figure jumped out of it, waving a gun and shouting. I heard the voice and knew.

"Reach, you bastards!" Frisky screamed at us.

George put his left hand on the wheel and I opened my door a little more. The little man in the street was bouncing up and down and yelling. Out of the small dark car from which he had jumped came no sound except the noise of its motor.

"This is a heist!" Frisky yelled. "Out of there and line up, you sons of bitches!"

I kicked my door open and started to get out, the Luger down at my side.

"You asked for it!" the little man yelled.

I dropped—fast. The gun in his hand belched flame. Somebody must have put a firing pin in it. Glass smashed behind my head. Out of the corner of my eye, which oughtn't to have had any corners at that particular moment, I saw George make a movement as smooth as a ripple of water. I brought the Luger up and started to squeeze the trigger, but a shot crashed beside me—George.

I held my fire. It wasn't needed now.

The dark car lurched forward and started down the hill furiously. It roared into the distance while the little man out in the middle of the pavement was still reeling grotesquely in the light reflected from the walls.

There was something dark on his face that spread. His gun bounded along the concrete. His little legs buckled and he plunged sideways and rolled and then, very suddenly, became still.

George said, "Yah!" and sniffed at the muzzle of his revolver.

"Nice shooting." I got out of the car, stood there looking at the little man—a crumpled nothing. The dirty white of his sneakers gleamed a little in the side glare of the car's lights.

George got out beside me. "Why me, brother?"

"I didn't fire. I was watching that pretty hip draw of yours. It was sweeter than honey."

"Thanks, pal. They were after Mister Gerald, of course. I usually ferry him home from the club about this time, full of liquor and bridge losses."

We went over to the little man and looked down at him. He wasn't anything to see. He was just a little man who was dead, with a big slug in his face and blood on him.

"Turn some of those damn lights off," I growled. "And let's get away from here fast."

"The house is just across the street." George sounded as casual as if he had just shot a nickel in a slot machine instead of a man.

"The Jeeters are out of this, if you like your job. You ought to know that. We'll go back to my place and start all over."

"I get it," he snapped, and jumped back into the big car. He cut the foglights and the sidelights and I got in beside him in the front seat.

We straightened out and started up the hill, over the brow. I looked back at the broken window. It was the small one at the extreme back of the car and it wasn't shatterproof. A large piece was gone from it. They could fit that, if they got around to it, and make some evidence. I didn't think it would matter, but it might.

At the crest of the hill a large limousine passed us going down. It's dome light was on and in the interior, as in a lighted showcase, an elderly couple sat stiffly, taking the royal salute. The man was in evening clothes, with a white scarf and a crush hat. The woman was in furs and diamonds.

George passed them casually, gunned the car and we made a fast right turn into a dark street. "There's a couple of good dinners all shot to hell," he drawled. "And I bet they don't even report it."

"Yeah. Let's get back home and have a drink," I said. "I never really got to like killing people."

5

We sat with some of Miss Harriet Huntress' Scotch in our glasses and looked at each other across the rims. George looked nice with his cap off. His head was clustered over with wavy dark brown hair and his teeth were very white and clean. He sipped his drink and nibbled a cigarette at the same time. His snappy black eyes had a cool glitter in them.

"Yale?" I asked.

"Dartmouth, if it's any of your business."

"Everything's my business. What's a college education worth these days?"

"Three squares and a uniform," he drawled.

"What kind of guy is young Jeeter?"

"Big blond bruiser, plays a fair game of golf, thinks he's hell with the women, drinks heavy but hasn't sicked up on the rugs so far."

"What kind of guy is old Jeeter?"

"He'd probably give you a dime—if he didn't have a nickel with him."

"Tsk, tsk, you're talking about your boss."

George grinned. "He's so tight his head squeaks when he takes his hat off. I always took chances. Maybe that's why I'm just somebody's driver. This is good Scotch."

I made another drink, which finished the bottle. I sat down again.

"You think those two gunnies were stashed out for Mister Gerald?"

"Why not? I usually drive him home about that time. Didn't today. He had a bad hangover and didn't go out until late. You're a dick, you know what it's all about, don't you?"

"Who told you I was a dick?"

"Nobody but a dick ever asked so goddam many questions."

I shook my head. "Uh-uh. I've asked you just six questions. Your boss has a lot of confidence in you. He must have told you."

The dark man nodded, grinned faintly and sipped. "The whole set-up is pretty obvious," he said. "When the car started to swing for the turn into the driveway these boys went to work. I don't figure they meant to kill anybody, somehow. It was just a scare. Only that little guy was nuts."

I looked at George's eyebrows. They were nice black eyebrows, with a gloss on them like horsehair.

"It doesn't sound like Marty Estel to pick that sort of helpers."

"Sure. Maybe that's why he picked that sort of helpers."

"You're smart. You and I can get along. But shooting that little punk makes it tougher. What will you do about that?"

"Nothing."

"Okay. If they get to you and tie it to your gun, if you still have the gun, which you probably won't, I suppose it will be passed off as an attempted stickup. There's just one thing."

"What?" George finished his second drink, laid the glass aside, lit a fresh cigarette and smiled.

"It's pretty hard to tell a car from in front—at night. Even with all those lights. It might have been a visitor."

He shrugged and nodded. "But if it's a scare, that would do just as well. Because the family would hear about it and the old man would guess whose boys they were —and why."

"Hell, you really are smart," I said admiringly, and the phone rang.

It was an English-butler voice, very clipped and precise, and it said that if I was Mr. Philip Marlowe, Mr. Jeeter would like to speak to me. He came on at once, with plenty of frost.

"I must say that you take your time about obeying orders," he barked. "Or hasn't that chauffeur of mine—"

"Yeah, he got here, Mr. Jeeter," I said. "But we ran into a little trouble. George will tell you."

"Young man, when I want something done—"

"Listen, Mr. Jeeter, I've had a hard day. Your son punched me on the jaw and I fell and cut my head open. When I staggered back to my apartment, more dead than alive, I was stuck up by a couple of hard guys with guns who told me to lay off the Jeeter case. I'm doing my best but I'm feeling a little frail, so don't scare me."

"Young man—"

"Listen," I told him earnestly, "If you want to call all the plays in this game, you can carry the ball yourself. Or you can save yourself a lot of money and hire an order taker. I have to do things my way. Any cops visit you tonight?"

"Cops?" he echoed in a sour voice. "You mean policemen?"

"By all means—I mean policemen."

"And why should I see any policemen?" he almost snarled.

"There was a stiff in front of your gates half an hour ago. Stiff meaning dead man. He's quite small. You could sweep him up in a dustpan, if he bothers you."

"My God! Are you serious?"

"Yes. What's more he took a shot at George and me. He recognized the car. He must have been all set for your son, Mr. Jeeter."

A silence with barbs on it. "I thought you said a dead man," Mr. Jeeter's voice said very coldly. "Now you say he shot at you."

"That was while he wasn't dead," I said. "George will tell you. George—"

"You come out here at once!" he yelled at me over the phone. "At once, do you hear? At once!"

"George will tell you," I said softly and hung up.

George looked at me coldly. He stood up and put his cap on. "Okay, pal," he said. "Maybe some day I can put you on to a soft thing." He started for the door.

"It had to be that way. It's up to him. He'll have to decide."

"Nuts," George said, looking back over his shoulder. "Save your breath, shamus. Anything you say to me is just so much noise in the wrong place."

He opened the door, went out, shut it, and I sat there still holding the telephone, with my mouth open and nothing in it but my tongue and a bad taste on that.

I went out to the kitchen and shook the Scotch bottle, but it was still empty. I opened some rye and swallowed a drink and it tasted sour. Something was bothering me. I had a feeling it was going to bother me a lot more before I was through.

They must have missed George by a whisker. I heard the elevator come up again almost as soon as it had stopped going down. Solid steps grew louder along the hallway. A fist hit the door. I went over and opened it.

One was in brown, one in blue, both large, hefty and bored.

The one in brown pushed his hat back on his head with a freckled hand and said: "You Philip Marlowe?"

"Me," I said.

They rode me back into the room without seeming to. The one in blue shut the door. The one in brown palmed a shield and let me catch a glint of the gold and enamel.

"Finlayson, Detective Lieutenant working out of Central Homicide," he said. "This is Sebold, my partner. We're a couple of swell guys not to get funny with. We hear you're kind of sharp with a gun."

Sebold took his hat off and dusted his salt-and-pepper hair back with the flat of his hand. He drifted noiselessly out to the kitchen.

Finlayson sat down on the edge of a chair and flicked his chin with a thumbnail as square as an ice cube and yellow as a mustard plaster. He was older than Sebold, but not so good-looking. He had the frowsy expression of a veteran cop who hadn't got very far.

I sat down. I said: "How do you mean, sharp with a gun?"

"Shooting people is how I mean."

I lit a cigarette. Sebold came out of the kitchen and went into the dressing room behind the wall bed.

"We understand you're a private-license guy," Finlayson said heavily.

"That's right."

"Give." He held his hand out. I gave him my wallet. He chewed it over and handed it back. "Carry a gun?"

I nodded. He held out his hand for it. Sebold came out of the dressing room. Finlayson sniffed at the Luger, snapped the magazine out, cleared the breech and held the gun so that a little light shone up through the magazine opening into the breech end of the barrel. He looked down the muzzle, squinting. He handed the gun to Sebold. Sebold did the same thing.

"Don't think so," Sebold said. "Clean, but not that clean. Couldn't have been cleaned within the hour. A little dust."

"Right."

Finlayson picked the ejected shell off the carpet, pressed it into the magazine and snapped the magazine back in place. He handed me the gun. I put it back under my arm.

"Been out anywhere tonight?" he asked tersely.

"Don't tell me the plot," I said. "I'm just a bit-player."

"Smart guy," Sebold said dispassionately. He dusted his hair again and opened a desk drawer. "Funny stuff. Good for a column. I like 'em that way—with my blackjack."

Finlayson sighed. "Been out tonight, shamus?"

"Sure. In and out all the time. Why?"

He ignored the question. "Where you been?"

"Out to dinner. Business call or two."

"Where at?"

"I'm sorry, boys. Every business has its private files."

"Had company, too," Sebold said, picking up George's glass and sniffing it. "Recent—within the hour."

"You're not that good," I told him sourly.

"Had a ride in a big Caddy?" Finlayson bored on, taking a deep breath. "Over West L.A. direction?"

"Had a ride in a Chrysler—over Vine Street direction."

"Maybe we better just take him down," Sebold said, looking at his fingernails.

"Maybe you better skip the gang-buster stuff and tell me what's stuck in your nose. I get along with cops—except when they act as if the law is only for citizens."

Finlayson studied me. Nothing I had said made an impression on him. Nothing Sebold said made any impression on him. He had an idea and he was holding it like a sick baby.

"You know a little rat named Frisky Lavon?" he sighed. "Used to be a dummy-chucker, then found out he could bug his way outa raps. Been doing that for say twelve years. Totes a gun and acts simple. But he quit acting tonight at seven-thirty about. Quit cold—with a slug in his head."

"Never heard of him," I said.

"You bumped anybody off tonight?"

"I'd have to look at my notebook."

Sebold leaned forward politely. "Would you care for a smack in the kisser?" he inquired.

Finlayson held his hand out sharply. "Cut it, Ben. Cut it. Listen, Marlowe. Maybe we're going at this wrong. We're not talking about murder. Could have been legitimate. This Frisky Lavon got froze off tonight on Calvello Drive in Bel-Air. Out in the middle of the street. Nobody seen or heard anything. So we kind of want to know."

"All right," I growled. "What makes it my business? And keep that piano tuner out of my hair. He has a nice suit and his nails are clean, but he bears down on his shield too hard."

"Nuts to you," Sebold said.

"We got a funny phone call," Finlayson said. "Which is where you come in. We ain't just throwing our weight around. And we want a forty-five. They ain't sure what kind yet."

"He's smart. He threw it under the bar at Levy's," Sebold sneered.

"I never had a forty-five," I said. "A guy who needs that much gun ought to use a pick."

Finlayson scowled at me and counted his thumbs. Then he took a deep breath and suddenly went human on me. "Sure, I'm just a dumb flatheel," he said. "Anybody could pull my ears off and I wouldn't even notice it. Let's all quit horsing around and talk sense.

"This Frisky was found dead after a no-name phone call to West L. A. police. Found dead outside a big house belonging to a man named Jeeter who owns a string of investment companies. He wouldn't use a guy like Frisky for a penwiper, so there's nothing in that. The servants didn't hear nothing, nor the servants at any of the four houses on the block. Frisky is lying in the street and somebody run over his foot, but what killed him was a forty-five slug smack in his face. West L.A. ain't hardly started the routine when some guy calls up Central and says to tell Homicide if they want to know who got Frisky Lavon, ask a private eye named Philip Marlowe, complete with address and everything, then a quick hang-up.

"Okay. The guy on the board gives me the dope and I don't know Frisky from a hole in my sock, but I ask Identification and sure enough they have him and just about the time I'm looking it over the flash comes from West L.A. and the description seems to check pretty close. So we get together and it's the same guy all right and the chief of detectives has us drop around here. So we drop around."

"So here you are," I said. "Will you have a drink?"

"Can we search the joint, if we do?

"Sure. It's a good lead—that phone call, I mean—if you put in about six months on it."

"We already got that idea," Finlayson growled. "A hundred guys could have chilled this little wart, and two-three of them maybe could have thought it was a smart rib to pin it on you. Them two-three is what interests us."

I shook my head.

"No ideas at all, huh?"

"Just for wisecracks," Sebold said.

Finlayson lumbered to his feet. "Well, we gotta look around."

"Maybe we had ought to have brought a search warrant," Sebold said, tickling his upper lip with the end of his tongue.

"I don't *have* to fight this guy, do I?" I asked Finlayson. "I mean, is it all right if I leave him his gag lines and just keep my temper?"

Finlayson looked at the ceiling and said dryly: "His wife left him day before yesterday. He's just trying to compensate, as the fellow says."

Sebold turned white and twisted his knuckles savagely. Then he laughed shortly and got to his feet.

They went at it. Ten minutes of opening and shutting drawers and looking at the backs of shelves and under seat cushions and letting the bed down and peering into the electric refrigerator and the garbage pail fed them up.

They came back and sat down again. "Just a nut," Finlayson said wearily. "Some guy that picked your name outa the directory maybe. Could be anything."

"Now I'll get that drink."

"I don't drink," Sebold snarled.

Finlayson crossed his hands on his stomach. "That don't mean any liquor gets poured in the flowerpot, son."

I got three drinks and put two of them beside Finlayson. He drank half of one of them and looked at the ceiling. "I got another killing, too," he said thoughtfully. "A guy in your racket, Marlowe. A fat guy on Sunset. Name of Arbogast. Ever hear of him?"

"I thought he was a handwriting expert," I said.

"You're talking about police business," Sebold told his partner coldly.

"Sure. Police business that's already in the morning paper. This Arbogast was shot three times with a twenty-two. Target gun. You know any crooks that pack that kind of heat?"

I held my glass tightly and took a long swallow. I hadn't thought Waxnose looked dangerous enough, but you never knew.

"I did," I said slowly. "A killer named Al Tessilore. But he's in Folsom. He used a Colt Woodsman."

Finlayson finished the first drink, used the second in about the same time, and stood up. Sebold stood up, still mad.

Finlayson opened the door. "Come on, Ben." They went out.

I heard their steps along the hall, the clang of the elevator once more. A car started just below in the street and growled off into the night.

"Clowns like that don't kill," I said out loud. But it looked as if they did.

I waited fifteen minutes before I went out again. The phone rang while I was waiting, but I didn't answer it.

I drove towards the El Milano and circled around enough to make sure I wasn't followed.

6

The lobby hadn't changed any. The blue carpet still tickled my ankles while I ambled over to the desk, the same pale clerk was handing a key to a couple of horse-faced females in tweeds, and when he saw me he put his weight on his left foot again and the door at the end of the desk popped open and out popped the fat and erotic Hawkins, with what looked like the same cigar stub in his face.

He hustled over and gave me a big warm smile this time, took hold of my arm. "Just the guy I was hoping to see," he chuckled. "Let's us go upstairs a minute."

"What's the matter?"

"Matter?" His smile became broad as the door to a two-car garage. "Nothing ain't the matter. This way."

He pushed me into the elevator and said, "Eight" in a fat cheerful voice and up we sailed and out we got and slid along the corridor. Hawkins had a hard hand and knew where to hold an arm. I was interested enough to let him get away with it. He pushed the buzzer beside Miss Huntress' door and Big Ben chimed inside and the door opened and I was looking at a deadpan in a derby hat and a dinner coat. He had his right hand in the side pocket of the coat, and under the derby a pair of scarred eyebrows and under the eyebrows a pair of eyes that had as much expression as the cap on a gas tank.

The mouth moved enough to say: "Yeah?"

"Company for the boss," Hawkins said expansively.

"What company?"

"Let me play too," I said. "Limited Liability Company. Gimme the apple."

"Huh?" The eyebrows went this way and that and the jaw came out. "Nobody ain't kiddin' nobody, I hope."

"Now, now, gents—" Hawkins began.

A voice behind the derby-hatted man interrupted him. "What's the matter, Beef?"

"He's in a stew," I said.

"Listen, mugg—"

"Now, now, gents—" as before.

"Ain't nothing the matter," Beef said, throwing his voice over his shoulder as it were a coil of rope. "The hotel dick got a guy up here and he says he's company."

"Show the company in, Beef." I liked this voice. It was smooth quiet, and you could have cut your name in it with a thirty-pound sledge and a cold chisel.

"Lift the dogs," Beef said, and stood to one side.

We went in. I went first, then Hawkins, then Beef wheeled neatly behind us like a door. We went in so close together that we must have looked like a three-decker sandwich.

Miss Huntress was not in the room. The log in the fireplace had almost stopped smoldering. There was still that smell of sandalwood on the air. With it cigarette smoke blended.

A man stood at the end of the davenport, both hands in the pockets of a blue camel's-hair coat with the collar high to a black snap-brim hat. A loose scarf hung outside his coat. He stood motionless, the cigarette in his mouth lisping smoke. He was tall, black-haired, suave, dangerous. He said nothing.

Hawkins ambled over to him. "This is the guy I was telling you about, Mr. Estel," the fat man burbled. "Come in earlier today and said he was from you. Kinda fooled me."

"Give him a ten, Beef."

The derby hat took its left hand from somewhere and there was a bill in it. It pushed the bill at Hawkins. Hawkins took the bill, blushing.

"This ain't necessary, Mr. Estel. Thanks a lot just the same."

"Scram."

"Huh?" Hawkins looked shocked.

"You heard him," Beef said truculently. "Want your fanny out the door first, huh?"

Hawkins drew himself up. "I gotta protect the tenants. You gentlemen know how it is. A man in a job like this."

"Yeah. Scram," Estel said without moving his lips.

Hawkins turned and went out quickly, softly. The door clicked gently shut behind him. Beef looked back at it, then moved behind me.

"See if he's rodded, Beef."

The derby hat saw if I was rodded. He took the Luger and went away from me. Estel looked casually at the Luger, back at me. His eyes held an expression of indifferent dislike.

"Name's Philip Marlowe, eh? A private dick."

"So what?" I said.

"Somebody's goin' to get somebody's face pushed into somebody's floor," Beef said coldly.

"Aw, keep that crap for the boiler room," I told him. "I'm sick of hard guys for this evening. I said 'so what,' and 'so what' is what I said."

Marty Estel looked mildly amused. "Hell, keep your shirt in. I've got to look after my friends, don't I? You know who I am. Okay, I know what you talked to

Miss Huntress about. And I know something about you that you don't know I know."

"All right," I said. "This fat slob Hawkins collected ten from me for letting me up here this afternoon—knowing perfectly well who I was—and he has just collected ten from your iron man for slipping me the nasty. Give me back my gun and tell me what makes my business your business."

"Plenty. First off, Harriet's not home. We're waiting for her on account of a thing that happened. I can't wait any longer. Got to go to work at the club. So what did you come after this time?"

"Looking for the Jeeter boy. Somebody shot at his car tonight. From now on he needs somebody to walk behind him."

"You think I play games like that?" Estel asked me coldly.

I walked over to a cabinet and opened it and found a bottle of Scotch. I twisted the cap off, lifted a glass from the tabouret and poured some out. I tasted it. It tasted all right.

I looked around for ice, but there wasn't any. It had all melted long since in the bucket.

"I asked you a question," Estel said gravely.

"I heard it. I'm making my mind up. The answer is, I wouldn't have thought it—no. But it happened. I was there. I was in the car—instead of young Jeeter. His father had sent for me to come to the house to talk things over."

"What things?"

I didn't bother to look surprised. "You hold fifty grand of the boy's paper. That looks bad for you, if anything happens to him."

"I don't figure it that way. Because that way I would lose my dough. The old man won't pay—granted. But I wait a couple of years and I collect from the kid. He gets his estate out of trust when he's twenty-eight. Right now he gets a grand a month and he can't even will anything, because it's still in trust. Savvy?"

"So you wouldn't knock him off," I said, using my Scotch. "But you might throw a scare into him."

Estel frowned. He discarded his cigarette into a tray and watched it smoke a moment before he picked it up again and snubbed it out. He shook his head.

"If you're going to bodyguard him, it would almost pay me to stand part of your salary, wouldn't it? Almost. A man in my racket can't take care of everything. He's of age and it's his business who he runs around with. For instance, women. Any reason why a nice girl shouldn't cut herself a piece of five million bucks?"

I said: "I think it's a swell idea. What was it you knew about me that I didn't know you knew?"

He smiled, faintly. "What was it you were waiting to tell Miss Huntress—the thing that happened?"

He smiled faintly again.

"Listen, Marlowe, there are lots of ways to play any game. I play mine on the house percentage, because that's all I need to win. What makes me get tough?"

I rolled a fresh cigarette around in my fingers and tried to roll it around my glass with two fingers. "Who said you were tough? I always heard the nicest things about you."

Marty Estel nodded and looked faintly amused. "I have sources of information," he said quietly. "When I have fifty grand invested in a guy, I'm apt to find out a little about him. Jeeter hired a man named Arbogast to do a little work. Arbogast was killed in his office today—with a twenty-two. That could have nothing to do with Jeeter's business. But there was a tail on you when you went there and you didn't give it to the law. Does that make you and me friends?"

I licked the edge of my glass, nodded. "It seems it does."

"From now on just forget about bothering Harriet, see?"

"Okay."

"So we understand each other real good, now."

"Yeah."

"Well, I'll be going. Give the guy back his Luger, Beef."

The derby hat came over and smacked my gun into my hand hard enough to break a bone.

"Staying?" Estel asked, moving towards the door.

"I guess I'll wait a little while. Until Hawkins comes up to touch me for another ten."

Estel grinned. Beef walked in front of him wooden-faced to the door and opened it. Estel went out. The door closed. The room was silent. I sniffed at the dying perfume of sandalwood and stood motionless, looking around.

Somebody was nuts. I was nuts. Everybody was nuts. None of it fitted together worth a nickel. Marty Estel, as he said, had no good motive for murdering anybody, because that would be the surest way to kill his chances to collect his money. Even if he had a motive for murdering anybody, Waxnose and Frisky didn't seem like the team he would select for the job. I was in bad with the police, I had spent ten dollars of my twenty expense money, and I didn't have enough leverage anywhere to lift a dime off a cigar counter.

I finished my drink, put the glass down, walked up and down the room, smoked a third cigarette, looked at my watch, shrugged and felt disgusted. The inner doors of the suite were closed. I went across to the one out of which young Jeeter must have sneaked that afternoon. Opening it I looked into a bedroom done in ivory and ashes of roses. There was a big double bed with no footboard, covered with figured brocade. Toilet articles glistened on a built-in dressing table with a panel light. The light was lit. A small lamp on a table beside the door was lit also. A door near the dressing table showed the cool green of bathroom tiles.

I went over and looked in there. Chromium, a glass stall shower, monogrammed towels on a rack, a glass shelf for perfume and bath salts at the foot of the tub, everything nice and refined. Miss Huntress did herself well. I hoped she was paying her own rent. It didn't make any difference to me—I just liked it that way.

I went back towards the living room, stopped in the doorway to take another pleasant look around, and noticed something I ought to have noticed the instant I stepped into the room. I noticed the sharp tang of cordite on the air, almost, but not quite gone. And then I noticed something else.

The bed had been moved over until its head overlapped the edge of a closet door which was not quite closed. The weight of the bed was holding it from opening. I went over there to find out why it wanted to open. I went slowly and about halfway there I noticed that I was holding a gun in my hand.

I leaned against the closet door. It didn't move. I threw more weight against it. It still didn't move. Braced against it I pushed the bed away with my foot, gave ground slowly.

A weight pushed against me hard. I had gone back a foot or so before anything else happened. Then it happened suddenly. He came out—sideways, in a sort of roll. I put some more weight back on the door and held him like that a moment, looking at him.

He was still big, still blond, still dressed in rough sporty material, with scarf and open-necked shirt. But his face wasn't red any more.

I gave ground again and he rolled down the back of the door, turning a little like a swimmer in the surf, thumped the floor and lay there, almost on his back, still looking at me. Light from the bedside lamp glittered on his head. There was a scorched and soggy stain on the rough coat—about where his heart would be. So he wouldn't get that five million after all. And nobody would get anything and Marty Estel wouldn't get his fifty grand. Because young Mister Gerald was dead.

I looked back into the closet where he had been. Its door hung wide open now. There were clothes on racks, feminine clothes, nice clothes. He had been backed in among them, probably with his hands in the air and a gun against his chest. And then he had been shot dead, and whoever did it hadn't been quite quick enough or quite strong enough to get the door shut. Or had been scared and had just yanked the bed over against the door and left it that way.

Something glittered down on the floor. I picked it up. A small automatic, .25 caliber, a woman's purse gun with a beautifully engraved butt inlaid with silver and ivory. I put the gun in my pocket. That seemed a funny thing to do, too.

I didn't touch him. He was as dead as John D. Arbogast and looked a whole lot deader. I left the door open and listened, walked quickly back across the room and into the living room and shut the bedroom door, smearing the knob as I did it.

A lock was being tinkled at with a key. Hawkins was back again, to see what delayed me. He was letting himself in with his passkey.

I was pouring a drink when he came in.

He came well into the room, stopped with his feet planted and surveyed me coldly.

"I seen Estel and his boy leave," he said. "I didn't see you leave. So I come up. I gotta—"

"You gotta protect the guests," I said.

"Yeah. I gotta protect the guests. You can't stay up here, pal. Not without the lady of the house is home."

"But Marty Estel and his hard boy can."

He came a little closer to me. He had a mean look in his eye. He had always had it, probably, but I noticed it more now.

"You don't want to make nothing of that, do you?" he asked me.

"No. Every man to his own chisel. Have a drink."

"That ain't your liquor."

"Miss Huntress gave me a bottle. We're pals. Marty Estel and I are pals. Everybody is pals. Don't you want to be pals?"

"You ain't trying to kid me, are you?"

"Have a drink and forget it."

I found a glass and poured him one. He took it.

"It's the job if anybody smells it on me," he said.

"Uh-huh."

He drank slowly, rolling it around on his tongue. "Good Scotch."

"Won't be the first time you tasted it, will it?"

He started to get hard again, then relaxed. "Hell, I guess you're just a kidder." He finished the drink, put the glass down, patted his lips with a large and very crumpled handkerchief and sighed.

"Okay," he said. "But we'll have to leave now."

"All set. I guess she won't be home for a while. You see them go out?"

"Her and the boy friend. Yeah, long time ago."

I nodded. We went towards the door and Hawkins saw me out. He saw me downstairs and off the premises. But he didn't see what was in Miss Huntress' bedroom. I wondered if he would go back up. If he did, the Scotch bottle would probably stop him.

I got into my car and drove off home—to talk to Anna Halsey on the phone. There wasn't any case any more—for us. I parked close to the curb this time. I wasn't feeling gay any more. I rode up in the elevator and unlocked the door and clicked the light on.

Waxnose sat in my best chair, an unlit hand-rolled brown cigarette between his fingers, his bony knees crossed, and his long Woodsman resting solidly on his leg. He was smiling. It wasn't the nicest smile I ever saw.

"Hi, pal," he drawled. "You still ain't had that door fixed. Kind of shut it, huh?" His voice, for all the drawl, was deadly.

I shut the door, stood looking across the room at him.

"So you killed my pal," he said.

He stood up slowly, came across the room slowly and leaned the .22 against my throat. His smiling thin-lipped mouth seemed as expressionless, for all its smile, as his wax-white nose. He reached quietly under my coat and took the Luger. I might as well leave it home from now on. Everybody in town seemed to be able to take it away from me.

He stepped back across the room and sat down again in the chair.

"Steady does it," he said almost gently. "Park the body, friend. No false moves. No moves at all. You and me are at the jumping-off place. The clock's tickin' and we're waiting to go."

I sat down and stared at him. A curious bird. I moistened my dry lips. "You told me his gun had no firing pin," I said.

"Yeah. He fooled me on that, the little so-and-so. And I told you to lay off the Jeeter kid. That's cold now. It's Frisky I'm thinking about. Crazy, ain't it? Me bothering about a dimwit like that, packin' him around with me, and letting him get hisself bumped off." He sighed and added simply, "He was my kid brother."

"I didn't kill him," I said.

He smiled a little more. He had never stopped smiling. The corners of his mouth just tucked in a little deeper.

"Yeah?"

He slid the safety catch off the Luger, laid it carefully on the arm of the chair at his right, and reached into his pocket. What he brought out made me as cold as an ice bucket.

It was a metal tube, dark and rough-looking, about four inches long and drilled with a lot of small holes. He held his woodsman in his left hand and began to screw the tube casually on the end of it.

"Silencer," he said. "They're the bunk, I guess you smart guys think. This one ain't the bunk—not for three shots. I oughta know. I made it myself."

I moistened my lips again. "It'll work for one shot," I said. "Then it jams the action. That one looks like cast-iron. It will probably blow your hand off."

He smiled his waxy smile, screwed it on, slowly, lovingly, gave it a last hard turn and sat back relaxed. "Not this baby. She's packed with steel wool and that's good for three shots, like I said. Then you got to repack it. And there ain't enough back pressure to jam the action of this gun. You feel good? I'd like you to feel good."

"I feel swell, you sadistic son of a bitch," I said.

"I'm having you lie down on the bed after a while. You won't feel nothing. I'm kind of fussy about my killings. Frisky didn't feel nothing, I guess. You got him neat."

"You don't see good," I sneered. "The chauffeur got him with a Smith and Wesson forty-four. I didn't even fire."

"Uh-huh."

"Okay, you don't believe me," I said. "What did you kill Arbogast for? There was nothing fussy about that killing. He was just shot at his desk, three times with a twenty-two and he fell down on the floor. What did he ever do to your filthy little brother?"

He jerked the gun up, but his smile held. "You got guts," he said. "Who is this here Arbogast?"

I told him. I told him slowly and carefully, in detail. I told him a lot of things. And he began in some vague way to look worried. His eyes flickered at me, away, back again, restlessly, like a hummingbird.

"I don't know any party named Arbogast, pal," he said slowly. "Never heard of him. And I ain't shot any fat guys today."

"You killed him," I said. "And you killed young Jeeter—in the girl's apartment at the El Milano. He's lying there dead right now. You're working for Marty Estel. He's going to be awfully damn sorry about that kill. Go ahead and make it three in a row."

His face froze. The smile went away at last. His whole face looked waxy now. He opened his mouth and breathed through it, and his breath made a restless worrying sound. I could see the faint glitter of sweat on his forehead, and I could feel the cold from the evaporation of sweat on mine.

Waxnose said very gently: "I ain't killed anybody at all, friend. Not anybody. I wasn't hired to kill people. Until Frisky stopped that slug I didn't have no such ideas. That's straight."

I tried not to stare at the metal tube on the end of the Woodsman.

A flame flickered at the back of his eyes, a small, weak, smoky flame. It seemed to grow larger and clearer. He looked down at the floor between his feet. I looked around at the light switch, but it was too far away. He looked up again. Very slowly he began to unscrew the silencer. He had it loose in his hand. He dropped it back into his pocket, stood up, holding the two guns, one in each hand. Then he had another idea. He sat down again, took all the shells out of the Luger quickly and threw it on the floor after them.

He came towards me softly across the room. "I guess this is your lucky day," he said. "I got to go a place and see a guy."

"I knew all along it was my lucky day. I've been feeling so good."

He moved delicately around me to the door and opened it a foot and started through the narrow opening, smiling again.

"I gotta see a guy," he said very gently, and his tongue moved along his lips.

"Not yet," I said, and jumped.

His gun hand was at the edge of the door, almost beyond the edge. I hit the door hard and he couldn't bring it in quickly enough. He couldn't get out of the way. I pinned him in the doorway and used all the strength I had. It was a crazy thing. He had given me a break and all I had to do was stand still and let him go. But I had a guy to see too—and I wanted to see him first.

Waxnose leered at me. He grunted. He fought with his hand beyond the door edge. I shifted and hit his jaw with all I had. It was enough. He went limp. I hit him again. His head bounced against the wood. I heard a light thud beyond the door edge. I hit him a third time. I never hit anything harder.

I took my weight back from the door then and he slid towards me, blank-eyed, rubber-kneed, and I caught him and twisted his empty hands behind him and let him fall. I stood over him panting. I went to the door. His Woodsman lay almost on the sill. I picked it up, dropped it into my pocket—not the pocket that held Miss Huntress' gun. He hadn't even found that.

There he lay on the floor. He was thin, he had no weight, but I panted just the same. In a little while his eyes flickered open and looked up at me.

"Greedy guy," he whispered wearily. "Why did I ever leave Saint Looey?"

I snapped handcuffs on his wrists and pulled him by the shoulders into the dressing room and tied his ankles with a piece of rope. I left him lying on his back, a little sideways, his nose as white as ever, his eyes empty now, his lips moving a little as if he were talking to himself. A funny lad, not all bad, but not so pure I had to weep over him either.

I put my Luger together and left with my three guns. There was nobody outside the apartment house.

7

The Jeeter mansion was on a nine- or ten-acre knoll, a big colonial pile with fat white columns and dormer windows and magnolias and a four-car garage. There was a circular parking space at the top of the driveway with two cars parked in it— one was the big dreadnought in which I'd ridden and the other a canary-yellow sports convertible I had seen before.

I rang a bell the size of a silver dollar. The door opened and a tall narrow cold-eyed bird in dark clothes looked out at me.

"Mr. Jeeter home? Mr. Jeeter, senior?"

"May I arsk who is calling?" The accent was a little too thick, like cut Scotch.

"Philip Marlowe. I'm working for him. Maybe I had ought to of gone to the servant's entrance."

He hitched a finger at a wing collar and looked at me without pleasure. "Aw, possibly. You may step in. I shall inform Mr. Jeeter. I believe he is engaged at the moment. Kindly wait 'ere in the 'all."

"The act stinks," I said. "English butlers aren't dropping their h's this year."

"Smart guy, huh?" he snarled, in a voice from not any farther across the Atlantic than Hoboken. "Wait here." He slid away.

I sat down in a carved chair and felt thirsty. After a while the butler came cat-footing back along the hall and jerked his chin at me unpleasantly.

. He seemed to have a few enemies. It even seemed that he was supposed
the car this evening when Frisky Lavon shot at it—but of course that was
lant."

Jeeter drew his white eyebrows together in an expression of puzzlement.
didn't look puzzled. He didn't look anything. He was as wooden-faced as a
re Indian. The girl looked a little white now, a little tense. I plowed on.
ck at the El Milano I found that Hawkins had let Marty Estel and his
ard into Miss Huntress' apartment to wait for her. Marty had something to
—that Arbogast had been killed. That made it a good idea for her to lay off
eeter for a while—until the cops quieted down anyhow. A thoughtful guy,
A much more thoughtful guy than you would suppose. For instance, he
bout Arbogast and he knew Mr. Jeeter went to Anna Halsey's office this
g and he knew somehow—Anna might have told him herself, I wouldn't
past her—that I was working on the case now. So he had me tailed to
t's place and away, and he found out later from his cop friends that Arbogast
en murdered, and he knew I hadn't given it out. So he had me there and
ade us pals. He went away after telling me this and once more I was left
n Miss Huntress' apartment. But this time for no reason at all I poked
. And I found young Mister Gerald, in the bedroom, in a closet."
epped quickly over to the girl and reached into my pocket and took out the
ancy .25 automatic and laid it down on her knee.
er see this before?"
r voice had a curious tight sound, but her dark blue eyes looked at me

es. It's mine."

ou kept it where?"

the drawer of a small table beside the bed."

ure about that?"

e thought. Neither of the two men stirred.

orge began to twitch the corner of his mouth. She shook her head suddenly,
ys.

o. I have an idea now I took it out to show somebody—because I don't know
about guns—and left it lying on the mantel in the living room. In fact, I'm
sure I did. It was Gerald I showed it to."

o he might have reached for it there, if anybody tried to make a wrong play
?"

e nodded, troubled. "What do you mean—he's in the closet?" she asked in
l quick voice.

ou know. Everybody in this room knows what I mean. They know that I
d you that gun for a purpose." I stepped away from her and faced George
s boss. "He's dead, of course. Shot through the heart—probably with this
was left there with him. That's why it would be left."

We went along a mile of hallway. At the end it broadened without any doors
into a huge sunroom. On the far side of the sunroom the butler opened a wide
door and I stepped past him into an oval room with a black-and-silver oval rug, a
black marble table in the middle of the rug, stiff high-backed carved chairs against
the walls, a huge oval mirror with a rounded surface that made me look like a
pygmy with water on the brain, and in the room three people.

By the door opposite where I came in, George the chauffeur stood stiffly in his
neat dark uniform, with his peaked cap in his hand. In the least uncomfortable of
the chairs sat Miss Harriet Huntress holding a glass in which there was half a drink.
And around the silver margin of the oval rug, Mr. Jeeter, senior, was trying his
legs out in a brisk canter, still under wraps, but mad inside. His face was red and
the veins on his nose were distended. His hands were in the pockets of a velvet
smoking jacket. He wore a pleated shirt with a black pearl in the bosom, a batwing
black tie and one of his patent-leather oxfords was unlaced.

He whirled and yelled at the butler behind me: "Get out and keep those doors
shut! And I'm not at home to anybody, understand? Nobody!"

The butler closed the doors. Presumably, he went away. I didn't hear him go.

George gave me a cool one-sided smile and Miss Huntress gave me a bland
stare over her glass. "You made a nice comeback," she said demurely.

"You took a chance leaving me alone in your apartment," I told her. "I might
have sneaked some of your perfume."

"Well, what do you want?" Jeeter yelled at me. "A nice sort of detective you
turned out to be. I put you on a confidential job and you walk right in on Miss
Huntress and explain the whole thing to her."

"It worked, didn't it?"

He stared. They all stared. "How do you know that?" he barked.

"I know a nice girl when I see one. She's here telling you she had an idea she
got not to like, and for you to quit worrying about it. Where's Mister Gerald?"

Old Man Jeeter stopped and gave me a hard level stare. "I still regard you as
incompetent," he said. "My son is missing."

"I'm not working for you. I'm working for Anna Halsey. Any complaints
you have to make should be addressed to her. Do I pour my own drink or do you
have a flunky in a purple suit to do it? And what do you mean, your son is
missing?"

"Should I give him the heave, sir?" George asked quietly.

Jeeter waved his hand at a decanter and siphon and glasses on the black marble
table and started around the rug again. "Don't be silly," he snapped at George.

George flushed a little, high on his cheekbones, His mouth looked tough.

I mixed myself a drink and sat down with it and tasted it and asked again: "What
do you mean your son is missing, Mr. Jeeter?"

"I'm paying you good money," he started to yell at me, still mad.

"When?"

He stopped dead in his canter and looked at me again. Miss Huntress laughed lightly. George scowled.

"What do you suppose I mean—my son is missing?" he snapped. "I should have thought that would be clear enough even to you. Nobody knows where he is. Miss Huntress doesn't know. I don't know. No one at any of the places where he might be known."

"But I'm smarter than they are," I said. "I know."

Nobody moved for a long minute. Jeeter stared at me fish-eyed. George stared at me. The girl stared at me. She looked puzzled. The other two just stared.

I looked at her. "Where did you go when you went out, if you're telling?"

Her dark blue eyes were water-clear. "There's no secret about it. We went out together—in a taxi. Gerald had had his driving license suspended for a month. Too many tickets. We went down towards the beach and I had a change of heart, as you guessed. I decided I was just being a chiseler after all. I didn't want Gerald's money really. What I wanted was revenge. On Mr. Jeeter here for ruining my father. Done all legally of course, but done just the same. But I got myself in a spot where I couldn't have my revenge and not look like a cheap chiseler. So I told George to find some other girl to play with. He was sore and we quarreled. I stopped the taxi and got out in Beverly Hills. He went on. I don't know where. Later I went back to the El Milano and got my car out of the garage and came here. To tell Mr. Jeeter to forget the whole thing and not bother to sic sleuths on to me."

"You say you went with him in a taxi," I said. "Why wasn't George driving him, if he couldn't drive himself?"

I stared at her, but I wasn't talking to her. Jeeter answered me, frostily. "George drove me home from the office, of course. At that time Gerald had already gone out. Is there anything important about that?"

I turned to him. "Yeah. There's going to be. Mister Gerald is at the El Milano. Hawkins the house dick told me. He went back there to wait for Miss Huntress and Hawkins let him into her apartment. Hawkins will do you those little favors—for ten bucks. He may be there still and he may not."

I kept on watching them. It was hard to watch all three of them. But they didn't move. They just looked at me.

"Well—I'm glad to hear it," Old Man Jeeter said. "I was afraid he was off somewhere getting drunk."

"No. He's not off anywhere getting drunk," I said. "By the way, among these places you called to see if he was there, you didn't call the El Milano?"

George nodded. "Yes, I did. They said he wasn't there. Looks like the house peeper tipped the phone girl off not to say anything."

"He wouldn't have to do that. She'd just ring the apartment and he wouldn't answer—naturally." I watched Old Man Jeeter hard then, with a lot of interest. It was going to be hard for him to take that up, but he was going to have to do it.

He did. He licked his lips first. "Why—naturally, [...]

I put my glass down on the marble table and stoo[...] hands hanging free. I still tried to watch them—all thr[...]

"Let's go back over this thing a little," I said. "We [...] know George is, although he shouldn't be, being j[...] Huntress is. And of course you are, Mr. Jeeter. So let [...] have a lot of things that don't add up, but I'm smart[...] anyhow. First-off a handful of photostats of notes from [...] having given these and Mr. Jeeter won't pay them, bu[...] named Arbogast check the signatures, to see if they lo[...] are. This Arbogast may have done other things. I don'[...] When I went to see him, he was dead—shot three ti[...] with a twenty-two. No, I didn't tell the police, Mr. Jee[...]

The tall silver-haired man looked horribly shocked[...] bulrush. "Dead?" he whispered. "Murdered?"

I looked at George. George didn't move a muscle. [...] quietly, waiting, tight-lipped.

I said: "There's only one reason to suppose his killi[...] Mr. Jeeter's affairs. He was shot with a twenty-two—and [...] who wears a twenty-two."

I still had their attention. And their silence.

"Why he was shot I haven't the faintest idea. He w[...] Miss Huntress or Marty Estel. He was too fat to get arou[...] was a little too smart. He got a simple case of signature [...] on from there to find out more than he should. And aft[...] than he should—he guessed more than he ought—and r[...] blackmail. And somebody rubbed him out this afternoon [...] I can stand it. I never knew him.

"So I went over to see Miss Huntress and after a lo[...] this itchy-handed house dick I got to see her and we ha[...] Gerald stepped neatly out of hiding and bopped me a r[...] over I went and hit my head on a chair leg. And when I [...] was empty. So I·went on home.

"And home I found the man with the twenty-two and [...] Frisky Lavon, with a bad breath and a very large gun, [...] now as he was shot dead in front of your house tonight, N[...] stick up your car. The cops know about that one—they c[...] because the other guy, the one that packs the twenty-t[...] brother and he thought I shot Dimwit and tried to put the [...] work. That's two killings.

"We now come to the third and most important. I we[...] because it no longer seemed a good idea for Mister Gera[...]

The old man took a step and stopped and braced himself against the table. I wasn't sure whether he had turned white or whether he had been white already. He stared stonily at the girl. He said very slowly, between his teeth: "You damned murderess!"

"Couldn't it have been suicide?" I sneered.

He turned his head enough to look at me. I could see that the idea interested him. He half nodded.

"No," I said. "It couldn't have been suicide."

He didn't like that so well. His face congested with blood and the veins on his nose thickened. The girl touched the gun lying on her knee, then put her hand loosely around the butt. I saw her thumb slide very gently towards the safety catch. She didn't know much about guns, but she knew that much.

"It couldn't be suicide," I said again, very slowly. "As an isolated event—maybe. But not with all the other stuff that's been happening. Arbogast, the stick-up down on Calvello Drive outside this house, the thugs planted in my apartment, the job with the twenty-two."

I reached into my pocket again and pulled out Waxnose's Woodsman. I held it carelessly on the flat of my left hand. "And curiously enough, I don't think it was *this* twenty-two—although this happens to be the gunman's twenty-two. Yeah, I have the gunman, too. He's tied up in my apartment. He came back to knock me off, but I talked him out of it. I'm a swell talker."

"Except that you overdo it," the girl said coolly, and lifted the gun a little.

"It's obvious who killed him, Miss Huntress," I said. "It's simply a matter of motive and opportunity. Marty Estel didn't, and didn't have it done. That would spoil his chances to get his fifty grand. Frisky Lavon's pal didn't, regardless of who he was working for, and I don't think he was working for Marty Estel. He couldn't have got into the El Milano to do the job, and certainly not into Miss Huntress' apartment. Whoever did it had something to gain by it and an opportunity to get to the place where it was done. Well, who had something to gain? Gerald had five million coming to him in two years out of a trust fund. He couldn't will it until he got it. So if he died, his natural heir got it. Who's his natural heir? You'd be surprised. Did you know that in the state of California and some others, but not in all, a man can by his own act become a natural heir? Just by adopting somebody who has money and no heirs!"

George moved then. His movement was once more as smooth as a ripple of water. The Smith & Wesson gleamed dully in his hand, but he didn't fire it. The small automatic in the girl's hand cracked. Blood spurted from George's brown hard hand. The Smith & Wesson dropped to the floor. He cursed. She didn't know much about guns—not very much.

"Of course!" she said grimly. "George could get into the apartment without any trouble, if Gerald was there. He would go in through the garage, a chauffeur in uniform, ride up in the elevator and knock at the door. And when Gerald opened it, George would back him in with that Smith and Wesson. But how did he know Gerald was there?"

I said: "He must have followed your taxi. We don't know where he has been all evening since he left me. He had a car with him. The cops will find out. How much was in it for you, George?"

George held his right wrist with his left hand, held it tightly, and his face was twisted, savage. He said nothing.

"George would back him in with the Smith and Wesson," the girl said wearily. "Then he would see my gun on the mantelpiece. That would be better. He would use that. He would back Gerald into the bedroom, away from the corridor, into the closet, and there, quietly, calmly, he would kill him and drop the gun on the floor."

"George killed Arbogast, too. He killed him with a twenty-two because he knew that Frisky Lavon's brother had a twenty-two, and he knew that because he had hired Frisky and his brother to put over a big scare on Gerald—so that when he was murdered it would look as if Marty Estel had had it done. That was why I was brought out here tonight in the Jeeter car—so that the two thugs who had been warned and planted could pull their act and maybe knock me off, if I got too tough. Only George likes to kill people. He made a neat shot at Frisky. He hit him in the face. It was so good a shot I think he meant it to be a miss. How about it, George?"

Silence.

I looked at old Jeeter at last. I had been expecting him to pull a gun himself, but he hadn't. He just stood there, open-mouthed, appalled, leaning against the black marble table, shaking.

"My God!" he whispered. "My God!"

"You don't have one—except money."

A door squeaked behind me. I whirled, but I needn't have bothered. A hard voice, about as English as Amos and Andy, said: "Put 'em up, bud."

The butler, the very English butler, stood there in the doorway, a gun in his hand, tight-lipped. The girl turned her wrist and shot him just kind of casually, in the shoulder or something. He squealed like a stuck pig.

"Go away, you're intruding," she said coldly.

He ran. We heard his steps running.

"He's going to fall," she said.

I was wearing my Luger in my right hand now, a little late in the season, as usual. I came around with it. Old Man Jeeter was holding on to the table, his face gray as a paving block. His knees were giving. George stood cynically, holding a handkerchief around his bleeding wrist, watching him.

"Let him fall," I said. "Down is where he belongs."

He fell. His head twisted. His mouth went slack. He hit the carpet on his side

We went along a mile of hallway. At the end it broadened without any doors into a huge sunroom. On the far side of the sunroom the butler opened a wide door and I stepped past him into an oval room with a black-and-silver oval rug, a black marble table in the middle of the rug, stiff high-backed carved chairs against the walls, a huge oval mirror with a rounded surface that made me look like a pygmy with water on the brain, and in the room three people.

By the door opposite where I came in, George the chauffeur stood stiffly in his neat dark uniform, with his peaked cap in his hand. In the least uncomfortable of the chairs sat Miss Harriet Huntress holding a glass in which there was half a drink. And around the silver margin of the oval rug, Mr. Jeeter, senior, was trying his legs out in a brisk canter, still under wraps, but mad inside. His face was red and the veins on his nose were distended. His hands were in the pockets of a velvet smoking jacket. He wore a pleated shirt with a black pearl in the bosom, a batwing black tie and one of his patent-leather oxfords was unlaced.

He whirled and yelled at the butler behind me: "Get out and keep those doors shut! And I'm not at home to anybody, understand? Nobody!"

The butler closed the doors. Presumably, he went away. I didn't hear him go.

George gave me a cool one-sided smile and Miss Huntress gave me a bland stare over her glass. "You made a nice comeback," she said demurely.

"You took a chance leaving me alone in your apartment," I told her. "I might have sneaked some of your perfume."

"Well, what do you want?" Jeeter yelled at me. "A nice sort of detective you turned out to be. I put you on a confidential job and you walk right in on Miss Huntress and explain the whole thing to her."

"It worked, didn't it?"

He stared. They all stared. "How do you know that?" he barked.

"I know a nice girl when I see one. She's here telling you she had an idea she got not to like, and for you to quit worrying about it. Where's Mister Gerald?"

Old Man Jeeter stopped and gave me a hard level stare. "I still regard you as incompetent," he said. "My son is missing."

"I'm not working for you. I'm working for Anna Halsey. Any complaints you have to make should be addressed to her. Do I pour my own drink or do you have a flunky in a purple suit to do it? And what do you mean, your son is missing?"

"Should I give him the heave, sir?" George asked quietly.

Jeeter waved his hand at a decanter and siphon and glasses on the black marble table and started around the rug again. "Don't be silly," he snapped at George.

George flushed a little, high on his cheekbones, His mouth looked tough.

I mixed myself a drink and sat down with it and tasted it and asked again: "What do you mean your son is missing, Mr. Jeeter?"

"I'm paying you good money," he started to yell at me, still mad.

"When?"

He stopped dead in his canter and looked at me again. Miss Huntress laughed lightly. George scowled.

"What do you suppose I mean—my son is missing?" he snapped. "I should have thought that would be clear enough even to you. Nobody knows where he is. Miss Huntress doesn't know. I don't know. No one at any of the places where he might be known."

"But I'm smarter than they are," I said. "*I* know."

Nobody moved for a long minute. Jeeter stared at me fish-eyed. George stared at me. The girl stared at me. She looked puzzled. The other two just stared.

I looked at her. "Where did you go when you went out, if you're telling?"

Her dark blue eyes were water-clear. "There's no secret about it. We went out together—in a taxi. Gerald had had his driving license suspended for a month. Too many tickets. We went down towards the beach and I had a change of heart, as you guessed. I decided I was just being a chiseler after all. I didn't want Gerald's money really. What I wanted was revenge. On Mr. Jeeter here for ruining my father. Done all legally of course, but done just the same. But I got myself in a spot where I couldn't have my revenge and not look like a cheap chiseler. So I told George to find some other girl to play with. He was sore and we quarreled. I stopped the taxi and got out in Beverly Hills. He went on. I don't know where. Later I went back to the El Milano and got my car out of the garage and came here. To tell Mr. Jeeter to forget the whole thing and not bother to sic sleuths on to me."

"You say you went with him in a taxi," I said. "Why wasn't George driving him, if he couldn't drive himself?"

I stared at her, but I wasn't talking to her. Jeeter answered me, frostily. "George drove me home from the office, of course. At that time Gerald had already gone out. Is there anything important about that?"

I turned to him. "Yeah. There's going to be. Mister Gerald is at the El Milano. Hawkins the house dick told me. He went back there to wait for Miss Huntress and Hawkins let him into her apartment. Hawkins will do you those little favors—for ten bucks. He may be there still and he may not."

I kept on watching them. It was hard to watch all three of them. But they didn't move. They just looked at me.

"Well—I'm glad to hear it," Old Man Jeeter said. "I was afraid he was off somewhere getting drunk."

"No. He's not off anywhere getting drunk," I said. "By the way, among these places you called to see if he was there, you didn't call the El Milano?"

George nodded. "Yes, I did. They said he wasn't there. Looks like the house peeper tipped the phone girl off not to say anything."

"He wouldn't have to do that. She'd just ring the apartment and he wouldn't answer—naturally." I watched Old Man Jeeter hard then, with a lot of interest. It was going to be hard for him to take that up, but he was going to have to do it.

He did. He licked his lips first. "Why—naturally, if I may ask?"

I put my glass down on the marble table and stood against the wall, with my hands hanging free. I still tried to watch them—all three of them.

"Let's go back over this thing a little," I said. "We're all wise to the situation. I know George is, although he shouldn't be, being just a servant. I know Miss Huntress is. And of course *you* are, Mr. Jeeter. So let's see what we have got. We have a lot of things that don't add up, but I'm smart. I'm going to add them up anyhow. First-off a handful of photostats of notes from Marty Estel. Gerald denies having given these and Mr. Jeeter won't pay them, but he has a handwriting man named Arbogast check the signatures, to see if they look genuine. They do. They are. This Arbogast may have done other things. I don't know. I couldn't ask him. When I went to see him, he was dead—shot three times—as I've since heard— with a twenty-two. No, I didn't tell the police, Mr. Jeeter."

The tall silver-haired man looked horribly shocked. His lean body shook like a bulrush. "Dead?" he whispered. "Murdered?"

I looked at George. George didn't move a muscle. I looked at the girl. She sat quietly, waiting, tight-lipped.

I said: "There's only one reason to suppose his killing had anything to do with Mr. Jeeter's affairs. He was shot with a twenty-two—and there is a man in this case who wears a twenty-two."

I still had their attention. And their silence.

"Why he was shot I haven't the faintest idea. He was not a dangerous man to Miss Huntress or Marty Estel. He was too fat to get around much. My guess is he was a little too smart. He got a simple case of signature identification and he went on from there to find out more than he should. And after he had found out more than he should—he guessed more than he ought—and maybe he even tried a little blackmail. And somebody rubbed him out this afternoon with a twenty-two. Okay, I can stand it. I never knew him.

"So I went over to see Miss Huntress and after a lot of finagling around with this itchy-handed house dick I got to see her and we had a chat, and then Mister Gerald stepped neatly out of hiding and bopped me a nice one on the chin and over I went and hit my head on a chair leg. And when I came out of that the joint was empty. So I went on home.

"And home I found the man with the twenty-two and with him a dimwit called Frisky Lavon, with a bad breath and a very large gun, neither of which matters now as he was shot dead in front of your house tonight, Mr. Jeeter—shot trying to stick up your car. The cops know about that one—they came to see me about it— because the other guy, the one that packs the twenty-two, is the little dimwit's brother and he thought I shot Dimwit and tried to put the bee on me. But it didn't work. That's two killings.

"We now come to the third and most important. I went back to the El Milano because it no longer seemed a good idea for Mister Gerald to be running around casually. He seemed to have a few enemies. It even seemed that he was supposed to be in the car this evening when Frisky Lavon shot at it—but of course that was just a plant."

Old Jeeter drew his white eyebrows together in an expression of puzzlement. George didn't look puzzled. He didn't look anything. He was as wooden-faced as a cigar-store Indian. The girl looked a little white now, a little tense. I plowed on.

"Back at the El Milano I found that Hawkins had let Marty Estel and his bodyguard into Miss Huntress' apartment to wait for her. Marty had something to tell her—that Arbogast had been killed. That made it a good idea for her to lay off young Jeeter for a while—until the cops quieted down anyhow. A thoughtful guy, Marty. A much more thoughtful guy than you would suppose. For instance, he knew about Arbogast and he knew Mr. Jeeter went to Anna Halsey's office this morning and he knew somehow—Anna might have told him herself, I wouldn't put it past her—that I was working on the case now. So he had me tailed to Arbogast's place and away, and he found out later from his cop friends that Arbogast had been murdered, and he knew I hadn't given it out. So he had me there and that made us pals. He went away after telling me this and once more I was left alone in Miss Huntress' apartment. But this time for no reason at all I poked around. And I found young Mister Gerald, in the bedroom, in a closet."

I stepped quickly over to the girl and reached into my pocket and took out the small fancy .25 automatic and laid it down on her knee.

"Ever see this before?"

Her voice had a curious tight sound, but her dark blue eyes looked at me levelly.

"Yes. It's mine."

"You kept it where?"

"In the drawer of a small table beside the bed."

"Sure about that?"

She thought. Neither of the two men stirred.

George began to twitch the corner of his mouth. She shook her head suddenly, sideways.

"No. I have an idea now I took it out to show somebody—because I don't know much about guns—and left it lying on the mantel in the living room. In fact, I'm almost sure I did. It was Gerald I showed it to."

"So he might have reached for it there, if anybody tried to make a wrong play at him?"

She nodded, troubled. "What do you mean—he's in the closet?" she asked in a small quick voice.

"You know. Everybody in this room knows what I mean. They know that I showed you that gun for a purpose." I stepped away from her and faced George and his boss. "He's dead, of course. Shot through the heart—probably with this gun. It was left there with him. That's why it would be left."

The old man took a step and stopped and braced himself against the table. I wasn't sure whether he had turned white or whether he had been white already. He stared stonily at the girl. He said very slowly, between his teeth: "You damned murderess!"

"Couldn't it have been suicide?" I sneered.

He turned his head enough to look at me. I could see that the idea interested him. He half nodded.

"No," I said. "It couldn't have been suicide."

He didn't like that so well. His face congested with blood and the veins on his nose thickened. The girl touched the gun lying on her knee, then put her hand loosely around the butt. I saw her thumb slide very gently towards the safety catch. She didn't know much about guns, but she knew that much.

"It couldn't be suicide," I said again, very slowly. "As an isolated event— maybe. But not with all the other stuff that's been happening. Arbogast, the stick-up down on Calvello Drive outside this house, the thugs planted in my apartment, the job with the twenty-two."

I reached into my pocket again and pulled out Waxnose's Woodsman. I held it carelessly on the flat of my left hand. "And curiously enough, I don't think it was *this* twenty-two—although this happens to be the gunman's twenty-two. Yeah, I have the gunman, too. He's tied up in my apartment. He came back to knock me off, but I talked him out of it. I'm a swell talker."

"Except that you overdo it," the girl said coolly, and lifted the gun a little.

"It's obvious who killed him, Miss Huntress," I said. "It's simply a matter of motive and opportunity. Marty Estel didn't, and didn't have it done. That would spoil his chances to get his fifty grand. Frisky Lavon's pal didn't, regardless of who he was working for, and I don't think he was working for Marty Estel. He couldn't have got into the El Milano to do the job, and certainly not into Miss Huntress' apartment. Whoever did it had something to gain by it and an opportunity to get to the place where it was done. Well, who had something to gain? Gerald had five million coming to him in two years out of a trust fund. He couldn't will it until he got it. So if he died, his natural heir got it. Who's his natural heir? You'd be surprised. Did you know that in the state of California and some others, but not in all, a man can by his own act become a natural heir? Just by adopting somebody who has money and no heirs!"

George moved then. His movement was once more as smooth as a ripple of water. The Smith & Wesson gleamed dully in his hand, but he didn't fire it. The small automatic in the girl's hand cracked. Blood spurted from George's brown hard hand. The Smith & Wesson dropped to the floor. He cursed. She didn't know much about guns—not very much.

"Of course!" she said grimly. "George could get into the apartment without any trouble, if Gerald was there. He would go in through the garage, a chauffeur in uniform, ride up in the elevator and knock at the door. And when Gerald opened it, George would back him in with that Smith and Wesson. But how did he know Gerald was there?"

I said: "He must have followed your taxi. We don't know where he has been all evening since he left me. He had a car with him. The cops will find out. How much was in it for you, George?"

George held his right wrist with his left hand, held it tightly, and his face was twisted, savage. He said nothing.

"George would back him in with the Smith and Wesson," the girl said wearily. "Then he would see my gun on the mantelpiece. That would be better. He would use that. He would back Gerald into the bedroom, away from the corridor, into the closet, and there, quietly, calmly, he would kill him and drop the gun on the floor."

"George killed Arbogast, too. He killed him with a twenty-two because he knew that Frisky Lavon's brother had a twenty-two, and he knew that because he had hired Frisky and his brother to put over a big scare on Gerald—so that when he was murdered it would look as if Marty Estel had had it done. That was why I was brought out here tonight in the Jeeter car—so that the two thugs who had been warned and planted could pull their act and maybe knock me off, if I got too tough. Only George likes to kill people. He made a neat shot at Frisky. He hit him in the face. It was so good a shot I think he meant it to be a miss. How about it, George?"

Silence.

I looked at old Jeeter at last. I had been expecting him to pull a gun himself, but he hadn't. He just stood there, open-mouthed, appalled, leaning against the black marble table, shaking.

"My God!" he whispered. "My God!"

"You don't have one—except money."

A door squeaked behind me. I whirled, but I needn't have bothered. A hard voice, about as English as Amos and Andy, said: "Put 'em up, bud."

The butler, the very English butler, stood there in the doorway, a gun in his hand, tight-lipped. The girl turned her wrist and shot him just kind of casually, in the shoulder or something. He squealed like a stuck pig.

"Go away, you're intruding," she said coldly.

He ran. We heard his steps running.

"He's going to fall," she said.

I was wearing my Luger in my right hand now, a little late in the season, as usual. I came around with it. Old Man Jeeter was holding on to the table, his face gray as a paving block. His knees were giving. George stood cynically, holding a handkerchief around his bleeding wrist, watching him.

"Let him fall," I said. "Down is where he belongs."

He fell. His head twisted. His mouth went slack. He hit the carpet on his side and rolled a little and his knees came up. His mouth drooled a little. His skin turned violet.

"Go call the law, angel," I said. "I'll watch them now."

"All right," she said standing up. "But you certainly need a lot of help in your private-detecting business, Mr. Marlowe."

8

I had been in there for a solid hour, alone. There was the scarred desk in the middle, another against the wall, a brass spittoon on a mat, a police loudspeaker box on the wall, three squashed flies, a smell of cold cigars and old clothes. There were two hard armchairs with felt pads and two hard straight chairs without pads. The electric-light fixture had been dusted about Coolidge's first term.

The door opened with a jerk and Finlayson and Sebold came in. Sebold looked as spruce and nasty as ever, but Finlayson looked older, more worn, mousier. He held a sheaf of papers in his hand. He sat down across the desk from me and gave me a hard bleak stare.

"Guys like you get in a lot of trouble," Finlayson said sourly. Sebold sat down against the wall and tilted his hat over his eyes and yawned and looked at his new stainless-steel wrist watch.

"Trouble is my business," I said. "How else would I make a nickel?"

"We oughta throw you in the can for all this cover-up stuff. How much you making on this one?"

"I was working for Anna Halsey who was working for Old Man Jeeter. I guess I made a bad debt."

Sebold smiled his blackjack smile at me. Finlayson lit a cigar and licked at a tear on the side of it and pasted it down, but it leaked smoke just the same when he drew on it. He pushed papers across the desk at me.

"Sign three copies."

I signed three copies.

He took them back, yawned and rumpled his old gray head. "The old man's had a stroke," he said. "No dice there. Probably won't know what time it is when he comes out. This George Hasterman, this chauffeur guy, he just laughs at us. Too bad he got pinked. I'd like to wrastle him a bit."

"He's tough," I said.

"Yeah. Okay, you can beat it for now."

I got up and nodded to them and went to the door. "Well, good night, boys."

Neither of them spoke to me.

I went out, along the corridor and down in the night elevator to the City Hall lobby. I went out the Spring Street side and down the long flight of empty steps and the wind blew cold. I lit a cigarette at the bottom. My car was still out at the Jeeter place. I lifted a foot to start walking to a taxi half a block down across the street. A voice spoke sharply from a parked car.

"Come here a minute."

It was a man's voice, tight, hard. It was Marty Estel's voice. It came from a big sedan with two men in the front seat. I went over there. The rear window was down and Marty Estel leaned a gloved hand on it.

"Get in." He pushed the door open. I got in. I was too tired to argue. "Take it away, Skin."

The car drove west through dark, almost quiet streets, almost clean streets. The night air was not pure but it was cool. We went up over a hill and began to pick up speed.

"What they get?" Estel asked coolly.

"They didn't tell me. They didn't break the chauffeur yet."

"You can't convict a couple million bucks of murder in this man's town." The driver called Skin laughed without turning his head. "Maybe I don't even touch my fifty grand now . . . she likes you."

"Uh-huh. So what?"

"Lay off her."

"What will it get me?"

"It's what it'll get you if you don't."

"Yeah, sure," I said. "Go to hell, will you please. I'm tired." I shut my eyes and leaned in the corner of the car and just like that went to sleep. I can do that sometimes, after a strain.

A hand shaking my shoulder woke me. The car had stopped. I looked out at the front of my apartment house.

"Home," Martey Estel said. "And remember. Lay off her."

"Why the ride home? Just to tell me that?"

"She asked me to look out for you. That's why you're loose. She likes you. I like her. See? You don't want any more trouble."

"Trouble—" I started to say, and stopped. I was tired of that gag for that night. "Thanks for the ride, and apart from that, nuts to you." I turned away and went into the apartment house and up.

The door lock was still loose but nobody waited for me this time. They had taken Waxnose away long since. I left the door open and threw the windows up and I was still sniffing at policemen's cigar butts when the phone rang. It was her voice, cool, a little hard, not touched by anything, almost amused. Well, she'd been through enough to make her that way, probably.

"Hello, brown eyes. Make it home all right?"

"Your pal Marty brought me home. He told me to lay off you. Thanks with all my heart, if I have any, but don't call me up any more."

"A little scared, Mr. Marlowe?"

"No. Wait for me to call you," I said. "Goodnight, angel."

"Goodnight, brown eyes."

The phone clicked. I put it away and shut the door and pulled the bed down. I undressed and lay on it for a while in the cold air.

Then I got up and had a drink and a shower and went to sleep.

They broke George at last, but not enough. He said there had been a fight over the girl and young Jeeter had grabbed the gun off the mantel and George had fought with him and it had gone off. All of which, of course, looked possible—in the papers. They never pinned the Arbogast killing on him or on anybody. They never found the gun that did it, but it was not Waxnose's gun. Waxnose disappeared—I never heard where. They didn't touch Old Man Jeeter, because he never came out of his stroke, except to lie on his back and have nurses and tell people how he hadn't lost a nickel in the depression.

Marty Estel called me up four times to tell me to lay off Harriet Huntress. I felt kind of sorry for the poor guy. He had it bad. I went out with her twice and sat with her twice more at home, drinking her Scotch. It was nice, but I didn't have the money, the clothes, the time or the manners. Then she stopped being at the El Milano and I heard she had gone to New York.

I was glad when she left—even though she didn't bother to tell me goodbye.

Ellery Queen

THE ADVENTURE OF ABRAHAM LINCOLN'S CLUE

Ellery Queen is—or is it "are"?—a detective, a writer, and an editor.

Let's begin with the detective, the dapper son of Inspector Richard Queen of the NYPD. Ellery and his father share an apartment on West Eighty-Seventh Street in Manhattan (just fifty-two blocks north of Nero Wolfe's place, a fact neither detective mentions), although he also has extended visits to Hollywood (where he works as a screenwriter) and Wrightsville (a little New England village with a rather appalling crime rate). Ellery is a writer, and although he now and then frets about deadlines, he spends more time sniffing out ingenious murderers than sitting at a typewriter.

Ellery Queen, the writer, the real *writer, is two men, Brooklyn-born cousins Frederic Dannay (1905–1982) and Manfred B. Lee (1905–1971) who made up their pseudonym and wrote their first Ellery Queen mystery in 1928 to enter a novel contest sponsored by McClure's magazine. They didn't win, but* The Roman Hat Mystery *(in which the murder takes place in a Broadway theater while a play is in progress) was published in book form a year later. By the time Lee died, the partners had published thirty-nine novels and seven collections of short stories. Although they always refused to talk about their working methods, Dannay once said, "We're not so much collaborators as competitors. It has produced a sharper edge." One of the trademarks of their early novels was a "Challenge to the Reader" that appeared toward the end of the book announcing that all the information needed to solve the crime had been presented.*

The editor Ellery Queen, of all the EQs, has probably had the most profound and longest-lasting influence on American detective fiction.

Ellery Queen's Mystery Magazine, *which is more the creation of Dannay than Lee, has been the country's primary—and for some years only— outlet for the detective story. Since it first came on the newsstands in 1941, it has had a unique record in being the first publisher of many of the now-standard names in American crime fiction.*

The Adventure of
Abraham Lincoln's Clue

THE CASE BEGAN on the outskirts of an upstate New York city with the dreadful name of Eulalia, behind the flaking shutters of a fat and curlicued house with architectural dandruff, recalling for all the world some blowsy ex-Bloomer Girl from the Gay Nineties of its origin.

The owner, a formerly wealthy man named DiCampo, possessed a grandeur not shared by his property, although it was no less fallen into ruin. His falcon's face, more Florentine then Victorian, was—like the house—ravaged by time and the inclemencies of fortune; but haughtily so, and indeed DiCampo wore his scurfy purple velvet house jacket like the prince he was entitled to call himself, but did not. He was proud, and stubborn, and useless; and he had a lovely daughter named Bianca, who taught at a Eulalia grade school and, through marvels of economy, supported them both.

How Lorenzo San Marco Borghese-Ruffo DiCampo came to this decayed estate is no concern of ours. The presence there this day of a man named Harbidger and a man named Tungston, however, is to the point: they had come, Harbidger from Chicago, Tungston from Philadelphia, to buy something each wanted very much, and DiCampo had summoned them in order to sell it. The two visitors were collectors, Harbidger's passion being Lincoln, Tungston's Poe.

The Lincoln collector, an elderly man who looked like a migrant fruit picker, had plucked his fruits well: Harbidger was worth about $40,000,000, every dollar of which was at the beck of his mania for Lincolniana. Tungston, who was almost as rich, had the aging body of a poet and the eyes of a starving panther, armament that had served him well in the wars of Poeana.

"I must say, Mr. DiCampo," remarked Harbidger, "that your letter surprised me." He paused to savor the wine his host had poured from an ancient and honorable bottle (DiCampo had filled it with California claret before their arrival). "May I ask what has finally induced you to offer the book and document for sale?"

"To quote Lincoln in another context, Mr. Harbidger," said DiCampo with a shrug of his wasted shoulders, " 'the dogmas of the quiet past are inadequate to the stormy present.' In short, a hungry man sells his blood."

"Only if it's of the right type," said old Tungston, unmoved. "You've made that book and document less accessible to collectors and historians, DiCampo, than the gold in Fort Knox. Have you got them here? I'd like to examine them."

"No other hand will ever touch them except by right of ownership," Lorenzo

267

DiCampo replied bitterly. He had taken a miser's glee in his lucky finds, vowing never to part with them; now forced by his need to sell them, he was like a suspicion-caked old prospector who, stumbling at last on pay dirt, draws cryptic maps to keep the world from stealing the secret of its location. "As I informed you gentlemen, I represent the book as bearing the signatures of Poe and Lincoln, and the document as being in Lincoln's hand; I am offering them with the customary proviso that they are returnable if they should prove to be not as represented; and if this does not satisfy you," and the old prince actually rose, "let us terminate our business here and now."

"Sit down, sit down, Mr. DiCampo," Harbidger said.

"No one is questioning your integrity," snapped old Tungston. "It's just that I'm not used to buying sight unseen. If there's a money-back guarantee, we'll do it your way."

Lorenzo DiCampo reseated himself stiffly. "Very well, gentlemen. Then I take it you are both prepared to buy?"

"Oh, yes!" said Harbidger. "What is your price?"

"Oh, no," said DiCampo. "What is your bid?"

The Lincoln collector cleared his throat, which was full of slaver. "If the book and document are as represented, Mr. DiCampo, you might hope to get from a dealer or realize at auction—oh—$50,000. I offer you $55,000."

"$56,000," said Tungston.

"$57,000," said Harbidger.

"$58,000," said Tungston.

"$59,000," said Harbidger.

Tungston showed his fangs. "$60,000," he said.

Harbidger fell silent, and DiCampo waited. He did not expect miracles. To these men, five times $60,000 was of less moment than the undistinguished wine they were smacking their lips over; but they were veterans of many a hard auction-room campaign, and a collector's victory tasted very nearly as sweet for the price as for the prize.

So the impoverished prince was not surprised when the Lincoln collector suddenly said, "Would you be good enough to allow Mr. Tungston and me to talk privately for a moment?"

DiCampo rose and strolled out of the room, to gaze somberly through a cracked window at the jungle growth that had once been his Italian formal gardens.

It was the Poe collector who summoned him back. "Harbidger has convinced me that for the two of us to try to outbid each other would simply run the price up out of all reason. We're going to make you a sporting proposition."

"I've proposed to Mr. Tungston, and he has agreed," nodded Harbidger, "that our bid for the book and document be $65,000. Each of us is prepared to pay that sum, and not a penny more."

"So that is how the screws are turned," said DiCampo, smiling. "But I do not understand. If each of you makes the identical bid, which of you gets the book and document?"

"Ah," grinned the Poe man, "that's where the sporting proposition comes in."

"You see, Mr. DiCampo," said the Lincoln man, "we are going to leave that decision to you."

Even the old prince, who had seen more than his share of the astonishing, was astonished. He looked at the two rich men really for the first time. "I must confess," he murmured, "that your compact is an amusement. Permit me?" He sank into thought while the two collectors sat expectantly. When the old man looked up he was smiling like a fox. "The very thing, gentlemen! From the typewritten copies of the document I sent you, you both know that Lincoln himself left a clue to a theoretical hiding place for the book which he never explained. Some time ago I arrived at a possible solution to the President's little mystery. I propose to hide the book and document in accordance with it."

"You mean whichever of us figures out your interpretation of the Lincoln clue and finds the book and document where you will hide them, Mr. DiCampo, gets both for the agreed price?"

"That is it exactly."

The Lincoln collector looked dubious. "I don't know . . ."

"Oh, come, Harbidger," said Tungston, eyes glittering. "A deal is a deal. We accept, DiCampo! Now what?"

"You gentlemen will of course have to give me a little time. Shall we say three days?"

Ellery let himself into the Queen apartment, tossed his suitcase aside, and set about opening windows. He had been out of town for a week on a case, and Inspector Queen was in Atlantic City attending a police convention.

Breathable air having been restored, Ellery sat down to the week's accumulation of mail. One envelope made him pause. It had come by airmail special delivery, it was postmarked four days earlier, and in the lower left corner, in red, flamed the word URGENT. The printed return address on the flap said: L.S.M.B.-R DICAMPO, POST OFFICE BOX 69, SOUTHERN DISTRICT, EULALIA, N.Y. The initials of the name had been crossed out and "Bianca" written above them.

The enclosure, in a large agitated female hand on inexpensive notepaper, said:

Dear Mr. Queen,

The most important detective book in the world has disappeared. Will you please find it for me?

Phone me on arrival at the Eulalia RR station or airport and I will pick you up.

Bianca DiCampo

A yellow envelope then caught his eye. It was a telegram, dated the previous day:

WHY HAVE I NOT HEARD FROM YOU STOP AM IN DESPERATE NEED
YOUR SERVICES

> BIANCA DICAMPO

He had no sooner finished reading the telegram than the telephone on his desk trilled. It was a long-distance call.

"Mr. Queen?" throbbed a contralto voice. "Thank heaven I've finally got through to you! I've been calling all day—"

"I've been away," said Ellery, "and you would be Miss Bianca DiCampo of Eulalia. In two words, Miss DiCampo: Why me?"

"In two words, Mr. Queen: Abraham Lincoln."

Ellery was startled. "You plead a persuasive case," he chuckled. "It's true, I'm an incurable Lincoln addict. How did you find out? Well, never mind. Your letter refers to a book, Miss DiCampo. Which book?"

The husky voice told him, and certain other provocative things as well. "So will you come, Mr. Queen?"

"Tonight if I could! Suppose I drive up first thing in the morning. I ought to make Eulalia by noon. Harbidger and Tungston are still around, I take it?"

"Oh, yes. They're staying at a motel downtown."

"Would you ask them to be there?"

The moment he hung up, Ellery leaped to his bookshelves. He snatched out his volume of *Murder for Pleasure*, the historical work on detective stories by his good friend Howard Haycraft, and found what he was looking for on page 26:

> And . . . young William Dean Howells thought it significant praise to assert of a nominee for President of the United States:
>
>> The bent of his mind is mathematical and metaphysical, and he is therefore pleased with the absolute and logical method of Poe's tales and sketches, in which the problem of mystery is given, and wrought out into everyday facts by processes of cunning analysis. It is said that he suffers no year to pass without a perusal of this author.
>
> Abraham Lincoln subsequently confirmed this statement, which appeared in his little-known "campaign biography" by Howells in 1860. . . . The instance is chiefly notable, of course, for its revelation of a little-suspected affinity between two great Americans. . . .

Very early the next morning Ellery gathered some papers from his files, stuffed them into his brief case, scribbled a note for his father, and ran for his car, Eulalia-bound.

He was enchanted by the DiCampo house, which looked like something out of Poe by Charles Addams; and, for other reasons, by Bianca, who turned out to be a genetic product supreme of northern Italy, with titian hair and Mediterranean blue eyes and a figure that needed only some solid steaks to qualify her for Miss Universe competition. Also, she was in deep mourning; so her conquest of the Queen heart was immediate and complete.

"He died of a cerebral hemorrhage, Mr. Queen," Bianca said, dabbing at her absurd little nose. "In the middle of the second night after his session with Mr. Harbidger and Mr. Tungston."

So Lorenzo San Marco Borghese-Ruffo DiCampo was unexpectedly dead, bequeathing the lovely Bianca near-destitution and a mystery.

"The only things of value Father really left me are that book and the Lincoln document. The $65,000 they now represent would pay off Father's debts and give me a fresh start. But I can't find them, Mr. Queen, and neither can Mr. Harbidger and Mr. Tungston—who'll be here soon, by the way. Father hid the two things, as he told them he would; but where? We've ransacked the place."

"Tell me more about the book, Miss DiCampo."

"As I said over the phone, it's called *The Gift: 1845*. The Christmas annual that contained the earliest appearance of Edgar Allan Poe's 'The Purloined Letter.'"

"Published in Philadelphia by Carey & Hart? Bound in red?" At Bianca's nod Ellery said, "You understand that an ordinary copy of *The Gift: 1845* isn't worth more than about $50. What makes your father's copy unique is that double autograph you mentioned."

"That's what he said, Mr. Queen. I wish I had the book here to show you— that beautifully handwritten *Edgar Allan Poe* on the flyleaf, and under Poe's signature the signature *Abraham Lincoln*."

"Poe's own copy, once owned, signed and read by Lincoln," Ellery said slowly. "Yes, that would be a collector's item for the ages. By the way, Miss DiCampo, what's the story behind the other piece—the Lincoln document?"

Bianca told him what her father had told her.

One morning in the spring of 1865, Abraham Lincoln opened the rosewood door of his bedroom in the southwest corner of the second floor of the White House and stepped out into the redcarpeted hall at the unusually late hour—for him—of 7:00 a.m.; he was more accustomed to beginning his workday at six.

But (as Lorenzo DiCampo had reconstructed events) Mr. Lincoln that morning had lingered in his bedchamber. He had awakened at his usual hour but, instead of leaving immediately on dressing for his office, he had pulled one of the cane chairs over to the round table, with its gas-fed reading lamp, and sat down to reread Poe's "The Purloined Letter" in his copy of the 1845 annual; it was a dreary morning, and the natural light was poor. The President was alone; the folding doors to Mrs. Lincoln's bedroom remained closed.

Impressed as always with Poe's tale, Mr. Lincoln on this occasion was struck by a whimsical thought; and, apparently finding no paper handy, he took an envelope from his pocket, discarded its enclosure, slit the two short edges so that the envelope opened out into a single sheet, and began to write on the blank side . . .

"Describe it to me, please."

"It's a long envelope, one that must have contained a bulky letter. It is addressed to the White House, but there is no return address, and Father was never able to identify the sender from the handwriting. We do know that the letter came through the regular mails, because there are two Lincoln stamps on it, lightly but unmistakably canceled."

"May I see your father's transcript of what Lincoln wrote out that morning on the inside of the envelope?"

Bianca handed him a typewritten copy and, in spite of himself, Ellery felt goose flesh rise as he read:

Apr. 14, 1865

Mr. Poe's The Purloined Letter is a work of singular originality. Its simplicity is a master-stroke of cunning, which never fails to arouse my wonder.

Reading the tale over this morning has given me a "notion." Suppose I wished to hide a book, this very book, perhaps? Where best to do so? Well, as Mr. Poe in his tale hid a letter *among letters*, might not a book be hidden *among books*? Why, if this very copy of the tale were to be deposited in a library and on purpose not recorded—would not the Library of Congress make a prime depository!—well might it repose there, undiscovered, for a generation.

On the other hand, let us regard Mr. Poe's "notion" turn-about: suppose the book were to be placed, not amongst other books, but *where no book would reasonably be expected?* (I may follow the example of Mr. Poe, and, myself, compose a tale of "ratiocination"!)

The "notion" beguiles me, it is nearly seven o'clock. Later to-day, if the vultures and my appointments leave me a few moments of leisure, I may write further of my imagined hiding-place.

In self-reminder: the hiding place of the book is in 30d, which

Ellery looked up. "The document ends there?"

"Father said that Mr. Lincoln must have glanced again at his watch, and shamefacedly jumped up to go to his office, leaving the sentence unfinished. Evidently he never found the time to get back to it."

Ellery brooded. Evidently indeed. From the moment when Abraham Lincoln stepped from his bedroom that Good Friday morning, fingering his thick gold watch on its vest chain, to bid the still-unrelieved night guard his customary courteous "Good morning" and make for his office at the other end of the hall, his day was spoken for. The usual patient push through the clutching crowd of favor seekers, many of whom had bedded down all night on the hall carpet; sanctuary in his sprawling office, where he read official correspondence; by 8:00 a.m. having breakfast with his family—Mrs. Lincoln chattering away about plans for the evening, twelve-year-old Tad of the cleft palate lisping a complaint that "nobody asked me to go," and young Robert Lincoln, just returned from duty, bubbling with stories about his hero Ulysses Grant and the last days of the war; then back to the presidential office to look over the morning newspapers (which Lincoln had once remarked he "never" read, but these were happy days, with good news everywhere), sign two documents, and signal the soldier at the door to admit the morning's first caller, Speaker of the House Schuyler Colfax (who was angling for a Cabinet post and had to be tactfully handled); and so on throughout the day—the historic Cabinet meeting at 11:00 a.m., attended by General Grant himself, that stretched well into the afternoon; a hurried lunch at almost half past two with Mrs. Lincoln (had this forty-five-pounds-underweight man eaten his usual midday meal of a biscuit, a glass of milk, and an apple?); more visitors to see in his office (including the unscheduled Mrs. Nancy Bushrod, escaped slave and wife of an escaped slave and mother of three small children, weeping that Tom, a soldier in the Army of the Potomac, was no longer getting his pay: "You are entitled to your husband's pay. Come this time tomorrow," and the tall President escorted her to the door, bowing her out "like I was a natural-born lady"; the late afternoon drive in the barouche to the Navy Yard and back with Mrs. Lincoln; more work, more visitors, into the evening . . . until finally, at five minutes past 8:00 p.m., Abraham Lincoln stepped into the White House formal coach after his wife, waved, and sank back to be driven off to see a play he did not much want to see, *Our American Cousin*, at Ford's Theatre . . .

Ellery mused over the black day in silence. And, like a relative hanging on the specialist's yet undelivered diagnosis, Bianca DiCampo sat watching him with anxiety.

Harbidger and Tungston arrived in a taxi to greet Ellery with the fervor of castaways grasping at a smudge of smoke on the horizon.

"As I understand it, gentlemen," Ellery said when he had calmed them down, "neither of you has been able to solve Mr. DiCampo's interpretation of the Lincoln clue. If I succeed in finding the book and paper where DiCampo hid them, which of you gets them?"

"We intend to split the $65,000 payment to Miss DiCampo," said Harbidger, "and take joint ownership of the two pieces."

"An arrangement," growled old Tungston, "I'm against on principle, in practice, and by plain horse sense."

"So am I," sighed the Lincoln collector, "but what else can we do?"

"Well," and the Poe man regarded Bianca DiCampo with the icy intimacy of the cat that long ago marked the bird as its prey, "Miss DiCampo, who now owns the two pieces, is quite free to renegotiate a sale on her own terms."

"Miss DiCampo," said Miss DiCampo, giving Tungston stare for stare, "considers herself bound by her father's wishes. His terms stand."

"In all likelihood, then," said the other millionaire, "one of us will retain the book, the other the document, and we'll exchange them every year, or some such thing." Harbidger sounded unhappy.

"Only practical arrangement under the circumstances," grunted Tungston, and *he* sounded unhappy. "But all this is academic, Queen, unless and until the book and document are found."

Ellery nodded. "The problem, then, is to fathom DiCampo's interpretation of that 30*d* in the document. 30d . . . I notice, Miss DiCampo—or, may I? Bianca? —that your father's typewritten copy of the Lincoln holograph text runs the 3 and *o* and *d* together—no spacing in between. Is that the way it occurs in the longhand?"

"Yes."

"Hmm. Still . . . 30d . . . Could *d* stand for *days* . . . or the British *pence* . . . or *died*, as used in obituaries? Does any of these make sense to you, Bianca?"

"No."

"Did your father have any special interest in, say, pharmacology? chemistry? physics? algebra? electricity? Small *d* is an abbreviation used in all those." But Bianca shook her splendid head. "Banking? Small *d* for *dollars, dividends?*"

"Hardly," the girl said with a sad smile.

"How about theatricals? Was your father ever involved in a play production? Small *d* stands for *door* in playscript stage directions."

"Mr. Queen, I've gone through every darned abbreviation my dictionary lists, and I haven't found one that has a point of contact with any interest of my father's."

Ellery scowled. "At that—I assume the typewritten copy is accurate—the manuscript shows no period after the *d*, making an abbreviation unlikely. 30d . . . let's concentrate on the number. Does the number 30 have any significance for you?"

"Yes, indeed," said Bianca, making all three men sit up. But then they sank back. "In a few years it will represent my age, and that has enormous significance. But only for me, I'm afraid."

"You'll be drawing wolf whistles at twice thirty," quoth Ellery warmly. "However! Could the number have cross-referred to anything in your father's life or habits?"

"None that I can think of, Mr. Queen. And," Bianca said, having grown roses in her cheeks, "thank you."

"I think," said old Tungston testily, "we had better stick to the subject."

"Just the same, Bianca, let me run over some 'thirty' associations as they come to mind. Stop me if one of them hits a nerve. The Thirty Tyrants—was your father interested in classical Athens? Thirty Years' War—in seventeenth-century European history? Thirty all—did he play or follow tennis? Or . . . did he ever live at an address that included the number 30?" Ellery went on and on, but to each suggestion Bianca DiCampo could only shake her head.

"The lack of spacing, come to think of it, doesn't necessarily mean that Mr. DiCampo chose to view the clue that way," said Ellery thoughtfully. "He might have interpreted it arbitrarily as 3-space-o-d."

"Three od?" echoed old Tungston. "What the devil could that mean?"

"Od? Od is the hypothetical force or power claimed by Baron von Reichenbach —in 1850, wasn't it?—to pervade the whole of nature. Manifests itself in magnets, crystals and such, which according to the excited Baron explained animal magnetism and mesmerism. Was your father by any chance interested in hypnosis, Bianca? Or the occult?"

"Not in the slightest."

"Mr. Queen," exclaimed Harbidger, "are you serious about all this—this semantic sludge?"

"Why, I don't know," said Ellery. "I never know till I stumble over something. Od . . . the word was used with prefixes, too—*biod*, the force of animal life; *elod*, the force of electricity; and so forth. *Three* od . . . or *triod*, the triune force—it's all right, Mr. Harbidger, it's not ignorance on your part, I just coined the word. But it does rather suggest the Trinity, doesn't it? Bianca, did your father tie up to the Church in a personal, scholarly, or any other way? No? That's too bad, really, because Od—capitalized—has been a minced form of the word God since the sixteenth century. Or . . . you wouldn't happen to have three Bibles on the premises, would you? Because—"

Ellery stopped with the smashing abruptness of an ordinary force meeting an absolutely immovable object. The girl and the two collectors gawped. Bianca had idly picked up the typewritten copy of the Lincoln document. She was not reading it; she was simply holding it on her knees; but Ellery, sitting opposite her, had shot forward in a crouch, rather like a pointer, and he was regarding the paper in her lap with a glare of pure discovery.

"That's it!" he cried.

"What's it, Mr. Queen?" the girl asked, bewildered.

"Please—the transcript!" He plucked the paper from her. "Of course. Hear this: '*On the other hand, let us regard Mr. Poe's "notion" turn-about.*' Turn-about. Look at the 30d 'turn-about'—as I just saw it!"

He turned the Lincoln message upside down for their inspection. In that position the 30d became:

poɛ

"*Poe!*" exploded Tungston.

"Yes, crude but recognizable," Ellery said swiftly. "So now we read the Lincoln clue as: '*The hiding-place of the book is in* Poe!' "

There was a silence.

"In Poe," said Harbidger blankly.

"In Poe?" muttered Tungston. "There are only a couple of trade editions of Poe in DiCampo's library, Harbidger, and we went through those. We looked in every book here."

"He might have meant among the Poe books in the *public* library. Miss Di-Campo—"

"Wait." Bianca sped away. But when she came back she was drooping. "It isn't. We have two public libraries in Eulalia, and I know the head librarian in both. I just called them. Father didn't visit either library."

Ellery gnawed a fingernail. "Is there a bust of Poe in the house, Bianca? Or any other Poe-associated object, aside from books?"

"I'm afraid not."

"Queer," he mumbled. "Yet I'm positive your father interpreted '*the hiding-place of the book*' as being '*in Poe.*' So he'd have hidden it '*in Poe*' . . ." Ellery's mumbling dribbled away into a tormented sort of silence: his eyebrows worked up and down, Groucho Marx fashion; he pinched the tip of his nose until it was scarlet; he yanked at his unoffending ears; he munched on his lip . . . until, all at once, his face cleared; and he sprang to his feet. "Bianca, may I use your phone?"

The girl could only nod, and Ellery dashed. They heard him telephoning in the entrance hall, although they could not make out the words. He was back in two minutes.

"One thing more," he said briskly, "and we're out of the woods. I suppose your father used a key ring or a key case, Bianca? May I have it, please?"

She fetched a key case. To the two millionaires it seemed the sorriest of objects, a scuffed and dirty tan leatherette case. But Ellery received it from the girl as if it were an artifact of historic importance from a newly discovered Fourth Dynasty tomb. He unsnapped it with concentrated love; he fingered its contents like a scientist. Finally he decided on a certain key.

"Wait here!" Thus Mr. Queen; and exit, running.

"I can't decide," old Tungston said after a while, "whether that fellow is a genius or an escaped lunatic."

Neither Harbidger nor Bianca replied. Apparently they could not decide, either.

They waited through twenty elongated minutes; at the twenty-first, they heard his car, champing. All three were in the front doorway as Ellery strode up the walk.

He was carrying a book with a red cover, and smiling. It was a compassionate smile, but none of them noticed.

"You—" said Bianca. "—found—" said Tungston. "—the book!" shouted Harbidger. "Is the Lincoln holograph in it?"

"It is," said Ellery. "Shall we all go into the house, where we may mourn in decent privacy?"

"Because," Ellery said to Bianca and the two quivering collectors as they sat across a refectory table from him, "I have foul news. Mr. Tungston, I believe you have never actually seen Mr. DiCampo's book. Will you now look at the Poe signature on the flyleaf?"

The panther claws leaped. There, toward the top of the flyleaf, in faded ink-script, ran the signature *Edgar Allan Poe*.

The claws curled, and old Tungston looked up sharply. "DiCampo never mentioned that it's a full autograph—he kept referring to it as 'the Poe signature.' Edgar *Allan* Poe . . . Why, I don't know of a single instance after his West Point days when Poe wrote out his middle name in an autograph! And the earliest he could have signed this 1845 edition is obviously when it was published, which was around the fall of 1844. In 1844 he'd surely have abbreviated the 'Allan,' signing 'Edgar A. Poe,' the way he signed everything! This is a forgery."

"My God," murmured Bianca, clearly intending no impiety; she was as pale as Poe's Lenore. "Is that true, Mr. Queen?"

"I'm afraid it is," Ellery said sadly. "I was suspicious the moment you told me the Poe signature on the flyleaf contained the 'Allan.' And if the Poe signature is a forgery, the book itself can hardly be considered Poe's own copy."

Harbidger was moaning. "And the Lincoln signature underneath the Poe, Mr. Queen! DiCampo never told me it reads *Abraham* Lincoln—the full Christian name. Except on official documents, Lincoln practically always signed his name 'A. Lincoln.' Don't tell me this Lincoln autograph is a forgery, too?"

Ellery forbore to look at poor Bianca. "I was struck by the 'Abraham' as well, Mr. Harbidger, when Miss DiCampo mentioned it to me, and I came equipped to test it. I have here"—and Ellery tapped the pile of documents he had taken from his briefcase—"facsimiles of Lincoln signatures from the most frequently repro-duced of the historic documents he signed. Now I'm going to make a precise tracing of the Lincoln signature on the flyleaf of the book"—he proceeded to do so

—"and I shall superimpose the tracing on the various signatures of the authentic Lincoln documents. So." He worked rapidly. On his third superimposition Ellery looked up. "Yes. See here. The tracing of the purported Lincoln signature from the flyleaf fits in minutest detail over the authentic Lincoln signature on this facsimile of the Emancipation Proclamation. It's a fact of life that's tripped many a forger that *nobody ever writes his name exactly the same way twice.* There are always variations. If two signatures are identical, then one must be a tracing of the other. So the 'Abraham Lincoln' signed on this flyleaf can be dismissed without further consideration as a forgery also. It's a tracing of the Emancipation Proclamation signature.

"Not only was this book not Poe's own copy; it was never signed—and therefore probably never owned—by Lincoln. However your father came into possession of the book, Bianca, he was swindled."

It was the measure of Bianca DiCampo's quality that she said quietly, "Poor, poor Father," nothing more.

Harbidger was poring over the worn old envelope on whose inside appeared the dearly beloved handscript of the Martyr President. "At least," he muttered, "we have *this*."

"Do we?" asked Ellery gently. "Turn it over, Mr. Harbidger."

Harbidger looked up, scowling. "No! You're not going to deprive me of this, too!"

"Turn it over," Ellery repeated in the same gentle way. The Lincoln collector obeyed reluctantly. "What do you see?"

"An authentic envelope of the period! With two authentic Lincoln stamps!"

"Exactly. And the United States has never issued postage stamps depicting living Americans; you have to be dead to qualify. The earliest U.S. stamp showing a portrait of Lincoln went on sale April 15, 1866—a year to the day after his death. Then a living Lincoln could scarcely have used this envelope, with these stamps on it, as writing paper. The document is spurious, too. I am so very sorry, Bianca."

Incredibly, Lorenzo DiCampo's daughter managed a smile with her "*Non importa, signor.*" He could have wept for her. As for the two collectors, Harbidger was in shock; but old Tungston managed to croak, "Where the devil did DiCampo hide the book, Queen? And how did you know?"

"Oh, that," said Ellery, wishing the two old men would go away so that he might comfort this admirable creature. "I was convinced that DiCampo interpreted what we now know was the forger's, not Lincoln's, clue, as 30d read upside down; or, crudely, *Poe*. But '*the hiding-place of the book is in Poe*' led nowhere.

"So I reconsidered, P, o, e. If those three letters of the alphabet didn't mean Poe, what could they mean? Then I remembered something about the letter you wrote me, Bianca. You'd used one of your father's envelopes, on the flap of which appeared his address: *Post Office Box 69, Southern District, Eulalia, N.Y.* If there was a Southern District in Eulalia, it seemed reasonable to conclude that there were post offices for other points of the compass, too. As, for instance, an Eastern District. Post Office Eastern. P.O. East. P.O.E."

"Poe!" cried Bianca.

"To answer your question, Mr. Tungston: I phoned the main post office, confirmed the existence of a Post Office East, got directions as to how to get there, looked for a postal box key in Mr. DiCampo's key case, found the right one, located the box DiCampo had rented especially for the occasion, unlocked it— and there was the book." He added, hopefully, "And that is that."

"And that *is* that," Bianca said when she returned from seeing the two collectors off. "I'm not going to cry over an empty milk bottle, Mr. Queen. I'll straighten out Father's affairs somehow. Right now all I can think of is how glad I am he didn't live to see the signatures and documents declared forgeries publicly, as they would surely have been when they were expertized."

"I think you'll find there's still some milk in the bottle, Bianca."

"I beg your pardon?" said Bianca.

Ellery tapped the pseudo-Lincolnian envelope. "You know, you didn't do a very good job describing this envelope to me. All you said was that there were two canceled Lincoln stamps on it."

"Well, there are."

"I can see you misspent your childhood. No, little girls don't collect things, do they? Why, if you'll examine these 'two canceled Lincoln stamps,' you'll see that they're a great deal more than that. In the first place, they're not separate stamps. They're a vertical pair—that is, one stamp is joined to the other at the horizontal edges. Now look at this upper stamp of the pair."

The Mediterranean eyes widened. "It's upside down, isn't it?"

"Yes, it's upside down," said Ellery, "and what's more, while the pair have perforations all around, there are no perforations between them, where they're joined.

"What you have here, young lady—and what our unknown forger didn't realize when he fished around for an authentic White House cover of the period on which to perpetrate the Lincoln forgery—is what's known to stamp collectors as a double printing error: a pair of 1866 black 15-cent Lincolns imperforate horizontally, with one of the pair printed upside down. No such error of the Lincoln issue has ever been reported. You're the owner, Bianca, of what may well be the rarest item in U.S. philately, and the most valuable."

The world will little note, nor long remember.

But don't try to prove it by Bianca DiCampo.

Rex Stout

SEE NO EVIL

Life at Nero Wolfe's brownstone on West Thirty-Fifth Street in Manhattan follows a rigid schedule. At 9:00 a.m. and again at 4:00 p.m. Wolfe (5 feet, 11 inches and weight "a seventh of a ton") takes his private elevator to the roof where he and his personal botanist Theodore Horstmann spend two-hour sessions tending a collection of ten thousand orchids. Breakfast is at 8:00, lunch 1:15, dinner 7:15, all prepared by master chef Fritz Brenner. Wolfe's working hours are spent in his library sitting in a specially built chair, sipping beer and listening to his assistant Archie Goodwin report on whatever case is currently under consideration. Archie is sometimes assisted by Saul Panzer, who might be called a private-eye subcontractor employed on a freelance basis.

The British writer and historian of the detective story Julian Symons has noted "something sexually ambiguous about the household" and wonders if when Rex Stout (1886–1975) began the series in 1934 he might have been "guying a little, in the gentlest way," the Holmes-Watson tradition. But if it all began as a mild joke, Wolfe and Archie became serious—and popular—and over the years the pair tidily dealt with over fifty major cases. Much is made in these adventures over the belief that Wolfe never leaves his house, but in fact he gets around more than everyone—even Stout—likes to admit. In one novel he manages to get chased across a pasture by a fractious bull (an event that so unnerves him that he later confesses, "I am lazy and conceited") and in another he returns to his native Montenegro to clear up a few things.

In "See No Evil," which has also been published under the title "The Squirt and the Monkey," the catching of a murderer is no less important than the rivalry between Wolfe and Inspector Cramer of the NYPD. Cramer's loathing of Wolfe is as much a continuing part of the series as is the cultivation of orchids, but friction between the established policeman and the private detective is, of course, another tradition as old as Holmes and Inspector Lestrade.

See No Evil

I WAS DOING two things at once. With my hands I was getting my armpit holster and the Marley .32 from a drawer of my desk, and with my tongue I was giving Nero Wolfe a lecture on economics.

"The most you can hope to soak him," I stated, "is five hundred bucks. Deduct a C for twenty per cent for overhead and another C for expenses incurred, that leaves three hundred. Eighty-five per cent for income tax will leave you with forty-five bucks clear for the wear and tear on your brain and my legs, not to mention the risk. That wouldn't buy—"

"Risk of what?" He muttered that only to be courteous, to show that he had heard what I said, though actually he wasn't listening. Seated behind his desk, he was scowling, not at me but at the crossword puzzle in the London *Times*.

"Complications," I said darkly. "You heard him explain it. Playing games with a gun is sappy." I was contorted, buckling the strap of the holster. That done, I picked up my coat. "Since you're listed in the red book as a detective, and since I draw pay, such as it is, as your licensed assistant, I'm all for detecting for people on request. But this bozo wants to do it himself, using our firearm as a prop." I felt my tie to see if it was straight. I didn't cross to the large mirror on the far wall of the office for a look, because whenever I did so in Wolfe's presence he snorted. "We might just as well," I declared, "send it up to him by messenger."

"Pfui," Wolfe muttered. "It is a thoroughly conventional proceeding. You are merely out of humor because you don't like Dazzle Dan. If it were Pleistocene Polly you would be zealous."

"Nuts. I look at the comics occasionally just to be cultured. It wouldn't hurt any if you did."

I went to the hall for my things, let myself out, descended the stoop, and headed toward Tenth Avenue for a taxi. A cold gusty wind came at my back from across the Hudson, and I made it brisk, swinging my arms, to get my blood going.

It was true that I did not care for Dazzle Dan, the hero of the comic strip that was syndicated to two thousand newspapers—or was it two million?—throughout the land. Also I did not care for his creator, Harry Koven, who had called at the office Saturday evening, forty hours ago. He had kept chewing his upper lip with jagged yellow teeth, and it had seemed to me that he might at least have chewed the lower lip instead of the upper, which doesn't show teeth. Moreover, I had not cared for his job as he outlined it. Not that I was getting snooty about the renown of Nero Wolfe—a guy who has had a gun lifted has got as much right to buy good detective work as a rich duchess accused of murder—but the way this Harry Koven had programmed it he was going to do the detecting himself, so the only difference between me and a messenger boy was that I was taking a taxi instead of the subway.

Anyhow Wolfe had taken the job and there I was. I pulled a slip of paper from my pocket, typed on by me from notes taken of the talk with Harry Koven, and gave it a look.

MARCELLE KOVEN, wife
ADRIAN GETZ, friend or camp follower, maybe both
PATRICIA LOWELL, agent (manager?), promoter
PETE JORDAN, artist, draws Dazzle Dan
BYRAM HILDEBRAND, artist, also draws D.D.

One of those five, according to Harry Koven, had stolen his gun, a Marley .32, and he wanted to know which one. As he had told it, that was all there was to it, but it was a cinch that if the missing object had been an electric shaver or a pair of cufflinks it would not have called for all that lip-chewing, not to mention other signs of strain. He had gone out of his way, not once but twice, to declare that he had no reason to suspect any of the five of wanting to do any shooting. The second time he had made it so emphatic that Wolfe had grunted and I had lifted a brow.

Since a Marley .32 is by no means a collector's item, it was no great coincidence that there was one in our arsenal and that therefore we were equipped to furnish Koven with the prop he wanted for his performance. As for the performance itself, the judicious thing to do was wait and see, but there was no point in being judicious about something I didn't like, so I had already checked it off as a dud.

I dismissed the taxi at the address on Seventy-sixth Street, east of Lexington Avenue. The house had had its front done over for the current century, unlike Nero Wolfe's old brownstone on West Thirty-fifth Street, which still sported the same front stoop it had started with. To enter this one you went down four steps instead of up seven, and I did so, after noting the pink shutters at the windows of all four floors and the tubs of evergreens flanking the entrance.

I was let in by a maid in uniform, with a pug nose and lipstick about as thick as Wolfe spreads Camembert on a wafer. I told her I had an appointment with Mr. Koven. She said Mr. Koven was not yet available and seemed to think that settled it, making me no offer for my hat and coat.

I said, "Our old brownstone, run by men only, is run better. When Fritz or I admit someone with an appointment we take his things."

"What's your name?" she demanded in a tone indicating that she doubted if I had one.

A loud male voice came from somewhere within. "Is that the man from Fur-nari's?"

A loud female voice came from up above. "Cora, is that my dress?"

I called out, "It's Archie Goodwin, expected by Mr. Koven at noon! It is now two minutes past twelve!"

That got action. The female voice, not quite so loud, told me to come up. The maid, looking frustrated, beat it. I took off my coat and put it on a chair, and my hat. A man came through a doorway at the rear of the hall and approached, speaking.

"More noise. Noisiest goddam place. Up this way." He started up the stairs. "When you have an appointment with Sir Harry, always add an hour."

I followed him. At the top of the flight there was a large square hall with wide archways to rooms at right and left. He led me through the one at the left.

There are few rooms I can't take in at a glance, but that was one of them. Two huge TV cabinets, a monkey in a cage in a corner, chairs of all sizes and colors, rugs overlapping, a fireplace blazing away, the temperature around eighty—I gave it up and focused on the inhabitant. That was not only simpler but pleasanter. She was smaller than I would specify by choice, but otherwise acceptable, especially the wide smooth brow above the serious gray eyes, and the cheekbones. She must have been part salamander, to look so cool and silky in that oven.

"Dearest Pete," she said, "you are going to stop calling my husband Sir Harry."

I admired that as a time-saver. Instead of the usual pronouncement of names, she let me know that she was Marcelle, Mrs. Harry Koven, and that the young man was Pete Jordan, and at the same time told him something.

Pete Jordan walked across to her as for a purpose. He might have been going to take her in his arms or slap her or anything in between. But a pace short of her he stopped.

"You're wrong," he told her in his aggressive baritone. "It's according to plan. It's the only way I can prove I'm not a louse. No one but a louse would stick at this, doing this crap month after month, and here look at me just because I like to eat. I haven't got the guts to quit and starve a while, so I call him Sir Harry to make you sore, working myself up to calling him something that will make him sore, and eventually I'll come to a boil and figure out a way to make Getz sore, and then I'll get bounced and I can start starving and be an artist. It's a plan."

He turned and glared at me. "I'm more apt to go through with it if I announce it in front of a witness. You're the witness. My name's Jordan, Pete Jordan."

He shouldn't have tried glaring because he wasn't built for it. He wasn't much bigger than Mrs. Koven, and he had narrow shoulders and broad hips. An aggressive baritone and a defiant glare coming from that make-up just couldn't have the effect he was after. He needed coaching.

"You have already made me sore," she told his back in a nice low voice, but not a weak one. "You act like a brat and you're too old to be a brat. Why not grow up?"

He wheeled and snapped at her, "I look on you as a mother!"

That was a foul. They were both younger than me, and she couldn't have had more than three or four years on him.

I spoke. "Excuse me," I said, "but I am not a professional witness. I came to see Mr. Koven at his request. Shall I go hunt for him?"

A thin squeak came from behind me. "Good morning, Mrs. Koven. Am I early?"

As she answered I turned for a look at the owner of the squeak, who was advancing from the archway. He should have traded voices with Pete Jordan. He had both the size and presence for a deep baritone, with a well-made head topped by a healthy mat of gray hair nearly white. Everything about him was impressive and masterful, including the way he carried himself, but the squeak spoiled it completely. It continued as he joined us.

"I heard Mr. Goodwin, and Pete left, so I thought—"

Mrs. Koven and Pete were both talking too, and it didn't seem worth the effort to sort it out, especially when the monkey decided to join in and started chattering. Also I could feel sweat coming on my forehead and neck, overdressed as I was with a coat and vest, since Pete and the newcomer were in shirt sleeves. I couldn't follow their example without displaying my holster. They kept it up, including the monkey, ignoring me completely but informing me incidentally that the squeaker was not Adrian Getz as I had first supposed, but Byram Hildebrand, Pete's co-worker in the grind of drawing Dazzle Dan.

It was all very informal and homey, but I was starting to sizzle and I crossed to the far side of the room and opened a window wide. I expected an immediate reaction but got none. Disappointed at that but relieved by the rush of fresh air, I filled my chest, used my handkerchief on the brow and neck, and, turning, saw that we had company. Coming through the archway was a pink-cheeked creature in a mink coat with a dark green slab of cork or something perched on her brown hair at a cocky slant. With no one bothering to glance at her except me, she moved across toward the fireplace, slid the coat off onto a couch, displaying a tricky plaid suit with an assortment of restrained colors, and said in a throaty voice that carried without being raised, "Rookaloo will be dead in an hour."

They were all shocked into silence except the monkey. Mrs. Koven looked at her, looked around, saw the open window, and demanded, "Who did that?"

"I did," I said manfully.

Byram Hildebrand strode to the window like a general in front of troops and pulled it shut. The monkey stopped talking and started to cough.

"Listen to him," Pete Jordan said. His baritone mellowed when he was pleased. "Pneumonia already! That's an idea! That's what I'll do when I work up to making Getz sore."

Three of them went to the cage to take a look at Rookaloo, not bothering to
greet or thank her who had come just in time to save the monkey's life. She stepped
to me, asking cordially, "You're Archie Goodwin? I'm Pat Lowell." She put out a
hand, and I took it. She had talent as a handclasper and backed it up with a good
straight look out of clear brown eyes. "I was going to phone you this morning to
warn you that Mr. Koven is never ready on time for an appointment, but he
arranged this himself so I didn't."

"Never again," I told her, "pass up an excuse for phoning me."

"I won't." She took her hand back and glanced at her wrist. "You're early
anyway. He told us the conference would be at twelve-thirty."

"I was to come at twelve."

"Oh." She was taking me in—nothing offensive, but she sure was rating me.
"To talk with him first?"

I shrugged. "I guess so."

She nodded, frowning a little. "This is a new one on me. I've been his agent
and manager for three years now, handling all his business, everything from en-
dorsements of cough drops to putting Dazzle Dan on scooters, and this is the first
time a thing like this has happened, him getting someone in for a conference
without consulting me—and Nero Wolfe, no less! I understand it's about a tie-up
of Nero Wolfe and Dazzle Dan, having Dan start a detective agency?"

I put that question mark there, though her inflection left it to me whether to
call it a question or merely a statement. I was caught off guard, so it probably
showed on my face—my glee at the prospect of telling Wolfe about a tie-up
between him and Dazzle Dan, with full details. I tried to erase it.

"We'd better wait," I said discreetly, "and let Mr. Koven tell it. As I understand
it, I'm only here as a technical adviser, representing Mr. Wolfe because he never
goes out on business. Of course you would handle the business end, and if that
means you and I will have to have a lot of talks—"

I stopped because I had lost her. Her eyes were aimed past my left shoulder
toward the archway, and their expression had suddenly and completely changed.
They weren't exactly more alive or alert, but more concentrated. I turned, and
there was Harry Koven crossing to us. His mop of black hair hadn't been combed,
and he hadn't shaved. His big frame was enclosed in a red silk robe embroidered
with yellow Dazzle Dans. A little guy in a dark blue suit was with him, at his
elbow.

"Good morning, my little dazzlers!" Koven boomed.

"It seems cool in here," the little guy said in a gentle worried voice.

In some mysterious way the gentle little voice seemed to make more noise than
the big boom. Certainly it was the gentle little voice that chopped off the return
greetings from the dazzlers, but it could have been the combination of the two, the
big man and the small one, that had so abruptly changed the atmosphere of the

room. Before they had all been screwy perhaps, but all free and easy; now they were all tightened up. They even seemed to be tongue-tied, so I spoke.

"I opened a window," I said.

"Good heavens," the little guy mildly reproached me and trotted over to the monkey's cage. Mrs. Koven and Pete Jordan were in his path, and they hastily moved out of it, as if afraid of getting trampled, though he didn't look up to trampling anything bigger than a cricket. Not only was he too little and too old, but also he was vaguely deformed and trotted with a jerk.

Koven boomed at me, "So you got here! Don't mind the Squirt and his damn monkey. He loves that damn monkey. I call this the steam room." He let out a laugh. "How is it, Squirt, okay?"

"I think so, Harry. I hope so." The low gentle voice filled the room again.

"I hope so too, or God help Goodwin." Koven turned on Byram Hildebrand. "Has seven-twenty-eight come, By?"

"No," Hildebrand squeaked. "I phoned Furnari, and he said it would be right over."

"Late again. We may have to change. When it comes, do a revise on the third frame. Where Dan says, 'Not tonight, my dear,' make it, 'Not today, my dear.' Got it?"

"But we discussed that—"

"I know, but change it. We'll change seven-twenty-nine to fit. Have you finished seven-thirty-three?"

"No. It's only—"

"Then what are you doing up here?"

"Why, Goodwin came, and you said you wanted us at twelve-thirty—"

"I'll let you know when we're ready—sometime after lunch. Show me the revise on seven-twenty-eight." Koven glanced around masterfully. "How is everybody? Blooming? See you all later. Come along, Goodwin, sorry you had to wait. Come with me."

He headed for the archway, and I followed, across the hall and up the next flight of stairs. There the arrangement was different; instead of a big square hall there was a narrow corridor with four doors, all closed. He turned left, to the door at that end, opened it, held it for me to pass through, and shut it again. This room was an improvement in several ways: it was ten degrees cooler, it had no monkey, and the furniture left more room to move around. The most prominent item was a big old scarred desk over by a window. After inviting me to sit, Koven went and sat at the desk and removed covers from dishes that were there on a tray.

"Breakfast," he said. "You had yours."

It wasn't a question, but I said yes to be sociable. He needed all the sociability he could get, from the looks of the tray. There was one dejected poached egg, one wavy thin piece of toast, three undersized prunes with about a teaspoonful of juice, a split of tonic water, and a glass. It was an awful sight. He waded into the prunes. When they were gone he poured the tonic water into the glass, took a sip, and demanded, "Did you bring it?"

"The gun? Sure."

"Let me see it."

"It's the one we showed you at the office." I moved to another chair, closer to him. "I'm supposed to check with you before we proceed. Is that the desk you kept your gun in?"

He nodded and swallowed a nibble of toast. "Here in this left-hand drawer, in the back."

"Loaded."

"Yes. I told you so."

"So you did. You also told us that you bought it two years ago in Montana, when you were there at a dude ranch, and brought it home with you and never bothered to get a license for it, and it's been there in the drawer right along. You saw it there a week or ten days ago, and last Friday you saw it was gone. You didn't want to call the cops for two reasons, because you have no license for it, and because you think it was taken by one of the five people whose names you gave—"

"I think it *may* have been."

"You didn't put it like that. However, skip it. You gave us the five names. By the way, was that Adrian Getz, the one you called Squirt?"

"Yes."

"Then they're all five here, and we can go ahead and get it over with. As I understand it, I am to put my gun there in the drawer where yours was, and you get them up here for a conference, with me present. You were to cook up something to account for me. Have you done that?"

He swallowed another nibble of toast and egg. Wolfe would have had that meal down in five seconds flat—or rather, he would have had it out the window. "I thought this might do," Koven said. "I can say that I'm considering a new stunt for Dan, have him start a detective agency, and I've called Nero Wolfe in for consultation, and he sent you up for a conference. We can discuss it a little, and I ask you to show us how a detective searches a room to give us an idea of the picture potential. You shouldn't start with the desk; start maybe with the shelves back of me. When you come to do the desk I'll push my chair back to be out of the way, and I'll have them right in front of me. When you open the drawer and take the gun out and they see it—"

"I thought you were going to do that."

"I know, that's what I said, but this is better because this way they'll be looking at the gun and you, and I'll be watching their faces. I'll have my eye right on them, and the one that took my gun, if one of them did it—when he or she suddenly sees you pull a gun out of the drawer that's exactly like it, it's going to show on his face, and I'm going to see it. We'll do it that way."

I admit it sounded better there on the spot than it had in Wolfe's office—and besides, he had revised it. This way he might really get what he wanted. I considered it, watching him finish the tonic water. The toast and egg were gone.

"It sounds all right," I conceded, "except for one thing. You'll be expecting a look of surprise, but what if there are five looks of surprise? At seeing me take a gun out of your desk—those who don't know you had a gun there."

"But they do know."

"All of them?"

"Certainly. I thought I told you that. Anyhow, they all know. Everybody knows everything around this place. They thought I ought to get rid of it, and now I wish I had. You understand, Goodwin, all there is to this—I just want to know where the damn thing is, I want to know who took it, and I'll handle it myself from there. I told Wolfe that."

"I know you did." I got up and went to his side of the desk, at his left, and pulled a drawer open. "In here?"

"Yes."

"The rear compartment?"

"Yes."

I reached to my holster for the Marley, broke it, removed the cartridges and dropped them into my vest pocket, put the gun in the drawer, shut the drawer, and returned to my chair.

"Okay," I said, "get them up here. We can ad lib it all right without any rehearsing."

He looked at me. He opened the drawer for a peek at the gun, not touching it, and pushed the drawer to. He shoved the tray away, leaned back, and began working on his upper lip with the jagged yellow teeth.

"I'm going to have to get my nerve up," he said, as if appealing to me. "I'm never much good until late afternoon."

I grunted. "What the hell. You told me to be here at noon and called the conference for twelve-thirty."

"I know I did. I do things like that." He chewed the lip some more. "And I've got to dress." Suddenly his voice went high in protest. "Don't try to rush me, understand?"

I was fed up, but had already invested a lot of time and a dollar for a taxi on the case, so kept calm. "I know," I told him, "artists are temperamental. But I'll explain how Mr. Wolfe charges. He sets a fee, depending on the job, and if it takes more of my time than he thinks reasonable he adds an extra hundred dollars an hour. Keeping me here until late afternoon would be expensive. I could go and come back."

He didn't like that and said so, explaining why, the idea being that with me there in the house it would be easier for him to get his nerve up and it might only take an hour or so. He got up and walked to the door and opened it, then turned and demanded, "Do you know how much I make an hour? The time I spend on my work? Over a thousand dollars. More than a thousand an hour! I'll go get some clothes on."

He went, shutting the door.

My wristwatch said 1:17. My stomach agreed. I sat maybe ten minutes, then went to the phone on the desk, dialed, got Wolfe, and told him how it was. He told me to go out and get some lunch, naturally, and I said I would, but after hanging up I went back to my chair. If I went out, sure as hell Koven would get his nerve up in my absence, and by the time I got back he would have lost it again and have to start over. I explained the situation to my stomach, and it made a polite sound of protest, but I was the boss. I was glancing at my watch again and seeing 1:42 when the door opened and Mrs. Koven was with me.

When I stood, her serious gray eyes beneath the wide smooth brow were level with the knot in my four-in-hand. She said her husband had told her that I was staying for a conference at a later hour. I confirmed it. She said I ought to have something to eat. I agreed that it was not a bad notion.

"Won't you," she invited, "come down and have a sandwich with us? We don't do any cooking, we even have our breakfast sent in, but there are some sandwiches."

"I don't want to be rude," I told her, "but are they in the room with the monkey?"

"Oh, no." She stayed serious. "Wouldn't that be awful? Downstairs in the workroom." She touched my arm. "Come on, do."

I went downstairs with her.

2

In a large room at the rear on the ground floor the other four suspects were seated around a plain wooden table, dealing with the sandwiches. The room was a mess —drawing tables under fluorescent lights, open shelves crammed with papers, cans of all sizes, and miscellaneous objects, chairs scattered around, other shelves with books and portfolios, and tables with more stacks of papers. Messy as it was to the eye, it was even messier to the ear, for two radios were going full blast.

Marcelle Koven and I joined them at the lunch table, and I perked up at once. There was a basket of French bread and pumpernickel, paper platters filled with slices of ham, smoked turkey, sturgeon, and hot corned beef, a big slab of butter, mustard and other accessories, bottles of milk, a pot of steaming coffee, and a one-pound jar of fresh caviar. Seeing Pete Jordan spooning caviar onto a piece of bread crust, I got what he meant about liking to eat.

"Help yourself!" Pat Lowell yelled into my ear.

I reached for the bread with one hand and the corned beef with the other and yelled back, "Why doesn't someone turn them down or even off?"

She took a sip of coffee from a paper cup and shook her head. "One's By Hildebrand's and one's Pete Jordan's! They like different programs when they're working! They have to go for volume!"

It was a hell of a din, but the corned beef was wonderful and the bread must have been from Rusterman's, nor was there anything wrong with the turkey and sturgeon. Since the radio duel precluded table talk, I used my eyes for diversion and was impressed by Adrian Getz, whom Koven called the Squirt. He would break off a rectangle of bread crust, place a rectangle of sturgeon on it, arrange a mound of caviar on top, and pop it in. When it was down he would take three sips of coffee and then start over. He was doing that when Mrs. Koven and I arrived and he was still doing it when I was full and reaching for another paper napkin.

Eventually, though, he stopped. He pushed back his chair, left it, went over to a sink at the wall, held his fingers under the faucet, and dried them with his handkerchief. Then he trotted over to a radio and turned it off, and to the other one and turned that off. Then he trotted back to us and spoke apologetically.

"That was uncivil, I know."

No one contradicted him.

"It was only," he went on, "that I wanted to ask Mr. Goodwin something before going up for my nap." His eyes settled on me. "Did you know when you opened that window that sudden cold drafts are dangerous for tropical monkeys?"

His tone was more than mild, it was wistful. But something about him—I didn't know what and didn't ask for time out to go into it—got my goat.

"Sure," I said cheerfully. "I was trying it out."

"That was thoughtless," he said, not complaining, just giving his modest opinion, and turned and trotted out of the room.

There was a strained silence. Pat Lowell reached for the pot to pour some coffee.

"Goodwin, God help you," Pete Jordan muttered.

"Why? Does he sting?"

"Don't ask me why, but watch your step. I think he's a kobold." He tossed his paper napkin onto the table. "Want to see an artist create? Come and look." He marched to one of the radios and turned it on, then to a drawing table and sat.

"I'll clean up," Pat Lowell offered.

Byram Hildebrand, who had not squeaked once that I heard, went and turned on the other radio before he took his place at another drawing table.

Mrs. Koven left us. I helped Pat Lowell clear up the lunch table, but all that did was pass time, since both radios were going and I rely mostly on talk to develop an acquaintance in the early stages. Then she left, and I strolled over to watch the artists. So far nothing had occured to change my opinion of Dazzle Dan, but I had to admire the way they did him. Working from rough sketches which all looked alike to me, they turned out the finished product in three colors so fast I could barely keep up, walking back and forth. The only interruptions for a long stretch were when Hildebrand jumped up to go and turn his radio louder, and a minute later Pete Jordan did likewise. I sat down and concentrated on the experiment of listening to two stations at once, but after a while my brain started to curdle and I got out of there.

A door toward the front of the lower hall was standing open, and I looked in and stepped inside when I saw Pat Lowell at a desk, working with papers. She looked up to nod and went on working.

"Listen a minute," I said. "We're here on a desert island, and for months you have been holding me at arm's length, and I'm desperate. It is not mere propinquity. In rags and tatters as you are, without make-up, I have come to look upon you—"

"I'm busy," she said emphatically. "Go play with a coconut."

"You'll regret this," I said savagely and went to the hall and looked through the glass of the front door at the outside world. The view was nothing to brag about, and the radios were still at my eardrums, so I went upstairs. Looking through the archway into the room at the left, and seeing no one but the monkey in its cage, I crossed to the other room and entered. It was full of furniture, but there was no sign of life. As I went up the second flight of stairs it seemed that the sound of the radios was getting louder instead of softer, and at the top I knew why. A radio was going the other side of one of the closed doors. I went and opened the door to the room where I had talked with Koven; not there. I tried another door and was faced by shelves stacked with linen. I knocked on another, got no response, opened it, and stepped in. It was a large bedroom, very fancy, with an oversized bed. The furniture and fittings showed that it was co-ed. A radio on a stand was giving with a soap opera, and stretched out on a couch was Mrs. Koven, sound asleep. She looked softer and not so serious, with her lips parted a little and relaxed fingers curled on the cushion, in spite of the yapping radio on the bedside table. I damn well intended to find Koven, and took a couple of steps with a vague notion of looking under the bed for him, when a glance through an open door at the right into the next room discovered him. He was standing at a window with his back to me. Thinking it might seem a little familiar on short acquaintance for me to enter from the bedroom where his wife was snoozing, I backed out to the hall, pulling the door to, moved to the next door, and knocked. Getting no reaction, I turned the knob and entered.

The radio had drowned out my noise. He remained at the window. I banged the door shut. He jerked around. He said something, but I didn't get it on account of the radio. I went and closed the door to the bedroom, and that helped some.

"Well?" he demanded, as if he couldn't imagine who I was or what I wanted.

He had shaved and combed and had on a well-made brown homespun suit, with a tan shirt and red tie.

"It's going on four o'clock," I said, "and I'll be going soon and taking my gun with me."

He took his hands from his pockets and dropped into a chair. Evidently this was the Koven personal living room, from the way it was furnished, and it looked fairly livable.

He spoke. "I was standing at the window thinking."

"Yeah. Any luck?"

He sighed and stretched his legs out. "Fame and fortune," he said, "are not all a man needs for happiness."

I sat down. Obviously the only alternatives were to wrangle him into it or call it off.

"What else would you suggest?" I asked brightly.

He undertook to tell me. He went on and on, but I won't report it verbatim because I doubt if it contained any helpful hints for you—I know it didn't for me. I grunted from time to time to be polite. I listened to him for a while and then got a little relief by listening to the soap opera on the radio, which was muffled some by the closed door but by no means inaudible. Eventually, of course, he got around to his wife, first briefing me by explaining that she was his third and they had been married only two years. To my surprise he didn't tear her apart. He said she was wonderful. His point was that even when you added to fame and fortune the companionship of a beloved and loving wife who was fourteen years younger than you, that still wasn't all you needed for happiness.

There was one interruption—a knock on the door and the appearance of Byram Hildebrand. He had come to show the revise on the third frame of Number 728. They discussed art some, and Koven okayed the revise, and Hildebrand departed. I hoped that the intermission had sidetracked Koven, but no; he took up again where he had left off.

I can take a lot when I'm working on a case, even a kindergarten problem like that one, but finally, after the twentieth sidewise glance at my wrist, I called a halt.

"Look," I said, "this has given me a new slant on life entirely, and don't think I don't appreciate it, but it's a quarter past four and it's getting dark. I would call it late afternoon. What do you say we go ahead with our act?"

He closed his trap and frowned at me. He started chewing his lip. After some of that he suddenly arose, went to a cabinet, and got out a bottle.

"Will you join me?" He produced two glasses. "I'm not supposed to drink until five o'clock, but I'll make this an exception." He came to me. "Bourbon all right? Say when."

I would have liked to plug him. He had known from the beginning that he would have to drink himself up to it but had sucked me in with a noon appointment. Anything I felt like saying would have been justified, but I held in. I accepted mine and raised it with him, to encourage him, and took a swallow. He took a dainty sip, raised his eyes to the ceiling, and then emptied the glass at a gulp. He picked up the bottle and poured a refill.

"Why don't we go in there with the refreshment," I suggested, "and go over it a little?"

"Don't rush me," he said gloomily. He took a deep breath, swelling his chest, and suddenly grinned at me, showing the teeth. He lifted the glass and drained it, reached for the bottle and tilted it to pour, and changed his mind.

"Come on," he said, heading for the door. I stepped around him to open the door, since both his hands were occupied, closed it behind us, and followed him down the hall. At the farther end we entered the room where we were to stage it. He went to the desk and sat, poured himself a drink, and put the bottle down. I went to the desk too, but not to sit. I had taken the precaution of removing the cartridges from my gun, but even so a glance at it wouldn't hurt any. I pulled the drawer open and was relieved to see that it was still there. I shut the drawer.

"I'll go get them," I offered.

"I said don't rush me," Koven protested, but no longer gloomy.

Thinking that two more drinks would surely do it, I moved to a chair. But I didn't sit. Something wasn't right, and it came to me what it was: I had placed the gun with the muzzle pointing to the right, and it wasn't that way now. I returned to the desk, took the gun out, and gave it a look.

It was a Marley .32 all right, but not mine.

3

I put my eye on Koven. The gun was in my left hand, and my right hand was a fist. If I had hit him that first second, which I nearly did, mad as I was, I would have cracked some knuckles.

"What's the matter?" he demanded.

My eyes were on him and through him. I kept them there for five pulse beats. It wasn't possible, I decided, that he was that good. Nobody could be.

I backed up a pace. "We've found your gun."

He gawked at me. "What?"

I broke it, saw that the cylinder was empty, and held it out. "Take a look."

He took it. "It looks the same—no, it doesn't."

"Certainly it doesn't. Mine was clean and bright. Is it yours?"

"I don't know. It looks like it. But how in the name of God—"

I reached and took it from him. "How do you think?" I was so damn mad I nearly stuttered. "Someone with hands took mine out and put yours in. It could have been you. Was it?"

"No. Me?" Suddenly he got indignant. "How the hell could it have been me when I didn't know where mine was?"

"You said you didn't. I ought to stretch you out and tamp you down. Keeping me here the whole goddam day, and now this! If you ever talk straight and to the point, now is the time. Did you touch my gun?"

"No. But you're—"

"Do you know who did?"

"No. But you're—"

"Shut up!" I went around the desk to the phone, lifted it, and dialed. At that hour Wolfe would be up in the plant rooms for his afternoon shift with the orchids, where he was not to be disturbed except in emergency, but this was one. When Fritz answered I asked him to buzz the extension, and in a moment I had Wolfe.

"Yes, Archie?" Naturally he was peevish.

"Sorry to bother you, but. I'm at Koven's. I put my gun in his desk, and we were all set for his stunt, but he kept putting it off until now. His will power sticks and has to be primed with alcohol. I roamed around. We just came in here where his desk is, and I opened the drawer for a look. Someone has taken my gun and substituted his—his that was stolen, you know? It's back where it belongs, but mine is gone."

"You shouldn't have left it there."

"Okay, you can have that, and you sure will, but I need instructions for now. Three choices: I can call a cop, or I can bring the whole bunch down there to you, don't think I can't the way I feel, or I can handle it myself. Which?"

"Confound it, not the police. They would enjoy it too much. And why bring them here? The gun's there, not here."

"Then that leaves me. I go ahead?"

"Certainly—with due discretion. It's a prank." He chuckled. "I would like to see your face. Try to get home for dinner." He hung up.

"My God, don't call a cop!" Koven protested.

"I don't intend to," I said grimly. I slipped his gun into my armpit holster. "Not if I can help it. It depends partly on you. You stay put, right here. I'm going down and get them. Your wife's asleep in the bedroom. If I find when I get back that you've gone and started chatting with her I'll either slap you down with your own gun or phone the police, I don't know which, maybe both. Stay put."

"This is my house, Goodwin, and—"

"Goddam it, don't you know a raving maniac when you see one?" I tapped my chest with a forefinger. "Me. When I'm as sore as I am now the safest thing would be for you to call a cop. I want my gun."

As I made for the door he was reaching for the bottle. By the time I got down to the ground floor I had myself well enough in hand to speak to them without betraying any special urgency, telling them that Koven was ready for them upstairs, for the conference. I found Pat Lowell still at the desk in the room in front and

Hildebrand and Jordan still at their drawing tables in the workroom. I even replied appropriately when Pat Lowell asked how I had made out with the coconut. As Hildebrand and Jordan left their tables and turned off their radios I had a keener eye on them than before; someone here had swiped my gun. As we ascended the first flight of stairs, with me in the rear, I asked their backs where I would find Adrian Getz.

Pat Lowell answered. "He may be in his room on the top floor." They halted at the landing, the edge of the big square hall, and I joined them. We could hear the radio going upstairs. She indicated the room to the left. "He takes his afternoon nap in there with Rookaloo, but not this late usually."

I thought I might as well glance in, and moved to the archway. A draft of cold air hit me, and I went on in. A window was wide open! I marched over and closed it, then went to take a look at the monkey. It was huddled on the floor in a corner of the cage, making angry little noises, with something clutched in its fingers against its chest. The light was dim, but I have good eyes, and not only was the something unmistakably a gun, but it was my Marley on a bet. Needing light, and looking for a wall switch, I was passing the large couch which faced the fireplace when suddenly I stopped and froze. Adrian Getz, the Squirt, was lying on the couch but he wasn't taking a nap.

I bent over him for a close-up and saw a hole in his skull northeast of his right ear, and some red juice. I stuck a hand inside the V of his vest and flattened it against him and held my breath for eight seconds. He was through taking naps.

I straightened up and called, "Come in here, all three of you, and switch on a light as you come!"

They appeared through the archway, and one of them put a hand to the wall. Lights shone. The back of the couch hid Getz from their view as they approached.

"It's cold in here," Pat Lowell was saying. "Did you open another—"

Seeing Getz stopped her, and the others too. They goggled.

"Don't touch him," I warned them. "He's dead, so you can't help him any. Don't touch anything. You three stay here together, right here in this room, while I—"

"Christ Almighty," Pete Jordan blurted. Hildebrand squeaked something. Pat Lowell put out a hand, found the couch back, and gripped it. She asked something, but I wasn't listening. I was at the cage, with my back to them, peering at the monkey. It was my Marley the monkey was clutching. I had to curl my fingers until the nails sank in to keep from opening the cage door and grabbing that gun.

I whirled. "Stick here together. Understand?" I was on my way. "I'm going up and phone."

Ignoring their noises, I left them. I mounted the stairs in no hurry, because if I had been a raving maniac before, I was now stiff with fury and I needed a few seconds to get under control. In the room upstairs Harry Koven was still seated at the desk, staring at the open drawer. He looked up and fired a question at me but got no answer. I went to the phone, lifted it, and dialed a number. When I got Wolfe he started to sputter at being disturbed again.

"I'm sorry," I told him, "but I wish to report that I have found my gun. It's in the cage with the monkey, who is—"

"What monkey?"

"Its name is Rookaloo, but please don't interrupt. It is holding my gun to its breast, I suspect because it is cold and the gun is warm, having recently been fired. Lying there on a couch is the body of a man, Adrian Getz, with a bullet hole in the head. It is no longer a question whether I call a cop, I merely wanted to report the situation to you before I do so. A thousand to one Getz was shot and killed with my gun. I will not be—hold it—"

I dropped the phone and jumped. Koven had made a dive for the door. I caught him before he reached it, got an arm and his chin, and heaved. There was a lot of feeling in it, and big as he was he sailed to a wall, bounced off, and went to the floor.

"I would love to do it again," I said, meaning it, and returned to the phone and told Wolfe, "Excuse me, Koven tried to interrupt. I was only going to say I will not be home to dinner."

"The man is dead."

"Yes, sir."

"Have you anything satisfactory for the police?"

"Sure. My apologies for bringing my gun here to oblige a murderer. That's all."

"We haven't answered today's mail."

"I know. It's a damn shame. I'll get away as soon as I can."

"Very well."

The connection went. I held the button down a moment, with an eye on Koven, who was upright again but not asking for an encore, then released it and dialed RE 7-5260.

4

I haven't kept anything like an accurate score, but I would say that over the years I haven't told the cops more than a couple of dozen barefaced lies, maybe not that many. They are seldom practical. On the other hand, I can't recall any murder case Wolfe and I were in on and I've had my story gone into at length where I have simply opened the bag and given them all I had, with no dodging and no withholding, except one, and this is it. On the murder of Adrian Getz I didn't have a single thing on my mind that I wasn't willing and eager to shovel out, so I let them have it.

It worked fine. They called me a liar.

Not right away, of course. At first even Inspector Cramer appreciated my cooperation, knowing as he did that there wasn't a man in his army who could shade me at seeing and hearing, remembering, and reporting. It was generously conceded that upon finding the body I had performed properly and promptly, herding the trio into the room and keeping the Kovens from holding a family council until the law arrived. From there on, of course, everyone had been under surveillance, including me.

At six-thirty, when the scientists were still monopolizing the room where Getz had got it, and city employees were wandering all over the place, and the various inmates were still in various rooms conversing privately with Homicide men, and I had typed and signed my own frank and full statement, I was confidently expecting that I would soon be out on the sidewalk unattended, flagging a taxi. I was in the front room on the ground floor, seated at Pat Lowell's desk, having used her typewriter, and Sergeant Purley Stebbins was sitting across from me, looking over my statement.

He lifted his head and regarded me, perfectly friendly. A perfectly friendly look from Stebbins would, from almost anyone else, cause you to get your guard up and be ready to either duck or counter, but Purley wasn't responsible for the design of his big bony face and his pig-bristle eyebrows.

"I guess you got it all in," he admitted. "As you told it."

"I suggest," I said modestly, "that when this case is put away you send that to the school to be used as a model report."

"Yeah." He stood up. "You're a good typist." He turned to go.

I arose too, saying casually, "I can run along now?"

The door opened, and Inspector Cramer entered. I didn't like his expression as he darted a glance at me. Knowing him well in all his moods, I didn't like the way his broad shoulders were hunched, or his clamped jaw, or the glint in his eye.

"Here's Goodwin's statement," Purley said. "Okay."

"As he told it?"

"Yes."

"Send him downtown and hold him."

It caught me completely off balance. "Hold *me?*" I demanded, squeaking almost like Hildebrand.

"Yes, sir." Nothing could catch Purley off balance. "On your order."

"No, charge him. Sullivan Act. He has no license for the gun we found on him."

"Ha, ha," I said. "Ha, ha, and ha, ha. There you got your laugh. A very fine gag. Ha."

"You're going down, Goodwin. I'll be down to see you later."

As I said, I knew him well. He meant it. I had his eyes. "This," I said, "is way out of my reach. I've told you where and how and why I got that gun." I pointed to the paper in Purley's hand. "Read it. It's all down, punctuated."

"You had the gun in your holster and you have no license for it."

"Nuts. But I get it. You've been hoping for years to hang something on Nero Wolfe, and to you I'm just a part of him, and you think here's your chance. Of course it won't stick. Wouldn't you rather have something that will? Like resisting arrest and assaulting an officer? Glad to oblige. Watch it—"

Tipping forward, I started a left hook for his jaw, fast and vicious, then jerked it down and went back on my heels. It didn't create a panic, but I had the satisfaction of seeing Cramer take a quick step back and Stebbins one forward. They bumped.

"There," I said. "With both of you to swear to it, that ought to be good for at least two years. I'll throw the typewriter at you if you'll promise to catch it."

"Cut the clowning," Purley growled.

"You lied about that gun," Cramer snapped. "If you don't want to get taken down to think it over, think now. Tell me what you came here for and what happened.

"I've told you."

"A string of lies."

"No, sir."

"You can have 'em back. I'm not trying to hang something on Wolfe, or you either. I want to know why you came here and what happened."

"Oh, for God's sake." I moved my eyes. "Okay, Purley, where's my escort?"

Cramer strode four paces to the door, opened it, and called, "Bring Mr. Koven in here!"

Harry Koven entered with a dick at his elbow. He looked as if he was even farther away from happiness than before.

"We'll sit down," Cramer said.

He left me behind the desk. Purley and the dick took chairs in the background. Cramer stationed himself across the desk from me, where Purley had been, with Koven on a chair at his left. He opened up.

"I told you, Mr. Koven, that I would ask you to repeat your story in Goodwin's presence, and you said you would."

Koven nodded. "That's right." He was hoarse.

"We won't need all the details. Just answer me briefly. When you called on Nero Wolfe last Saturday evening, what did you ask him to do?"

"I told him I was going to have Dazzle Dan start a detective agency in a new series." The hoarseness bothered Koven, and he cleared his throat explosively. "I told him I needed technical assistance, and possibly a tie-up, if we could arrange—"

There was a pad of ruled paper on the desk. I reached for it, and a pencil, and started doing shorthand. Cramer leaned over, stretched an arm, grabbed a corner of the pad, and jerked it away. I could feel the blood coming to my head, which was silly of it with an inspector, a sergeant, and a private all in the room.

"We need your full attention," Cramer growled. He went to Koven. "Did you say anything to Wolfe about your gun being taken from your desk?"

"Certainly not. It hadn't been taken. I did mention that I had a gun in my desk for which I had no license, but that I never carried it, and I asked if that was risky. I told them what make it was, a Marley thirty-two. I asked how much trouble it would be to get a license, and if—"

"We'll keep it brief. Just cover the points. What arrangement did you make with Wolfe?"

"He agreed to send Goodwin to my place on Monday for a conference with my staff and me."

"About what?"

"About the technical problems of having Dazzle Dan do detective work, and possibly a tie-up."

"And Goodwin came?"

"Yes, today around noon." Koven's hoarseness kept interfering with him, and he kept clearing his throat. My eyes were at his face, but he hadn't met them. Of course he was talking to Cramer and had to be polite. He went on, "The conference was for twelve-thirty, but I had a little talk with Goodwin and asked him to wait. I have to be careful what I do with Dan and I wanted to think it over some more. Anyway I'm like that, I put things off. It was after four o'clock when he—"

"Was your talk with Goodwin about your gun being gone?"

"Certainly not. We might have mentioned the gun, about my not having a license for it, I don't remember—no, wait a minute, we must have, because I pulled the drawer open and we glanced in at it. Except for that, we only talked—"

"Did you or Goodwin take your gun out of the drawer?"

"No. Absolutely not."

"Did he put his gun in the drawer?"

"Absolutely not."

I slid in, "When I took my gun from my holster to show it to you, did you—"

"Nothing doing," Cramer snapped at me. "You're listening. Just the high spots for now." He returned to Koven. "Did you have another talk with Goodwin later?"

Koven nodded. "Yes, around half-past three he came up to my room—the living room. We talked until after four, there and in my office, and then—"

"In your office did Goodwin open the drawer of the desk and take the gun out and say it had been changed?"

"Certainly not!"

"What did he do?"

"Nothing, only we talked, and then he left to go down and get the others to come up for the conference. After a while he came back alone, and without saying anything he came to the desk and took my gun from the drawer and put it under his coat. Then he went to the phone and called Nero Wolfe. When I heard him tell Wolfe that Adrian Getz had been shot, that he was on a couch downstairs dead, I got up to go down there, and Goodwin jumped me from behind and knocked me out. When I came to he was still talking to Wolfe, I don't know what he was telling him, and then he called the police. He wouldn't let me—"

"Hold it," Cramer said curtly. "That covers that. One more point. Do you know of any motive for Goodwin's wanting to murder Adrian Getz?"

"No, I don't. I told—"

"Then if Getz was shot with Goodwin's gun how would you account for it? You're not obliged to account for it, but if you don't mind just repeat what you told me."

"Well—" Koven hesitated. He cleared his throat for the twentieth time. "I told you about the monkey. Goodwin opened a window, and that's enough to kill that kind of a monkey, and Getz was very fond of it. He didn't show how upset he was but Getz was very quiet and didn't show things much. I understand Goodwin likes to kid people. Of course I don't know what happened, but if Goodwin went in there later when Getz was there, and started to open a window, you can't tell. When Getz once got aroused he was apt to do anything. He couldn't have hurt Goodwin any, but Goodwin might have got out his gun just for a gag, and Getz tried to take it away, and it went off accidentally. That wouldn't be murder, would it?"

"No," Cramer said, "that would only be a regrettable accident. That's all for now, Mr. Koven. Take him out, Sol, and bring Hildebrand."

As Koven arose and the dick came forward I reached for the phone on Pat Lowell's desk. My hand got there, but so did Cramer's, hard on top of mine.

"The lines here are busy," he stated. "There'll be a phone you can use downtown. Do you want to hear Hildebrand before you comment?"

"I'm crazy to hear Hildebrand," I assured him. "No doubt he'll explain that I tossed the gun in the monkey's cage to frame the monkey. Let's just wait for Hildebrand."

It wasn't much of a wait; the Homicide boys are snappy. Byram Hildebrand, ushered in by Sol, stood and gave me a long straight look before he took the chair Koven had vacated. He still had good presence, with his fine mat of nearly white hair, but his extremities were nervous. When he sat he couldn't find comfortable spots for either his hands or his feet.

"This will only take a minute," Cramer told him. "I just want to check on Sunday morning. Yesterday. You were here working?"

Hildebrand nodded, and the squeak came. "I was putting on some touches. I often work Sundays."

"You were in there in the workroom?"

"Yes. Mr. Getz was there, making some suggestions. I was doubtful about one of his suggestions and went upstairs to consult Mr. Koven, but Mrs. Koven was there in the hall and—"

"You mean the big hall one flight up?"

"Yes. She said Mr. Koven wasn't up yet and Miss Lowell was in his office waiting to see him. Miss Lowell has extremely good judgment, and I went up to consult her. She disapproved of Mr. Getz's suggestion, and we discussed various matters, and mention was made of the gun Mr. Koven kept in his desk drawer. I pulled the drawer open just to look at it, with no special purpose, merely to look at it, and closed the drawer again. Shortly afterward I returned downstairs."

"Was the gun there in the drawer?"

"Yes."

"Did you take it out?"

"No. Neither did Miss Lowell. We didn't touch it."

"But you recognized it as the same gun?"

"I can't say that I did, no. I had never examined the gun, never had it in my hand. I can only say that it looked the same as before. It was my opinion that our concern about the gun being kept there was quite childish, but I see now that I was wrong. After what happened today—"

"Yeah." Cramer cut him off. "Concern about a loaded gun is never childish. That's all I'm after now. Sunday morning, in Miss Lowell's presence, you opened the drawer of Koven's desk and saw the gun which you took to be the gun you had seen there before. Is that correct?"

"That's correct," Hildebrand squeaked.

"Okay, that's all." Cramer nodded to Sol. "Take him back to Rowcliff."

I treated myself to a good deep breath. Purley was squinting at me, not gloating, just concentrating. Cramer turned his head to see that the door was closed after the dick and the artist and then turned back to me.

"Your turn," he growled.

I shook my head. "Lost my voice," I whispered, hissing.

"You're not funny, Goodwin. You're never as funny as you think you are. This time you're not funny at all. You can have five minutes to go over it and realize how complicated it is. When you phoned Wolfe *before* you phoned us, you couldn't possibly have arranged all the details. I've got you. I'll be leaving here before long to join you downtown, and on my way I'll stop in at Wolfe's place for a talk. He won't clam up on this one. At the very least I've got you good on the Sullivan Act. Want five minutes?"

"No, sir." I was calm but emphatic. "I want five days and I would advise you to take a full week. Complicated doesn't begin to describe it. Before I leave for downtown, if you're actually going to crawl out on that one, I wish to remind you of something, and don't forget it. When I voluntarily took Koven's gun from my holster and turned it over—it wasn't 'found on me,' as you put it—I also turned over six nice clean cartridges which I had in my vest pocket, having previously removed them from my gun. I hope none of your heroes gets careless and mixes them up with the cartridges found in my gun, if any, when you retrieved it from the monkey. That would be a mistake. The point is, if I removed the cartridges from my gun in order to insert one or more from Koven's gun, when and why did I do it? There's a day's work for you right there. And if I did do it, then Koven's friendly effort to fix me up for justifiable manslaughter is wasted, much as I appreciate it, because I must have been premeditating something, and you know what. Why fiddle around with the Sullivan Act? Make it the big one, and I can't get bail. Now I button up."

I set my jaw.

Cramer eyed me. "Even a suspended sentence," he said, "you lose your license."

I grinned at him.

"You goddam mule," Purley rumbled.

I included him in the grin.

"Send him down," Cramer rasped and got up and left.

5

Even when a man is caught smack in the middle of a felony, as I had been, there is a certain amount of red tape to getting him behind bars, and in my case not only red tape but also other activities postponed my attainment of privacy. First I had a long conversation with an assistant district attorney, who was the suave and subtle type and even ate sandwiches with me. When it was over, a little after nine o'clock, both of us were only slightly more confused than when we started. He left me in a room with a specimen in uniform with slick brown hair and a wart on his cheek. I told him how to get rid of the wart, recommending Doc Vollmer.

I was expecting the promised visit by Inspector Cramer any minute. Naturally I was nursing an assorted collection of resentments, but the one on top was at not being there to see and hear the talk between Cramer and Wolfe. Any chat those two had was always worth listening to, and that one must have been outstanding, with Wolfe learning not only that his client was lying five ways from Sunday, which was bad enough, but also that I had been tossed in the can and the day's mail would have to go unanswered.

When the door finally opened and a visitor entered it wasn't Inspector Cramer. It was Lieutenant Rowcliff, whose murder I will not have to premeditate when I get around to it because I have already done the premeditating. There are not many murderers so vicious and inhuman that I would enjoy seeing them caught by Rowcliff. He jerked a chair around to sit facing me and said with oily satisfaction, "At last we've got you, by God."

That set the tone for the interview.

I would enjoy recording in full that two-hour session with Rowcliff, but it would sound like bragging, and therefore I don't suppose you would enjoy it too. His biggest handicap is that when he gets irritated to a certain point he can't help stuttering, and I'm onto him enough to tell when he's just about there, and then I start stuttering before he does. Even with a close watch and careful timing it takes luck to do it right, and that evening I was lucky. He came closer than ever before to plugging me, but didn't, because he wants to be a captain so bad he can taste it and he's not absolutely sure that Wolfe hasn't got a solid in with the Commissioner or the Mayor or possibly Grover Whalen himself.

Cramer never showed up, and that added another resentment to my healthy pile. I knew he had been to see Wolfe, because when they had finally let me make my phone call, around eight o'clock, and I had got Wolfe and started to tell him about it, he had interrupted me in a voice as cold as an Eskimo's nose.

"I know where you are and how you got there. Mr. Cramer is here. I have phoned Mr. Parker, but it's too late to do anything tonight. Have you had anything to eat?"

"No, sir. I'm afraid of poison and I'm on a hunger strike."

"You should eat something. Mr. Cramer is worse than a jackass, he's demented. I intend to persuade him, if possible, of the desirability of releasing you at once."

He hung up.

When, shortly after eleven, Rowcliff called it off and I was shown to my room, there had been no sign of Cramer. The room was in no way remarkable, merely what was to be expected in a structure of that type, but it was fairly clean, strongly scented with disinfectant, and was in a favorable location since the nearest corridor light was six paces away and therefore did not glare through the bars of my door. Also it was a single, which I appreciated. Alone at last, away from telephones and other interruptions, I undressed and arranged my gray pinstripe on the chair, draped my shirt over the end of the blankets, got in, stretched, and settled down for a complete survey of the complications. But my brain and nerves had other plans, and in twenty seconds I was asleep.

In the morning there was a certain amount of activity, with the check-off and a trip to the lavatory and breakfast, but after that I had more privacy than I really cared for. My watch had slowed down. I tested the second hand by counting, with no decisive result. By noon I would almost have welcomed a visit from Rowcliff and was beginning to suspect that someone had lost a paper and there was no record of me anywhere and everyone was too busy to stop and think. Lunch, which I will not describe, broke the monotony some, but then, back in my room, I was alone with my wristwatch. For the tenth time I decided to spread all the pieces out, sort them, and have a look at the picture as it had been drawn to date, and for the tenth time it got so damn jumbled that I couldn't make first base, let alone on around.

At 1:09 my door swung open and the floorwalker, a chunky short guy with only half an ear on the right side, told me to come along. I went willingly, on out of the block to an elevator, and along a ground-floor corridor to an office. There I was pleased to see the tall lanky figure and long pale face of Henry George Parker, the only lawyer Wolfe would admit to the bar if he had the say. He came to shake my hand and said he'd have me out of there in a minute now.

"No rush," I said stiffly. "Don't let it interfere with anything important."

He laughed, Haw-haw, and took me inside the gate. All the formalities but one which required my presence had already been attended to, and he made good on his minute. On the way up in the taxi he explained why I had been left to rot until past noon. Getting bail on the Sullivan Act charge had been simple, but I had also been tagged with a material witness warrant, and the DA had asked the judge to put it at fifty grand! He had been stubborn about it, and the best Parker could do was talk it down to twenty, and he had had to report back to Wolfe before closing the deal. I was not to leave the jurisdiction. As the taxi crossed Thirty-fourth Street I looked west across the river. I had never cared much for New Jersey, but now the idea of driving through the tunnel and on among the billboards seemed attractive.

I preceded Parker up the stoop at the old brownstone on West Thirty-fifth, used my key but found that the chain bolt was on, which was normal but not invariable when I was out of the house, and had to push the button. Fritz Brenne, chef and house manager, let us in and stood while we disposed of our coats and hats.

"Are you all right, Archie?" he inquired.

"No," I said frankly. "Don't you smell me?"

As we went down the hall Wolfe appeared, coming from the door to the dining room. He stopped and regarded me. I returned his gaze with my chin up.

"I'll go up and rinse off," I said, "while you're finishing lunch."

"I've finished," he said grimly. "Have you eaten?"

"Enough to hold me."

"Then we'll get started."

He marched into the office, across the hall from the dining room, went to his oversized chair behind his desk, sat, and got himself adjusted for comfort. Parker took the red leather chair. As I crossed my desk I started talking, to get the jump on him.

"It will help," I said, not aggressively but pointedly, "if we first get it settled about my leaving that room with my gun there in the drawer. I do not—"

"Shut up!" Wolfe snapped.

"In that case," I demanded, "why didn't you leave me in the coop? I'll go back and—"

"Sit down!"

I sat.

"I deny," he said, "that you were in the slightest degree imprudent. Even if you were, this has transcended such petty considerations." He picked up a sheet of paper from his desk. "This is a letter which came yesterday from a Mrs. E. R. Baumgarten. She wants me to investigate the activities of a nephew who is employed by the business she owns. I wish to reply. Your notebook."

He was using what I call his conclusive tone, leaving no room for questions, let alone argument. I got my notebook and pen.

"Dear Mrs. Baumgarten." He went at it as if he had already composed it in his mind. "Thank you very much for your letter of the thirteenth, requesting me to undertake an investigation for you. Paragraph. I am sorry that I cannot be of service to you. I am compelled to decline because I have been informed by an official of the New York Police Department that my license to operate a private detective agency is about to be taken away from me. Sincerely yours."

Parker ejaculated something and got ignored. I stayed deadpan, but among my emotions were renewed regret that I had missed Wolfe's and Cramer's talk.

Wolfe was saying, "Type it at once and send Fritz to mail it. If any requests for appointments come by telephone refuse them, giving the reason and keeping a record."

"The reason given in the letter?"

"Yes."

I swiveled the typewriter to me, got paper and carbon in, and hit the keys. I had to concentrate. This was Cramer's farthest north. Parker was asking questions, and Wolfe was grunting at him. I finished the letter and envelope, had Wolfe sign it, went to the kitchen and told Fritz to take it to Eighth Avenue immediately, and returned to the office.

"Now," Wolfe said, "I want all of it. Go ahead."

Ordinarily when I start giving Wolfe a full report of an event, no matter how extended and involved, I just glide in and keep going with no effort at all, thanks to my long and hard training. That time, having just got a severe jolt, I wasn't so hot at the beginning, since I was supposed to include every word and movement, but by the time I had got to where I opened the window it was coming smooth and easy. As usual, Wolfe soaked it all in without making any interruptions.

It took all of an hour and a half, and then came questions, but not many. I rate a report by the number of questions he has when I'm through, and by that test this was up toward the top. Wolfe leaned back and closed his eyes.

Parker spoke. "It could have been any of them, but it must have been Koven. Or why his string of lies, knowing that you and Goodwin would both contradict him?" The lawyer haw-hawed. "That is, if they're lies—considering your settled policy of telling your counselor only what you think he should know."

"Pfui." Wolfe's eyes came open. "This is extraordinarily intricate, Archie. Have you examined it any?"

"I've started. When I pick at it, it gets worse instead of better."

"Yes. I'm afraid you'll have to type it out. By eleven tomorrow morning?"

"I guess so, but I need a bath first. Anyway, what for? What can we do with it without a license? I suppose it's suspended?"

He ignored it. "What the devil is that smell?" he demanded.

"Disinfectant. It's for the bloodhounds in case you escape." I arose. "I'll go scrub."

"No." He glanced at the wall clock, which said 3:45—fifteen minutes to go until he was due to join Theodore and the orchids up on the roof. "An errand first. I believe it's the *Gazette* that carries the Dazzle Dan comic strip?"

"Yes, sir."

"Daily and Sunday?"

"Yes, sir."

"I want all of them for the past three years. Can you get them?"

"I can try."

"Do so."

"Now?"

"Yes. Wait a minute—confound it, don't be a cyclone! You should hear my instructions for Mr. Parker, but first one for you. Mail Mr. Koven a bill for recovery of his gun, five hundred dollars. It should go today."

"Any extras, under the circumstances?"

"No. Five hundred flat." Wolfe turned to the lawyer. "Mr. Parker, how long will it take to enter a suit for damages and serve a summons on the defendant?"

"That depends." Parker sounded like a lawyer. "If it's rushed all possible and there are no unforeseen obstacles and the defendant is accessible for service, it could be merely a matter of hours."

"By noon tomorrow?"

"Quite possibly, yes."

"Then proceed, please. Mr. Koven has destroyed, by slander, my means of livelihood. I wish to bring an action demanding payment by him of the sum of one million dollars."

"M-m-m-m," Parker said. He was frowning.

I addressed Wolfe. "I want to apologize," I told him, "for jumping to a conclusion. I was supposing you had lost control for once and buried it too deep in Cramer. Whereas you did it purposely, getting set for this. I'll be damned."

Wolfe grunted.

"In this sort of thing," Parker said, "it is usual, and desirable, to first send a written request for recompense, by your attorney if you prefer. It looks better."

"I don't care how it looks. I want immediate action."

"Then we'll act." That was one of the reasons Wolfe stuck to Parker; he was no dilly-dallier. "But I must ask, isn't the sum a little flamboyant? A full million?"

"It is not flamboyant. At a hundred thousand a year, a modest expectation, my income would be a million in ten years. A detective license once lost in this fashion is not easily regained."

"All right. A million. I'll need all the facts for drafting a complaint."

"You have them. You've just heard Archie recount them. Must you stickle for more?"

"No. I'll manage." Parker got to his feet. "One thing, though, service of process may be a problem. Policemen may still be around, and even if they aren't I doubt if strangers will be getting into that house tomorrow."

"Archie will send Saul Panzer to you. Saul can get in anywhere and do anything." Wolfe wiggled a finger. "I want Mr. Koven to get that. I want to see him in this room. Five times this morning I tried to get him on the phone, without success. If that doesn't get him I'll devise something that will."

"He'll give it to his attorney."

"Then the attorney will come, and if he's not an imbecile I'll give myself thirty minutes to make him send for his client or go and get him. Well?"

Parker turned and left, not loitering. I got at the typewriter to make out a bill for half a grand, which seemed like a waste of paper after what I had just heard.

6

At midnight that Tuesday the office was a sight. It has often been a mess, one way and another, including the time the strangled Cynthia Brown was lying on the floor with her tongue protruding, but this was something new. Dazzle Dan, both black-and-white and color, was all over the place. On account of our shortage of manpower, with me tied up on my typing job, Fritz and Theodore had been drafted for the chore of tearing out the pages and stacking them chronologically, ready for Wolfe to study. With Wolfe's permission, I had bribed Lon Cohen of the *Gazette* to have three years of Dazzle Dan assembled and delivered to us, by offering him an exclusive. Naturally he demanded specifications.

"Nothing much," I told him on the phone. "Only that Nero Wolfe is out of the detective business because Inspector Cramer is taking away his license."

"Quite a gag," Lon conceded.

"No gag. Straight."

"You mean it?"

"We're offering it for publication. Exclusive, unless Cramer's office spills it, and I don't think they will."

"The Getz murder?"

"Yes. Only a couple of paragraphs, because details are not yet available, even to you. I'm out on bail."

"I know you are. This is pie. We'll raid the files and get it over there as soon as we can."

He hung up without pressing for details. Of course that meant he would send Dazzle Dan COD, with a reporter. When the reporter arrived a couple of hours later, shortly after Wolfe had come down from the plant rooms at six o'clock, it wasn't just a man with a notebook, it was Lon Cohen himself. He came to the office with me, dumped a big heavy carton on the floor by my desk, removed his coat and dropped it on the carton to show that Dazzle Dan was his property until paid for, and demanded, "I want the works. What Wolfe said and what Cramer said. A picture of Wolfe studying Dazzle Dan—"

I pushed him into a chair, courteously, and gave him all we were ready to turn loose of. Naturally that wasn't enough; it never is. I let him fire questions up to a dozen or so, even answering one or two, and then made it clear that that was all for now and I had work to do. He admitted it was a bargain, stuck his notebook in his pocket, and got up and picked up his coat.

"If you're not in a hurry, Mr. Cohen," muttered Wolfe, who had left the interview to me.

Lon dropped the coat and sat down. "I have nineteen years, Mr. Wolfe. Before I retire."

"I won't detain you that long." Wolfe sighed. "I am no longer a detective, but I'm a primate and therefore curious. The function of a newspaperman is to satisfy curiosity. Who killed Mr. Getz?"

Lon's brows went up. "Archie Goodwin? It was his gun."

"Nonsense. I'm quite serious. Also I'm discreet. I am excluded from the customary sources of information by the jackassery of Mr. Cramer. I—"

"May I print that?"

"No. None of this. Nor shall I quote you. This is a private conversation. I would like to know what your colleagues are saying but not printing. Who killed Mr. Getz? Miss Lowell? If so, why?"

Lon pulled his lower lip down and let it up again. "You mean we're just talking."

"Yes."

"This might possibly lead to another talk that could be printed."

"It might. I make no commitment." Wolfe wasn't eager.

"You wouldn't. As for Miss Lowell, she has not been scratched. It is said that Getz learned she was chiseling on royalties from makers of Dazzle Dan products and intended to hang it on her. That could have been big money."

"Any names or dates?"

"None that are repeatable. By me. Yet."

"Any evidence?"

"I haven't seen any."

Wolfe grunted. "Mr. Hildebrand. If so, why?"

"That's shorter and sadder. He has told friends about it. He has been with Koven for eight years and was told last week he could leave at the end of the month, and he blamed it on Getz. He might or might not get another job at his age."

Wolfe nodded. "Mr. Jordan?"

Lon hesitated. "This I don't like, but others are talking, so why not us? They say Jordan has painted some pictures, modern stuff, and twice he has tried to get a gallery to show them, two different galleries, and both times Getz has somehow kiboshed it. This has names and dates, but whether because Getz was born a louse or whether he wanted to keep Jordan?"

"I'll do my own speculating, thank you. Mr. Getz may not have liked the pictures. Mr. Koven?"

Lon turned a hand over. "Well? What better could you ask? Getz had him buffaloed, no doubt about it. Getz ruled the roost, plenty of evidence on that, and nobody knows why, so the only question is what he had on Koven. It must have been good, but what was it? You say this is a private conversation?"

"Yes."

"Then here's something we got started on just this afternoon. It has to be checked before we print it. That house on Seventy-sixth Street is in Getz's name."

"Indeed." Wolfe shut his eyes and opened them again. "And Mrs. Koven?"

Lon turned his other hand over. "Husband and wife are one, aren't they?"

"Yes. Man and wife make one fool."

Lon's chin jerked up. "I want to print that. Why not?"

"It was printed more than three hundred years ago. Ben Jonson wrote it." Wolfe sighed. "Confound it, what can I do with only a few scraps?" He pointed at the carton. "You want that stuff back, I suppose?"

Lon said he did. He also said he would be glad to go on with the private conversation in the interest of justice and the public welfare, but apparently Wolfe had all the scraps he could use at the moment. After ushering Lon to the door I went up to my room to spend an hour attending to purely personal matters, a detail that had been too long postponed. I was out of the shower, selecting a shirt, when a call came from Saul Panzer in response to the message I had left. I gave him all the features of the picture that would help and told him to report to Parker's law office in the morning.

After dinner that evening we were all hard at it in the office. Fritz and Theodore were unfolding Gazettes, finding the right page and tearing it out, and carrying off the leavings. I was banging away at my machine, three pages an hour. Wolfe was at his desk, concentrating on a methodical and exhaustive study of three years of Dazzle Dan. It was well after midnight when he pushed back his chair, arose, stretched, rubbed his eyes, and told us, "It's bedtime. This morass of fatuity has given me indigestion. Good night."

Wednesday morning he tried to put one over. His routine was breakfast in his room, with the morning paper, at eight; then shaving and dressing; then, from nine to eleven, his morning shift up in the plant rooms. He never went to the office before eleven, and the detective business was never allowed to mingle with the orchids. But that Wednesday he fudged. While I was in the kitchen with Fritz, enjoying griddle cakes, Darst's sausage, honey, and plenty of coffee, and going through the morning papers, with two readings for the Gazette's account of Wolfe's enforced retirement, Wolfe sneaked downstairs into the office and made off with a

stack of Dazzle Dan. The way I knew, before breakfast I had gone in there to
straighten up a little, and I am trained to observe. Returning after breakfast, and
glancing around before starting at my typewriter, I saw that half of a pile of Dan
was gone. I don't think I had ever seen him quite so hot under the collar. I admit
I fully approved. Not only did I not make an excuse for a trip up to the roof to
catch him at it, but I even took the trouble to be out of the office when he came
down at eleven o'clock, to give him a chance to get Dan back unseen.

My first job after breakfast had been to carry out some instructions Wolfe had
given me the evening before. Manhattan office hours being what they are, I got no
answer at the number of Levay Recorders, Inc., until 9:35. Then it took some
talking to get a promise of immediate action, and if it hadn't been for the name of
Nero Wolfe I wouldn't have made it. But I got both the promise and the action. A
little after ten two men arrived with cartons of equipment and tool kits, and in less
than an hour they were through and gone, and it was a neat and nifty job. It would
have taken an expert search to reveal anything suspicious in the office, and the wire
to the kitchen, running around the baseboard and on through, wouldn't be suspicious even if seen.

It was hard going at the typewriter on account of the phone ringing, chiefly
reporters wanting to talk to Wolfe, or at least me, and finally I had to ask Fritz in
to answer the damn thing and give everybody a brush-off. A call he switched to me
was one from the DA's office. They had the nerve to ask me to come down there
so they could ask me something. I told them I was busy answering Help Wanted
ads and couldn't spare the time. Half an hour later Fritz switched another one to
me. It was Sergeant Purley Stebbins. He was good and sore, beefing about Wolfe
having no authority to break the news about losing his license, and it wasn't official
yet, and where did I think it would get me refusing to cooperate with the DA on a
murder when I had discovered the body, and I could have my choice of coming
down quick or having a PD car come and get me. I let him use up his breath.

"Listen, brother," I told him, "I hadn't heard that the name of this city has
been changed to Moscow. If Mr. Wolfe wants to publish it that he's out of business,
hoping that someone will pass the hat or offer him a job as a doorman, that's his
affair. As for my cooperating, nuts. You have already got me sewed up on two
charges, and on advice of counsel and my doctor I am staying home, taking aspirin
and gargling with prune juice and gin. If you come here, no matter who, you won't
get in without a search warrant. If you come with another warrant for me, say for
cruelty to animals because I opened that window, you can either wait on the stoop
until I emerge or shoot the door down, whichever you prefer. I am now hanging
up."

"If you'll listen a minute, damn it."

"Good-by, you double-breasted nitwit."

I cradled the phone, sat thirty seconds to calm down, and resumed at the typewriter. The next interruption came not from the outside but from Wolfe, a little before noon. He was back at his desk, analyzing Dazzle Dan. Suddenly he pronounced my name, and I swiveled.

"Yes, sir."

"Look at this."

He slid a sheet of the *Gazette* across his desk, and I got up and took it. It was a Sunday half-page, in color, from four months back. In the first frame Dazzle Dan was scooting along a country road on a motorcycle, passing a roadside sign that read:

PEACHES RIGHT FROM THE TREE!
AGGIE GHOOL AND HAGGIE KROOL

Frame two, D.D. had stopped his bike alongside a peach tree full of red and yellow fruit. Standing there were two females, presumably Aggie Ghool and Haggie Krool. One was old and bent, dressed in burlap as near as I could tell; the other was young and pink-cheeked, wearing a mink coat. If you say surely not a mink coat, I say I'm telling what I saw. D.D. was saying, in his balloon, "Gimme a dozen."

Frame three, the young female was handing D.D. the peaches, and the old one was extending her hand for payment. Frame four, the old one was giving D.D. his change from a bill. Frame five, the old one was handing the young one a coin and saying, "Here's your ten percent, Haggie," and the young one was saying, "Thank you very much, Aggie." Frame six, D.D. was asking Aggie, "Why don't you split it even?" and Aggie was telling him, "Because it's my tree." Frame seven, D.D. was off again on the bike, but I felt I had had enough and looked at Wolfe inquiringly.

"Am I supposed to comment?"

"If it would help, yes."

"I pass. If it's a feed from the National Industrialists' League it's the wrong angle. If you mean the mink coat, Pat Lowell's may not be paid for."

He grunted. "There have been two similar episodes, one each year, with the same characters."

"Then it may be paid for."

"Is that all?"

"It's all for now. I'm not a brain, I'm a typist. I've got to finish this damn report."

I tossed the art back to him and returned to work.

At 12:28 I handed him the finished report, and he dropped D.D. and started on it. I went to the kitchen to tell Fritz I would take on the phone again, and as I reentered the office it was ringing. I crossed my desk and got it. My daytime formula was, "Nero Wolfe's office, Archie Goodwin speaking," but with our license gone it was presumably illegal to have an office, so I said, "Nero Wolfe's residence, Archie Goodwin speaking," and heard Saul Panzer's husky voice.

"Reporting in, Archie. No trouble at all. Koven is served. Put it in his hand five minutes ago."

"In the house?"

"Yes. I'll call Parker—"

"How did you get in?"

"Oh, simple. The man that delivers stuff from that Furnari's you told me about has got the itch bad, and it only took ten bucks. Of course after I got inside I had to use my head and legs both, but with your sketch of the layout it was a cinch."

"For you, yes. Mr. Wolfe says satisfactory, which as you know is as far as he ever goes. I say you show promise. You'll call Parker?"

"Yes. I have to go there to sign a paper."

"Okay. Be seeing you."

I hung up and told Wolfe. He lifted his eyes, said, "Ah!" and returned to the report.

After lunch there was an important chore, involving Wolfe, me, our memory of the talk Saturday evening with Koven, and the equipment that had been installed by Levay Recorders, Inc. We spent nearly an hour at it, with three separate tries, before we got it done to Wolfe's satisfaction.

After that it dragged along, at least for me. The phone calls had fallen off. Wolfe, at his desk, finished with the report, put it in a drawer, leaned back, and closed his eyes. I would just as soon have opened a conversation, but pretty soon his lips started working—pushing out, drawing back, and pushing out again—and I knew his brain was busy so I went to the cabinet for a batch of the germination records and settled down to making entries. He didn't need a license to go on growing orchids, though the question would soon arise of how to pay the bills. At four o'clock he left to go up to the plant rooms, and I went on with the records. During the next two hours there were a few phone calls, but none from Koven or his lawyer or Parker. At two minutes past six I was telling myself that Koven was probably drinking himself up to something, no telling what, when two things happened at once: the sound came from the hall of Wolfe's elevator jerking to a stop, and the doorbell rang.

I went to the hall, switched on the stoop light, and took a look through the panel of one-way glass in the front door. It was a mink coat all right, but the hat was different. I went closer, passing Wolfe on his way to the office, got a view of the face, and saw that she was alone. I marched to the office door and announced, "Miss Patricia Lowell. Will she do?"

He made a face. He seldom welcomes a man crossing his threshold; he never welcomes a woman. "Let her in," he muttered.

I stepped to the front, slid the bolt off, and opened up. "This is the kind of surprise I like," I said heartily. She entered, and I shut the door and bolted it. "Couldn't you find a coconut?"

"I want to see Nero Wolfe," she said in a voice so hard that it was out of character, considering her pink cheeks.

"Sure. This way." I ushered her down the hall and on in. Once in a while Wolfe rises when a woman enters his office, but this time he kept not only his chair but also his tongue. He inclined his head a quarter of an inch when I pronounced her name, but said nothing. I gave her the red leather chair, helped her throw her coat back, and went to my desk.

"So you're Nero Wolfe," she said.

That called for no comment and got none.

"I'm scared to death," she said.

"You don't look it," Wolfe growled.

"I hope I don't; I'm trying not to." She started to put her bag on the little table at her elbow, changed her mind, and kept it in her lap. She took off a glove. "I was sent here by Mr. Koven."

No comment. We were looking at her. She looked at me, then back at Wolfe, and protested, "My God, don't you ever say anything?"

"Only on occasion." Wolfe leaned back. "Give me one. You say something."

She compressed her lips. She was sitting forward and erect in the big roomy chair, with no contact with the upholstered back. "Mr. Koven sent me," she said, clipping it, "about the ridiculous suit for damages you brought. He intends to enter a counterclaim for damage to his reputation through actions of your acknowledged agent, Archie Goodwin. Of course he denies that there is any basis for your suit."

She stopped. Wolfe met her gaze and kept his trap shut.

"That's the situation," she said belligerently.

"Thank you for coming to tell me," Wolfe murmured. "If you'll show Miss Lowell the way out, please, Archie?"

I stood up. She looked at me as if I had offered her a deadly insult, and looked back at Wolfe. "I don't think," she said, "that your attitude is very sensible. I think you and Mr. Koven should come to an agreement on this. Why wouldn't this be the way to do it—say the claims cancel each other, and you abandon yours and he abandons his?"

"Because," Wolfe said dryly, "my claim is valid and his isn't. If you're a member of the bar, Miss Lowell, you should know that this is a little improper, or anyway unconventional. You should be talking with my attorney, not with me."

"I'm not a lawyer, Mr. Wolfe. I'm Mr. Koven's agent and business manager. He thinks lawyers would just make this more of a mess than it is, and I agree with him. He thinks you and he should settle between you. Isn't that possible?"

"I don't know. We can try. There's a phone. Get him down here."

She shook her head. "He's not—he's too upset. I'm sure you'll find it more practical to deal with me, and if we come to an understanding he'll approve, I guarantee that. Why don't we go into it—the two claims?"

"I doubt if it will get us anywhere." Wolfe sounded perfectly willing to come halfway. "For one thing, a factor in both claims is the question who killed Adrian Getz and why? If it was Mr. Goodwin, Mr. Koven's claim has a footing, and I freely concede it; if it was someone else I concede nothing. If I discussed it with you I would have to begin by considering that aspect; I would have to ask you some pointed questions; and I doubt if you would dare to risk answering them."

"I can always button up. What kind of questions?"

"Well—" Wolfe pursed his lips. "For example, how's the monkey?"

"I can risk answering that. It's sick. It's at the Speyer Hospital. They don't expect it to live."

"Exposure from the open window?"

"Yes. They're very delicate, that kind."

Wolfe nodded. "That table over there by the globe—that pile of stuff on it is Dazzle Dan for the past three years. I've been looking through it. Last August and September a monkey had a prominent role. It was drawn by two different persons, or at least with two different conceptions. In its first seventeen appearances it was depicted maliciously—on a conjecture, by someone with a distaste for monkeys. Thereafter it was drawn sympathetically and humorously. The change was abrupt and noticeable. Why? On instructions from Mr. Koven?"

Pat Lowell was frowning. Her lips parted and went together again.

"You have four choices," Wolfe said bluntly. "The truth, a lie, evasion, or refusal to answer. Either of the last two would make me curious, and I would get my curiosity satisfied somehow. If you try a lie it may work, but I'm an expert on lies and liars."

"There's nothing to lie about. I was thinking back. Mr. Getz objected to the way the monkey was drawn, and Mr. Koven had Mr. Jordan do it instead of Mr. Hildebrand."

"Mr. Jordan likes monkeys?"

"He likes animals. He said the monkey looked like Napoleon."

"Mr. Hildebrand does not like monkeys?"

"He didn't like that one. Rookaloo knew it, of course, and bit him once. Isn't this pretty silly, Mr. Wolfe? Are you going on with this?"

"Unless you walk out, yes. I'm investigating Mr. Koven's counterclaim, and this is how I do it. With any question you have your four choices—and a fifth too, of course: get up and go. How did you feel about the monkey?"

"I thought it was an awful nuisance, but it had its points as a diversion. It was my fault it was there, since I gave it to Mr. Getz."

"Indeed. When?"

"About a year ago. A friend returning from South America gave it to me, and I couldn't take care of it so I gave it to him."

"Mr. Getz lives at the Koven house?"

"Yes."

"Then actually you were dumping it onto Mrs. Koven. Did she appreciate it?"

"She has never said so. I didn't—I know I should have considered that. I apologized to her, and she was nice about it."

"Did Mr. Koven like the monkey?"

"He liked to tease it. But he didn't dislike it; he teased it just to annoy Mr. Getz."

Wolfe leaned back and clasped his hands behind his head. "You know, Miss Lowell, I did not find the Dazzle Dan saga hopelessly inane. There is a sustained sardonic tone, some fertility of invention, and even an occasional touch of imagination. Monday evening, while Mr. Goodwin was in jail, I telephoned a couple of people who are supposed to know things and was referred by them to others. I was told that it is generally believed, though not published, that the conception of Dazzle Dan was originally supplied to Mr. Koven by Mr. Getz, that Mr. Getz was the continuing source of inspiration for the story and pictures, and that without him Mr. Koven will be up a stump. What about it?"

Pat Lowell had stiffened. "Talk." She was scornful. "Just cheap talk."

"You should know." Wolfe sounded relieved. "If that belief could be validated I admit I would be up a stump myself. To support my claim against Mr. Koven, and to discredit his against me, I need to demonstrate that Mr. Goodwin did not kill Mr. Getz, either accidentally or otherwise. If he didn't, then who did? One of you five. But all of you had a direct personal interest in the continued success of Dazzle Dan, sharing as you did in the prodigious proceeds; and if Mr. Getz was responsible for the success, why kill him?" Wolfe chuckled. "So you see I'm not silly at all. We've been at it only twenty minutes, and already you've helped me enormously. Give us another four or five hours, and we'll see. By the way."

He leaned forward to press a button at the edge of his desk, and in a moment Fritz appeared.

"There'll be a guest for dinner, Fritz."

"Yes, sir." Fritz went.

"Four or five hours?" Pat Lowell demanded.

"At least that. With a recess for dinner; I banish business from the table. Half for me and half for you. This affair is extremely complicated, and if you came here to get an agreement we'll have to cover it all. Let's see, where were we?"

She regarded him. "About Getz, I didn't say he had nothing to do with the success of Dazzle Dan. After all, so do I. I didn't say he won't be a loss. Everyone knows he was Mr. Koven's oldest and closest friend. We were all quite aware that Mr. Koven relied on him—"

Wolfe showed her a palm. "Please, Miss Lowell, don't spoil it for me. Don't give me a point and then try to snatch it back. Next you'll be saying that Koven called Getz 'the Squirt' to show his affection, as a man will call his dearest friend an old bastard, whereas I prefer to regard it as an inferiority complex, deeply resentful, showing its biceps. Or telling me that all of you, without exception, were inordinately fond of Mr. Getz and submissively grateful to him. Don't forget that Mr. Goodwin spent hours in that house among you and has fully reported to me; also you should know that I had a talk with Inspector Cramer Monday evening and learned from him some of the plain facts, such as the pillow lying on the floor, scorched and pierced, showing that it had been used to muffle the sound of the shot, and the failure of all of you to prove lack of opportunity."

Wolfe kept going. "But if you insist on minimizing Koven's dependence as a fact, let me assume it as a hypothesis in order to put a question. Say, just for my question, that Koven felt strongly about his debt to Getz and his reliance on him, that he proposed to do something about it, and that he found it necessary to confide in one of you people, to get help or advice. Which of you would he have come to? We must of course put his wife first, ex officio and to sustain convention—and anyway, out of courtesy I must suppose you incapable of revealing your employer's conjugal privities. Which of you three would he have come to—Mr. Hildebrand, Mr. Jordan, or you?"

Miss Lowell was wary. "On your hypothesis, you mean."

"Yes."

"None of us."

"But if he felt he had to?"

"Not with anything as intimate as that. He wouldn't have let himself have to. None of us three has ever got within miles of him on anything really personal."

"Surely he confides in you, his agent and manager?"

"On business matters, yes. Not on personal things, except superficialities."

"Why were all of you so concerned about the gun in his desk?"

"We weren't concerned, not *really* concerned—at least I wasn't. I just didn't like it's being there, loaded, so easy to get at, and I knew he didn't have a license for it."

Wolfe kept on about the gun for a good ten minutes—how often had she seen it, had she ever picked it up, and so forth, with special emphasis on Sunday morning, when she and Hildebrand had opened the drawer and looked at it. On that detail she corroborated Hildebrand as I had heard him tell it to Cramer. Finally she balked. She said they weren't getting anywhere, and she certainly wasn't going to stay for dinner if afterward it was only going to be more of the same.

Wolfe nodded in agreement. "You're quite right," he told her. "We've gone as far as we can, you and I. We need all of them. It's time for you to call Mr. Koven and tell him so. Tell him to be here at eight-thirty with Mrs. Koven, Mr. Jordan, and Mr. Hildebrand."

She was staring at him. "Are you trying to be funny?" she demanded.

He skipped it. "I don't know," he said, "whether you can handle it properly; if not, I'll talk to him. The validity of my claim, and of his, depends primarily on who killed Mr. Getz. I now know who killed him. I'll have to tell the police but first I want to settle the matter of my claim with Mr. Koven. Tell him that. Tell him that if I have to inform the police before I have a talk with him and the others there will be no compromise on my claim, and I'll collect it."

"This is a bluff."

"Then call it."

"I'm going to." She left the chair and got the coat around her. Her eyes blazed at him. "I'm not such a sap!" She started for the door.

"Get Inspector Cramer, Archie!" Wolfe snapped. He called, "They'll be there by the time you are!"

I lifted the phone and dialed. She was out in the hall, but I heard neither footsteps nor the door opening.

"Hello," I told the transmitter, loud enough. "Manhattan Homicide West? Inspector Cramer, please. This is—"

A hand darted past me, and a finger pressed the button down, and a mink coat dropped to the floor. "Damn you!" she said, hard and cold, but the hand was shaking so that the finger slipped off the button. I cradled the phone.

"Get Mr. Koven's number for her, Archie," Wolfe purred.

7

At twenty minutes to nine Wolfe's eyes moved slowly from left to right, to take in the faces of our assembled visitors. He was in a nasty humor. He hated to work right after dinner, and from the way he kept his chin down and a slight twitch of a muscle in his cheek I knew it was going to be real work. Whether he had got them there with a bluff or not, and my guess was that he had, it would take more than a bluff to rake in the pot he was after now.

Pat Lowell had not dined with us. Not only had she declined to come along to the dining room; she had also left untouched the tray which Fritz had taken to her in the office. Of course that got Wolfe's goat and probably got some pointed remarks from him, but I wasn't there to hear them because I had gone to the kitchen to check with Fritz on the operation of the installation that had been made by Levay Recorders, Inc. That was the one part of the program that I clearly understood. I was still in the kitchen, rehearsing with Fritz, when the doorbell rang and I went to the front and found them there in a body. They got better hall service than I had got at their place, and also better chair service in the office.

When they were seated Wolfe took them in from left to right—Harry Koven in the red leather chair, then his wife, then Pat Lowell, and, after a gap, Pete Jordan and Byram Hildebrand over toward me. I don't know what impression Wolfe got from his survey, but from where I sat it looked as if he was up against a united front.

"This time," Koven blurted, "you can't cook up a fancy lie with Goodwin. There are witnesses."

He was keyed up. I would have said he had had six drinks, but it might have been more.

"We won't get anywhere that way, Mr. Koven," Wolfe objected. "We're all tangled up, and it will take more than blather to get us loose. You don't want to pay me a million dollars. I don't want to lose my license. The police don't want to add another unsolved murder to the long list. The central and dominant factor is the violent death of Mr. Getz, and I propose to deal with that at length. If we can get that settled—"

"You told Miss Lowell you know who killed him. If so, why don't you tell the police? That ought to settle it."

Wolfe's eyes narrowed. "You don't mean that, Mr. Koven—"

"You're damn right I mean it!"

"Then there's a misunderstanding. I heard Miss Lowell's talk with you on the phone, both ends of it. I got the impression that my threat to inform the police about Mr. Getz's death was what brought you down here. Now you seem—"

"It wasn't any threat that brought me here! It's that blackmailing suit you started! I want to make you eat it and I'm going to!"

"Indeed. Then I gather that you don't care who. gets my information first, you or the police. But I do. For one thing, when I talk to the police I like to be able—"

The doorbell rang. When visitors were present Fritz usually answered the door, but he had orders to stick to his post in the kitchen, so I got up and went to the hall, circling behind the arc of the chairs. I switched on the stoop light for a look through the one-way glass. One glance was enough. Stepping back into the office, I stood until Wolfe caught my eye.

"The man about the chair," I told him.

He frowned. "Tell him I'm—" He stopped, and the frown cleared. "No. I'll see him. If you'll excuse me a moment?" He pushed his chair back, made it to his feet, and came, detouring around Koven. I let him precede me into the hall and closed that door before joining him. He strode to the front, peered through the glass, and opened the door. The chain bolt stopped it at a crack of two inches.

Wolfe spoke through the crack. "Well, sir?"

Inspector Cramer's voice was anything but friendly. "I'm coming in."

"I doubt it. What for?"

"Patricia Lowell entered here at six o'clock and is still here. The other four entered fifteen minutes ago. I told you Monday evening to lay off. I told you your license was suspended, and here you are with your office full. I'm coming in."

"I still doubt it. I have no client. My job for Mr. Koven, which you know about, has been finished, and I have sent him a bill. These people are here to discuss an action for damages which I have brought against Mr. Koven. I don't need a license for that. I'm shutting the door."

He tried to, but it didn't budge. I could see the tip of Cramer's toe at the bottom of the crack.

"By God, this does it," Cramer said savagely. "You're through."

"I thought I was already through. But this—"

"I can't hear you! The wind."

"This is preposterous, talking through a crack. Descend to the sidewalk, and I'll come out. Did you hear that?"

"Yes."

"Very well. To the sidewalk."

Wolfe marched to the big old walnut rack and reached for his overcoat. After I had held it for him and handed him his hat I got my coat and slipped into it and then took a look through the glass. The stoop was empty. A burly figure was at the bottom of the steps. I unbolted the door and opened it, followed Wolfe over the sill, pulled the door shut, and made sure it was locked. A gust of wind pounced on us, slashing at us with sleet. I wanted to take Wolfe's elbow as we went down the steps, thinking where it would leave me if he fell and cracked his skull, but knew I hadn't better.

He made it safely, got his back to the sleety wind, which meant that Cramer had to face it, and raised his voice. "I don't like fighting a blizzard, so let's get to the point. You don't want these people talking with me, but there's nothing you can do about it. You have blundered and you know it. You arrested Mr. Goodwin on a trumpery charge. You came and blustered me and went too far. Now you're afraid I'm going to explode Mr. Koven's lies. More, you're afraid I'm going to catch a murderer and toss him to the district attorney. So you—"

"I'm not afraid of a goddam thing." Cramer was squinting to protect his eyes from the cutting sleet. "I told you to lay off, and by God you're going to. Your suit against Koven is a phony."

"It isn't, but let's stick to the point. I'm uncomfortable. I am not an outdoors man. You want to enter my house. You may, under a condition. The five callers are in my office. There is a hole in the wall, concealed from view in the office by what is apparently a picture. Standing, or on a stool, in a nook at the end of the hall, you can see and hear us in the office. The condition is that you enter quietly —confound it!"

The wind had taken his hat. I made a quick dive and stab but missed, and away it went. He had only had it fourteen years.

"The condition," he repeated, "is that you enter quietly, take your post in the nook, oversee from there, and give me half an hour. Thereafter you will be free to join us if you think you should. I warn you not to be impetuous. Up to a certain point your presence would make it harder for me, if not impossible, and I doubt if you'll know when that point is reached. I'm after a murderer, and there's one chance in five, I should say, that I'll get him. I want—"

"I thought you said you were discussing an action for damages."

"We are. I'll get either the murderer or the damages. Do you want to harp on that?"

"No."

"You've cooled off, and no wonder, in this hurricane. My hair will go next. I'm going in. If you come along it must be under the condition as stated. Are you coming?"

"Yes."

"You accept the condition?"

"Yes."

Wolfe headed for the steps. I passed him to go ahead and unlock the door. When they were inside I closed it and put the bolt back on. They hung up their coats, and Wolfe took Cramer down the hall and around the corner to the nook. I brought a stool from the kitchen, but Cramer shook his head. Wolfe slid the panel aside, making no sound, looked through, and nodded to Cramer. Cramer took a look and nodded back, and we left him. At the door to the office Wolfe muttered about his hair, and I let him use my pocket comb.

From the way they looked at us as we entered you might have thought they suspected we had been in the cellar fusing a bomb, but one more suspicion wouldn't make it any harder. I circled to my desk and sat. Wolfe got himself back in place, took a deep breath, and passed his eyes over them.

"I'm sorry," he said politely, "but that was unavoidable. Suppose we start over" —he looked at Koven—"say with your surmise to the police that Getz was shot by Mr. Goodwin accidentally in a scuffle. That's absurd. Getz was shot with a cartridge that had been taken from your gun and put into Goodwin's gun. Manifestly Goodwin couldn't have done that, since when he first saw your gun Getz was already dead. Therefore—"

"That's not true!" Koven cut in. "He had seen it before, when he came to my office. He could have gone back later and got the cartridges."

Wolfe glared at him in astonishment. "Do you really dare, sir, in front of me, to my face, to cling to that fantastic tale you told the police? That rigmarole?"

"You're damn right I do!"

"Pfui." Wolfe was disgusted. "I had hoped, here together, we were prepared to get down to reality. It would have been better to adopt your suggestion to take my information to the police. Perhaps—"

"I made no such suggestion!"

"In this room, Mr. Koven, some fifteen minutes ago?"

"No!"

Wolfe made a face. "I see," he said quietly. "It's impossible to get on solid ground with a man like you, but I still have to try. Archie, bring the tape from the kitchen, please?"

I went. I didn't like it. I thought he was rushing it. Granting that he had been jostled off his stride by Cramer's arrival, I felt that it was far from one of his best performances, and this looked like a situation where nothing less than his best would do. So I went to the kitchen, passing Cramer in his nook without a glance, told Fritz to stop the machine and wind, and stood and scowled at it turning. When it stopped I removed the wheel and slipped it into a carton and, carton in hand, returned to the office.

"We're waiting," Wolfe said curtly.

That hurried me. There was a stack of similar cartons on my desk, and in my haste I knocked them over as I was putting down the one I had brought. It was embarrassing with all eyes on me, and I gave them a cold look as I crossed to the cabinet to get the player. It needed a whole corner of my desk, and I had to shove the tumbled cartons aside to make room. Finally I had the player in position and connected, and the wheel of tape, taken from the carton, in place.

"All right?" I asked Wolfe.

"Go ahead."

I flipped the switch. There was a crackle and a little spitting, and then Wolfe's voice came:

"It's not that, Mr. Koven, not at all, I only doubt if it's worth it to you, considering the size of my minimum fee, to hire me for anything so trivial as finding a stolen gun, or even discovering the thief. I should think—"

"No!" Wolfe bellowed.

I switched it off. I was flustered. "Excuse it," I said. "The wrong one."

"Must I do it myself?" Wolfe asked sarcastically.

I muttered something, turning the wheel to rewind. I removed it, pawed among the cartons, picked one, took out the wheel, put it on, and turned the switch. This time the voice that came on was not Wolfe's but Koven's—loud and clear.

"This time you can't cook up a fancy lie with Goodwin. There are witnesses."

Then WOLFE'S: "We won't get anywhere that way, Mr. Koven. We're all tangled up, and it will take more than blather to get us loose. You don't want to pay me a million dollars. I don't want to lose my license. The police don't want to add another unsolved murder to the long list. The central and dominant factor is the violent death of Mr. Getz, and I propose to deal with that at length. If we can get that settled—"

KOVEN'S: "You told Miss Lowell you know who killed him. If so, why don't you tell the police? That ought to settle it."

WOLFE: "You don't mean that, Mr. Koven—"

KOVEN: "You're damn right I mean it!"

WOLFE: "Then there's a misunderstanding. I heard Miss Lowell's talk with you on the phone, both ends of it. I got the impression that my threat to inform the police—"

"That's enough!" Wolfe called. I turned it off. Wolfe looked at Koven. "I would call that," he said dryly, "a suggestion that I take my information to the police. Wouldn't you?"

Koven wasn't saying. Wolfe's eyes moved. "Wouldn't you, Miss Lowell?"

She shook her head. "I'm not an expert on suggestions."

Wolfe left her. "We won't quarrel over terms, Mr. Koven. You heard it. Incidentally, about the other tape you heard the start of through Mr. Goodwin's clumsiness, you may wonder why I haven't given it to the police to refute you. Monday evening, when Inspector Cramer came to see me, I still considered you as my client and I didn't want to discomfit you until I heard what you had to say. Before Mr. Cramer left he had made himself so offensive that I was disinclined to tell him anything whatever. Now you are no longer my client. We'll discuss this matter realistically or not at all. I don't care to badger you into an explicit statement that you lied to the police; I'll leave that to you and them; I merely insist that we proceed on the basis of what we both know to be the truth. With that understood—"

"Wait a minute," Pat Lowell put in. "The gun was in the drawer Sunday morning. I saw it."

"I know you did. That's one of the knots in the tangle, and we'll come to it." His eyes swept the arc. "We want to know who killed Adrian Getz. Let's get at it. What do we know about him or her? We know a lot.

"First, he took Koven's gun from the drawer sometime previous to last Friday and kept it somewhere. For that gun was put back in the drawer when Goodwin's was removed shortly before Getz was killed, and cartridges from it were placed in Goodwin's gun.

"Second, the thought of Getz continuing to live was for some reason so repugnant to him as to be intolerable.

"Third, he knew the purpose of Koven's visit here Saturday evening, and of Goodwin's errand at the Koven house on Monday, and he knew the details of the procedure planned by Koven and Goodwin. Only with—"

"I don't know them even yet," Hildebrand squeaked.

"Neither do I," Pete Jordan declared.

"The innocent can afford ignorance," Wolfe told them. "Enjoy it if you have it. Only with that knowledge could he have devised his intricate scheme and carried it out.

"Fourth, his mental processes are devious but defective. His deliberate and spectacular plan to make it appear that Goodwin had killed Getz, while ingenious in some respects, was in others witless. Going to Koven's office to get Goodwin's gun from the drawer and placing Koven's gun there, transferring the cartridges from Koven's gun to Goodwin's, proceeding to the room below to find Getz asleep, shooting him in the head, using a pillow to muffle the sound—all that was well enough, competently conceived and daringly executed, but then what? Wanting to make sure that the gun would be quickly found on the spot, a quite unnecessary precaution, he slipped it into the monkey's cage. That was probably improvisation and utterly brainless. Mr. Goodwin couldn't possibly be such a vapid fool.

"Fifth, he hated the monkey deeply and bitterly, either on its own account or because of its association with Getz. Having just killed a man, and needing to leave the spot with all possible speed, he went and opened a window, from only one conceivable motive. That took a peculiar, indeed an unexampled, malevolence. I admit it was effective. Miss Lowell tells me the monkey is dying.

"Sixth, he placed Koven's gun in the drawer Sunday morning and, after it had been seen there, took it out again. That was the most remarkable stratagem of all. Since there was no point in putting it there unless it was to be seen, he arranged that it should be seen. Why? It could only have been that he already knew what was to happen on Monday when Mr. Goodwin came, he had already conceived his scheme for framing Goodwin for the homicide, and he thought he was arranging in advance to discredit Goodwin's story. So he not only put the gun in the drawer Sunday morning, he also made sure its presence would be noted—and not, of course, by Mr. Koven."

Wolfe focused on one of them. "You saw the gun in the drawer Sunday morning, Mr. Hildebrand?"

"Yes." The squeak was off pitch. "But I didn't put it there!"

"I didn't say you did. Your claim to innocence has not yet been challenged. You were in the workroom, went up to consult Mr. Koven, encountered Mrs. Koven one flight up, were told by her that Mr. Koven was still in bed, ascended to the office, found Miss Lowell there, and you pulled the drawer open and both of you saw the gun there. Is that correct?"

"I didn't go up there to look in that drawer. We just—"

"Stop meeting accusations that haven't been made. It's a bad habit. Had you been upstairs earlier that morning?"

"No!"

"Had he, Miss Lowell?"

"Not that I know of." She spoke slowly, with a drag, as if she had only so many words and had to count them. "Our looking into the drawer was only incidental."

"Had he, Mrs. Koven?"

The wife jerked her head up. "Had what?" she demanded.

"Had Mr. Hildebrand been upstairs earlier that morning?"

She looked bewildered. "Earlier than what?"

"You met him in the second-floor hall and told him that your husband was still in bed and that Miss Lowell was up in the office. Had he been upstairs before that? That morning?"

"I haven't the slightest idea."

"Then you don't say that he had been?"

"I know nothing about it."

"There's nothing as safe as ignorance—or as dangerous." Wolfe spread his gaze again. "To complete the list of what we know about the murderer. Seventh and last, his repugnance to Getz was so extreme that he even scorned the risk that by killing Getz he might be killing Dazzle Dan. How essential Getz was to Dazzle Dan—"

"I make Dazzle Dan!" Harry Koven roared. "Dazzle Dan is mine!" He was glaring at everybody. "I am Dazzle Dan!"

"For God's sake shut up, Harry!" Pat Lowell said sharply.

Koven's chin was quivering. He needed three drinks.

"I was saying," Wolfe went on, "that I do not know how essential Getz was to Dazzle Dan. The testimony conflicts. In any case the murderer wanted him dead. I've identified the murderer for you by now, surely?"

"You have not," Pat Lowell said aggressively.

"Then I'll specify." Wolfe leaned forward at them. "But first let me say a word for the police, particularly Mr. Cramer. He is quite capable of unraveling a tangle like this, with its superficial complexities. What flummoxed him was Mr. Koven's elaborate lie, apparently corroborated by Miss Lowell and Mr. Hildebrand. If he had had the gumption to proceed on the assumption that Mr. Goodwin and I were telling the truth and all of it, he would have found it simple. This should be a lesson to him."

Wolfe considered a moment. "It might be better to specify by elimination. If you recall my list of seven facts about the murderer, that is child's play. Mr. Jordan, for instance, is eliminated by Number Six; he wasn't there Sunday morning. Mr. Hildebrand is eliminated by three or four of them, especially Number Six again; he had made no earlier trip upstairs. Miss Lowell is eliminated, for me, by Numbers Four and Five; and I am convinced that none of the three I have named can meet the requirements of Number Three. I do not believe that Mr. Koven would have confided in any of them so intimately. Nor do I—"

"Hold it!" The gruff voice came from the doorway.

Heads jerked around. Cramer advanced and stopped at Koven's left, between him and his wife. There was dead silence. Koven had his neck twisted to stare up at Cramer, then suddenly he fell apart and buried his face in his hands.

Cramer, scowling at Wolfe, boiling with rage, spoke. "Damn you, if you had given it to us! You and your numbers game!"

"I can't give you what you won't take," Wolfe said bitingly. "You can have her now. Do you want more help? Mr. Koven was still in bed Sunday morning when two of them saw the gun in the drawer. More? Spend the night with Mr. Hildebrand. I'll stake my license against your badge that he'll remember that when he spoke with Mrs. Koven in the hall she said something that caused him to open the drawer and look at the gun. Still more? Take all the contents of her room to your laboratory. She must have hid the gun among her intimate things, and you should find evidence. You can't put him on the stand and ask him if and when he told her what he was doing; he can't testify against his wife; but surely—"

Mrs. Koven stood up. She was pale but under control, perfectly steady. She looked down at the back of her husband's bent head.

"Take me home, Harry," she said.

Cramer, in one short step, was at her elbow.

"Harry!" she said, softly insistent. "Take me home."

His head lifted and turned to look at her. I couldn't see his face. "Sit down, Marcy," he said. "I'll handle this." He looked at Wolfe. "If you've got a record of what I said here Saturday, all right. I lied to the cops. So what? I didn't want—"

"Be quiet, Harry," Pat Lowell blurted at him. "Get a lawyer and let him talk. Don't say anything."

Wolfe nodded. "That's good advice. Especially, Mr. Koven, since I hadn't quite finished. It is a matter of record that Mr. Getz not only owned the house you live in but also that he owned Dazzle Dan and permitted you to take only ten per cent of the proceeds."

Mrs. Koven dropped back into the chair and froze, staring at him. Wolfe spoke to her. "I suppose, madam, that after you killed him you went to his room to look for documents and possibly found some and destroyed them. That must have been part of your plan last week when you first took the gun from the drawer—to destroy all evidence of his ownership of Dazzle Dan after killing him. That was foolish, since a man like Mr. Getz would surely not leave invaluable papers in so accessible a spot, and they will certainly be found; we can leave that to Mr. Cramer. When I said it is a matter oi record I meant a record that I have inspected and have in my possession."

Wolfe pointed. "That stack of stuff on that table is Dazzle Dan for the past three years. In one episode, repeated annually with variations, he buys peaches from two characters named Aggie Ghool and Haggie Krool, and Aggie Ghool, saying that she owns the tree, gives Haggie Krool ten per cent of the amount received and pockets the rest. A.G. are the initials of Adrian Getz; H.K. are the initials of Harry Koven. It is not credible that that is coincidence or merely a prank, especially since the episode was repeated annually. Mr. Getz must have had a singularly contorted psyche, taking delight as he did in hiding the fact of his ownership and control of that monster, but compelling the nominal owner to publish it each year in a childish allegory. For a meager ten per cent—"

"Not of the net," Koven objected. "Ten per cent of the gross. Over four hundred a week clear, and I—"

He stopped. His wife had said, "You worm." Leaving her chair, she stood looking down at him, stiff and towering, overwhelming, small as she was.

"You worm!" she said in bitter contempt. "Not even a worm. Worms have guts, don't they?"

She whirled to face Wolfe. "All right, you've got him. The one time he ever acted like a man, and he didn't have the guts to see it through. Getz owned Dazzle Dan, that's right. When he got the idea and sold it, years ago, and took Harry in to draw it and front it, Harry should have insisted on an even split right then and didn't. He never had it in him to insist on anything, and never would, and Getz knew it. When Dazzle Dan caught on, and the years went by and it kept getting bigger and bigger, Getz didn't mind Harry having the name and the fame as long as he owned it and got the money. You said he had a contorted psyche, maybe that was it, only that's not what I'd call it. Getz was a vampire."

"I'll accept that," Wolfe murmured.

"That's the way it was when I met Harry, but I didn't know it until we were married, two years ago. I admit Getz might not have got killed if it hadn't been for me. When I found out how it was I tried to talk sense into Harry. I told him his name had been connected with Dazzle Dan so long that Getz would have to give him a bigger share, at least half, if he demanded it. He claimed he tried, but he just wasn't man enough. I told him his name was so well known that he could cut loose and start another one on his own, but he wasn't man enough for that either. He's not a man, he's a worm. I didn't let up. I kept after him, I admit that. I'll admit it on the witness stand if I have to. And I admit I didn't know him as well as I thought I did. I didn't know there was any danger of making him desperate enough to commit murder. I didn't know he had it in him. Of course he'll break down, but if he says I knew that he had decided to kill Getz I'll have to deny it because it's not true. I didn't."

Her husband was staring up at the back of her head, his mouth hanging open.

"I see." Wolfe's voice was hard and cold. "First you plan to put it on a stranger, Mr. Goodwin—indeed, two strangers, for I am in it too. That failing, you put it on your husband." He shook his head. "No, madam. Your silliest mistake was opening the window to kill the monkey, but there were others. Mr. Cramer?"

Cramer had to take only one step to get her arm.

"Good God!" Koven groaned.

Pat Lowell said to Wolfe in a thin sharp voice, "So this is what you worked me for."

She was a tough baby too, that girl.

Ray Bradbury

YESTERDAY I
LIVED!

Ray Bradbury (1920–   ) is probably the first person a nonreader of science fiction would mention if asked to name a science-fiction writer. Of course, a number of science-fiction purists claim that although his stories may be set in the future or on Mars, he doesn't write science fiction at all, but fantasy or even old-fashioned horror. Bradbury himself claims that as far as sales are concerned his most successful book is not The Martian Chronicles *or* Fahrenheit 451, *but* Dandelion Wine, *a romantic and utterly nonscientific novel about the summer of 1928 in a small Illinois city.*

Whatever sort of writer Ray Bradbury turned out to be, in the early 1940s he was producing—at the rate of a story a week—fiction published in pulp magazines such as Detective Tales, Flynn's Detective Fiction, *and* Dime Mystery Magazine. *The stories had titles—usually made up by a magazine editor, not the author—like "Corpse Carnival," "Hell's Half Hour," and "Four-Way Funeral."*

Bradbury has said that to be a good writer you have to write at least a thousand words a day. "That's just to get the junk out of your system." He still writes, he says, at the same rate he did in the forties, "somewhere between eighteen and thirty-two pages a week."

Looking back on his pulp days, Bradbury admits he was no challenger of Hammett's, Chandler's or James M. Caine's. But "Yesterday I Lived!" published in 1944, is an example of everyday pulp fiction at its peppery and wise-guy best.

Yesterday I Lived!

Y EARS WENT BY and after all the years of raining and cold and fog going and coming through Hollywood Cemetery over a stone with the name Diana Coyle on it, Cleve Morris walked into the studio projection room out of the storm and looked up at the screen.

She was there. The long, lazy body of hers, the shining red hair and bright complementary green eyes.

And Cleve thought, *Is it cold out there, Diana? Is it cold out there tonight? Is the rain to you yet? Have the years pierced the bronze walls of your resting place and are you still—beautiful?*

He watched her glide across the screen, heard her laughter, and his wet eyes shimmered her into bright quivering color streaks.

It's so warm in here tonight, Diana. You're here, all the warmth of you, and yet it's only so much illusion. They buried you three years ago, and now the autograph hunters are crazy over some new actress here at the studio.

He choked on that. No reason for this feeling, but everyone felt that way about her. Everyone loved her, hated her for being so lovely. But maybe *you* loved her more than the others.

Who in hell are you? She hardly ever saw you. Cleve Morris, a desk sergeant spending two hours a day at the front desk buzzing people through locked doors and six hours strolling around dim sound stages, checking things. She hardly knew you. It was always, "Hello, Diana," and "Hi, Sarge!" and "Good night, Diana," when her long evening gown rustled from the stages, and over her smooth shoulder one eye winking. "Night, Sarge; be a good boy!"

Three years ago. Cleve slid down in his projection room loge. The watch on his wrist ticked eight o'clock. The studio was dead, lights fading one by one. Tomorrow, action lots of it. But now, tonight, he was alone in this room, looking over the old films of Diana Coyle. In the projection booth behind him, checking the compact spools of film, Jamie Winters, the studio's A-1 cameraman, did the honors of projection.

So here you are, the two of you, late at night. The film flickers, marring her lovely face. It flickers again, and you're irritated. It flickers twice more, a long time, then smooths out. Bad print. Cleve sinks lower in his seat, thinking back three years ago, along about this same hour of night, just about the same day of the month . . . three years ago . . . same hour . . . rain in the dark sky . . . three years ago . . .

.   .   .

Cleve was at his desk that night. People strode through doors, rain-spangled, never seeing him. He felt like a mummy in a museum where the attendants had long ago tired of noticing him. Just a fixture to buzz doors open for them.

"Good evening, Mr. Guilding."

R. J. Guilding thought it over and vetoed the suggestion with a jerk of one gray-gloved hand. His white head jerked too. "Is it?" he wanted to know. You get that way being a producer.

Buzz. Door open. *Slam.*

"Good evening, Diana!"

"What?" She walked from the rainy night with it shining in little clear gems on her white oval face. He'd like to have kissed them away. She looked lost and alone. "Oh, hello, Cleve. Working late. The darn picture's almost finished. Gosh, I'm tired."

Buzz. Door open. *Slam.*

He looked after her and kept her perfume as long as he could.

"Ah, flatfoot," somebody said. Leaning over the desk, smiling ironically, was a pretty man named Robert Denim. "Open the door for me, country boy. They never should've put you on this job. You're glamor-struck. Poor kid."

Cleve looked at him strangely. "She doesn't belong to you anymore, does she?"

Denim's face was suddenly not pretty. He didn't say anything for a moment, but by the look in his eyes Cleve's doubts were removed. Denim grabbed the door and jerked it viciously.

Cleve purposely left the buzzer untouched. Denim swore and turned around, one gloved hand balled into a fist. Cleve buzzed the buzzer, smiling. It was the kind of smile that drained Denim's hesitation, made him decide to pull the knob again and stride off down away into the halls, into the studio.

A few minutes later Jamie Winters entered, shaking off rain, but holding onto a man-sized peeve. "That Diana Coyle woman; I tell you, Cleve. She stays up late at night and expects me to photograph her like a twelve-year-old kid! What a job I got! Fooey."

Behind Jamie Winters came Georgie Kroll, and Tally Durham hanging onto him so that Diana couldn't get him. But it was too late. By Georgie's face he was already got; and by Tally's she knew it but couldn't believe it.

Slam.

Cleve checked his name chart, found that everybody who was working tonight was already in. He relaxed. This was a dark hive, and Diana was the queen bee with all the other bees humming around her. The studio worked late tonight, just for her, all the lights, sound, color, activity. Cleve smoked a cigarette quietly, leaning back, smiling over his thoughts. *Diana, let's just you and me buy a little home in San Fernando where the flood washes you out every year, and the wild flowers spring up when the flood is gone. Nice paddling in a canoe with you, Diana, even in a flood. We got flowers, hay, sunlight, and peace in the valley, Diana.*

The only sound to Cleve was the rain beating at the windows, an occasional flare of thunder, and his watch ticking like a termite boring a hole in the structure of silence.

Tictictictictic . . .

The scream pulled him out of his chair and half across the reception room, echoed through the building. A script girl burst into view, shambling with dead feet, babbling. Cleve grabbed her and held her still.

"She's dead! She's dead!"

The watch went *tic, tic, tic* all over again.

Lightning blew up around the place, and a cold wind hit Cleve's neck. His stomach turned over and he was afraid to ask the simple question he would eventually have to ask. Instead he stalled the inevitable, locking the bronze front doors and making secure any windows that were open. When he turned, the script girl was leaning against his desk, a tremble in her like something shattered in a finely integrated machine, shaking it to pieces.

"On stage twelve. Just now," she gasped. "Diana Coyle."

Cleve ran through the dim alleys of the studio, the sound of his running lonely in the big empty spaces. Ahead of him brilliant lights poured from opened stage doors; people stood framed in the vast square, shocked, not moving.

He ran onto the set and stopped, his heart pounding, to look down.

She was the most beautiful person who ever died.

Her silver evening gown was a small lake around her. Her fingernails were five scarlet beetles dead and shining on either side of her slumped body.

All the hot lights looked down, trying to keep her warm when she was fast cooling. My blood too, thought Cleve. Keep me warm, lights!

The shock of it held everybody as in a still photo.

Denim, fumbling with a cigarette, spoke first.

"We were in the middle of a scene. She just fell down and that was all."

Tally Durham, about the size of a salt shaker, wandered blindly about the stage telling everybody, "We thought she fainted, that's all! I got the smelling salts!"

Denim sucked, deeply nervous, on his smoke. "The smelling salts didn't work . . ."

For the first time in his life Cleve touched Diana Coyle.

But it was too late now. What good to touch cold clay that didn't laugh back at you using green eyes and curved lips?

He touched her and said, "She's been poisoned."

The word "poison" spread out through the dim sound stage behind the glaring lights. Echoes came back with it.

Georgie Kroll stuttered. "She—she got a drink—from the soft drinks—box— a couple minutes ago. Maybe—"

Cleve found the soft drinks dispenser blindly. He smelled one bottle and tucked it aside carefully, using a handkerchief, into a lunchbox that was studio property. "Nobody touch that."

The floor was rubbery to walk on. "Anybody see anybody else touch that bottle before Diana drank out of it?"

Way up in the glaring electrical heaven, a guy looked down like a short-circuited god and called, "Hey, Cleve, just before the last scene we had light trouble. Somebody conked a main switch. The lights were doused for about a minute and a half. Plenty time for someone to fix that bottle!"

"Thanks." Cleve turned to Jamie Winters, the cameraman. "You got film in your camera? Got a picture of—her—dying?"

"I guess so. Sure!"

"How soon can you have it developed?"

"Two, three hours. Got to call Juke Davis and have him come to the studio, though.

"Phone him, then. Take two watchmen with you to guard that film. Beat it!"

Far away the sirens were singing and Hollywood was going to sleep. Somebody onstage suddenly realized Diana was dead and started sobbing.

I wish I could do that, thought Cleve. *I wish I could cry. What am I supposed to do now, act tough, be a Sherlock? Question everyone, when my heart isn't working?* Cleve heard his voice going on alone.

"We'll be working late tonight, everybody. We'll be working until we get this scene right. And if we don't get it right, I guess we don't go home. Before the homicide squad gets here, everyone to their places. We'll do the scene over. Places everybody."

They did the scene over.

The homicide squad arrived. There was one detective named Foley and another named Sadlowe. One was small, the other big. One talked a lot, and the other listened. Foley did the talking and it gave Cleve a sick headache.

R. J. Guilding, the director and producer of the film, slumped in his canvas chair, wiping his face and trying to tell Foley that he wanted this whole mess kept out of the papers and quiet.

Foley told him to shut up. Foley glared at Cleve as if he were also a suspect. "What've you found out, son?"

"There was film in the camera. Film of Diana—Miss Coyle's death."

Foley's eyebrows went like that. "Well, hell, let's see it!"

They walked over into the film laboratory to get the film. Cleve was frankly afraid of the place. Always had been. It was a huge dark mortuary building with dead-end passages and labyrinths of black walls to cut the light. You stumbled through pitch dark, touching the walls, careening, turning, cursing, twisting around cutouts; walked south, east, west, south again and suddenly found yourself in a green-freckled space as big as the universe. Nothing to see but green welts and splashes of light, dim snakes of film climbing, winding over spools from floor to high ceiling and back down. The one brilliant light was a printing light that shot from a projector and printed negtative to positive as they slid by in parallel slots. The positive then coiled over and down into a long series of developing baths. The place was a whining morgue. Juke Davis moved around in it with ghoullike movements.

"There's no soundtrack. I'll develop it and splice it in later," said Davis. "Here you are, Mr. Foley. Here's your film."

They took the film and retreated back through the labyrinth.

In the projection room Cleve and the detectives Foley and Sadlowe, with Jamie Winters operating the projector in the booth, watched the death scene printed on the screen for them. Stage twelve had been slammed shut, and other officers were back there, talking, grilling everyone in alphabetical order.

On the screen Diana laughed. Robert Denim laughed back. It was very silent. They opened their mouths but no sounds came out. People danced behind them. Diana and Robert Denim danced now, gracefully, quietly, leisurely. When they stopped dancing they talked seriously with—Tally Durham and Georgie Kroll.

Foley spoke. "You say that this fellow Kroll loved Diana too?"

Cleve nodded, "Who didn't?"

Foley said, "Yeah. Who didn't. Well—" He stared with suspicion at the screen. "How about this Tally Durham woman. Was she jealous?"

Was there any woman in Hollywood who didn't hate Diana because she was perfect? Cleve spoke of Tally's love for Georgie Kroll.

"It never fails," replied Foley with a shake of his head.

Cleve said, "Tally may have killed Diana. Who knows. Georgie'd have a motive too. Diana treated him like a rag doll. He wanted her and couldn't have her. That happened to a lot of men in Diana's life. If she ever loved anybody, it was Robert Denim, and that didn't last. Denim is a little too—tough, I guess that's how you'd put it."

Foley snorted. "Good going. We got three suspects in one scene. Any one of them could have dosed that pop bottle with nicotine. The lights were out for a minute and a half. In that time any guy who ever bought Black Leaf Forty nicotine sulfate at the corner garden store could have tossed twenty drops of it in her drink and gone back playing innocent when the lights bloomed again. Nuts."

Sadlowe spoke for the first time that evening. "There ought to be some way to splice out the innocents from this film." A brilliant observation.

Cleve caught his breath. *She* was dying.

She died like she had done everything in her life. You had to admire the way she did it, with the grace, fire, and control of a fine cat-animal. In the middle of the scene she forgot her lines. Her fingers crawled slowly to her throat and she turned. Her face changed. She looked straight out at you from the screen as if she knew this was her biggest and, to a cynic, her best scene.

Then she fell, like a silken canopy from which the supports had been instantly withdrawn.

Denim crouched over her, mouthing the word, "Diana!"

And Tally Durham screamed a silent scream as the film shivered and fluttered into blackness, numbers, amber colors, and then nothing but glaring light.

Oh, God, press a button somewhere! Run the reel backward and bring her back to life! Press a button as you see in those comic newsreels; in which smashed trains are reintegrated, fallen emperors are enthroned, the sun rises in the west and—Diana Coyle rises from the dead!

From the booth Jamie Winters's voice said, "That's it. That's all of it. You want to see it again?"

Foley said, "Yeah. Show it to us half a dozen times."

"Excuse me," gasped Cleve.

"Where are you going?"

He went out into the rain. It beat cold on him. Behind him, inside, Diana was dying again and again and again, like a trained puppet. Cleve clenched his jaw and looked straight up at the sky and let the night cry on him, all over him, soaking him through and through; in perfect harmony, the night and he and the crying dark . . .

The storm lasted until morning both inside and outside the studio. Foley yelled at everybody. Everybody answered back calmly that they weren't guilty; yes, they had hated Diana, but at the same time loved her, yes, they were jealous of her, but she was a good girl too.

Foley evolved a colossal idea, invited all suspects to the projection room and scared hell out of everyone, proving nothing, by showing them Diana's last scene. R. J. Guilding broke down and sobbed, Georgie squeaked, and Tally screamed. Cleve got sick to his stomach, and the night went on and on.

Georgie said yes, yes, he'd loved Diana; Tally said yes, yes, she'd hated her; Guilding reaffirmed the fact that Diana had stalled production, causing trouble; and Robert Denim admitted to an attempted reconciliation between himself and his former wife. Jamie Winters told how Diana had stayed up late nights, ruining her face for proper photography. And R. J. Guilding snapped, "Diana told me you were photographing her poorly, on purpose!"

Jamie Winters was calm. "That's not true. She was trying to shove the blame for her complexion off on someone else, me."

Foley said, "You were in love with her too?"

Winters replied, "Why do you think I became her photographer?"

So when dawn came Diana was still dead as the night before. Big stage doors thundered aside and the suspects wearily shambled out to climb into their cars and start home.

Cleve watched them through aching eyes. Silently he walked around the studio, checking everything when it didn't need checking. He smelled the sweet green odor of the cemetery over the wall.

Funny Hollywood. It builds a studio next door to a graveyard. Right over that wall there. Sometimes it seemed everyone in movietown tried to scale that wall. Some poured themselves over in a whiskey tide, some smoked themselves over; all of them looked forward to an office in Hollywood Cemetery—with no phones. Well, Diana didn't have to climb that wall.

Someone had pushed her over. . . .

Cleve held on to the steering wheel, tight, hard, wanting to break it, telling the world to get out of the way dammit! He was beginning to get mad!

They buried her on a bright California day with a stiff wind blowing and too many red and yellow and blue flowers and the wrong kind of tears.

That was the first day Cleve ever drank enough to get drunk. He would always remember that day.

The studio phoned three days later.

"Say, Morris, what's eating you? Where you been?"

"In my apartment," said Cleve dully.

He kept the radio off, he didn't walk the streets like he used to at night, dreaming. He neglected the newspapers; they had big pictures of her in them. The radio talked about her, so he almost wrecked the thing. When the week was over she was safely in the earth, and the newspapers had tapered off the black ink wreaths, were telling her life story on page two the following Wednesday; page four Thursday; page five Friday; page ten Saturday; and by the following Monday they wrote the concluding chapter and slipped it among the stock-market reports on page twenty-nine.

You're slipping, Diana! Slipping! You used to make page one!

Cleve went back to work.

By Friday there was nothing left but that new stone in Hollywood Cemetery. Papers rotted in the flooded gutters, washing away the ink of her name; the radio blatted war, and Cleve worked with his eyes looking funny and changed.

He buzzed doors all day, and people went in and out. He watched Tally dance in every morning, smaller and chipper, and happy now that Diana was gone, holding on to Georgie, who was all hers now, except his mind and soul. He watched Robert Denim walk in, and they never spoke to each other. He waved hello to Jamie Winters and was courteous to R. J. Guilding.

But he watched them all, like a dialogue director waiting for one muffed line or missed cue.

And finally the papers announced casually that her death had been attributed to suicide, and it was a closed chapter.

A couple of weeks later Cleve was still sticking to his apartment, reading and thinking, when the phone rang.

"Cleve? This is Jamie Winters. Look, cop-man, come out of it. You're wanted at a party, now, tonight. I got some film clips from Gable's last picture."

There was argument. In the end Cleve gave in and went to the party. They sat in Jamie Winters's parlor facing a small-size screen. Winters showed them scenes from pictures that never reached the theater. Garbo tripping over a light cord and falling on her platform. Spencer Tracy blowing his lines and swearing. William Powell sticking his tongue out at the camera when he forgot his next cue. Cleve laughed for the first time in a million years.

Jamie Winters had an endless collection of film clips of famous stars blowing up and saying censorable things.

And when Diane Coyle showed up, it was like a kick in the stomach. Like being shot with two barrels of a shotgun! Cleve jerked and gasped, and shut his eyes, clenching the chair.

Then, suddenly, he was very cool. He had an idea. Looking at the screen, it came to him, like cold rain on his cheeks.

"Jamie!" he said.

In the sprocketing darkness, Jamie replied, "Yes?"

"I've got to see you in the kitchen, Jamie."

"Why?"

"Never mind why. Let the camera run itself and come on."

In the kitchen Cleve held on to Jamie. "It's about those films you're showing us. The mistakes. The censored clips. Have you any clips from Diana's last picture? Spoiled scenes, blow-ups, I mean?"

"Yeah. At the studio. I collect them. It's a hobby. That stuff usually goes in the trash can. I keep them for laughs."

Cleve sucked in his breath. "Can you get that film for me; all of it; bring it here tomorrow night and go over it with me?"

"Sure, if you want me to. I don't see—"

"Never mind, Jamie. Just do like I say, huh? Bring me all the cutouts, the scenes that were bad. I want to see who spoiled the scenes, who caused the most trouble, and why! Will you do it, Jamie?"

"Sure. Sure I will, Cleve. Take it easy. Here, sit down. Have a drink."

Cleve didn't eat much the next day. The hours went too slowly. At night he ate a little supper and swallowed four aspirins. Then he drove in a mechanical nightmare to Jamie Winters's house.

Jamie was waiting with drinks and film in the camera.

"Thanks, Jamie." Cleve sat down and drank nervously. "All right. Shall we see them?"

"Action!" said Jamie.

Light on the screen. "Take one, scene seven, *The Gilded Virgin:* Diana Coyle, Robert Denim."

Clack!

The scene faded in. There was a terrace by an ocean scene in moonlight. Diana was talking.

"It's a lovely night. So lovely I can't believe in it."

Robert Denim, holding her hands in his, looked at her and said, "I think I can make you believe in it. I'll—damn it!"

"Cut!" cried Guilding's voice offscreen.

The film ran on. Denim's face was ugly, getting dark and lined.

"There you go, hogging the camera again!"

"Me?" Diana wasn't beautiful anymore. Not *this* way. She shook the gilt off her wings in an angry powder. "Me, you two-bit thespian, you loud-mouthed, dirty—"

Flick. Dark. End of film.

Cleve sat there, staring. After a while he said, "They didn't get along, did they?" And then, to himself, almost, "I'm glad."

"Here's another one," said Winters. The camera ticked rapidly.

Another scene. A party scene. Laughter and music; and cutting across it, dark, snapping, bitter and accusative:

"—damn you!"

"—if you fed me the wrong cue on purpose! Of all the cheap, common little—"

Diana and Robert Denim, at it again!

Another scene, and another, and another. Six, seven, eight!

Here was one of Denim saying, "Honest to God, someone ought to shut you up for good, lady!"

"Who?" cried Diana, eyes flashing like little green stones. "You? You snivel-nosed ham!"

And Denim, glaring back, saying quietly, "Yes. Maybe me. Why not? It's an idea."

There were some bristling hot scenes with Tally Durham too. And one in which Diana browbeat little Georgie Kroll until he was nervous and sweating out an apology. All on film; all good evidence. But the ratio was seven of Denim's blow-ups to one of Tally's or Georgie's. On and on and on and on!

"Stop it, stop it!" Cleve got up from his chair. His figure cut the light, threw a shadow on the screen, swaying.

"Thanks for the trouble, Jamie. I'm tired too. Can—can I have these film clips of Denim?"

"Sure."

"I'm going downtown to police headquarters tonight and turn in Robert Denim for the murder of Diana Coyle. Thanks again, Jamie. You been a great help. Night."

Five, ten, fifteen, twenty hours. Count 'em by twos, by fours, by sixes. Rush the hours by. Argue with the cops and go home and flop in bed.

Toddle off to your gas chamber, Robert Denim; that's a good little killer!

And then in the middle of deep slumber, your phone rang.

"Hullo."

And a voice said over the phone in the night, "Cleve?"

"Yeah?"

And the voice said, "This is Juke Davis at the film laboratory. Come quick, Cleve. I been hurt, I been hurt, oh, I been hurt . . ." A body fell at the other end of the line.

Silence.

He found Juke lying in a chemical bath. Red chemical from his own body where a knife had dug out his dreams and his living and his talking forever and spread it around in a scarlet lake.

A phone receiver hung dangling on one greenish wall. It was dark in the laboratory. Someone had shuffled in through the dim tunnels, come out of the dark, and now, standing there, Cleve heard nothing but the film moving forever on its trellises, like some vine going up through the midnight room trying to find the sun. Numbly, Cleve knelt beside Juke. The man lay half propped against the film machinery where the printing light shot out and imprinted negative to positive. He had crawled there, across the room.

In one clenched fist, Cleve found a frame of film; the faces of Tally, Georgie, Diana, and Robert Denim on it. Juke had found out something, something about this film, something about a killer; and his reward had come swiftly to him through the studio dark.

Cleve used the phone.

"This is Cleve Morris. Is Robert Denim still being held at Central Jail?"

"He's in his cell, and he won't talk. I tell you, Morris, you gave us a bum steer with them film clips . . ."

"Thanks." Cleve hung up. He looked at Juke lying there by the machinery. "Well, who was it, Juke? It wasn't Denim. That leaves Georgie and Tally? Well?"

Juke said nothing and the machinery sang a low sad song.

One year went by. Another year followed. And then a third.

Robert Denim contracted out to another studio. Tally married Georgie, Guilding died at a New Year's party of overdrinking and a bad heart, time went on, everybody forgot. Well, almost everybody . . .

Diana, child, is it cold out there tonight—?

Cleve rose in his seat. Three years ago. He blinked his eyes. Same kind of night as this, cold and raining.

The screen flickered.

Cleve paid little attention. It kept flickering strangely. Cleve stiffened. His heart beat with the sprocketing noise of the machine. He bent forward.

"Jamie, will you run that last one hundred feet over again?"

"Sure thing, Cleve."

Flickers on film. Imperfections. Long blotches, short blobs. Cleve spelled it out. W . . . I . . . N. . . .

Cleve opened the door of the projection room so softly Jamie Winters didn't hear him. Winters was glaring out at the film on the screen, and there was a strange, happy look on his face. The look of a saint seeing a new miracle.

"Enjoying yourself, Jamie boy?"

Jamie Winters shook himself and turned and smiled uneasily.

Cleve locked the door. He gave a little soft lecture: "It's been a long time. I haven't slept well many nights. Three years, Jamie. And tonight you had nothing to do so you ran off some film so you could gloat over it. Gloat over Diana and think how clever you were. Maybe it was fun to see me suffer too; you knew how much I liked her. Have you come here often in the past three years to gloat over her, Jamie?" he asked softly.

Winters laughed good-naturedly.

Cleve said, "She didn't love you, did she? You were her photographer. So to even things up, you began photographing her badly. It fits in. Her last two films were poor. She looked tired. It wasn't her fault; you did things with your camera. So Diana threatened to tell on you. You would've been blackballed at every studio. You couldn't have her love, and she threatened your career, so what did you do, Jamie Winters? You killed her."

"This is a poor idea of a joke," said Winters, hardening.

Cleve went on, "Diana looked at the camera when she died. She looked at you. We never thought of that. In a theater you always feel as if she were looking at the audience, not the man behind the camera. She died. You took a picture of her dying. Then, later, you invited me to a party, fed me the bait, with those film clips showing Denim in a suspicious light. I fell for it. You destroyed all the other film that put Denim in a good position. Juke Davis found out what you were doing.

He worked with film all the time, he knew you were juggling clips. You wanted to frame Denim because there had to be a fall guy and you'd be clear. Juke questioned you, you stabbed him. You stole and destroyed the few extra clips Juke had discovered. Juke couldn't talk over the phone, but he shoved his hand in the printing light of the developing machine and printed your name W-I-N-T-E-R-S in black splotches as the film moved. He happened to be printing the negative of Diana's last film that night! And you began running it off to me ten minutes ago, thinking it was only a damaged film!"

Jamie Winters moved quickly, like a cat. He ripped open the projector and tore the film out in one vicious animal movement.

Cleve hit him. He pulled way back and blasted loose.

The case was really over now. But he wasn't happy or glad or anything but blind red angry, flooded with hot fury.

All he could think of now while he hit the face of Winters again and again and again, holding him tight with one hand, beating him over and over with the other, all he could think of was—

A stone in the yard of the cemetery just over the wall from the studio; a stone sweating blue rain over her bronzed name. All he could say in a hoarse, choked whisper was:

"Is it cold out there tonight, Diana; is it cold, little girl?"

And Cleve hit him again and again and again!

Ross Macdonald

THE CHILL

The entry on Ross Macdonald (1915–1983) in the Encyclopedia of Crime and Detection, *edited by Chris Steinbrunner and Otto Penzler, begins with the evaluation, "One of the few mystery writers also regarded as a major American novelist." That, perhaps, should read, "The only . . . ," for while other major writers may have dabbled in the detective-story format, Ross Macdonald began there and stayed there and won recognition in unlikely places (front-page reviews in* The New York Times Book Review, *a* Newsweek *cover story) as a detective writer.*

His first novels were written under his real name, Kenneth Millar, but in 1949, to avoid confusion with his wife, Margaret Millar, who was also making a reputation in the mystery field (at the time, a greater reputation), he borrowed his grandfather's name and published the first Lew Archer novel under the pseudonym John Macdonald. That, however, led to confusion with another new detective writer named John D. MacDonald, so the name was again changed first to John Ross Macdonald (for five novels) and finally to just plain Ross. (When Macdonald published The Blue Hammer, *in 1976, MacDonald complained to the publisher that Ross was again causing confusion because all of John D.'s Travis McGee novels have colors in their titles.)*

As for Lew Archer's name, it's tempting to say he was christened after Sam Spade's murdered partner, Miles Archer, but Macdonald claimed it came from his zodiac sign, Sagittarius. Archer's name, too, has gone through some curious changes. In the movies he was called Lew Harper because Paul Newman, who played the part, liked characters whose names began with H; and in England, for some reason, Archer in the early novels was changed to Arless.

Lew Archer, to Macdonald, "is less a doer than a questioner, a consciousness in which the meanings of other lives emerge." For Eudora Welty Archer "is at heart a champion, but a self-questioning, often a self-deriding champion." His "talking voice," Macdonald has said, is patterned on the one James M. Caine used in The Postman Always Rings Twice. *"You can say almost anything about anything with a tone like that," he once said.*

The Chill, *published in 1946, was, Macdonald wrote, "one of the stronger single plot ideas that ever came to me." But he was somewhat surprised to find himself using an academic setting. When I took up the hardboiled novel, beginning in 1946 with Blue City, I was writing in reaction against a number of things, among them my strict academic background. [Macdonald has a Ph.D. from the University of Michigan, his thesis subject being Coleridge's psychological criticism.] The world of gamblers and gunmen and crooked politicians and their floozies seemed realer, somehow, more central to experience, than the cool university life I knew. In these later books, the academic life keeps creeping back in. Its privileged upper world, like the subworld of professional crime, does have of course its plots and counterplots, its knifings and its bloodless assassinations, its politicians and players for high stakes, its guilty lover."*

The Chill

T HE HEAVY RED-FIGURED DRAPES over the courtroom windows were incompletely closed against the sun. Yellow daylight leaked in and dimmed the electric bulbs in the high ceiling. It picked out random details in the room: the glass water cooler standing against the paneled wall opposite the jury box, the court reporter's carmine-tipped fingers playing over her stenotype machine, Mrs. Perrine's experienced eyes watching me across the defense table.

It was nearly noon on the second and last day of her trial. I was the final witness for the defense. Her attorney had finished questioning me. The deputy D.A. waived cross-examination, and several of the jurors looked at him with puzzled frowns. The judge said I could go.

From my place on the witness stand I'd noticed the young man sitting in the front row of spectators. He wasn't one of the regular trial-watchers, housewives and pensioners filling an empty morning with other people's troubles. This one had troubles of his own. His brooding blue gaze stayed on my face, and I had the uncomfortable feeling that he might be willing to share his troubles with me.

He rose from his seat as I stepped down and intercepted me at the door. "Mr. Archer, may I talk to you?"

"All right."

The bailiff opened the door and gestured urgently. "Outside, gentlemen. Court is still in session."

We moved out into the corridor. The young man scowled at the automatically closing door. "I don't like being pushed around."

"I'd hardly describe that as being pushed around. What's eating you, friend?"

I shouldn't have asked him. I should have walked briskly out to my car and driven back to Los Angeles. But he had that clean, crewcut All-American look, and that blur of pain in his eyes.

"I just got thrown out of the Sheriff's office. It came on top of a couple of other brushoffs from the local authorities, and I'm not used to that kind of treatment."

"They don't mean it personally."

"You've had a lot of detective experience, haven't you? I gathered that from what you said on the witness stand. Incidentally, you did a wonderful job for Mrs. Perrine. I'm sure the jury will acquit her."

"We'll see. Never bet on a jury." I distrusted his compliment, which probably meant he wanted something more substantial from me. The trial in which I had just testified marked the end of a long uninteresting case, and I was planning a fishing trip to La Paz. "Is that all you wanted to say to me?"

"I have a lot to say, if you'll only listen. I mean, I've got this problem about my wife. She left me."

"I don't ordinarily do divorce work, if that's what you have in mind."

"Divorce?" Without making a sound, he went through the motions of laughing hollowly, once. "I was only married one day—less than one day. Everybody including my father keeps telling me I should get an annulment. But I don't want an annulment or a divorce. I want her back."

"Where is your wife now?"

"I don't know." He lit a cigarette with unsteady hands. "Dolly left in the middle of our honeymoon weekend, the day after we were married. She may have met with foul play."

"Or she may have decided she didn't want to be married, or not to you. It happens all the time."

"That's what the police keep saying: it happens all the time. As if that's any comfort! Anyway, I know that wasn't the case. Dolly loved me, and I loved—I love her."

He said this very intensely, with the entire force of his nature behind the words. I didn't know his nature but there was sensitivity and feeling there, more feeling than he could handle easily.

"You haven't told me your name."

"I'm sorry. My name is Kincaid. Alex Kincaid."

"What do you do for a living?"

"I haven't been doing much lately, since Dolly—since this thing happened. Theoretically I work for the Channel Oil Corporation. My father is in charge of their Long Beach office. You may have heard of him. Frederick Kincaid?"

I hadn't. The bailiff opened the door of the courtroom, and held it open. Court had adjourned for lunch, and the jurors filed out past him. Their movements were solemn, part of the ritual of the trial. Alex Kincaid watched them as if they were going out to sit in judgment on him.

"We can't talk here," he said. "Let me buy you lunch."

"I'll have lunch with you. Dutch." I didn't want to owe him anything, at least till I'd heard his story.

There was a restaurant across the street. Its main room was filled with smoke and the roar of conversation. The red-checkered tables were all occupied, mainly with the courthouse people, lawyers and sheriff's men and probation officers. Though Pacific Point was fifty miles south of my normal beat, I recognized ten or a dozen of them.

Alex and I went into the bar and found a couple of stools in a dim corner. He ordered a double scotch on the rocks. I went along with it. He drank his down like medicine and tried to order a second round immediately.

"You set quite a pace. Slow down."

"Are you telling me what to do?" he said distinctly and unpleasantly.

"I'm willing to listen to your story. I want you to be able to tell it."

"You think I'm an alcoholic or something?"

"I think you're a bundle of nerves. Pour alcohol on a bundle of nerves and it generally turns into a can of worms. While I'm making suggestions you might as well get rid of those chips you're wearing on both shoulders. Somebody's liable to knock them off and take a piece of you with them."

He sat for a while with his head down. His face had an almost fluorescent pallor, and a faint humming tremor went through him.

"I'm not my usual self, I admit that. I didn't know things like this could happen to people."

"It's about time you told me what did happen. Why not start at the beginning?"

"You mean when she left the hotel?"

"All right. Start with the hotel."

"We were staying at the Surf House," he said, "right here in Pacific Point. I couldn't really afford it but Dolly wanted the experience of staying there—she never had. I figured a three-day weekend wouldn't break me. It was the Labor Day weekend. I'd already used my vacation time, and we got married that Saturday so that we could have at least a three-day honeymoon."

"Where were you married?"

"In Long Beach, by a judge."

"It sounds like one of these spur-of-the-moment weddings."

"I suppose it was, in a way. We hadn't known each other too long. Dolly was the one, really, who wanted to get married right now. Don't think I wasn't eager. I was. But my parents thought we should wait a bit, until we could find a house and have it furnished and so on. They would have liked a church wedding. But Dolly wanted to be married by a judge."

"What about her parents?"

"They're dead. She has no living relatives." He turned his head slowly and met my eyes. "Or so she claims."

"You seem to have your doubts about it."

"Not really. It's just that she got so upset when I asked her about her parents. I naturally wanted to meet them, but she treated my request as though I was prying. Finally she told me her entire family was dead, wiped out in an auto accident."

"Where?"

"I don't know where. When it comes right down to it, I don't know too much about my wife. Except that she's a wonderful girl," he added in a rush of loyal feeling slightly flavored with whisky. "She's beautiful and intelligent and good and I know she loves me." He was almost chanting, as though by wishful thinking or sheer incantation he could bend reality back into shape around him.

"What was her maiden name?"

"Dolly McGee. Her name is really Dorothy. She was working in the university library and I was taking a summer course in Business Ad—"

"Just this summer?"

"That's correct." He swallowed, and his adam's apple throbbed like a grief in his throat. "We only knew each other for six weeks—six-and-a-half weeks—before we were married. But we saw each other every day of those six-and-a-half weeks."

"What did you do together?"

"I don't see that it matters."

"It could. I'm trying to get a line on her personal habits."

"She had no *bad* habits, if that's what you're looking for. She never let me drink when we were out together. She wasn't very keen on the coffee houses, either, or the movies. She was—she's a very serious girl. Most of our time we talked—we talked and walked. We must have covered most of West Los Angeles."

"What did you talk about?"

"The meaning of life," he said, as if this went without saying. "We were trying to work out a plan to live by, a set of rules for our marriage and our children. The main thing for Dolly was the children. She wanted to bring them up to be real people. She thought it was more important to be an honest individual than to have security and worldly possessions and so on. I don't want to bore you with all this."

"You're not. I take it she was completely sincere?"

"Nobody was ever more sincere. I mean it. She actually wanted me to give up my job and go back and finish my M.A. She didn't think I should take money from my family. She was willing to go on working to help me through. But we decided against that plan, when we made up our minds to get married."

"It wasn't a forced marriage?"

He looked at me stonily. "There was nothing like that between us. As a matter of fact we didn't even—I mean, I didn't touch her on our wedding night. The Surf House and Pacific Point seemed to get on her nerves, even though she was the one who wanted to come here. So we decided to postpone the physical bit. A lot of couples do that nowadays."

"How does Dolly feel about sex?"

"Fine. We talked about it very frankly. If you think she left me because she's afraid of it, you're way off the beam. She's a warm person."

"Why did she leave you, Alex?"

His eyes clouded with pain, which had scarcely left them. "I haven't been able to figure it out. It wasn't anything between me and Dolly, I'm sure of that. The man with the beard must have had something to do with it."

"How does he get into the picture?"

"He came to the hotel that afternoon—the day she left. I was down on the beach having a swim, and afterward I went to sleep in the sun. I must have been away from the room for a couple of hours. She was gone, bag and baggage, when

I got back. The desk clerk told me she had this visitor before she left, a man with a short gray beard who stayed in the room about an hour."

"No name?"

"He didn't mention his name."

"Did he and your wife leave together?"

"The desk clerk said they didn't. The man left first. Then Dolly took a taxi to the bus station, but so far as I could find out she didn't buy a ticket. She didn't buy a railroad ticket or an airline ticket, either. She had no car. So I've been going on the assumption that she's still here in Pacific Point. She couldn't walk down the freeway."

"She could hitchhike."

"Not Dolly."

"Where did she live before you were married?"

"In Westwood, in a furnished apartment. She gave it up and we moved her typewriter and things into my apartment on Saturday morning just before the ceremony. All the stuff is still there, and it's one of the things that worry me. I've been over it with a fine-toothed comb for clues, but she didn't leave any behind— nothing really personal at all."

"Do you think she planned to marry you and leave you?"

"No, I don't. What would be the point?"

"I can think of several possibilities. Do you carry much insurance, for example?"

"A fair amount. Dad insured me when I was born. But he's still the beneficiary."

"Does your family have money?"

"Not that much. Dad makes a good living, but he works for it. Anyway, what you're hinting at is out of the question. Dolly's completely honest, and she doesn't even care about money."

"What does she care about?"

"I thought she cared about me," he said with his head down. "I still believe she does. Something must have happened to her. She may have gone out of her mind."

"Is she mentally unstable?"

He considered the question, and his answer to it. "I don't think so. She had her black spells. I guess most people do. I was talking loosely."

"Keep on talking loosely. You can't tell what may be important. You've been making a search for her, of course?"

"As much of a search as I could. But I can't do it all by myself, without any cooperation from the police. They write down what I say on little pieces of paper and put them away in a drawer and give me pitying looks. They seem to think Dolly found out something shameful about me on our wedding night."

"Could there be any truth in that?"

"No! We're crazy about each other. I tried to tell that to the Sheriff this morning. He gave me one of those knowing leers and said he couldn't act unless there was some indication of a breach of the peace. I asked him if a missing woman wasn't some indication, and he said no. She was free and twenty-one and she left under her own power and I had no legal right to force her to come back. He advised me to get an annulment. I told him what he could do with his advice, and he ordered two of his men to throw me out of his office. I found out where the deputy D.A. was, in court, and I was waiting to put in a complaint when I saw you on the stand."

"Nobody sent you to me, then?"

"No, but I can give you references. My father—"

"You told me about your father. He thinks you should get an annulment, too."

Alex nodded dolefully. "Dad thinks I'm wasting my time, on a girl who isn't worth it."

"He could be right."

"He couldn't be more wrong. Dolly is the only one I've ever loved and the only one I ever will love. If you won't help me, I'll find somebody who will!"

I liked his insistence. "My rates are high. A hundred a day and expenses."

"I've got enough to pay you for at least a week." He reached for his billfold and slammed it down on the bar, so hard that the bartender looked at him suspiciously. "Do you want a cash advance?"

"There's no hurry," I said. "Do you have a picture of Dolly?"

He removed a folded piece of newspaper from the billfold and handed it to me with a certain reluctance, as if it was more valuable than money. It was a reproduction of a photograph which had been unfolded and refolded many times.

"Among happy honeymooners at the Surf House," the caption said, "are Mr. and Mrs. Alex Kincaid of Long Beach." Alex and his bride smiled up at me through the murky light. Her face was oval and lovely in a way of its own, with a kind of hooded intelligence in the eyes and humor like a bittersweet taste on the mouth.

"When was this taken?"

"Three weeks ago Saturday, when we arrived at the Surf House. They do it for everybody. They printed it in the Sunday morning paper, and I clipped it. I'm glad I did. It's the only picture I have of her."

"You could get copies."

"Where?"

"From whoever took it."

"I never thought of that. I'll see the photographer at the hotel about it. How many pictures do you think I should ask him for?"

"Two or three dozen, anyway. It's better to have too many than too few."

"That will run into money."

"I know, and so will I."

"Are you trying to talk yourself out of a job?"

"I don't need the work, and I could use a rest."

"To hell with you then."

He snatched at the flimsy picture between my fingers. It tore across the middle. We faced each other like enemies, each of us holding a piece of the happy honeymooners.

Alex burst into tears.

2

I agreed over lunch to help him find his wife. That and the chicken pot pie calmed him down. He couldn't remember when he had eaten last, and he ate ravenously.

We drove out to the Surf House in separate cars. It was on the sea at the good end of town: a pueblo hotel whose Spanish gardens were dotted with hundred-dollar-a-day cottages. The terraces in front of the main building descended in wide green steps to its own marina. Yachts and launches were bobbing at the slips. Further out on the water, beyond the curving promontory that gave Pacific Point its name, white sails leaned against a low gray wall of fog.

The desk clerk in the Ivy League suit was very polite, but he wasn't the one who had been on duty on the Sunday I was interested in. That one had been a summer replacement, a college boy who had gone back to school in the East. He himself, he regretted to say, knew nothing about Mrs. Kincaid's bearded visitor or her departure.

"I'd like to talk to the hotel photographer. Is he around today?"

"Yes, sir. I believe he's out by the swimming pool."

We found him, a thin spry man wearing a heavy camera like an albatross around his neck. Among the colored beach clothes and bathing costumes, his dark business suit made him look like an undertaker. He was taking some very candid pictures of a middle-aged woman in a bikini who didn't belong in one. Her umbilicus glared at the camera like an eyeless socket.

When he had done his dreadful work, the photographer turned to Alex with a smile. "Hi. How's the wife?"

"I haven't seen her recently," Alex said glumly.

"Weren't you on your honeymoon a couple of weeks ago? Didn't I take your picture?"

Alex didn't answer him. He was peering around at the poolside loungers like a ghost trying to remember how it felt to be human. I said:

"We'd like to get some copies made of that picture you took. Mrs. Kincaid is on the missing list, and I'm a private detective. My name is Archer."

"Fargo. Simmy Fargo." He gave me a quick handshake, and the kind of glance a camera gives you when it records you for posterity. "In what sense on the missing list?"

"We don't know. She left here in a taxi on the afternoon of September the second. Kincaid has been looking for her ever since."

"That's tough," Fargo said. "I suppose you want the prints for circularization. How many do you think you'll be needing?"

"Three dozen?"

He whistled, and slapped himself on his narrow wrinkled forehead. "I've got a busy weekend coming up, and it's already started. This is Friday. I could let you have them by Monday. But I suppose you want them yesterday?"

"Today will do."

"Sorry." He shrugged loosely, making his camera bob against his chest.

"It could be important, Fargo. What do you say we settle for a dozen, in two hours?"

"I'd like to help you. But I've got a job." Slowly, almost against his will, he turned and looked at Alex. "Tell you what I'll do. I'll call the wife in, and you can have your pictures. Only don't stand me up, the way the other one did."

"What other one?" I said.

"Big guy with a beard. He ordered a print of the same picture and never came back for it. I can let you have that print now if you like."

Alex came out of his dark trance. He took hold of Fargo's arm with both hands and shook it. "You saw him then. Who is he?"

"I thought maybe you knew him." Fargo disengaged himself and stepped back. "As a matter of fact, I thought I knew him, too. I could have sworn I took his picture once. But I couldn't quite place the face. I see too many faces."

"Did he give you his name?"

"He must have. I don't take orders without a name. I'll see if I can find it for you, eh?"

We followed him into the hotel and through a maze of corridors to his small cluttered windowless office. He phoned his wife, then burrowed into the pile of papers on his desk and came up with a photographer's envelope. Inside, between two sheets of corrugated paper, was a glossy print of the newlyweds. On the front of the envelope Fargo had written in pencil: "Chuck Begley, Wine Cellar."

"I remember now," he said. "He told me he was working at the Wine Cellar. That's a liquor store not too far from here. When Begley didn't claim his picture I called them. They said Begley wasn't working for them any more." Fargo looked from me to Alex. "Does the name Begley mean anything to you?"

We both said that it didn't. "Can you describe him, Mr. Fargo?"

"I can describe the part of him that wasn't covered with seaweed, I mean the beard. His hair is gray, like the beard, and very thick and wavy. Gray eyebrows and gray eyes, an ordinary kind of straight nose, I noticed it was peeling from the sun. He's not bad-looking for an older man, apart from his teeth, which aren't good. And he looks as though he's taken a beating or two in his time. Personally I wouldn't want to go up against him. He's a big man, and he looks pretty rough."

"How big?"

"Three or four inches taller than I am. That would make him six feet one or two. He was wearing a short-sleeve sport shirt, and I noticed the muscles in his arms."

"How did he talk?"

"Nothing special. He didn't have a Harvard accent, and he didn't say ain't."

"Did he give you any reason for wanting the picture?"

"He said he had a sentimental interest. He saw it in the paper, and it reminded him of somebody. I remember thinking he must have dashed right over. The paper with the picture in it came out Sunday morning, and he came in around Sunday noon."

"He must have gone to see your wife immediately afterward," I said to Alex. And to Fargo: "How did this particular picture happen to be used by the newspaper?"

"They picked it out of a batch I sent over. The *Press* often uses my pictures, as a matter of fact I used to work for them. Why they used this one instead of some of the others I couldn't say." He held up the print in the fluorescent light, then handed it to me. "It did turn out well, and Mr. Kincaid and his wife make an attractive couple."

"Thanks very much," Alex said sardonically.

"I was paying you a compliment, fellow."

"Sure you were."

I took the print from Fargo and shunted Alex out of the place before it got too small for him. Black grief kept flooding up in him, changing to anger when it reached the air. It wasn't just grief for a one-day wife, it was also grief for himself. He didn't seem to know if he was a man or not.

I couldn't blame him or his feelings, but they made him no asset to the kind of work I was trying to do. When I found the Wine Cellar, on a motel strip a few blocks inland, I left him outside in his little red sports car.

The interior of the liquor store was pleasantly cool. I was the only potential customer, and the man behind the counter came out from behind it to greet me.

"What can I do for you, sir?"

He wore a plaid waistcoat, and he had the slightly muzzy voice and liquid eyes and dense complexion of a man who drank all day and into the night.

"I'd like to see Chuck Begley."

He looked vaguely pained, and his voice took on a note of mild complaint. "I had to fire Chuck. I'd send him out with a delivery, and sometimes it'd arrive when it was supposed to, and sometimes it wouldn't."

"How long ago did you fire him?"

"Couple of weeks. He only worked for me a couple of weeks. He isn't cut out for that kind of work. I told him more than once it was beneath his capacity. Chuck Begley is a fairly bright man if he'd straighten up, you know."

"I don't know."

"I thought perhaps you were an acquaintance of his."

I showed him my photostat.

He blew the smell of peppermint in my face. "Is Begley on the run?"

"He may be. Why?"

"I wondered when he first came in why a man like him would take a part-time delivery job. What's he wanted for?"

"I wouldn't know. Can you give me his home address?"

"I think I can at that." He stroked his veined nose, watching me over his fingers. "Don't tell Begley I gave you the word. I don't want him bouncing back on me."

"I won't."

"He spends a lot of time in the home of one of my customers. You might say he's a non-paying guest of hers. I certainly wouldn't want to make trouble for her. But then," he reasoned, "if Begley's on the run I'm doing her a favor in seeing that he's picked up. Isn't that right?"

"I'd say so. Where does she live?"

"On Shearwater Beach, cottage number seventeen. Her name's Madge Gerhardi. Take the freeway south and you'll see the Shearwater turnoff about two miles down the line. Only just don't tell either of them that it was me sent you. Okay?"

"Okay." I left him with his bottles.

3

We parked our cars at the top of the access lane, and I persuaded Alex to stay in his, out of sight. Shearwater Beach turned out to be a kind of expensive slum where several dozen cottages stood in a row. The changing blue reflection of the sea glared through the narrow gaps between them. Beyond their peaked rooftops, out over the water, a tern circled on flashing wings, looking for fish.

Number seventeen needed paint, and leaned on its pilings like a man on crutches. I knocked on the scabbed gray door. Slowly, like bodies being dragged, footsteps approached the other side. The bearded man opened it.

He was a man of fifty or so wearing an open-necked black shirt from which his head jutted like weathered stone. The sunlight struck mica glints from his eyes. The fingers with which he was holding the edge of the door were bitten down to the quick. He saw me looking at them and curled them into a fist.

"I'm searching for a missing girl, Mr. Begley." I had decided on the direct approach. "She may have met with foul play and if she did, you may have been one of the last people who saw her alive."

He rubbed the side of his face with his clenched knuckles. His face bore marks of old trouble, some of them done by hand: faintly quilted patches around the eyes, a thin scar on his temple divided like a miniature ruler by stitch-marks. Old trouble and the promise of further trouble.

"You must be crazy. I don't even know any girls."

"You know *me*," a woman said behind him.

She appeared at his shoulder and leaned on him, waiting for somebody to second the self-administered flattery. She was about Begley's age, and may have been older. Her body was very assertive in shorts and a halter. Frizzled by repeated dyeings and bleachings, her hair stuck up on her head like a yellow fright wig. Between their deep blue artificial shadows, her eyes were the color of gin.

"I'm very much afraid that you must be mistaken," she said to me with a cultivated Eastern-seaboard accent which lapsed immediately. "I swear by all that's holy that Chuck had nothing to do with any girl. He's been too busy looking after little old me." She draped a plump white arm across the back of his neck. "Haven't you, darling?"

Begley was immobilized between the woman and me. I showed him Fargo's glossy print of the honeymooners.

"You know this girl, don't you? Her name, her married name, is Dolly Kincaid."

"I never heard of her in my life."

"Witnesses tell me different. They say you went to see her at the Surf House three weeks ago this coming Sunday. You saw this picture of her in the paper and ordered a copy of it from the photographer at the Surf House."

The woman tightened her arm around his neck, more like a wrestling partner than a lover. "Who is she, Chuck?"

"I have no idea." But he muttered to himself: "So it's started all over again."

"What has started all over again?"

She was stealing my lines. "Could I please talk to Mr. Begley alone?"

"He has no secrets from me." She looked up at him proudly, with a wilted edge of anxiety on her pride. "Have you, darling? We're going to be married, aren't we, darling?"

"Could you stop calling me darling? Just for five minutes? Please?"

She backed away from him, ready to cry, her downturned red mouth making a lugubrious clown face.

"Please go inside," he said. "Let me talk to the man."

"This is my place. I have a right to know what goes on in my own place."

"Sure you do, Madge. But I have squatter's privileges, at least. Go in and drink some coffee."

"Are you in trouble?"

"No. Of course I'm not." But there was resignation in his voice. "Beat it, eh, like a good girl?"

His last word seemed to mollify her. Dawdling and turning, she disappeared down the hallway. Begley closed the door and leaned on it.

"Now you can tell me the truth," I said.

"All right, so I went to see her at the hotel. It was a stupid impulse. It doesn't make me a murderer."

"Nobody suggested that, except you."

"I thought I'd save you the trouble." He spread out his arms as if for instant crucifixion. "You're the local law, I gather."

"I'm working with them," I said hopefully. "My name is Archer. You haven't explained why you went to see Mrs. Kincaid. How well did you know her?"

"I didn't know her at all." He dropped his outspread arms in emphasis. The sensitive areas around his mouth were hidden by his beard, and I couldn't tell what he was doing with them. His gray eyes were unrevealing. "I thought I knew her, but I didn't."

"What do you mean?"

"I thought she might be my daughter. There was quite a resemblance to her in the newspaper picture, but not so much in the flesh. The mistake on my part was natural. I haven't seen my daughter for so long."

"What's your daughter's name?"

He hesitated. "Mary. Mary Begley. We haven't been in touch for over ten years. I've been out of the country, on the other side of the world." He made it sound as remote as the far side of the moon.

"Your daughter must have been quite young when you left."

"Yeah. Ten or eleven."

"And you must have been quite fond of her," I said, "to order a picture just because it reminded you of her."

"I was fond of her."

"Why didn't you go back for the picture then?"

He went into a long silence. I became aware of something impressive in the man, the untouchable still quality of an aging animal.

"I was afraid that Madge would be jealous," he said. "I happen to be living on Madge."

I suspected he was using the bald statement to tell a lie. But it may have come from a deeper source. Some men spend their lives looking for ways to punish themselves for having been born, and Begley had some of the stigmata of the trouble-prone. He said:

"What do you think happened to Mrs. Kincaid?" His question was cold and formal, disclaiming all interest in the answer to it.

"I was hoping you'd have some ideas on the subject. She's been missing for nearly three weeks. I don't like it. It's true that girls are always disappearing, but not on their honeymoons—not when they love their husbands."

"She loves hers, does she?"

"He thinks so. How was she feeling when you saw her? Was she depressed?"

"I wouldn't say that. She was surprised to see me."

"Because she hadn't seen you for so long?"

He sneered at me hairily. "Don't bother trying to trap me. I told you she wasn't my daughter. She didn't know me from Adam."

"What did you find to talk about with her?"

"We didn't talk." He paused. "Maybe I asked her a few questions."

"Such as?"

"Who her father was. Who her mother was. Where she came from. She said she came from Los Angeles. Her maiden name was Dolly something—I forget the name. Her parents were both dead. That's about all."

"It took you quite a while to get that much out of her."

"I was only there five or ten minutes, maybe fifteen."

"The desk clerk said an hour."

"He made a mistake."

"Or maybe you did, Mr. Begley. Time passes very rapidly sometimes."

He clutched at this dubious excuse. "Maybe I did stay longer than I realized. I remember now, she wanted me to stay and meet her husband." His eyes held steady, but they had taken on a faint lying sheen. "He didn't come and didn't come, so I left."

"Did you suggest seeing her again?"

"No. She wasn't that interested in my story."

"You told her your story?"

"I told her about my daughter, naturally, just like I told you."

"I don't understand it. You say you were out of the country for ten years. Where?"

"In New Caledonia, mostly. I worked for a chrome mine there. They shut it down last spring and shipped us home."

"And now you're looking for your daughter?"

"I'd certainly like to put my hands on her."

"So she can be a bridesmaid at your wedding?" I wanted to see how sharp a needle he would take.

He took this one without a word.

"What happened to your wife?"

"She died." His eyes were no longer steady. "Look, do we have to go into all this? It's bad enough losing your loved ones without having it raked up and pushed in your face." I couldn't tell if his self-pity was false: self-pity always is to some extent.

"It's too bad you lost your family," I said. "But what did you expect when you left the country for ten years?"

"It wasn't my choice. How would you like to get shanghaied and not be able to get back?"

"Is that your story? It isn't a likely one."

"My story is wilder than that, but we won't go into it. You wouldn't believe me, anyway. Nobody else has."

"You could always try me."

"It would take all day. You've got better things to do than talk to me."

"Name one."

"You said there's a young lady missing. Go and find her."

"I was hoping you could help me. I still am hoping, Mr. Begley."

He looked down at his feet. He was wearing huaraches. "I've told you all I know about her. I should never have gone to that hotel in the first place. Okay, so I made a mistake. You can't hang a man for a little mistake in judgment."

"You've mentioned murder once, and hanging once. I wonder why."

"It was just a manner of speaking." But the confidence was seeping out of him through the holes my needle had made. He said with a rising inflection: "You think I murdered her?"

"No. I do think this. Something happened between you, or something was said, that might explain why she left so suddenly. Give it some thought, will you?"

Slowly, perhaps involuntarily, he raised his head and looked up at the sun. Under his tilted beard his neck was pale and scrawny. It gave the impression that he was wearing the kind of mask Greek actors wore, covering him completely from my eyes.

"No. Nothing was said like that."

"Was there any trouble between you?"

"No."

"Why did she let you come to her room?"

"I guess she was interested in my story. I talked to her on the house phone, said she resembled my daughter. It was just a foolish impulse. I knew as soon as I saw her that she wasn't."

"Did you make arrangements to see her again?"

"No. I'd certainly like to."

"Did you wait outside the hotel for her, or agree to meet her at the bus station?"

"I did not. What are you trying to nail me for? What do you want?"

"Just the truth. I'm not satisfied I've been getting it from you."

He said in a sudden spurt of fury: "You've got as much as—" He began to regret the outburst before it was over, and swallowed the rest of the words.

But he turned his back on me and went inside, slamming the door. I waited for a little while, and gave up on him. I walked back along the sandy access lane to our cars.

The blonde woman, Madge Gerhardi, was sitting beside Alex in his red Porsche. He looked up with shining eyes.

"Mrs. Gerhardi has seen her. She's seen Dolly."

"With Begley?"

"No, not with him." She opened the door and squeezed out of the little car. "It was at that garage that specializes in fixing foreign cars. I drive an MG myself, and I had it in for a lube job. The girl was there with an old woman. They went away together in an old brown Rolls. The girl was doing the driving."

"Are you certain of the identification?" I showed her the picture again.

She nodded over it emphatically. "I'm certain, unless she has a twin. I noticed her because she was so stunning."

"Do you know who the old woman was?"

"No, but the man at the garage ought to be able to tell you." She gave us directions, and started to edge away. "I better get back to the house. I snuck out along the beach, and Chuck will be wondering where I am."

4

A mechanic lying face up on a creeper rolled out from under the raised front end of a Jaguar sedan. I saw when he stood up that he was a plump Mediterranean type with "Mario" embroidered on his coverall. He nodded enthusiastically when I asked him about the old Rolls and the old lady.

"That's Mrs. Bradshaw. I been looking after her Rolls for the last twelve years, ever since she bought it. It's running as good now as the day she bought it." He looked at his greasy hands with some satisfaction, like a surgeon recalling a series of difficult but successful operations. "Some of the girls she gets to drive her don't know how to treat a good car."

"Do you know the girl who's driving her at present?"

"I don't know her name. Mrs. Bradshaw has quite a turnover with her drivers. She gets them from the college mostly. Her son is Dean at the college, and he won't let the old lady do her own driving. She's crippled with rheumatics, and I think she was in a smashup at one time."

I cut in on Mario's complicated explanations and showed him the print. "This girl?"

"Yeah. She was here with Mrs. Bradshaw the other day. She's a new one. Like I said, Mrs. Bradshaw has quite a turnover. She likes to have her own way, and these college girls don't take orders too well. Personally I always hit it off with Mrs. Bradshaw—"

"Where does she live?"

Alex sounded anxious, and Mario was slightly infected by his anxiety. "What is it you want with her?"

"She's not the one I'm interested in. The girl is my wife."

"You and her are on the outs?"

"I don't know. I have to talk to her."

Mario looked up at the high corrugated-iron roof of the garage. "My wife divorced me a couple years ago. I been putting on weight ever since. A man don't have the same motivation."

"Where does Mrs. Bradshaw live?" I said.

"Foothill Drive, not too far from here. Take the first cross street to the right, it runs into it. You can look up the house number in the phone book, on the desk there. It's in her son's name, Roy Bradshaw."

I thanked him. He lay down on the creeper and slid back under the Jaguar. The directory was under the telephone on top of the battered desk which stood in a corner. I found the listing: "Roy Bradshaw, 311 Foothill Drive."

"We could phone from here," Alex said.

"It's always better in person."

In spite of the housing tracts and the smokeless industries proliferating around it, Pacific Point had kept its identity. Foothill Drive was lined with trees, and had a dusty changeless quality. Settled old families still lived here behind mortised walls that had resisted earthquakes, or hedges that had outlived generations of gardeners.

The towering cypress hedge of 311 masked the house completely from the road. I turned in through the open iron gates with Alex following me. We passed a small white gatehouse with a green door and green shutters, rounded a bend in the driveway, and came in sight of the white Colonial house.

A woman with a wide straw hat tied under her chin was kneeling shoulder deep among the flowers in front of it. She had a pair of clippers in her gloved hands. They snicked in the silence when our engines died.

She rose cumbrously to her feet and came toward us, tucking wisps of gray hair under her hat. She was just an old lady in dirty tennis shoes but her body, indeterminate in a loose blue smock, carried itself with heavy authority, as if it recalled that it had once been powerful or handsome. The architecture of her face had collapsed under the weight of flesh and years. Still her black eyes were alert, like unexpected animal or bird life in the ruins of a building.

"Mrs. Bradshaw?" Alex said eagerly.

"I am Mrs. Bradshaw. What do you gentlemen want? I'm very busy, as you can see." She flourished the clippers. "I never trust anyone else to clip my roses. And still they die, poor things." Regret rustled in her voice.

"They look very beautiful to me," I said in an encouraging way. "Mr. Kincaid and I hate to bother you. But he seems to have misplaced his wife, and we have reason to think she's working for you."

"For me? I employ no one but my Spanish couple. My son," she added with a trace of pride, "keeps me to a strict budget."

"Don't you have a girl driving for you?"

She smiled. "I completely forgot about her. She's just on a part-time basis. What's her name? Molly? Dolly? I never can remember the girls' names."

"Dolly," I said, and showed her the print. "Is this Dolly?"

She removed one gardening glove to take the picture. Her hand was gnarled with arthritis.

"I do believe it is. But she said nothing to me about being married. I'd never have hired her if I'd known, it makes for too much involvement. I like to take my little drives on schedule."

Alex interrupted her rather garrulous chatter. "Where is she now?"

"I couldn't say. She's done her day's stint for me. She may have walked over to the college, or she may be in the gatehouse. I let my girls use the gatehouse. Sometimes they abuse the privilege, but so far this one hasn't." She gave Alex a sharp black glance. "I hope she won't begin to, now that you've turned up."

"I don't expect she'll be going on—"

I cut him short. "Go and see if she's in the gatehouse." I turned back to Mrs. Bradshaw: "How long has she been with you?"

"About two weeks. The semester started two weeks ago."

"Is she attending the college?"

"Yes. I get all my girls from there, except when I have to have a regular attendant, as I did when my son was abroad last summer. I hope I don't lose Dolly. She's brighter than most of them. But if she goes I suppose there are always others. You'll realize, when you've lived as long as I have, that the young ones leave the old ones . . ."

She turned to her roses, glowing red and yellow in the sunlight. She seemed to be looking for some way to finish the thought. None occurred to her. I said:

"What name is she using? What surname?"

"I'm afraid I don't remember. I call them by their first names. My son could tell you."

"Is he here?"

"Roy is at the college. He happens to be the Dean there."

"Is it far from here?"

"You can see it from where you stand."

Her arthritic hand curled on my elbow and turned me gently. Through a gap in the trees I could make out the metal cupola of a small observatory. The old lady spoke close to my ear, in a gossipy way:

"What happened between your young friend and his wife?"

"They came here on their honeymoon and she walked out on him. He's trying to find out why."

"What a strange thing to do," she said. "I'd never have acted like that on my honeymoon, I had too much respect for my husband. But girls are different nowadays, aren't they? Loyalty and respect mean nothing to them. Are you married, young man?"

"I have been."

"I see. Are you the boy's father?"

"No. My name is Archer. I'm a private detective."

"Really? What do you make of all this?" She gestured vaguely with her clippers toward the gatehouse.

"Nothing so far. She may have left him on account of a girlish whim. Or she may have had deep dark reasons. All I can do is ask her. By the way, Mrs. Bradshaw, have you ever heard her mention a man named Begley?"

"Begley?"

"He's a big man with a short gray beard. He visited her at the Surf House the day she left her husband. There's some possibility that he's her father."

She wet her seamed lips with the purple tip of her tongue. "She didn't mention him to me. I don't encourage the girls to unburden themselves to me. Perhaps I should."

"What kind of a mood has Dolly been in lately?"

"It's hard to say. She's always the same. Quiet. She thinks her own thoughts."

Alex appeared, walking rapidly around the bend in the driveway. His face was bright.

"It's her definitely. I found her things in the closet."

"You weren't authorized to go in there," Mrs. Bradshaw said.

"It's her house, isn't it?"

"It happens to be mine."

"But she has the use of it, hasn't she?"

"She does. You don't."

A quarrel with Dolly's employer was the last thing Alex needed. I stepped between them, turned him around, and walked him away from the trouble for the second time.

"Get lost," I said when he was in his car. "You're in my way."

"But I have to see her."

"You'll see her. Go and check in at the Mariner's Rest Motel for both of us. It's on the strip between here and the Surf House—"

"I know where it is. But what about Dolly?"

"I'm going over to the college to talk to her. I'll bring her back with me, if she's willing."

"Why can't I go along to the college?" he said like a spoiled child.

"Because I don't want you to. Dolly has a separate life of her own. You may not like it, but you have no right to jump in and wreck it for her. I'll see you at the motel."

"He drove away rapidly and angrily, spinning the wheels of his car. Mrs. Bradshaw was back among her roses. I asked her very politely for permission to examine Dolly's things. She said that would have to be up to Dolly.

5

The campus was an oasis of vivid green under the brown September foothills. Most of the buildings were new and very modern, ornamented with pierced concrete screens and semi-tropical plantings. A barefoot boy sitting under a roadside palm took time out from his Salinger to show me where the Administration Building was.

I parked in the lot behind it, among a scattering of transportation clunks with faculty stickers. A new black Thunderbird stood out among them. It was late Friday afternoon by now, and the long collegiate weekend was setting in. The glass information booth opposite the entrance of the building was empty. The corridors were practically deserted.

I found the Dean's office without much trouble. The paneled anteroom was furnished with convertible Danish pieces, and with a blond secretary who sat at a typewriter guarding the closed inner door. She had a pale thin face, strained blue eyes that had worked too long under fluorescent light, and a suspicious voice:

"Can I help you, sir?"

"I'd like to see the Dean."

"Dean Bradshaw is very busy, I'm afraid. Perhaps I can assist you?"

"Perhaps. I'm trying to get in touch with one of your girl students. Her name is Dolly McGee, or Dolly Kincaid."

"Which?" she said with a little gasp of irritation.

"Her maiden name is McGee, her married name is Kincaid. I don't know which she's using."

"Are you a parent?" she said delicately.

"No. I'm not her father. But I have good reason for wanting to see her."

She looked at me as if I was a self-confessed kingpin in the white slave traffic. "We have a policy of not giving out information about students, except to parents."

"What about husbands?"

"You're her husband?"

"I represent her husband. I think you'd better let me talk to the Dean about her."

"I can't do that," she said in a final tone. "Dean Bradshaw is in conference with the department heads. About what do you wish to see Miss McGee?"

"It's a private matter."

"I see."

We had reached an impasse. I said in the hope of making her smile: "We have a policy of not giving out information."

She looked insulted, and went back to her typewriter. I stood and waited. Voices rose and fell behind the door of the inner office. "Budget" was the word I caught most frequently. After a while the secretary said:

"I suppose you could try Dean Sutherland, if she's in. Dean Sutherland is Dean of Women. Her office is just across the hall."

Its door was standing open. The woman in it was the well-scrubbed ageless type who looks old in her twenties and young in her forties. She wore her brown hair rolled in a bun at the back of her neck. Her only concession to glamour was a thin pink line of lipstick accenting her straight mouth.

She was a good-looking woman in spite of this. Her face was finely chiseled. The front of her blouse curved out over her desk like a spinnaker going downwind.

"Come in," she said with a severity that I was getting used to. "What are you waiting for?"

Her fine eyes had me hypnotized. Looking into them was like looking into the beautiful core of an iceberg, all green ice and cold blazing light.

"Sit down," she said. "What is your problem?"

I told her who I was and why I was there.

"But we have no Dolly McGee or Dolly Kincaid on campus."

"She must be using a third name, then. I know she's a student here. She has a job driving for Dean Bradshaw's mother." I showed her my photograph.

"But this is Dorothy Smith. Why would she register with us under a false name?"

"That's what her husband would like to know."

"Is this her husband in the picture with her?"

"Yes."

"He appears to be a nice enough boy."

"Apparently she didn't think so."

"I wonder why." Her eyes were looking past me, and I felt cheated. "As a matter of fact, I don't see how she *could* register under a false name, unless she came to us with forged credentials." She rose abruptly. "Excuse me for a minute, Mr. Archer."

She went into the next room, where filing cabinets stood like upended metal coffins, and came back with a folder which she opened on her desk. There wasn't much in it.

"I see," she said more or less to herself. "She's been admitted provisionally. There's a note here to the effect that her transcript is on the way."

"How long is provisional admission good for?"

"Until the end of September." She consulted her desk calendar. "That gives her nine days to come up with a transcript. But she'll have to come up with an explanation rather sooner. We don't look with favor on this sort of deception. And I had the impression that she was a straightforward girl." Her mouth turned down at the corners.

"You know her personally, Dean Sutherland?"

"I make a point of contacting all the new girls. I went out of my way to be useful to Miss or Mrs. Smith-Kincaid. In fact I helped her get her part-time job in the library."

"And the job with old Mrs. Bradshaw?"

She nodded. "She heard that there was an opening there, and I recommended her." She looked at her watch. "She may be over there now."

"She isn't. I just came from Mrs. Bradshaw's. Your Dean lives pretty high on the hog, by the way. I thought academic salaries were too low."

"They are. Dean Bradshaw comes from a wealthy old family. What was his mother's reaction to this?" She made an impatient gesture which somehow included me.

"She seemed to take it in stride. She's a smart old woman."

"I'm glad you found her so," she said, as if she had had other kinds of experience with Mrs. Bradshaw. "Well, I suppose I'd better see if Mrs. Smith-Kincaid is in the library."

"I could go over there and ask."

"I think not. I had better talk to her first, and try to find out what's going on in her little head."

"I didn't want to make trouble for her."

"Of course not, and you didn't. The trouble is and was there. You merely uncovered it. I'm grateful to you for that."

"Could your gratitude," I said carefully, "possibly take the form of letting me talk to her first?"

"I'm afraid not."

"I've had a lot of experience getting the facts out of people."

It was the wrong thing to say. Her mouth turned down at the corners again. Her bosom changed from a promise to a threat.

"I've had experience, too, a good many years of it, and I am a trained counselor. If you'll be good enough to wait outside, I'm going to try and phone her at the library." She flung a last shaft as I went out: "And please don't try to intercept her on the way here."

"I wouldn't dream of it, Miss Sutherland."

"Dean Sutherland, if you please."

I went and read the bulletin board beside the information booth. The jolly promises of student activities, dances and get-togethers and poetry clubs and breakfasts where French was spoken, only saddened me. It was partly because my own attempt at college hadn't worked out, partly because I'd just put the kibosh on Dolly's.

A girl wearing horn-rimmed glasses, and a big young fellow in a varsity sweater drifted in from outside and leaned against the wall. She was explaining something to him, something about Achilles and the tortoise. Achilles was chasing the tortoise, it seemed, but according to Zeno he would never catch it. The space between them was divisible into an infinite number of parts; therefore it would take Achilles an infinite period of time to traverse it. By that time the tortoise would be some-where else.

The young man nodded, "I see that."

"But it isn't so," the girl cried. "The infinite divisibility of space is merely theoretical. It doesn't affect actual *movement* across space."

"I don't get it, Heidi."

"Of course you do. Imagine yourself on the football field. You're on the twenty-yard line and there's a tortoise crawling away from you toward the thirty-yard line."

I stopped listening. Dolly was coming up the outside steps toward the glass door, a dark-haired girl in a plaid skirt and a cardigan. She leaned on the door for a moment before she pushed it open. She seemed to have gone to pieces to some extent since Fargo had taken her picture. Her skin was sallow, her hair not recently brushed. Her dark uncertain glance slid over me without appearing to take me in.

She stopped short before she reached Dean Sutherland's office. Turning in a sudden movement, she started for the front door. She stopped again, between me and the two philosophers, and stood considering. I was struck by her faintly sullen beauty, her eyes dark and blind with thought. She turned around once more and trudged back along the hallway to meet her fate.

The office door closed behind her. I strolled past it after a while and heard the murmur of female voices inside, but nothing intelligible. From Dean Bradshaw's office across the hall the heads of departments emerged as a body. In spite of their glasses and their foreheads and their scholars' stoops, they looked a little like schoolboys let out for recess.

A woman with a short razorblade haircut came into the building and drew all their eyes. Her ash-blonde hair shone against the deep tan of her face. She attached herself to a man standing by himself in the doorway of the Dean's office.

He seemed less interested in her than she was in him. His good looks were rather gentle and melancholy, the kind that excite maternal passions in women. Though his brown wavy hair was graying at the temples, he looked rather like a college boy who twenty years after graduation glanced up from his books and found himself middle-aged.

Dean Sutherland opened the door of her office and made a sign to him. "Can you spare me a minute, Dr. Bradshaw? Something serious has come up." She was pale and grim, like a reluctant executioner.

He excused himself. The two Deans shut themselves up with Dolly. The woman with the short and shining haircut frowned at the closed door. Then she gave me an appraising glance, as if she was looking for a substitute for Bradshaw. She had a promising mouth and good legs and a restless predatory air. Her clothes had style.

"Looking for someone?" she said.

"Just waiting."

"For Lefty or for Godot? It makes a difference."

"For Lefty Godot. The pitcher."

"The pitcher in the rye?"

"He prefers bourbon."

"So do I," she said. "You sound like an anti-intellectual to me, Mr.—"

"Archer. Didn't I pass the test?"

"It depends on who does the grading."

"I've been thinking maybe I ought to go back to school. You make it seem attractive, and besides I feel so out of things when my intellectual friends are talking about Jack Kerouac and Eugene Burdick and other great writers, and I can't read. Seriously, if I were thinking of going back to college, would you recommend this place?"

She gave me another of her appraising looks. "Not for you, Mr. Archer. I think you'd feel more at home in some larger urban university, like Berkeley or Chicago. I went to Chicago myself. This college presents quite a contrast."

"In what way?"

"Innumerable ways. The quotient of sophistication here is very low, for one thing. This used to be a denominational college, and the moral atmosphere is still in Victorian stays." As if to demonstrate that she was not, she shifted her pelvis. "They tell me when Dylan Thomas visited here—but perhaps we'd better not go into that. *De mortuis nil nisi bonum.*"

"Do you teach Latin?"

"No, I have small Latin and less Greek. I try to teach modern languages. My name is Helen Haggerty, by the way. As I was saying, I wouldn't really recommend Pacific Point to you. The standards are improving every year, but there's still a great deal of dead wood around. You can see some of it from here."

She cast a sardonic glance toward the entrance, where five or six of her fellow professors were conducting a post-mortem of their conference with the Dean.

"That was Dean Bradshaw you were talking to, wasn't it?"

"Yes. Is he the one you want to see?"

"Among others."

"Don't be put off by his rather forbidding exterior. He's a fine scholar—the only Harvard doctor on the faculty—and he can advise you better than I ever could. But tell me honestly, are you really serious about going back to college? Aren't you kidding me a little?"

"Maybe a little."

"You could kid me more effectively over a drink. And I could use a drink, preferably bourbon."

"It's a handsome offer." And a sudden one, I thought. "Give me a rain check, will you? Right now I have to wait for Lefty Godot."

She looked more disappointed than she had any right to be. We parted on fairly good, mutually suspicious terms.

The fatal door I was watching opened at last. Dolly backed out thanking the two Deans effusively, and practically curtsying. But I saw when she turned around and headed for the entrance that her face was white and set.

I went after her, feeling a little foolish. The situation reminded me of a girl I used to follow home from Junior High. I never did work up enough nerve to ask her for the privilege of carrying her books. But I began to identify Dolly with that unattainable girl whose name I couldn't even remember now.

She hurried along the mall that bisected the campus, and started up the steps of the library building. I caught up with her.

"Mrs. Kincaid?"

She stopped as though I had shot her. I took her arm instinctively. She flung away my hand, and opened her mouth as if to call out for help. No sound came out. The other students around us, passing on the wide mall or chatting on the steps, paid no attention to her silent scream.

"I'd like very much to talk to you, Mrs. Kincaid."

She pushed her hair back, so forcefully that one of her eyes slanted up and gave her an Eurasian look. "Who are you?"

"A friend of your husband's. You've given Alex a bad three weeks."

"I suppose I have," she said, as if she had only just thought of it.

"You must have had a bad three weeks yourself, if you're fond of him at all. Are you?"

"Am I what?" She seemed to be slightly dazed.

"Fond of Alex."

"I don't know. I haven't had time to think about it. I don't wish to discuss it, with you or anyone. Are you really a friend of Alex's?"

"I think I can claim to be. He doesn't understand what you're doing to him. He's a pretty sad young man."

"No doubt he caught it from me. Spreading ruin is my specialty."

"It doesn't have to be. Why don't you call it off, whatever you're doing, and give it another try with Alex? He's waiting for you here in town right now."

"He can wait till doomsday, I'm not going back to him."

Her young voice was surprisingly firm, almost harsh. There was something about her eyes I didn't like. They were wide and dry and fixed, eyes which had forgotten how to cry.

"Did Alex hurt you in some way?"

"He wouldn't hurt a fly. You know that, if you're really a friend of his. He's a nice harmless boy, and I don't want to hurt him." She added with conscious drama: "Tell him to congratulate himself on his narrow escape."

"Is that the only message you have for your husband?"

"He isn't my husband, not really. Tell him to get an annulment. Tell him I'm not ready to settle down. Tell him I've decided to finish my education."

She made it sound like a solitary trip to the moon, one-way.

I went back to the Administration Building. The imitation flagstone pavement of the mall was flat and smooth, but I had the feeling that I was walking knee-deep in gopher holes. Dean Sutherland's door was closed and, when I knocked, her "Come in" was delayed and rather muffled.

Dean Bradshaw was still with her, looking more than ever like a college student on whom light frost had fallen during the night.

She was flushed, and her eyes were bright emerald green. "This is Mr. Archer, Brad, the detective I told you about."

He gave my hand a fiercely competitive grip. "It's a pleasure to meet you, sir. Actually," he said with an attempt to a smile, "it's rather a mixed pleasure under the circumstances. I very much regret the necessity of your coming here to our campus."

"The kind of work I do has to be done," I said a little defensively. "Mrs. Kincaid ran out on her husband, and some explanation is due him. Did she give any to you?"

Dean Sutherland put on her grim face. "She's not returning to him. She found out something on their wedding night so dreadful—"

Bradshaw raised his hand. "Wait a minute, Laura. The facts she divulged to you are in the nature of professional confidences. We certainly don't want this chap running back to her husband with them. The poor girl is frightened enough as it is."

"Frightened of her husband? I find that hard to believe," I said.

"She didn't pour out her heart to you," Laura Sutherland cried warmly. "Why do you suppose the poor child used a fake name? She was mortally afraid that he would track her down."

"You're being melodramatic, you know." Bradshaw's tone was indulgent. "The boy can't be as bad as all that."

"You didn't hear her, Brad. She told me things, as woman to woman, that I haven't even told you, and I don't intend to."

I said: "Perhaps she was lying."

"She most assuredly was not! I know the truth when I hear it. And my advice to you is to go back to that husband of hers, wherever he is, and tell him that you haven't been able to find her. She'll be safer and happier if you do."

"She seems to be safe enough. She certainly isn't happy. I talked to her outside for a minute."

Bradshaw tilted his head in my direction. "What did she say?"

"Nothing sensational. She made no accusations against Kincaid. In fact she blamed herself for the breakup. She says she wants to go on with her education."

"Good."

"Are you going to let her stay here?"

Bradshaw nodded. "We've decided to overlook her little deception. We believe in giving young people a certain amount of leeway, so long as it doesn't impinge on the rights of others. She can stay, at least for the present, and continue to use her pseudonym if she likes." He added with dry academic humor: " 'A rose by any other name,' you know."

"She's going to have her transcripts sent to us right away," Dean Sutherland said. "Apparently she's had two years of junior college and a semester at the university."

"What's she planning to study here?"

"Dolly is majoring in psychology. According to Professor Haggerty, she has a flair for it."

"How would Professor Haggerty know that?"

"She's Dolly's academic counselor. Apparently Dolly is deeply interested in criminal and abnormal psychology."

For some reason I thought of Chuck Begley's bearded head, with eyes opaque as a statue's. "When you were talking with Dolly, did she say anything about a man named Begley?"

"Begley?" They looked at each other and then at me. "Who," she asked, "is Begley?"

"It's possible he's her father. At any rate he had something to do with her leaving her husband. Incidentally I wouldn't put too much stock in her husband's Asiatic perversions or whatever it was she accused him of. He's a clean boy, and he respects her."

"You're entitled to your opinion," Laura Sutherland said, as though I wasn't. "But please don't act on it precipitately. Dolly is a sensitive young woman, and something has happened to shake her very deeply. You'll be doing them both a service by keeping them apart."

"I agree," Bradshaw said solemnly.

"The trouble is, I'm being paid to bring them together. But I'll think about it, and talk it over with Alex."

6

In the parking lot behind the building Professor Helen Haggerty was sitting at the wheel of the new black Thunderbird convertible. She had put the top down and parked it beside my car, as if for contrast. The late afternoon sunlight slanting across the foothills glinted on her hair and eyes and teeth.

"Hello again."

"Hello again," I said. "Are you waiting for me?"

"Only if you're left-handed."

"I'm ambidextrous."

"You would be. You threw me a bit of a curve just now."

"I did?"

"I know who you are." She patted a folded newspaper on the leather seat beside her. The visible headline said: "Mrs. Perrine Acquitted." Helen Haggerty said: "I think it's very exciting. The paper credits you with getting her off. But it's not quite clear how you do it."

"I simply told the truth, and evidently the jury believed me. At the time the alleged larceny was committed here in Pacific Point, I had Mrs. Perrine under close surveillance in Oakland."

"What for? Another larceny?"

"It wouldn't be fair to say."

She made a mock-sorrowful mouth, which fitted the lines of her face too well. "All the interesting facts are confidential. But I happen to be checked out for security. In fact my father is a policeman. So get in and tell me all about Mrs. Perrine."

"I can't do that."

"Or I have a better idea," she said with her bright unnatural smile. "Why don't you come over to my house for a drink?"

"I'm sorry, I have work to do."

"Detective work?"

"Call it that."

"Come *on*." With a subtle movement, her body joined in the invitation. "All work and no play makes Jack a dull boy. You don't want to be a dull boy and make me feel rejected. Besides, we have things to talk about."

"The Perrine case is over. Nothing could interest me less."

"It was the Dorothy Smith case I had in mind. Isn't that why you're on campus?"

"Who told you that?"

"The grapevine. Colleges have the most marvelously efficient grapevines, second only to penitentiaries."

"Are you familiar with penitentiaries?"

"Not intimately. But I wasn't lying when I told you my father was a policeman." A gray pinched expression touched her face. She covered it over with another smile. "We do have things in common. Why don't you come along?"

"All right. I'll follow you. It will save you driving me back."

"Wonderful."

She drove as rapidly as she operated, with a jerky nervousness and a total disregard for the rules of the road. Fortunately the campus was almost empty of cars and people. Diminished by the foothills and by their own long shadows, the buildings resembled a movie lot which had shut down for the night.

She lived back of Foothill Drive in a hillside house made out of aluminum and glass and black enameled steel. The nearest rooftop floated among the scrub oaks a quarter of a mile down the slope. You could stand in the living room by the central fireplace and see the blue mountains rising up on one side, the gray ocean falling away on the other. The offshore fog was pushing in to the land.

"Do you like my little eyrie?"

"Very much."

"It isn't really mine, alas, I'm only renting at present, though I have hopes. Sit down. What will you drink? I'm going to have a tonic."

"That will do nicely."

The polished tile floor was almost bare of furniture. I strolled around the large room, pausing by one of the glass walls to look out. A wild pigeon lay on the patio with its iridescent neck broken. Its faint spreadeagled image outlined in dust showed where it had flown against the glass.

I sat on a rope chair which probably belonged on the patio. Helen Haggerty brought our drinks and disposed herself on a canvas chaise, where the sunlight would catch her hair again, and shine on her polished brown legs.

"I'm really just camping for now," she said. "I haven't sent for my furniture, because I don't know if I want it around me any more. I may just leave it in storage and start all over, and to hell with the history. Do you think that's a good idea, Curveball Lefty Lew?"

"Call me anything, I don't mind. I'd have to know the history."

"Ha. You never will." She looked at me sternly for a minute, and sipped her drink. "You might as well call me Helen."

"All right, Helen."

"You make it sound so formal. I'm not a formal person, and neither are you. Why should we be formal with each other?"

"You live in a glass house, for one thing," I said smiling. "I take it you haven't been in it long."

"A month. Less than a month. It seems longer. You're the first really interesting man I've met since I arrived here."

I dodged the compliment. "Where did you live before?"

"Here and there. There and here. We academic people are such nomads. It doesn't suit me. I'd like to settle down permanently. I'm getting old."

"It doesn't show."

"You're being gallant. Old for a woman, I mean. Men never grow old."

Now that she had me where she apparently wanted me, she wasn't crowding so hard, but she was working. I wished that she would stop, because I liked her. I downed my drink. She brought me a second tonic with all the speed and efficiency of a cocktail waitress. I couldn't get rid of the dismal feeling that each of us was there to use the other.

With the second tonic she let me look down her dress. She was smooth and brown as far as I could see. She arranged herself on the chaise with one hip up. so that I could admire the curve. The sun, in its final yellow flareup before setting, took possession of the room.

"Shall I pull the drapes?" she said.

"Don't bother for me. It'll be down soon. You were going to tell me about Dolly Kincaid alias Dorothy Smith."

"Was I?"

"You brought the subject of her up. I understand you're her academic counselor."

"And that's why you're interested in me, *n'est-ce pas?*" Her tone was mocking.

"I was interested in you before I knew of your connection with Dolly."

"Really?"

"Really. Here I am to prove it."

"Here you are because I lured you with the magic words Dorothy Smith. What's she doing on this campus anyway?" She sounded almost jealous of the girl.

"I was sort of hoping you knew the answer to that."

"Don't you?"

"Dolly gives conflicting stories, probably derived from romantic fiction—"

"I don't think so," she said. "She's a romantic all right—one of these romantic idealists who are always a jump or two behind her unconscious mind. I ought to know, I used to be one myself. But I also think she has some real trouble—appalling trouble."

"What was her story to you?"

"It was no story. It was the lousy truth. We'll come to it later on, if you're a good boy." She stirred like an odalisque in the dying light, and recrossed her polished legs. "How brave are you, Mr. Lew?"

"Men don't talk about how brave they are."

"You're full of copybook maxims," she said with some malice. "I want a serious answer."

"You could always try me."

"I may at that. I have a use—I mean, I need a man."

"Is that a proposal, or a business proposition, or are you thinking about some third party?"

"You're the man I have in mind. What would you say if I told you that I'm likely to be killed this weekend?"

"I'd advise you to go away for the weekend."

She leaned sideways toward me. Her breast hardly sagged. "Will you take me?"

"I have a prior commitment."

"If you mean little Mr. Alex Kincaid, I can pay you better than he can. Not to mention fringe benefits," she added irrepressibly.

"That college grapevine is working overtime. Or is Dolly the source of your information?"

"She's one of them. I could tell you things about that girl that would curl your hair."

"Go ahead. I've always wanted curly hair."

"Why should I? You don't offer a *quid pro quo*. You don't even take me seriously. I'm not used to being turned down flat, by the way."

"It's nothing personal. I'm just the phlegmatic type. Anyway, you don't need me. There are roads going in three directions—Mexico, the desert, or Los Angeles —and you have a nice fast car."

"I'm too nervous to drive any distance."

"Scared?"

She nodded.

"You put up a good front."

"A good front is all I have."

Her face looked closed and dark, perhaps because the sunlight had faded from the room. Only her hair seemed to hold the light. Beyond the slopes of her body I could see the mountains darkening down.

"Who wants to kill you, Helen?"

"I don't know exactly. But I've been threatened."

"How?"

"Over the telephone. I didn't recognize the voice. I couldn't tell if it was a man or a woman, or something in between." She shuddered.

"Why would anybody threaten you?"

"I don't know," she said without meeting my eyes.

"Teachers do get threatened from time to time. It usually isn't serious. Have you had a run-in with any local crackpots?"

"I don't even know any local people. Except the ones at the college, of course."

"You may have a psychoneurotic in one of your classes."

She shook her head. "It's nothing like that. This is serious."

"How do you know?"

"I have my ways of knowing."

"Is it anything to do with Dolly Kincaid?"

"Perhaps. I can't say for sure. The situation is so complicated."

"Tell me about the complicated situation."

"It goes a long way back," she said, "all the way back to Bridgeton."

"Bridgeton?"

"The city where I was born and raised. The city where everything happened. I ran away, but you can't run away from the landscape of your dreams. My nightmares are still set in the streets of Bridgeton. That voice on the telephone threatening to kill me was Bridgeton catching up with me. It was the voice of Bridgeton talking out of the past."

She was unconscious of herself, caught in a waking nightmare, but her description of it sounded false. I still didn't know whether to take her seriously.

"Are you sure you're not talking nonsense out of the present?"

"I'm not making this up," she said. "Bridgeton will be the death of me. Actually I've always known it would."

"Towns don't kill people."

"You don't know the proud city of my birth. It has quite a record along those lines."

"Where is it?"

"In Illinois, south of Chicago."

"You say that everything happened there. What do you mean?"

"Everything important—it was all over before I knew it had started. But I don't want to go into the subject."

"I can't very well help you unless you do."

"I don't believe you have any intention of helping me. You're simply trying to pump me for information."

It was true. I didn't care for her as she wished to be cared for by someone. I didn't entirely trust her. Her handsome body seemed to contain two alternating persons, one sensitive and candid, one hard and evasive.

She rose and went to the glass wall that faced the mountains. They had turned lavender and plum, with dark nocturnal blue in their clefts and groins. The entire evening, mountains and sky and city, was inundated with blue.

"*Die blaue Stunde,*" she said more or less to herself. "I used to love this hour. Now it gives me the mortal shivers."

I got up and stood behind her. "You're deliberately working on your own emotions."

"You know so much about me."

"I know you're an intelligent woman. Act like one. If the place is getting you down leave it, or stay here and take precautions. Ask for police protection."

"You're very free with brilliant suggestions not involving you. I asked for protection yesterday after I got the threatening telephone call. The Sheriff sent a man out. He said such calls were common, and usually involved teenagers."

"Could it have been a teenager?"

"I don't think so. But the deputy said they sometimes disguise their voices. He told me not to worry."

"So don't worry."

"I can't help it. I'm afraid, Lew. Stay with me?"

She turned and leaned on my chest, moving her body tentatively against me. The only real feeling I had for her was pity. She was trying to use me, and using herself in order to use me.

"I have to run along," I said. "I told you at the start I have a prior commitment. But I'll check back on you."

"Thanks so much!"

She pulled away from me, so violently that she thudded like a bird against the glass wall.

7

I drove downhill through deepening twilight toward the Mariner's Rest Motel, telling myself in various tones of voice that I had done the right thing. The trouble was, in the scene I had just walked out of, there was no right thing to do—only sins of commission or omission.

A keyboy wearing a gold-braided yachting cap who looked as though he had never set foot on a dock told me that Alex Kincaid had registered and gone out again. I went to the Surf House for dinner. The spotlit front of the big hotel reminded me of Fargo and all the useless pictures I had ordered from him.

He was in the dark room adjoining his little office. When he came out he was wearing rectangular dark glasses against the light. I couldn't see his eyes, but his mouth was hostile. He picked up a bulky manila envelope from the desk and thrust it at me.

"I thought you were in a hurry for these prints."

"I was. Things came up. We found her."

"So now you don't want 'em? My wife worked in this sweat-box half the afternoon to get 'em ready."

"I'll take them. Kincaid will have use for them if I don't. How much?"

"Twenty-five dollars including tax. It's actually $24.96."

I gave him two tens and a five, and his mouth went through three stages of softening. "Are they getting back together?"

"I don't know yet."

"Where did you find her?"

"Attending the local college. She has a job driving for an old lady named Bradshaw."

"The one with the Rolls?"

"Yes. You know her?"

"I wouldn't say that. She and her son generally eat Sunday buffet lunch in the dining room. She's quite a character. I took a candid picture of them once, on the chance they'd order some copies, and she threatened to smash my camera with her cane. I felt like telling the old biddy her face was enough to smash it."

"But you didn't?"

"I can't afford such luxuries." He spread out his chemical-stained hands. "She's a local institution, and she could get me fired."

"I understand she's loaded."

"Not only that. Her son is a big wheel in educational circles. He seems like a nice enough joe, in spite of the Harvard lah-de-dah. As a matter of fact he calmed her down when she wanted to smash my Leica. But it's hard to figure a guy like that, a good-looking guy in his forties still tied to his old lady's apron-strings."

"It happens in the best of families."

"Yeah, especially in the best. I see a lot of these sad cookies waiting around for the money, and by the time they inherit it's too late. At least Bradshaw had the guts to go out and make a career for himself." Fargo looked at his watch. "Speaking of careers, I've already put in a twelve-hour day and I've got about two hours of developing to do. See you."

I started toward the hotel coffee shop. Fargo came running after me along the corridor. The rectangular dark glasses lent his face a robotlike calm which went oddly with the movements of his legs and arms.

"I almost forgot to ask you. You get a line on this Begley?"

"I talked to him for quite a while. He didn't give too much. He's living with a woman on Shearwater Beach."

"Who's the lucky woman?" Fargo said.

"Madge Gerhardi is her name. Do you know her?"

"No, but I think I know who he is. If I could take another look at him—"

"Come over there now."

"I can't. I'll tell you who I *think* he is under all that seaweed, if you promise not to quote me. There's such a thing as accidental resemblance, and a libel suit is the last thing I need."

"I promise not to quote you."

"See that you don't." He took a deep breath like a skin diver getting ready to go for the bottom. "I think he's a fellow named Thomas McGee who murdered his wife in Indian Springs about ten years ago. I took a picture of McGee when I was a cub reporter on the paper, but they never used the picture. They never play up those Valley cases."

"You're sure he murdered his wife?"

"Yeah, it was an open-and-shut case. I don't have time to go into details, in fact they're getting pretty hazy at this late date. But most of the people around the courthouse thought he should have been given first degree. Gil Stevens convinced the jury to go for second degree, which explains how he's out so quick."

Remembering Begley's story about his ten years on the other side of the world, the other side of the moon, I thought that ten years wasn't so very quick.

The fog was dense along Shearwater Beach. It must have been high tide: I could hear the surf roaring up under the cottages and sucking at their pilings. The smell of iodine hung in the chilly air.

Madge Gerhardi answered the door and looked at me rather vaguely. The paint on her eyelids couldn't hide the fact that they were swollen.

"You're the detective, aren't you?"

"Yes. May I come in?"

"Come in if you want. It won't do any good. He's gone."

I'd already guessed it from her orphaned air. I followed her along a musty hallway into the main room, which was high and raftered. Spiders had been busy in the angles of the rafters, which were webbed and blurred as if fog had seeped in at the corners. The rattan furniture was coming apart at the joints. The glasses and empty bottles and half-empty bottles standing around on the tables and the floor suggested that a party had been going on for some days and might erupt again if I wasn't careful.

The woman kicked over an empty bottle on the way to the settee, where she flung herself down.

"It's your fault he's gone," she complained. "He started to pack right after you were here this afternoon."

I sat on a rattan chair facing her. "Did Begley say where he was going?"

"Not to me he didn't. He did say I wasn't to expect him back, that it was all off. Why did you have to scare him, anyway? Chuck never did anybody any harm."

"He scares very easily."

"Chuck is sensitive. He's had a great deal of trouble. Many's the time he told me that all he wanted was a quiet nook where he could write about his experiences. He's writing an autobiographical novel about his experiences."

"His experiences in New Caledonia?"

She said with surprising candor: "I don't think Chuck ever set foot in New Caledonia. He got that business about the chrome mine out of an old *National Geographic* magazine. I don't believe he ever left this country."

"Where has he been?"

"In the pen," she said. "You know that, or you wouldn't be after him. I think it's a dirty crying shame, when a man has paid his debt to society and proved that he can rehabilitate himself—"

It was Begley she was quoting, Begley's anger she was expressing, but she couldn't sustain the anger or remember the end of the quotation. She looked around the wreckage of the room in dim alarm, as if she had begun to suspect that his rehabilitation was not complete.

"Did he tell you what he was in for, Mrs. Gerhardi?"

"Not in so many words. He read me a piece from his book the other night. This character in the book was in the pen and he was thinking about the past and how they framed him for a murder he didn't commit. I asked him if the character stood for him. He wouldn't say. He went into one of his deep dark silences."

She went into one of her own. I could feel the floor trembling under my feet. The sea was surging among the pilings like the blithe mindless forces of dissolution. The woman said:

"Was Chuck in the pen for murder?"

"I was told tonight that he murdered his wife ten years ago. I haven't confirmed it. Can you?"

She shook her head. Her face had lengthened as if by its own weight, like unbaked dough. "It must be a mistake."

"I hope so. I was also told that his real name is Thomas McGee. Did he ever use that name?"

"No."

"It does tie in with another fact," I said, thinking aloud. "The girl he went to visit at the Surf House had the same name before she was married. He said the girl resembled his daughter. I think she is his daughter. Did he ever talk about her?"

"Never."

"Or bring her here?"

"No. If she's his daughter, he wouldn't bring her here." She reached for the empty bottle she had kicked over, set it on its base, and slumped back onto the settee, as if morally exhausted by the effort.

"How long did Begley, or McGee, live here with you?"

"A couple of weeks is all. We were going to be married. It's lonely living here without a man."

"I can imagine."

She drew a little life from the sympathy in my voice: "They just don't stay with me. I try to make things nice for them, but they don't stay. I should have stuck with my first husband." Her eyes were far away and long ago. "He treated me like a queen but I was young and foolish. I didn't know any better than to leave him."

We listened to the water under the house.

"Do you think Chuck went away with this girl you call his daughter?"

"I doubt it," I said. "How did he leave here, Mrs. Gerhardi? By car?"

"He wouldn't let me drive him. He said he was going up to the corner and catch the L.A. bus. It stops at the corner if you signal it. He walked up the road with his suitcase and out of sight." She sounded both regretful and relieved.

"About what time?"

"Around three o'clock."

"Did he have any money?"

"He must have had some for the bus fare. He couldn't have had much. I've been giving him a little money, but he would only take what he needed from me, and then it always had to be a loan. Which he said he would pay back when he got his book of experiences on the market. But I don't care if he never pays me back. He was nice to have around."

"Really?"

"Really he was. Chuck is a smart man. I don't care what he's done in the course of his life. A man can change for the better. He never gave me a bad time once." She made a further breakthrough into candor: "I was the one who gave him the bad times. I have a drinking problem. He only drank with me to be sociable. He didn't want me to drink alone." She blinked her gin-colored eyes. "Would you like a drink?"

"No thanks. I have to be on my way." I got up and stood over her. "You're sure he didn't tell you where he was going?"

"Los Angeles is all I know. He promised I'd hear from him but I don't expect it. It's over."

"If he should write or phone will you let me know?"

She nodded. I gave her my card, and told her where I was staying. When I went out, the fog had moved inland as far as the highway.

8

I stopped at the motel again on my way to the Bradshaw house. The keyboy told me that Alex was still out. I wasn't surprised when I found his red Porsche parked under the Bradshaws' hedge beside the road.

The moon was rising behind the trees. I let my thoughts rise with it, imagining that Alex had got together with his bride and they were snug in the gatehouse, talking out their troubles. The sound of the girl's crying wiped out the hopeful image. Her voice was loud and terrible, almost inhuman. Its compulsive rhythms rose and fell like the ululations of a hurt cat.

The door of the gatehouse was slightly ajar. Light spilled around its edges, as if extruded by the pressure of the noise inside. I pushed it open.

"Get out of here," Alex said.

They were on a studio bed in the tiny sitting room. He had his arms around her, but the scene was not domestic. She seemed to be fighting him, trying to struggle out of his embrace. It was more like a scene in a closed ward where psychiatric nurses will hold their violent patients, sometimes for hours on end, rather than strap them in canvas jackets.

Her blouse was torn, so that one of her breasts was almost naked. She twisted her unkempt head around and let me see her face. It was gray and stunned, and it hardly changed expression when she screamed at me:

"Get out!"

"I think I better stick around," I said to the both of them.

I closed the door and crossed the room. The rhythm of her crying was running down. It wasn't really crying. Her eyes were dry and fixed in her gray flesh. She hid them against her husband's body.

His face was shining white.

"What happened, Alex?"

"I don't really know. I was waiting for her when she got home a few minutes ago. I couldn't get much sense out of her. She's awfully upset about something."

"She's in shock," I said, thinking that he was close to it himself. "Was she in an accident?"

"Something like that."

His voice trailed off in a mumble. His look was inward, as if he was groping for the strength to handle this new problem.

"Is she hurt, Alex?"

"I don't think so. She came running down the road, and then she tried to run away again. She put up quite a battle when I tried to stop her."

As if to demonstrate her prowess as a battler, she freed her hands and beat at his chest. There was blood on her hands. It left red dabs on his shirt-front.

"Let me go," she pleaded. "I want to die. I deserve to."

"She's bleeding, Alex."

He shook his head. "It's somebody else's blood. A friend of hers was killed."

"And it's all my fault," she said in a flat voice.

He caught her wrists and held her. I could see manhood biting into his face. "Be quiet Dolly. You're talking nonsense."

"Am I? She's lying in her blood, and I'm the one who put her there."

"Who is she talking about?" I said to Alex.

"Somebody called Helen. I've never heard of her."

I had.

The girl began to talk in her wispy monotone, so rapidly and imprecisely that I could hardly follow. She was a devil and so was her father before her and so was Helen's father and they had the bond of murder between them which made them blood sisters and she had betrayed her blood sister and done her in.

"What did you do to Helen?"

"I should have kept away from her. They die when I go near them."

"That's crazy talk," Alex said softly. "You never hurt anybody."

"What do you know about me?"

"All I need to. I'm in love with you."

"Don't say that. It only makes me want to kill myself." Sitting upright in the circle of his arms, she looked at her bloody hands and cried some more of her terrible dry tears. "I'm a criminal."

Alex looked up at me, his eyes blue-black. "Can you make any sense of it?"

"Not much."

"You can't really think she killed this Helen person?" We were talking past Dolly as if she was deaf or out of her head, and she accepted this status.

"We don't even know that anybody's been killed," I said. "Your wife is loaded with some kind of guilt, but it may belong to somebody else. I found out a little tonight about her background, or I think I did." I sat on the shabby brown studio bed beside them and said to Dolly: "What's your father's name?"

She didn't seem to hear me.

"Thomas McGee?"

She nodded abruptly, as if she'd been struck from behind. "He's a lying monster. He made me into a monster."

"How did he do that?"

The question triggered another nonstop sentence. "He shot her," she said with her chin on her shoulder, "and left her lying in her blood but I told Aunt

Alice and the policemen and the court took care of him but now he's done it again."

"To Helen?"

"Yes, and I'm responsible. I caused it to happen."

She seemed to take a weird pleasure in acknowledging her guilt. Her gray and jaded looks, her tearless crying, her breathless run-on talking and her silences, were signs of an explosive emotional crisis. Under the raw melodrama of her self-accusations, I had the sense of something valuable and fragile in danger of being permanently broken.

"We'd better not try to question her any more," I said. "I doubt right now she can tell the difference between true and false."

"Can't I?" she said malignly. "Everything I remember is true and I can remember everything from year one, the quarrels and the beatings, and then he finally shot her in her blood—"

I cut in: "Shut up, Dolly, or change the record. You need a doctor. Do you have one in town here?"

"No. I don't need a doctor. Call the police. I want to make a confession."

She was playing a game with us and her own mind, I thought, performing dangerous stunts on the cliff edge of reality, daring the long cloudy fall.

"You want to confess that you're a monster," I said.

It didn't work. She answered matter-of-factly: "I am a monster."

The worst of it was, it was happening physically before my eyes. The chaotic pressures in her were changing the shape of her mouth and jaw. She peered at me dully through a fringe of hair. I'd hardly have recognized her as the girl I talked to on the library steps that day.

I turned to Alex. "Do you know any doctors in town?"

He shook his head. His short hair stood up straight as if live electricity was running through him from his contact with his wife. He never let go of her.

"I could call Dad in Long Beach."

"That might be a good idea, later."

"Couldn't we take her to the hospital?"

"Not without a private doctor to protect her."

"Protect her from what?"

"The police, or the psycho ward. I don't want her answering any official questions until I have a chance to check on Helen."

The girl whimpered. "I don't want to go to the psycho ward. I had a doctor in town here a long time ago." She was sane enough to be frightened, and frightened enough to cooperate.

"What's his name?"

"Dr. Godwin. Dr. James Godwin. He's a psychiatrist. I used to come in and see him when I was a little girl."

"Do you have a phone in the gatehouse?"

"Mrs. Bradshaw lets me use her phone."

I left them and walked up the driveway to the main house. I could smell fog even at this level now. It was rolling down from the mountains, flooding out the moon, as well as rising from the sea.

The big white house was quiet, but there was light behind some of the windows. I pressed the bell push. Chimes tinkled faintly behind the heavy door. It was opened by a large dark woman in a cotton print dress. She was crudely handsome, in spite of the pitted acne scars on her cheekbones. Before I could say anything she volunteered that Dr. Bradshaw was out and Mrs. Bradshaw was on her way to bed.

"I just want to use the phone. I'm a friend of the young lady in the gatehouse."

She looked me over doubtfully. I wondered if Dolly's contagion had given me a wild irrational look.

"It's important," I said. "She needs a doctor."

"Is she sick?"

"Quite sick."

"You shouldn't ought to leave her alone."

"She isn't alone. Her husband's with her."

"But she is not married."

"We won't argue about it. Are you going to let me call a doctor?"

She stepped back reluctantly and ushered me past the foot of a curved staircase into a book-lined study where a lamp burned like a night light on the desk. She indicated the telephone beside it, and took up a watchful position by the door.

"Could I have a little privacy, please? You can search me on the way out."

She sniffed, and withdrew out of sight. I thought of calling Helen's house, but she wasn't in the telephone directory. Dr. James Godwin fortunately was. I dialed his number. The voice that eventually answered was so quiet and neutral that I couldn't tell if it was male or female.

"May I speak to Dr. Godwin?"

"This is Dr. Godwin." He sounded weary of his identity.

"My name is Lew Archer. I've just been talking to a girl who says she used to be your patient. Her maiden name was Dolly or Dorothy McGee. She's not in a good way."

"Dolly? I haven't seen her for ten or eleven years. What's troubling her?"

"You're the doctor, and I think you'd better see her. She's hysterical, to put it mildly, talking incoherently about murder."

He groaned. With my other ear I could hear Mrs. Bradshaw call hoarsely down the stairs:

"What's going on down there, Maria?"

"The girl Dolly is sick, he says."

"Who says?"

"I dunno. Some man."

"Why didn't you tell me she was sick?"

"I just did."

Dr. Godwin was talking in a small dead voice that sounded like the whispering ghost of the past: "I'm not surprised this material should come up. There was a violent death in her family when she was a child, and she was violently exposed to it. She was in the immediate pre-pubic period, and already in a vulnerable state."

I tried to cut through the medical jargon: "Her father killed her mother, is that right?"

"Yes." The word was like a sigh. "The poor child found the body. Then they made her testify in court. We permit such barbarous things—" He broke off, and said in a sharply different tone: "Where are you calling from?"

"Roy Bradshaw's house. Dolly is in the gatehouse with her husband. It's on Foothill Drive—"

"I know where it is. In fact I just got in from attending a dinner with Dean Bradshaw. I have another call to make, and then I'll be right with you."

I hung up and sat quite still for a moment in Bradshaw's leather-cushioned swivel chair. The walls of books around me, dense with the past, formed a kind of insulation against the present world and its disasters. I hated to get up.

Mrs. Bradshaw was waiting in the hallway. Maria had disappeared. The old woman was breathing audibly, as if the excitement was a strain on her heart. She clutched the front of her pink wool bathrobe against her loosely heaving bosom.

"What's the trouble with the girl?"

"She's emotionally upset."

"Did she have a fight with her husband? He's a hothead, I could hardly blame her."

"The trouble goes a little deeper than that. I just called Dr. Godwin the psychiatrist. She's been his patient before."

"You mean to tell me the girl is—?" She tapped her veined temple with a swollen knuckle.

A car had stopped in the driveway, and I didn't have to answer her question. Roy Bradshaw came in the front door. The fog had curled his hair tight, and his thin face was open. It closed up when he saw us standing together at the foot of the stairs.

"You're late," Mrs. Bradshaw said in an accusing tone. "You go out wining and dining and leave me here to cope all by myself. Where were you, anyway?"

"The Alumni banquet. You can't have forgotten that. You know how those banquets drag on, and I'm afraid I made my own contribution to the general boredom." He hesitated, becoming aware of something in the scene more serious than an old woman's possessiveness. "What's up, Mother?"

"This man tells me the little girl in the gatehouse has gone out of her mind. Why did you have to send me a girl like that, a psychiatric patient?"

"I didn't send her."

"Who did?"

I tried to break in on their foolishness, but neither of them heard me. They were intent on their game of emotional ping-pong, which had probably been going on since Roy Bradshaw was a boy.

"It was either Laura Sutherland or Helen Haggerty," he was saying. "Professor Haggerty is her counselor, and it was probably she."

"Whichever one it was, I want you to instruct her to be more careful next time. If you don't care about my personal safety—"

"I *do* care about your safety. I care very much about your safety." His voice was strained thin between anger and submissiveness. "I had no idea there was anything the matter with the girl."

"There probably wasn't," I said. "She's had a shock. I just called a doctor for her. Dr. Godwin."

Bradshaw turned slowly in my direction. His face was strangely soft and empty, like a sleeping boy's.

"I know Dr. Godwin," he said. "What kind of a shock did she sustain?"

"It isn't clear. I'd like to talk to you in private."

Mrs. Bradshaw announced in a trembling voice: "This is my house, young man."

She was telling me, but she was also reminding Bradshaw, flicking the economic whip at him. He felt its sting:

"I live here, too. I have my duties to you, and I try to perform them satisfactorily. I also have my duties to the students."

"You and your precious students." Her bright black eyes were scornful. "Very well. You can have your privacy. I'll go outside."

She actually started for the front door, drawing her bathrobe around her lumpy body as if she was being cast out into a blizzard. Bradshaw went after her. There were pullings and haulings and cajolings and a final goodnight embrace, from which I averted my eyes, before she climbed heavily up the stairs, with his assistance.

"You mustn't judge Mother too harshly," he said when he came down. "She's getting old, and it makes it hard for her to adjust to crises. She's really a generous-hearted soul, as I have good reason to know."

I didn't argue with him. He knew her better than I did.

"Well, Mr. Archer, shall we go into my study?"

"We can save time if we talk on the road."

"On the road?"

"I want you to take me to Helen Haggerty's place if you know where it is. I'm not sure I can find it in the dark."

"Why on earth? Surely you're not taking Mother seriously? She was simply talking to hear herself talk."

"I know. But Dolly's been doing some talking, too. She says that Helen

Haggerty is dead. She has blood on her hands, by way of supporting evidence. I think we'd better go up there and see where the blood came from."

He gulped. "Yes. Of course. It isn't far from here. In fact it's only a few minutes by the bridle path. But at night we'll probably get there faster in my car."

We went out to his car. I asked him to stop at the gatehouse, and glanced in. Dolly was lying on the studio bed with her face turned to the wall. Alex had covered her with a blanket. He was standing by the bed with his hands loose.

"Dr. Godwin is on his way," I said in a low voice. "Keep him here till I get back, will you?"

He nodded, but he hardly appeared to see me. His look was still inward, peering into depths he hadn't begun to imagine until tonight.

9

Bradshaw's compact car was equipped with seat-belts, and he made me fasten mine before we set out. Between his house and Helen's I told him as much as I thought he needed to know about Dolly's outpourings. His response was sympathetic. At my suggestion, he left his car by the mailbox at the foot of Helen's lane. When we got out I could hear a foghorn moaning from the low sea.

Another car, a dark convertible whose shape I could barely make out through the thickening air, was parked without lights down the road. I ought to have shaken it down. But I was pressed by my own private guilt, and eager to see if Helen was alive.

Her house was a faint blur of light high among the trees. We started up the hairpinning gravel driveway. An owl flew low over our heads, silent as a traveling piece of fog. It lit somewhere in the gray darkness, called to its mate, and was answered. The two invisible birds seemed to be mocking us with their sad distant foghorn voices.

I heard a repeated crunching up ahead. It resolved itself into footsteps approaching in the gravel. I touched Bradshaw's sleeve, and we stood still. A man loomed up above us. He had on a topcoat and a snap-brim hat. I couldn't quite see his face.

"Hello."

He didn't answer me. He must have been young and bold. He ran straight at us, shouldering me, spinning Bradshaw into the bushes. I tried to hold him but his downhill momentum carried him away.

I chased his running footfalls down to the road, and got there in time to see him climbing into the convertible. Its engine roared and its parking lights came on as I ran toward it. Before it leaped away, I caught a glimpse of a Nevada license and the first four figures of the license number. I went back to Bradshaw's car and wrote them down in my notebook: FT37.

I climbed up the driveway a second time. Bradshaw had reached the house. He was sitting on the doorstep with a sick look on his face. Light poured over him from the open door and cast his bowed shadow brokenly on the flagstones.

"She *is* dead, Mr. Archer."

I looked in. Helen was lying on her side behind the door. Blood had run from a round bullet hole in her forehead and formed a pool on the tiles. It was coagulating at the edges, like frost on a dark puddle. I touched her sad face. She was already turning cold. It was nine-seventeen by my watch.

Between the door and the pool of blood I found a faint brown hand-print still sticky to the touch. It was about the size of Dolly's hand. She could have fallen accidentally, but the thought twisted through my head that she was doing her best to be tried for murder. Which didn't necessarily mean that she was innocent.

Bradshaw leaned like a convalescent in the doorway. "Poor Helen. This is a heinous thing. Do you suppose the fellow who attacked us—?"

"I'd say she's been dead for at least two hours. Of course he may have come back to wipe out his traces or retrieve his gun. He acted guilty."

"He certainly did."

"Did Helen Haggerty ever mention Nevada?"

He looked surprised. "I don't believe so. Why?"

"The car our friend drove away in had a Nevada license."

"I see. Well, I suppose we must call the police."

"They'll resent it if we don't."

"Will you? I'm afraid I'm feeling rather shaken."

"It's better if you do, Bradshaw. She worked for the college, and you can keep the scandal to a minimum."

"Scandal? I hadn't even thought of that."

He forced himself to walk past her to the telephone on the far side of the room. I went through the other rooms quickly. One bedroom was completely bare except for a kitchen chair and a plain table which she had been using as a working desk. A sheaf of test papers conjugating French irregular verbs lay on top of the table. Piles of books, French and German dictionaries and grammars and collections of poetry and prose, stood around it. I opened one at the flyleaf. It was rubber-stamped in purple ink: Professor Helen Haggerty, Maple Park College, Maple Park, Illinois.

The other bedroom was furnished in rather fussy elegance with new French Provincial pieces, lambswool rugs on the polished tile floor, soft heavy handwoven drapes at the enormous window. The wardrobe contained a row of dresses and skirts with Magnin and Bullocks labels, and under them a row of new shoes to match. The chest of drawers was stuffed with sweaters and more intimate garments, but nothing really intimate. No letters, no snapshots.

The bathroom had wall-to-wall carpeting and a triangular sunken tub. The medicine chest was well supplied with beauty cream and cosmetics and sleeping pills. The latter had been prescribed by a Dr. Otto Schrenk and dispensed by Thompson's Drug Store in Bridgeton, Illinois, on June 17 of this year.

I turned out the bathroom wastebasket on the carpet. Under crumpled wads of used tissue I found a letter in an airmail envelope postmarked in Bridgeton, Illinois, a week ago and addressed to Mrs. Helen Haggerty. The single sheet inside was signed simply "Mother," and gave no return address.

Dear Helen

It was thoughtful of you to send me a card from sunny Cal my favorite state of the union even though it is years since I was out there. Your father keeps promising to make the trip with me on his vacation but something always comes up to put it off. Anyway his blood pressure is some better and that is a blessing. I'm glad you're well. I wish you would reconsider about the divorce but I suppose that's all over and done with. It's a pity you and Bert couldn't stay together. He is a good man in his way. But I suppose distant pastures look greenest.

Your father is still furious of course. He won't let me mention your name. He hasn't really forgiven you for when you left home in the first place, or forgiven himself either I guess, it takes two to make a quarrel. Still you are his daughter and you shouldn't have talked to him the way you did. I don't mean to recriminate. I keep hoping for a reconcilement between you two before he dies. He is not getting any younger, you know, and I'm not either, Helen. You're a smart girl with a good education and if you wanted to you could write him a letter that would make him feel different about "things." You are his only daughter after all and you've never taken it back that he was a crooked stormtrooper. That is a hard word for a policeman to swallow from anybody and it still rankles him after more than twenty years. Please write.

I put the letter back in the wastebasket with the other discarded paper. Then I washed my hands and returned to the main room. Bradshaw was sitting in the rope chair, stiffly formal even when alone. I wondered if this was his first experience of death. It wasn't mine by a long shot, but this death had hit me especially hard. I could have prevented it.

The fog outside was getting denser. It moved against the glass wall of the house, and gave me the queer sensation that the world had dropped away, and Bradshaw and I were floating together in space, unlikely *gemini* encapsulated with the dead woman.

"What did you tell the police?"

"I talked to the Sheriff personally. He'll be here shortly. I gave him only the necessary minimum. I didn't know whether or not to say anything about Mrs. Kincaid."

"We have to explain our discovery of the body. But you don't have to repeat anything she said. It's purely hearsay so far as you're concerned."

"Do you seriously regard her as a suspect in this?"

"I have no opinion yet. We'll see what Dr. Godwin has to say about her mental condition. I hope Godwin is good at his job."

"He's the best we have in town. I saw him tonight, oddly enough. He sat at the speaker's table with me at the Alumni dinner, until he was called away."

"He mentioned seeing you at dinner."

"Yes. Jim Godwin and I are old friends." He seemed to lean on the thought.

I looked around for something to sit on, but there was only Helen's canvas chaise. I squatted on my heels. One of the things in the house that puzzled me was the combination of lavish spending and bare poverty, as if two different women had taken turns furnishing it. A princess and a pauper.

I pointed this out to Bradshaw, and he nodded: "It struck me when I was here the other evening. She seems to have spent her money on inessentials."

"Where did the money come from?"

"She gave me to understand she had a private income. Heaven knows she didn't dress as she did on an assistant professor's salary."

"Did you know Professor Haggerty well?"

"Hardly. I did escort her to one or two college functions, as well as the opening concert of the fall season. We discovered a common passion for Hindemith." He made a steeple of his fingers. "She's a—she was a very presentable woman. But I wasn't close to her, in any sense. She didn't encourage intimacy."

I raised my eyebrows. Bradshaw colored slightly.

"I don't mean sexual intimacy, for heaven's sake. She wasn't my type at all. I mean that she didn't talk about herself to any extent."

"Where did she come from?"

"Some small college in the Middle West, Maple Park I believe. She'd already left there and come out here when we appointed her. It was an emergency appointment, necessitated by Dr. Farrand's coronary. Fortunately Helen was available. I don't know what our Department of Modern Languages will do now, with the semester already under way."

He sounded faintly resentful of the dead woman's absenteeism. While it was natural enough for him to be thinking of the college and its problems, I didn't like it. I said with deliberate intent to jolt him:

"You and the college are probably going to have worse problems than finding a teacher to take her place."

"What do you mean?"

"She wasn't an ordinary female professor. I spent some time with her this afternoon. She told me among other things that her life had been threatened."

"How dreadful," he said, as though the threat of murder were somehow worse than the fact. "Who on earth—?"

"She had no idea, and neither have I. I thought perhaps you might. Did she have enemies on the campus?"

"I certainly can't think of any. You understand, I didn't know Helen at all well."

"I got to know her pretty well, in a hurry. I gathered she'd had her share of experience, not all of it picked up in graduate seminars and faculty teas. Did you go into her background before you hired her?"

"Not too thoroughly. It was an emergency appointment, as I said, and in any case it wasn't my responsibility. The head of her department, Dr. Geisman, was favorably impressed by her credentials and made the appointment."

Bradshaw seemed to be delicately letting himself off the hook. I wrote down Geisman's name in my notebook.

"Her background ought to be gone into," I said. "It seems she was married, and recently divorced. I also want to find out more about her relations with Dolly. Apparently they were close."

"You're not suggesting a Lesbian attachment? We have had—" He decided not to finish the sentence.

"I'm not suggesting anything. I'm looking for information. How did Professor Haggerty happen to become Dolly's counselor?"

"In the normal way, I suppose."

"What is the normal way of acquiring a counselor?"

"It varies. Mrs. Kincaid was an upperclassman, and we usually permit upperclassmen to choose their own counselors, so long as the counselor in question has an opening in his or her schedule."

"Then Dolly probably chose Professor Haggerty, and initiated the friendship herself?"

"She had every chance to. Of course it may have been pure accident."

As if we had each received a signal on a common wavelength, we turned and looked at Helen Haggerty's body. It seemed small and lonely at the far end of the room. Our joint flight with it through cloudy space had been going on for a long time. I looked at my watch. It was only nine-thirty-one, fourteen minutes since our arrival. Time seemed to have slowed down, dividing itself into innumerable fractions, like Zeno's space or marijuana hours.

With a visible effort, Bradshaw detached his gaze from the body. His moment of communion with it had cost him the last of his boyish look. He leaned toward me with deep lines of puzzlement radiating from his eyes and mouth:

"I don't understand what Mrs. Kincaid said to you. Do you mean to say she actually confessed this—this murder?"

"A cop or a prosecutor might say so. Fortunately none was present. I've heard a lot of confessions, good ones and phony ones. Hers was a phony one, in my opinion."

"What about the blood?"

"She may have slipped and fallen in it."

"Then you don't think we should mention any of it to the Sheriff?"

"If you don't mind stretching a point."

His face showed that he minded, but after some hesitation he said: "We'll keep it to ourselves, at least for the present. After all she was a student of ours, however briefly."

Bradshaw didn't notice his use of the past tense, but I did, and it depressed me. I think we were both relieved by the sound of the Sheriff's car coming up the hill. It was accompanied by a mobile laboratory. Within a few minutes a fingerprint man and a deputy coroner and a photographer had taken over the room and changed its character. It became impersonal and drab like any room anywhere in which murder had been committed. In a curious way the men in uniform seemed to be doing the murder a second and final time, annulling Helen's rather garish aura, converting her into laboratory meat and courtroom exhibits. My raw nerves jumped when the bulbs flashed in her corner.

Sheriff Herman Crane was a thick-shouldered man in a tan gabardine suit. His only suggestion of uniform was a slightly broad-brimmed hat with a woven leather band. His voice had an administrative ring, and his manner had the heavy ease of a politician, poised between bullying and flattery. He treated Bradshaw with noisy deference, as if Bradshaw was a sensitive plant of undetermined value but some importance.

Me he treated the way cops always treated me, with occupational suspicion. They suspected me of the misdemeanor of doing my own thinking. I did succeed in getting Sheriff Crane to dispatch a patrol car in pursuit of the convertible with the Nevada license. He complained that his department was seriously understaffed, and he didn't think road blocks were indicated at this stage of the game. At this stage of the game I made up my mind not to cooperate fully with him.

The Sheriff and I sat in the chaise and the rope chair respectively and had a talk while a deputy who knew speed-writing took notes. I told him that Dolly Kincaid, the wife of a client of mine, had discovered the body of her college counselor Professor Haggerty and reported the discovery to me. She had been badly shocked, and was under a doctor's care.

Before the Sheriff could press me for further details, I gave him a *verbatim* account, or as close to *verbatim* as I could make it, of my conversation with Helen about the death threat. I mentioned that she had reported it to his office, and he seemed to take this as a criticism:

"We're understaffed, like I said. I can't keep experienced men. Los Angeles lures 'em away with salaries we can't pay and pie in the sky." I was from Los Angeles, as he knew, and the implication was that I was obscurely to blame. "If I put a man on guard duty in every house that got a crank telephone call, I wouldn't have anybody left to run the department."

"I understand that."

"I'm glad you do. Something I don't understand—how did this conversation you had with the decedent happen to take place?"

"Professor Haggerty approached me and asked me to come up here with her."

"What time was this?"

"I didn't check the time. It was shortly before sundown. I was here for about an hour."

"What did she have in mind?"

"She wanted me to stay with her, for protection. I'm sorry I didn't." Simply having the chance to say this made me feel better.

"You mean she wanted to hire you, as a bodyguard?"

"That was the idea." There was no use going into the complex interchange that had taken place between Helen and me, and failed.

"How did she know you were in the bodyguard business?"

"I'm not, exactly. She knew I was an investigator because she saw my name in the paper."

"Sure enough," he said. "You testified in the Perrine case this morning. Maybe I ought to congratulate you because Perrine got off."

"Don't bother."

"No, I don't think I will. The Perrine broad was guilty as hell and you know it and I know it."

"The jury didn't think so," I said mildly.

"Juries can be fooled and witnesses can be bought. Suddenly you're very active in our local crime circles, Mr. Archer." The words had the weight of an implied threat. He flung out a heavy careless hand toward the body. "This woman, this Professor Haggerty here, you're sure she wasn't a friend of yours?"

"We became friends to a certain extent."

"In an hour?"

"It can happen in an hour. Anyway, we had a previous conversation at the college today."

"What about before today? Did you have other previous conversations?"

"No. I met her today for the first time."

Bradshaw, who had been hanging around us in various anxious attitudes, spoke up: "I can vouch for the truth of that, Sheriff, if it will save you any time."

Sheriff Crane thanked him and turned back to me: "So it was a purely business proposition between her and you?"

"It would have been if I had been interested." I wasn't telling the precise truth, but there was no way to tell it to Crane without sounding foolish.

"You weren't interested. Why not?"

"I had other business."

"What other business?"

"Mrs. Kincaid had left her husband. He employed me to locate her."

"I heard something about that this morning. Did you find out why she left him?"

"No. My job was to locate her. I did."

"Where?"

I glanced up at Bradshaw. He gave me a reluctant nod. I said: "She's a student at the college."

"And now you say she's under a doctor's care? What doctor?"

"Dr. Godwin."

"The psychiatrist, eh?" The Sheriff uncrossed his heavy legs and leaned toward me confidentially. "What does she need a psychiatrist for? Is she out of her head?"

"She was hysterical. It seemed like a good idea to call one."

"Where is she now?"

I looked at Bradshaw again. He said: "At my house. My mother employed her as a driver."

The Sheriff got up with a rowing motion of his arms. "Let's get over there and talk to her."

"I'm afraid that won't be possible," Bradshaw said.

"Who says so?"

"I do, and I'm sure the doctor would concur."

"Naturally Godwin says what his patients pay him to say. I've had trouble with him before."

"I know that." Bradshaw had turned pale, but his voice was under rigid control. "You're not a professional man, Sheriff, and I rather doubt that you understand Dr. Godwin's code of ethics."

Crane reddened under the insult. He couldn't think of anything to say. Bradshaw went on:

"I very seriously doubt that Mrs. Kincaid can or should be questioned at the present time. What's the point of it? If she had anything to hide, she wouldn't have rushed to the nearest detective with her dreadful news. I'm sure we don't want to subject the girl to cruel and unusual punishment, simply for doing her duty as a citizen."

"What do you mean, cruel and unusual punishment? I'm not planning to third-degree her."

"I hope and trust you're not planning to go near the child tonight. That would be cruel and unusual punishment in my opinion, Sheriff, and I believe I speak for informed opinion in this county."

Crane opened his mouth to expostulate, perhaps realized the hopelessness of trying to outtalk Bradshaw, and shut it again. Bradshaw and I walked out unaccompanied. I said when we were out of hearing of the house:

"That was quite a job you did of facing down the Sheriff."

"I've always disliked that blustering bag of wind. Fortunately he's vulnerable. His majority slipped badly in the last election. A great many people in this county, including Dr. Godwin and myself, would like to see more enlightened and efficient law enforcement. And we may get it yet."

Nothing had changed visibly in the gatehouse. Dolly was still lying on the studio bed with her face turned to the wall. Bradshaw and I hesitated at the door. Walking with his head down, Alex crossed the room to speak to us.

"Dr. Godwin went up to the house to make a phone call. He thinks she ought to be in a nursing home, temporarily."

Dolly spoke in a monotone: "I know what you're saying. You might as well say it out loud. You want to put me away."

"Hush, darling." It was a brave word.

The girl relapsed into silence. She hadn't moved at all. Alex drew us outside, keeping the door open so that he could watch her. He said in a low voice:

"Dr. Godwin doesn't want to run the risk of suicide."

"It's that bad, eh?" I said.

"I don't think so. Neither does Dr. Godwin, really. He says it's simply a matter of taking reasonable security precautions. I told him I could sit up with her, but he doesn't think I should try to do it myself."

"You shouldn't," Bradshaw said. "You'll need to have something left for to-morrow."

"Yeah. Tomorrow." Alex kicked at the rusty boot-scraper attached to the side of the doorstep. "I better call Dad. Tomorrow's a Saturday, he ought to be able to come."

Footsteps approached from the direction of the main house. A big man in an alligator coat emerged from the fog, his bald head gleaming in the light from the doorway. He greeted Bradshaw warmly:

"Hello, Roy. I enjoyed your speech, what I heard of it. You'll elevate us yet into the Athens of the West. Unfortunately a patient dragged me out in the middle of it. She wanted to know if it was safe for her to see a Tennessee Williams movie all by herself. She really wanted me to go along with her and protect her from bad thoughts." He turned to me. "Mr. Archer? I'm Dr. Godwin."

We shook hands. He gave me a look of lingering intensity, as if he was going to paint my portrait from memory. Godwin had a heavy, powerful face, with eyes that changed from bright to dark like lamps being turned down. He had authority, which he was being careful not to use.

"I'm glad you called me. Miss McGee—Mrs. Kincaid needed something to calm her down." He glanced in through the doorway. "I hope she's feeling better now."

"She's much quieter," Alex said. "Don't you think it will be all right for her to stay here with me?"

Godwin made a commiserating face. His mouth was very flexible, like an actor's. "It wouldn't be wise, Mr. Kincaid. I've made arrangements for a bed in a nursing home I use. We don't want to take any chances with her life."

"But why should she try to kill herself?"

"She has a lot on her mind, poor girl. I always pay attention to suicide threats, or even the slightest hint of them."

"Have you found out just what she does have on her mind?" Bradshaw said.

"She didn't want to talk much. She's very tired. It can wait till morning."

"I hope so," Bradshaw said. "The Sheriff wants to question her about the shooting. I did my best to hold him off."

Godwin's mobile face became grave. "There actually has been a murder then? Another murder?"

"One of our new professors, Helen Haggerty, was shot in her home tonight. Mrs. Kincaid apparently stumbled on the body."

"She's had dreadful luck." Godwin looked up at the low sky. "I sometimes feel as though the gods have turned their backs on certain people."

I asked him to explain what he meant. He shook his head: "I'm much too tired to tell you the bloody saga of the McGees. A lot of it has faded out of my memory, mercifully. Why don't you ask the courthouse people for the details?"

"That wouldn't be a good idea, under the circumstances."

"It wouldn't, would it? You can see how tired I am. By the time I get my patient safely disposed of for the night I'll have just enough energy left to make it home and to bed."

"We still need to talk, doctor."

"What about?"

I didn't like to say it in front of Alex but I said it, watching him: "The possibility that she committed this second murder, or let's say the possibility that she'll be accused of it. She seems to want to be."

Alex rose to her defense: "She was out of her head, temporarily, and you can't use what she said—"

Godwin laid a hand on his shoulder. "Take it easy, Mr. Kincaid. We can't settle anything now. What we all need is a night's sleep—especially your wife. I want you to come along with me to the nursing home in case I need help with her on the way. You," he said to me, "can follow along in your car and bring him back. You'll want to know where the nursing home is, anyway, because I'll meet you there tomorrow morning at eight, after I've had an opportunity to talk to Mrs. Kincaid. Got that?"

"Tomorrow morning at eight."

He turned to Bradshaw. "Roy, if I were you I'd go and see how Mrs. Bradshaw is feeling. I gave her a sedative, but she's alarmed. She thinks, or pretends to think, that she's surrounded by maniacal assassins. You can talk her out of it better than I could."

Godwin seemed to be a wise and careful man. At any rate, his authority imposed itself. All three of us did as he said.

So did Dolly. Propped between him and Alex, she came out to his car. She didn't struggle or make a sound, but she walked as though she was on her way to the execution chamber.

10

An hour later I was sitting on one of the twin beds in my motel room. There was nothing more I could do right now, except possibly stir up trouble if I went for information to the local authorities. But my mind kept projecting on the plaster wall rapid movies of actions I could be performing. Run down Begley-McGee. Capture the man from Nevada.

I shut off the violent images with an effort of will and forced myself to think about Zeno, who said that Achilles could never traverse the space between him and the tortoise. It was a soothing thought, if you were a tortoise, or maybe even if you were Achilles.

I had a pint of whisky in my bag. I was getting it out of its sock when I thought of Arnie Walters, a Reno colleague of mine who had split more than one pint with me. I put in a long-distance call to his office, which happened to be the front room of his house. Arnie was at home.

"Walters Detective Agency," he said in a reluctant midnight voice.

"This is Lew Archer."

"Oh. Good. I didn't really want to go to bed. I was only modeling my pajamas."

"Irony isn't your forte, so drop it. All I'm asking for is a small service which I will repay in kind at the earliest opportunity. Are you recording?"

I heard the click of the machine, and told it and Arnie about Helen's death. "A couple of hours after the shooting, the man I'm interested in came out of the murder house and drove away in a black or dark blue convertible, I think a late-model Ford, with a Nevada license. I think I got the first four figures—"

"You think?"

"It's foggy here, and it was dark. First four figures are probably FT37. The subject is young and athletic, height about five-eleven, wearing a dark topcoat and dark snap-brim fedora. I couldn't make out his face."

"Have you seen your oculist lately?"

"You can do better than that, Arnie. Try."

"I hear senior citizens can get free glaucoma tests nowadays."

Arnie was older than I was, but he didn't like to have this pointed out. "What's bugging you? Trouble with the wife?"

"No trouble," he said cheerfully. "She's waiting for me in bed."

"Give Phyllis my love."

"I'll give her my own. In case I come up with anything, which seems unlikely in view of the fragmentary information, where do I contact you?"

"I'm staying at the Mariner's Rest Motel in Pacific Point. But you better call my answering service in Hollywood."

He said he would. As I hung up, I heard a gentle tapping on my door. It turned out to be Alex. He had pulled on his trousers over his pajamas.

"I heard you talking in here."

"I was on the phone."

"I didn't mean to interrupt."

"I'm through phoning. Come in and have a drink."

He entered the room cautiously, as if it might be boobytrapped. In the last few hours his movements had become very tentative. His bare feet made no sound on the carpet.

The bathroom cupboard contained two glasses wrapped in wax paper. I unwrapped and filled them. We sat on the twin beds, drinking to nothing in particular. We faced each other like mirror images separated by an invisible wall of glass.

I was conscious of the differences between us, particularly of Alex's youth and lack of experience. He was at the age when everything hurts.

"I was thinking of calling Dad," he said. "Now I don't know whether I should or not."

There was another silence.

"He won't say 'I told you so,' in so many words. But that will be the general idea. Fools rush in where angels fear to tread and all that jazz."

"I think it makes just as much sense if you reverse it. Angels rush in where fools are afraid to tread. Not that I know any angels."

He got the message. "You don't think I'm a fool?"

"You've handled yourself very well."

"Thank you," he said formally. "Even if it isn't actually true."

"It is, though. It must have taken some doing."

Whisky and the beginnings of human warmth had dissolved the glass wall between us. "The worst of it," he said, "was when I put her in the nursing home just now. I felt as if I was—you know, consigning her to oblivion. The place is like something out of Dante, with people crying and groaning. Dolly's a sensitive girl. I don't see how she'll be able to take it."

"She can take it better than some other things, such as wandering around loose in her condition."

"You think she's insane, don't you?"

"What I think doesn't matter. We'll get an expert opinion tomorrow. There's no doubt she's temporarily off base. I've seen people further off, and I've seen them come back."

"You think she'll be all right then?"

He'd grabbed at what I said like a flying trapeze and swung up into hopefulness. Which I didn't think ought to be encouraged:

"I'm more concerned about the legal situation than the psychiatric one."

"You can't really believe she killed this friend of hers—Helen? I know she said so, but it isn't possible. You see, I know Dolly. She isn't aggressive at all. She's one of the really pro-life people. She doesn't even like to kill a spider."

"It is possible, Alex, and that was all I said. I wanted Godwin to be aware of the possibility from the start. He's in a position to do a lot for your wife."

Alex said, "My wife," with a kind of wonder.

"She is your wife, legally. But nobody would consider that you owe her much. You have an out, if you want to use it."

The whisky slopped in his glass. I think he barely restrained himself from throwing it in my face.

"I'm not going to ditch her," he said. "If you think I ought to, you can go to hell."

I hadn't liked him thoroughly until now. "Somebody had to mention the fact that you have an out. A lot of people would take it."

"I'm not a lot of people."

"So I gather."

"Dad would probably call me a fool, but I don't care if she's guilty of murder. I'm staying."

"It's going to cost money."

"You want more money, is that it?"

"I can wait. So can Godwin. I was thinking about the future. Also there's the strong possibility that you'll need a lawyer tomorrow."

"What for?" He was a good boy, but a little slow on the uptake.

"Judging by tonight, your main problem is going to be to prevent Dolly from talking herself into deep trouble. That means keeping her out of the hands of the authorities, in a place where she can be properly looked after. A good lawyer can be a help in that. Lawyers generally don't wait for their money in criminal cases."

"Do you really think she's in such danger—such legal jeopardy? Or are you just trying to put the iron in my soul?"

"I talked to the local sheriff tonight, and I didn't like the gleam in his eye when we got on the subject of Dolly. Sheriff Crane isn't stupid. He knew that I was holding back on him. He's going to bear down on her when he catches on to the family connection."

"The family connection?"

"The fact that her father murdered her mother." It was cruel to hit him with it again, on top of everything else. Still it was better for him to hear it from me than from the dreary voice that talks from under the twisted pillow at three o'clock in the morning. "Apparently he was tried and convicted in the local courts. Sheriff Crane probably gathered the evidence for the prosecution."

"It's almost as though history is repeating itself." There was something approaching awe in Alex's voice. "Did I hear you say that this Chuck Begley character, the man with the beard, is actually her father?"

"He seems to be."

"He was the one who started the whole thing off," he said, as much to himself as to me. "It was after he visited her that Sunday that she walked out on me. What do you think happened between them, to make her do that?"

"I don't know, Alex. Maybe he bawled her out for testifying against him. In any case he brought back the past. She couldn't handle the old mess and her new marriage together, so she left you."

"I still don't get it," he said. "How could Dolly have a father like that?"

"I'm not a geneticist. But I do know most non-professional killers aren't criminal types. I intend to find out more about Begley-McGee and his murder. I suppose it's no use asking if Dolly ever talked about it to you?"

"She never said a word about either of her parents, except that they were dead. Now I can understand why. I don't blame her for lying—" He cut the sentence short, and amended it: "I mean, for not telling me certain things."

"She made up for it tonight."

"Yeah. It's been quite a night." He nodded several times, as though he was still absorbing its repercussions. "Tell me the honest truth, Mr. Archer. Do you believe the things she said about being responsible for this woman's death? And her mother?"

"I can't even remember half of them."

"That's not an answer."

"Maybe we'll get some better answers tomorrow. It's a complex world. The human mind is the most complex thing in it."

"You don't give me much comfort."

"It's not my job to."

Making a bitter face over this and the last of his whisky, he rose slowly. "Well, you need your sleep, and I have a phone call to make. Thanks for the drink." He turned with his hand on the doorknob. "And thanks for the conversation."

"Any time. Are you going to call your father?"

"No. I've decided not to."

I felt vaguely gratified. I was old enough to be his father, with no son of my own, and that may have had something to do with my feeling.

"Who are you going to call, or is that a private matter?"

"Dolly asked me to try and get in touch with her Aunt Alice. I guess I've been putting it off. I don't know what to say to her aunt. I didn't even know she had an Aunt Alice until tonight."

"I remember she mentioned her. When did Dolly ask you to make the call?"

"In the nursing home, the last thing. She wants her aunt to come and see her. I didn't know if that was a good idea or not."

"It would depend on the aunt. Does she live here in town?"

"She lives in the Valley, in Indian Springs. Dolly said she's in the county directory. Miss Alice Jenks."

"Let's try her."

I found her name and number in the phone book, placed the toll call, and handed the receiver to Alex. He sat on the bed, looking at the instrument as if he had never seen one before.

"What am I going to say to her?"

"You'll know what to say. I want to talk to her when you're finished."

A voice rasped from the receiver: "Yes? Who is this?"

"I'm Alex Kincaid. Is that Miss Jenks? . . . We don't know each other, Miss Jenks, but I married your niece a few weeks ago . . . Your niece, Dolly McGee. We were married a few weeks ago, and she's come down with a rather serious illness . . . No, it's more emotional. She's emotionally disturbed, and she wants to see you. She's in the Whitmore Nursing Home here in Pacific Point. Dr. Godwin is looking after her."

He paused again. There was sweat on his forehead. The voice at the other end went on for some time.

"She says she can't come tomorrow," he said to me; and into the receiver: "Perhaps Sunday would be possible? . . . Yes, fine. You can contact me at the Mariner's Rest Motel, or . . . Alex Kincaid. I'll look forward to meeting you."

"Let me talk to her," I said.

"Just a minute, Miss Jenks. The gentleman here with me, Mr. Archer, has something to say to you." He handed over the receiver.

"Hello, Miss Jenks."

"Hello, Mr. Archer. And who are you, may I ask, at one o'clock in the morning?" It wasn't a light question. The woman sounded anxious and irritated, but she had both feelings under reasonable control.

"I'm a private detective. I'm sorry to disrupt your sleep with this, but there's more to the situation than simple emotional illness. A woman has been murdered here."

She gasped, but made no other comment.

"Your niece is a material witness to the murder. She may be more deeply involved than that, and in any case she's going to need support. So far as I know you're her only relative, apart from her father—"

"You can leave him out. He doesn't count. He never has, except in a negative way." Her voice was flat and harsh. "Who was killed?"

"A friend and counselor of your niece's, Professor Helen Haggerty."

"I never heard of the woman," she said with combined impatience and relief.

"You'll be hearing a great deal about her, if you're at all interested in your niece. Are you close to her?"

"I was, before she grew away from me. I brought her up after her mother's death." Her voice became flat again: "Does Tom McGee have anything to do with this new killing?"

"He may have. He's in town here, or he was."

"I knew it!" she cried in bleak triumph. "They had no business letting him out. They should have put him in the gas chamber for what he did to my little sister."

She was choked with sudden emotion. I waited for her to go on. When she didn't, I said:

"I'm anxious to go into the details of that case with you, but I don't think we should do it over the phone. It really would be helpful if you could come here tomorrow."

"I simply can't. There's no use badgering me. I have a terribly important meeting tomorrow afternoon. Several state officials will be here from Sacramento, and it will probably go on into the evening."

"What about the morning?"

"I have to prepare for them in the morning. We're shifting over to a new state-county welfare program." Latent hysteria buzzed in her voice, the hysteria of a middle-aged spinster who has to make a change. "If I walked out on this project, I could lose my position."

"We don't want that to happen, Miss Jenks. How far is it from there to Pacific Point?"

"Seventy miles, but I tell you I can't make it."

"I can. Will you give me an hour in the morning, say around eleven?"

She hesitated. "Yes, if it's important. I'll get up an hour earlier and do my paperwork. I'll be home at eleven. You have my address? It's just off the main street of Indian Springs."

I thanked her and got rid of Alex and went to bed, setting my mental alarm for six-thirty.

11

Alex was still sleeping when I was ready to leave in the morning. I let him sleep, partly for selfish reasons, and partly because sleep was kinder to him than waking was likely to be.

The fog was thick outside. Its watery mass overlay Pacific Point and transformed it into a kind of suburb of the sea. I drove out of the motel enclosure into a gray world without perspective, came abruptly to an access ramp, descended onto the freeway where headlights swam in pairs like deep-sea fish, and arrived at a truck stop on the east side without any real sense that I had driven across the city.

I'd been having a little too much talk with people whose business was talking. It was good to sit at the counter of a working-class restaurant where men spoke when they wanted something, or simply to kid the waitress. I kidded her a little myself. Her name was Stella, and she was so efficient that she threatened to take the place of automation. She said with a flashing smile that this was her aim in life.

My destination was near the highway, on a heavily used thoroughfare lined mainly with new apartment buildings. Their faddish pastel colors and scant transplanted palms seemed dingy and desolate in the fog.

The nursing home was a beige stucco one-storied building taking up most of a narrow deep lot. I rang the bell at eight o'clock precisely. Dr. Godwin must have been waiting behind the door. He unlocked it and let me in himself.

"You're a punctual man, Mr. Archer."

His changeable eyes had taken the stony color of the morning. I noticed when he turned to shut the door behind us that his shoulders were permanently stooped. He was wearing a fresh white smock.

"Sit down, won't you? This is as good a place to talk as any."

We were in a small reception room or lounge. I sat in one of several worn armchairs aimed at a silent television set in one corner. Through the inner door I could hear the rattle of dishes and the bright voices of nurses beginning the day.

"Is this your place, doctor?"

"I have an interest in it. Most of the patients here are mine. I've just been giving some shock treatments." He smoothed the front of his smock. "I'd feel less like a witch-doctor if I knew why electric shocks make depressed people feel better. So much of our science, or art, is still in the empirical stage. But the people do get better," he said with a sudden grin, too sudden to touch his watching, waiting eyes.

"Is Dolly?"

"Yes, I think she's somewhat better. We don't have overnight cures, of course. I want to keep an eye on her for at least a week. Here."

"Is she fit to be questioned?"

"I don't want you to question her, or anyone else remotely connected with the —the world of crime and punishment." As if to remove the curse from his refusal, he flung himself loosely into the armchair beside me, asked me for a cigarette and let me light it.

"Why not?"

"I do not love the law in its current primitive state, where sick people are trapped into betraying themselves in their sickness and then treated by the courts as if they were well. I've been fighting the situation for a long time." He rested his ponderous bald head on the back of the chair, and blew smoke toward the ceiling.

"What you say suggests that Dolly is in danger from the law."

"I was making a general statement."

"Which applied specifically to Dolly. We don't have to play games, doctor. We're both on the same side. I don't assume the girl is guilty of anything. I do think she has information which may help me to clear up a murder."

"But what if she's guilty?" he said, watching for my reaction.

"Then I'd want to cooperate with you in getting charges reduced, finding mitigating circumstances, making a case for merciful treatment by the court. Remember I'm working for her husband. Is she guilty?"

"I don't know."

"You have talked to her this morning?"

"She did most of the talking. I don't ask many questions. I wait and I listen. In the end you learn more that way." He gave me a meaningful look, as if I should start applying this principle.

I waited and listened. Nothing happened. A plump woman with long black hair straggling down the back of her cotton robe appeared in the inside doorway. She stretched out her arms to the doctor.

He lifted his hand like a weary king. "Good morning, Nell."

She gave him a bright agonized smile and softly withdrew, like a woman walking backward in her sleep. Her outstretched arms were the last I saw of her.

"It would be helpful if you told me what Dolly had to say this morning."

"And possibly dangerous." Godwin crushed out his cigarette in a blue ceramic ashtray which looked homemade. "There is after all a difference between you and me. What a patient says to me is a professional confidence. You have no professional standing. If you refused to repeat information in court you could be jailed for contempt. I could, under the law, but I'm not likely to be."

"I've sweated out contempt before. And the police won't get anything out of me that I don't choose to tell them. That's a guarantee."

"Very well." Godwin nodded his head once, decisively. "I'm concerned about Dolly and I'll try to tell you why without any professional jargon. You may be able to put together the objective jigsaw puzzle while I'm reconstructing the subjective one."

"You said no professional jargon, doctor."

"Sorry. First there's her history. Her mother Constance McGee brought her to me at the instigation of her sister Alice, a woman I know slightly, when Dolly was ten years old. She wasn't a happy child. In fact she was in some danger of becoming really withdrawn, for good reason. There's always good reason. Her father McGee was an irresponsible and violent man who couldn't handle the duties of fatherhood. He blew hot and cold on the child, spoiled her and punished her, constantly fought with his wife and eventually left her, or was left, it hardly matters. I would have preferred to treat him instead of Dolly, since he was the main source of the trouble in the family. But he was unreachable."

"Did you ever see him?"

"He wouldn't even come in for an interview," Godwin said with regret. "If I could have reached him, I might have been able to prevent a murder. Perhaps not. From what I've been told he was a severely maladjusted man who needed help but never got it. You can understand my bitterness about the gap between psychiatry and the law. People like McGee are allowed to run around loose, without preventive action of any kind, until they commit a crime. Then of course they're hauled into court and sent away for ten or twenty years. But not to a hospital. To a prison."

"McGee's out now. He's been in town here. Did you know that?"

"Dolly told me this morning. It's one of the many severe pressures on her. You can understand how a sensitive child brought up in an atmosphere of violence and instability would be plagued by anxiety and guilt. The worst guilt often arises when a child is forced, by sheer instinctive self-preservation, to turn against her parents. A clinical psychologist I work with helped Dolly to express her feelings in clay and doll-play and so on. There wasn't too much I could do for her myself, since children don't have the mental equipment to be analyzed. But I did try to assume the role of the calm and patient father, provide some of the stability that was missing in her young life. And she was doing pretty well, until the disaster occurred."

"You mean the murder?"

He swung his head in sorrow. "McGee worked himself into a self-pitying rage one night, came to the aunt's house in Indian Springs where they were staying, and shot Constance through the heart. Dolly was alone in the house with her mother. She heard the shot and saw McGee taking off. Then she discovered the body."

His head went on swinging slowly like a heavy silent bell. I said:

"What was her reaction at the time?"

"I don't know. One of the peculiar difficulties of my work is that I often have to perform a public function with private means. I can't go out and lasso patients. Dolly never came back to me. She no longer had her mother to bring her in from the Valley, and Miss Jenks, her aunt, is a busy woman."

"But didn't you say that Alice Jenks suggested treatment for Dolly in the first place?"

"She did. She also paid for it. Perhaps with all the trouble in the family she felt she couldn't afford it any longer. At any rate, I didn't see Dolly again until last night, with one exception. I went to court the day she testified against McGee. As a matter of fact I bearded the judge in his chambers and told him that it shouldn't be allowed. But she was a key witness, and they had her aunt's permission, and they put her through her sad little paces. She acted like a pale little automaton lost in a world of hostile adults."

His large body trembled with feeling. His hands burrowed under his smock, searching for a cigarette. I gave him one and lit it, and lit one for myself.

"What did she say in court?"

"It was very short and simple. I suspect that she was thoroughly rehearsed. She heard the shot and looked out her bedroom window and saw her father running away with the gun in his hand. One other question had to do with whether McGee had threatened Constance with bodily harm. He had. That was all."

"You're sure?"

"Yes. This isn't my unaided recollection, as they say. I took written notes at the time, and I scanned them this morning."

"Why?"

"They're part of her history, evidently a crucial part." He blew out smoke and looked at me through it, long and cautiously.

I said: "Does she tell a different story now?"

His face was working with complex passions. He was a man of feeling, and Dolly was his office daughter lost for many years.

"She tells an absurd story," he burst out. "I not only can't believe it, I can't believe that she believes it. She isn't that sick."

He paused, drawing deep on his cigarette, trying to get himself under full control. I waited and listened. This time he did go on:

"She claims now that she didn't see McGee that night, and that in fact he had nothing to do with the murder. She says she lied on the witness stand because the various adults wanted her to."

"Why would she say that now?"

"I don't pretend to understand her. After an interval of ten years we've naturally lost what rapport we had. And of course she hasn't forgiven me for what she considers my betrayal—my failure to look after her in the disaster. But what could I do? I couldn't go to Indian Springs and kidnap her out of her aunt's house."

"You care about your patients, doctor."

"Yes. I care. It keeps me tired." He stubbed his cigarette in the ceramic ashtray. "Nell made this ashtray, by the way. It's rather good for a first attempt."

I murmured something in agreement. Above the subsiding clamor of dishes, a wild old complaining voice rose in the depths of the building.

"That story of hers," I said, "may not be so very absurd. It fits in with the fact that McGee visited her on the second day of her honeymoon and hit her so hard with something that it knocked her right off the tracks."

"You're acute, Mr. Archer. That's precisely what happened. He treated her to a long tirade on the subject of his innocence. You mustn't forget that she loved her father, however ambivalently. He was able to convince her that her memory was at fault, that he was innocent and she was guilty. Childhood memories are powerfully influenced by emotion."

"That she was guilty of perjury, you mean?"

"Murder." He leaned toward me. "She told me this morning she killed her mother herself."

"With a gun?"

"With her tongue. That's the absurd part. She claims she killed her mother and her friend, Helen, and sent her father to prison into the bargain, all with her poisonous tongue."

"Does she explain what she means by that?"

"She hasn't yet. It's an expression of guilt which may be only superficially connected with these murders."

"You mean she's using the murders to unload guilt which she feels about something else?"

"More or less. It's a common enough mechanism. I know for a fact that she didn't kill her mother, or lie about her father, essentially. I'm certain McGee was guilty."

"Courts can make mistakes, even in a capital case."

He said with a kind of muted arrogance: "I know more about that case than ever came out in court."

"From Dolly?"

"From various sources."

"I'd be obliged if you'd let me in on it."

His eyes veiled themselves. "I can't do that. I have to respect the confidences of my patients. But you can take my word for it that McGee killed his wife."

"Then what's Dolly feeling so guilty about?"

"I'm sure that will come out, in time. It probably has to do with her resentment against her parents. It's natural she'd want to punish them for the ugly failure of their marriage. She may well have fantasied her mother's death, her father's imprisonment, before those things emerged into reality. When the poor child's vengeful dreams came true, how else could she feel but guilty? McGee's tirade the other weekend stirred up the old feelings, and then this dreadful accident last night—" He ran out of words and spread his hands, palms upward and fingers curling, on his heavy thighs.

"The Haggerty shooting was no accident, doctor. The gun is missing, for one thing."

"I realize that. I was referring to Dolly's discovery of the body, which was certainly accidental."

"I wonder. She blames herself for that killing, too. I don't see how you can explain that in terms of childhood resentments."

"I wasn't attempting to." There was irritation in his voice. It made him pull a little professional rank on me: "Nor is there any need for you to understand the psychic situation. You stick to the objective facts, and I'll handle the subjective." He softened this with a bit of philosophy: "Objective and subjective, the outer world and the inner, do correspond of course. But sometimes you have to follow the parallel lines almost to infinity before they touch."

"Let's stick to the objective facts then. Dolly said she killed Helen Haggerty with her poisonous tongue. Is that all she said on the subject?"

"There was more, a good deal more, of a rather confused nature. Dolly seems to feel that her friendship with Miss Haggerty was somehow responsible for the latter's death."

"The two women were friends?"

"I'd say so, yes, though there was twenty years' difference in their ages. Dolly confided in her, poured out everything, and Miss Haggerty reciprocated. Apparently she'd had severe emotional problems involving her own father, and she couldn't resist the parallel with Dolly. They both let down their back hair. It wasn't a healthy situation," he said dryly.

"Does she have anything to say about Helen's father?"

"Dolly seems to think he was a crooked policeman involved in a murder, but that may be sheer fantasy—a kind of secondary image of her own father."

"It isn't. Helen's father is a policeman, and Helen at least regarded him as a crook."

"How in the world would you know that?"

"I read a letter from her mother on the subject. I'd like to have a chance to talk to her parents."

"Why don't you?"

"They live in Bridgeton, Illinois."

It was a long jump, but not so long as the jump my mind made into blank possibility. I had handled cases which opened up gradually like fissures in the firm ground of the present, cleaving far down through the strata of the past. Perhaps Helen's murder was connected with an obscure murder in Illinois more than twenty years ago, before Dolly was born. It was a wishful thought, and I didn't mention it to Dr. Godwin.

"I'm sorry I can't be more help to you," he was saying. "I have to go now, I'm already overdue for my hospital rounds."

The sound of a motor detached itself from the traffic in the street, and slowed down. A car door was opened and closed. Men's footsteps came up the walk. Moving quickly for a big man, Godwin opened the door before they rang.

I couldn't see who his visitors were, but they were unwelcome ones. Godwin went rigid with hostility.

"Good morning, Sheriff," he said.

Crane responded folksily: "It's a hell of a morning and you know it. September's supposed to be our best month, but the bloody fog's so thick the airport's socked in."

"You didn't come here to discuss the weather."

"That's right, I didn't. I heard you got a fugitive from justice holed up here."

"Where did you hear that?"

"I have my sources."

"You'd better fire them, Sheriff. They're giving you misleading information."

"Somebody is, doctor. Are you denying that Mrs. Dolly Kincaid née McGee is in this building?"

Godwin hesitated. His heavy jaw got heavier. "She is."

"You said a minute ago she wasn't. What are you trying to pull, doc?"

"What are you trying to pull? Mrs. Kincaid is not a fugitive. She's here because she's ill."

"I wonder what made her ill. Can't she stand the sight of blood?"

Godwin's lips curled outward. He looked ready to spit in the other man's face. I couldn't see the Sheriff from where I sat, and I made no attempt to. I thought it was best for me to stay out of sight.

"It isn't just the weather that makes it a lousy day, doc. We had a lousy murder in town last night. I guess you know that, too. Probably Mrs. Kincaid told you all about it."

"Are you accusing her?" Godwin said.

"I wouldn't say that. Not yet, anyway."

"Then beat it."

"You can't talk like that to me."

Godwin held himself motionless but his breath shook him as though he had a racing engine inside of him. "You accused me in the presence of witnesses of harboring a fugitive from justice. I could sue you for slander and by God I will if you don't stop harassing me and my patients."

"I didn't mean it that way." Crane's voice was much less confident. "Anyway, I got a right to question a witness."

"At some later time perhaps you have. At the present time Mrs. Kincaid is under heavy sedation. I can't permit her to be questioned for at least a week."

"A week?"

"It may be longer. I strongly advise you not to press the point. I'm prepared to go before a judge and certify that police questioning at the present time would endanger her health and perhaps her life."

"I don't believe it."

"I don't care what you believe."

Godwin slammed the door and leaned on it, breathing like a runner. A couple of white-uniformed nurses who had been peeking through the inner door tried to look as if they had business there. He waved them away.

I said with unfeigned admiration: "You really went to bat for her."

"They did enough damage to her when she was a child. They're not going to compound it if I can help it."

"How did they know she was here?"

"I have no idea. I can usually trust the staff to keep their mouths shut." He gave me a probing look. "Did you tell anyone?"

"Nobody connected with the law. Alex did mention to Alice Jenks that Dolly was here."

"Perhaps he shouldn't have. Miss Jenks has worked for the county a long time, and Crane and she were old acquaintances."

"She wouldn't tattle on her own niece, would she?"

"I don't know what she'd do." Godwin tore off his smock and threw it at the chair where I had been sitting. "Well, shall I let you out?"

He shook his keys like a jailer.

12

About halfway up the pass road I came out into sunlight. The fog below was like a sea of white water surging into the inlets of the mountains. From the summit of the pass, where I paused for a moment, further mountains were visible on the inland horizon.

The wide valley between was full of light. Cattle grazed among the live oaks on the hillsides. A covey of quail marched across the road in front of my car like small plumed tipsy soldiers. I could smell newmown hay, and had the feeling that I had dropped down into a pastoral scene where nothing much had changed in a hundred years.

The town of Indian Springs didn't entirely dispel the feeling, though it had its service stations and its drive-ins offering hamburgers and tacos. It had a bit of old-time Western atmosphere, and more than a bit of the old-time sun-baked poverty of the West. Prematurely aging women watched over their brown children in the dooryards of crumbling adobes. Most of the loiterers in the main street had Indian faces under their broad-brimmed hats. Banners advertising Old Rodeo Days hung limply over their heads.

Alice Jenks lived in one of the best houses on what appeared to be the best street. It was a two-storied white frame house, with deep porches upstairs and down, standing far back from the street behind a smooth green lawn. I stepped onto the grass and leaned on a pepper tree, fanning myself with my hat. I was five minutes early.

A rather imposing woman in a blue dress came out on the veranda. She looked me over as if I might possibly be a burglar cleverly creeping up on her house at eleven o'clock in the morning. She came down the steps and along the walk toward me. The sun flashed on her glasses and lent her searchlight eyes.

Close up, she wasn't so alarming. The brown eyes behind the glasses were strained and anxious. Her hair was streaked with gray. Her mouth was unexpectedly generous and even soft, but it was tweezered like a live thing between the harsh lines that thrust down from the base of her nose. The stiff blue dress that curved like armor plate over her monolithic bosom was old-fashioned in cut, and gave her a dowdy look. The valley sun had parched and roughened her skin.

"Are you Mr. Archer?"

"Yes. How are you, Miss Jenks?"

"I'll survive." Her handshake was like a man's. "Come up on the porch, we can talk there."

Her movements, like her speech, were so abrupt that they suggested the jitters. The jitters under firm, perhaps lifelong, control. She motioned me into a canvas glider and sat on a reed chair facing me, her back to the street. Three Mexican boys on one battered bicycle rode by precariously like high-wire artists.

"I don't know just what you want from me, Mr. Archer. My niece appears to be in very serious trouble. I talked to a friend in the courthouse this morning—"

"The Sheriff?"

"Yes. He seems to think that Dolly is hiding from him."

"Did you tell Sheriff Crane where she was?"

"Yes. Shouldn't I have?"

"He trotted right over to the nursing home to question her. Dr. Godwin wouldn't let him."

"Dr. Godwin is a great one for taking matters into his own hands. I don't believe myself that people in trouble should be coddled and swaddled in cotton wool, and what I believe for the rest of the world holds true for my own family. We've always been a law-abiding family, and if Dolly is holding something back, she ought to come out with it. I say let the truth be told, and the chips fall where they may."

It was quite a speech. She seemed to be renewing her old disagreement with Godwin about Dolly's testimony at the trial.

"Those chips can fall pretty hard, sometimes, when they fall on people you love."

She watched me, her sensitive mouth held tight, as if I had accused her of a weakness. "People I love?"

I had only an hour, and no sure intuition of how to reach her. "I'm assuming you love Dolly."

"I haven't seen her lately—she seems to have turned against me—but I'll always be fond of her. That doesn't mean"—and the deep lines reasserted themselves at the corners of her mouth—"that I'll condone any wrongdoing on her part. I have a public position—"

"Just what is your position?"

"I'm senior county welfare worker for this area," she announced. Then she looked anxiously behind her at the empty street, as if a posse might be on its way to relieve her of her post.

"Welfare begins at home."

"Are you instructing me in the conduct of my private life?" She didn't wait for an answer. "Let me tell you, you don't have to. Who do you think took the child in when my sister's marriage broke up? I did, of course. I gave them both a home, and after my sister was killed I brought my niece up as if she was my own daughter. I gave her the best of food and clothes, the best of education. When she wanted her own independence, I gave her that, too. I gave her the money to go and study in Los Angeles. What more could I do for her?"

"You can give her the benefit of the doubt right now. I don't know what the Sheriff said to you, but I'm pretty sure he was talking through his little pointed hat."

Her face hardened. "Sheriff Crane does not make mistakes."

I had the sense of doubleness again, of talking on two levels. On the surface we were talking about Dolly's connection with the Haggerty killing but underneath this, though McGee had not been mentioned, we were arguing the question of McGee's guilt.

"All policemen make mistakes," I said. "All human beings make mistakes. It's even possible that you and Sheriff Crane and the judge and the twelve jurors and everybody else were mistaken about Thomas McGee, and convicted an innocent man."

She laughed in my face, not riotously. "That's ridiculous, you didn't know Tom McGee. He was capable of anything. Ask anybody in this town. He used to get drunk and come home and beat her. More than once I had to stand him off with a gun, with the child holding onto my legs. More than once, after Constance left him, he came to this house and battered on the door and said he would drag her out of here by the hair. But I wouldn't let him." She shook her head vehemently, and a strand of iron-gray hair fell like twisted wire across her cheek.

"What did he want from her?"

"He wanted domination. He wanted her under his thumb. But he had no right to her. We Jenks are the oldest family in town. The McGees across the river are the scum of the earth, most of them are on welfare to this day. He was one of the worst of them but my sister couldn't see it when he came courting her in his white sailor suit. He married her against Father's bitter objections. He gave her a dozen years of hell on earth and then he finally killed her. Don't tell me he was innocent. You don't know him."

A scrub jay in the pepper tree heard her harsh obsessive voice and raised his own voice in counter-complaint. I said under his noise:

"Why did he kill your sister?"

"Out of sheer diabolical devilment. What he couldn't have he chose to destroy. It was as simple as that. It wasn't true that there was another man. She was faithful to him to the day she died. Even though they were living in separate houses, my sister kept herself pure."

"Who said there was another man?"

She looked at me. The hot blood left her face. She seemed to lose the confidence that her righteous anger had given her.

"There were rumors," she said weakly. "Foul, dirty rumors. There always are when there's bad blood between a husband and wife. Tom McGee may have started them himself. I know his lawyer kept hammering away at the idea of another man. It was all I could do to sit there and listen to him, trying to destroy my sister's reputation after that murdering client of his had already destroyed her life. But Judge Gahagan made it clear in his instructions to the jury that it was just a story he invented, with no basis in fact."

"Who was McGee's lawyer?"

"An old fox named Gil Stevens. People don't go to him unless they're guilty, and he takes everything they have to get them off."

"But he didn't get McGee off."

"He practically did. Ten years is a small price to pay for first-degree murder. It should have been first-degree. He should have been executed."

The woman was implacable. With a firm hand she pressed her stray lock of hair back into place. Her graying head was marcelled in neat little waves, all alike, like the sea in old steel engravings. Such implacability as hers, I thought, could rise from either one of two sources: righteous certainty, or a guilty dubious fear that she was wrong. I hesitated to tell her what Dolly had said, that she had lied her father into prison. But I intended to tell her before I left.

"I'm interested in the details of the murder. Would it be too painful for you to go into them?"

"I can stand a lot of pain. What do you want to know?"

"Just how it happened."

"I wasn't here myself. I was at a meeting of the Native Daughters. I was president of the local group that year." The memory of this helped to restore her composure.

"Still I'm sure you know as much about it as anyone."

"No doubt I do. Except Tom McGee," she reminded me.

"And Dolly."

"Yes, and Dolly. The child was here in the house with Constance. They'd been living with me for some months. It was past nine o'clock and she'd already gone to bed. Constance was downstairs sewing. My sister was a fine seamstress, and she made most of the child's clothes. She was making a dress for her that night. It got all spotted with blood. They made it an exhibit at the trial."

Miss Jenks couldn't seem to forget the trial. Her eyes went vague, as if she could see it like a ritual continually being repeated in the courtroom of her mind.

"What were the circumstances of the shooting?"

"It was simple enough. He came to the front door. He talked her into opening it."

"It's strange that he could do that, after her bad experiences with him."

She brushed my objection aside with a flat movement of her hand. "He could talk a bird out of a tree when he wanted to. At any rate, they had an argument. I suppose he wanted her to come back with him, as usual, and she refused. Dolly heard their voices raised in anger."

"Where was she?"

"Upstairs in the front bedroom, which she shared with her mother." Miss Jenks pointed upward at the boarded ceiling of the veranda. "The argument woke the child up, and then she heard the shot. She went to the window and saw him run out to the street with the smoking gun in his hand. She came downstairs and found her mother in her blood."

"Was she still alive?"

"She was dead. She died instantaneously, shot through the heart."

"With what kind of a gun?"

"A medium-caliber hand-gun, the Sheriff thought. It was never found. McGee probably threw it in the sea. He was in Pacific Point when they arrested him next day."

"On Dolly's word?"

"She was the only witness, poor child."

We seemed to have an unspoken agreement that Dolly existed only in the past. Perhaps because we were both avoiding the problem of Dolly's present situation, some of the tension between us had evaporated. I took advantage of this to ask Miss Jenks if I could look over the house.

"I don't see what for."

"You've given me a very clear account of the murder. I want to try and relate it to the physical layout."

She said doubtfully: "I don't have much more time, and frankly I don't know how much more of this I can stand. My sister was very dear to me."

"I know."

"What are you trying to prove?"

"Nothing. I just want to understand what happened. It's my job."

A job and its imperatives meant something to her. She got up, opened the front door, and pointed out the place just inside it where her sister's body had lain. There was of course no trace of the ten-year-old crime on the braided rag rug in the hall. No trace of it anywhere, except for the blind red smear it had left in Dolly's mind, and possibly in her aunt's.

I was struck by the fact that Dolly's mother and her friend Helen had both been shot at the front door of their homes by the same caliber gun, possibly held by the same person. I didn't mention this to Miss Jenks. It would only bring on another outburst against her brother-in-law McGee.

"Would you like a cup of tea?" she said unexpectedly.

"No thanks."

"Or coffee? I use instant. It won't take long."

"All right. You're very kind."

She left me in the living room. It was divided by sliding doors from the dining room, and furnished with stiff old dark pieces reminiscent of a nineteenth-century parlor. There were mottoes on the walls instead of pictures, and one of them brought back with a rush and a pang my grandmother's house in Martinez. It said: "He is the Silent Listener at Every Conversation." My grandmother had hand-embroidered the same motto and hung it in her bedroom. She always whispered.

An upright grand piano with a closed keyboard stood in one corner of the room. I tried to open it, but it was locked. A photograph of two women and a child stood in the place of honor on the piano top. One of the women was Miss Jenks, younger but just as stout and overbearing. The other woman was still younger and much prettier. She held herself with the naïve sophistication of a small-town belle. The child between them, with one hand in each of theirs, was Dolly aged about ten.

Miss Jenks had come through the sliding doors with a coffee tray. "That's the three of us." As if two women and a little girl made a complete family. "And that's my sister's piano. She played beautifully. I never could master the instrument myself."

She wiped her glasses. I didn't know whether they were clouded by emotion or by the steam from the coffee. Over it she related some of Constance's girlhood triumphs. She had won a prize for piano, another for voice. She did extremely well in high school, especially in French, and she was all set to go to college, as Alice had gone before her, when that smooth-talking devil of a Tom McGee—

I left most of my coffee and went out into the hallway. It smelled of the mold that invades old houses. I caught a glimpse of myself in the clouded mirror beside the deer-horn hatrack. I looked like a ghost from the present haunting a bloody moment in the past. Even the woman behind me had an insubstantial quality, as if her large body was a husk or shell from which the essential being had departed. I found myself associating the smell of mold with her.

A rubber-treaded staircase rose at the rear of the hall. I was moving toward it as I said:

"Do you mind if I look at the room Dolly occupied?"

She allowed my momentum to carry her along and up the stairs. "It's my room now."

"I won't disturb anything."

The blinds were drawn, and she turned on the overhead light for me. It had a pink shade which suffused the room with pinkness. The floor was thickly carpeted with a soft loose pink material. A pink decorator spread covered the queen-sized bed. The elaborate three-mirrored dressing-table was trimmed with pink silk flounces, and so was the upholstered chair in front of it.

A quilted pink long chair stood by the window with an open magazine across its foot. Miss Jenks picked up the magazine and rolled it in her hands so that its cover wasn't visible. But I knew a *True Romance* when I saw one.

I crossed the room, sinking to the ankles in the deep pink pile of her fantasy, and raised the blind over the front window. I could see the wide flat second-story porch, and through its railings the pepper tree, and my car in the street. The three Mexican boys came by on their bicycle, one on the handlebars, one on the seat, one on the carrier, trailed by a red mongrel which had joined the act.

"They have no right to be riding like that," Miss Jenks said at my shoulder. "I have a good mind to report them to the deputy. And that dog shouldn't be running around loose."

"He's doing no harm."

"Maybe not, but we had a case of hydrophobia two years ago."

"I'm more interested in ten years ago. How tall was your niece at that time?"

"She was a good big girl for her age. About four feet and a half. Why?"

I adjusted my height by getting down on my knees. From this position I could see the lacy branches of the pepper tree, and through them most of my car, but nothing nearer. A man leaving the house would scarcely be visible until he passed the pepper tree, at least forty feet away. A gun in his hand could not be seen until he reached the street. It was a hasty and haphazard experiment, but its result underlined the question in my mind.

I got up off my knees. "Was it dark that night?"

She knew which night I meant. "Yes. It was dark."

"I don't see any street lights."

"No. We have none. This is a poor town, Mr. Archer."

"Was there a moon?"

"No. I don't believe so. But my niece has excellent eyesight. She can spot the markings on a bird—"

"At night?"

"There's always some light. Anyway, she'd know her own father." Miss Jenks corrected herself: "She *knew* her own father."

"Did she tell you this?"

"Yes. I was the first one she told."

"Did you question her about it in any detail?"

"I didn't, no. She was quite broken up, naturally. I didn't want to subject her to the strain."

"But you didn't mind subjecting her to the strain of testifying to these things in court."

"It was necessary, necessary to the prosecution's case. And it did her no harm."

"Dr. Godwin thinks it did her a lot of harm, that the strain she went through then is partly responsible for her breakdown."

"Dr. Godwin has his ideas and I have mine. If you want my opinion, he's a dangerous man, a troublemaker. He has no respect for authority, and I have no respect for a man like that."

"You used to respect him. You sent your niece to him for treatment."

"I know more about him now than I did then."

"Do you mind telling me why she needed treatment?"

"No. I don't mind." She was still trying to preserve a friendly surface, though we were both conscious of the disagreement simmering under it. "Dolly wasn't doing well in school. She wasn't happy or popular. Which was natural enough with her parents—I mean, her father, making a shambles of their home together.

"This isn't the backwoods," she said as if she suspected maybe it was, "and I thought the least I could do was see that she got a little help. Even the people on welfare get family counseling when they need it. So I persuaded my sister to take her into Pacific Point to see Dr. Godwin. He was the best we had at that time. Constance drove her in every Saturday morning for about a year. The child showed considerable improvement, I'll say that much for Godwin. So did Constance. She seemed brighter and happier and surer of herself."

"Was she getting treatment, too?"

"I guess she had a little, and of course it did her good to get into town every Saturday. She wanted to move into town but there was no money for it. She left McGee and moved in with me instead. That took some of the strain off her. He couldn't stand to see that. He couldn't stand to see her getting her dignity back. He killed her like a dog in the manger."

After ten years her mind was still buzzing like a fly around the bloody moment.

"Why didn't you continue Dolly's therapy? She probably needed it more than ever afterward."

"It wasn't possible. I work Saturday mornings. I have to get my paperwork done some time." She fell silent, confused and tongue-tied as honest people can be by their own deviousness.

"Also you had a disagreement with Godwin about your niece's testimony at the trial."

"I'm not ashamed of it, no matter what *he* says. It did her no harm to speak out about her father. It probably did her good. She had to get it out of her system somehow."

"It isn't out of her system, though. She's still hung up on it." Just as you are, Miss Jenks. "But now she's changed her story."

"Changed her story?"

"She says now that she didn't see her father the night of the murder. She denies that he had anything to do with it."

"Who told you that?"

"Godwin. He'd just been talking to her. She told him she lied in court to please the adults." I was tempted to say more, but remembered in time that it would almost certainly be relayed to her friend the Sheriff.

She was looking at me as if I had questioned a basic faith of her life. "He's twisting what she said, I'm sure. He's using her to prove that he was right when he was wrong."

"I doubt that, Miss Jenks. Godwin doesn't believe her new story himself."

"You see! She's either crazy or she's lying! Don't forget she's got McGee blood in her!" She was appalled by her own outburst. She turned her eyes away, glancing around the pink room as though it might somehow vouch for the girlish innocence of her intentions. "I didn't really mean that," she said. "I love my niece. It's just —it's harder than I thought to rake over the past like this."

"I'm sorry, and I'm sure you love your niece. Feeling about her the way you do, and did, you couldn't have fed her a false story to tell in court."

"Who says I did?"

"No one. I'm saying you couldn't have. You're not the sort of woman who could bring herself to corrupt the mind of a twelve-year-old child."

"No," she said. "I had nothing to do with Dolly's accusation against her father. She came to me with it, the night it happened, within half-an-hour of the *time* it happened. I never questioned it for a minute. It had all the accents of truth."

But she had not. I didn't think she was lying, exactly. More likely she was suppressing something. She spoke carefully and in a low voice, so that the motto in the living room wouldn't hear her. She still wasn't meeting my eyes. A slow dull flush rose from her heavy neck to her face. I said:

"I doubt that it was physically possible for her to identify anyone, even her own father, at this distance on a dark night—let alone pick out a smoking gun in his hand."

"But the police accepted it. Sheriff Crane and the D.A. both believed her."

"Policemen and prosecutors are usually glad to accept the facts, or the pseudo-facts, that fit their case."

"But Tom McGee was guilty. He was guilty."

"He may have been."

"Then why are you trying to convince me that he wasn't?" The flush of shame in her face was going through the usual conversion into a flush of anger. "I won't listen."

"You might as well listen. What can you lose? I'm trying to open up that old case because it's connected, through Dolly, with the Haggerty case."

"Do you believe she killed Miss Haggerty?" she said.

"No. Do you?"

"Sheriff Crane seems to regard her as the main suspect."

"Did he say so to you, Miss Jenks?"

"He as much as said so. He was feeling me out on what my reaction would be if he took her in for questioning."

"And what was your reaction?"

"I hardly know, I was so upset. I haven't seen Dolly for some time. She went and married behind my back. She was always a good girl, but she may have changed."

I had the feeling that Miss Jenks was talking out of her deepest sense of herself: She had always been a good girl, but she might have changed.

"Why don't you call Crane up and tell him to lay off? Your niece needs delicate handling."

"You don't believe she's guilty of this murder?"

"I said I didn't. Tell him to lay off or he'll lose the next election."

"I couldn't do that. He's my senior in county work." But she was thinking about it. She shook the thought off. "Speaking of which, I've given you all the time I possibly can. It must be past twelve."

I was ready to leave. It had been a long hour. She followed me downstairs and out onto the veranda. I had the impression as we said goodbye that she wanted to say something more. Her face was expectant. But nothing came.

13

The fog had thinned out a little along the coastline, but you still couldn't see the sun, only a sourceless white glare that hurt the eyes. The keyboy at the Mariner's Rest told me that Alex had driven away with an older man in a new Chrysler. His own red sports car was still in the parking enclosure, and he hadn't checked out.

I bought a sandwich at a drive-in down the street and ate it in my room. Then I made a couple of frustrating phone calls. The switchboard operator at the courthouse said there wasn't a chance of getting hold of a trial transcript this afternoon: everything was locked up tight for the weekend. I called the office of Gil Stevens, the lawyer who had unsuccessfully defended Tom McGee. His answering service said he was in Balboa. No, I couldn't reach him there. Mr. Stevens was racing his yacht today and tomorrow.

I decided to drop in on Jerry Marks, the young lawyer who had acted as Mrs. Perrine's defense counsel. His office was in a new shopping center not too far from the motel strip. Jerry was unmarried and ambitious, and he might be in it, even on a Saturday afternoon.

The front door was open and I walked into the waiting room, which was furnished with maple and chintz. The secretary's cubicle behind the glass half-wall on the left was deserted for the weekend, but Jerry Marks was in the inner office.

"How are you, Jerry?"

"I'm all right."

He looked at me guardedly over the book he was reading, an enormous tome entitled *Rules of Evidence*. He wasn't very experienced in criminal practice, but he was competent and honest. His homely Middle-European face was warmed and lit by intelligent brown eyes.

"How's Mrs. Perrine?" I said.

"I haven't seen her since she was released, and I don't expect to. I seldom see much of my ex-clients. I smell of the courtroom to them."

"I have the same experience. Are you free?"

"Yeah, and I'm going to stay that way. I promised myself a clear weekend of study, murder or no murder."

"You know about the Haggerty murder then."

"Naturally, it's all over town."

"What have you heard?"

"Really not very much. Somebody at the courthouse told my secretary that this lady professor was shot by a girl student at the college. I forget her name."

"Dolly Kincaid. Her husband is my client. She's in a nursing home, under a doctor's care."

"Psycho?"

"It depends on your definition of psycho. It's a complex situation, Jerry. I doubt that she's legally insane under the McNaghten rule. On the other hand I very much doubt that she did the shooting at all."

"You're trying to get me interested in the case," he said suspiciously.

"I'm not trying to do anything to you. Actually I came to you for information. What's your opinion of Gil Stevens?"

"He's the local old master. Get him."

"He's out of town. Seriously, is he a good lawyer?"

"Stevens is the most successful criminal lawyer in the country. He has to be good. He knows law, and he knows juries. He does pull some old-fashioned courtroom shenanigans that I wouldn't use myself. He's quite an actor, heavy with the emotion. It works, though. I can't remember when he's lost an important case."

"I can. About ten years ago he defended a man named Tom McGee who was convicted of shooting his wife."

"That was before my time."

"Dolly Kincaid is McGee's daughter. Also, she was the key witness for the prosecution at her father's trial."

Jerry whistled. "I see what you mean by complex." After a pause, he said: "Who's her doctor?"

"Godwin."

He pushed out his heavy lips. "I'd go easy with him."

"What do you mean?"

"I'm sure he's a good psychiatrist, but maybe not so much in the forensic department. He's a very bright man and he doesn't hide his light under a bushel, in fact he sometimes acts like a mastermind. Which puts people's backs up, especially if their name is Gahagan and they're sitting on the Superior Court bench. So I'd use him sparingly."

"I can't control the use that's made of him."

"No, but you can warn her attorney—"

"It would be a lot simpler if you were her attorney. I haven't had a chance to talk to her husband today, but I think he'll go along with my recommendation. His family isn't poverty-stricken, by the way."

"It wasn't the money I was thinking about," Jerry said coldly. "I promised myself that I'd spend this weekend with my books."

"Helen Haggerty should have picked another weekend to get herself shot."

It came out harsher than I intended. My own failure to do anything for Helen was eating me.

Jerry regarded me quizzically. "This case is a personal matter with you?"

"It seems to be."

"Okay, okay," he said. "What do you want me to do?"

"Just hold yourself in readiness for the present."

"I'll be here all afternoon. After that my answering service will be able to contact me."

I thanked him and went back to the motel. Alex's room next to mine was still empty. I checked with my own answering service in Hollywood. Arnie Walters had left his number for me and I called Reno.

Arnie was out of the office, but his wife and partner Phyllis took the call. Her exuberant femininity bounced along the wires:

"I never *see* you, Lew. All I hear is your voice on the telephone. For all I know you don't exist any more, but simply made some tapes a number of years ago and somebody plays them to me from time to time."

"How do you explain the fact that I'm responsive? Like now."

"Electronics. I explain everything I don't understand electronically. It saves me no end of trouble. But when am I going to *see* you?"

"This weekend, if Arnie's tabbed the driver of the convertible."

"He hasn't quite done that, but he does have a line on the owner. She's a Mrs. Sally Burke and she lives right here in Reno. She claims her car was stolen a couple of days ago. But Arnie doesn't believe her."

"Why not?"

"He's very intuitive. Also she didn't report the alleged theft. Also she has boy friends of various types. Arnie's out doing legwork on them now."

"Good."

"I gather this is important," Phyllis said.

"It's a double murder case, maybe a triple. My client's a young girl with emotional problems. She's probably going to be arrested today or tomorrow, for something she almost certainly didn't do."

"You sound very intense."

"This case has gotten under my skin. Also I don't know where I'm at."

"I never heard you admit that before, Lew. Anyway, I was thinking before you called, maybe I could strike up an acquaintance with Mrs. Sally Burke. Does that sound like a good idea to you?"

"An excellent idea." Phyllis was an ex-Pinkerton operative who looked like an ex-chorus girl. "Remember Mrs. Burke and her playmates may be highly danger-ous. They may have killed a woman last night."

"Not this woman. I've got too much to live for." She meant Arnie.

We exchanged some further pleasantries in the course of which I heard people coming into Alex's room next door. After I said goodbye to Phyllis I stood by the wall and listened. Alex's voice and the voice of another man were raised in argu-ment, and I didn't need a contact mike to tell what the argument was about. The other man wanted Alex to clear out of this unfortunate mess and come home.

I knocked on his door.

"Let me handle them," the other man said, as if he was expecting the police.

He stepped outside, a man of about my age, good-looking in a grayish way, with a thin face, narrow light eyes, a pugnacious chin. The mark of organization was on him, like an invisible harness worn under his conservative gray suit.

There was some kind of desperation in him, too. He didn't even ask who I was before he said: "I'm Frederick Kincaid and you have no right to chivvy my son around. He has nothing to do with that girl and her crimes. She married him under false pretenses. The marriage didn't last twenty-four hours. My son is a respectable boy—"

Alex stepped out and pulled at the older man's arm. His face was miserable with embarrassment. "You'd better come inside, Dad. This is Mr. Archer."

"Archer, eh? I understand you've involved my son in this thing—"

"On the contrary, he hired me."

"I'm firing you." His voice sounded as if it had often performed this function.

"We'll talk it over," I said.

The three of us jostled each other in the doorway. Kincaid senior didn't want me to come in. It was very close to turning into a brawl. Each of us was ready to hit at least one of the others.

I bulled my way into the room and sat down in a chair with my back to the wall. "What's happened, Alex?"

"Dad heard about me on the radio. He phoned the Sheriff and found out where I was. The Sheriff called us over there just now. They found the murder gun."

"Where?"

Alex was slow in answering, as though the words in his mouth would make the whole thing realer when he let them out. His father answered for him:

"Where she hid it, under the mattress of the bed in that little hut she's been living in—"

"It isn't a hut," Alex said. "It's a gatehouse."

"Don't contradict me, Alex."

"Did you see the gun?" I said.

"We did. The Sheriff wanted Alex to identify it, which naturally he couldn't do. He didn't even know she had a gun."

"What kind of a gun is it?"

"It's a Smith and Wesson revolver, .38 caliber, with walnut grips. Old, but in pretty fair condition. She probably bought it at a pawn shop."

"Is this the police theory?"

"The Sheriff mentioned the possibility."

"How does he know it's hers?"

"They found it under her mattress, didn't they?" Kincaid talked like a prosecutor making a case, using it to bring his son into line. "Who else could have hidden it there?"

"Practically anybody else. The gatehouse was standing open last night, wasn't it, Alex?"

"It was when I got there."

"Let me do the talking," his father said. "I've had more experience in these matters."

"It hasn't done you a hell of a lot of good. Your son is a witness, and I'm trying to get at the facts."

He stood over me with his hands on his hips, vibrating. "My son has nothing whatever to do with this case."

"Don't kid yourself. He's married to the girl."

"The marriage is meaningless—a boyish impulse that didn't last one full day. I'm having it annulled. It wasn't even consummated, he tells me."

"You can't annul it."

"Don't tell me what I can do."

"I think I will, though. All you can do is annul yourself and your son. There's more to a marriage than sexual consummation or legal technicalities. The marriage is real because it's real for Alex."

"He wants out of it now."

"I don't believe you."

"It's true, isn't it, Alex, you want to come home with me and Mother? She's terribly worried about you. Her heart is kicking up again." Kincaid was throwing everything but the kitchen sink.

Alex looked from him to me. "I don't know. I just want to do what's right."

Kincaid started to say something, probably having to do with the kitchen sink, but I talked over him:

"Then answer another question or two, Alex. Was Dolly carrying a gun when she came running back to the gatehouse last night?"

"I didn't see one."

Kincaid said: "She probably had it concealed under her clothes."

"Shut up, Kincaid," I said calmly from my sitting position. "I don't object to the fact that you're a bloodless bastard. You obviously can't help it. I do object to your trying to make Alex into one. Leave him a choice, at least."

Kincaid sputtered a couple of times, and walked away from me. Alex said without looking at either of us: "Don't talk to my father that way, Mr. Archer."

"All right. She was wearing a cardigan and a blouse and skirt. Anything else?"

"No."

"Carrying a bag?"

"I don't think so."

"Think."

"She wasn't."

"Then she couldn't have been carrying a concealed .38 revolver. You didn't see her hide it under the mattress?"

"No."

"And were you with her all the time, between the time she got back and the time she left for the nursing home?"

"Yes. I was with her all the time."

"Then it's pretty clear it isn't Dolly's gun, or at least it wasn't Dolly who hid it under the mattress. Do you have any idea who it could have been?"

"No."

"You said it was the murder gun. How did they establish that? They haven't had time for ballistics tests."

Kincaid spoke up from the far corner where he had been sulking: "It's the right caliber to fit the wound, and one shell had been fired, recently. It stands to reason it's the gun she used."

"Do you believe that, Alex?"

"I don't know."

"Have they questioned her?"

"They intend to. The Sheriff said something about waiting until they nailed it down with ballistic evidence, Monday."

That gave me a little time, if I could believe Alex. The pressures of the night and morning, on top of the uncertainties of the last three weeks, had left him punchy. He looked almost out on his feet.

"I think we all should wait," I said, "before we make up our minds about your wife. Even if she's guilty, which I very strongly doubt, you owe her all the help and support you can give her."

"He owes her nothing," Kincaid said. "Not a thing. She married him fraudulently. She lied to him again and again."

I kept my voice and temper down, for contrast. "She still needs medical care, and she needs a lawyer. I have a good local lawyer waiting to step in, but I can't retain him myself."

"You're taking quite a lot into your hands, aren't you?"

"Somebody has to assume responsibility. There's a lot of it floating around loose at the moment. You can't avoid it by crawling into a hole and pulling the hole in after you. The girl's in trouble, and whether you like it or not she's a member of your family."

Alex appeared to be listening. I didn't know if he was hearing me. His father shook his narrow gray head:

"She's no member of my family, and I'll tell you one thing for certain. She's not going to drag my son down into the underworld. And neither are you." He turned to Alex. "How much have you already paid this man?"

"A couple of hundred."

Kincaid said to me: "You've been amply paid, exorbitantly paid. You heard me fire you. This is a private room and if you persist in intruding I'll call the management. If they can't handle you I'll call the police."

Alex looked at me and lifted his hands, not very far, in a helpless movement. His father put an arm around his shoulders:

"I'm only doing what's best for you, son. You don't belong with these people. We'll go home and cheer up Mother. After all you don't want to drive her into her grave."

It came out smooth and pat, and it was the clincher. Alex didn't look at me again. I went back to my own room and phoned Jerry Marks and told him I had lost a client and so had he. Jerry seemed disappointed.

14

Alex and his father vacated their room and drove away. I didn't go out to see them off but I could hear the sound of their engines, quickly muffled by the fog. I sat and let my stomach unknot, telling myself I should have handled them better. Kincaid was a frightened man who valued his status the way some previous generations valued their souls.

I drove up Foothill to the Bradshaw house. The Dean was probably another breakable reed, but he had money, and he had shown some sympathy for Dolly, over and above his official interest in the case. I had no desire to continue it on my own. I needed a principal, preferably one who swung some weight locally. Alice Jenks met this requirement, more or less, but I didn't want her for a client.

A deputy was standing guard at the gatehouse. He wouldn't let me in to look around but he didn't object to my going up to the main house. The Spanish woman Maria answered the door.

"Is Dr. Bradshaw home?"

"No sir."

"Where can I find him?"

She shrugged. "I dunno. I think Mrs. Bradshaw said he's gone for the weekend."

"That's queer. I'd like to talk to Mrs. Bradshaw."

"I'll see if she's busy."

I stepped inside uninvited and sat down on a gilt chair in the entrance hall while Maria went upstairs. She came down and told me that Mrs. Bradshaw would be with me shortly.

It was at least half-an-hour before she came limping down. She had primped her gray head and rouged her cheeks and put on a dress with lace at her slack throat held in place by a diamond brooch. I wondered, as she made me the dubious gift of her hand, if all this had been done for my benefit.

The old lady seemed glad to see me. "How are you, Mr.—it's Mr. Archer, isn't it? I've been so hoping somebody would call. This fog makes one feel so isolated, and with my driver gone—" She seemed to hear the note of complaint rising in her voice, and cut it off. "How is the girl?" she said briskly.

"She's being taken care of. Dr. Godwin thinks she's better than she was last night."

"Good. You'll be glad to know," she said with a bright ironic stare, "that I'm somewhat better myself than I was last night. My son informed me this morning that I staged one of my exhibitions, as he calls them. Frankly, I was upset. Nights aren't my best season."

"It was a rough night for everybody."

"And I'm a selfish old woman. Isn't that what you're thinking?"

"People don't seem to change much as they get older."

"That has all the earmarks of an insult." But she was smiling, almost flirtatiously. "You imply that I've always been this way."

"You'd know better than I would."

She laughed outright. It wasn't a joyous sound, but there was humor in it. "You're a bold young man, and a bright one. I like bright young men. Come into the study and I'll see that you get a drink."

"Thank you, but I can't stay—"

"Then I'll sit here." She lowered herself carefully onto the gilt chair. "My moral qualities may not have altered for the worse. My physical capabilities certainly have. This fog is very bad for my arthritis." She added, with a gingerly shake of her head: "But I mustn't complain. I promised my son, in penance for last night, that I would go through an entire day without uttering a word of complaint."

"How are you doing?"

"Not so well," she said with her wry and wrinkled smile. "It's like solitaire, you always cheat a little. Or don't you?"

"I don't play the game."

"You're not missing a great deal, but it helps to pass the days for me. Well, I won't keep you if you have business."

"I have business with Dr. Bradshaw. Do you know where I can contact him?"

"Roy flew to Reno this morning."

"Reno?"

"Not to gamble, I assure you. He hasn't an iota of gambling instinct. In fact I sometimes think he's excessively cautious. Roy is a bit of a mother's boy, wouldn't you say?" She looked up at me with complex irony, unembarrassed by his condition or her complicity in it.

"I'm a little surprised that he'd go away in the middle of this murder case."

"So was I, but there was no stopping him. He isn't exactly running away from it. They're holding a conference of small-college deans at the University of Nevada. It's been planned for months, and Roy is slated as one of the principal speakers. He felt it was his duty to be there. But I could see very well that he was eager to go. He loved the public eye, you know—he's always been a bit of an actor—but he isn't so terribly fond of the responsibilities that go with it."

I was amused and intrigued and a little appalled by her realism. She seemed to be enjoying it herself. Conversation was better than solitaire.

Mrs. Bradshaw rose creakingly and leaned on my arm. "You might as well come into the study. It's drafty here. I've taken a fancy to you, young man."

I didn't know if this was a blessing or a curse. She grinned up into my face as if she could read my doubts there. "Don't worry, I won't eat you." She placed the emphasis on the final word, as though she had already eaten her son for breakfast.

We went into the study together and sat in facing highbacked leather chairs. She rang for Maria and ordered me a highball. Then she leaned back and scanned the bookshelves. The phalanxes of books seemed to remind her of Bradshaw's importance.

"Don't misunderstand me. I love my son profoundly and I'm proud of him. I'm proud of his good looks and I'm proud of his brains. He graduated *summa cum laude* from Harvard and went on to take a most distinguished doctorate. One of these days he's going to be the president of a major university or a great foundation."

"Is he ambitious, or are you?"

"I used to be, for him. As Roy became more ambitious, I became less so. There are better things in life than climbing an endless ladder. I haven't entirely given up hope that he'll marry." She cocked a bright old eye at me. "He *likes* women, you know."

"I'm sure he does."

"In fact I was beginning to persuade myself that he was interested in Miss Haggerty. I've never known him to pay so much attention to any other woman." She dropped the statement so that it became a question.

"He mentioned to me that he took her out several times. But he also said that they were never close in any way. His reaction to her death confirmed that."

"What was his reaction to her death?"

I'd done a lot of pumping in my time, and I knew when it was being done to me. "I mean his general reaction. He wouldn't have flown to Reno this morning, deans' conference or no deans' conference, if he had been really fond of Helen Haggerty. He'd be here in Pacific Point trying to find out who did her in."

"You seem quite let down about it."

"I was looking for his help. He seemed genuinely concerned about Dolly Kincaid."

"He is. We both are. In fact Roy asked me at breakfast to do what I could for the girl. But what can I do?" She displayed her crumpled hands, making a show of her helplessness.

Maria came in with my clinking highball, handed it to me unceremoniously, and asked her employer if there was anything else. There wasn't. I sipped my drink, wondering if Mrs. Bradshaw was a client I could possibly handle, if she became my client. She had the money, all right. The diamonds winking at her throat would have bought my services for several years.

"You can hire me," I said.

"Hire you?"

"If you really want to do something for Dolly, and not just sit there paying lip-service to the idea. Do you think we could get along?"

"I was getting along with men when you were in the cradle, Mr. Archer. Are you implying I can't get along with people?"

"I seem to be the one who can't. Alex Kincaid just fired me, with a strong assist from his father. They want no part of Dolly and her problems, now that the chips are down."

Her black eyes flashed. "I saw through that boy immediately. He's a molly-coddle."

"I don't have the resources to go on by myself. It isn't good practice, anyway. I need somebody to back me, preferably somebody with local standing and—I'll be frank—a substantial bank balance."

"How much would it cost me?"

"It depends on how long the case goes on and how many ramifications develop. I get a hundred a day and expenses. Also I have a team of detectives in Reno working on a lead that may be a hot one."

"A lead in Reno?"

"It originated here, last night."

I told her about the man in the convertible which belonged to Mrs. Sally Burke, a woman with many boy friends. She leaned forward in her chair in mounting interest:

"Why aren't the police working on that lead?"

"They may be. If they are, I don't know about it. They seem to have settled for the idea that Dolly's guilty and everything else is irrelevant. It's simpler that way."

"You don't accept that idea?"

"No."

"In spite of the gun they found in her bed?"

"You know about that, then."

"Sheriff Crane showed it to me this morning. He wanted to know if I recognized it. Of course I didn't. I abhor the very sight of guns myself. I've never permitted Roy to own a gun."

"And you have no idea who owned that one?"

"No, but the Sheriff appeared to take it for granted that it was Dolly's, and that it tied her to the murder."

"We have no reason to think it was hers. If it was, the last place she'd put it would be under her own mattress. Her husband denies she did, and he was with

her continuously once she got back to the gatehouse. There's the further point that
there's no definite proof it's the murder weapon."

"Really?"

"Really. It will take ballistics tests and they're not scheduled until Monday. If
my luck holds, I think I can throw more light on the situation by then."

"Do you have a definite theory of your own, Mr. Archer?"

"I have an idea that the ramifications of this thing go far back beyond Dolly. It
wasn't Dolly who threatened Miss Haggerty's life. She would have recognized her
voice, they were close friends. I think Dolly walked up to her house simply to ask
her advice about whether to go back to her husband. She stumbled over the body
and panicked. She's still in panic."

"Why?"

"I'm not prepared to explain it. I want to go into her background further. I also
want to go into Miss Haggerty's background."

"That might be interesting," she said, as if she was considering attending a
double-feature movie. "How much is all this going to cost me?"

"I'll keep it as low as I can. But it could mount up in the thousands, two or
three or even four."

"That's rather an expensive penance."

"Penance?"

"For all my selfishness, past and present and future. I'll think about it, Mr.
Archer."

"How long do you need to think about it?"

"Call me tonight. Roy will be telephoning me around dinnertime—he telephones me every night when he's away—and I couldn't possibly give you an answer
before I discuss it with him. We live on a tighter budget than you might think,"
she said earnestly, fingering the diamonds at her throat.

15

I drove up under the dripping trees to Helen Haggerty's place. Two deputies
messing around outside the front door wouldn't let me in or answer any questions.
It was turning out to be a bad day.

I drifted over to the campus and into the Administration Building. I had some
idea of talking to Laura Sutherland, the Dean of Women, but her office was locked.
All the offices were locked. The building was deserted except for a white-headed
man in blue jeans who was sweeping the corridor with a long-handled push-broom.
He looked like Father Time, and I had a nightmare moment of thinking that he
was sweeping Helen's last vestiges away.

In a kind of defensive reflex I got my notebook and looked up the name of the

chairman of the modern languages department. Dr. Geisman. The old man with
the push-broom knew where his office was:

"It's in the new Humanity Building, down the line." He pointed. "But he won't
be there on a Saturday afternoon."

The old man was mistaken. I found Geisman in the department office on the
first floor of the Humanities Building, sitting with a telephone receiver in one hand
and a pencil in the other. I had seen him coming out of Bradshaw's conference the
day before, a heavy middle-aged man with thick spectacles imperfectly masking
anxious little eyes.

"One moment," he said to me; and into the telephone: "I'm sorry you can't
help us, Mrs. Bass. I realize you have your family responsibilities and of course the
remuneration is not great for a special lecturer."

He sounded foreign, though he had no accent. His voice was denatured, as if
English was just another language he had learned.

"I am Dr. Geisman," he said as he hung up and stroked out a name on the list
in front of him. "Are you Dr. de Falla?"

"No. My name is Archer."

"What are your qualifications? Do you have an advanced degree?"

"In the university of hard knocks."

He didn't respond to my smile. "A member of our faculty is defunct, as you
must know, and I've had to give up my Saturday in an attempt to find a replacement
for her. If you expect me to take your application seriously—"

"I'm not applying for anything, doctor, except possibly a little information. I'm
a private detective investigating Professor Haggerty's death, and I'm interested in
how she happened to land here."

"I have no time to go into all that again. There are classes which must be met
on Monday. If this Dr. de Falla doesn't arrive, or proves impossible, I don't know
what to do." He peered at his wristwatch. "I'm due at the Los Angeles airport at
six-thirty."

"You can spare five minutes, anybody can."

"Very well. Five minutes." He tapped the crystal of his watch. "You wish to
know how Miss Haggerty came here? I can't say, except that she appeared in my
office one day and asked for a position. She had heard about Professor Farrand's
heart attack. This is our second emergency in a month."

"Who told her about the heart attack?"

"I don't know. Perhaps Dean Sutherland. She gave Dean Sutherland as a local
reference. But it was common knowledge, it was in the paper."

"Was she living here before she applied for a job with you?"

"I believe so. Yes, she was. She told me she already had a house. She liked the
place, and wished to remain. She was very eager for the post. Frankly, I had some
doubts about her. She had a master's degree from Chicago but she wasn't fully

qualified. The school where she had been teaching, Maple Park, is not credentialed on our level. But Dean Sutherland told me she needed the position and I let her have it, unfortunately."

"I understood she had a private income."

He pursed his lips and shook his head. "Ladies with a private income don't take on four sections of French and German, plus counseling duties, at a salary of less than five thousand dollars. Perhaps she meant her alimony. She told me she was having difficulty collecting her alimony." His spectacles glinted as he looked up. "You knew that she had been recently divorced?"

"I heard that. Do you know where her ex-husband is?"

"No. I had very few words with her at any time. Do you suspect him?"

"I have no reason to. But when a woman is killed you normally look for a man who had a motive to kill her. The local police have other ideas."

"You don't agree with them?"

"I'm keeping my mind open, doctor."

"I see. They tell me one of our students is under suspicion."

"So I hear. Do you know the girl?"

"No. She was registered for none of our departmental courses, fortunately."

"Why 'fortunately'?"

"She is psychoneurotic, they tell me." His myopic eyes looked as vulnerable as open oysters under the thick lenses of his glasses. "If the administration employed proper screening procedures we would not have students of that sort on the campus, endangering our lives. But we are very backward here in some respects." He tapped the crystal of his watch again. "You've had your five minutes."

"One more question, doctor. Have you been in touch with Helen Haggerty's family?"

"Yes, I phoned her mother early this morning. Dean Bradshaw asked me to perform that duty, though properly I should think it was his duty. The mother, Mrs. Hoffman, is flying out here and I have to meet her at the Los Angeles airport."

"At six-thirty?"

He nodded dismally. "There seems to be no one else available. Both of our deans are out of town—"

"Dean Sutherland, too?"

"Dean Sutherland, too. They've gone off and left the whole business on my shoulders." His glasses blurred with self-pity, and he took them off to wipe them. "It's foggy, and I can't see to drive properly. My eyesight is so poor that without my glasses I can't tell the difference between you and the Good Lord himself."

"There isn't much difference."

He put on his glasses, saw that this was a joke, and emitted a short barking laugh.

"What plane is Mrs. Hoffman coming in on, doctor?"

"United, from Chicago. I promised to meet her at the United baggage counter."

"Let me."

"Are you serious?"

"It will give me a chance to talk to her. Where do you want me to bring her?"

"I reserved her a room at the Pacific Hotel. I could meet you there, at eight, say."

"Fine."

He got up and came around the desk and shook my hand vigorously. As I was leaving the building, a small, old man in a black hat and a greenish black cloak came sidling out of the fog. He had a dyed-looking black mustache, hectic black eyes, a wine flush on his hollow cheeks.

"Dr. de Falla?"

He nodded. I held the door for him. He swept off his hat and bowed.

"*Merci beaucoup.*"

His rubber-soled shoes made no more sound than a spider. I had another one of my little nightmare moments. This one was Doctor Death.

16

It was a slow drive up the coast but the fog lifted before I reached the airport, leaving a thickish twilight in the air. I parked my car at the United building. It was exactly six-twenty-five, according to the ticket the girl in the parking lot handed me. I crossed the road to the bright enormous building and found the baggage carrousel, besieged by travelers.

A woman who looked like a dried-up older Helen was standing on the edge of the crowd beside her suitcase. She had on a black dress under a black coat with a ratty fur collar, black hat, and black gloves.

Only her garish red hair was out of keeping with the occasion. Her eyes were swollen, and she seemed dazed, as if a part of her mind was still back in Illinois.

"Mrs. Hoffman?"

"Yes. I'm Mrs. Earl Hoffman."

"My name is Archer. Your daughter's department head, Dr. Geisman, asked me to pick you up."

"That was nice of him," she said with a poor vague smile. "And nice of you."

I picked up her suitcase, which was small and light. "Would you like something to eat, or drink? There's a pretty good restaurant here."

"Oh no thanks. I had dinner on the plane. Swiss steak. It was a very interesting flight. I never flew in a jet before. But I wasn't the least bit frightened."

She didn't know what she was. She stared around at the bright lights and the people. The muscles of her face were tensing up as if she might be getting ready to cry some more. I got hold of her thin upper arm and hustled her out of there and across the road to my car. We circled the parking lot and got onto the freeway.

"They didn't have this when I was here before. I'm glad you decided to meet me. I'd get lost," she said in a lost voice.

"How long is it since you were here before?"

"Nearly twenty years. It was when Hoffman was in the Navy, he was a warrant officer in the Shore Patrol. They assigned him to San Diego and Helen had already run—left home, and I thought I might as well get the benefit of the travel. We lived in San Diego for over a year, and it was very nice." I could hear her breathing as if she was struggling up to the rim of the present. She said carefully: "Pacific Point is quite near San Diego, isn't it?"

"About fifty miles."

"Is that right?" After another pause, she said: " Are you with the college?"

"I happen to be a detective."

"Isn't that interesting? My husband is a detective. He's been on the Bridgeton force for thirty-four years. He's due to retire next year. We've talked about retiring in California but this will probably turn him against it. He pretends not to care, but he cares. I think he cares just as much as I do." Her voice floated along above the highway noises like a disembodied spirit talking to itself.

"It's too bad he couldn't fly out with you today."

"He could have, if he'd wanted to. He could have taken time off. I think he was afraid he couldn't face it. And he has his blood pressure to consider." She hesitated again. "Are you investigating my daughter's murder?"

"Yes."

"Dr. Geisman said on the phone that you have a suspect, a young girl. What would make a student shoot one of her teachers? I never heard of such a thing."

"I don't think she did, Mrs. Hoffman."

"But Dr. Geisman said it was practically open and shut." The sorrow in her voice had changed into a kind of vengeful justice.

"That may be." I had no desire to argue with a potentially valuable witness. "I'm investigating other angles, and you may be able to help me."

"How is that?"

"Your daughter's life was threatened. She talked to me about it before she was shot. Somebody called her on the telephone. It was a voice she didn't recognize, but she said a strange thing about it. She said it sounded like the voice of Bridgeton."

"Bridgeton? That's where we live."

"I know that, Mrs. Hoffman. Helen said it was Bridgeton catching up with her. Do you have any idea what she meant?"

"She always hated Bridgeton. From the time that she was in high school she blamed it for everything that went wrong with her life. She couldn't wait to get out of Bridgeton."

"I understand she ran away from home."

"I wouldn't put it that way," although she almost had. "She only dropped out of sight for one summer, and she was working all the time. She had a job with a newspaper in Chicago. Then she started in at the University, and she let me know where she was. It was just her father—" She cut this sentence off short. "I used to help her out of my housekeeping money until we went into the Navy."

"What was the trouble between her and her father?"

"It had to do with his professional work. At least that was what the final big battle was about."

"When Helen called him a crooked stormtrooper?"

She turned in the seat to look at me. "Helen told you that, eh? Are you—were you her boy friend or something like that?"

"We were friends." I found that I could say it with some conviction. We had spent a single angry hour together but her death had turned a light on it which hurt my eyes.

She leaned closer to study my face. "What else did she tell you?"

"There was murder involved in her quarrel with her father."

"That's a lie. I don't mean Helen was lying, but she was mistaken. The Deloney shooting was an accident pure and simple. If Helen thought she knew more about it than her father, she was dead wrong."

"Dead" and "wrong" were heavy words to lay on the dead. Her black-gloved hand flew up to her mouth. She rode for a while in hunched and fearful silence, a thin dry cricket of a woman who had lost her chirp.

"Tell me about the Deloney shooting, Mrs. Hoffman."

"I don't see the point of doing that. I never talk about my husband's cases. He doesn't like me to."

"But he isn't here."

"In a way he is. We've been together so long. Anyway it's all past history."

"History is always connected with the present. That case may have something to do with Helen's death."

"How could that be? It was twenty years ago, longer than that, and it didn't amount to anything at the time. The only reason it made an impression on Helen was that it happened in our apartment building. Mr. Deloney was cleaning a gun, and it went off and shot him, and that was the whole story."

"Are you sure?"

"Hoffman said so, and Hoffman doesn't lie." It sounded like an incantation which she had used before.

"What made Helen think he was lying?"

"Imagination pure and simple. She said she talked to a witness who saw somebody shoot Mr. Deloney, but I say she dreamed it. No witness ever turned up, and Hoffman said there couldn't have been a witness. Mr. Deloney was alone in the apartment when it happened. He tried to clean a loaded gun and shot himself in the face. Helen must have dreamed the other. She had a bit of a crush on Mr. Deloney. He was a good-looking man, and you know how young girls are."

"How old was she?"

"Nineteen. That was the summer she left home."

It was full dark now. Away off to the right the lights of Long Beach, where I had spent my own uneasy youth, were reflected like a dying red fire from the overcast.

"Who was Mr. Deloney?"

"Luke Deloney," she said. "He was a very successful contractor in Bridgeton and throughout the state. He owned our apartment building and other buildings in town. Mrs. Deloney still owns them. They're worth a lot more than they were then, and even then he was close to a millionaire."

"Deloney has a surviving widow?"

"Yes, but don't go jumping to conclusions. She was miles away, in their main house, when it happened. Sure there was a lot of talk in town, but she was as innocent as a newborn babe. She came from a very good family. She was one of the famous Osborne sisters in Bridgeton."

"What were they famous for?"

"Their father was the U.S. Senator. I remember when I was in grade school, back before the World War One, they used to ride to hounds in red coats. But they were always very democratic."

"Good for them." I brought her back to the Deloney case. "You say Deloney was shot in the building where you had your own apartment?"

"Yes. We were in an apartment on the ground floor. We got it dirt cheap because we used to collect the rent for Mr. Deloney. He kept the roof apartment for himself. He used it for a kind of private office, and a place to throw parties for visiting firemen and so on. A lot of big men from the state house were friends of his. We used to see them coming and going," she said in a privileged way.

"And he shot himself in this penthouse apartment?"

"The gun shot him," she corrected me. "It was an accident."

"What sort of a man was Deloney?"

"He was a self-made man, I guess you'd say. He came from the same section of town Hoffman and I did, which is how we got the job collecting rent for him, and that *helped*, in the depression. The depression didn't faze Luke Deloney. He borrowed the money to start his own contracting business and came up fast on his own initiative, and married Senator Osborne's oldest daughter. There's no telling where he might have got to. He was only a young man of forty when he died."

"Helen was interested in him, you say?"

"Not seriously, I don't mean that. I doubt if they ever said two words to each other. But you know how young girls are, dreaming about older men. He was the most successful man around, and Helen was always very ambitious. It's funny, she blamed her father for being a failure, which he isn't. But when she finally got around to marrying she had to pick Bert Haggerty, and he's a failure if there ever was one."

She was talking much more freely, but her loquacity tended to fly off in all directions. It was natural enough. Her daughter's murder had dropped a depth charge into her life.

"Assume there is a connection," I said, "between Helen's death and the Deloney shooting—do you have any notion what it could be?"

"No, she must have been imagining things. She was always a great one for that."

"But she said she knew a witness who saw Deloney shot by someone else?"

"She was talking foolishness."

"Why?"

"You mean why would she say such things to her father? To get under his skin. There was always bad blood between them, from the time that Hoffman first raised his hand to her. Once they got arguing, there wasn't anything she wouldn't say."

"Did she name the witness?"

"How could she? There was no such person. Her father challenged her to mention a name. She admitted that she couldn't, that she was just talking."

"She admitted it?"

"She had to. Hoffman made her. But she never took back the hard words she spoke to him."

"Is it possible that Helen herself was the witness?"

"That's crazy and you know it. How could she be a witness to something that never happened?" But there was a shrill edge on her certitude.

"Deloney's dead, remember. So is she. It tends to confirm the things she told her friends before she died."

"About Bridgeton, you mean?"

"Yes."

She lapsed into silence again. Below the harbor cities we entered the fog zone. I was afraid of running into a pileup and I slowed down. Mrs. Hoffman kept looking back as if she could feel Bridgeton catching up.

"I hope Hoffman isn't drinking," she said after a while. "It isn't good for his blood pressure. I'll blame myself if anything happens to him."

"One of you had to come out here."

"I suppose so. Anyway Bert is with him and whatever else he may be Bert is no drunk."

"Helen's ex-husband is staying with her father?"

"Yes. He come over from Maple Park this morning and drove me to the airport. Bert's a good boy. I shouldn't call him a boy, he's a grown man in his forties, but he always seems younger than he is."

"Does he teach at Maple Park?"

"That's right, only he hasn't got his degree. He's been working on it for years. He teaches journalism and English, and he helps put out the school paper. He used to be a newspaperman, that was how Helen met him."

"When she was nineteen?"

"You have a good memory. You and Hoffman would get along. Hoffman's middle name is memory. There was a time before we got our wartime expansion when he knew every building in Bridgeton. Every factory, every warehouse, every residence. Pick any house on any street and he could tell you who built it and who owned it. He could tell you who lived there and who used to live there and how many children they had and how much income and anything else you wanted to know about them. I'm not exaggerating, ask any of his fellow officers. They used to predict great things for him, but he never made it higher than Lieutenant."

I wondered why the great things hadn't materialized. She gave me a kind of answer, which I suspected was more of a legend than a fact:

"Helen got her memory from him. They were more alike than either of them admitted. And they were crazy about each other, under all the trouble there was between them. It broke his heart when Helen left home and never wrote. He never asked about her, either, but he did a lot of brooding. He was never the same man again."

"Did she marry Bert Haggerty right away?"

"No, she kept him dangling for five or six years. He was away in the army part of that time. Bert did well in the war—a lot of men did well in the war that never did so well before or since—and he was full of confidence for a while. He was going to write a book, start his own newspaper, take her to Europe on their honeymoon. They did get to Europe, on the G. I. Bill—I gave them part of the money to make the trip—but that was all that ever came of his plans. He never could settle down to any one thing, and when he finally did it was too late. Last spring they came to the parting of the ways. I didn't like it, but I can hardly blame her. She always did better than he did, from the time that they were married. And one thing I'll say for Helen, she always had class."

"I agree."

"But maybe she should have stuck with Bert. Who knows? Maybe this wouldn't have happened. I sometimes think that any man is better than no man at all."

Later, as we were entering Pacific Point, she said: "Why couldn't Helen marry an upstanding husband? It's funny. She had brains and looks *and* class, but she never could attract an upstanding man."

I could feel her eyes on my profile, trying to chart the lost continent of her daughter's life.

17

The Pacific Hotel stood on a corner just above the economic equator that divided the main street into a prosperous section and a not so prosperous one. The lobby was almost empty on this Saturday night. Four old men were playing bridge in the light of a standing lamp. The only other human being in sight was Dr. Geisman, if he qualified.

He got up out of a shabby green plastic armchair and shook hands formally with Mrs. Hoffman.

"I see that you've arrived safely. How are you?"

"I'm all right, thanks."

"Your daughter's unexpected demise came as quite a blow to us."

"To me, too."

"In fact I've been endeavoring all day to find a replacement for her. I still haven't succeeded. This is the worst possible time of year to try to recruit teaching personnel."

"That's too bad."

I left them trying to breathe life into their stillborn conversation and went into the bar for a drink. A single customer sat trading sorrows with the fat lugubrious bartender. Her hair was dyed black, with a greenish sheen on it like certain ducks.

I recognized the woman—I could have spotted Mrs. Perrine at a thousand yards—and I started to back out of the room. She turned and saw me.

"Fancy meeting you here." She made a large gesture which almost upset the empty glass in front of her, and said to the bartender: "This is my friend Mr. Archer. Pour my friend a drink."

"What'll you have?"

"Bourbon. I'm paying. What is the lady drinking?"

"Planter's punch," she said, "and thanks for the 'lady.' Thanks for everything in fact. I'm celebrating, been celebrating all day."

I wished she hadn't been. The granite front she had kept up at her trial had eroded, and the inner ruin of her life showed through. While I didn't know all of Mrs. Perrine's secrets, I knew the record she had left on the police blotters of twenty cities. She had been innocent of this one particular crime, but she was a hustler who had worked the coasts from Acapulco to Seattle and from Montreal to Key West.

The bartender limped away to make our drinks. I sat on the stool beside her. "You should pick another town to celebrate in."

"I know. This town is a graveyard. I felt like the last living inhabitant, until you sashayed in."

"That isn't what I mean, Mrs. Perrine."

"Hell, call me Bridget, you're my pal, you've earned the right."

"Okay, Bridget. The police didn't like your acquittal, you couldn't expect them to. They'll pick you up for any little thing."

"I haven't stepped out of line. I have my own money."

"I'm thinking about what you might do if you go on celebrating. You can't afford to jaywalk in this town."

She considered this problem, and her twisting face mimicked the efforts of her mind. "You may be right at that. I been thinking of going to Vegas in the morning. I have a friend in Vegas."

The bartender brought our drinks. Mrs. Perrine sipped at hers, making a sour face, as if she'd suddenly lost her taste for it. Her gaze strayed to the mirror behind the bar.

"My gosh," she said, "is that me? I look like the wrath of God."

"Take a bath and get some sleep."

"It isn't so easy to sleep. I get lonely at night." She ogled me, more or less automatically.

She wasn't my baby. I finished my drink and put two dollar bills on the bar.

"Good night, Bridget. Take it easy. I have to make a phone call."

"Sure you do. See you at the Epworth League."

The bartender limped toward her as I walked out. Mrs. Hoffman and Dr. Geisman were no longer in the lobby. I found the telephone booths in a cul-de-sac behind the main desk and called the Bradshaw house.

Before the phone had rung more than once, the old lady's voice came quavering over the line. "Roy? Is that you, Roy?"

"This is Archer."

"I was so hoping it would be Roy. He always telephones by this time. You don't suppose something has happened to him?"

"No. I don't."

"Have you seen the paper?"

"No."

"There's an item to the effect that Laura Sutherland went to the Reno conference with him. Roy didn't tell me that. Do you suppose he's interested in Laura?"

"I wouldn't know."

"She's a lovely young woman, don't you think?"

I wondered if she'd had some wine at dinner that made her silly. "I have no opinion on the subject, Mrs. Bradshaw. I called to see if you're willing to follow through on our conversation this afternoon."

"I'm afraid I couldn't possibly, not without Roy's consent. He handles the money in the family, you know. Now I'm going to ask you to cut this short, Mr. Archer. I'm expecting to hear from Roy at any moment."

She hung up on me. I seemed to be losing my touch with little old ladies. I went into the washroom and looked at my face in the mirror above the row of basins. Someone had written in pencil on the wall: Support Mental Health or I'll kill you.

A small brown newsboy came into the washroom and caught me grinning at my reflection. I pretended to be examining my teeth. He looked about ten years old, and conducted himself like a miniature adult.

"Read all about the murder," he suggested.

I bought a local paper from him. The lead story was headlined: "PPC Teacher

Shot," with the subhead: "Mystery Student to be Questioned." In effect, it tried and convicted Dolly. She had "registered fraudulently, using an alias." Her friendship with Helen was described as "a strange relationship." The S and W thirty-eight found in her bed was "the murder weapon." She had "a dark secret in her past"—the McGee killing—and was "avoiding questioning by the police."

No other possible suspect was mentioned. The man from Reno didn't appear in the story.

In lieu of doing something constructive I tore the paper to pieces and dropped the pieces in the trash basket. Then I went back to the telephone booths. Dr. Godwin's answering service wanted to know if it was an emergency.

"Yes. It has to do with a patient of Dr. Godwin's."

"Are you the patient, sir?"

"Yes," I lied, wondering if this meant I needed help.

The switchboard girl said in a gentler voice: "The last time the doctor called in he was at home."

She recited his number but I didn't use it. I wanted to talk to Godwin face to face. I got his address out of the directory and drove across town to his house.

It was one of a number of large houses set on the edge of the mesa which normally overlooked the harbor and the city. Tonight it was islanded by the fog.

Behind the Arizona fieldstone front of the house a tenor and a soprano were singing a heartbreaking duet from *La Bohème*.

The door was answered by a handsome woman wearing a red silk brocade coat and the semi-professional smile that doctors' wives acquire. She seemed to recognize my name.

"I'm sorry, Mr. Archer. My husband was here until just a few minutes ago. We were actually listening to music for a change. Then a young man called—the husband of one of his patients—and he agreed to meet him at the nursing home."

"It wasn't Alex Kincaid who called?"

"I believe it was, Mr. Archer." She stepped outside, a brilliant and very feminine figure in her red coat. "My husband has spoken of you. I understand you're working on this criminal case he's involved with."

"Yes."

Her hand touched my arm. "I'm worried about him. He's taking this thing so seriously. He seems to think that he let the girl down when she was his patient before, and that it makes him responsible for everything that's happened." Her fine long eyes looked up at me, asking for reassurance.

"He isn't," I said.

"Will you tell him so? He won't listen to me. There are very few people he will listen to. But he seems to have some respect for you, Mr. Archer."

"It's mutual. I doubt that he'd want my opinion on the subject of his responsibility, though. He's a very powerful and temperamental man, easy to cross."

"You're telling me," she said. "I suppose I had no right to ask you to speak to him. But the way he pours his life away into those patients of his—" Her hand moved from her breast in an outward gesture.

"He seems to thrive on it."

"I don't." She made a wry face. "Physician's wife, heal thyself, eh?"

"You're thriving by all appearances," I said. "That's a nice coat, by the way."

"Thank you. Jim bought it for me in Paris last summer."

I left her smiling less professionally, and went to the nursing home. Alex's red Porsche was standing at the curb in front of the big plain stucco building. I felt my heartbeat pounding in my ears. Something good could still happen.

A Spanish American nurse's aide in a blue and white uniform unlocked the door and let me into the front room to wait for Dr. Godwin. Nell and several other bathrobed patients were watching a television drama about a pair of lawyers, father and son. They paid no attention to me. I was only a real-life detective, unemployed at the moment. But not, I hoped, for long.

I sat in an empty chair to one side. The drama was well directed and well played but I couldn't keep my mind on it. I began to watch the four people who were watching it. Nell the somnambulist, her black hair hanging like tangled sorrows down her back, held cupped in her hands the blue ceramic ashtray she had made. A young man with an untrimmed beard and rebellious eyes looked like a conscientious objector to everything. A thin-haired man, who was trembling with excitement, went on trembling right through the commercial. An old woman had a translucent face through which her life burned like a guttering candle. Step back a little and you could almost imagine that they were three generations of one family, grandmother, parents, and son, at home on a Saturday night.

Dr. Godwin appeared in the inner doorway and crooked his finger at me. I followed him down the hallway through a thickening hospital odor, into a small cramped office. He switched on a lamp over the desk and sat behind it. I took the only other chair.

"Is Alex Kincaid with his wife?"

"Yes. He called me at home and seemed very eager to see her, though he hasn't been around all day. He also wanted to talk to me."

"Did he say anything about running out on her?"

"No."

"I hope he's changed his mind." I told Godwin about my meeting with Kincaid senior, and Alex's departure with his father.

"You can't entirely blame him for falling by the wayside momentarily. He's young, and under great strain." Godwin's changeable eyes lit up. "The important thing, for him as well as Dolly, is that he decided to come back."

"How is she?"

"Calmer, I think. She didn't want to talk tonight, at least not to me."

"Will you let me have a try at her?"

"No."

"I almost regret bringing you into this case, doctor."

"I've been told that before, and less politely," he said with a stubborn smile. "But once I'm in I'm in, and I'll continue to do as I think best."

"I'm sure you will. Did you see the evening paper?"

"I saw it."

"Does Dolly know what's going on outside? About the gun, for instance?"

"No."

"Don't you think she should be told?"

He spread out his hands on the scarred desk-top. "I'm trying to simplify her problems, not add to them. She had so many pressures on her last night, from both the past and the present, that she was on the verge of a psychotic breakdown. We don't want that to happen."

"Will you be able to protect her from police questioning?"

"Not indefinitely. The best possible protection would be a solution to this case absolving her."

"I'm working on it. I talked to her Aunt Alice this morning, and looked over the scene of the McGee killing. I became pretty well convinced that even if McGee did kill his wife, which I doubt, Dolly couldn't have identified him as he left the house. In other words her testimony at his trial was cooked."

"Alice Jenks convinced you of this?"

"The physical layout did. Miss Jenks did her best to convince me of the opposite, that McGee was guilty. I wouldn't be surprised if she was the main motive power behind the case against him."

"He *was* guilty."

"So you've said. I wish you'd go into your reasons for believing that."

"I'm afraid I can't. It has to do with the confidences of a patient."

"Constance McGee?"

"Mrs. McGee wasn't formally a patient. But you can't treat a child without treating the parents."

"And she confided in you?"

"Naturally, to some extent. For the most part we talked about her family problems." Godwin was feeling his way carefully. His face was bland. Under the lamp his bald head gleamed like a metal dome in moonlight.

"Her sister Alice made an interesting slip. She said there was no other man in Constance's life. I didn't ask her. Alice volunteered the information."

"Interesting."

"I thought so. Was Constance in love with another man at the time she was shot?"

Godwin nodded almost imperceptibly.

"Who was he?"

"I have no intention of telling you. He's suffered enough." A shadow of the suffering passed across his own face. "I've told you this much because I want you to understand that McGee had a motive, and was certainly guilty."

"I think he was framed, just as Dolly is being framed."

"We agree on the latter point. Why can't we settle for that?"

"Because there have been three killings, and they're connected. They're connected subjectively, as you would say, in Dolly's mind. I believe they're objectively connected, too. They may all have been done by the same person."

Godwin didn't ask me who. It was just as well. I was talking over my head, and I had no suspect.

"What third killing are you referring to?"

"The death of Luke Deloney, a man I never heard of until tonight. I met Helen Haggerty's mother at the L.A. airport and had a talk with her on the way down here. According to her, Deloney shot himself by accident while cleaning a gun. But Helen claimed he was murdered and said she knew a witness. The witness may have been herself. At any rate she quarreled with her father on the issue—he seems to have been the detective in charge of the case—and ran away from home. All this was over twenty years ago."

"You seriously think it's connected with the present case?"

"Helen thought so. Her death makes her an authority on the subject."

"What do you propose to do about it?"

"I'd like to fly to Illinois tonight and talk to Helen's father. But I can't afford to do it on my own hook."

"You could phone him."

"I could. My sense of the situation is that it would do more harm than good. He may be a tough nut to crack."

Godwin said after a minute's thought: "I might consider backing you."

"You're a generous man."

"A curious one," he said. "Remember I've been living with this case for over ten years. I'd give a good deal to see it ended."

"Let me talk to Alex first, and ask him how he feels about laying out more money."

Godwin inclined his head and remained bowing as he stood up. He wasn't bowing to me. It was more of a general and habitual bow, as if he could feel the weight of the stars and was asking their permission to take part of the weight on human shoulders.

"I'll get him out of there. He's stayed long enough."

Godwin disappeared down the hallway. A few minutes later Alex came back alone. He walked like a man in a tunnel underground, but his face was more serene than I'd ever seen it.

He paused in the doorway. "Dr. Godwin said you were here."

"I'm surprised to see you."

Hurt and embarrassment flickered across the upper part of his face. He brushed at it impatiently with his fingers. Then he stepped into the office, shutting the door behind him and leaning on it.

"I made a fool of myself today. I tried to chicken out."

"It takes guts to admit it."

"Don't gloss it over," he said sharply. "I was really lousy. It's funny, when Dad gets upset it has a peculiar effect on me. It's like sympathetic vibrations: he goes to pieces, I go to pieces. Not that I'm blaming *him*."

"I'm blaming him."

"Please don't. You have no right to." His eyebrows knitted. "The company's talking about bringing in computers to handle most of the work in the office. Dad's afraid he can't adjust, and I guess it makes him afraid of things in general."

"You've been doing some thinking."

"I had to. You started me off with what you said about annulling myself. I felt that way when I went home with Dad—as though I wasn't a man any more." He pushed himself clear of the door and balanced himself on his feet, his arms swinging slightly at his sides. "It's really amazing, you know? You really can make a decision inside yourself. You can decide to be one thing or another."

The only trouble was that you had to make the decision every hour on the hour. But he would have to find that out for himself.

"How is your wife?" I said.

"She actually seemed glad to see me. Have you talked to her?"

"Dr. Godwin wouldn't let me."

"He wouldn't let me either, till I promised not to ask her any questions. I didn't, but the subject of the revolver came up. She'd heard two of the aides talking about some newspaper story—"

"It's in the local paper. What did she have to say about the gun?"

"It isn't hers. Somebody must have hidden it under her mattress. She asked me to describe it, and she said it sounded like her Aunt Alice's revolver. Her aunt used to keep it on her bedside table at night. Dolly was sort of fascinated by it when she was a little girl." He breathed deeply. "Apparently she saw her aunt threaten her father with it. I didn't want her to go into all that stuff but I couldn't prevent her. She calmed down again after a while."

"At least she's stopped blaming herself for Helen Haggerty's death."

"She hasn't though. She still says it was her fault. Everything's her fault."

"In what way?"

"She didn't go into it. I didn't want her to."

"You mean Dr. Godwin didn't want you to."

"That's right. He's calling the shots. I guess he knows more about her than I ever will."

"I take it you're going on with your marriage?" I said.

"We have to. I realized that today. People can't walk out on each other when they're in this kind of trouble. I think maybe Dolly realizes it, too. She didn't turn her back on me or anything."

"What else did you talk about?"

"Nothing important. The other patients, mostly. There's one old lady with a broken hip who doesn't want to stay in bed. Dolly's been sort of looking after her." It seemed important to him. "She can't be so very sick herself." It was an implied question.

"You'll have to take that up with the doctor."

"He isn't saying much. He wants to give her some psychological tests tomorrow. I told him to go ahead."

"Do I have your go-ahead, too?"

"Naturally. I was hoping that you'd take that for granted. I want you to do everything you can to settle this thing. I'll give you a written contract—"

"That won't be necessary. But it's going to cost you money."

"How much money?"

"A couple of thousand, maybe a good deal more."

I told him about the Reno end of the case, which Arnie and Phyllis Walters were handling, and about the Bridgeton situation which I wanted to explore. I also advised him to talk to Jerry Marks first thing in the morning.

"Will Mr. Marks be available on a Sunday?"

"Yes. I've already set him up for you. Of course you're going to have to give him a retainer."

"I have some savings bonds," he said thoughtfully, "and I can borrow on my insurance policy. Meantime I can sell the car. It's paid for, and I've been offered two five for it. I was getting pretty tired of sports car rallies and all that jazz. It's kid stuff."

18

The front doorbell rang. Someone trotted past the office door to answer it. It was getting late for visitors, and I went out and followed the aide along the hallway. The four patients were still watching the television screen as if it was a window on the outside world.

Whoever had rung the bell was knocking now, rather violently.

"Just a minute," the aide said through the door. She got her key into the lock and opened it partly. "Who is it? Who do you want to see?"

It was Alice Jenks. She tried to push her way in, but the aide had her white shoe against the door.

"I wish to see my niece, Dolly McGee."

"We have no such patient."

"She calls herself Dolly Kincaid now."

"I can't let you in to see anyone without doctor's permission."

"Is Godwin here?"

"I think so."

"Get him," Miss Jenks said peremptorily.

The girl's Latin temper flared. "I don't take orders from you," she said in a hissing whisper. "And keep your voice down. We have people trying to rest."

"Get Dr. Godwin."

"Don't worry, I intend to. But you'll have to wait outside."

"It will be a pleasure."

I stepped between them before the nurse closed the door and said to Miss Jenks: "May I speak to you for a minute?"

She peered at me through fogged glasses. "So you're here, too."

"I'm here, too."

I stepped out under the outside light and heard the door shut behind me. The air was chilly after the hot-house atmosphere of the nursing home. Miss Jenks had on a thick fur-collared coat which made her figure massive in the gloom. Droplets of water glistened in the fur, and in her graying hair.

"What do you want with Dolly?"

"It's none of your business. She's my flesh and blood, not yours."

"Dolly has a husband. I represent him."

"You can go and represent him in some other constituency. I'm not interested in you or her husband."

"But suddenly you're interested in Dolly. Does it have anything to do with the story in the paper?"

"Maybe it has and maybe it hasn't." In her language, that meant yes. She added defensively: "I've been interested in Dolly since she was born. I know better than a lot of strangers what's good for her."

"Dr. Godwin isn't a stranger."

"No. I wish he was."

"I hope you're not thinking of taking her out of here."

"Maybe I am and maybe I'm not." She dug some Kleenex out of her purse and used it to clean her glasses. I could see a newspaper folded small in the purse.

"Miss Jenks, did you read the description of the revolver that was found in Dolly's bed?"

She replaced her glasses quickly, as though to cover the startled look in her eyes. "Naturally I read it."

"Did it ring any bell with you?"

"Yes. It sounded like the revolver I used to have, so I came into town to the courthouse to have a look at it. It looks like mine all right."

"You admit that?"

"Why shouldn't I? I haven't seen it for over ten years."

"Can you prove it?"

"Of course I can prove it. It was stolen from my house before Constance was shot. Sheriff Crane theorized at the time that it might have been the gun McGee used on her. He still thinks so. McGee could easily have taken it. He knew where it was, in my bedroom."

"You didn't tell me all this this morning."

"I didn't think of it. It was only theory, anyway. You were interested in facts."

"I'm interested in both, Miss Jenks. What's the police theory now? That McGee killed Miss Haggerty and tried to frame his daughter?"

"I wouldn't put it past him. A man who would do what he did to his wife—" Her voice sank out of hearing in her throat.

"And they want to use his daughter to nail McGee again?"

She didn't answer me. Lights went on inside, and there were sounds of movement culminating in Godwin's opening the door. He shook his keys at us, grinning fiercely.

"Come inside, Miss Jenks."

She stamped up the concrete steps. Godwin had cleared the front room of everyone but Alex, who was sitting on a chair against the wall. I stood unobtrusively in the corner beside the silent television set.

She faced him, almost as tall in heels as he was, almost as wide in her coat, almost as stubborn in her pride. "I don't approve of what you're doing, Dr. Godwin."

"What am I doing?" He sat on the arm of a chair and crossed his legs.

"You know what I'm referring to. My niece. Keeping her cooped up here in defiance of the constituted authorities."

"There's no defiance involved. I try to do my duty, the Sheriff tries to do his. Sometimes we come into conflict. It doesn't necessarily mean that Sheriff Crane is right and I'm wrong."

"It does to me."

"I'm not surprised. We've disagreed before, on a similar issue. You and your friend the Sheriff had your way on that occasion, unfortunately for your niece."

"It did her no harm to testify. Truth is truth."

"And trauma is trauma. It did her incalculable harm, which she's still suffering under."

"I'd like to see that for myself."

"So you can make a full report to the Sheriff?"

"Good citizens cooperate with the law," she said sententiously. "But I'm not here on the Sheriff's behalf. I came here to help my niece."

"How do you propose to help her?"

"I'm going to take her home with me."

Godwin stood up shaking his head.

"You can't stop me. I've been her guardian since her mother died. The law will back me up."

"I think not," Godwin said coldly. "Dolly's of age, and she's here of her own free will."

"I'd like to ask her that question for myself."

"You're not going to ask her any questions."

The woman took a step toward him and thrust her head forward on her neck. "You think you're a little tin god, don't you, masterminding my family's affairs? I say you've got no right to keep her here under duress, making us all look bad. I've got a position to keep up in this county. I spent the day with some very high-level people from Sacramento."

"I'm afraid I don't follow your logic. But keep your voice down, please." Godwin himself was using the slow weary monotone that I had first heard on the telephone twenty-four hours before. "And let me assure you again, your niece is here of her own free will."

"That's right." Alex came forward into the verbal line of fire. "I don't believe we've met. I'm Alex Kincaid, Dolly's husband."

She disregarded his hand.

"I think it's important for her to stay here," he said. "I have confidence in the doctor, and so has my wife."

"I'm sorry for you then. He had me bamboozled, too, until I found out what went on in his office."

Alex looked inquiringly at Godwin. The doctor turned his hands out as if he was feeling for rain. He said to Miss Jenks:

"You graduated in sociology, I believe."

"What if I did?"

"From a woman of your training and background, I'd expect a more professional attitude toward the practice of psychiatry."

"I'm not talking about the practice of psychiatry. I'm talking about the practice of other things."

"What other things?"

"I wouldn't soil my tongue with them. But please don't think I didn't know my sister and what went on in her life. I've been remembering things—the way she used to primp and preen Saturday mornings before she came in to town. And then she wanted to move here, to be closer."

"Closer to me?"

"So she told me."

Godwin's face was white, as if all its color had been drawn into the darkness of his eyes. "You're a silly woman, Miss Jenks, and I've had enough of you. I'll ask you to leave now."

"I'm staying here till I see my niece. I want to know what you're practicing on her."

"It would do her no good. In your present mood you'd do no good to anyone." He moved around her to the door and held it open. "Good night."

She didn't move or look at him. She stood with her head down, a little dazed by the anger that had gone through her like a storm.

"Do you wish to be forcibly removed?"

"Try it. You'll end up in court."

But a kind of shame had begun to invade her face. Her mouth was twitching like a small injured thing. It had said more than she intended.

When I took her by the arm and said, "Come on, Miss Jenks," she let me lead her to the door. Godwin closed it on her.

"I have no patience with fools," he said.

"Have a little patience with me, though, will you, doctor?"

"I'll give it a try, Archer." He took a deep breath and let it out as a sigh. "You want to know if there's any truth in her innuendo."

"You make it easy for me."

"Why not? I love the truth. My entire life is a search for it."

"Okay, was Constance McGee in love with you?"

"I suppose she was, in a way. Women patients traditionally fall in love with their doctors, particularly in my field. It didn't persist in her case."

"This may strike you as a foolish question, but did you love her?"

"I'll give you a foolish answer, Mr. Archer. Of course I loved her. I loved her the way a doctor loves his patients, if he's any good. It's a love that's more maternal than erotic." He spread his large hands on his chest, and spoke from there: "I wanted to serve her. I didn't succeed too well."

I was silenced.

"And now, gentlemen, if you'll excuse me, I have hospital rounds in the morning." He swung his keys.

Alex said to me in the street: "Do you believe him?"

"Unless or until I have proof that he's lying. He's not telling all he knows but people seldom do, let alone doctors. I'd take his word ahead of Alice Jenks's."

He started to climb into his car, then turned back toward me, gesturing in the direction of the nursing home. Its plain rectangular façade loomed in the fog like a blockhouse, the visible part of an underground fortress.

"You think she's safe there, Mr. Archer?"

"Safer than she'd be on the streets, or in jail, or in a psycho ward with a police psychiatrist quizzing her."

"Or at her aunt's?"

"Or at her aunt's. Miss Jenks is one of these righteous women who doesn't let her left lobe know what her right lobe is doing. She's quite a tiger."

His eyes were still on the front of the nursing home.

Deep inside the building, the wild old voice I had heard that morning rose again. It faded like the cry of a seabird flying away, intermitted by wind.

"I wish I could stay with Dolly, and protect her," Alex said.

He was a good boy.

I broached the subject of money. He gave me most of the money in his wallet. I used it to buy an airline ticket to Chicago and return, and caught a late flight from International Airport.

19

I left the toll road, which bypassed Bridgeton, and drove my rented car through the blocks of housing tracts on the outskirts of the city. I could see the clumps of sawed-off skyscrapers in the business district ahead, and off to the left, across the whole south side, the factories. It was Sunday morning, and only one of their stacks was pouring smoke into the deep blue sky.

I stopped for gas at a service station and looked up Earl Hoffman's address in the telephone directory. When I asked the attendant how to get to Cherry Street, where Hoffman lived, he pointed in the general direction of the factories.

It was a middle-class street of substantial two-story houses which had been touched but not destroyed by the blight that creeps outward from the centers of cities. Hoffman's house was of grimy white brick like the others, but the front porch had been painted within living memory. An old Chevrolet coupé stood at the curb in front of it.

The doorbell didn't work. I knocked on the screen door. An old young man with more nose than chin opened the inner door and looked at me through the screen in a sad way.

"Mr. Haggerty?"

"Yes."

I told him my name and trade and where I was from. "I was with your wife—your ex-wife—shortly before she was killed."

"It's a dreadful thing."

He stood absently in the doorway, forgetting to ask me in. He had a frowzy sleepless look as if he'd been up most of the night. Though there was no gray on his head, white hairs glistened in his day-old beard. His small eyes had the kind of incandescence that goes with conscious suffering.

"May I come in, Mr. Haggerty?"

"I don't know if it's such a good idea. Earl's pretty broken up."

"I thought he and his daughter had been on the outs for a long time."

"They were. It only makes it harder for him, I think. When you're angry with someone you love, you always expect at the back of your mind there'll be a reconciliation some day. But now there will never be anything."

He was speaking for his father-in-law but also for himself. His empty hands moved aimlessly at his sides. The fingers of his right hand were stained dark yellow by nicotine.

"I'm sorry," I said, "that Mr. Hoffman isn't feeling well. I'm afraid I'll have to talk to him anyway. I didn't come from California for the ride."

"No. Obviously not. What is it you have to discuss with him?"

"His daughter's murder. He may be able to help me understand it."

"I thought it was already solved."

"It isn't."

"Has the girl student been cleared?"

"She's in process of being cleared," I said with deliberate vagueness. "You and I can go into all that later. Right now I'm very eager to talk to Hoffman."

"If you insist. I only hope you can get some sense out of him."

I saw what he meant when he took me through the house to "Earl's den," as Haggerty called it. It was furnished with a closed roll-top desk, an armchair, a studio couch. Through a haze compounded of whisky fumes and smoke I could see a big old man sprawled in orange pajamas on the couch, his head propped up by bolsters. A strong reading light shone on his stunned face. His eyes seemed out of focus, but he was holding a magazine with an orange cover that almost matched his pajamas. The wall above him was decorated with rifles and shotguns and hand guns.

"When I recall the loss of all my perished years," he said huskily.

Old cops didn't talk like that, and Earl Hoffman looked like no exception to the rule. His body was massive, and could have belonged to a professional football player or a wrestler gone to pot. His nose had once been broken. He had a clipped gray head and a mouth like bent iron.

"That's beautiful poetry, Bert," the iron mouth said.

"I suppose it is."

"Who's your friend, Bert?"

"Mr. Archer, from California."

"California, eh? That's where my poor little Helen got knocked off."

He sobbed, or hiccupped, once. Then he swung himself onto the edge of the couch, letting his bare feet fall heavily to the floor.

"Do you know—did you know my little daughter Helen?"

"I knew her."

"Isn't that remarkable." He rose swaying and clasped my hands in both of his, using me to support him. "Helen was a remarkable girl. I've just been reading over one of her poems. Wrote it when she was just a teen-age girl at City College. Here, I'll show you."

He made a fairly elaborate search for the orange-covered magazine, which was lying in plain sight on the floor where he had dropped it. The name of it was the *Bridgeton Blazer*, and it looked like a school production.

Haggerty picked it up and handed it to him: "Please don't bother with it, Earl. Helen didn't write it anyway."

"Didn't write it? 'Course she wrote it. It's got her initials on it." Hoffman flipped through the pages. "See?"

"But she was only translating from Verlaine."

"Never heard of him." Hoffman turned to me, thrusting the magazine into my hands. "Here, read this. See what a remarkable gift poor little Helen had."
I read:

> When the violins
> Of the autumn winds
> Begin to sigh
> My heart is torn
> With their forlorn
> Monotony.
>
> And when the hour
> Sounds from the tower
> I weep tears
> For I recall
> The loss of all
> My perished years.
>
> And then I go
> With the winds that blow
> And carry me
> There and here
> Like a withered and sere
> Leaf from a tree.
>   —H.H.

Hoffman looked at me with one of his unfocused eyes. "Isn't that beautiful poetry, Mr. Arthur?"

"Beautiful."

"I only wisht I understood it. Do you understand it?"

"I think so."

"Then keep it. Keep it in memory of poor little Helen."

"I couldn't do that."

"Sure you can. Keep it." He snatched it out of my hands, rolled it up, and thrust it into my jacket pocket, breathing whisky in my face.

"Keep it," Haggerty whispered at my shoulder. "You don't want to cross him."

"You heard him. You don't want to cross me."

Hoffman grinned loosely at me. He clenched his left fist, examined it for defects, then used it to strike himself on the chest. He walked on spraddled legs to the roll-top desk and opened it. There were bottles and a single smeared tumbler inside. He half-filled the tumbler from a fifth of bourbon and drank most of it down. His son-in-law said something under his breath, but made no move to stop him.

The heavy jolt squeezed sweat out of Hoffman's face. It seemed to sober him a little. His eyes focused on me.

"Have a drink?"

"All right. I'll take water and ice in mine, please." I didn't normally drink in the morning but this was an abnormal occasion.

"Get some ice and a glass, Bert. Mr. Arthur wants a drink. If you're too mucky-muck to drink with me, Mr. Arthur isn't."

"The name is Archer."

"Get *two* glasses," he said with his foolish grin. "Mr. Archer wants a drink, too. Sit down," he said to me. "Take the load off your feet. Tell me about poor little Helen."

We sat on the couch. I filled him in quickly on the circumstances of the murder, including the threat that preceded it, and Helen's feeling that Bridgeton was catching up with her.

"What did she mean by that?" The lines of the grin were still on his face like clown marks but the grin had become a rictus.

"I've come a long way to see if you can help me answer that question."

"Me? Why come to me? I never knew what went on in her mind, she never *let* me know. She was too bright for me." His mood swayed into heavy drunken self-pity. "I sweated and slaved to buy her an education like I never had, but she wouldn't give her poor old father the time of day."

"I understand you had a bad quarrel and she left home."

"She told you, eh?"

I nodded. I had decided to keep Mrs. Hoffman out of it. He was the kind of man who wouldn't want his wife ahead of him in anything.

"She tell you the names she called me, crook and Nazi, when all I was doing was my bounden duty? You're a cop, you know how a man feels when your own family undermines you." He peered at me sideways. "You are a cop, aren't you?"

"I have been."

"What do you do for a living now?"

"Private investigation."

"Who for?"

"A man named Kincaid, nobody you know. I knew your daughter slightly, and I have a personal interest in finding out who killed her. I think the answer may be here in Bridgeton."

"I don't see how. She never set foot in this town for twenty years, until last spring. She only came home then to tell her mother she was getting a divorce.

From *him*." He gestured toward the back of the house, where I could hear ice being chipped.

"Did she do any talking to you?"

"I only saw her the once. She said hello-how-are-you and that was about it. She told her mother that she'd had it with Bert and her mother couldn't talk her out of it. Bert even followed her out to Reno to try and convince her to come back, but it was no go. He isn't enough of a man to hold a woman."

Hoffman finished his drink and set his tumbler down on the floor. He remained slumped forward for about a minute, and I was afraid he was going to get sick or pass out on me. But he came back up to a sitting position and muttered something about wanting to help me.

"Fine. Who was Luke Deloney?"

"Friend of mine. Big man in town back before the war. She told you about him, too, eh?"

"You could tell me more, Lieutenant. I hear you have a memory like an elephant."

"Did Helen say that?"

"Yes." The lie didn't cost me anything, not even a pang of conscience.

"At least she had some respect for her old man, eh?"

"A good deal."

He breathed with enormous relief. It would pass, as everything passes when a man is drinking seriously to kill awareness. But for the moment he was feeling good. He believed his daughter had conceded a point in their bitter life-long struggle.

"Luke was born in nineteen-oh-three on Spring Street," he said with great care, "in the twenty-one-hundred block, way out on the south side—two blocks over from where I lived when I was a kid. I knew him in grade school. He was the kind of a kid who saved up his paper-route money to buy a Valentine for everybody in his class. He actually did that. The principal used to take him around to the various rooms to show off his mental arithmetic. He did have a good head on his shoulders, I'll give him that. He skipped two grades. He was a comer.

"Old man Deloney was a cement finisher, and cement started to come in strong for construction after the World War. Luke bought himself a mixer with the money he'd saved and went into business for himself. He did real well in the twenties. At his peak he had over five hundred men working for him all over the state. Even the depression didn't cramp his style. He was a wheeler and a dealer as well as a builder. The only things going up in those days were public works, so he went out in a big way for the federal and state contracts. He married Senator Osborne's daughter, and that didn't do him any harm, either."

"I hear Mrs. Deloney's still alive."

"Sure she is. She lives in the house the Senator built in nineteen-oh-one on

Glenview Avenue on the north side. Number one-oh-three, I think." He was straining to live up to his encyclopedic reputation.

I made a mental note of the address. Preceded by clinking, Bert Haggerty came into the room with ice and water and glasses on a tin tray. I cleared a space on the desk and he set the tray down. It had originally belonged to the Bridgeton Inn.

"You took long enough," Hoffman said offhandedly.

Haggerty stiffened. His eyes seemed to regroup themselves more closely at the sides of his nose.

"Don't talk to me like that, Earl. I'm not a servant."

"If you don't like it you know what you can do."

"I realize you're tight, but there's a limit—"

"Who's tight? I'm not tight."

"You've been drinking for twenty-four hours."

"So what? A man has a right to drown his sorrows. But my brain is as clear as a bell. Ask Mr. Arthur here. Mr. Archer."

Haggerty laughed, mirthlessly, falsetto. It was a very queer sound, and I tried to cover it over with a broad flourish:

"The Lieutenant's been filling me in on some ancient history. He has a memory like an elephant."

But Hoffman wasn't feeling good any more. He rose cumbrously and advanced on Haggerty and me. One of his eyes looked at each of us. I felt like a man in a cage with a sick bear and his keeper.

"What's funny, Bert? You think my sorrow is funny, is that it? She wouldn't be dead if you were man enough to keep her at home. Why didn't you bring her home from Reno with you?"

"You can't blame me for everything," Haggerty said a little wildly. "I got along with her better than you did. If she hadn't had a father-fixation—"

"Don't give me that, you lousy intellectual. Ineffectual. Ineffectual intellectual. You're not the only one that can use four-bit words. And stop calling me Earl. We're not related. We never would have been if I had any say in the matter. We're not even related and you come into my house spying on my personal habits. What are you, an old woman?"

Haggerty was speechless. He looked at me helplessly.

"I'll break your neck," his father-in-law said.

I stepped between them. "Let's have no violence, Lieutenant. It wouldn't look good on the blotter."

"The little pipsqueak accused me. He said I'm drunk. You tell him he's mistaken. Make him apologize."

I turned to Haggerty, closing one eye. "Lieutenant Hoffman is sober, Bert. He can carry his liquor. Now you better get out of here before something happens."

He was glad to. I followed him out into the hall.

"This is the third or fourth time," he said in a low voice. "I didn't mean to set him off again."

"Let him cool for a bit. I'll sit with him. I'd like to talk to you afterward."

"I'll wait outside in my car."

I went back into the bear cage. Hoffman was sitting on the edge of the couch with his head supported by his hands.

"Everything's gone to hell in a hand-car." he said. "That pussy willow of a Bert Haggerty gets under my skin. I dunno what he thinks he's sucking around for." His mood changed. "You haven't deserted me, anyway. Go ahead, make yourself a drink."

I manufactured a light highball and brought it back to the couch. I didn't offer Hoffman any. In wine was truth, perhaps, but in whisky, the way Hoffman sluiced it down, was an army of imaginary rats climbing your legs.

"You were telling me about Luke Deloney and how he grew."

He squinted at me. "I don't know why you're so interested in Deloney. He's been dead for twenty-two years. Twenty-two years and three months. He shot himself, but I guess you know that, eh?" A hard intelligence glinted momentarily in his eyes and drew them into focus on my face.

I spoke to the hard intelligence: "Was there anything between Helen and Deloney?"

"No, she wasn't interested in *him*. She had a crush on the elevator boy, George. I ought to know, she made me get him the job. I was sort of managing the Deloney Apartments at the time. Luke Deloney and me, we were like that."

He tried to cross his second finger over his forefinger. It kept slipping. He finally completed the maneuver with the help of his other hand. His fingers were thick and mottled like uncooked breakfast sausages.

"Luke Deloney was a bit of a womanizer," he said indulgently, "but he didn't mess around with the daughters of his friends. He never cared for the young stuff, anyway. His wife must of been ten years older than he was. Anyway, he wouldn't touch my daughter. He knew I'd kill him."

"Did you?"

"That's a lousy question, mister. If I didn't happen to like you I'd knock your block off."

"No offense."

"I had nothing against Luke Deloney. He treated me fair and square. Anyway, I told you he shot himself."

"Suicide?"

"Naw. Why would he commit suicide? He had everything, money and women and a hunting lodge in Wisconsin. He took me up there personally more than once. The shooting was an accident. That's the way it went into the books and that's the way it stays."

"How did it happen, Lieutenant?"

"He was cleaning his .32 automatic. He had a permit to tote it on his person —I helped him get it myself—because he used to carry large sums of money. He took the clip out all right but he must of forgot the shell that was in the chamber. It went off and shot him in the face."

"Where?"

"Through the right eye."

"I mean where did the accident occur?"

"In one of the bedrooms in his apartment. He kept the roof apartment in the Deloney building for his private use. More than once I drank with him up there. Prewar Green River, boy." He slapped my knee, and noticed the full glass in my hand. "Drink up your drink."

I knocked back about half of it. It wasn't prewar Green River. "Was Deloney drinking at the time of the shooting?"

"Yeah, I think so. He knew guns. He wouldn't of made that mistake if he was sober."

"Was anybody with him in the apartment?"

"No."

"Can you be sure?"

"I can be sure. I was in charge of the investigation."

"Did anybody share the apartment with him?"

"Not on a permanent basis, you might say. Luke Deloney had various women on the string. I checked them out, but none of them was within a mile of the place at the time it happened."

"What kind of women?"

"All the way from floozies to one respectable married woman here in town. Their names didn't go into the record then and they're not going to now."

There was a growl in his voice. I didn't pursue the subject. Not that I was afraid of Hoffman exactly. I had at least fifteen years on him, and a low alcohol content. But if he went for me I might have to hurt him badly.

"What about Mrs. Deloney?" I said.

"What about her?"

"Where was she when all this was going on?"

"At home, out on Glenview. They were sort of separated. She didn't believe in divorce."

"People who don't believe in divorce sometimes believe in murder."

Hoffman moved his shoulders belligerently. "You trying to say that I hushed up a murder?"

"I'm not accusing you of anything, Lieutenant."

"You better not. I'm a cop, remember, first, last and always." He raised his fist and rotated it before his eyes like a hypnotic device. "I been a good cop all my life. In my prime I was the best damn cop this burg ever saw. I'll have a drink on that." He picked up his tumbler. "Join me?"

I said I would. We were moving obscurely on a collision course. Alcohol might soften the collision, or sink him. I finished my drink and handed him my glass. He filled it to the brim with neat whisky. Then he filled his own. He sat down and stared into the brown liquid as if it was a well where his life had drowned.

"Bottoms up," he said.

"Take it easy, Lieutenant. You don't want to kill yourself." It occurred to me as I said it that maybe he did.

"What are you, another pussy willow? Bottoms up."

He drained his glass and shuddered. I held mine in my hand. After a while he noticed this.

"You didn't drink your drink. What you trying to do, pull a fast one on me? Insult my hosh—my hoshpit—?" His lips were too numb to frame the word.

"No insult intended. I didn't come here for a drinking party, Lieutenant. I'm seriously interested in who killed your daughter. Assuming Deloney was murdered—"

"He wasn't."

"Assuming he was, the same person may have killed Helen. In view of everything I've heard, from her and other people, I think it's likely. Don't you?"

I was trying to get his mind under my control: the sloppy drunken sentimental part, and the drunken violent part, and the hard intelligent part hidden at the core.

"Deloney was an accident," he said clearly and stubbornly.

"Helen didn't think so. She claimed it was murder, and that she knew a witness to the murder."

"She was lying, trying to make me look bad. All she ever wanted to do was make her old man look bad."

His voice had risen. We sat and listened to its echoes. He dropped his empty glass, which bounced on the rug, and clenched the fist which seemed to be his main instrument of expression. I got ready to block it, but he didn't throw it at me.

Heavily and repeatedly, he struck himself in the face, on the eyes and cheeks, on the mouth, under the jaw. The blows left dull red welts in his clay-colored flesh. His lower lip split.

Hoffman said through the blood: "I clobbered my poor little daughter. I chased her out of the house. She never came back."

Large tears the color of pure distilled alcohol or grief rolled from his puffing eyes and down his damaged face. He fell sideways on the couch. He wasn't dead. His heart was beating strongly. I straightened him out—his legs were as heavy as sandbags—and put a bolster under his head. With blind eyes staring straight up into the light, he began to snore.

I closed the roll-top desk. The key was in it, and I turned it on the liquor and switched off the light and took the key outside with me.

20

Bert Haggerty was sitting in the Chevrolet coupé, wearing a stalled expression. I got in beside him and handed him the key.

"What's this?"

"The key to the liquor. You better keep it. Hoffman's had as much as he can take."

"Did he throw you out?"

"No. He passed out, while hitting himself in the face. Hard."

Haggerty thrust his long sensitive nose toward me. "Why would Earl do a thing like that?"

"He seemed to be punishing himself for hitting his daughter a long time ago."

"Helen told me about that. Earl treated her brutally before she left home. It's one thing I can't forgive him for."

"He can't forgive himself. Did Helen tell you what they quarreled about?"

"Vaguely. It was something to do with a murder here in Bridgeton. Helen believed, or pretended to believe, that her father deliberately let the murderer go free."

"Why do you say she pretended to believe it?"

"My dear dead wife," he said, wincing at the phrase, "had quite a flair for the dramatic, especially in her younger days."

"Did you know her before she left Bridgeton?"

"For a few months. I met her in Chicago at a party in Hyde Park. After she left home I helped her to get a job as a cub reporter. I was working for the City News Bureau then. But as I was saying, Helen always had this dramatic flair and when nothing happened in her life for it to feed on she'd *make* something happen or pretend that it had happened. Her favorite character was Mata Hari," he said with a chuckle that was half a sob.

"So you think she invented this murder?"

"I suppose I thought so at the time, because I certainly didn't take it seriously. I have no opinion now. Does it matter?"

"It could matter very much. Did Helen ever talk to you about Luke Deloney?"

"Who?"

"Luke Deloney, the man who was killed. He owned the apartment building they lived in, and occupied the penthouse himself."

Haggerty lit a cigarette before he answered. His first few words came out as visible puffs of smoke: "I don't recall the name. If she talked about him, it couldn't have made much of an impression on me."

"Her mother seems to think Helen had a crush on Deloney."

"Mrs. Hoffman's a pretty good woman, and I love her like a mother, but she gets some wild ideas."

"How do you know that this one is so wild? Was Helen in love with *you* then?"

He took a deep drag on his cigarette, like an unweaned child sucking on a dry bottle. It burned down to his yellow fingers. He tossed it into the street with a sudden angry gesture.

"She never was in love with me. I was useful to her, for a while. Later, in some sense, I was the last chance. The faithful follower. The last chance for gas before the desert."

"The desert?"

"The desert of love. The desert of unlove. But I don't think I'll go into the long and dreary chronicle of my marriage. It wasn't a lucky one, for either of us. I loved her, as far as I'm able to love, but she didn't love me. Proust says it's always that way. I'm teaching Proust to my sophomore class this fall, if I can summon up the élan to go on teaching."

"Who did Helen love?"

"It depends on which year you're talking about. Which month of which year." He didn't move, but he was hurting himself, hitting himself in the face with bitter words.

"Right at the beginning, before she left Bridgeton."

"I don't know if you'd call it love, but she was deeply involved with a fellow-student at the City College. It was a Platonic affair, the kind bright young people have, or used to have. It consisted largely of reading aloud to each other from their own works and others'. According to Helen, she never went to bed with him. I'm pretty sure she was a virgin when I met her."

"What was his name?"

"I'm afraid I don't remember. It's a clear case of Freudian repression."

"Can you describe him?"

"I never met him. He's a purely legendary figure in my life. But obviously he isn't the elusive murderer you're searching for. Helen would have been happy to see him go free." He had withdrawn from the pain of memory and was using an almost flippant tone, as if he was talking about people in a play, or watching ceiling movies at the dentist's. "Speaking of murder, as we seem to be doing, you were going to tell me about my ex-wife's death. She's completely ex now, isn't she, exed out?"

I cut in on his sad nonsense and gave him the story in some detail, including the man from Reno who ran away in the fog, and my attempts to get him identified. "Earl tells me you went to Reno last summer to see your wife. Did you run into any of her acquaintances there?"

"Did I not. Helen played a trick on me involving a couple of them. Her purpose was to stall off any chance for an intimate talk with me. Anyway, the one evening we spent together she insisted on making it a foursome with this woman named Sally something and her alleged brother."

"Sally Burke?"

"I believe that was her name. The hell of it was, Helen arranged it so that I was the Burke woman's escort. She wasn't a bad-looking woman, but we had nothing in common, and in any case it was Helen I wanted to talk to. But she spent the entire evening dancing with the brother. I'm always suspicious of men who dance too well."

"Tell me more about this brother. He may be our man."

"Well, he struck me as a rather sleazy customer. That may be projected envy. He was younger than I am, and healthier, and better looking. Also, Helen seemed to be fascinated by his line of chatter, which I thought was pointless—all about cars and horses and gambling odds. How a highly educated woman like Helen could be interested in such a man—" He tired of the sentence, and dropped it.

"Were they lovers?"

"How would I know? She wasn't confiding in me."

"But you know your own wife, surely."

He lit another cigarette and smoked half of it. "I'd say they weren't lovers. They were simply playmates. Of course she was using him to hit at me."

"For what?"

"For being her husband. For having been her husband. Helen and I parted on bad terms. I tried to put the marriage together again in Reno, but she wasn't even remotely interested."

"What broke up your marriage?"

"It had a major fracture in it from the beginning." He looked past me at the house where Earl Hoffman was lying senseless under the past. "And it got worse. It was both our faults. I couldn't stop nagging her and she couldn't stop—doing what she was doing."

I waited and listened. The church-bells were ringing, in different parts of the city.

"She was a tramp," Haggerty said. "A campus tramp. I started her on it when she was a nineteen-year-old babe in the woods in Hyde Park. Then she went on without me. Toward the end she was even taking money."

"Who from?"

"Men with money, naturally. My wife was a corrupt woman, Mr. Archer. I played a part in making her what she was, so I have no right to judge her." His eyes were brilliant with the pain that came and went like truth in him.

I felt sorry for the man. It didn't prevent me from saying: "Where were you Friday night?"

"At home in Maple Park in our—in my apartment, grading themes."

"Can you prove it?"

"I have the marked papers to prove it. They were turned in to me on Friday, and I marked them Friday night. I hope you're not imagining I did something fantastic like flying to California and back?"

"When a woman is murdered, you ask her estranged husband where he was at the time. It's the corollary of *cherchez la femme.*"

"Well, you have my answer. Check it out if you like. But you'll save yourself time and trouble simply by believing me. I've been completely frank with you— inordinately frank."

"I appreciate that."

"But then you turn around and accuse me—"

"A question isn't an accusation, Mr. Haggerty."

"It carried that implication," he said in an aggrieved and slightly nagging tone. "I thought the man in Reno was your suspect."

"He's one of them."

"And I'm another?"

"Let's drop it, shall we?"

"You brought it up."

"Now I'm dropping it. Getting back to the man in Reno, can you remember his name?"

"I was introduced to him, of course, but I don't recall his surname. The women called him Jud. I'm not sure whether it was a given name or a nickname."

"Why did you refer to him as Mrs. Burke's alleged brother?"

"They didn't strike me as brother and sister. They acted toward each other more like—oh—intimate friends who were simply going along with Helen's gag. I inter- cepted a couple of knowing glances, for example."

"Will you describe the man in detail for me?"

"I'll try. My visual memory isn't too good. I'm strictly the verbal type."

But under repeated questions, he built up an image of the man: age about thirty-two or -three, height just under six feet, weight about 175; muscular and active, good-looking in an undistinguished way; thinning black hair, brown eyes, no scars. He had worn a light gray silk or imitation silk suit and pointed low black shoes in the Italian style. Haggerty had gathered that the man Jud worked in some undetermined capacity for one of the gambling clubs in the Reno-Tahoe area.

It was time I went to Reno. I looked at my watch—nearly eleven—and remem- bered that I would gain time on the flight west. I could still have a talk with Luke Deloney's widow, if she was available, and get to Reno at a reasonable hour.

I went into the house with Haggerty, called O'Hare Airport, and made a reservation on a late afternoon flight. Then I called Mrs. Deloney. She was at home, and would see me.

Bert Haggerty offered to drive me out to her house. I told him he'd better stay with his father-in-law. Hoffman's snores were sounding through the house like muffled lamentations, but he could wake up at any time and go on the rampage.

21

Glenview Avenue wound through the north side of the north side, in a region of estates so large that it almost qualified as country. Trees lined the road and sometimes met above it. The light that filtered through their turning leaves onto the great lawns was the color of sublimated money.

I turned in between the brick gate-posts of 103 and shortly came in sight of an imposing old red brick mansion. The driveway led to a brick-columned *porte-cochère* on the right. I was hardly out of my car when a Negro maid in uniform opened the door.

"Mr. Archer?"

"Yes."

"Mrs. Deloney is expecting you, in the downstairs sitting-room."

She was sitting by a window looking out on a countryside where red sumac blazed among less brilliant colors. Her hair was white, and bobbed short. Her blue silk suit looked like Lily Daché. Her face was a mass of wrinkles but its fine bones remained in all their delicacy. She was handsome in the way an antique object can be handsome without regard to the condition of the materials. Her mind must have been very deep in the past, because she didn't notice us until the maid spoke.

"Mr. Archer is here, Mrs. Deloney."

She rose with the ease of a younger woman, putting down a book she was holding. She gave me her hand and a long look. Her eyes were the same color as her blue silk suit, unfaded and intelligent.

"So you've come all the way from California to see me. You must be disappointed."

"On the contrary."

"You don't need to flatter me. When I was twenty I looked like everybody else. Now I'm past seventy, I look like myself. It's a liberating fact. But do sit down. This chair is the most comfortable. My father Senator Osborne preferred it to any other."

She indicated a red leather armchair polished and dark with use. The chair she sat in opposite me was a ladder-backed rocker with worn cushions attached to it. The rest of the furnishings in the room were equally old and unpretentious, and I wondered if she used it as a place to keep the past.

"You've had a journey," she reminded herself. "Can I give you something to eat or drink?"

"No thanks."

She dismissed the maid. "I'm afraid you're going to be doubly disappointed. I can add very little to the official account of my husband's suicide. Luke and I hadn't been in close touch for some time before it occurred."

"You already have added something," I said. "According to the official account it was an accident."

"So it was. I'd almost forgotten. It was thought best to omit the fact of suicide from the public reports."

"Who thought it best?"

"I did, among others. Given my late husband's position in the state, his suicide was bound to have business and political repercussions. Not to mention personal ugliness."

"Some people might think it was uglier to alter the facts of a man's death."

"Some people might think it," she said with a *grande dame* expression. "Not many of them would say it in my presence. In any case the fact was not altered, only the report of it. I've had to live with the fact of my husband's suicide."

"Are you perfectly certain that it is a fact?"

"Perfectly."

"I've just been talking to the man who handled the case, Lieutenant Hoffman. He says your husband shot himself by accident while he was cleaning an automatic pistol."

"That was the story we agreed upon. Lieutenant Hoffman naturally sticks to it. I see no point in your trying to change it at this late date."

"Unless Mr. Deloney was murdered. Then there would be some point."

"No doubt, but he was *not* murdered." Her eyes came up to mine, and they hadn't changed, except that they may have become a little harder.

"I've heard rumors that he was, as far away as California."

"Who's been spreading such nonsense?"

"Lieutenant Hoffman's daughter Helen. She claimed she knew a witness to the killing. The witness may have been herself."

The insecurity that had touched her face changed into cold anger. "She has no right to tell such lies. I'll have her stopped!"

"She's been stopped," I said. "Somebody stopped her Friday night, with a gun. Which is why I'm here."

"I see. Where in California was she killed?"

"Pacific Point. It's on the coast south of Los Angeles."

Her eyes flinched, ever so slightly. "I'm afraid I never heard of it. I'm naturally sorry that the girl is dead, though I never knew her. But I can assure you that her death had nothing to do with Luke. You're barking up the wrong tree, Mr. Archer."

"I wonder."

"There's no need to. My husband wrote me a note before he shot himself which made the whole thing very clear. Detective Hoffman brought it to me himself. No one knew it existed except him and his superiors. I hadn't intended to tell you."

"Why?"

"Because it was ugly. In effect he blamed me and my family for what he intended to do. He was in financial hot water, he'd been gambling in stocks and other things, his business was overextended. We refused to help him, for reasons both personal and practical. His suicide was an attempt to strike back at us. It succeeded, even though we altered the facts, as you put it." She touched her flat chest. "I was hurt, as I was meant to be."

"Was Senator Osborne alive at the time?"

"I'm afraid you don't know your history," she chided me. "My father died on December 14, 1936, three-and-a-half years before my husband killed himself. At least my father was spared the humiliation."

"You referred to family."

"I meant my sister Tish and my late Uncle Scott, the guardian of our trust. He and I were responsible for refusing further assistance to Luke. The decision was essentially mine. Our marriage had ended."

"Why?"

"The usual reason, I believe. I don't care to discuss it." She rose and went to the window and stood there straight as a soldier looking out. "A number of things ended for me in 1940. My marriage, and then my husband's life, and then my sister's. Tish died in the summer of that same year, and I cried for her all that fall. And now it's fall again," she said with a sigh. "We used to ride together in the fall. I taught her to ride when she was five years old and I was ten. That was before the turn of the century."

Her mind was wandering off into remoter and less painful times. I said:

"Forgive me for laboring the point, Mrs. Deloney, but I have to ask you if that suicide note still exists."

She turned, trying to smooth the marks of grief from her face. They persisted. "Of course not. I burned it. You can take my word as to its contents."

"It isn't your word that concerns me so much. Are you absolutely certain your husband wrote it?"

"Yes. I can't be mistaken about his handwriting."

"A clever forgery can fool almost anybody."

"That's absurd. You're talking the language of melodrama."

"We live it every day, Mrs. Deloney."

"But who would forge a suicide note?"

"It's been done, by other murderers."

She flung back her white head and looked at me down her delicate curved nose. She resembled a bird, even in the sound of her voice:

"My husband was not murdered."

"It seems to me you're resting a great deal of weight on a single handwritten note which might have been forged."

"It was not forged. I know that by internal evidence. It referred to matters that only Luke and I were privy to."

"Such as?"

"I have no intention of telling you, or anyone. Besides, Luke had been talking for months about killing himself, especially when he was in his cups."

"You said you hadn't been close to him for months."

"No, but I got reports, from mutual friends."

"Was Hoffman one of them?"

"Hardly. I didn't consider him a friend."

"Yet he hushed up your husband's suicide for you. Your husband's alleged suicide."

"He was ordered to. He had no choice."

"Who gave the order?"

"Presumably the Commissioner of Police. He *was* a friend of mine, and a friend of Luke's."

"And that made it all right for him to order the falsification of records?"

"It's done every day," she said, "in every city in the land. Spare me your moralizing, Mr. Archer. Commissioner Robertson is long since dead. The case itself is a dead issue."

"Maybe it is to you. It's very much on Hoffman's mind. His daughter's murder revived it."

"I'm sorry for both of them. But I can't very well alter the past to accommodate some theory you may have. What are you trying to prove, Mr. Archer?"

"Nothing specific. I'm trying to find out what the dead woman meant when she said that Bridgeton had caught up with her."

"No doubt she meant something quite private and personal. Women usually do. But as I said, I never knew Helen Hoffman."

"Was she involved with your husband?"

"No. She was not. And please don't ask me how I can be sure. We've scratched enough at Luke's grave, don't you think? There's nothing hidden there but a poor suicide. I helped to put him there, in a way."

"By cutting off his funds?"

"Precisely. You didn't think I was confessing to shooting him?"

"No," I said. "Would you like to?"

Her face crinkled up in a rather savage smile. "Very well. I shot him. What do you propose to do about it?"

"Nothing. I don't believe you."

"Why would I say it if it wasn't true?" She was playing the kind of fantastic girlish game old women sometimes revert to.

"Maybe you wanted to shoot your husband. I have no doubt you did want to. But if you actually had, you wouldn't be talking about it."

"Why not? There's nothing you could possibly do. I have too many good friends in this city, official and otherwise. Who incidentally would be greatly disturbed if you persisted in stirring up that old mess."

"Am I to take that as a threat?"

"No, Mr. Archer," she said with her tight smile, "I have nothing against you except that you're a zealot in your trade, or do you call it a profession? Does it really matter so much how people died? They're dead, as we all shall be, sooner or later. Some of us sooner. And I feel I've given you enough of my remaining time on earth."

She rang for the maid.

22

I still had time for another try at Earl Hoffman. I drove back toward his house, through downtown streets depopulated by the Sabbath. The questions Mrs. Deloney had raised, or failed to answer, stuck in my mind like fishhooks which trailed their broken lines into the past.

I was almost certain Deloney hadn't killed himself, by accident or intent. I was almost certain somebody else had, and that Mrs. Deloney knew it. As for the suicide note, it could have been forged, it could have been invented, it could have been misread or misremembered. Hoffman would probably know which.

As I turned into Cherry Street, I saw a man in the next block walking away from me. He had on a blue suit and he moved with the heavy forcefulness of an old cop, except that every now and then he staggered and caught himself. I saw when I got closer that it was Hoffman. The orange cuffs of his pajama legs hung below his blue trousers.

I let him stay ahead of me, through slums that became more blighted as we went south. We entered a Negro district. The adult men and women on the sidewalk gave Hoffman a wide berth. He was walking trouble.

He wasn't walking too well. He stumbled and fell on his hands and knees by a gap-toothed picket fence. Some children came out from behind the fence and followed him, prancing and hooting, until he turned on them with upraised arms. He turned again and went on.

We left the Negro district and came to a district of very old three-storied frame houses converted into rooming houses and business buildings. A few newer apartment buildings stood among them, and Hoffman's destination was one of these.

It was a six-story concrete structure with a slightly rundown aspect: cracked and yellowing blinds in the rows of windows, brown watermarks below them. Hoffman went in the front entrance. I could see the inscription in the concrete arch above it: Deloney Apartments, 1928. I parked my car and followed Hoffman into the building.

He had evidently taken the elevator up. The tarnished brass arrow above the elevator door slowly turned clockwise to seven and stuck there. I gave up pushing the button after a while—Hoffman had probably left the door ajar—and found the fire stairs. I was breathing hard by the time I reached the metal door that let out onto the roof.

I opened the door a crack. Except for some pigeons coohooing on a neighboring rooftop, everything outside seemed very quiet. A few potted shrubs and a green plexiglas windscreen jutting out at right angles from the wall of the penthouse had converted a corner of the roof into a terrace.

A man and a woman were sunning themselves there. She was lying face down on an air mattress with the brassière of her bikini unfastened. She was blonde and nicely made. He sat in a deck chair, with a half-empty cola bottle on the table beside him. He was broad and dark, with coarse black hair matting his chest and shoulders. He wore a diamond ring on the little finger of his left hand, and had a faint Greek accent.

"So you think the restaurant business is low class? When you say that you're biting the hand that feeds you. The restaurant business put mink on your back."

"I didn't say it. What I said, the insurance business is a nice clean business for a man."

"And restaurants are dirty? Not my restaurants. I even got violet rays in the toilets—"

"Don't talk filthy," she said.

"Toilet is not a filthy word."

"It is in my family."

"I'm sick of hearing about your family. I'm sick of hearing about your good-for-nothing brother Theo."

"Good-for-nothing?" She sat up, exposing a pearly flash of breast before she fastened its moorings. "Theo made the Million Dollar Magic Circle last year."

"Who bought the policy that put him over the top? I did. Who set him up in the insurance agency in the first place? I did."

"Mr. God." Her face was a beautiful blank mask. It didn't change when she said: "Who's that moving around in the house? I sent Rosie home after breakfast."

"She came back maybe."

"It doesn't sound like Rosie. It sounds like a man."

"Could be Theo coming to sell me this year's Magic Circle policy."

"That isn't funny."

"I think it's very funny."

He laughed to prove it. He stopped laughing when Earl Hoffman came out from behind the plexiglas windscreen. Every mark on his face was distinct in the sunlight. His orange pajamas were down over his shoes.

The dark man got out of his deck chair and pushed air toward Hoffman with his hands. "Beat it. This is a private roof."

"I can't do that," Hoffman said reasonably. "We got a report of a dead body. Where is it?"

"Down in the basement. You'll find it there." The man winked at the woman.

"The basement? They said the penthouse." Hoffman's damaged mouth opened and shut mechanically, like a dummy's as if the past was ventriloquizing through him. "You moved it, eh? It's against the law to move it."

"*You* move yourself out of here." The man turned to the woman, who had covered herself with a yellow terrycloth robe: "Go in and phone the you-know-who."

"I am the you-know-who," Hoffman said. "And the woman stays. I have some questions to ask her. What's your name?"

"None of your business," she said.

"Everything's my business." Hoffman flung one arm out and almost lost his balance. "I'm detective invesgating murder."

"Let's see your badge, detective."

The man held out his hand, but he didn't move toward Hoffman. Neither of them had moved. The woman was on her knees, with her beautiful scared face slanting up at Hoffman.

He fumbled in his clothes, produced a fifty-cent piece, looked at it in a frustrated way, and flung it spinning over the parapet. Faintly, I heard it ring on the pavement six stories down.

"Must of left it home," he said mildly.

The woman gathered herself together and made a dash for the penthouse. Moving clumsily and swiftly, Hoffman caught her around the waist. She didn't struggle, but stood stiff and white-faced in the circle of his arm.

"Not so fast now, baby. Got some questions to ask you. You the broad that's been sleeping with Deloney?"

She said to the man: "Are you going to let him talk to me this way? Tell him to take his hands off me."

"Take your hands off my wife," the man said without force.

"Then tell her to sit down and cooperate."

"Sit down and cooperate," the man said.

"Are you crazy? He smells like a still. He's crazy drunk."

"I know that."

"Then *do* something."

"I am doing something. You got to humor them."

Hoffman smiled at him like a public servant who was used to weathering unjust criticism. His hurt mouth and mind made the smile grotesque. The woman tried to pull away from him. He only held her closer, his belly nudging her flank.

"You look a little bit like my dau'er Helen. You know my dau'er Helen?"

The woman shook her head frantically. Her hair fluffed out.

"She says there was a witness to the killing. Were you there when it happened, baby?"

"I don't even know what you're talking about."

"Sure you do. Luke Deloney. Somebody drilled him in the eye and tried to make it look like suicide."

"I remember Deloney," the man said. "I waited on him in my father's hamburg joint once or twice. He died before the war."

"Before the war?"

"That's what I said. Where you been the last twenty years, detective?"

Hoffman didn't know. He looked around at the rooftops of his city as if it was a strange place. The woman cried out:

"Let me go, fatso."

He seemed to hear her from a long way off. "You speak with some respect to your old man."

"If you were my old man I'd kill myself."

"Don't give me no more of your lip. I've had as much of your lip as I'm going to take. You hear me?"

"Yes I hear you. You're a crazy old man and take your filthy paws off me."

Her hooked fingers raked at his face, leaving three bright parallel tracks. He slapped her. She sat down on the gravel roof. The man picked up the half-empty cola bottle. Its brown contents gushed down his arm as he raised it, advancing on Hoffman.

Hoffman reached under the back of his coat and took a revolver out of his belt. He fired it over the man's head. The pigeons flew up from the neighboring rooftop, whirling in great spirals. The man dropped the bottle and stood still with his hands raised. The woman, who had been whimpering, fell silent.

Hoffman glared at the glaring sky. The pigeons diminished into it. He looked at the revolver in his hand. With my eyes focused on the same object, I stepped out into the sunlight.

"You need any help with these witnesses, Earl?"

"Naw, I can handle 'em. Everythin's under control." He squinted at me. "What was the name again? Arthur?"

"Archer." I walked toward him, pushing my squat shadow ahead of me across the uneven surface of the gravel. "You'll get some nice publicity out of this, Earl. Solving the Deloney killing singlehanded."

"Yeah. Sure." His eyes were deeply puzzled. He knew I was talking nonsense, as he knew he had been acting nonsense out, but he couldn't admit it, even to himself. "They hid the body in the basement."

"That means we'll probably have to dig."

"Is everybody crazy?" the man said between his upraised arms.

"Keep quiet, you," I said. "You better call for reinforcements, Earl. I'll hold the gun on these characters."

He hesitated for a stretching moment. Then he handed me the revolver and went into the penthouse, bumping the doorframe heavily with his shoulder.

"Who are you?" the man said.

"I'm his keeper. Relax."

"Did he escape from the insane asylum?"

"Not yet."

The man's eyes were like raisins thumbed deep into dough. He helped his wife to her feet, awkwardly brushing off the seat of her robe. Suddenly she was crying in his arms and he was patting her back with his diamonded hand and saying something emotional in Greek.

Through the open door I could hear Hoffman talking on the phone: "Six men with shovels an' a drill for concrete. Her body's under the basement floor. Want 'em here in ten minutes or somebody gets reamed!"

The receiver crashed down, but he went on talking. His voice rose and fell like a wind, taking up scattered fragments of the past and blowing them together in a whirl. "He never touched her. Wouldn't do that to the daughter of a friend. She was a good girl, too, a clean little daddy's girl. 'Member when she was a little baby, I used to give her her bath. She was soft as a rabbit. I held her in my arms, she called me da." His voice broke. "What happened?"

He was silent. Then he screamed. I heard him fall to the floor with a thud that shook the penthouse. I went inside. He was sitting with his back against the kitchen stove, trying to remove his trousers. He waved me back.

"Keep away from me. There's spiders on me."

"I don't see any spiders."

"They're under my clothes. Black Widows. The killer's trying to poison me with spiders."

"Who is the killer, Earl?"

His face worked. "Never found out who put the chill on Deloney. Word came down from the top, close off the case. What can a man—?" Another scream issued from his throat. "My God, there's hundreds of 'em crawling on me."

He tore at his clothes. They were in blue and orange rags when the police arrived, and his old wrestler's body was naked and writhing on the linoleum.

The two patrolmen knew Earl Hoffman. I didn't even have to explain.

23

The red sun sank abruptly when the plane came down into the shadow of the mountains. I had wired my ETA to the Walters agency, and Phyllis was waiting for me at the airport.

She took my hand and offered me her cheek. She had a peaches-and-cream complexion, a little the worse for the sun, and opaque smiling eyes the color of Indian enamel.

"You look tired, Lew. But you do exist."

"Don't tell me. It makes me feel tireder. You look wonderful."

"It gets more difficult as I get older. But then some other things get easier." She didn't say what things. We walked toward her car in the sudden evening. "What were you doing in Illinois, anyway? I thought you were working on a case in Pacific Point."

"It's in both places. I found an old pre-war murder in Illinois which seems to be closely tied in with the current ones. Don't ask me how. It would take all night to explain, and we have more important things to do."

"You do, anyway. You have a dinner date at eighty-thirty with Mrs. Sally Burke. You're an old friend of mine from Los Angeles, business unspecified. You take it from there."

"How did you fix it?"

"It wasn't hard. Sally dotes on free dinners and unattached men. She wants to get married again."

"But how did you get to know her?"

"I sort of happened into her at the bar where she hangs out and we got drunk together last night. One of us got drunk, anyway. She did some talking about her brother Judson, who may be the man you want."

"He is. Where does he live?"

"Somewhere on the South Shore. It's a hard place to find people, as you know. Arnie's out there looking for him now."

"Lead me to his sister."

"You sound like a lamb asking to be led to the slaughter. Actually she's a pretty nice gal," she said with female solidarity. "Not bright, but she has her heart in the right place. She's very fond of her brother."

"So was Lucrezia Borgia."

Phyllis slammed the car door. We drove toward Reno, a city where nothing good had ever happened to me, but I kept hoping.

Mrs. Sally Burke lived close in on Riley Street, in the upper flat of an old two-story house. Phyllis dropped me off in front of it at eight-twenty-nine, having extracted my promise to come back and spend the night with Arnie and her. Mrs. Burke was waiting in full panoply on the upper landing: tight black sheath with foxes, pearls and earrings, four-inch heels. Her hair was mingled brown and blonde, as if to express the complexity of her personality. Her brown eyes appraised me, as I came up to her level, the way an antebellum plantation owner might look over an able-bodied slave on the auction block.

She smelled nice, anyway, and she had a pleasant friendly anxious smile. We exchanged greetings and names. I was to call her Sally right away.

"I'm afraid I can't ask you in, the place is a mess. I never seem to get anything done on Sunday. You know the old song, 'Gloomy Sunday'? That is, since my divorce. Phyllis says you're divorced."

"Phyllis is right."

"It's different for a man," she said with some faint resentment. "But I can see you could use a woman to look after you."

She was one of the fastest and least efficient workers I'd ever met. My heart went down toward my boots. She was looking at my boots, and at the clothes I had slept in on the plane. On the other hand I was able-bodied. I had climbed the stairs unaided.

"Where shall we eat?" she said. "The Riverside is nice."

It was nice and expensive. After a couple of drinks I ceased to care about spending Alex's money. I began to be fascinated, in a way, by Sally Burke's conversation. Her ex-husband, if I could believe her, was a combination of Dracula, Hitler, and Uriah Heep. He made at least twenty-five thousand a year as a salesman in the Northwest, but more than once she had to attach his salary to collect her measly six hundred a month alimony. She was having a rough time making ends meet, especially now that her little brother had lost his job at the club.

I ordered her another drink and indicated mild sympathy.

"Jud's a good boy," she said, as if somebody had just denied it. "He played football at Washington State and led the team in rushing. A lot of people in Spokane thought he would have made All-American if he'd played for a better-known school. But he never got due recognition, he never has. He lost his coaching job out of sheer politics pure and simple. The charges they made were a lot of poppycock, he told me so himself."

"What charges?"

"Nothing. They were a lot of poppycock, I mean it." She finished her fourth martini and regarded me with simple cunning over the empty glass. "I don't believe you told me what kind of business that you're in, Lew?"

"I don't believe I did. I run a small agency in Hollywood."

"Isn't that interesting? Jud has always been interested in acting. He hasn't done any, actually, but he's said to be a very handsome boy. Jud was down in Hollywood last week."

"Looking for an acting job?"

"Anything," she said. "He's a willing worker, but the trouble is he isn't trained for anything, I mean after he lost his teaching credentials, and then the dance studio folded. Do you think you could get him something to do in Hollywood?"

"I'd certainly like to talk to him," I said truthfully.

She was tipsy and hopeful, and she wasn't surprised by my interest in her brother.

"*That* can be arranged," she said. "As a matter of fact he's at my apartment right now. I could call him and tell him to come over here."

"Let's have dinner first."

"*I* don't mind paying for Jud's dinner." She realized she had made a tactical error, and quickly back-tracked: "But I guess three's company, eh? I mean two."

She talked so much about her brother at dinner that it was almost like having him there. She recited his old football statistics. She told me, with a kind of vicarious enthusiasm, all about his prowess with ladies. She explained about the brilliant ideas Jud was always hatching. The one I liked best was a plan for a condensed version of the Bible, with all the offensive passages removed, for family reading.

Sally couldn't drink. She was coming apart by the time we finished eating. She wanted to pick up her brother and go and hell around in the clubs, but my heart wasn't in it. I took her home. In the cab she went to sleep on my shoulder. This I didn't mind.

I woke her up on Riley Street and got her into the house and up the stairs. She seemed very large and loosely put together, and the foxes kept slipping. I felt as if I'd been nursing drunks all weekend.

A man in shirtsleeves and form-fitting trousers opened the door of her flat. With Sally leaning on me, I got a quick impression of him: a man of half-qualities who lived in a half-world: he was half-handsome, half-lost, half-spoiled, half-smart, half-dangerous. His pointed Italian shoes were scuffed at the toes.

"Need any help?" he said to me.

"Don't be ridic," Sally said. "I'm in perfect control. Mr. Archer, meet brother Jud, Judson Foley."

"Hello," he said. "You shouldn't have let her drink. She's got a weak head for liquor. Here, I'll take her."

With weary skill he looped her arm over his shoulders, clasped her around the waist, walked her through the front room into a lighted bedroom, laid her out on the Hollywood bed, and turned off the light.

He seemed unpleasantly surprised to find me still in the front room. "Good night, Mr. Archer, or whatever your name is. We're closing up for the night now."

"You're not very hospitable."

"No. My sister is the hospitable one." He cast a sour glance around the little room, at overflowing ashtrays, clouded glasses, scattered newspapers. "I never saw you before, I'll never see you again. Why should I be hospitable?"

"You're sure you never saw me before? Think hard."

His brown eyes studied my face, and then my body. He scratched nervously at the front of his thinning hair. He shook his head.

"If I ever saw you before I must have been drunk at the time. Did Sally bring you here when I was drunk?"

"No. Were you drinking last Friday night?"

"Let's see, what night was that? I think I was out of town. Yeah. I didn't get back here until Saturday morning." He was trying to sound casual and look unconcerned. "It must have been two other guys."

"I don't think so, Jud. I ran into you, or you ran into me, about nine last Friday night in Pacific Point."

Panic brightened his face like a flash of lightning. "Who are you?"

"I chased you down Helen Haggerty's driveway, remember? You were too fast for me. It took me two days to catch up."

He was breathing as if he'd just finished the run. "Are you from the police?"

"I'm a private detective."

He sat down in a Danish chair, gripping the fragile arms so hard I thought they might break. He snickered. It was very close to a sob.

"This is Bradshaw's idea, isn't it?"

I didn't answer him. I cleared a chair and sat in it.

"Bradshaw said he was satisfied with my story. Now he sends you up against me." His eyes narrowed. "I suppose you were pumping my sister about me."

"She doesn't need much priming."

Twisting in the chair, he threw a wicked look in the direction of her bedroom. "I wish she'd keep her mouth shut about my business."

"Don't blame her for what you did yourself."

"But the hell of it is I didn't *do* anything. I *told* Bradshaw that, and he believed me, at least he said he did."

"Are you talking about Roy Bradshaw?"

"Who else? He recognized me the other night, or thought he did. I didn't know who it was I bumped in the dark. I just wanted out of there."

"Why?"

He lifted his heavy shoulders and sat with them lifted, head down between them. "I didn't want trouble with the law."

"What were you doing at Helen's?"

"She *asked* me to come. Hell, I went there as a good Samaritan. She called me at the motel in Santa Monica and practically begged me to come and spend the night. It wasn't my beautiful blue eyes. She was frightened, she wanted company."

"What time did she call you?"

"Around seven or seven-thirty. I was just coming in from getting something to eat." He dropped his shoulders. "Listen, you know all this, you got it from Bradshaw, didn't you? What are you trying to do, trap me into a mistake?"

"It's an idea. What sort of a mistake did you have in mind?"

He shook his head, and went on shaking it as he spoke. "I didn't have anything particular in mind. I mean, I can't afford to make any mistakes."

"You already made the big one, when you ran."

"I know. I panicked." He shook his head some more. "There she was with a bullet hole in her skull and there I was a natural setup for a patsy. I heard you fellows coming, and I panicked. You've got to believe me."

They always said that. "Why do I have to believe you?"

"Because I'm telling the truth. I'm innocent as a little child."

"That's pretty innocent."

"I didn't mean in general, I meant in this particular situation. I went a long way out of my way to give Helen a helping hand. It doesn't make sense I'd go there to knock her off. I *liked* the girl. She and I had a lot in common."

I didn't know if this was a compliment to either of them. Bert Haggerty had described his ex-wife as corrupt. The man in front of me was a dubious character. Behind the mask of his good looks he seemed dilapidated, as if he'd painfully bumped down several steps in the social scale. In spite of this, I half-believed his story. I would never more than half-believe anything he said.

"What did you and Helen have in common?"

He gave me a quick sharp up-from-under look. This wasn't the usual line of questioning. He thought about his answer. "Sports. Dancing. Fun and games. We had some real fun times, I mean it. I almost died when I found her the other night."

"How did you happen to meet her?"

"You *know* all this," he said impatiently. "You're working for Bradshaw, aren't you?"

"Put it this way: Bradshaw and I are on the same side." I wanted to know why Roy Bradshaw loomed so large in Foley's mind, but other questions had priority. "Now why don't you humor me and tell me how you knew Helen?"

"It's simple enough." He jabbed his thumb downward like a decadent emperor decreeing death. "She rented the downstairs apartment when she was putting in her six weeks this summer. She and my sister hit it off, and eventually I got into the act. The three of us used to go places together."

"In Sally's car?"

"I had my own car then—sixty-two Galaxie five hundred," he said earnestly. "This was back in August before I lost my job and couldn't keep up with the payments."

"How did you happen to lose your job?"

"That wouldn't interest you. It had nothing to do with Helen Haggerty, nothing whatever."

His overinsistence on the point made me suspicious. "What were you working at?"

"I said you wouldn't be interested."

"I can easily find out where you were working. You might as well tell me."

He said with his eyes down: "I was in the cashier's cage at the Solitaire in Stateline. I guess I made one mistake too many." He looked at his strong square fumbling hands.

"So you were looking for work in Los Angeles?"

"Correcto." He seemed relieved to get away from the subject of his job and why he lost it. "I didn't make a connection, but I've got to get out of this place."

"Why?"

He scratched his hair. "I can't go on living on my sister. It *cuts* me, being on the ding. I'm going down to L.A. again and have another look around."

"Let's get back to the first time. You say Helen called you at your motel Friday night. How did she know you were there?"

"I already called her earlier in the week."

"What for?"

"The usual. I mean, I thought we could get together, have some fun." He kept talking about having fun but he looked as if he hadn't had any for years. "Helen already had a date that night, Wednesday night. As a matter of fact she had a date with Bradshaw. They were going to some concert. She said she'd call me back another time. Which she did, Friday night."

"What did she say on the telephone?"

"That somebody threatened to kill her, and she was scared. I never heard her talk like that before. She said that she had nobody to turn to but me. And I got there too late." There seemed to be grief in him, but even this was ambiguous, as if he felt defrauded by Helen's death.

"Were Helen and Bradshaw close?"

He answered cautiously: "I wouldn't say that. I guess they lucked into each other last summer the same way Helen and I did. Anyway, he was busy Friday night. He had to give a speech at some big dinner. At least that's what he told me this morning."

"He wasn't lying. Did Bradshaw and Helen meet here in Reno?"

"Where else?"

"I thought Bradshaw spent the summer in Europe."

"You thought wrong. He was here all through August, anyway."

"What was he doing here?"

"He told me once he was doing some kind of research at the University of Nevada. He didn't say what kind. I hardly knew him, actually. I ran into him a couple of times with Helen, and that was it. I didn't see him again until today."

"And you say he recognized you Friday night and came here to question you?"

"That's the truth. He came here this morning, gave me quite a grilling. *He* believed I didn't do that murder. I don't see why you can't believe me."

"I'll want to talk to Bradshaw before I make up my mind. Where is he now, do you know?"

"He said he was staying at the Lakeview Inn, on the North Shore. I don't know if he's still there or not."

I stood up and opened the door. "I think I'll go and see."

I suggested to Jud that he stay where he was, because a second runout would make him look very bad. He nodded. He was still nodding when a counter-impulse took hold of him and he rushed me. His heavy shoulder caught me under the ribs and slammed me against the doorframe wheezing for air.

He threw a punch at my face. I shifted my head. His fist crunched into the plaster wall. He yipped in pain. He hit me low in the belly with his other hand. I slid down the doorframe. He kneed me, a glancing blow on the side of the jaw.

This impelled me to get up. He rushed me again, head down. I stepped to one side and chopped the back of his neck as he went by. He staggered rapidly through the door and across the landing, and plunged down. At the foot of the stairs he lay still.

But he was conscious when the police arrived. I rode along to the station to make sure they nailed him down. We hadn't been there five minutes when Arnie came in. He had an understanding with the officers. They booked Foley for assault and related charges, and promised to hold him.

24

Arnie drove me out to the Lakeview Inn, a rambling California Gothic pile which must have dated from the early years of the century. Generations of summer visitors had marched through the lobby and trampled out any old-world charm it might once have had. It seemed an unlikely place for Roy Bradshaw to be staying.

But Bradshaw was there, the elderly night clerk said. He took a railroad watch out of his vest pocket and consulted it. "It's getting pretty late, though. They may be asleep."

"They?"

"Him and his wife. I can go up and call him, if you want me to. We never did put telephones in the rooms."

"I'll go up. I'm a friend of Dr. Bradshaw's."

"I didn't know he was a doctor."

"A doctor of philosophy," I said. "What's his room number?"

"Thirty-one, on the top floor." The old man seemed relieved at not having to make the climb.

I left Arnie with him and went up to the third floor. Light shone through the transom of 31, and I could hear the indistinct murmur of voices. I knocked. There was a silence, followed by the noise of slippered feet.

Roy Bradshaw spoke through the door. "Who is it?"

"Archer."

He hesitated. A sleeper in the room across the hall, perhaps disturbed by our voices, began to snore. Bradshaw said:

"What are you doing here?"

"I have to see you."

"Can't it wait till morning?" His voice was impatient, and he had temporarily mislaid his Harvard accent.

"No. It can't. I need your advice on what to do about Judson Foley."

"Very well. I'll get dressed."

I waited in the narrow ill-lit hallway. It had the faintly acrid smell which old buildings seem to absorb from the people who pass through them night by night, the smell of transient life. The snoring man was uttering terrible moans between his snores. A woman told him to turn over, and he subsided.

I could hear a quick interchange of voices in Bradshaw's room. The woman's voice seemed to want something, which Bradshaw's voice denied. I thought I recognized the woman's voice, but I couldn't be sure.

I was sure when Bradshaw finally opened the door. He tried to slip out without letting me see in, but I caught a glimpse of Laura Sutherland. She was sitting upright on the edge of the unmade bed in a severely cut Paisley robe. Her hair was down around her shoulders, and she was rosy and beautiful.

Bradshaw jerked the door shut. "So now you know."

He had pulled on slacks and a black turtleneck sweater which made him look more undergraduate than ever. In spite of the tension in him, he seemed quite happy.

"I don't know what I know," I said.

"This is not an illicit liaison, believe me. Laura and I were married some time ago. We're keeping our marriage secret, for the present. I'm going to ask you to go along with that."

I didn't say whether I would or not. "Why all the secrecy?"

"We have our reasons. For one thing, under the college regulations, Laura would have to give up her post. She intends to, of course, but not immediately. And then there's Mother. I don't know how I'm going to break it to her."

"You could just tell her. She'll survive."

"It's easy enough to say. It isn't possible."

The thing that made it impossible, I thought, was Mother's money. Having money and looking forward to inheriting more were difficult habits for a man to break in early middle age. But I felt a sneaking admiration for Bradshaw. He had more life in him than I'd suspected.

We went downstairs and through the lobby, where Arnie was playing gin rummy with the night clerk. The bar was a gloomy cavern with antlers on the walls instead of stalactites and customers instead of stalagmites. One of the customers, a local man wearing a cap and windbreaker and carrying a load, wanted to buy Bradshaw and me a drink. The bartender told him it was time to go home. Surprisingly, he went, and most of the others drifted out after him.

We sat at the bar. Bradshaw ordered a double bourbon and insisted on one for me, though I didn't need it. There was some aggression in his insistence. He hadn't forgiven me for stumbling on his secret, or for dragging him away from his wife's bed.

"Well," he said, "what about Judson Foley?"

"He tells me you recognized him Friday night."

"I had an intuition that it was he." Bradshaw had recovered his accent, and was using it as a kind of vocal mask.

"Why didn't you say so? You could have saved a lot of legwork and expense."

He looked at me solemnly over his drink. "I had to be certain and I was very far from being that. I couldn't accuse a man, and set the police on his trail, unless I were certain."

"So you came here to make certain?"

"It happened to work out that way. There are times in a man's life when everything seems to fall together into place, have you noticed?" A momentary flash of glee broke through his earnestness. "Laura and I had been planning to steal a weekend here for some time, and the conference gave us the opportunity. Foley was a side issue, but of course a very important one. I looked him up this morning and questioned him thoroughly. He seems completely innocent to me."

"Innocent of what?"

"Of Helen's murder. Foley went to her house to give her what protection he could, but she was already beyond protection when he got there. He lost his nerve and ran."

"What was he afraid of?"

"A false accusation, what he calls a frameup. He's had some trouble with the law in the past. It had to do with shaving points, as they call it, in football games."

"How do you know?"

"He told me. I have," he said with a chuckle of vanity, "a certain capacity to inspire confidence in these—ah—disaffiliates. The man was utterly forthright with me, and in my considered opinion he had nothing to do with Helen's murder."

"You're probably right. I'd still like to find out more about him."

"I know very little about him. He was a friend of Helen's. I saw him once or twice in her company."

"In Reno."

"Yes. I spent a part of the summer in Nevada. It's another fact about myself that I'm not publicizing." He added rather vaguely: "A man has a right to some private life, surely."

"You mean you were here with Laura?"

He dropped his eyes. "She was with me a part of the time. We hadn't quite made up our minds to get married. It was quite a decision. It meant the end of her career and the end of my—life with Mother," he concluded lamely.

"I can understand your reason for keeping it quiet. Still I wish you'd told me that you met Foley and Helen last month in Reno."

"I should have. I apologize. One acquires the habit of secrecy." He added in a different, passionate voice: "I'm deeply in love with Laura. I'm jealous of anything that threatens to disturb our idyl." His words were formal and old-fashioned, but the feeling behind them seemed real.

"What was the relationship between Foley and Helen?"

"They were friends, nothing more, I'd say. Frankly I was a little surprised at her choice of companion. But he was younger than she, and I suppose that was the attraction. Presentable escorts are at a premium in Reno, you know. I had quite a time myself fending off the onslaughts of various predatory females."

"Does that include Helen?"

"I suppose it does." Through the gloom I thought I could discern a faint blush on his cheek. "Of course she didn't know about my—my *thing* with Laura. I've kept it a secret from everyone."

"Is that why you don't want Foley taken back for questioning?"

"I didn't say that."

"I'm asking you."

"I suppose that's partly it." There was a long silence. "But if you think it's necessary, I won't argue. Laura and I have nothing really to hide."

The bartender said: "Drink up, gentlemen. It's closing time."

We drank up. In the lobby Bradshaw gave me a quick nervous handshake, muttering something about getting back to his wife. He went up the stairs two at a time, on his toes.

I waited for Arnie to finish his game of gin. One of the things that made him a first-rate detective was his ability to merge with almost any group, nest into almost any situation, and start a conversation rolling. He and the night man shook hands when we left the hotel.

"The woman your friend registered with," he said in the car, "is a good-looking brownette type, well stacked, who talks like a book."

"She's his wife."

"You didn't tell me Bradshaw was married," he said rather irritably.

"I just found out. The marriage is *sub rosa*. The poor beggar has a dominating mother in the background. In the foreground. The old lady has money, and I think he's afraid of being disinherited."

"He better come clean with her, and take his chances."

"That's what I told him."

Arnie put the car in gear and as we drove west and south along the lakeshore, recounted a long story about a client he had handled for Pinkerton in San Francisco before the war. She was a well-heeled widow of sixty or so who lived in Hillsborough with her son, a man in his thirties. The son was always home by midnight, but seldom before, and the mother wanted to know what he was doing with his evenings. It turned out he had been married for five years to an ex-waitress whom he maintained, with their three small children, in a row house in South San Francisco.

Arnie seemed to think that this was the end of the story.

"What happened to the people?" I asked him.

"The old lady fell in love with her grandchildren and put up with the daughter-in-law for their sake. They all lived happily ever after, on her money."

"Too bad Bradshaw hasn't been married long enough to have any children."

We drove in silence for a while. The road left the shore and tunneled among trees which enclosed it like sweet green coagulated night. I kept thinking about Bradshaw and his unsuspected masculinity.

"I'd like you to do some checking on Bradshaw, Arnie."

"Has this marriage business escalated him into a suspect?"

"Not in my book. Not yet, anyway. But he did suppress the fact that he met Helen Haggerty in Reno last summer. I want to know exactly what he was doing here in the month of August. He told Judson Foley he was doing research at the University of Nevada, but that doesn't seem likely."

"Why not?"

"He's got a doctorate from Harvard, and he'd normally do his research there or at Berkeley or Stanford. I want you to do some checking on Foley, too. Find out if you can why Foley was fired by the Solitaire Club."

"That shouldn't be too hard. Their top security man is an old friend of mine." He looked at his watch in the light from the dash. "We could go by there now but he probably won't be on duty this late on a Sunday night."

"Tomorrow will do."

Phyllis was waiting for us with food and drink. We sat up in her kitchen foolishly late, getting mildly drunk on beer and shared memories and exhaustion. Eventually the conversation came full circle, back to Helen Haggerty and her death. At three o'clock in the morning I was reading aloud her translated poem in the *Bridgeton Blazer* about the violins of the autumn winds.

"It's terribly sad," Phyllis said. "She must have been a remarkable young girl, even if it is only a translation."

"That was her father's word for her. Remarkable. He's remarkable, too, in his own way."

I tried to tell them about the tough old drunken heartbroken cop who had sired Helen. Suddenly it was half-past three and Phyllis was asleep with her head resting like a tousled dahlia among the bottles on the kitchen table. Arnie began gathering up the bottles, carefully, so as not to wake her unnecessarily soon.

Alone in their guest room I had one of those intuitions that come sometimes when you're very tired and emotionally stirred up. I became convinced that Hoffman had given me the *Blazer* for a reason. There was something in it he wanted me to see.

I sat in my underwear on the edge of the open fresh-smelling bed and read the little magazine until my eyes crossed. I learned a good deal about student activities at Bridgeton City College twenty-two years ago, but nothing of any apparent consequence to my case.

I found another poem I liked, though. It was signed with the initials G.R.B., and it went:

> If light were dark
> and dark were light,
> Moon a black hole
> In the blaze of night,

A raven's wing
As bright as tin,
Then you, my love,
Would be darker than sin.

I read it aloud at breakfast. Phyllis said she envied the woman it had been written to. Arnie complained that his scrambled eggs weren't moist. He was older than Phyllis, and it made him touchy.

We decided after breakfast to leave Judson Foley sitting for the present. If Dolly Kincaid were arrested and arraigned, Foley would make a fairly good surprise witness for the defense. Arnie drove me to the airport, where I caught a Pacific flight to Los Angeles.

I picked up an L.A. paper at International Airport, and found a brief account of the Haggerty killing in the Southland News on an inside page. It informed me that the wife-slayer Thomas McGee, released from San Quentin earlier in the year, was being sought for questioning. Dolly Kincaid wasn't mentioned.

25

Around noon I walked into Jerry Marks's store-front office. His secretary told me that Monday was the day for the weekly criminal docket and Jerry had spent the morning in court. He was probably having lunch somewhere near the courthouse. Yes, Mr. Kincaid had got in touch with Mr. Marks on Sunday, and retained him.

I found them together in the restaurant where Alex and I had lunched the day it began. Alex made room for me on his side of the booth, facing the front. Business was roaring, and there was a short lineup inside the front door.

"I'm glad the two of you got together," I said.

Alex produced one of his rare smiles. "So am I. Mr. Marks has been wonderful."

Jerry flapped his hand in a depreciating way. "Actually I haven't been able to do anything yet. I had another case to dispose of this morning. I did make an attempt to pick Gil Stevens's brains, but he told me I'd better go to the transcript of the trial, which I plan to do this afternoon. Mrs. Kincaid," he said, with a sidelong glance at Alex, "was just as uncommunicative as Stevens."

"You've talked to Dolly then?"

He lowered his voice. "I tried, yesterday. We've got to know where we stand before the police get to her."

"Is that going to happen?"

Jerry glanced around him at the courthouse crowd, and lowered his voice still further. "According to the grapevine, they were planning to make their move today, when they completed their ballistics tests. But something's holding them up. The Sheriff and the experts he brought in are still down in the shooting gallery under the courthouse."

"The bullet may be fragmented. It often is in head wounds. Or they may have shifted their main attention to another suspect. I see in the paper they've put out an APB for Thomas McGee."

"Yes, it was done yesterday. He's probably over the Mexican border by now."

"Do you consider him a major suspect, Jerry?"

"I'll want to read that transcript before I form an opinion. Do you?"

It was a hard question. I was spared having to answer it by a diversion. Two elderly ladies, one in serviceable black and one in fashionable green, looked in through the glass front door. They saw the waiting queue and turned away. The one in black was Mrs. Hoffman, Helen's mother. The other was Luke Deloney's widow.

I excused myself and went out after them. They had crossed the street in the middle of the block and were headed downtown, moving through light and shadow under the giant yuccas that hedged the courthouse grounds. Though they seemed to keep up an incessant conversation, they walked together like strangers, out of step and out of sympathy. Mrs. Deloney was much the older, but she had a horsewoman's stride. Mrs. Hoffman stubbed along on tired feet.

I stayed on the other side of the street and followed them at a distance. My heart was thudding. Mrs. Deloney's arrival in California confirmed my belief that her husband's murder and Helen's were connected, and that she knew it.

They walked two blocks to the main street and went into the first restaurant they came to, a tourist trap with empty tables visible through its plate glass windows. There was an open-fronted cigar store diagonally across the street. I looked over its display of paperbacks, bought a pack of cigarettes, and smoked three or four which I lit at the old-fashioned gas flame, and eventually bought a book about ancient Greek philosophy. It had a chapter on Zeno which I read standing. The old ladies were a long time over lunch.

"Archer will never catch the old ladies," I said.

The man behind the counter cupped his ear. "What was that?"

"I was thinking aloud."

"It's a free country. I like to talk to myself when I'm off work. In the store here it wouldn't be appropriate." He smiled over the word, and his gold teeth flashed like jewelry.

The old ladies came out of the restaurant and separated. Mrs. Hoffman limped south, toward her hotel. Mrs. Deloney strode in the opposite direction, moving rapidly now that she was unencumbered by her companion. From the distance you could have taken her for a young woman who had unaccountably bleached her hair white.

She turned off the main street in the direction of the courthouse, and halfway down the block disappeared into a modern concrete and glass building. "Law Offices of Stevens and Ogilvy," said the brass sign beside the entrance. I walked on to the next corner, sat on a bench at a bus stop, and read in my new book about Heraclitus. All things flow like a river, he said; nothing abides. Parmenides, on the other hand, believed that nothing ever changed, it only seemed to. Both views appealed to me.

A cab pulled up in front of the Stevens and Ogilvy office. Mrs. Deloney came out, and the cab took her away. I made a note of its license number before I went into the building.

It was a large office, and a working one. Typewriters were clacking in a row of cubicles behind the waiting room. A very junior attorney in a flannel suit was telling the middle-aged woman at the front desk how he wanted a brief set up on her typewriter.

He went away. Her steel-gray glance met mine, and we happened to smile at each other. She said:

"I was typing briefs when he was just a gleam in his daddy's eye. Can I help you?"

"I'm very eager to see Mr. Gil Stevens. My name is Archer."

She looked in her appointment book, and then at her watch. "Mr. Stevens is due for lunch in ten minutes. He won't be coming back to the office today. I'm sorry."

"It has to do with a murder case."

"I see. I may be able to slip you in for five minutes if that will do any good."

"It might."

She talked to Stevens on the phone and waved me past the cubicles to an office at the end of the hall. It was large and sumptuous. Stevens sat on leather behind mahogany, flanked by a glass-faced cabinet of yachting trophies. He was lion-faced, with a big soft masterful mouth, a high brow overhung by broken wings of yellowish white hair, pale blue eyes that had seen everything at least once and were watching the second time around. He wore tweeds and a florid bow tie.

"Close the door behind you, Mr. Archer, and sit down."

I parked myself on a leather settee and started to tell him what I was doing there. His heavy voice interrupted me:

"I have only a very few minutes. I know who you are, sir, and I believe I know what you have in mind. You want to discuss the McGee case with me."

I threw him a curve: "And the Deloney case."

His eyebrows went up, forcing the flesh above them into multiple corrugations. Sometimes you have to give away information on the chance of gaining other information. I told him what had happened to Luke Deloney.

He leaned forward in his chair. "You say this is connected in some way with the Haggerty murder?"

"It has to be. Helen Haggerty lived in Deloney's apartment building. She said she knew a witness to Deloney's murder."

"Strange she didn't mention it." He wasn't talking to me. He was talking to himself about Mrs. Deloney. Then he remembered that I was there. "Why do you come to me with this?"

"I thought you'd be interested, since Mrs. Deloney is your client."

"Is she?"

"I assumed she was."

"You're welcome to your assumptions. I suppose you followed her here."

"I happened to see her come in. But I've wanted to get in touch with you for a couple of days."

"Why?"

"You defended Tom McGee. His wife's death was the second in a series of three related murders which started with Deloney and ended with Helen Haggerty. Now they're trying to pin the Haggerty death on McGee or his daughter, or both of them. I believe McGee is innocent, and has been all along."

"Twelve of his peers thought otherwise."

"Why did they, Mr. Stevens?"

"I get no pleasure from discussing past mistakes."

"This could be very relevant to the present. McGee's daughter admits she lied on the witness stand. She says she lied her father into prison."

"Does she now? The admission comes a little belatedly. I should have borne down on her in cross, but McGee didn't want me to. I made the mistake of respecting his wishes."

"What was the motive behind them?"

"Who can say? Paternal love, perhaps, or his feeling that the child had been made to suffer enough. Ten years in prison is a big price to pay for such delicacies of feeling."

"You're convinced that McGee was innocent?"

"Oh, yes. The daughter's admission that she was lying removes any possible doubt." Stevens took a blotched green cigar out of a glass tube, clipped it and lit it. "I take it that is highly confidential advice."

"On the contrary, I'd like to see it publicized. It might help to bring McGee in. He's on the run, as you probably know."

Stevens neither affirmed nor denied this. He sat like a mountain behind a blue haze of smoke.

"I'd like to ask him some questions," I said.

"What about?"

"The other man, for one thing—the man Constance McGee was in love with. I understand he played some part in your case."

"He was my hypothetical alternative." Steven's face crumpled in a rueful smile.

"But the judge wouldn't let him in, except in my summing-up, unless I put McGee on the stand. Which didn't seem advisable. That other man was a two-edged weapon. He was a motive for McGee, as well as an alternative suspect. I made the mistake of going for an outright acquittal."

"I don't quite follow."

"It doesn't matter. It's only history." He waved his hand, and the smoke shifted around him like strata of time in an old man's memory.

"Who was the other man?"

"Come now, Mr. Archer, you can't expect to walk in off the street and pump me dry. I've been practicing law for forty years."

"Why did you take McGee's case?"

"Tom used to do some work on my boats. I rather liked him."

"Aren't you interested in clearing him?"

"Not at the expense of another innocent man."

"You know who the other man is?"

"I know who he is, if Tom can be believed." While he still sat solidly in his chair, he was withdrawing from me like a magician through dissolving mirrors. "I don't divulge the secrets that come to me. I bury 'em, sir. That's why they come to me."

"It would be a hell of a thing if they put Tom back in San Quentin for the rest of his life, or gassed him."

"It certainly would. But I suspect you're trying to enlist me in your cause, rather than Tom's."

"We could certainly use you."

"Who are 'we'?"

"McGee's daughter Dolly and her husband Alex Kincaid, Jerry Marks and me."

"And what *is* your cause?"

"The solution of those three murders."

"You make it sound very simple and neat," he said. "Life never is. Life always has loose ends, and it's sometimes best to let them ravel out."

"Is that what Mrs. Deloney wants?"

"I wasn't speaking on behalf of Mrs. Deloney. I don't expect to." He worked a speck of tobacco onto the tip of his tongue, and spat it out.

"Did she come to you for information about the McGee case?"

"No comment."

"That probably means yes. It's a further indication that the McGee case and the Deloney killing are connected."

"We won't discuss it," he said shortly. "As for your suggestion that I join forces with you, Jerry Marks had the same idea this morning. As I told him, I'll think about it. In the meantime I want you and Jerry to think about something. Tom McGee and his daughter may be on opposite sides of this issue. They certainly were ten years ago."

"She was a child then, manipulated by adults."

"I know that." He rose, bulking huge in his light tweed suit. "It's been interesting talking to you but I'm overdue for a luncheon meeting." He moved past me to the door, gesturing with his cigar. "Come along."

26

I walked down the main street to the Pacific Hotel and asked for Mrs. Hoffman. She had just checked out, leaving no forwarding address. The bellhop who handled her bag said she had ridden away in a taxi with another old lady wearing a green coat. I gave him five dollars and my motel address, and told him it would be worth another five to find out where they'd gone.

It was past two o'clock, and my instinct told me this was the crucial day. I felt cut off from what was happening in the private offices of the courthouse, in the shooting gallery and laboratory where the ballistics tests were being conducted, behind the locked door of the nursing home. Time was slipping away, flowing past me like Heraclitus' river, while I was checking up on the vagaries of old ladies.

I went back to the telephone booths behind the hotel lobby and called Godwin's office. The doctor was with a patient, and wouldn't be available until ten minutes to three. I tried Jerry Marks. His secretary told me he was still out.

I made a collect call to the Walters agency in Reno. Arnie answered the phone:

"Nice timing, Lew. I just got the word on your boy."

"Which one? Bradshaw or Foley?"

"Both of them in a way. You wanted to know why Foley lost his job at the Solitaire Club. The answer is he used his position in the cashier's cage to find out how much Bradshaw was worth."

"How did he do that?"

"You know how the clubs check up on their customers when they open an account. They put in a query to the customer's bank, get an approximate figure on his bank balance, and set a limit to his credit accordingly. 'Low three' means a three-figure bank balance on the low side, and maybe a limit of a couple of hundred. A 'high four' might be seven or eight thousand, and a 'low five' maybe twenty or thirty thousand. Which incidentally is Bradshaw's bracket."

"Is he a gambler?"

"He isn't. That's the point. He never opened an account at the Solitaire, or anywhere else that I know of, but Foley put in a query on him anyway. The club caught it, did a double check on Foley, and got him out of there fast."

"It smells like possible blackmail, Arnie."

"More than possible," he said. "Foley admits to a bit of a record in that line."

"What else does he admit?"

"Nothing else yet. He claims he got the information for a friend."

"Helen Haggerty?"

"Foley isn't saying. He's holding back in the hope of making a deal."

"Go ahead and deal with him. He got hurt worse than I did. I'm willing to drop charges."

"It may not be necessary, Lew."

"Deal with him. Assuming blackmail, which I do, the question is what makes Bradshaw blackmailable."

"Could be his divorce," Arnie said smoothly. "You were interested in what Bradshaw was doing in Reno between the middle of July and the end of August. The answer is on the court record. He was establishing residence for a divorce from a woman named Letitia O. Macready."

"Letitia who?"

"Macready." He spelled it out. "I haven't been able to get any further information on the woman. According to the lawyer who handled the divorce, Bradshaw didn't know where she lived. Her last known address was in Boston. The official notice of the proceedings came back from there with a 'Gone—No Order' stamp."

"Is Bradshaw still at Tahoe?"

"He and his new wife checked out this morning. They were on their way back to Pacific Point. That makes him your baby."

"Baby isn't quite the word for Bradshaw. I wonder if his mother knows about the first marriage."

"You could always ask her."

I decided to try and talk to Bradshaw first. I got my car out of the courthouse lot and drove out to the college. The students on the mall and in the corridors, particularly the girls, wore subdued expressions. The threat of death and judgment had invaded the campus. I felt a little like its representative.

The blonde secretary in the Dean's outer office looked tense, as if only her will was holding her, and the whole institution, together.

"Dean Bradshaw isn't in."

"Not back from the weekend yet?"

"Of course he's back." She added in a defensive tone: "Dean Bradshaw was here this morning for over an hour."

"Where is he now?"

"I don't know. I guess he went home."

"You sound kind of worried about him."

She answered me with a machine-gun burst from her typewriter. I retreated, across the hall to Laura Sutherland's office. Her secretary told me she hadn't come in today. She'd phoned in the middle of the morning that she was afraid she was coming down with something. I hoped it wasn't something serious, like death and judgment.

I drove back to Foothill and along it to the Bradshaw house. Wind rustled in the trees. The fog had been completely dissipated, and the afternoon sky was a brilliant aching blue. The mountains rising into it were distinct in every scarred and wrinkled detail.

I was more aware than usual of these things, but I felt cut off from them. I must have had some empathy for Roy Bradshaw and his new wife and was afraid of being hurt in my empathy. I drove past his gate without seeing it and had to turn in the next driveway and come back to the Bradshaw house. I was somewhat relieved to be told by the Spanish woman, Maria, that Bradshaw wasn't there and hadn't been all day.

Mrs. Bradshaw called from the stairs in a cracked penetrating voice: "Is that you, Mr. Archer? I want to talk to you."

She came down the steps in a quilted dressing robe and cloth slippers. The weekend had aged her. She looked very old and haggard.

"My son hasn't been home for three days." she complained, "and he hasn't telephoned once. What do you suppose has happened to him?"

"I'd like to discuss that question with you, in private."

Maria, who had been listening with her entire body, went off in a hip-swinging dudgeon. Mrs. Bradshaw took me to a room I hadn't been in before, a small sitting room opening on a patio at the side of the house. Its furnishings were informal and old-fashioned, and they reminded me slightly of the room where I had interviewed Mrs. Deloney.

This room was dominated by an oil painting over the fireplace. It was a full-length portrait, almost life-size, of a handsome gentleman wearing sweeping white mustaches and a cutaway. His black eyes followed me across the room to the armchair which Mrs. Bradshaw indicated. She sat in an upholstered platform rocker with her slippered feet on a small petit point hassock.

"I've been a selfish old woman," she said unexpectedly. "I've been thinking it over, and I've decided to pay your expenses after all. I don't like what they're doing to that girl."

"You probably know more about it than I do."

"Probably. I have some good friends in this city." She didn't elaborate.

"I appreciate the offer," I said, "but my expenses are being taken care of. Dolly's husband came back."

"Really? I'm so glad." She tried to warm herself at the thought, and failed. "I'm deeply concerned about Roy."

"So am I, Mrs. Bradshaw." I decided to tell her what I knew, or part of it. She was bound to find out soon about his marriage, his marriages. "You don't have to worry about his physical safety. I saw him last night in Reno, and he was in good shape. He checked in at the college today."

"His secretary lied to me then. I don't know what they're trying to do to me out there, or what my son is up to. What was he really doing in Reno?"

"Attending a conference, as he said. He also went there to look into a suspect in Helen Haggerty's murder."

"He must have been very fond of her, after all, to go to such lengths."

"He was involved with Miss Haggerty. I don't think the involvement was romantic."

"What was it then?"

"Financial. I think he was paying her money, and incidentally he got her a job at the college, through Laura Sutherland. To put it bluntly, the Haggerty woman was blackmailing your son. She may have called it something different herself. But she used a crooked friend in Reno to check on his bank balance before she ever came here. This was the same man Roy went to Reno to talk to."

Mrs. Bradshaw didn't throw a fit, as I was afraid she might. She said in a grave tone: "Are these facts, Mr. Archer, or are you exercising your imagination?"

"I wish I were. I'm not."

"But how could Roy be blackmailed? He's led a blameless life, a dedicated life. I'm his mother. I ought to know."

"That may be. But the standard varies for different people. A rising college administrator has to be lily-white. An unfortunate marriage, for instance, would queer his chances for that university presidency you were telling me about."

"An unfortunate marriage? But Roy has never been married."

"I'm afraid he has," I said. "Does the name Letitia Macready mean anything to you?"

"It does not."

She was lying. The name drew a net of lines across her face, reduced her eyes to bright black points and her mouth to a purse with a drawstring. She knew the name and hated it, I thought; perhaps she was even afraid of Letitia Macready.

"The name ought to mean something to you, Mrs. Bradshaw. The Macready woman was your daughter-in-law."

"You must be insane. My son has never married."

She spoke with such force and assurance that I had a moment of doubt. It wasn't likely that Arnie had made a mistake—he seldom did—but it was possible that there were two Roy Bradshaws. No, Arnie had talked to Bradshaw's lawyer in Reno, and must have made a positive identification.

"You have to get married," I said, "before you can get a divorce. Roy got a Reno divorce a few weeks ago. He was in Nevada establishing residence for it from the middle of July till the end of August."

"Now I know you're insane. He was in Europe all that time, and I can prove it." She got up, on creaking reluctant limbs, and went to the eighteenth-century secretary against one wall. She came back toward me with a sheaf of letters and postcards in her shaking hands. "He sent me these. You can see for yourself that he was in Europe."

I looked over the postcards. There were about fifteen of them, arranged in order: The Tower of London (postmarked London, July 18), the Bodleian Library (Oxford, July 21), York Cathedral (York, July 25), Edinburgh Castle (Edinburgh,

July 29), The Giant's Causeway (Londonderry, August 3), The Abbey Theatre (Dublin, August 6), Land's End (St. Ives, August 8), The Arc de Triomphe (Paris, August 12), and so on through Switzerland and Italy and Germany. I read the card from Munich (a view of the English Gardens, postmarked August 25):

Dear Moms:
Yesterday I visited Hitler's eyrie at Berchtesgaden—a beautiful setting made grim by its associations—and today, by way of contrast, I took a bus to Oberammergau, where the Passion Play is performed. I was struck by the almost Biblical simplicity of the villagers. This whole Bavarian countryside is studded with the most stunning little churches. How I wish you could enjoy them with me! I'm sorry to hear that your summer companion is presenting certain prickly aspects. Well, the summer will soon be over and I for one will be happy to turn my back on the splendors of Europe and come home. All my love.

Roy

I turned to Mrs. Bradshaw. "Is this your son's handwriting?"
"Yes. It's unmistakable. I know he wrote those cards, and these letters, too."
She brandished several letters under my nose. I looked at the postmarks: London, July 19; Dublin, August 7; Geneva, August 15; Rome, August 20; Berlin, August 27; Amsterdam, August 30. I started to read the last one ("Dear Moms: Just a hasty note, which may arrive after I do, to tell you how I loved your letter about the blackbirds . . .") but Mrs. Bradshaw snatched it out of my hand.
"Please don't *read* the letters. My son and I are very close, and he wouldn't like me to show our correspondence to a stranger." She gathered all the letters and cards and locked them up in the secretary. "I believe I've proved my point, that Roy couldn't have been in Nevada when you say he was."
For all her assurance, her voice was questioning. I said:
"Did you write letters to him while he was away?"
"I did. That is to say, I dictated them to Miss What's-her-name, except for once or twice when my arthritis allowed me to write. I had a nurse-companion during the summer. Miss Wadley, her name was. She was one of these completely self-centered young women—"
I cut in: "Did you write a letter about the blackbirds?"
"Yes. We had an invasion of them last month. It was more of a fanciful little tale than a letter, having to do with blackbirds baked in a pie."
"Where did you send the blackbird letter?"
"Where? I think to Rome, to American Express in Rome. Roy gave me an itinerary before he left here."
"He was supposed to be in Rome on August 20. The blackbird letter was answered from Amsterdam on August 30."

"You have an impressive memory, Mr. Archer, but I fail to see what you're getting at."

"Just this. There was a lapse of at least ten days between the receiving and the answering of that letter—time enough for an accomplice to pick it up in Rome, airmail it to Roy in Reno, get his airmail reply in Amsterdam, and remail it to you here."

"I don't believe it." But she half-believed it. "Why would he go to such lengths to deceive his mother?"

"Because he was ashamed of what he was actually doing—divorcing the Macready woman in Reno—and he didn't want you, or anyone else, to know about it. Has he been to Europe before?"

"Of course. I took him there soon after the war, when he was in graduate school at Harvard."

"And did you visit many of these same places?"

"Yes. We did. Not Germany, but most of the others."

"Then it wouldn't have been hard for him to fake the letters. As for the postcards, his accomplice must have bought them in Europe and mailed them to him."

"I dislike your use of the word 'accomplice' in connection with my son. There is, after all, nothing criminal about this—this deception. It's a purely personal matter."

"I hope so, Mrs. Bradshaw."

She must have known what I meant. Her face went through the motions of swallowing pain. She turned her back on me and went to the window. Several white-eyed blackbirds were walking around on the tiles of the patio. I don't suppose she saw them. One of her hands combed roughly at her hair, over and over, until it stuck up like molting thistles. When she turned around at last, her eyes were half-closed, and her face seemed tormented by the light.

"I'm going to ask you to keep all this in confidence, Mr. Archer."

Roy Bradshaw had used very similar language last night, about his marriage to Laura.

"I can try," I said.

"Please do. It would be tragic if Roy's career were to be ruined by a youthful indiscretion. That's all it was, you know—a youthful indiscretion. It would never have happened if his father had lived to give him a father's guidance." She gestured toward the portrait over the fireplace.

"By 'it' you mean the Macready woman?"

"Yes."

"You know her then?"

"I know her."

As if the admission had exhausted her, she collapsed in the platform rocker, leaning her head on the high cushioned back. Her loose throat seemed very vulnerable.

"Miss Macready came to see me once," she said. "It was before we left Boston, during the war. She wanted money."

"Blackmail money?"

"That's what it amounted to. She asked me to finance a Nevada divorce for her. She'd picked Roy up on Scollay Square and tricked the boy into marrying her. She was in a position to wreck his future. I gave her two thousand dollars. Apparently she spent it on herself and never bothered getting a divorce." She sighed. "Poor Roy."

"Did he know that you knew about her?"

"I never told him. I thought I had ended the threat by paying her money. I wanted it over with and forgotten, with no recriminations between my son and me. But apparently she's been haunting him all these years."

"Haunting him in the flesh?"

"Who knows? I thought I understood my son, and all the details of his life. It turns out that I don't."

"What sort of a woman is she?"

"I saw her only once, when she came to my house in Belmont. I formed a most unfavorable impression. She claimed to be an actress, unemployed, but she dressed and talked like a member of an older profession than that." Her voice rasped with irony. "I suppose I have to admit that the redheaded hussy was handsome, in a crude way. But she was utterly unsuitable for Roy, and of course she knew it. He was an innocent lad, hardly out of his teens. She was obviously an experienced woman."

"How old was she?"

"Much older than Roy, thirty at least."

"So she'd be pushing fifty now."

"At least," she said.

"Have you ever seen her in California?"

She shook her head so hard that her face went loose and wobbly.

"Has Roy?"

"He's never mentioned her to me. We've lived together on the assumption that the Macready woman never existed. And I beg you not to tell him what I've told you. It would destroy all confidence between us."

"There may be more important considerations, Mrs. Bradshaw."

"What could be more important?"

"His neck."

She sat with her thick ankles crossed, more stunned than impassive. Her broad sexless body made her resemble a dilapidated Buddha. She said in a hushed voice:

"Surely you can't suspect my son of murder?"

I said something vague and soothing. The eyes of the man in the portrait followed me out. I was glad the father wasn't alive, in view of what I might have to do to Roy.

27

I hadn't eaten since breakfast, and on my way into town I stopped at a drive-in. While I was waiting for my sandwich, I made another call to Arnie Walters from an outside booth.

Arnie had made his deal with Judson Foley. It was Helen Haggerty who had wanted the word on Bradshaw's financial status. Foley couldn't or wouldn't swear that she had blackmail in mind. But shortly after he sold her the information she came into sudden wealth, by Foley's standards.

"How much did she pay Foley?"

"Fifty dollars, he says. Now he feels cheated."

"He always will," I said. "Did she tell Foley what she had on Bradshaw?"

"No. She was very careful not to, apparently. But there's a piece of negative evidence: She didn't mention to Foley that Bradshaw had been married, or was getting a divorce. Which probably means that that information was worth money to her."

"It probably does."

"One other fact came out, Lew. The Haggerty woman knew Bradshaw long before they met in Reno."

"Where and how?"

"Foley says he doesn't know, and I believe him. I offered to pay him for any information that checked out. It broke his heart when he couldn't do business with me."

I found Jerry Marks in the law library on the second floor of the courthouse. Several bound volumes of typescript were piled on the table in front of him. There was dust on his hands, and a smudge on the side of his nose.

"Have you turned up anything, Jerry?"

"I've come to one conclusion. The case against McGee was weak. It consisted of two things, mainly: prior abuse of his wife, and the little girl's testimony, which some judges would have thrown out of court. I've been concentrating on her testimony, because I'm going to have a chance to question her under pentothal."

"When?"

"Tonight at eight, at the nursing home. Dr. Godwin isn't free till then."

"I want to be there."

"That suits me, if Godwin can be persuaded. It was all I could do to get myself invited, and I'm her lawyer."

"I think Godwin is sitting on something. There's a job that needs doing between now and eight. It's properly my job but this is your town and you can do it faster. Find out if Roy Bradshaw's alibi for Helen Haggerty's murder is waterproof and dustproof and antimagnetic."

Jerry sat up straight and used his forefinger to smudge his nose some more. "How should I go about it?"

"Bradshaw addressed an alumni banquet Friday evening. I want to know if he could have slipped out during one of the other speeches, or left in time to kill her. You have a right to any facts the sheriff's men and the pathologist can provide about time of death."

"I'll do my best," he said, pushing his chair back.

"One other thing, Jerry. Is there any word on the ballistics tests?"

"The rumor says they're still going on. The rumor doesn't say why. Do you suppose they're trying to fake something?"

"No, I don't. Ballistics experts don't go in for fakery."

I left him gathering up his transcripts and walked downtown to the Pacific Hotel. My bellhop had contacted Mrs. Deloney's cab-driver, and told me in return for a second five that the two elderly ladies had checked in at the Surf House. I bought a drip-dry shirt and some underwear and socks and went back to my motel to shower and change. I needed that before I tackled Mrs. Deloney again.

Someone was knocking as I stepped out of the shower, tapping ever so gently as if the door was fragile.

"Who's there?"

"Madge Gerhardi. Let me in."

"As soon as I'm dressed."

It took a little time. I had to pick the pins out of my new shirt, and my hands were jerking.

"*Please* let me in," the woman said at the door. "I don't want to be seen."

I pulled on my trousers and went to the door in my bare feet. She pressed in past me as if there was a storm at her back. Her garish blonde hair was windblown. She took hold of my hands with both of her clammy ones.

"The police are watching my house. I don't know if they followed me here or not. I came along the beach."

"Sit down," I said, and placed a chair for her. "I'm sure the police aren't after you. They're looking for your friend Begley-McGee."

"Don't call him that. It sounds as though you're making fun of him." It was an avowal of love.

"What do you want me to call him?"

"I still call him Chuck. A man has a right to change his name, after what they did to him, and what they're doing. Anyway, he's a writer, and writers use pen names."

"Okay. I'll call him Chuck. But you didn't come here to argue about a name."

She fingered her mouth, pushing her full lower lip from side to side. She wasn't wearing lipstick or any other makeup. Without it she looked younger and more innocent.

"Have you heard from Chuck?" I said.

She nodded almost imperceptibly, as if too great a movement would endanger him.

"Where is he, Madge?"

"In a safe place. I'm not to tell you where unless you promise not to tell the police."

"I promise."

Her pale eyes brightened. "He wants to talk to you."

"Did he say what about?"

"I didn't talk to him personally. A friend of his down at the harbor telephoned the message."

"I take it he's somewhere around the harbor then."

She gave me another of her barely visible nods.

"You've told me this much," I said. "You might as well tell me the rest. I'd give a lot for an interview with Chuck."

"And you won't lead the police to him?"

"Not if I can help it. Where is he, Madge?"

She screwed up her face and made the plunge: "He's on Mr. Stevens's yacht, the *Revenant*."

"How did he get aboard her?"

"I'm not sure. He knew that Mr. Stevens was racing her at Balboa over the weekend. I think he went there and surrendered to Mr. Stevens."

I left Madge in my room. She didn't want to go out again by herself, or ride along with me. I took the waterfront boulevard to the harbor. While a few tugboats and tuna-fishers used its outer reaches, most of the boats moored at the slips or anchored within the long arm of the jetty were the private yachts and cruisers of weekend sailors.

On a Monday, not many of them were at sea, but I noticed a few white sails on the horizon. They were headed shoreward, like homing dreams.

A man in the harbormaster's glass-enclosed lookout pointed out Stevens's yacht to me. Though she rode at the far end of the outer slip, she was easy to spot because of her towering mast. I walked out along the floating dock to her.

Revenant was long and sleek, with a low streamlined cabin and a racing cockpit. Her varnish was smooth and clear, her brass was bright. She rocked ever so slightly on the enclosed water, like an animal trembling to run.

I stepped aboard and knocked on the hatch. No answer, but it opened when I pushed. I climbed down the short ladder and made my way past some short-wave radio equipment, and a tiny galley smelling of burned coffee, into the sleeping quarters. An oval of sunlight from one of the ports, moving reciprocally with the motion of the yacht, fluttered against the bulkhead like a bright and living soul. I said to it:

"McGee?"

Something stirred in an upper bunk. A face appeared at eye level. It was a suitable face for the crew of a boat named *Revenant*. McGee had shaved off his beard, and the lower part of his face had a beard-shaped pallor. He looked older and thinner and much less sure of himself.

"Did you come here by yourself?" he whispered.

"Naturally I did."

"That means you don't think I'm guilty, either." He was reduced to such small momentary hopefulnesses.

"Who else doesn't think you're guilty?"

"Mr. Stevens."

"Was this his idea?" I said, with a gesture that included McGee and myself.

"He didn't say I *shouldn't* talk to you."

"Okay, McGee, what's on your mind?"

He lay still watching me. His mouth was twitching, and his eyes held a kind of beseeching brightness. "I don't know where to start. I've been living in my thoughts for ten years—so long it hardly seems real. I know what happened to me but I don't know why. Ten years in the pen, with no chance of parole because I wouldn't admit that I was guilty. How could I? I was bum-rapped. And now they're getting ready to do it again."

He gripped the polished mahogany edge of the bunk. "I can't go back to 'Q,' brother. I did ten years and it was *hard* time. There's no time as hard as the time you do for somebody else's mistake. God, but the days crawled. There weren't enough jobs to go round and half the time I had nothing to do but sit and think.

"I'll kill myself," he said, "before I let them send me back again."

He meant it, and I meant what I said in reply: "It won't happen, McGee. That's a promise."

"I only wish I could believe you. You get out of the habit of believing people. They don't believe you, you don't believe them."

"Who killed your wife?"

"I don't know."

"Who do you think killed her?"

"I'm not saying."

"You've gone to a lot of trouble, and taken quite a risk, to get me out here and tell me you're not saying. Let's go back to where it started, McGee. Why did your wife leave you?"

"I left her. We had been separated for months when she was killed. I wasn't even in Indian Springs that night, I was here in the Point."

"Why did you leave her?"

"Because she asked me to. We weren't getting along. We never did get along after I came back from the service. Constance and the kid spent the war years living with her sister, and she couldn't adjust to me after that. I admit I was a wild man for a while then. But her sister Alice promoted the trouble between us."

"Why?"

"She thought the marriage was a mistake. I guess she wanted Constance all to herself. I just got in the way."

"Did anybody else get in the way?"

"Not if Alice could help it."

I phrased my question more explicitly: "Was there another man in Constance's life?"

"Yeah. There was." He seemed ashamed, as if the infidelity had been his. "I've given it a lot of thought over the years, and I don't see much point in opening it up now. The guy had nothing to do with her death, I'm sure of that. He was crazy about her. He wouldn't hurt her."

"How do you know?"

"I talked to him about her, not long before she was killed. The kid told me what was going on between him and her."

"You mean your daughter Dolly?"

"That's right. Constance used to meet the guy every Saturday, when she brought Dolly in to see the doctor. On one of my visiting days with the kid—the last one we ever had together, in fact—she told me about those meetings. She was only eleven or twelve and she didn't grasp the full significance, but she knew something fishy was going on.

"Every Saturday afternoon Constance and the guy used to park her in a double-feature movie and go off by themselves someplace, probably some motel. Constance asked the kid to cover for her, and she did. The guy even gave her money to tell Alice that Constance went to those movies with her. I thought that was a lousy trick." McGee tried to warm over his old anger but he had suffered too much, and thought too much, to be able to. His face hung like a cold moon over the edge of the bunk.

"We might as well use his name," I said. "Was it Godwin?"

"Hell no. It was Roy Bradshaw. He used to be a professor at the college." He added with a kind of mournful pride: "Now he's the Dean out there."

He wouldn't be for long, I thought; his sky was black with chickens coming home to roost.

"Bradshaw was one of Dr. Godwin's patients," McGee was saying. "That's where he and Connie met, in Godwin's waiting room. I think the doctor kind of encouraged the thing between them."

"What makes you think that?"

"Bradshaw told me himself the doctor said it was good for them, for their emotional health. It's a funny thing, I went to Bradshaw's house to get him to lay off Connie, even if I had to beat him up. But by the time he was finished talking he had me half-convinced that he and Connie were right, and I was wrong. I still don't know who was right and who was wrong. I know I never gave her any real happiness, after the first year. Maybe Bradshaw did."

"Is that why you didn't inject him into your trial?"

"That was one reason. Anyway, what was the use of fouling it up? It would only make me look worse." He paused. A deeper tone rose from a deeper level of his nature: "Besides, I loved her. I loved Connie. It was the one way I had to prove I loved her."

"Did you know that Bradshaw was married to another woman?"

"When?"

"For the last twenty years. He divorced her a few weeks ago."

McGee looked shocked. He'd been living on illusions for a long time, and I was threatening his sustenance. He pulled himself back into the bunk, almost out of sight.

"Her name was Letitia Macready—Letitia Macready Bradshaw. Have you ever heard of her?"

"No. How could he be married? He was living at home with his mother."

"There are all kinds of marriages," I said. "He may not have seen his wife in years, and then again he may have. He may have had her living here in town, unknown to his mother or any of his friends. I suspect that was the case, judging from the lengths he went to to cover up his divorce."

McGee said in a confused and shaken voice: "I don't see what it has to do with me."

"It may have a very great deal. If the Macready woman was in town ten years ago, she had a motive for killing your wife—a motive as strong as your own."

He didn't want to think about the woman. He was too used to thinking about himself. "I *had* no motive. I wouldn't hurt a hair of her head."

"You did, though, once or twice."

He was silent. All I could see of him was his wavy gray hair, like a dusty wig, and his large dishonest eyes trying to be honest:

"I hit her a couple of times, I admit it. I suffered the tortures of the damned afterward. You've got to understand, I used to get mean when I got plastered. That's why Connie sent me away. I don't blame her. I don't blame her for anything. I blame myself." He drew in a long breath and let it out slowly.

I offered him a cigarette, which he refused. I lit one for myself. The bright trembling patch of sunlight was climbing the bulkhead. It would soon be evening.

"So Bradshaw had a wife," McGee said. He had had time to absorb the information. "And he told me he intended to marry Connie."

"Maybe he did intend to. It would strengthen the woman's motive."

"You honestly think she did it?"

"She's a prime suspect. Bradshaw is another. He must have been a suspect to your daughter, too. She enrolled in his college and took a job in his household to check on him. Was that your idea, McGee?"

He shook his head.

"I don't understand her part in all this. She hasn't been much help in explaining it, either."

"I know," he said. "Dolly's done a lot of lying, starting away back when. But when a little kid lies you don't put the same construction on it as you would an adult."

"You're a forgiving man."

"Oh no I'm not. I went to her with anger in my heart that Sunday I saw her picture in the paper, with her husband. What right did she have to a happy marriage after what she did to me? That's what was on my mind."

"Did you tell her what was on your mind?"

"Yessir, I did. But my anger didn't last. She reminded me so of her mother in appearance. It was like going back twenty years to happier times, when we were first married. We had a real good year when I was in the Navy and Connie was pregnant, with her."

His mind kept veering away from his current troubles. I could hardly blame him, but I urged him back to them:

"You gave your daughter a hard time the other Sunday, didn't you?"

"I did at first. I admit that. I asked her why she lied about me in court. That was a legitimate question, wasn't it?"

"I should say so. What was her reaction?"

"She went into hysterics and said she wasn't lying, that she saw me with the gun and everything and heard me arguing with her mother. Which was false, and I told her so. I wasn't even in Indian Springs that night. That stopped her cold."

"Then what?"

"I asked her why she had lied about me." He licked his lips and said in a hushed voice: "I asked her if she shot her mother herself, maybe by accident, the way Alice kept that revolver lying around loose. It was a terrible question, but it had to come out. It's been on my mind for a long time."

"As long ago as your trial?"

"Yeah. Before that."

"And that's why you wouldn't let Stevens cross-examine her?"

"Yeah. I should have let him go ahead. I ended up cross-questioning her myself ten years later."

"What was the result?"

"More hysterics. She was laughing and crying at the same time. I never felt so sorry for anybody. She was as white as a sheet and the tears popped out of her eyes and ran down her face. Her tears looked so *pure*."

"What did she say?"

"She said she didn't do it, naturally."

"Could she have? Did she know how to handle a gun?"

"A little. I gave her a little training, and so did Alice. It doesn't take much gun-handling to pull a trigger, especially by accident."

"You still think it could have happened that way?"

"I don't know. It's mainly what I wanted to talk to you about."

These words seemed to release him from an obscure bondage. He climbed down out of the upper bunk and stood facing me in the narrow aisle. He had on a seaman's black turtleneck, levis, and rubber-soled deck shoes.

"You're in a position to go and talk to her," he said. "I'm not. Mr. Stevens won't. But you can go and ask her what really happened."

"She may not know."

"I realize that. She got pretty mixed up the other Sunday. God knows I wasn't trying to mix her up. I only asked her some questions. But she didn't seem to know the difference between what happened and what she said in court."

"That story she told in court—did she definitely admit she made it up?"

"She made it up with a lot of help from Alice. I can imagine how it went. 'This is the way it happened, isn't it?' Alice would say. 'You saw your old man with the gun, didn't you?' And after a while the kid had her story laid out for her."

"Would Alice deliberately try to frame you?"

"She wouldn't put it that way herself. She'd know for a fact I was guilty. All she was doing was making sure I got punished for my crime. She probably fed the kid her lines without knowing she was faking evidence. My dear sister-in-law was always out to get me, anyway."

"Was she out to get Connie, too?"

"Connie? She doted on Connie. Alice was more like her mother than her sister. There was fourteen-fifteen years' difference in their ages."

"You said she wanted Connie to herself. Her feelings for Connie could have changed if she found out about Bradshaw."

"Not *that* much. Anyway, who would tell her?"

"Your daughter might have. If she told you, she'd tell Alice."

McGee shook his head. "You're really reaching."

"I have to. This is a deep case, and I can't see the bottom of it yet. Did Alice ever live in Boston, do you know?"

"I think she always lived here. She's a Native Daughter. I'm a native son, but nobody ever gave me a medal for it."

"Even Native Daughters have been known to go to Boston. Did Alice ever go on the stage, or marry a man named Macready, or dye her hair red?"

"None of those things sound like Alice."

I thought of her pink fantastic bedroom, and wondered.

"They sound more," McGee was saying, and then he stopped. He was silent for a watching moment. "I'll take that cigarette you offered me."

I gave him a cigarette and lighted it. "What were you going to say?"

"Nothing. I must have been thinking aloud."

"Who were you thinking about?"

"Nobody you know. Forget it, eh?"

"Come on, McGee. You're supposed to be leveling with me."

"I still have a right to my private thoughts. It kept me alive in prison."

"You're out of prison now. Don't you want to stay out?"

"Not if somebody else has to go in."

"Sucker," I said. "Who are you covering for now?"

"Nobody."

"Madge Gerhardi?"

"You must be off your rocker."

I couldn't get anything more out of him. The long slow weight of prison forces men into unusual shapes. McGee had become a sort of twisted saint.

28

He was about to be given another turn of the screw. When I climbed out into the cockpit I saw three men approaching along the floating dock. Their bodies, their hatted heads, were dark as iron against the exploding sunset.

One of them showed me a deputy's badge and a gun, which he held on me while the others went below. I heard McGee cry out once. He scrambled up through the hatch with blue handcuffs on his wrists and a blue gun at his back. The single look he gave me was full of fear and loathing.

They didn't handcuff me, but they made me ride to the courthouse with McGee in the screened rear compartment of the Sheriff's car. I tried to talk to him. He wouldn't speak to me or look in my direction. He believed I had turned him in, and perhaps I had without intending to.

I sat under guard outside the interrogation room while they questioned him in tones that rose and fell and growled and palavered and yelled and threatened and promised and refused and wheedled. Sheriff Crane arrived, looking tired but important. He stood over me smiling, with his belly thrust out.

"Your friend's in real trouble now."

"He's been in real trouble for the last ten years. You ought to know, you helped to cook it for him."

The veins in his cheeks lit up like intricate little networks of infra-red tubing. He leaned toward me spewing martini-scented words:

"I could put you in jail for loose talk like that. You know where your friend is going? He's going all the way to the green room this time."

"He wouldn't be the first innocent man who was gassed."

"Innocent? McGee's a mass murderer, and we've got the evidence to prove it.

It took my experts all day to nail it down: The bullet in the Haggerty corpse came from the same gun as the bullet we found in McGee's wife—the same gun he stole from Alice Jenks in Indian Springs."

I'd succeeded in provoking the Sheriff into an indiscretion. I tried for another. "You have no proof he stole it. You have no proof he fired it either time. Where's he been keeping the gun for the last ten years?"

"He cached it someplace, maybe on Stevens's boat. Or maybe an accomplice kept it for him."

"Then he hid it in his daughter's bed to frame her?"

"That's the kind of man he is."

"Nuts!"

"Don't talk to me like that!" He menaced me with the cannon ball of his belly.

"Don't talk like that to the Sheriff," the guard said.

"I don't know of any law against the use of the word 'nuts.' And incidentally I wasn't violating anything in the California Code when I went to the yacht to talk to McGee. I'm cooperating with a local attorney in this investigation and I have a right to get my information where I can and keep it confidential."

"How did you know he was there?"

"I got a tip."

"From Stevens?"

"Not from Stevens. You and I could trade information, Sheriff. How did *you* know he was there?"

"I don't make deals with suspects."

"What do you suspect me of? Illegal use of the word 'nuts'?"

"It isn't so funny. You were taken with McGee. I have a right to hold you."

"I have a right to call an attorney. Try kicking my rights around and see where it gets you. I have friends in Sacramento."

They didn't include the Attorney General or anybody close to him, but I liked the sound of the phrase. Sheriff Crane did not. He was half a politician, and like most of his kind he was an insecure man. He said after a moment's thought:

"You can make your call."

The Sheriff went into the interrogation room—I caught a glimpse of McGee hunched gray-faced under a light—and added his voice to the difficult harmony there. My guard took me into a small adjoining room and left me by myself with a telephone. I used it to call Jerry Marks. He was about to leave for his appointment with Dr. Godwin and Dolly, but he said he'd come right over to the courthouse and bring Gil Stevens with him if Stevens was available.

They arrived together in less than fifteen minutes. Stevens shot me a glance from under the broken white wings of his hair. It was a covert and complex glance which seemed to mean that for the record we were strangers. I suspected the old lawyer had advised McGee to talk to me, and probably set up the interview. I was in a position to use McGee's facts in ways that he couldn't.

With soft threats of *habeas corpus* proceedings, Jerry Marks sprung me out. Stevens remained behind with the Sheriff and a Deputy D.A. It was going to take longer to spring his client.

A moon like a fallen fruit reversing gravity was hoisting itself above the rooftops. It was huge and slightly squashed.

"Pretty," Jerry said in the parking lot.

"It looks like a rotten orange to me."

"Ugliness is in the eye of the beholder. I learned that at my mother's knee and other low joints, as a well-known statesman said." Jerry always felt good when he tried something he learned in law school, and it worked. He walked to his car swiftly, on the balls of his feet, and made the engine roar. "We're late for our appointment with Godwin."

"Did you have time to check on Bradshaw's alibi?"

"I did. It seems to be impregnable." He gave me the details as we drove across town. "Judging by temperature loss, rate of blood coagulation, and so on, the Deputy Coroner places the time of Miss Haggerty's death as no later than eight-thirty. From about seven until about nine-thirty Dean Bradshaw was sitting, or standing up talking, in front of over a hundred witnesses. I talked to three of them, three alumni picked more or less at random, and they all agreed he didn't leave the speaker's table during that period. Which lets him out."

"Apparently it does."

"You sound disappointed, Lew."

"I'm partly that, and partly relieved. I rather like Bradshaw. But I was pretty certain he was our man."

In the remaining minutes before we reached the nursing home, I told him briefly what I'd learned from McGee, and from the Sheriff. Jerry whistled, but made no other comment.

Dr. Godwin opened the door for us. He wore a clean white smock and an aggrieved expression.

"You're late, Mr. Marks. I was just about ready to call the whole thing off."

"We had a little emergency. Thomas McGee was arrested about seven o'clock tonight. Mr. Archer happened to be with him, and he was arrested, also."

Godwin turned to me. "*You* were with McGee?"

"He sent for me, and he talked. I'm looking forward to comparing his story with his daughter's."

"I'm afraid you aren't—ah—co-opted to this session," Godwin said with some embarrassment. "As I pointed out to you before, you don't have professional immunity."

"I do if I'm acting on Mr. Marks's instructions. Which I am."

"Mr. Archer is correct, on both counts," Jerry said.

Godwin let us in reluctantly. We were outsiders, interlopers in his shadowy kingdom. I had lost some of my confidence in his benevolent despotism, but I kept it to myself for the present.

He took us to the examination room where Dolly was waiting. She was sitting on the end of a padded table, wearing a sleeveless white hospital gown. Alex stood in front of her, holding both her hands. His eyes stayed on her face, hungry and worshipping, as if she was the priestess or the goddess of a strange one-member cult.

Her hair was shining and smooth. Her face was composed. Only her eyes had a sullen restlessness and inwardness. They moved across me and failed to give any sign of recognition.

Godwin touched her shoulder. "Are you ready, Dolly?"

"I suppose I am."

She lay back on the padded table. Alex held on to one of her hands.

"You can stay if you like, Mr. Kincaid. It might be easier if you didn't."

"Not for me," the girl said. "I feel safer when he's with me. I want Alex to know all about—everything."

"Yes. I want to stay."

Godwin filled a hypodermic needle, inserted it in her arm, and taped it to the white skin. He told her to count backward from one hundred. At ninety-six the tension left her body and an inner light left her face. It flowed back in a diffused form when the doctor spoke to her:

"Do you hear me, Dolly?"

"I hear you," she murmured.

"Speak louder. I can't hear you."

"I hear you," she repeated. Her voice was faintly slurred.

"Who am I?"

"Dr. Godwin."

"Do you remember when you were a little girl you used to come and visit me in my office?"

"I remember."

"Who used to bring you to see me?"

"Mommy did. She used to bring me in in Aunt Alice's car."

"Where were you living then?"

"In Indian Springs, in Aunt Alice's house."

"And Mommy was living there, too?"

"Mommy was living there, too. She lived there, too."

She was flushed, and talking like a drunken child. The doctor turned to Jerry Marks with a handing-over gesture. Jerry's dark eyes were mournful.

"Do you remember a certain night," he said, "when your Mommy was killed?"

"I remember. Who are you?"

"I'm Jerry Marks, your lawyer. It's all right to talk to me."

"It's all right," Alex said.

The girl looked up at Jerry sleepily. "What do you want me to tell you?"

"Just the truth. It doesn't matter what I want, or anybody else. Just tell me what you remember."

"I'll try."

"Did you hear the gun go off?"

"I heard it." She screwed up her face as if she was hearing it now. "I am—it frightened me."

"Did you see anyone?"

"I didn't go downstairs right away. I was scared."

"Did you see anyone out the window?"

"No. I heard a car drive away. Before that I heard her running."

"You heard *who* running?" Jerry said.

"I thought it was Aunt Alice at first, when she was talking to Mommy at the door. But it couldn't have been Aunt Alice. She wouldn't shoot Mommy. Besides, her gun was missing."

"How do you know?"

"She said I took it from her room. She spanked me with a hairbrush for stealing it."

"When did she spank you?"

"Sunday night, when she came home from church. Mommy said she had no right to spank me. Aunt Alice asked Mommy if *she* took the gun."

"Did she?"

"She didn't say—not while I was there. They sent me to bed."

"*Did* you take the gun?"

"No. I never touched it. I was afraid of it."

"Why?"

"I was afraid of Aunt Alice."

She was rosy and sweating. She tried to struggle up onto her elbows. The doctor eased her back into her supine position, and made an adjustment to the needle. The girl relaxed again, and Jerry said:

"Was it Aunt Alice talking to your Mommy at the door?"

"I thought it was at first. It sounded like her. She had a big scary voice. But it couldn't have been Aunt Alice."

"Why couldn't it?"

"It just couldn't."

She turned her head in a listening attitude. A lock of hair fell over her half-closed eyes. Alex pushed it back with a gentle hand. She said:

"The lady at the door said it had to be true, about Mommy and Mr. Bradshaw. She said she got it from Daddy's own lips, and Daddy got it from me. And then she shot my Mommy and ran away."

There was silence in the room, except for the girl's heavy breathing. A tear as slow as honey was exuded from the corner of one eye. It fell down her temple. Alex wiped the blue-veined hollow with his handkerchief. Jerry leaned across her from the other side of the table:

"Why did you say your Daddy shot your Mommy?"

"Aunt Alice wanted me to. She didn't say so, but I could tell. And I was afraid she'd think that I did it. She spanked me for taking the gun, and I *didn't* take it. I said it was Daddy. She made me say it over and over and over."

There were more tears than one now. Tears for the child she had been, frightened and lying, and tears for the woman she was painfully becoming. Alex wiped her eyes. He looked close to tears himself.

"Why," I said, "did you try to tell us that you killed your mother?"

"Who are you?"

"I'm Alex's friend Lew Archer."

"That's right," Alex said.

She lifted her head and let it fall back. "I forget what you asked me."

"Why did you say you killed your mother?"

"Because it was all my fault. I told my Daddy about her and Mr. Bradshaw, and that's what started everything."

"How do you know?"

"The lady at the door said so. She came to shoot Mommy because of what Daddy told her."

"Do you know who she was?"

"No."

"Was it your Aunt Alice?"

"No."

"Was it anyone you knew?"

"No."

"Did your mother know her?"

"I don't know. Maybe she did."

"Did she talk as if she knew her?"

"She called her by name."

"What name?"

"Tish. She called her Tish. I could tell Mommy didn't like her, though. She was afraid of her, too."

"Why haven't you ever told anyone this before?"

"Because it was all my fault."

"It wasn't," Alex said. "You were only a child. You weren't responsible for what the adults did."

Godwin shushed him with his finger to his lips. Dolly rolled her head from side to side:

"It was all my fault."

"This has gone on long enough," Godwin whispered to Jerry. "She's made some gains. I want to have a chance to consolidate them."

"But we haven't even got to the Haggerty case."

"Make it short then." Godwin said to the girl: "Dolly, are you willing to talk about last Friday night?"

"Not about finding her." She screwed up her face until her eyes were hidden.

"You needn't go into the details of finding the body," Jerry said. "But what were you doing there?"

"I wanted to talk to Helen. I often walked up the hill to talk to her. We were friends."

"How did that happen to be?"

"I ingratiated myself with Helen," she said with queer blank candor. "I thought at first she might be the lady—the woman who shot my mother. The rumor was going around the campus that she was close to Dean Bradshaw."

"And you were on the campus to find that woman?"

"Yes. But it wasn't Helen. I found out she was new in town, and she told me herself there was nothing between her and Bradshaw. I had no right to drag her into this."

"How did you drag her in?"

"I told her everything, about my mother and Bradshaw and the murder and the woman at the door. Helen was killed because she knew too much."

"That may be," I said, "but she didn't learn it from you."

"She did! I told her everything."

Godwin pulled at my sleeve. "Don't argue with her. She's coming out of it fast, but her mind is still operating below the conscious level."

"Did Helen ask you questions?" I said to the girl.

"Yes. She asked me questions."

"Then you didn't force the information on her."

"No. She wanted to know."

"What did she want to know?"

"All about Dean Bradshaw and my mother."

"Did she say why?"

"She wanted to help me in my crusade. I went on a sort of crusade after I talked to Daddy in the hotel. A children's crusade." Her giggle turned into a sob before it left her throat. "The only thing it accomplished was the death of my good friend Helen. And when I found her body—"

Her eyes opened wide. Then her mouth opened wide. Her body went rigid, as if it was imitating the rigor of the dead. She stayed like that for fifteen or twenty seconds.

"It was like finding Mommy again," she said in a small voice, and came fully awake. "Is it all right?"

"It's all right," Alex said.

He helped her up to a sitting position. She leaned on him, her hair mantling his shoulder. A few minutes later, still leaning on him, she walked across the hallway to her room. They walked like husband and wife.

Godwin closed the door of the examination room. "I hope you gentlemen got what you wanted," he said with some distaste. "She talked very freely," Jerry said. The experience had left him drained.

"It was no accident. I've been preparing her for the last three days. Pentothal, as I've told you before, is no guarantee of truth. If a patient is determined to lie, the drug can't stop him."

"Are you implying she wasn't telling the truth?"

"No. I believe she was, so far as she knows the truth. My problem now is to enlarge her awareness and make it fully conscious. If you gentlemen will excuse me?"

"Wait a minute," I said. "You can spare me a minute, doctor. I've spent three days and a lot of Kincaid's money developing facts that you already had in your possession."

"Have you indeed?" he said coldly.

"I have indeed. You could have saved me a good deal of work by filling me in on Bradshaw's affair with Constance McGee."

"I'm afraid I don't exist for the purpose of saving detectives work. There's a question of ethics involved here which you probably wouldn't understand. Mr. Marks probably would."

"I don't understand the issue," Jerry said, but he edged between us as if he expected trouble. He touched my shoulder. "Let's get out of here, Lew, and let the doctor get about his business. He's cooperated beautifully and you know it."

"Who with? Bradshaw?"

Godwin's face turned pale. "My first duty is to my patients."

"Even when they murder people?"

"Even then. But I know Roy Bradshaw intimately and I can assure you he's incapable of killing anyone. Certainly he didn't kill Constance McGee. He was passionately in love with her."

"Passion can cut two ways."

"He didn't kill her."

"A couple of days ago you were telling me McGee did. You can be mistaken, doctor."

"I know that, but not about Roy Bradshaw. The man has lived a tragic life."

"Tell me about it."

"He'll have to tell you himself. I'm not a junior G-man, Mr. Archer. I'm a doctor."

"What about the woman he recently divorced, Tish or Letitia? Do you know her?"

He looked at me without speaking. There was sad knowledge in his eyes. "You'll have to ask Roy about her," he said finally.

29

On his way to the courthouse to question McGee, Jerry dropped me at the harbor, where my car had been left sitting. The moon was higher now, and had regained its proper shape and color. Its light converted the yachts in the slips into a ghostly fleet of Flying Dutchmen.

I went back to my motel to talk to Madge Gerhardi. She had evaporated, along with the rest of the whisky in my pint bottle. I sat on the edge of the bed and tried her number and got no answer.

I called the Bradshaw house. Old Mrs. Bradshaw seemed to have taken up a permanent position beside the telephone. She picked up the receiver on the first ring and quavered into it:

"Who is that, please?"

"It's only Archer. Roy hasn't come home, has he?"

"No, and I'm worried about him, deeply worried. I haven't seen him or heard from him since early Saturday morning. I've been calling his friends—"

"I wouldn't do that, Mrs. Bradshaw."

"I have to do something."

"There are times when it's better to do nothing. Keep still and wait."

"I can't. You're telling me there's something terribly wrong, aren't you?"

"I think you know it."

"Does it have to do with that dreadful woman—that Macready woman?"

"Yes. We have to find out where she is. I'm pretty sure your son could tell me, but he's made himself unavailable. Are you sure you haven't seen the woman since Boston?"

"I'm quite certain. I saw her only once, when she came to me for money."

"Can you describe her for me?"

"I thought I had."

"In more detail, please. It's very important."

She paused to think. I could hear her breathing over the line, a faint rhythmic huskiness. "Well, she was quite a large woman, taller than I, red-haired. She wore her hair bobbed. She had quite a good figure, rather lush, and quite good features, too—a kind of brassy good looks. And she had green eyes, murky green eyes which I didn't like at all. She wore very heavy makeup, more appropriate for the stage than the street, and she was hideously overdressed."

"What was she wearing?"

"It hardly seems relevant, after twenty years. But she had on a leopardskin—an imitation leopardskin coat, as I recall, and under it something striped. Sheer hose, with runs in them. Ridiculously high heels. A good deal of costume jewelry."

"How did she talk?"

"Like a woman of the streets. A greedy, pushing, lustful woman." The moral indignation in her voice hardly surprised me. She had almost lost Roy to the woman, and might yet.

"Would you know her if you saw her again, in different clothes, with her hair perhaps a different color?"

"I think so, if I had a chance to study her."

"You'll have that chance when we find her."

I was thinking that the color of a woman's eyes was harder to change than her hair. The only green-eyed woman connected with the case was Laura Sutherland. She had a conspicuously good figure and good features, but nothing else that seemed to jibe with the description of the Macready woman. Still, she might have changed. I'd seen other women change unrecognizably in half the time.

"You know Laura Sutherland, Mrs. Bradshaw?"

"I know her slightly."

"Does she resemble the Macready woman?"

"Why do you ask that?" she said on a rising note. "Do you suspect Laura?"

"I wouldn't go that far. But you haven't answered my question."

"She couldn't possibly be the same woman. She's a wholly different type."

"What about her basic physical characteristics?"

"I suppose there is some resemblance," she said dubiously. "Roy has always been attracted to women who are obviously mammals."

And obviously mother figures, I thought. "I have to ask you one other question, a more personal question."

"Yes?" She seemed to be bracing herself for a blow.

"I suppose you're aware that Roy was Dr. Godwin's patient."

"Dr. Godwin's patient? I don't believe it. He wouldn't go behind my back." For all her half-cynical insight into his nature she seemed to know very little about him.

"Dr. Godwin says he did, apparently for some years."

"There must be a mistake. Roy has nothing the matter with his mind." There was a vibrating silence. "Has he?"

"I was going to ask you, but I'm sorry I brought it up. Take it easy, Mrs. Bradshaw."

"How can I, with my boy in jeopardy?"

She wanted to hold me on the line, siphoning comfort into her frightened old ears, but I said good night and hung up. One suspect had been eliminated: Madge Gerhardi; the description didn't fit her and never could have. Laura was still in the running.

It wouldn't make sense, of course, for Bradshaw to divorce her and remarry her immediately. But I had only Bradshaw's word for his recent marriage to Laura. I was gradually realizing that his word stretched like an elastic band, and was as easily broken. I looked up Laura's address—she lived in College Heights—and was copying it into my notebook when the phone rang.

It was Jerry Marks. McGee denied having told the woman Tish or anyone else about the affair between Bradshaw and his wife. The only one he had discussed the subject with was Bradshaw.

"Bradshaw may have told the woman himself," I said. "Or possibly the woman overheard McGee."

"Possibly, but hardly likely. McGee says his conversation with Bradshaw took place in Bradshaw's house."

"He could have had the woman there while his mother was away."

"You think she lives around here?"

"Somewhere in Southern California, anyway. I believe Bradshaw's been leading a split-level life with her, and that she's responsible for both the McGee and the Haggerty killings. I just got an improved description of her from Bradshaw's mother. Better pass it along to the police. Do you have something to write on?"

"Yes. I'm sitting at the Sheriff's desk."

I recited Letitia Macready's description, but I didn't say anything about Laura Sutherland. I wanted to talk to her myself.

College Heights was a detached suburb on the far side of the campus from the city. It was a hodgepodge of tract houses and fraternity houses, duplexes and apartment buildings, interspersed with vacant lots sprouting for-sale signs. A boy with a guitar in one of the lighted fraternity houses was singing that this land belongs to you and me.

Laura lived in one of the better apartments, a garden apartment built around an open court with a swimming pool. A shirt-sleeved man slapping mosquitoes in a deck chair by the pool pointed out her door to me and mentioned with some complacency that he owned the place.

"Is anybody with her?"

"I don't think so. She did have a visitor, but he went home."

"Who was he?"

The man peered up at my face. "That's her private business, mister."

"I expect it was Dean Bradshaw, from the college."

"If you know, why ask?"

I walked to the back of the court and knocked on her door. She opened it on a chain. Her face had lost a good deal of its rosy beauty. She had on a dark suit, as if she was in mourning.

"What do you want? It's late."

"Too late for us to have a talk, Mrs. Bradshaw?"

"I'm not Mrs. Bradshaw," she said without much conviction. "I'm not married."

"Roy said you were last night. Which one of you is lying?"

"Please, my landlord's out there." She unchained the door and stepped back out of the widening light. "Come inside if you must."

She closed the door and chained it behind me. I was looking at her instead of the room, but I had the impression of a tastefully decorated place where shaded lights gleamed peacefully on wooden and ceramic surfaces. I was searching her face for traces of a past wholly different from her present. There were no visible traces, no cruel lines or pouches of dissipation. But she hadn't much peace in her. She was watching me as though I was a burglar.

"What are you afraid of?"

"I'm not afraid," she said in a frightened voice. She tried to control it with her hand at her throat. "I resent your barging into my home and making personal remarks."

"You invited me in, more or less."

"Only because you were talking indiscreetly."

"I called you by your married name. What's your objection to it?"

"I *have* no objection," she said with a wan smile. "I'm very proud of it. But my husband and I are keeping it a secret."

"A secret from Letitia Macready?"

She showed no particular reaction to the name. I'd already given up on the idea that it could be hers. No matter how well preserved her body or her skin might be, she was clearly too young. When Bradshaw married Letitia, Laura couldn't have been more than a girl in her teens.

"Letitia who?" she said.

"Letitia Macready. She's also known as Tish."

"I have no idea who you're talking about."

"I'll tell you if you really want to know. May I sit down?"

"Please do," she said without much warmth. I was the messenger who brought bad tidings, the kind they used to kill in the old days.

I sat on a soft leather hassock with my back against the wall. She remained standing.

"You're in love with Roy Bradshaw, aren't you?"

"I wouldn't have married him if I weren't."

"Just when did you marry him?"

"Two weeks ago last Saturday, September the tenth." A little color returned to her cheeks with the memory of the day. "He'd just got back from his European tour. We decided to go to Reno on the spur of the moment."

"Had you spent some time with him there earlier in the summer?"

She frowned in a puzzled way, and shook her head.

"Whose idea was it to go to Reno?"

"Roy's of course, but I was willing. I've been willing for some time," she added in a spurt of candor.

"What held up the marriage?"

"It wasn't held *up*, exactly. We postponed it, for various reasons. Mrs. Bradshaw is a very possessive mother, and Roy has nothing of his own except his salary. It may sound mercenary—" She paused in some embarrassment, and tried to think of a better way to phrase it.

"How old is his mother?"

"Somewhere in her sixties. Why?"

"She's a vigorous woman, in spite of her infirmities. She may be around for a long time yet."

Her eyes flashed with some of their fine old iceberg fire. "We're not waiting for her to die, if that's what you think. We're simply waiting for the psychological moment. Roy hopes to persuade her to take a more reasonable view of—of me. In the meantime—" She broke off, and looked at me distrustfully. "But none of this is any concern of yours. You promised to tell me about the Macready person, whoever she is. Tish Macready? The name sounds fictitious."

"I assure you the woman isn't. Your husband divorced her in Reno shortly before he married you."

She moved to a chair and sat down very suddenly, as if her legs had lost their strength. "I don't believe it. Roy has never been married before."

"He has, though. Even his mother admitted it, after a struggle. It was an unfortunate marriage, contracted when he was a student at Harvard. But he waited until this summer to end it. He spent part of July and all of August establishing residence in Nevada."

"Now I know you're mistaken. Roy was in Europe all that time."

"I suppose you have letters and postcards to prove it?"

"Yes, I do," she said with a relieved smile.

She went into another room and came back with a handful of mail tied with a red ribbon. I riffled through the postcards and put them in chronological order: Tower of London (postmarked London, July 18), Bodleian Library (Oxford, July 21), and so on down to the view of the English Gardens (Munich, August 25). Bradshaw had written on the back of this last card:

Dear Laura:

Yesterday I visited Hitler's eyrie at Berchtesgaden—a beautiful setting made grim by its associations—and today, by way of contrast, I took a bus to Oberammergau, where the Passion Play is performed. I was struck by the almost Biblical simplicity of the villagers. This whole Bavarian countryside is studded with the most stunning little churches. How I wish you could enjoy them with me! I'm sorry to hear that your summer has turned out to be a lonely one. Well, the summer will soon be over and I for one will be happy to turn my back on the splendors of Europe and come home. All my love.

Roy

I sat and reread the incredible message. It was almost word by word the same as the one Mrs. Bradshaw had shown me. I tried to put myself in Bradshaw's place, to understand his motive. But I couldn't imagine what helpless division in a man's nature, what weary self-mockery or self-use, would make him send identical lying postcards to his mother and his fiancée.

"What's the matter?" Laura said.

"Merely everything."

I gave her back her documents. She handled them lovingly. "Don't try to tell me Roy didn't write these. They're in his writing and his style."

"He wrote them in Reno," I said, "and shipped them for remailing to a friend or accomplice who was traveling in Europe."

"Do you *know* this?"

"I'm afraid I do. Can you think of any friend of his who might have helped him?"

She bit her lower lip. "Dr. Godwin spent the late summer traveling in Europe. He and Roy are very close. In fact Roy was his patient for a long time."

"What was Godwin treating him for?"

"We haven't discussed it, really, but I expect it had something to do with his excessive—his excessive dependence on his mother." A slow angry flush mounted from her neck to her cheekbones. She turned away from the subject. "But why would two grown men collaborate in such a silly letter-writing game?"

"It isn't clear. Your husband's professional ambitions probably enter into it. He obviously didn't want anyone to know about his previous, bad marriage, or his divorce, and he went to great lengths to keep everything quiet. He got off a similar set of European postcards and letters to his mother. He may have sent a third set to Letitia."

"Who *is* she? *Where* is she?"

"I think she's here in town, or was as recently as last Friday night. She's very likely been here for the last ten years. I'm surprised your husband never gave it away, even to someone as close as you."

She was still standing over me, and I looked up into her face. Her eyes were heavy. She shook her head.

"Or maybe it isn't so surprising. He's very good at deceiving people, living on several levels, maybe deceiving himself to a certain extent. Mother's boys get that way sometimes. They need their little escape hatches from the hothouse."

Her bosom rose. "He isn't a mother's boy. He may have had a problem when he was younger, but now he's a virile man, and I *know* he loves me. There must be a reason for all this." She looked down at the cards and letters in her hand.

"I'm sure there is. I suspect the reason has to do with our two murders. Tish Macready is the leading suspect for both of them."

"*Two* murders?"

"Actually there have been three, spaced over a period of twenty-two years: Helen Haggerty on Friday night, Constance McGee ten years ago, Luke Deloney in Illinois before the war."

"Deloney?"

"Luke Deloney. You wouldn't know about him, but I think Tish Macready does."

"Is he connected with the Mrs. Deloney at the Surf House?"

"She's his widow. You know her?"

"Not personally. But Roy was talking to her on the telephone shortly before he left here."

"What did he say?"

"Simply that he was coming over to see her. I asked him who she was, but he was in too great a hurry to explain."

I got up. "If you'll excuse me, I'll see if I can catch him at the hotel. I've been trying to catch him all day."

"He was here, with me." She smiled slightly, involuntarily, but her eyes were confused. "Please don't tell him I told you. Don't tell him I told you anything."

"I'll try, but it may come out."

I moved to the door and tried to open it. The chain delayed my exit.

"Wait," she said behind me. "I've remembered something—something he wrote in a book of poems he lent me."

"What did he write?"

"Her name."

She started into the other room. Her hip bumped the doorframe, and Bradshaw's cards and letters fell from her hands. She didn't pause to pick them up.

She returned with an open book and thrust it at me a little blindly. It was a well-worn copy of Yeats's *Collected Poems*, open to the poem "Among School Children." The first four lines of the fourth stanza were underlined in pencil, and Bradshaw had written in the margin beside them the single word, "Tish."

I read the four lines to myself:

> Her present image floats into the mind—
> Did Quattrocento finger fashion it
> Hollow of cheek as though it drank the wind
> And took a mess of shadows for its meat?

I wasn't certain what they meant, and said so.

Laura answered bitterly: "It means that Roy still loves her. Yeats was writing about Maud Gonne—the woman he loved all his life. Roy may even have lent me the Yeats to let me know about Tish. He's very subtle."

"He probably wrote her name there long ago, and forgot about it. If he still loved her, he wouldn't have divorced her and married you. I have to warn you, though, that your marriage may not be legal."

"Not legal?" She was a conventional woman, and the possibility jarred her. "But we were married in Reno by a judge."

"His divorce from Tish," I said, "is probably voidable. I gather she wasn't properly informed of Bradshaw's action. Which means that under California law he's still married to her if she wants it that way."

Shaking her head, she took the book of poems from my hands and tossed it with some violence into a chair. A piece of paper fluttered from between the leaves. I picked it up from the floor.

It was another poem, in Bradshaw's handwriting:

> *To Laura*
>
> If light were dark
> And dark were light,
> Moon a black hole
> In the blaze of night,
>
> A raven's wing
> As bright as tin,
> Then you, my love,
> Would be darker than sin.

At breakfast I had read the same poem aloud to Arnie and Phyllis. It had been printed twenty-odd years ago in the Bridgeton *Blazer*, over the initials G.R.B. I had a gestalt, and Bridgeton and Pacific Point came together in a roaring traffic of time. G.R.B. George Roy Bradshaw.

"When did he write this poem to you, Laura?"

"Last spring, when he lent me the Yeats."

I left her reading it over to herself, trying to recapture the spring.

3o

Passing through the lobby of the Surf House, I noticed Helen's mother sitting by herself in a far corner. She was deep in thought and she didn't look up until I spoke:

"You're sitting up late, Mrs. Hoffman."

"I don't have much choice," she said resentfully. "I'm supposed to be sharing a cottage with Mrs. Deloney, and it was entirely her idea. But she put me out so she can entertain her friend in private."

"You mean Roy Bradshaw?"

"That's what he calls himself now. I knew George Bradshaw when he was glad to be given a good hot meal, and I served him more than one in my own kitchen."

I pulled up a chair beside hers. "All this adds up to an interesting coincidence."

"I think it does, too. But I'm not supposed to talk about it."

"Who says so?"

"Mrs. Deloney."

"Does she tell you what to do?"

"No, but it was nice of her to take me out of that crummy room in the Pacific Hotel and—" She paused, considering.

"And stash you in the lobby here?"

"It's only temporary."

"So is life. Are you and your husband going to take orders from people like the Deloneys until the day you die? You get nothing out of it, you know, except the privilege of being pushed around."

"Nobody pushes Earl around," she said defensively. "You leave Earl out of this."

"Have you heard from him?"

"I haven't, and I'm worried about Earl. I tried to phone home two nights in a row, and nobody answered. I'm afraid he's drinking."

"He's in the hospital," I said.

"Is he sick?"

"He made himself sick with too much whisky."

"How do you know that?"

"I helped to get him to the hospital. I was in Bridgeton yesterday morning. Your husband talked to me, quite freely toward the end. He admitted Luke Deloney had been murdered but he had orders from the top to let it go as an accident."

Her eyes darted around the lobby, shyly and shamefully. There was no one in sight but the night clerk and a couple who didn't look married renting a room from him. But Mrs. Hoffman was as nervous as a cricket on a crowded floor.

"You might as well tell me what you know," I said. "Let me buy you a cup of coffee."

"I'd be up all night."

"A cup of cocoa then."

"Cocoa sounds good."

We went into the coffee shop. Several orchestra members in mauve jackets were drinking coffee at the counter and complaining in the language of their tribe about the pay. I sat in a booth facing Mrs. Hoffman and the plate glass door, so that I could see Bradshaw if he came out through the lobby.

"How did you come to know Bradshaw, Mrs. Hoffman?"

"Helen brought him home from City College. I think she was stuck on him for a while, but I could see that he wasn't stuck on her. They were more friends. They had interests in common."

"Like poetry?"

"Like poetry and play-acting. Helen said he was very talented for a boy his age, but he was having a hard time staying in college. We wangled him a part-time job running the elevator in the apartments. All it paid was five a week, but he was glad to have it. He was as thin as a rake and as poor as Job's turkey when we knew him. He claimed he came from a wealthy family in Boston, that he ran away from his freshman year at Harvard to be on his own. I never really believed him at the time —I thought he was maybe ashamed of his folks and putting on the dog—but I guess it was true after all. They tell me his mother is loaded." She gave me a questioning look.

"Yes. I know her."

"Why would a young fellow run away from all that money? I spent most of my own life trying to get a little to stick to my fingers."

"Money usually has strings attached to it."

I didn't go into a fuller explanation. The waitress brought Mrs. Hoffman's cocoa and my coffee. I said when she had retreated behind the counter:

"Have you ever known a woman named Macready? Letitia O. Macready?"

Mrs. Hoffman's hand fumbled with her cup and spilled some brown liquid in the saucer. I was fleetingly conscious that her hair was dyed an unlikely shade of red and that she might once have been a handsome woman with a good figure and a gaudy taste in clothes. But she couldn't be Tish Macready. She'd been married to Earl Hoffman for over forty years.

She put a folded paper napkin under her cup to absorb the spillage. "I knew her to say hello to."

"In Bridgeton?"

"I'm not supposed to talk about Letitia. Mrs. Deloney—"

"Your daughter's in a refrigerated drawer and all you give me is Mrs. Deloney."

She bowed her head over the shiny formica table. "I'm afraid of her," she said, "of what she can do to Earl."

"Be afraid of what she's already done to him. She and her political pals made him seal up the Deloney case, and it's been festering inside of him ever since."

"I know. It's the first time Earl ever laid down on the job deliberately."

"You admit that?"

"I guess I have to. Earl never said it out in so many words, but I knew, and Helen knew. It's why she left us."

And why, perhaps, in the long run Helen couldn't stay honest.

"Earl had a great respect for Luke Deloney," the woman was saying, "even if Luke did have his human failings. He was the one who made good for all of us in a manner of speaking. His death hit Earl real hard, and he started drinking right after, seriously I mean. I'm worried about Earl." She reached across the table and touched the back of my hand with her dry fingertips. "Do you think he'll be all right?"

"Not if he keeps on drinking. He ought to survive this bout. I'm sure he's being well taken care of. But Helen isn't."

"Helen? What can anybody do for Helen?"

"You can do something for her by telling the truth. Her death deserves an explanation at least."

"But I don't know who killed her. If I did I'd shout it from the housetops. I thought the police were after that man McGee who killed his wife."

"McGee has been cleared. Tish Macready killed his wife, and probably your daughter as well."

She shook her head solemnly. "You're mistaken, mister. What you say isn't possible. Tish Macready—Tish Osborne that was—she died long ago before either of those tragedies happened. I admit there were rumors about her at the time of Luke Deloney's death, but then she had her own tragedy, poor thing."

"You said 'Tish Osborne that was.' "

"That's right. She was one of Senator Osborne's girls—Mrs. Deloney's sister. I told you about them the other night when we were driving down here from the airport, how they used to ride to hounds." She smiled faintly, nostalgically, as if she had caught a flash of red coats from her childhood.

"What were the rumors about her, Mrs. Hoffman?"

"That she was carrying on with Luke Deloney before his death. Some people said she shot him herself, but I never believed that."

"Was she having an affair with Luke Deloney?"

"She used to spend some time in his apartment, that was no secret. She was kind of his unofficial hostess when Luke and Mrs. Deloney were separated. I didn't think too much about it. She was already divorced from Val Macready. And she was Luke's sister-in-law after all, I guess she had a right to be in his penthouse."

"Did she have red hair?"

"More auburn, I'd say. She had beautiful auburn hair." Mrs. Hoffman absently stroked her own dyed curls. "Tish Osborne had a lot of life in her. I was sorry to hear when she died."

"What happened to her?"

"I don't know exactly. She died in Europe when the Nazis ran over France. Mrs. Deloney still hasn't got over it. She was talking about her sister's death today."

Something that felt like a spider with wet feet climbed up the back of my neck into the short hairs and made them bristle. The ghost of Tish or a woman (or a man?) using her name had come to the door of the house in Indian Springs ten years ago, more than ten years after the Germans overran France.

"Are you certain she's dead, Mrs. Hoffman?"

She nodded. "There was quite a writeup in the papers, even the Chicago papers. Tish Osborne was the belle of Bridgeton in her time. I can remember back in the early twenties her parties were famous. The man she married, Val Macready, had meat-packing money on his mother's side."

"Is he still alive?"

"The last I heard of him, he married an Englishwoman during the war and was living in England. He wasn't a Bridgeton boy and I never really knew him. I just read the society pages, and the obituaries."

She sipped her cocoa. Her look, her self-enclosed posture, seemed to be telling me that she had survived. Her daughter Helen had been brighter, Tish Osborne had been wealthier, but she was the one who had survived. She would survive Earl, too, and probably make a shrine of the study where he kept his liquor in the roll-top desk.

Well, I had caught one of the old ladies. The other one would be tougher.

"Why did Mrs. Deloney fly out here?"

"I guess it was just a rich woman's whim. She said she wanted to help me out in my time of trouble."

"Were you ever close to her?"

"I hardly knew her. Earl knows her better."

"Was Helen close to her?"

"No. If they ever met each other, it's news to me."

"Mrs. Deloney came a long way to help out a comparative stranger. Has she given you any particular help, apart from changing hotels?"

"She bought me lunch and dinner. I didn't want her to pay, but she insisted."

"What were you to do in return for the free room and board?"

"Nothing."

"Didn't she ask you not to talk about her sister Tish?"

"That's true, she did. I wasn't to say anything about her carrying on with Luke Deloney, or the rumors that went around about his death. She's very sensitive about her sister's reputation."

"Abnormally sensitive, if Tish has really been dead for over twenty years. Who weren't you supposed to mention these things to?"

"Anybody, especially you."

She drowned her nervous little giggle in the remains of her cocoa.

31

I went out into the grounds of the hotel. The high moon floated steadily in the sky and in the ornamental pools of the Spanish garden. There was yellower light behind the shutters of Mrs. Deloney's cottage, and the sound of voices too low to be eavesdropped on.

I knocked on the door.

"What is it?" she said.

"Service." Detective service.

"I didn't order anything."

But she opened the door. I slipped in past her and stood against the wall. Bradshaw was sitting on an English sofa beside the fireplace in the opposite wall. A low fire burned in the grate, and gleamed on the brass fittings.

"Hello," he said.

"Hello, George."

He jumped visibly.

Mrs. Deloney said: "Get out of here." She seemed to have perfectly round blue eyes in a perfectly square white face, all bone and will. "I'll call the house detective."

"Go ahead, if you want to spread the dirt around."

She shut the door.

"We might as well tell him," Bradshaw said. "We have to tell someone."

The negative jerk of her head was so violent it threw her off balance. She took a couple of backward steps and regrouped her forces, looking from me to Bradshaw as if we were both her enemies.

"I absolutely forbid it," she said to him. "Nothing is to be said."

"It's going to come out anyway. It will be better if we bring it out ourselves."

"It is *not* going to come out. Why should it?"

"Partly," I said, "because you made the mistake of coming here. This isn't your town, Mrs. Deloney. You can't put a lid on events the way you could in Bridgeton."

She turned her straight back on me. "Pay no attention to him, George."

"My name is Roy."

"Roy," she corrected herself. "This man tried to bluff me yesterday in Bridgeton, but he doesn't know a thing. All we have to do is remain quiet."

"What will that get us?"

"Peace."

"I've had my fill of that sort of peace," he said. "I've been living close up to it all these years. You've been out of contact. You have no conception of what I've been through." He rested his head on the back of the sofa and lifted his eyes to the ceiling.

"You'll go through worse," she said roughly, "if you let down your back hair now."

"At least it will be different."

"You're a spineless fool. But I'm not going to let you ruin what remains of my life. If you do, you'll get no financial help from me."

"Even that I can do without."

But he was being careful to say nothing I wanted to know. He'd been wearing a mask so long that it stuck to his face and controlled his speech and perhaps his habits of thought. Even the old woman with her back turned was playing to me as if I was an audience.

"This argument is academic, in more than one sense," I said. "The body isn't buried any longer. I know your sister Letitia shot your husband, Mrs. Deloney. I know she later married Bradshaw in Boston. I have his mother's word for it—"

"His mother?"

Bradshaw sat up straight. "I do have a mother after all." He added in his earnest cultivated voice, with his eyes intent on the woman's: "I'm still living with her, and she has to be considered in this matter, too."

"You lead a very complicated life," she said.

"I have a very complicated nature."

"Very well, young Mr. Complexity, the ball is yours. Carry it." She went to a love-seat in a neutral corner of the room and sat down there.

"I thought the ball was mine," I said, "but you're welcome to it, Bradshaw. You can start where everything started, with the Deloney killing. You were Helen's witness, weren't you?"

He nodded once. "I shouldn't have gone to Helen with that heavy knowledge. But I was deeply upset and she was the only friend I had in the world."

"Except Letitia."

"Yes. Except Letitia."

"What was your part in the murder?"

"I was simply there. And it wasn't a murder, properly speaking. Deloney was killed in self-defense, virtually by accident."

"This is where I came in."

"It's true. He caught us in bed together in his penthouse."

"Did you and Letitia make a habit of going to bed together?"

"It was the first time. I'd written a poem about her, which the college magazine printed, and I showed it to her in the elevator. I'd been watching her, admiring her, all through the spring. She was much older than I was, but she was fascinating. She was the first woman I ever had." He spoke of her with a kind of awe still.

"What happened in the penthouse bedroom, Bradshaw?"

"He caught us, as I said. He got a gun out of the chest of drawers and hit me with the butt of it. Tish tried to stop him. He beat her face in with the gun. She got her hands on it somehow, and it went off and killed him."

He touched the lid of his right eye, and nodded toward the old woman. She was watching us from the corner, from the distance of her years.

"Mrs. Deloney hushed the matter up, or had it hushed up. You can hardly blame her, under the circumstances. Or blame us. We went to Boston, where Tish spent months in and out of the hospital having her face rebuilt. Then we were married. I was in love with her, in spite of the discrepancy in our ages. I suppose my feeling for my own mother prepared me to love Tish."

His hooded intelligence flared up in his eyes so bright it was half-insane. His mouth was wry.

"We went to Europe on our honeymoon. My mother put French detectives on our trail. I had to leave Tish in Paris and come home to make my peace with Mother and start my sophomore year at Harvard. The war broke out in Europe that same month. I never saw Tish again. She fell sick and died before I knew it."

"I don't believe you. There wasn't time for all that."

"It happened very rapidly, as tragedy does."

"Not yours, it's been dragging on for twenty-two years."

"No," Mrs. Deloney said. "He's telling the truth, and I can prove it to you."

She went into another room of the cottage and came back with a heavily creased document which she handed me. It was an *acte de décès* issued in Bordeaux and dated July 16, 1940. It stated in French that Letitia Osborne Macready, aged 45, had died of pneumonia.

I gave it back to Mrs. Deloney. "You carry this with you wherever you go?"

"I happened to bring it with me."

"Why?"

She couldn't think of an answer.

"I'll tell you why. Because your sister is very much alive and you're afraid she'll be punished for her crimes."

"My sister committed no crime. The death of my husband was either justifiable homicide or accident. The police commissioner realized that or he'd never have quashed the case."

"That may be. But Constance McGee and Helen Haggerty weren't shot by accident."

"My sister died long before either of those women."

"Your own actions deny it, and they mean more than this phony death certificate. For instance, you visited Gil Stevens today and tried to pump him about the McGee case."

"He broke my confidence, did he?"

"There was nothing there to be broken. You're not Stevens's client. He's still representing McGee."

"He didn't tell me."

"Why should he? This isn't your town."

She turned in confusion to Bradshaw. He shook his head. I crossed the room and stood over him:

"If Tish is safely buried in France, why did you go to such elaborate trouble to divorce her?"

"So you know about the divorce. You're quite a digger for facts, aren't you, quite a Digger Indian? I begin to wonder if there's anything you don't know about my private life."

He sat there, looking up at me brightly and warily. I was a little carried away by the collapse of his defenses, and I said:

"Your private life, or your private lives, are something for the book. Have you been keeping up two establishments, dividing your time between your mother and your wife?"

"I suppose it's obvious that I have," he said tonelessly.

"Does Tish live here in town?"

"She lived in the Los Angeles area. I have no intention of telling you where, and I can assure you you'll never find the place. There'd be no point in it, anyway, since she's no longer there."

"Where and how did she die this time?"

"She isn't dead. That French death certificate is a fake, as you guessed. But she is beyond your reach. I put her on a plane to Rio de Janeiro on Saturday, and she'll be there by now."

Mrs. Deloney said: "You didn't tell me that!"

"I hadn't intended to tell anyone. However, I have to make Mr. Archer see that there's no point in pressing this thing any further. My wife—my ex-wife—is an old woman, and a sick one, and she's beyond extradition. I've arranged for her to have medical care, psychiatric care in a South American city which I won't name."

"You're admitting that she killed Helen Haggerty?"

"Yes. She confessed to me when I went to see her in Los Angeles early Saturday morning. She shot Helen and hid the gun in my gatehouse. I contacted Foley in Reno primarily to find out if he had witnessed anything. I didn't want him black-mailing me—"

"I thought he already was."

"Helen was," he said. "She learned about my pending divorce in Reno, and she jumped to a number of conclusions, including the fact that Tish was still alive. I gave her a good deal of money, and got her a job here, in order to protect Tish."

"And yourself."

"And myself. I do have a reputation to protect, though I've done nothing illegal."

"No. You're very good at arranging for other people to do your dirty work. You brought Helen here as a kind of decoy, didn't you?"

"I'm afraid I don't understand you." But he shifted uneasily.

"You took Helen out a few times and passed the word that she was your intended. She wasn't, of course. You were already married to Laura and you hated Helen, with good reason."

"That's not true. We were on quite a friendly basis, in spite of her demands. She was a very old friend, after all, and I couldn't help sympathizing with her feeling that she deserved something from the world."

"I know what she got—a bullet in the head. The same thing Constance McGee got. The same thing Laura would have got if you hadn't set Helen up as a substitute victim for Tish."

"I'm afraid you're getting much too complicated."

"For a complicated nature like yours?"

He looked around the room as if he felt imprisoned in it, or in the maze of his own nature. "You'll never prove any complicity on my part in Helen's death. It came as a fearful shock to me. Letitia's confession was another shock."

"Why? You must have known she killed Constance McGee."

"I didn't know it till Saturday. I admit I had my suspicions. Tish was always savagely jealous. I've lived with the dreadful possibility for ten years, hoping and praying that my suspicions were unfounded—"

"Why didn't you ask her?"

"I suppose I couldn't face it. Things were already so difficult between us. It would have meant admitting my love for Connie." He heard his own words, and sat quiet for a moment, his eyes downcast, as if he was peering down into a chasm in himself. "I really did love her, you know. Her death almost finished me."

"But you survived to love again."

"Men do," he said. "I'm not the sort of man who can live without love. I loved even Tish as long and as well as I could. But she got *old*, and sick."

Mrs. Deloney made a spitting sound. He said to her:

"I wanted a wife, one who could give me children."

"God help any children of yours, you'd probably abandon them. You broke all your promises to my sister."

"Everyone breaks promises. I didn't intend to fall in love with Connie. It simply happened. I met her in a doctor's waiting room quite by accident. But I didn't turn my back on your sister. I never have. I've done more for her than she ever did for me."

She sneered at him with the arrogance of a second-generation aristocrat. "My sister lifted you out of the gutter. What were you—an elevator boy?"

"I was a college student, and an elevator boy by my own choice."

"Very likely."

He leaned toward her, fixing her with his bright eyes. "I had family resources to draw on if I had wished."

"Ah yes, your precious mother."

"Be careful what you say about my mother."

There was an edge on his words, the quality of a cold threat, and it silenced her. This was one of several moments when I sensed that the two of them were playing a game as complex as chess, a game of power on a hidden board. I should have tried to force it open. But I was clearing up my case, and as long as Bradshaw was willing to talk I didn't care about apparent side issues.

"I don't understand the business of the gun," I said. "The police have established that Connie McGee and Helen were shot with the same gun—a revolver that belonged originally to Connie's sister Alice. How did Tish get hold of it?"

"I don't really know."

"You must have some idea. Did Alice Jenks give it to her?"

"She very well may have."

"That's nonsense, Bradshaw, and you know it. The revolver was stolen from Alice's house. Who stole it?"

He made a steeple of his fingers and admired its symmetry. "I'm willing to tell you if Mrs. Deloney will leave the room."

"Why should I?" she said from her corner. "Anything my sister could endure to live through I can endure to hear."

"I'm not trying to spare your sensibilities," Bradshaw said. "I'm trying to spare myself."

She hesitated. It became a test of wills. Bradshaw got up and opened the inner door. Through it I could see across a hall into a bedroom furnished in dull luxury. The bedside table held an ivory telephone and a leather-framed photograph of a white-mustached gentleman who looked vaguely familiar.

Mrs. Deloney marched into the bedroom like a recalcitrant soldier under orders. Bradshaw closed the door sharply behind her.

"I'm beginning to hate old women," he said.

"You were going to tell me about the gun."

"I was, wasn't I?" He returned to the sofa. "It's not a pretty story. None of it is. I'm telling you the whole thing in the hope that you'll be completely satisfied."

"And not bring in the authorities?"

"Don't you see there's nothing to be gained by bringing them in? The sole effect would be to turn the town on its ear, wreck the standing of the college which I've worked so hard to build up, and ruin more than one life."

"Especially yours and Laura's?"

"Especially mine and Laura's. She's waited for me, God knows. And even I deserve something more than I've had. I've lived my entire adult life with the consequences of a neurotic involvement that I got into when I was just a boy."

"Is that what Godwin was treating you for?"

"I needed *some* support. Tish hasn't been easy to deal with. She drove me half out of my mind sometimes with her animal violence and her demands. But now it's over." His eyes changed the statement into a question and a plea.

"I can't make any promises," I said. "Let's have the entire story, then we'll think about the next step. How did Tish get hold of Alice's revolver?"

"Connie took it from her sister's room and gave it to me. We had some wild idea of using it to cut the Gordian knot."

"Do you mean kill Tish with it?"

"It was sheer fantasy," he said, *"folie à deux.* Connie and I would never have carried it out, desperate as we were. You'll never know the agony I went through dividing myself between two wives, two lovers—one old and rapacious, the other young and passionate. Jim Godwin warned me that I was in danger of spiritual death."

"For which murder is known to be a sure cure."

"I'd never have done it. I couldn't. Actually Jim made me see that. I'm not a violent man."

But there was violence in him now, pressing against the conventional fears that corseted his nature and held him still, almost formal, under my eyes. I sensed his murderous hatred for me. I was forcing all his secrets into the open, as I thought.

"What happend to the gun Connie stole for you?"

"I put it away in what I thought was a safe place, but Tish must have found it."

"In your house?"

"In my mother's house. I sometimes took her there when Mother was away."

"Was she there the day McGee called on you?"

"Yes." He met my eyes. "I'm amazed that you should know about that day. You're very thorough. It was the day when everything came to a head. Tish must have found the gun in the lockbox in my study where I'd hidden it. Before that she must have heard McGee complaining to me about my interest in his wife. She took the gun and turned it against Constance. I suppose there was a certain poetic justice in that."

Bradshaw might have been talking about an event in someone else's past, the death of a character in history or fiction. He no longer cared for the meaning of his own life. Perhaps that was what Godwin meant by spiritual death.

"Do you still maintain you didn't know Tish killed her until she confessed it last Saturday?"

"I suppose I didn't let myself realize. So far as I knew the gun had simply disappeared. McGee might very well have taken it from my study when he was in the house. The official case against him seemed very strong."

"It was put together with old pieces of string, and you know it. McGee and his daughter are my main concern. I won't be satisfied until they're completely cleared."

"But surely that can be accomplished without dragging Letitia back from Brazil."

"I have only your word that she's in Brazil," I said. "Even Mrs. Deloney was surprised to hear it."

"Good heavens, don't you believe me? I've literally exposed my entrails to you."

"You wouldn't do that unless you had a reason. I think you're a liar, Bradshaw, one of those virtuosos who use real facts and feelings to make their stories plausible. But there's a basic implausibility in this one. If Tish was safe in Brazil, it's the last thing you'd ever tell me. I think she's hiding out here in California."

"You're quite mistaken."

His eyes came to mine, candid and earnest as only an actor's can be. A telephone chirring behind the bedroom door interrupted our staring contest. Bradshaw moved toward the sound. I was on my feet and I moved more rapidly, shouldering him against the doorframe, picking up the bedside phone before it rang a third time.

"Hello."

"Is that you, darling?" It was Laura's voice. "Roy, I'm frightened. She *knows* about us. She called here just a minute ago and said she was coming over."

"Keep the door locked and chained. And you better call the police."

"That isn't Roy. Is it?"

Roy was behind me. I turned in time to see the flash of brass as the poker in his fist came down on my head.

32

Mrs. Deloney was slapping my face with a wet towel. I told her to quit it. The first thing I saw when I got up was the leather-framed photograph beside her telephone. It seemed to my blurred vision to be a photograph of the handsome old black-eyed gentleman whose portrait hung over the fireplace in Mrs. Bradshaw's sitting room.

"What are you doing with a picture of Bradshaw's father?"

"It happens to be my own father, Senator Osborne."

I said: "So Mrs. Bradshaw's a virtuoso, too."

Mrs. Deloney looked at me as if my brains had been addled by the poker. But the blow had been a glancing one, and I couldn't have been out for more than a few seconds. Bradshaw was leaving the hotel parking lot when I got there.

His light car turned uphill away from the ocean. I followed him to Foothill Drive and caught him long before he reached his house. He made it easy for me by braking suddenly. His car slewed sideways and came to a shuddering halt broadside across the road.

It wasn't me he was trying to stop. Another car was coming downhill toward us. I could see its headlights approaching under the trees like large calm insane eyes, and Bradshaw silhouetted in their beam. He seemed to be fumbling with his seat-belt. I recognized Mrs. Bradshaw's Rolls in the moment before, with screeching brakes, it crashed into the smaller car.

I pulled off the road, set out a red blinker, and ran uphill toward the point of impact. My footsteps were loud in the silence after the crash. The crumpled nose of the Rolls was nuzzled deep in the caved-in side of Bradshaw's car. He lolled in the driver's seat. Blood ran down his face from his forehead and nose and the corners of his mouth.

I went in through the undamaged door and got his seat-belt unbuckled. He toppled limply into my arms. I laid him down in the road. The jagged lines of blood across his face resembled cracks in a mask through which live tissue showed. But he was dead. He lay pulseless and breathless under the iron shadows of the tree branches.

Old Mrs. Bradshaw had climbed down out of her high protected seat. She seemed unhurt. I remember thinking at the moment that she was an elemental power which nothing could ever kill.

"It's Roy, isn't it? Is he all right?"

"In a sense he is. He wanted out. He's out."

"What do you mean?"

"I'm afraid you've killed him, too."

"But I didn't mean to hurt him. I wouldn't hurt my own son, the child of my womb."

Her voice cracked with maternal grief. I think she half-believed she was his mother, she had lived the rôle so long. Reality had grown dim as the moonlit countryside around her.

She flung herself on the dead man, holding him close, as if her old body could somehow warm him back to life and rekindle his love for her. She wheedled and cooed in his ear, calling him a naughty malingering boy for trying to scare her.

She shook him. "Wake up! It's Moms."

As she had told me, night wasn't her best season. But she had a doubleness in her matching Roy's, and there was an element of play-acting in her frenzy.

"Leave him alone," I said. "And let's drop the mother bit. The situation is ugly enough without that."

She turned in queer slow furtiveness and looked up at me. "The mother bit?"

"Roy Bradshaw wasn't your son. The two of you put on a pretty good act— Godwin would probably say it fitted both your neurotic needs—but it's over."

She got up in a surge of anger which brought her close to me. I could smell her lavender, and feel her force.

"I *am* his mother. I have his birth certificate to prove it."

"I bet you do. Your sister showed me a death certificate which proves that you died in France in 1940. With your kind of money you can document anything. But you can't change the facts by changing them on paper. Roy married you in Boston after you killed Deloney. Eventually he fell in love with Constance McGee. You killed her. Roy lived with you for another ten years, if you can call it living, terrified that you'd kill again if he ever dared to love anyone again. But finally he dared, with Laura Sutherland. He managed to convince you that it was Helen Haggerty he was interested in. So you went up the bridle path on Friday night and shot her. Those are all facts you can't change."

Silence set in between us, thin and bleak like a quality of the moonlight. The woman said:

"I was only protecting my rights. Roy owed me faithfulness at least. I gave him money and background, I sent him to Harvard, I made all his dreams come true."

We both looked down at the dreamless man lying in the road.

"Are you ready to come downtown with me and make a formal statement about how you protected your rights over the years? Poor Tom McGee is back in jail, still sweating out your rap."

She pulled herself erect. "I won't permit you to use such language to me. I'm not a criminal."

"You were on your way to Laura Sutherland's, weren't you? What were you planning to do to her, old woman?"

She covered the lower part of her face with her hand. I thought she was ill, or overcome with shame. But she said:

"You mustn't call me that. I'm not old. Don't look at my face, look into my eyes. You can see how young I am."

It was true in a way. I couldn't see her eyes clearly, but I knew they were bright and black and vital. She was still greedy for life, like the imaginary Letitia, the weird projection of herself in imitation leopardskin she had used to hide behind.

She shifted her hand to her heavy chin and said: "I'll give you money."

"Roy took your money. Look what happened to him."

She turned abruptly and started for her car. I guessed what was in her mind— another death, another shadow to feed on—and got to the open door of the Rolls before her. Her black leather bag was on the floor where it had fallen in the collision. Inside the bag I found the new revolver which she had intended to use on Roy's new wife.

"Give me that."

She spoke with the authority of a Senator's daughter and the more terrible authority of a woman who had killed two other women and two men.

"No more guns for you," I said.

No more anything, Letitia.

P. D. James

THE MURDER OF SANTA CLAUS

Until now Phyllis Dorothy James (1920–   ) has been associated with two detectives: Adam Dalgliesh, Chief Superintendent of Scotland Yard, and Cordelia Gray, proprietor of Pryde's Detective Agency. In "The Murder of Santa Claus," which is published here for the first time, P. D. James introduces a new detective, Charles Mickledore, a none-too-prosperous writer of unfashionably old-fashioned detective stories who asks, frankly enough, "Why should I expect my writing to be any more successful than my life?"

Dalgliesh—then a lowly inspector—appeared in P. D. James's first novel, Cover Her Face (1962). A widower, the son of a clergyman, a published poet (who, considering his line of work, meets an unusual number of people who know about his poetry), Adam has been described by a marriage counselor as "self-sufficient, uninvolved, a professional detective dedicated to his job, totally unused to the claims, emotional and domestic, which a wife and family would make on him." The counselor was describing him to Cordelia Gray (they tend to pop up in each other's novels), who has been called "slight but tough." Cordelia made her debut in the ironically titled An Unsuitable Job for a Woman (1973), in which she takes over a down-at-the-heels detective agency after the death of her boss, Bernie Pryde.

P. D. James has written eight novels featuring either Dalgliesh or Gray, and a serious, nondetective one, Innocent Blood. Cordelia's books tend to be more whimsical than Adam's, as he is apt to brood on human frailty, while she, being self-employed with a payroll to meet, is more concerned with giving her clients good value for their money. The settings of many of the novels are medical or institutional, reflecting the years the author worked in hospital administration and later as a civil servant in the British Home Office criminal division.

With Charles Mickledore—who is, we're told, "no Dick Francis, not even a P. D. James"—P. D. James herself seems to be having a bit of fun with some of the hoarier traditions of detective fiction.

The Murder of Santa Claus

1

IF YOU'RE AN ADDICT of detective fiction you may have heard of me, Charles Mickledore. I say "addict" advisedly; no occasional or highly discriminating reader of the genre is likely to ask for my latest offering at his public library. I'm no H. R. F. Keating, no Dick Francis, not even a P. D. James. But I do a workmanlike job on the old conventions, for those who like their murders cozy, and although my amateur detective the Hon. Martin Carstairs has been described as a pallid copy of Peter Wimsey at least I haven't burdened him with a monocle, or with Harriet Vane for that matter. I make enough to augment a modest private income. Unmarried, solitary, unsociable—why should I expect my writing to be any more successful than my life?

Sometimes I'm even asked to do a radio chat show when one of the more distinguished practitioners of death isn't available. I've gotten used to the old question: Have you ever, Mr. Mickledore, had personal experience of murder? Invariably I lie. For one thing, interviewers never expect the truth; there isn't time. And for another, they wouldn't believe me. The murder I was involved with was as complicated, as bizarre, as histrionic as any fictional mayhem I've managed to concoct even in my more inspired moments. If I were writing about it I'd call it the Murder of Santa Claus. And that, essentially, was what it was.

Appropriately enough it took place in the heyday of the cozy "whodunits," the Christmas of 1939, the first Christmas of the war. I was sixteen, an awkward age at the best of times and, as a sensitive and solitary only child, I was more awkward than most. My father was in the Colonial Service serving in Singapore and I usually spent the winter holiday with my housemaster and his family. But this year my parents wrote that my father's elder half-brother, Victor Mickledore, had invited me to his Cotswold manor house at Marston Turville. His instructions were precise. I was to arrive by the 4:15 train on Christmas Eve and would depart on the morning of Wednesday 27 December. I would be met at Marston station by his housekeeper/secretary, Miss Makepiece. There would be four other guests: Major and Mrs. Turville, from whom he had bought the Manor five years previously; his stepson Henry Caldwell, the famous amateur flyer; and the actress, Miss Gloria Belsize. I had, of course, heard of Caldwell and of Miss Belsize although I don't suppose that even I, naïve as I was, supposed it to be her real name.

My uncle—or should it be step-uncle?—apologized for the fact that there would be no other young guests to keep me company. That didn't worry me. But the thought of the visit did. I had only met my uncle once, when I was ten. I had the idea, gleaned as children do from half-spoken sentences and overheard remarks, that my parents and he were on bad terms. I think he had once wanted to marry my mother. Perhaps this was an attempt at reconciliation now that war, with its uncertainties, had started. My father had made it plain in his letter that I was expected to accept the invitation and that he was relying on me to make a good impression. I put out of my mind the treacherous thought that my uncle was very rich and that he had no children.

Miss Makepiece was waiting for me at Marston station. She greeted me with no particular warmth and as she led the way to the waiting Rover I was reminded of the school matron on one of her more repressive days. We drove through the village in silence. It lay somber and deserted in its pre-Christmas calm. I can remember the church half-hidden behind the great yews and the silent school with the children's Christmas chains of colored paper gleaming dully against the windows.

Marston Turville is a small seventeenth-century manor house, its three wings built round a courtyard. I saw it first as a mass of gray stone blacked out, as was the whole village, under low broken clouds. My uncle greeted me before a log fire in the great hall. I came in, blinking, from the December dusk into a blaze of color: candles sparkling on the huge Christmas tree, its tub piled with imitation snowballs of frosted cottonwool; the leaping fire; the gleam of firelight on silver. My fellow guests were taking tea and I see them as a tableau, cups half way to their lips, predestined victims waiting for the tragedy to begin.

Memory, perverse and selective, has even clothed them appropriately. When I picture that Christmas Eve, I see Henry Caldwell, that doomed hero, in his RAF uniform with his medal ribbons on his breast. But he couldn't have been wearing it. He was only then waiting to report for his RAF training. And I invariably picture Gloria Belsize in the slinky golden evening dress which she changed into for dinner, her nipples pointing the satin; I found it difficult to keep my eyes from them. I see the plain, intimidatingly efficient Miss Makepiece in her gray woolen dress severe as a uniform, the Turvilles in their shabby country tweeds, my uncle always in his immaculate dinner jacket.

He bent on me with his dark sardonic face. "So you're Alison's boy. I wondered how you'd turn out."

I thought I knew what he was thinking; that the right father would have made all the difference. I was aware of my lack of height besides his six foot two—only Henry could match him—and of my adolescent crop of pimples. He introduced me to my fellow guests. The Turvilles were a gentle-faced white-haired couple, older than I had expected and both rather deaf. I found Henry's austere good looks rather formidable; shyness and hero-worship made me dumb. Miss Belsize's face was known to me from the papers. Now I saw what tactful touching-up had concealed: the deepening lines under the eyes, the sagging jawline, the hectic flush under the remarkable eyes. Then I wondered why she should be so excited by Christmas. Now I realize that she was half-drunk for most of the day and that my uncle saw it, was amused by it, and made no attempt to curb her. We were an ill-assorted party. None of us was at ease, myself least of all. After that first greeting my uncle hardly spoke to me. But whenever we were together I was aware of his intense scrutiny, of being in some way under approval.

The first intimation of horror, the Christmas cracker with its message of menace, was delivered at seven o'clock. It was a long tradition at Marston Turville that carol singers from the village sang to their squire on Christmas Eve. They arrived promptly, sidling in under the blackout curtain one by one, as the lights in the great hall were lowered. There were ten of them, seven men and three women, cloaked against the cold of that frosty night, and each carrying a lantern which was lit as soon as the heavy door was closed. I stood, uneasy in my newly acquired dinner jacket, between Mrs. Turville and Henry to the right of the fire, and listened to the old innocently nostalgic carols resolutely sung in their hearty country voices. Afterwards the butler, Poole, and one of the maids brought in mince pies and hot punch. But there was an air of constraint. They should have been singing for the Turvilles. The manor was in alien hands. They ate and drank with almost un-seemly haste. The lights were put out, the door opened, and my uncle with Miss Makepiece at his side thanked them and said goodnight. Miss Belsize fluttered round them as they left almost as if she were chatelaine of the manor. The Turvilles had stood distanced at the far end of the room and, when the singing began, I saw her hand steal out to his.

We saw the cracker almost at once. It had been placed on a small table near the door. It was fashioned of red-and-yellow crepe paper, overlarge, obviously an amateur effort but made with some skill. Miss Belsize seized it and read:

" 'Victor Mickledore!' It's got your name on it, darling. Someone's left you a present. What fun! Do let's pull it!"

He didn't respond but pulled on his cigarette and gazed at her contemptuously through the smoke. She flushed, then held the cracker out to me and we pulled together. The paper tore apart without a bang and a small object fell out and rolled over the carpet. I bent and picked it up. Wrapped neatly in an oblong of paper was a small metal charm in the shape of a skull attached to a key ring; I had seen similar ones in gift shops. I opened the paper folded round it and saw a verse hand-printed in capitals. Gloria cried:

"Read it out, darling!"

I glanced at my uncle's impassive face and heard my nervous, overloud voice:

"Merry Christmas, Mickledore!
Go to bed and sleep no more.
Take this charm and hold it fast;
This night's sleep shall be your last.

Christmas bells ring merrily;
Bells of hell shall ring for thee.
Happy Christmas, Mickledore.
Go to bed and sleep no more."

There was a moment's silence. Then Henry said calmly:

"One of your neighbors doesn't like you, Victor. He's wrong about the bells, though. No Christmas bells in wartime. The bells of hell are another matter. No doubt they aren't subject to Defense Regulations."

Gloria's voice was high:

"It's a death threat! Someone wants to kill you. That woman was among the singers, wasn't she? The one whose child you ran over and killed last Christmas Eve. The village schoolmistress. Saunders. That's her name. Mrs. Saunders was here!"

There was a dreadful silence. My uncle spoke in a voice like a whiplash:

"A witness saw a dark Daimler but it wasn't mine. My Daimler never left the garage last Christmas Eve. Poole confirmed it."

"I know, darling. I didn't mean anything . . ."

"You seldom do." He turned to Poole:

"The best place for this is the kitchen grate."

Then Henry spoke:

"I shouldn't destroy it, not for a time anyway. It's harmless enough, but if you get another and the thing becomes a nuisance it might be as well to let the police see it."

Miss Makepiece said in her cool voice:

"I'll put it in the study desk."

She took it away and the rest of us followed her with our eyes. Gloria said:

"But you'll lock your door, darling. I think you ought to lock your bedroom door."

Victor said:

"I lock my door against no one in my house. If I have an enemy I meet him face to face. And now perhaps we could go in to dinner."

It was an uncomfortable meal. Gloria's loud, half-tipsy volubility served only to emphasize the general cheerlessness. And it was at dinner that she told me about another of my uncle's traditions. Promptly at one o'clock, "to give us time to get to sleep or at least be in our proper beds, darling," he would put on a Santa Claus costume and distribute gifts to each of his guests. We would find a stocking ready at the foot of each bed.

"See what I got last year," she exulted, stretching out her arm to me across the table. The diamond bracelet sparkled in the candlelight. My uncle cracked a walnut in his palm like a pistol shot.

"You may do better this year if you're a good girl."

The words and the tone were an insult.

I remember the rest of the evening in a series of brightly lit cameos. Dancing after dinner, the Turvilles staidly circling, Gloria clinging amorously to Henry, Miss Makepiece watching with contemptuous eyes from her seat by the fire. How evocative those records are now! Beer Barrel Polka, Deep Purple, Run Rabbit Run, Jeepers Creepers and Tiger Rag. Then the game of hunt the hare; according to Henry this was another of Victor's Christmas traditions, one in which the whole household was required to take part. I was chosen as hare. A balloon was tied to my arm and I was given five minutes to hide anywhere in the house. The aim was to regain the front door before I was caught and the balloon punctured. For me it was the only jolly part of the evening. I remember giggling housemaids; Gloria, chasing me round the kitchen table, making ineffectual lunges with a rolled magazine; my last mad rush to the door as Henry burst from the study and exploded the balloon with one swipe of a branch of holly. Later, I remember the dying firelight gleaming on crystal decanters as Poole brought in the drinks tray. The Turvilles went to bed first—she wanted to listen to the 10:45 Epilogue in her own room—and were shortly followed by Gloria and Miss Makepiece. I said my good-nights at 11:45, leaving my uncle alone with Henry, the drinks tray between them.

At my bedroom door I found Miss Makepiece waiting for me. She asked me to change rooms with Henry. He was in the red room with its curtained four-poster and, after his accident in June when he had been forced down in his flight to South America and had escaped in seconds from the blazing cockpit, she thought he might find the bed claustrophobic. She helped me move my few belongings into the new room on the back corridor and bade me goodnight. I can't say I was sorry to be farther from my uncle.

Christmas Eve was nearly over. I thought about my day as I undressed and made my way to the bathroom at the turn of the corridor. It hadn't been too bad, after all. Henry had been remote but amiable. Miss Makepiece was intimidating, but she had left me alone. I was still terrified of Victor, but Mrs. Turville had been a motherly and protective presence. Deaf and shabby, she yet had her own gentle authority. There was a small carved statue of the Virgin in a niche to the right of the fireplace. Before the game of hunt the hare, someone had tied a balloon to its neck. Quietly she had asked Poole to remove it and he had at once obeyed. Afterwards she had explained to me that the statue was called the Turville Grace and for three hundred years had protected the heir from harm. She told me that her only son was in a Guards regiment and asked about my own family. How glad I must be that they were in Singapore where the war could not touch them. Could not touch them! The irony stings even now.

The lined bed curtains and the canopy were of heavy crimson material, damask I suppose. Because of some defect in the rails they couldn't be fully drawn back except at the foot and there was barely space for my bedside table. Lying on the high and surprisingly hard mattress I had the impression of being enveloped in flames of blood, and I could understand Miss Makepiece's concern that Henry should sleep elsewhere. I don't think I realized then, child that I was, that she was in love with him any more than I accepted what I surely must have known, that Gloria had been my uncle's mistress.

I slept almost immediately, but that internal clock which regulates our waking made me stir after little more than two hours. I switched on my bedside lamp and looked at my watch. It was a minute to one o'clock. Santa Claus would be on his way. I put out the light and waited, feeling again some of the excitement I had felt as a young child on this most magical night of the year. He came promptly, gliding in soundlessly over the carpet. Curtained as I was I could hear nothing, not even the sound of his breathing. I half covered my head with the sheet, feigned sleep, and watched with one narrowed eye. He was holding a torch and the pool of light shone momentarily on his fur-trimmed robe, the peaked hood drawn forward over his face. A white-gloved hand slipped a package into the stocking. And then he was gone as silently as he had come.

At sixteen one has no patience. I waited until I was sure he had gone then crept down the bed. The present, wrapped in red striped paper, was slim. I untied the ribbon. Inside was a box containing a gold cigarette case carved with the initials H.R.C. How odd that I hadn't remembered! This present was, of course, meant for Henry. I should have to wait for mine until morning. On impulse I opened the case. Inside was a typed message.

Happy Christmas! No need to get it tested. It's gold all right. And in case you're beginning to hope, this is the only gold you'll get from me.

I wished I hadn't opened it, hadn't seen that offensive gibe.

I took some time replacing the wrapping and ribbon as neatly as I could, put the package back in the stocking, and settled myself to sleep.

I woke once again in the night. I needed to go to the lavatory. The corridor, like the whole house, was blacked out, but a small oil lamp was kept burning on a table and I groped my sleepy way by its light. I had regained my room when I heard footsteps. I slipped back into the recess of the door and watched. Major and Mrs. Turville, dressing-gowned, came silently down the corridor and slipped into the bathroom, furtively as if gaining a refuge. He was carrying what looked like a rolled-up towel. I waited, curious. In a few seconds she put her head round the door, glanced down the passage, then withdrew. Three seconds later they came out together, he still carrying the rolled towel as if it were a baby. Afraid of being detected in my spying, I closed the door. It was a curious incident. But I soon forgot it in oblivion.

I had drawn back my curtain before sleeping and was woken by the first light of dawn. A tall dressing-gowned figure was standing at the foot of the bed. It was Henry. He came up to me and handed me a gift-wrapped package, saying:

"Sorry if I disturbed you. I was trying to exchange presents before you woke."

He took his own but didn't open it, and watched while I tore the paper off mine. My uncle had given me a gold watch wrapped in a ten-pound note. The richness of it left me speechless but I knew that I was pink with pleasure. He watched my face, then said:

"I wonder what price he'll exact for that. Don't let him corrupt you. That's what he uses his money for, playing with people. Your parents are overseas, aren't they?"

I nodded.

"It might be sensible to write to them that you'd rather not holiday here. It's your affair. I don't want to interfere. But your uncle isn't good for the young. He isn't good for anyone."

I don't know what, if anything, I should have found to say. I recall my momentary resentment that he should have spoiled some of my pleasure in my present. But it was then that we heard the first scream.

It was high, horrible, a wild female screeching. Henry ran out and I scrambled out of bed and followed, down the corridor and round to the front of the house. The screams were coming from the open door of my uncle's bedroom. As we reached it, Gloria appeared in the doorway, disheveled in her mauve silk dressing gown, her hair loose. Clutching at Henry, she stopped screaming, caught her breath and gasped:

"He's dead! Murdered! Victor's murdered!"

We slackened our pace and walked almost slowly up to the bed. I was aware of Miss Makepiece behind us, of Poole coming down the corridor bearing a tray with early morning tea. My uncle lay stretched on his back, still in his Santa Claus costume, the hood framing his face. His mouth was half open in a parody of a grin; his nose was sharply beaked like a bird's; his hands, neatly disposed at his side, seemed unnaturally white and thin, too frail for the heavy signet ring. Everything about him was diminished, made harmless, almost pathetic. But my eyes came back and fixed themselves finally on the knife. It had been plunged into his chest, pinning to it the menacing rhyme from the Christmas cracker.

I felt a dreadful nausea, which, to my shame, gave way to a heady mixture of fear and excitement. I was aware of Major Turville coming up beside me. He said:

"I'll tell my wife; she mustn't come in here. Henry you'd better ring the police."

Miss Makepiece said:

"Is he dead?"

She might have been asking if breakfast was ready.

Henry answered:

"Oh yes, he's dead all right."

"But there's so little blood. Round the knife. Why didn't he bleed?"

"That means he was dead before the knife was put in."

I wondered that they could be so calm. Then Henry turned to Poole: "Is there a key to this room?"

"Yes, sir. On the keyboard in the business room."

"Fetch it please. We'd better lock up here and keep out until the police arrive."

They ignored Gloria, who crouched sniveling at the foot of the bed. And they seemed to have forgotten me. I stood there, shivering, my eyes fixed on that grotesque red-robed corpse which had been Victor Mickledore.

Then Poole coughed, ridiculously deferential:

"I'm wondering, sir, why he didn't defend himself. Mr. Mickledore always kept a gun in the drawer of the bedside table."

Henry went over and pulled it open.

It was then that Gloria stopped crying, gave a hysterical laugh, and sang out in a high quavering voice:

> "Happy Christmas, Mickledore,
> Go to bed and wake no more.
> Merry Christmas, sound the knell,
> Murdered, dead and gone to hell."

But all our eyes were on the drawer.

It was empty. The gun was missing.

2

A retired seventy-six-year-old police officer, even from a small country force, isn't short of memories to solace his fireside evenings and, until Charles Mickledore's letter arrived, I hadn't thought about the Marston Turville killing for years. Mickledore asked me to give my version of the case as part of a private account he was writing and I was surprised how vividly the memories came flooding back. I don't know how he managed to run me to earth. He mentioned that he wrote detective fiction and that may have helped. Not that I read it. In my experience police officers rarely do. Once you've had to cope with the real thing, you lose the taste for fantasy.

I was interested to learn what had happened to that shy, unattractive, secretive boy. At least he was still alive. Too many of that little group which had spent Christmas Eve 1939 with him at Marston Turville had come to violent ends. One murdered; one shot down in flames; one killed in a car smash; two caught in a London air raid; and one, largely due to my activities, ignominiously dead at the end of a rope. Not that I lose any sleep over that. You get on with your job and let the consequences look after themselves. That's the only way I know to do police work. But I'd better get on with my story.

My name is John Pollinger and in December 1939 I was a newly promoted Detective Inspector in the County Force. The Mickledore killing was my first murder. I arrived at the Manor with my sergeant at nine-thirty and old Doc McKay, the police surgeon, was hard on my heels. Henry Caldwell had taken charge and had done all the correct things. The death room was locked, no one had been allowed to leave the house and they had all kept together. Only Mrs. Turville was missing—locked in her bedroom and, according to her husband, too distressed to see me. But the Major was willing to let me in as soon as Doc MacKay had taken a look at her. He was their family doctor; but then, he was doctor to all the village. Most of us involved in the case knew one another. That was my strength; it was also my weakness.

Once we had parted the heavy Santa Claus robe, its inner fold stiffened and darkened with blood, it didn't need the missing gun to tell us that Mickledore had been shot. The bullet had been aimed at short range to the heart. And I couldn't see Mickledore lying there meekly waiting for it. There was an empty glass on his bedside table. Taking it up, I could just detect the faint smell of whisky. But I had an open mind on what else it might have contained.

Doc McKay pulled out the knife—an ordinary sharp-bladed kitchen knife— with one quick jerk of his gloved hand. He sniffed round the larger gunshot wound for signs of scorching, then checked the body temperature and the progress of rigor mortis. The timing of death is always chancy, but he finally estimated that Mickledore had been killed sometime between 11:30 and two o'clock. It was an opinion that the post-mortem examination subsequently confirmed.

We were short of manpower in that first winter of the phony war and I had to manage with one sergeant and a couple of detective constables new to the job. I interviewed the suspects myself. It wouldn't have been convincing if they'd pretended any grief and, to give them their due, they didn't try. They spoke the conventional platitudes and so did I; but we didn't fool one another.

Caldwell said that he had last seen Mickledore carrying a glass of whisky to his room when they parted in the corridor shortly before midnight. The Turvilles and Miss Belsize, who had retired earlier, claimed that they were asleep by midnight and hadn't stirred until morning. Charles Mickledore admitted that he had gone to the bathroom sometime after one—he hadn't looked at his watch—but insisted that he had seen no one and heard nothing. I had a strong impression he was lying but I didn't press him at that first interview. The young seldom lie convincingly. They haven't had time to practice like the rest of us.

Poole and the cook, Mrs. Banting, lived in separate flats in the stable block; Mickledore had a dislike of servants sleeping in the house. The other three maids were local girls who came in part-time from the village and had gone home after dinner. Mrs. Banting had put the turkey and Christmas pudding in the pantry before leaving for her bed at eleven and Poole had left with her. She had returned at six to begin her Christmas preparations and Poole had arrived at seven to take up the early morning tea trays. Both claimed to have spent a night of innocent oblivion and swore that their keys hadn't left their possession. No one heard the gunshot. The Turvilles were deaf, Miss Belsize probably half drunk and doped, the young sleep soundly, and Mickledore's door was of heavy oak. All the same, it was odd.

I may as well admit that my first suspect was Caldwell. This was a murder requiring nerve and that he had in plenty. I reckoned that his country had a better use for him than stringing him up·in a hangman's noose. But if the law found him guilty, he'd be for the drop war or no war. But one thing, in particular, puzzled me. His mother had died in 1934. Why wait five years to take his revenge? Why this Christmas? It didn't make sense.

Caldwell and Miss Makepiece were the only two, apart from the boy, who admitted having left their rooms that night. Miss Makepiece said that, shortly after one o'clock, she had been woken by a call on her bedside telephone; Mickledore never took night calls and the extension was in her room. The call was from Bill Sowers, our Air Raid Warden, complaining that a strip of light was showing from one of the first-floor windows. Miss Makepiece had roused Caldwell and they had taken torches, unbolted a side door from the kitchen quarters, and had gone out together to identify the source of the light and check that the rest of the house was properly blacked out. Afterwards they had taken a nip of whisky from the decanter still in the great hall—it was a cold night to go traipsing round in dressing gowns, and had decided to play a game of chess. It seemed a bit odd to me; but they said they were by now thoroughly awake and disinclined for sleep. Both were experienced players and they welcomed the chance of a peaceful game. They couldn't remember which of them had suggested it, but both agreed that the game had ended just before three, when they had gone to their rooms for what remained of the night.

And here I thought I had them. I play a reasonable game myself so I asked them to sit at different ends of the room and write down as many of the moves as they could remember. It's strange, but I can recall some of that game to this day. Miss Makepiece was white and opened with pawn to king four. Caldwell responded by playing the Sicilian. After about ninety minutes white managed to queen a pawn and black resigned. They were able to remember a remarkable number of moves and I was forced to accept that the game had been played. Caldwell had nerve. But had he nerve enough to play a complicated game of chess while his victim, still warm, lay murdered upstairs?

And that call from Bill Sowers was genuine, too. I had been with him when he made it from the village call box. We had come out of church together after

Midnight Service and had immediately seen the offending light, as had most of the congregation. And Bill, always punctilious, had looked at his watch. His call to the Manor had been made at six minutes past one.

It was four-thirty before I finally left the Manor to report to the Chief Constable. Those were the days of the old-fashioned chiefs—none of your university special entrants or Police College intellectuals. I loved old Colonel Maybricke. My own father had been killed at Ypres and I suppose he was some kind of substitute. He didn't start talking about the murder until his wife had settled me in front of their roaring fire with tea and a hefty slice of her homemade Christmas cake. He listened in silence to my account, then said:

"I've had Major Turville on the telephone. Perfectly proper. What you'd expect from a gentleman. He thinks he ought not to sit on the Bench until his business is cleared up. Must say I agree with him."

"Yes, sir."

"What's odd, although I didn't say so to him, is what he and Mrs. Turville are doing at the Manor. Hardly the sort of Christmas invitation you'd expect them to accept. Mickledore insisted on taking the place away from them complete, lock, stock and barrel, cheated them on the price if rumor's correct, and they choose to spend Christmas under his roof. Damned odd. And then there's the curious reaction of Mrs. Turville. You still haven't had a chance to question her or search the room?"

"She let me in after Doc McKay had examined her. She was upset, naturally enough, but perfectly calm. All she could tell me was that she'd gone to sleep shortly after listening to the Dvořák String Quartet at 10:55—they had twin beds —and didn't stir until her husband woke her with news of the murder."

"Which promptly threw her into a state of shock. Not very likely, not with Mary Turville. Ever see her in the hunting field?"

"No, sir."

"She was younger then, of course. A different world. But Mrs. Turville's not the kind to be thrown into shock by a body she didn't see."

I said nothing. But I reckon he guessed my thoughts. She could have seen it; been the first person to see it; seen it at that moment when it ceased to be Mickledore and became a body. The Chief went on:

"And that secretary cum housekeeper. Why does she stay? Rumor has it that he treats her like a slave."

"I doubt that, sir. She's too useful. It can't be easy to find a first-class secretary who'll also run your house."

"Even so, it can't be an agreeable job."

"She was quite frank about it. She has an invalid mother. Mickledore pays the nursing home fees."

"And a good salary in addition, no doubt."

It was odd, I thought, how we were speaking of him in the present tense.

"And Gloria Belsize. What attracts her to the Manor?"

I knew the answer to that one; it was to be found in a Christmas stocking. Last year, a diamond bracelet. This year an emerald clasp. Her story was that she had rushed impulsively into Mickledore's room to thank him for it and had found him dead. The Chief cut me another wedge of cake:

"That light we all saw after church. Anyone admit to that bit of carelessness?"

"It came from the back bathroom on the first floor. Only Charles Mickledore admits to visiting it in the night. He says he could have pulled back the curtain to look out over the fields, but he isn't sure."

"Odd thing to be vague about. Still, it was Christmas Eve. Excitement. A strange house. This Father Christmas nonsense of Mickledore's. You say that the boy was the only one to see him."

"The only one to admit it."

"Then he's a vital witness. Did he recognize his uncle?"

"Not definitely, sir. But he says it never occurred to him that it wasn't Mickledore. And then there's the fact that he was given the present intended for Caldwell. Miss Makepiece says that only the boy, Caldwell and herself knew about the change of rooms."

"Which suggests that Santa Claus didn't know, whoever he was. Or we are intended to believe just that?"

I said:

"What I can't understand is why the gun wasn't left by the body or replaced in the drawer. Why take it away and hide it?"

"Probably to cast doubt on whether it really is the weapon. We can't prove that until we find it. There are plenty of old Service revolvers still around from the last war. Come to that, Saunders still has his uncle's. He mentioned it to me last month when we were discussing civilian defense. I'd forgotten that. Saunders has a revolver!"

"Not now, he hasn't, sir. That's one thing I asked him when I went to question him and his wife about the cracker. He said he got rid of the weapon after his daughter was killed."

"Did he say why?"

"Because he was afraid that the temptation to shoot Mickledore might get too much for him."

"That's candid enough. What did he do with it?"

"Threw it in Potter's Pool, sir."

"Where it's now well down in the mud. Very convenient. No one has ever dredged anything from Potter's Pool. Still, you'd better try. We need that gun wherever it came from."

I hadn't enjoyed my interview with the Saunders. All the village respected Will and Edna—a decent, hardworking couple who had doted on their only daughter. We had been pretty friendly, but I knew that he and his wife resented the fact that we hadn't caught the hit-and-run driver of the Daimler that knocked down and killed their Dorothy. It wasn't for lack of trying. We knew, and they knew, that Mickledore was the suspect. He was the only owner of a Daimler in the neighborhood and the accident had happened in the narrow lane from the Manor. But there had been no identifiable damage to his car and Poole had been ready to swear that it had never left the garage. We couldn't arrest him on unsupported suspicion.

So I had to handle the interview with tact. They were just back from church when I arrived. We settled down in their neat sitting room and Mrs. Saunders made up the fire. But they didn't offer me a drink as they once would have done and I knew that they would be glad to see the back of me. And there was something else I knew. The murder of Mickledore wasn't news to them. They were on the telephone—Saunders ran the one village taxi—and I guessed that someone from the Manor had telephoned a warning. And I thought I knew who. Miss Makepiece and Edna Saunders were old college friends.

They denied any knowledge of the Christmas cracker or its message. After Mrs. Saunders had returned from the carol singing they had spent the evening by the fire listening to the wireless. The news at nine o'clock, *Robinson Crusoe* at 9:15 and the *Crime Wave at Blandings* at 10:00. Mrs. Saunders had particularly wanted to hear the Wodehouse play, as the actors Gladys Young and Carleton Hobbs were particular favorites.

They were able to tell me what had been on the nine o'clock news—the awards to officers and men of the submarine Ursula, the big IRA raid in Dublin, the Pope's Christmas message. I led them on gently to the crucial time. They said that they had listened to the Solemn Midnight Mass from Downside, which had ended at 12:45, and had then gone to their bed. They were even able to describe the music. But that didn't mean that both of them had been listening. It hadn't taken more than one hand to put that bullet into Mickledore.

I wrenched my mind back to the present. The Chief was saying:

"It looks as if the cracker must have been brought into the house by one of the carol singers. But I suppose it's not impossible for one of the house party to have planted it."

"Only those who were near the door."

"But if one or both of the Saunders shot Mickledore they must have had an accomplice. They couldn't have known where to find the cracker. And they couldn't have gotten in unless the door was opened for them."

"The back door was unbolted, sir, while Caldwell and Miss Makepiece checked the lights. That was at about ten past one."

But the murderer couldn't have depended on that. There was no difficulty in getting into Mickledore's bedroom, of course. I respect his refusal to lock his door. And the obvious time for the murder was while he was delivering the presents. They all knew that his room would be empty. The murderer sneaks in, takes the gun and hides—where?"

"There's a large clothes closet, sir."

"Very convenient. And so was this game of hunt the hare. It gave the murderer the chance to steal the cracker, check on the gun, select a knife. He could safely be seen anywhere, even in another person's bedroom. Silly kind of game, though, for grown men. Who suggested it?"

"Mickledore. It's part of his ritual family Christmas."

"Then the murderer could rely on its being played. All he had to do was conceal the knife and cracker on his person until he could hide them in his room."

"Not easy for Miss Belsize, sir. She was wearing a slinky evening dress. And somehow I can't picture her scampering about in the kitchen."

"Don't exclude her, John. If that will you found in the study still stands, she inherits £20,000. And so does Miss Makepiece. And Poole gets £10,000 you said. Men, and women, have killed for far less. Ah well, you'd better get back to it, I suppose. We must find that gun."

We were to find it all right. But more surprisingly and dramatically than either of us could have dreamed.

3

There are more agreeable ways of spending Christmas day than being interrogated by the police, particularly by Inspector Pottinger with his dogged, impassive persistence, his accusing eyes. With the impulsive chivalry of the young, I had decided to protect Mrs. Turville. I lied about seeing her and her husband in the night. I was deliberately vague when I described the visit of Santa Claus. I wasn't sure how far I managed to deceive Pottinger, but lying takes practice. I was to get better at it by the end of the case.

The questioning was ceaseless. Henry was even summoned to the study in the middle of Christmas dinner. It was an uncomfortable meal. Mrs. Banting had already put the huge turkey in the oven when the murder was discovered and there was a general feeling that, having been cooked, it might as well be eaten. But Henry said firmly that the combination of Christmas pudding and violent death would be intolerably indigestible; the pudding would keep until next year. So we ate mince pies instead. I had the healthy appetite of youth and was embarrassingly aware that I was eating with undisguised enjoyment while the adults toyed with their lukewarm turkey and shredded Brussels sprouts.

Afterwards Poole served coffee in the hall and we listened in silence to the three o'clock King's broadcast. Nineteen thirty-nine was the occasion on which he finished with the quotation about the man standing at the gate of the year and asking for a light to guide him into the unknown. I have heard it many times since, but it has never sounded so poignant as it did spoken in the King's slow and careful voice on that Christmas of 1939.

It was a relief to us all when, at four-thirty, Inspector Pottinger left the Manor, leaving his sergeant to continue the search for the gun. Poole, bringing in the tea, told us that the Inspector had gone to report to the Chief Constable; Poole had his own mysterious ways of discovering what the police were up to.

But we were not left in peace for long. Just before seven he returned. His imperious knock on the front door, clearly heard in the hall, was like the knock of doom. Poole showed him in with his usual insolent formality and I watched the eyes of my companions turn to him with a mixture of apprehension and inquiry. The drinks tray had been brought in early and Gloria was noisily mixing cocktails for herself and Henry. But she must have been drinking earlier; even my inexperienced eyes could see that she was half-drunk. Before the Inspector could say more than a stolid "Good evening" she swayed up to him glass in hand.

"Here comes our village Poirot with his little gray cells clicking away. But no handcuffs. Haven't you come to arrest poor little Gloria?"

Henry went quietly up to her. I heard him whisper urgently. But she laughed and advanced to the Christmas tree. Suddenly she began pulling off the decorations and throwing them wildly over him. A strand of tinsel caught on the Turville Grace, but Mrs. Turville seemed not to care. Gloria began chanting.

"Time for pressies, everyone. We always have pressies off the tree at seven. Mustn't break with tradition. Victor wouldn't like it. One for you, Poole, and one for Mrs. Banting. Catch!"

She tore the parcels from the tree and tossed them to Poole. He said an expressionless, "Thank you, Miss," and placed them on a side table. Henry moved forward and caught hold of her arm. But she wrenched herself free and seized another present from the tree.

"It's for you, darling. Henry, written in Victor's own hand."

Henry's voice was like ice. I had never heard him speak in that tone before.

"Leave it. This isn't the time for presents. I'll take it home with me."

"Don't be a spoilsport, darling! You want to see your pressie. Let Gloria open it for you."

There was one of those moments of absolute silence which seem in retrospect so portentous. Perhaps I only now imagine, forty-four years later, that the whole room froze and watched breathless as she tore off the gaudy Christmas paper. Inside was a further wrapping of red-and-yellow crepe; surely the paper from the Christmas cracker? This was wrapped round a couple of large linen handkerchiefs. But that wasn't all. Gloria unfolded them, gasped and let out a shrill scream. Her shaking hands parted. And the revolver, found at last, fell with a dull thud at Pottinger's feet.

After the discovery of the gun the atmosphere subtly changed. Before then we had comforted ourselves with the theory, which we all strenuously promoted, that a stranger had gained access to the Manor by the unbolted side door while Henry and Miss Makepiece were checking the windows. He had discovered the cracker while searching the study and had stabbed the message to the body as a bizarre gesture of contempt.

Now it was less easy to believe that the killer came from outside. We stopped discussing the murder, afraid of what we might say or suggest, wary of one another's eyes. Mrs. Turville, who looked suddenly like a very old woman, tried to reassure and comfort me. Relishing my shameful excitement in the face of murder, which has never left me, I was glad she didn't know how little I needed or deserved her kindness. The police questioning went on, more rigorous, more insistent. By the time Inspector Pottinger left we were all exhausted and glad of an excuse to seek an early bed.

It was ten o'clock when I heard a knock at my door. My heart thudded, I slipped out of bed and whispered "Who is it?" There was a second more insistent knock. Cautiously I opened the door. Gloria sidled in, trembling with fear and with cold.

"Charles, darling, could you bear to sleep in my room? There's a big armchair, and you could bring your eiderdown. I'm too terrified to be alone."

"Can't you lock the door?"

"There isn't a lock. And I daren't take my sleeping pill in case he comes when I'm unconscious."

"Who comes?"

"The murderer, of course."

What sixteen-year-old could resist that appeal to chivalry? Flattered to be asked, and not sorry to have company, I pattered along the corridor behind her. We pushed the heavy armchair against the door and I settled down in reasonable comfort. It was curiously cozy in her bedroom with the pool of light from the bedside lamp shining on her fair hair. We spoke in whispers like conspirators.

"They think Victor was doped with my sleeping pills and then shot while he slept. Pottinger keeps on asking me if any are missing. How can I tell? My Mayfair doctor lets me have what I ask. I've got a whole bottle here in my bedside drawer. Anyone could have helped himself. I don't count them."

I said:

"But wouldn't he taste the pills?"

"Not in his whisky. I never can."

She propped herself on her elbow and leaned towards me.

"Have you thought about Poole? Poole could have done it. He knows that Victor killed the Saunders child. He lied about the Daimler never leaving the garage. He had to. Victor had something on him."

"Had what on him?"

"He's been in prison for assaulting small girls. He wouldn't last long in the village if that came out. And it's very convenient for him that Victor died when he died. He was thinking of changing his will. That's why you're here. If he liked you, he was thinking of making you his heir and cutting the rest of us out."

It had been convenient for her, too, I thought, that my uncle had died when he had. I whispered:

"How do you know about the will?"

"Victor told me. He liked tormenting me. He could be terribly cruel. People say that he drove his wife to suicide."

Gloria had swallowed her sleeping pill by now and her voice was becoming blurred. I had to strain to hear her.

"And then there's the Turvilles."

"What about the Turvilles?"

I realized that my voice had betrayed me. She laughed sleepily.

"You like her, don't you? Everyone does. The perfect lady. Not like little Gloria. Must protect the dear Turvilles. But they're up to something. Their door was ajar. The deaf don't realize how loudly they whisper. He was saying 'We have to go through with it, darling. We've spent the money and we've planned it so carefully . . . So carefully.' " Gloria's voice faded into silence.

Spent what money and for what? I wondered as I lay there listening to Gloria's low guttural breathing. Wakeful, I relived all the events of that extraordinary Christmas. My arrival at Marston station, the silent drive through the darkening village, the school with the Christmas chains of colored paper gleaming against the windows. The first sight of my uncle's dark judgmental face. The carol singers creeping out under the blackout curtain. The game of hunt the hare. The silent figure of Santa Claus at the foot of my bed. Myself, standing by Victor's bed and noting every detail of that grotesquely clad, unreal corpse. Doctor McKay leaving Mrs. Turville's room with his old-fashioned Gladstone bag. The strand of tinsel thrown by Gloria over the Turville Grace. The gun thudding at Pottinger's feet.

The varied images flashed upon my inner eye like camera shots. And suddenly, the confused medley of sights and sounds fused into a coherent picture. Before I fell asleep I knew what I must do. Tomorrow I would first speak to Inspector Pottinger. And then I would confront the murderer.

I saw Inspector Pottinger first and told him what I had to tell. Then I sought out Henry. He was in the great hall with the Turvilles and I asked if I might speak to him alone. Tactful as ever they got up and silently left. I said:

"I know it was you."

That sixteen-year-old boy is a stranger to me now and memory is self-deluding. I couldn't, surely, have been so confident, so self-assured as I seem to recall. But there is no doubt about what I had to say. And I remember perfectly—how could I ever forget?—how he looked and the words he spoke to me.

He looked down at me calmly, unfrightened, a little sadly.

"Suppose you tell me how."

"When Santa Claus slipped your present into my stocking he was wearing a white glove. The murderer would have needed to wear gloves to avoid fingerprints. But the hands of the corpse were bare and I could see no gloves by the bed."

"And you kept this vital piece of evidence from the police?"

"I wanted to protect the Turvilles. I saw them creeping about suspiciously in the night. He was carrying a rolled towel. I thought it concealed the gun."

"And how did you imagine they got rid of it? Pottinger searched our rooms."

"Mrs. Turville feigned illness. I thought she gave the gun to Dr. McKay after he'd seen her. He could have taken it away in his Gladstone bag."

"But when the gun was found, you realized that your theory was wrong. The Turvilles were innocent."

"And last night I guessed the truth. Dr. McKay did take something away in his bag: the Turville Grace. That's what they were doing—substituting a fake statue for the one they believe will protect their son. They were desperate to regain it now that he's gone to war."

"So now you pick on me as suspect number one. Am I also supposed to have fabricated and planted the cracker?"

"No. You and I stood together during the carol singing. You were never near the door. I think you used it to complicate the crime—that's why you suggested keeping it—but it was Mrs. Saunders who made it. She could have taken some of the crepe paper her school children were provided with to make their Christmas decorations. I noticed, too, that the verse was written by someone who punctuated correctly as if by instinct. And it didn't threaten death. All they wanted was to harass Victor, to spoil his Christmas. It was a small, pathetic revenge for the death of their daughter."

"Well, go on. So far it's remarkably convincing."

"You took the cracker and the kitchen knife and stole some of Gloria's sleeping pills while we were playing hunt the hare. The game is traditional at the Manor. You could rely on its being played. And it was you who asked for a change of room. You wanted to be close to my uncle and to have me farther away in case I heard the shot. The Turvilles are deaf and Gloria takes sleeping pills. My young ears were the danger. But even I couldn't hear a shot in that heavily curtained bed. You can't really be claustrophobic, can you? The RAF wouldn't have accepted you if you were."

He looked down on me, his pale handsome face still calm, still unfrightened. And I realized again that he must have been Santa Claus. No one else in the house could match my uncle's height.

When he spoke, his voice was ironic, almost amused.

"Don't stop now. Aren't you getting to the exciting part?"

"You slipped the sleeping pills in Victor's whisky while you were drinking together or, perhaps, later while he was in the bathroom. Then you took his gun and shot him while he lay drugged and undressed on his bed, probably between twelve-fifteen and twelve-thirty. Promptly at one o'clock you took the part of Santa Claus, being careful to leave your present in my stocking. Then you dressed the corpse in the robes and drove in the knife through the menacing cracker rhyme. It was you who pulled aside that curtain in the bathroom, knowing that it would bring an immediate call. If Miss Makepiece hadn't woken you—but you were the natural choice—you would have pretended to hear her prowling about outside. There was no difficulty in persuading her to play chess with you and thus innocently provide you with that vital alibi for the hours after one o'clock."

He said calmly:

"Congratulations. You should write detective stories. Is there anything you don't know?"

"Yes. What you did with the white gloves and the death's head charm from the cracker."

He looked at me with a half smile, then bent and rummaged among the cotton wool snowballs round the foot of the Christmas tree. He brought one out, a rolled white ball with strands of cotton wool and tinsel still adhering to it. Deliberately he threw it into the fire. The flames licked at it, then blazed high.

"I've been waiting for the chance to do that. The fire had died by midnight and ever since it was relit this room has been occupied."

"And the charm?"

"Someone will break a tooth on it next Christmas. I took the cloth and grease-proof paper off the Christmas pudding and pressed it in among the sixpenny pieces. Even if it's found next year it will be too late to help Pottinger."

"And, immediately after the shooting, you wrapped the gun in the crepe paper and hid it in the Christmas tree present bearing your name. You would have taken it away with you when you left the Manor if Gloria hadn't found it so dramatically. No wonder you tried to restrain her."

He said:

"There's no witness to this conversation. I'm trusting you, but not perhaps as much as you suppose."

I looked at him full in the face.

"I'm trusting you, too. Five minutes ago I asked to see Inspector Pottinger and told him that I'd remembered something vital. I said that when Santa Claus slipped your present into my stocking I distinctly saw the gold of his signet ring. Your fingers are much thicker than Victor's. You couldn't have forced on that ring. If I stick to my lie—and I shall—they won't dare arrest you."

He didn't thank me. I didn't say anything. I cried out:

"But why? And why now, this Christmas?"

"Because he murdered my mother. Oh, not in any way I can prove. But she killed herself after only two years of marriage to him. I always meant to destory him, but the years pass and the will atrophies. And then came the war. This phony war won't last much longer and there will be nothing phony about the killing once it begins in earnest. I'll be shooting down young pilots, decent ordinary Germans with whom I've no quarrel. It has to be done. They'll do it to me if they can. But it will be more tolerable now that I've killed the one man who did deserve it. I've kept faith with her. If I have to go, I'll go more easily."

I picture that blazing Spitfire spiraling into the Channel and I wonder if he did.

5

I've posted my account of the Marston Turville murder to Charles Mickledore, but God knows why he wanted it. It was hardly my most successful case; I never made an arrest and the mystery remains to this day. Once the boy recalled seeing that ring on his uncle's finger my case against Caldwell collapsed. The medical evidence showed that Mickledore was dead before three o'clock, when Caldwell and Miss Makepiece finished their game of chess. Caldwell couldn't have shot him and done all that was necessary in those few minutes between the delivery of the presents and the warden's telephone call.

His alibi held.

The Turvilles were killed by a V2 rocket while on a day trip to London. Well, that's how they would have wanted to go, quickly and together. But there are Turvilles still at the Manor. Their son survived the war and bought back his ancestral home. I wonder if his grandchildren frighten themselves on Christmas Eve with tales of the murder of Santa Claus.

Neither Poole nor Miss Belsize benefitted long from their legacies. She bought herself a Bentley and killed herself in it, driving while drunk. He purchased a house in the village and played the gentleman. But within a year he was up to his old tricks with small girls. I was actually on my way to arrest him when he hanged himself in his garage, choked to death on the end of a washing line. The public hangman would have made a neater job of it.

I sometimes wonder if young Charles Mickledore lied about seeing that ring. Now that we're in touch, I'm tempted to ask him. But it was over forty years ago— an old crime, an old story. And if Henry Caldwell did owe a debt to society, he paid it at last and in full.

Donald E. Westlake

NEVER SHAKE A
FAMILY TREE

*Donald E. Westlake (1933–   ) is something of a genial gadfly in the
detective writer's world. He began, critic Anthony Boucher noted, as "one
of the ablest practitioners of the absolutely tough, hard-nosed novel of
crime, with an acute insight into criminal thinking" and then, after five
novels, shifted gears and began producing comic works—such as* The
Fugitive Pigeon, God Save the Mark, *and* The Hot Rock—*full of bum-
bling crooks, inept capers, and innocent bystanders who get roped into
off-the-wall adventures they never bargained for. Under various pseu-
donyms (Richard Stark probably being the best known) he has, however,
continued to write suitably respectable "serious" crime stories as well.*

*The heroine of this far-from-serious short story is hardly a traditional
detective, but genealogy, by its very nature, leads to detection and deduction and conclusions that are not always what the genealogist had in
mind.*

Never Shake a Family Tree

Actually, I was never so surprised in my life, and I seventy-three my last birthday and eleven times a grandmother and twice a great-grandmother. But never in my life did I see the like, and that's the truth.

It all began with my interest in genealogy, which I got from Mrs. Ernestine Simpson, a widow I met at Bay Arbor, in Florida, when I went there three summers ago. I certainly didn't like Florida—far too expensive, if you ask me, and far too bright, and with just too many mosquitoes and other insects to be believed—but I wouldn't say the trip was a total loss, since it did interest me in genealogical research, which is certainly a wonderful hobby, as well as being very valuable, what with one thing and another.

Actually, my genealogical researches have been valuable in more ways than one, since they have also been instrumental in my meeting some very pleasant ladies and gentlemen, although some of them only by postal, and of course it was through this hobby that I met Mr. Gerald Fowlkes in the first place.

But I'm getting far ahead of my story, and ought to begin at the beginning, except that I'm blessed if I know where the beginning actually is. In one way of looking at things, the beginning is my introduction to genealogy through Mrs. Ernestine Simpson, who has since passed on, but in another way the beginning is really almost two hundred years ago, and in still another way the story doesn't really begin until the first time I came across the name of Euphemia Barber.

Well. Actually, I suppose, I ought to begin by explaining just what genealogical research is. It is the study of one's family tree. One checks marriage and birth and death records, searches old family Bibles and talks to various members of one's family, and one gradually builds up a family tree, showing who fathered whom and what year, and when so-and-so got married, and when so-and-so died, and so on. It's really fascinating work, and there are any number of amateur genealogical societies throughout the country, and when one has one's family tree built up for as far as one wants—seven generations, or nine generations, or however long one wants—then it is possible to write this all up in a folder and bequeath it to the local library, and then there is a *record* of one's family for all time to come, and I for one think that's important and valuable to have even if my youngest boy, Tom, does laugh at it and say it's just a silly hobby. Well, it *isn't* a silly hobby. After all, I found evidence of murder that way, didn't I?

So, actually, I suppose the whole thing really begins when I first come across the name of Euphemia Barber. Euphemia Barber was John Anderson's second wife. John Anderson was born in Goochland County, Virginia, in 1754. He married Ethel Rita Mary Rayborn in 1777, just around the time of the Revolution, and they had seven children, which wasn't at all strange for that time, though large families have, I notice, gone out of style today, and I for one think it's a shame.

At any rate, it was John and Ethel Anderson's third child, a girl named Prudence, who is in my direct line on my mother's father's side, so of course I had them in my family tree. But then, in going through Appomattox County records —Goochland County being now a part of Appomattox, and no longer a separate county of its own—I came across the name of Euphemia Barber. It seems that Ethel Anderson died in 1793, in giving birth to her eighth child—who also died —and three years later, 1796, John Anderson remarried, this time marrying a widow named Euphemia Barber. At that time he was forty-two years of age, and her age was given as thirty-nine.

Of course, Euphemia Barber was not at all in my direct line, being John Anderson's second wife, but I was interested to some extent in her pedigree as well, wanting to add her parents' names and her place of birth to my family chart, and also because there were some Barbers fairly distantly related on my father's mother's side, and I was wondering if this Euphemia might be kin to them. But the records were very incomplete, and all I could learn was that Euphemia Barber was not a native of Virginia, and had apparently only been in the area for a year or two when she married John Anderson. Shortly after John's death in 1798, two years after their marriage, she sold the Anderson farm, which was apparently a somewhat prosperous location, and moved away again. So that I had neither birth nor death records on her, nor any record of her first husband, whose last name had apparently been Barber, but only the one lone record of her marriage to my great-great-great-great-great-grandfather on my mother's father's side.

Actually, there was no reason for me to pursue the question further, since Euphemia Barber wasn't in my direct line anyway, but I had worked diligently and, I think, well, on my family tree, and had it almost complete back nine generations, and there was really very little left to do with it, so I was glad to do some tracking down.

Which is why I included Euphemia Barber in my next entry in the *Genealogical Exchange*. Now, I suppose I ought to explain what the *Genealogical Exchange* is. There are any number of people throughout the country who are amateur genealogists, concerned primarily with their own family trees, but of course family trees do interlock, and any one of these people is liable to know about just the one record which has been eluding some other searcher for months. And so there are magazines devoted to the exchanging of such information, for nominal fees. In the last few years I had picked up all sorts of valuable leads in this way. And so my entry in the summer issue of the *Genealogical Exchange* read:

BUCKLEY, Mrs. Henrietta Rhodes, 119A Newbury St., Boston, Mass. Xch data on *Rhodes, Anderson, Richards, Pryor, Marshall, Lord*. Want any info Euphemia *Barber*, m. John Anderson, Va. 1796.

Well. The *Genealogical Exchange* had been helpful to me in the past, but I never received anywhere near the response caused by Euphemia Barber. And the first response of all came from Mr. Gerald Fowlkes.

It was a scant two days after I received my own copy of the summer issue of the *Exchange*. I was still poring over it myself, looking for people who might be linked to various branches of my family tree, when the telephone rang. Actually, I suppose I was somewhat irked at being taken from my studies, and perhaps I sounded a bit impatient when I answered the phone.

If so, the gentleman at the other end gave no sign of it. His voice was most pleasant, quite deep and masculine, and he said, "May I speak, please, with Mrs. Henrietta Buckley?"

"This is Mrs. Buckley," I told him.

"Ah," he said. "Forgive my telephoning, please, Mrs. Buckley. We have never met. But I noticed your entry in the current issue of the *Genealogical Exchange—*"

"Oh?" I was immediately excited, all thought of impatience gone. This was surely the fastest reply I'd ever had to date!

"Yes," he said. "I noticed the reference to Euphemia Barber. I do believe that may be the Euphemia Stover who married Jason Barber in Savannah, Georgia, in 1791. Jason Barber is in my direct line, on my mother's side. Jason and Euphemia had only the one child, Abner, and I am descended from him."

"Well," I said. "You certainly do seem to have complete information."

"Oh, yes," he said. "My own family chart is almost complete. For twelve generations, that is. I'm not sure whether I'll try to go back farther than that or not. The English records before 1600 are so incomplete, you know."

"Yes, of course," I said. I was, I admit, taken aback. Twelve generations! Surely that was the most ambitious family tree I had ever heard of, though I had read sometimes of people who had carried particular branches back as many as fifteen generations. But to actually be speaking to a person who had traced his entire family back twelve generations!

"Perhaps," he said, "it would be possible for us to meet, and I could give you the information I have on Euphemia Barber. There are also some Marshalls in one branch of my family; perhaps I can be of help to you there, as well." He laughed, a deep and pleasant sound, which reminded me of my late husband, Edward, when he was most particularly pleased. "And, of course," he said, "there is always the chance that you have some information on the Marshalls which can help me."

"I think that would be very nice," I said, and so I invited him to come to the apartment the very next afternoon.

At one point the next day, perhaps half an hour before Gerald Fowlkes was to arrive, I stopped my fluttering around to take stock of myself and to realize that if ever there were an indication of second childhood taking over, my thoughts and actions preparatory to Mr. Fowlkes' arrival were certainly it. I had been rushing hither and thither, dusting, rearranging, polishing, pausing incessantly to look in the mirror and touch my hair with fluttering fingers, all as though I were a flighty teenager before her very first date. "Henrietta," I told myself sharply, "you are seventy-three years old, and all that nonsense is well behind you now. Eleven times a grandmother, and just look at how you carry on!"

But poor Edward had been dead and gone these past nine years, my brothers and sisters were all in their graves, and as for my children, all but Tom, the youngest, were thousands of miles away, living their own lives—as of course they should—and only occasionally remembering to write a duty letter to Mother. And I am much too aware of the dangers of the clinging mother to force my presence too often upon Tom and his family. So I am very much alone, except of course for my friends in the various church activities and for those I have met, albeit only by postal, through my genealogical research.

So it *was* pleasant to be visited by a charming gentleman caller, and particularly so when that gentleman shared my own particular interests.

And Mr. Gerald Fowlkes, on his arrival, was surely no disappointment. He looked to be no more than fifty-five years of age, though he swore to sixty-two, and had a fine shock of gray hair above a strong and kindly face. He dressed very well, with that combination of expense and breeding so little found these days, when the well-bred seem invariably to be poor and the well-to-do seem invariably to be horribly plebeian. His manner was refined and gentlemanly, what we used to call courtly, and he had some very nice things to say about the appearance of my living room.

Actually, I make no unusual claims as a housekeeper. Living alone, and with quite a comfortable income having been left me by Edward, it is no problem at all to choose tasteful furnishings and keep them neat. (Besides, I had scrubbed the apartment from top to bottom in preparation for Mr. Fowlkes' visit.)

He had brought his pedigree along, and what a really beautiful job he had done. Pedigree charts, photostats of all sorts of records, a running history typed very neatly on bond paper and inserted in a loose-leaf notebook—all in all, the kind of careful, planned, well-thought-out perfection so unsuccessfully striven for by all amateur genealogists.

From Mr. Fowlkes, I got the missing information on Euphemia Barber. She was born in 1765, in Salem, Massachusetts, the fourth child of seven born to John and Alicia Stover. She married Jason Barber in Savannah in 1791. Jason, a well-to-do merchant, passed on in 1794, shortly after the birth of their first child, Abner. Abner was brought up by his paternal grandparents, and Euphemia moved away from Savannah. As I already knew, she had gone to Virginia, where she had married John Anderson. After that, Mr. Fowlkes had no record of her, until her death in Cincinnati, Ohio, in 1852. She was buried as Euphemia Stover Barber, apparently not having used the Anderson name after John Anderson's death.

This done, we went on to compare family histories and discover an Alan

Marshall of Liverpool, England, around 1680, common to both trees. I was able to give Mr. Fowlkes Alan Marshall's birth date. And then the specific purpose of our meeting was finished. I offered tea and cakes, it then being four-thirty in the afternoon, and Mr. Fowlkes graciously accepted.

Before leaving, Mr. Fowlkes asked me to accompany him to a concert on Friday evening, and I very readily agreed. And so began the strangest three months of my entire life.

It didn't take me long to realize that I was being courted. Actually, I couldn't believe it at first. Aftr all, at *my* age! But I myself did know some very nice couples who had married late in life—a widow and a widower, both lonely, sharing interests, and deciding to lighten their remaining years together—and looked at in that light it wasn't at all as ridiculous as it might appear at first.

Actually, I had expected my son Tom to laugh at the idea, and to dislike Mr. Fowlkes instantly upon meeting him. I suppose various fictional works that I have read had given me this expectation. So I was most pleasantly surprised when Tom and Mr. Fowlkes got along famously together from their very first meeting, and even more surprised when Tom came to me and told me Mr. Fowlkes had asked him if he would have any objection to his, Mr. Fowlkes', asking for my hand in matrimony. Tom said he had no objection at all, but actually thought it a wonderful idea, for he knew that both Mr. Fowlkes and myself were rather lonely, with nothing but our genealogical hobbies to occupy our minds.

As to Mr. Fowlkes' background, he very early gave me his entire history. He came from a fairly well-to-do family in upstate New York, and was himself now retired from his business, which had been a stock brokerage in Albany. He was a widower these last six years, and his first marriage had not been blessed with any children, so that he was completely alone in the world.

The next three months were certainly active ones. Mr. Fowlkes—Gerald— squired me everywhere, to concerts and to museums and even, after we had come to know one another well enough, to the theater. He was at all times most polite and thoughtful, and there was scarcely a day went by but what we were together.

During this entire time, of course, my own genealogical researches came to an absolute standstill. I was much too busy, and my mind was much too full of Gerald, for me to concern myself with family members who were long since gone to their rewards. Promising leads from the *Genealogical Exchange* were not followed up, for I didn't write a single letter. And though I did receive many in the *Exchange*, they all went unopened into a cubbyhole in my desk. And so the matter stayed, while the courtship progressed.

After three months Gerald at last proposed. "I am not a young man, Henrietta," he said. "Nor a particularly handsome man"—though he most certainly was very handsome, indeed—"nor even a very rich man, although I do have sufficient for my declining years. And I have little to offer you, Henrietta, save my own self, whatever poor companionship I can give you, and the assurance that I will be ever at your side."

What a beautiful proposal! After being nine years a widow, and never expecting even in fanciful daydreams to be once more a wife, what a beautiful proposal and from what a charming gentleman!

I agreed at once, of course, and telephoned Tom, the good news that very minute. Tom and his wife, Estelle, had a dinner party for us, and then we made our plans. We would be married three weeks hence. A short time? Yes, of course, it was, but there was really no reason to wait. And we would honeymoon in Washington, D.C., where my oldest boy, Roger, has quite a responsible position with the State Department. After which, we would return to Boston and take up our residence in a lovely old home on Beacon Hill, which was then for sale and which we would jointly purchase.

Ah, the plans! The preparations! How newly filled were my so recently empty days!

I spent most of the the last week closing my apartment on Newbury Street. The furnishings would be moved to our new home by Tom, while Gerald and I were in Washington. But, of course, there was ever so much packing to be done, and I got at it with a will.

And so at last I came to my desk, and my genealogical researches lying as I had left them. I sat down at the desk, somewhat weary, for it was late afternoon and I had been hard at work since sunup, and I decided to spend a short while getting my papers into order before packing them away. And so I opened the mail which had accumulated over the last three months.

There were twenty-three letters. Twelve asked for information on various family names mentioned in my entry in the *Exchange*, five offered to give me information, and six concerned Euphemia Barber. It was, after all, Euphemia Barber who had brought Gerald and me together in the first place, and so I took time out to read these letters.

And so came the shock. I read the six letters, and then I simply sat limp at the desk, staring into space, and watched the monstrous pattern as it grew in my mind. For there was no question of the truth, no question at all.

Consider: Before starting the letters, this is what I knew of Euphemia Barber: She had been born Euphemia Stover in Salem, Massachusetts, in 1765. In 1791 she married Jason Barber, a widower of Savannah, Georgia. Jason died two years later, in 1793, of a stomach upset. Three years later Euphemia appeared in Virginia and married John Anderson, also a widower. John Anderson died two years thereafter, in 1798, of stomach upset. In both cases Euphemia sold her late husband's property and moved on.

And here is what the letters added to that, in chronological order:

From Mrs. Winnie Mae Cuthbert, Dallas, Texas: Euphemia Barber, in 1800, two years after John Anderson's death, appeared in Harrisburg, Pennsylvania, and married one Andrew Cuthbert, a widower and a prosperous feed merchant. Andrew died in 1801, of a stomach upset. The widow sold his store, and moved on.

From Miss Ethel Sutton, Lousiville, Kentucky: Euphemia Barber, in 1804, married Samuel Nicholson of Louisville, a widower and a well-to-do tobacco farmer. Samuel Nicholson passed on in 1807, of a stomach upset. The widow sold his farm and moved on.

From Mrs. Isabelle Padgett, Concord, California: In 1808 Euphemia Barber married Thomas Norton, then Mayor of Dover, New Jersey, and a widower. In 1809 Thomas Norton died of a stomach upset.

From Mrs. Luella Miller, Bicknell, Utah: Euphemia Barber married Jonas Miller, a wealthy shipowner of Portsmouth, New Hampshire, a widower, in 1811. The same year Jonas Miller died of a stomach upset. The widow sold his property, and moved on.

From Mrs. Lola Hopkins, Vancouver, Washington: In 1813, in southern Indiana, Euphemia Barber married Edward Hopkins, a widower and a farmer. Edward Hopkins died in 1816 of a stomach upset. The widow sold the farm, and moved on.

From Mr. Roy Cumbie, Kansas City, Missouri: In 1819 Euphemia Barber married Stanley Thatcher of Kansas City, Missouri, a river barge owner and a widower. Stanley Thatcher died, of a stomach upset, in 1821. The widow sold his property, and moved on.

The evidence was clear, and complete. The intervals of time without dates could mean that there had been other widowers who had succumbed to Euphemia Barber's fatal charms, and whose descendants did not number among themselves an amateur genealogist. Who could tell just how many husbands Euphemia had murdered? For murder it quite clearly was, brutal murder, for profit. I had evidence of eight murders, and who knew but what there were eight more, or eighteen more? Who could tell, at this late date, just how many times Euphemia Barber had murdered for profit, and had never been caught?

Such a woman is inconceivable. Her husbands were always widowers, sure to be lonely, sure to be susceptible to a wily woman. She preyed on widowers, and left them all, a widow.

Gerald.

The thought came to me, and I pushed it firmly away. It couldn't possibly be true; it couldn't possibly have a single grain of truth.

But what did I know of Gerald Fowlkes, other than what he had told me? And wasn't I a widow, lonely and susceptible? And wasn't I financially well off?

Like father, like son, they say. Could it be also, like great-great-great-great-great-grandmother, like great-great-great-great-great-grandson?

What a thought! It came to me that there must be any number of widows in the country, like myself, who were interested in tracing their family trees. Women who had a bit of money and leisure, whose children were grown and gone out into the world to live their own lives, and who filled some of the empty hours with the hobby of genealogy. An unscrupulous man, preying on well-to-do widows, could find no better introduction than a common interest in genealogy.

What a terrible thought to have about Gerald! And yet I couldn't push it from my mind, and at last I decided that the only thing I could possibly do was try to substantiate the autobiography he had given me, for if he had told the truth about himself, then he could surely not be a beast of the type I was imagining.

A stockbroker, he had claimed to have been, in Albany, New York. I at once telephoned an old friend of my first husband's, who was himself a Boston stockbroker, and asked him if it would be possible for him to find out if there had been, at any time in the last fifteen or twenty years, an Albany stockbroker named Gerald Fowlkes. He said he could do so with ease, using some sort of directory he had, and would call me back. He did so, with the shattering news that no such individual was listed!

Still I refused to believe. Donning my coat and hat, I left the apartment at once and went directly to the telephone company, where, after an incredible number of white lies concerning genealogical research, I at last persuaded someone to search for an old Albany, New York, telephone book. I knew that the main office of the company kept books for other major cities, as a convenience for the public, but I wasn't sure they would have any from past years. Nor was the clerk I talked to, but at last she did go and search, and came back finally with the 1946 telephone book from Albany, dusty and somewhat ripped, but still intact, with both the normal listings and the yellow pages.

No Gerald Fowlkes was listed in the white pages, or in the yellow pages under Stocks & Bonds.

So. It was true. And I could see exactly what Gerald's method was. Whenever he was ready to find another victim, he searched one or another of the genealogical magazines until he found someone who shared one of his own past relations. He then proceeded to effect a meeting with that person, found out quickly enough whether or not the intended victim was a widow, of the proper age range, and with the properly large bank account, and then the courtship began.

I imagined that this was the first time he had made the mistake of using Euphemia Barber as the go-between. And I doubted that he even realized he was following in Euphemia's footsteps. Certainly, none of the six people who had written to me about Euphemia could possibly guess, knowing only of the one marriage and death, what Euphemia's role in life had actually been.

And what was I to do now? In the taxi, on the way back to my apartment, I sat huddled in a corner, and tried to think.

For this *was* a severe shock, and a terrible disappointment. And how could I face Tom, or my other children, or any of my friends, to whom I had already written the glad news of my impending marriage? And how could I return to the drabness of my days before Gerald had come to bring me gaiety and companionship and courtly grace?

Could I even call the police? I was sufficiently convinced myself, but could I possibly convince anyone else?

All at once, I made my decision. And, having made it, I immediately felt ten years younger, ten pounds lighter, and quite a bit less foolish. For, I might as well admit, in addition to everything else, this had been a terrible blow to my pride.

But the decision was made, and I returned to my apartment cheerful and happy.

And so we were married.

Married? Of course. Why not?

Because he will try to murder me? Well, of course, he *will* try to murder me. As a matter of fact, he has already tried, half a dozen times.

But Gerald is working at a terrible disadvantage. For he cannot murder me in any way that looks like murder. It must appear to be a natural death, or, at the very worst, an accident. Which means that he must be devious, and he must plot and plan, and never come at me openly to do me in.

And there is the source of his disadvantage. For I am forewarned, and forewarned is forearmed.

But what, really, do I have to lose? At seventy-three, how many days on this earth do I have left? And how *rich* life is these days! How rich compared to my life before Gerald came into it! Spiced with the thrill of danger, the excitement of cat and mouse, the intricate moves and countermoves of the most fascinating game of all.

And, of course, a pleasant and charming husband. Gerald *has* to be pleasant and charming. He can never disagree with me, at least not very forcefully, for he can't afford the danger of my leaving him. Nor can he afford to believe that I suspect him. I have never spoken of the matter to him, and so far as he is concerned I know nothing. We go to concerts and museums and the theater together. Gerald is attentive and gentlemanly, quite the best sort of companion at all times.

Of course, I can't allow him to feed me breakfast in bed, as he would so love to do. No, I told him, I was an old-fashioned woman, and believed that cooking was a woman's job, and so I won't let him near the kitchen. Poor Gerald!

And we don't take trips, no matter how much he suggests them.

And we've closed off the second story of our home, since I pointed out that the first floor was certainly spacious enough for just the two of us, and I felt I was getting a little old for climbing stairs. He could do nothing, of course, but agree.

And, in the meantime, I have found another hobby, though of course Gerald knows nothing of it. Through discreet inquiries, and careful perusal of past issues of the various genealogical magazines, and the use of the family names in Gerald's family tree, I am gradually compiling another sort of tree. Not a family tree, no.

One might facetiously call it a hanging tree. It is a list of Gerald's wives. It is in with my genealogical files, which I have willed to the Boston library. Should Gerald manage to catch me after all, what a surprise is in store for the librarian who sorts out those files of mine! Not as big a surprise as the one in store for Gerald, of course.

Ah, here comes Gerald now, in the automobile he bought last week. He's going to ask me again to go for a ride with him.

But I shan't go.

Ruth Rendell

DEATH NOTES

Ruth Rendell (1930–   ) is the sort of writer mystery fans appreciate: She writes well, but she also writes a lot (twenty-seven books in twenty years). Her first novel, published in 1964, was From Doon With Death and featured a detective named Chief Inspector Wexford from Kingsmarkham, a smallish place not all that far from London. A year later she published To Fear a Painted Devil, a mysterious psychological novel, but not a detective story. During her career Ruth Rendell has balanced these two different lines, her Wexford adventures and her dark, often Freudian tales of convoluted family life. It is safe to say that between them she has cultivated two distinct groups of readers, each of which, so far, has remained somewhat skeptical of the other.

Unlike many creators of detective series, Rendell has not "frozen" Wexford and his fellow residents of Kingsmarkham at some never-advancing age. Wexford grows older; the career of his actress daughter has its ups and downs; new men join the force; marriages fall apart; there are weddings, funerals, baptisms (the liturgy of the Anglican church fascinates Rendell, and quotations from The Book of Common Prayer often have more to do with a case than one might expect). With each new book basic lore on the life, times, and social history of Kingsmarkham grows until now the town itself is a leading component of the series.

It is a Sussex market town with about twelve thousand inhabitants and a raincoat factory. The downtown area has felt the heavy hand of urban renewal, but there are still picturesque back streets and at least one old coaching inn. Set in "agricultural country with neither seaside nor downs, castles nor cathedrals," the best the standard guidebooks can say about the place is that Kingsmarkham is only a short drive from Forby, which bears the official distinction of being "the fifth most beautiful village in England."

Over the course of the dozen Wexford novels (Death Notes, the eleventh, was published in 1981), the town has changed. Cracks have begun to develop in the walls of the "new" police station. The Carousel Café, where Wexford used to buy his morning coffee, has become the Pearl of Africa, serving authentic—or so it claims—Ugandan cuisine. But there is a difference between Kingsmarkham time and Greenwich Mean Time. Six years in Kingsmarkham equal twenty years in the "real" world, which means all of us are aging about three times as fast as Wexford.

Death Notes

Part One

1

AGAINST THE ANGELS and apostles in the windows the snow fluttered like plucked down. A big soft flake struck one of the Pre-Raphaelite halos and clung there, cotton wool on gold tinsel. It was something for an apathetic congregation to watch from the not much warmer interior as the rector of St. Peter's, Kingsmarkham, came to the end of the second lesson. St. Matthew, chapter fifteen, for 27 January.

"For out of the heart proceed evil thoughts, murders, adulteries, fornications, thefts, false witness, blasphemies. These are the things which defile a man . . ."

Two of his listeners turned their eyes from the pattern the snow was making on a red and blue and yellow and purple "Annunciation" and waited expectantly. The rector closed the heavy Bible with its dangling marker and opened an altogether more mundane-looking, small black book of the exercise variety. He cleared his throat.

"I publish the banns of marriage between Sheila Katherine Wexford, spinster, of this parish, and Andrew Paul Thorverton, bachelor, of the parish of St. John, Hampstead. This is the first time of asking. And between Manuel Camargue, widower, of this parish, and Dinah Baxter Sternhold, widow, of the parish of St. Mary, Forby. This is the third time of asking. If any of you know cause or just impediment why these persons should not be joined together in holy matrimony, ye are to declare it."

He closed the book. Manuel Camargue resigned himself, for the third week in succession, to the sermon. As the congregation settled itself, he looked about him. The same crowd of old faithfuls came each week. He saw only one newcomer, a beautiful fair-haired girl whom he instantly recognized without being able to put a name to her. He worried about this a good deal for the next half-hour, trying to place her, annoyed with himself because his memory had become so hopeless and glasses no longer did much for his eyes.

The name came to him just as everyone was getting up to leave. Sheila Wexford. Sheila Wexford, the actress. That was who it was. He and Dinah had seen her last autumn in that Somerset Maugham revival, though what the name of the play had been escaped him. She had been at school with Dinah, they still knew each other slightly. Her banns had been called before his but her name hadn't registered because of that insertion of Katherine. It was odd that two people as famous as they should have had their banns called simultaneously in this country parish church.

He looked at her again. She was dressed in a coat of sleek pale fur over a black wool dress. Her eye caught his and he saw that she also recognized him. She gave him a quick faint smile, a smile that was conspiratorial, rueful, gay, ever so slightly embarrassed, all those things expressed as only an actress of her calibre could express them. Camargue countered with a smile of his own, the best he could do.

It was still snowing. Sheila Wexford put an umbrella up and made an elegant dash towards the lychgate. Should he offer her a lift to wherever she lived? Camargue decided that his legs were inadequate to running after her, especially through six-inch-deep snow. When he reached the gate he saw her getting into a car driven by a man at least old enough to be her father. He felt a pang for her. Was this the bridegroom? And then the absurdity of such a thought, coming from him, struck him forcefully and with a sense which he often had of the folly of human beings and their blindness to their own selves.

Ted was waiting in the Mercedes. Reading the *News of the World*, hands in woolen gloves. He had the engine running to work the heater and the wipers and the demisters. When he saw Camargue he jumped out and opened the rear door.

"There you are, Sir Manuel. I put a rug in seeing it's got so perishing."

"What a kind chap you are," said Camargue. "It was jolly cold in church. Let's hope it'll warm up for the wedding."

Ted said he hoped so but the long-range weather forecast was as gloomy as per usual. If he hadn't held his employer in such honor and respect he would have said he'd have his love to keep him warm. Camargue knew this and smiled to himself. He pulled the rug over his knees. Dinah, he thought, my Dinah. Towards her he felt a desire as passionate, as youthful, as intense, as any he had known as a boy. But he would never touch her, he knew better than that, and his mouth curled with distaste at the idea of it, of him and her together. It would be enough for him that she should be his dear companion—for a little while.

They had entered the gates and were mounting the long curving drive that led up to the house. Ted drove in the two channels, now filling once more with snow, which he had dug out that morning. From the smooth, pure and radiant whiteness, flung like a soft and spotless cloth over the hillocks and little valleys of Camargue's garden, rose denuded silver birches, poplars and willows, and the spikes of conifers, dark green and slate-blue and golden-yellow, as snugly clothed as gnomes.

The jam factory came into view quite suddenly. Camargue called it the jam factory, or sometimes the shoebox, because it was unlike any of the houses around. Not mock or real Tudor, not fake or genuine Georgian, but a long box with lots of glass, and at one end, dividing the original building from the newer wing, a tower with a peaked roof like an oast house. Perched on the weathervane, a facsimile of a treble clef in wrought iron, was a seagull, driven inland in its quest for food. It looked as white as the snow itself against the cinder-dark sky.

Ted's wife, Muriel, opened the front door. You entered the house at the lower level, where it was built into the hillside. There was a wide hall here which led through an arch into the dining room.

"It's so cold, sir," said Muriel, "that I'm cooking you a proper lunch since you said you wouldn't be going to Mrs. Sternhold's."

"Jolly thoughtful of you," said Camargue, who no longer much cared what he ate. Muriel took his coat away to dry it. She and Ted lived in a house in the grounds, a period piece and as much unlike the jam factory as could be. Camargue liked her to have her afternoons off and all of her Sundays, but he couldn't be always checking her generous impulses. When he was half-way up the stairs the dog Nancy came down to meet him, wide smiling mouth and eager pink tongue and young strong paws capable of sending him flying. She was his fifth Alsatian, a rich roan color, just two years old.

The drawing room, two of its walls entirely glass, shone with the curious light that is uniquely reflected off snow. The phone began to ring as he stepped off the top stair.

"Were they well and truly called?"

"Yes, darling, the third time of asking. And at St. Peter's?"

"Yes. My word, it was cold, Dinah. Is it snowing in Forby?"

"Well, it is but not all that heavily. Won't you change your mind and come? The main roads are all right and you know Ted won't mind. I do wish you'd come."

"No. You'll have your parents. They've met me. Let them get over the shock a bit before Saturday." Camargue laughed at her exclamation of protest. "No, my dear, I won't come today. Muriel's cooking lunch for me. Just think, after Saturday you'll have to have all your meals with me, no excuses allowed."

"Manuel, shall I come over this evening?"

He laughed. "No, please." It was strange how his accent became more marked when he talked to her. Must be emotion, he supposed. "The villages will be cut off from Kingsmarkham by tonight, mark my words."

He went into the music room, the dog following him. Up inside the cone-shaped roof of the tower it was dark like twilight. He looked at the flute, which lay in its open case on the table, and then reflectively, no longer with pain, at his clawed hands. The flute had been exposed like that to show to Dinah's mother and Muriel would have been too much in awe of it to put it away. Camargue closed the lid of the case and sat down at the piano. He had never been much of a pianist, a second-class concert average, so it brought him no frustration or sadness to strum away occasionally with those (as he called them) silly old hands of his. He played *Für Elise* while Nancy, who adored piano music, thumped her tail on the marble floor.

Muriel called him to lunch. He went downstairs for it. She liked to lay the big mahogany table with lace and silver and glass just for him, and to wait on him. Far more than he had ever been or could ever be, she was aware of what was due to Sir Manuel Camargue. Ted came in as he was having coffee and said he would take Nancy out now, a good long hike in the snow, he said, she loved snow. And he'd break the ice at the edge of the lake. Hearing the chain on her lead rattle, Nancy nearly fell downstairs in her haste to be out.

Camargue sometimes tried to stop himself sleeping the afternoons away. He was rarely successful. He had a suite of rooms in the wing beyond the tower; bedroom, bathroom, small sitting room where Nancy's basket was, and he would sit determinedly in his armchair, reading or playing records—he was mad about James Galway at the moment. Galway, he thought, was heaps better than he had ever been—but he would always nod off. Often he slept till five or six. He put on the Flute Concerto, Köchel 313, and as the sweet, bright, liquid notes poured out, looked at himself in the long glass. He was still, at any rate, tall. He was thin. Thin like a ramshackle scarecrow, he thought, like an old junk-shop skeleton, with hands that looked as if every joint had been broken and put together again awry. *Tout casse, tout lasse, tout passe.* Now that he was so old he often thought in one or other of the two languages of his infancy. He sat down in the armchair and listened to the music Mozart wrote for a cantankerous Dutchman, and by the time the second movement had begun he was asleep.

Nancy woke him, laying her head in his lap. She had been back from her walk a long time, it was nearly five. Ted wouldn't come back to take her out again. Camargue would let her out himself and perhaps walk with her as far as the lake. It had stopped snowing, and the last of the daylight, a curious shade of yellow, gilded the whiteness and threw long blue shadows. Camargue took James Galway off the turntable and put him back in the sleeve. He walked along the passage and through the music room, pausing to straighten a crooked picture, a photograph of the building which housed the Camargue School of Music at Wellridge, and passed on into the drawing room. As he approached the tea tray Muriel had left for him, the phone rang. Dinah again.

"I phoned before, darling. Were you asleep?"

"What else?"

"I'll come over in the morning, shall I, and bring the rest of the presents? Mother and Dad have brought us silver pastry forks from my uncle, my godfather."

"I must say, people are jolly generous, the second time round for both of us. I'll have the drive specially cleared for you. Ted shall be up to do it by the crack of dawn."

"Poor Ted." He was sensitive to the slight change in her tone and he braced himself. "Manuel, you haven't heard any more from—Natalie?"

"From that woman," said Camargue evenly, "no."

"I shall have another go at you in the morning, you know, to make you see reason. You're quite wrong about her, I'm sure you are. And to take a step like changing your will without . . ."

His accent was strong as he interrupted her. "I saw her, Dinah, not you, and I know. Let's not speak of it again, eh?"

She said simply, "Whatever you wish. I only want what's best for you."

"I know that," he said. He talked to her a little longer and then he went downstairs to make his tea. The tranquillity of the day had been marred by Dinah's raising the subject of Natalie. It forced him to think of that business again when he had begun to shut it out.

He carried the teapot upstairs and lifted the folded napkin from the plate of cucumber sandwiches. That woman, whoever she was, had made the tea and brought the pot up, and it was after that that she had looked at Cazzini's golden gift on the wall and he had known. As is true of all honest and guileless people, Camargue resented attempts to practice deceit on him far more than do those who are themselves deceitful. It had been a hateful affront, and all the worse because it had taken advantage of an old man's weakness and a father's affection. Dinah's plea did not at all alter his feelings. It only made him think he should have told the police or his solicitors, after all. But no. He had told the woman that he had seen through her and he had told her what he meant to do, and now he must do his best to forget it. Dinah was what future he had, Dinah would be his daughter and more than daughter.

He sat by the window with the curtains undrawn, watching the snow turn blue, then glow dully white again as the darkness closed in. The moon was coming up, a full, cold, midwinter's moon, a glowing greenish-white orb. At seven he took the tea things down and fed Nancy a large can of dog meat.

By the light of the moon he could see the lake quite clearly from the drawing-room window. To call it a lake was to flatter it, it was just a big pond really. It lay on the other side of the drive, down a shallow slope and ringed with willow trees and hawthorn bushes. Camargue could see that Ted, as good as his word, had been down to the pond that afternoon and broken the ice for air to get in to the fish. There were carp in the pond, some of them very large and very old. Ted's footprints led down to the water's edge and back up again to the drive. He had cast the ice on to the bank in great gray blocks. The moon showed it all up as well as any arc lamp. Nancy's pawprints were everywhere, and in places in the drifts there were signs of where she had plunged and rolled. He stroked her smooth brown head, drawing her against him, gently pushing her to settle down and sleep at his feet. The moon sailed in a black and shining sky from which all the heavy cloud had gone. He opened his book, the biography of an obscure Romanian composer who had once written an étude especially for him, and read for an hour or so.

When it got to half-past eight he could feel himself nodding off again, so he got up and stretched and stood in the window. To his surprise he saw it was snowing once more, snow falling out of the wrack which was drifting slowly over the clear sky and towards where the moon was. The conifers were powdered again, all but one. Then he saw the tree move. He had often thought that by night and in the half-light and through his failing eyes those trees looked like men. Now he had actually mistaken a man for a tree. Or a woman for a tree. He couldn't tell whether it had been Ted or Muriel that he had seen, a trousered figure in a heavy coat moving up now where the path must be towards the birch copse. It must have been one of them. Camargue decided to postpone letting Nancy out for ten minutes. If Ted saw him he would take over and fuss and probably insist on giving the dog a proper walk, which she didn't need after all the exercise she had had. If Muriel saw him she would very likely want to come in and make him cocoa.

The figure in the garden had disappeared. Now the moon was no longer so bright. He couldn't remember that he had ever before seen such snow in all the years he had lived in Sussex. In his youth, in the Pyrenees, the snows had come like this with an even more bitter cold. It was remembering those days that had made him plant in this garden all the little fir trees and yews and junipers . . .

He could have sworn he saw another tree move. How grotesque was old age when the faculties one took for granted like trusted friends began to play on one malicious practical jokes. He called out:

"Nancy! Time to go out."

She was there at the head of the stairs long before he was. If he had gone first she would have knocked him over. He walked down behind her, propelling her with his toe when she looked anxiously back and up at him. At the foot of the stairs he switched on the outside light to illuminate the wide court into which the drive led. The snowflakes danced like sparks in the yellow light but when he opened the door the sharp cold of the night rushed in to meet him. Nancy bounded out into the whirling snow. Camargue took his sheepskin coat and gloves and a walking-stick from the cloaks cupboard and followed her out.

She was nowhere to be seen, though her paws had ploughed a path down the slope towards the lake. He fastened his coat and pulled the woolen scarf up around his throat. Nancy, though well aware this outing was no regular walk but merely for the purpose of stimulating and answering a call of nature, nevertheless would sometimes go off. If the weather conditions were right, damp and muggy, for instance, or like this, she had been known to go off for half an hour. It would be a nuisance were she to do that tonight when he felt so tired that even on his feet, even with this icy air stinging his face, he could feel drowsiness closing in on him.

"Nancy! Nancy, where are you?"

He could easily go back into the house and phone Ted and ask him to come over and await the dog's return. Ted wouldn't mind. On the other hand, wasn't that yielding to the very helplessness he was always striving against? What business had he to be getting married, to be setting up house again, even recommencing a social life, if he couldn't do such a little thing for himself as letting a dog out before he went to bed? What he would do was return to the house and sit in the chair in the hall and wait for Nancy to come back. If he fell asleep her scraping at the front door would awaken him.

Even as he decided this he did the very opposite. He followed the track she had made down the slope to the lake, calling her, irritably now, as he went.

The marks Ted had made when he broke the ice at the water's edge were already obliterated by snow, while Nancy's fresh tracks were fast becoming covered. Only the stacked ice showed where Ted had been. The area he had cleared was again iced over with a thin gray crust. The lake was a somber sheet of ice with a faint sheen on it that the clouded moon made, and the willows, which by daylight looked like so many crouched spiders or daddy-long-legs, were laden with snow that clung to them and changed their shape. Camargue called the dog again. Only last week she had done this to him and then had suddenly appeared out of nowhere and come skittering across the ice towards him.

He began breaking the new ice with his stick. Then he heard the dog behind him, a faint crunching on the snow. But when he turned round, ready to seize her collar in the hook of the walking-stick, there was no dog there, there was nothing there but the gnome conifers and the light shining down on the white sheet of the circular courtyard. He would break up the rest of the thin ice, clear an area a yard long and a foot wide as Ted had done, and then he would go back into the house and wait for Nancy indoors.

Again the foot crunched behind him, the tree walked. He stood up and turned and, raising his stick as if to defend himself, looked into the face of the tree that moved.

2

The music met Chief Inspector Wexford as he let himself into his house. A flute playing with an orchestra. This was one of Sheila's dramatic gestures, he supposed, contrived to time with his homecoming. It was beautiful music, slow, measured, secular, yet with a religious sound.

His wife was knitting, on her face the amused, dry, very slightly exasperated expression it often wore while Sheila was around. And Sheila would be very much around for the next three weeks, having unaccountably decided to be married from home, in her own parish church, and to establish the proper period of residence beforehand in her father's house. She sat on the floor, between the log fire and the record player, her cheek resting on one round white arm that trailed with grace upon a sofa cushion, her pale gold water-straight hair half covering her face. When she lifted her head and shook her hair back he saw that she had been crying.

"Oh, Pop, darling, isn't it sad? They've had this tremendous obituary program for him on the box. Even Mother shed a tear. And then we thought we'd mourn him with his own music."

Wexford doubted very much if Dora, a placid and eminently sensible woman, had expressed these extravagant sentiments. He picked up the record sleeve. Mozart, Concerto for Flute and Harp, K 229; the English Chamber Orchestra, conductor, Raymond Leppard; flute, Manuel Camargue; harp, Marisa Roblès.

"We actually heard him once," said Dora. "Do you remember? At the Wigmore Hall it was, all of thirty years ago."

"Yes."

But he could scarcely remember. The pictured face on the sleeve, too sensitive, too mobile to be handsome, the eyes alight with a kind of joyous humor, evoked no image from the past. The movement came to an end and now the music became bright, liquid, a singable tune, and Camargue, who was dead, alive again in his flute. Sheila wiped her eyes and got up to kiss her father. It was all of eight years since he and she had lived under the same roof. She had become a swan since then, a famous lady, a tele-face. But she still kissed him when he came and went, putting her arms around his neck like a nervous child. Wryly, he liked it.

He sat down, listening to the last movement while Dora finished her row in the Fair Isle and went to get his supper. Andrew's regular evening phone call prevented Sheila from getting full dramatic value out of her memorial to Camargue, and by the time she came back into the room the record was over and her father was eating his steak-and-kidney pie.

"You didn't actually know him, did you, Sheila?"

She thought he was reproaching her for her tears. "I'm sorry, Pop, I cry so easily. It's a matter of having to learn how, you know, and then not being able to unlearn."

He grinned at her. "Thus on the fatal bank of Nile weeps the deceitful crocodile? I didn't mean that, anyway. Let me put it more directly. Did you know him personally?"

She shook her head. "I think he recognized me in church. He must have known I come from round here." It was nothing that she should be recognized. She was recognized wherever she went. For five years the serial in which she played the most beautiful of the air hostesses had been on television twice a week at a peak-viewing time. Everybody watched *Runway*, even though a good many said shamefacedly that they "only saw the tail-end before the news" or "the kids have it on." Stewardess Curtis was famous for her smile. Sheila smiled it now, her head tilted reflectively. "I know his wife-that-was-to-be personally," she said. "Or I used to. We were at school together."

"A young girl?"

"Thank you kindly, father dear. Let's say young to be marrying Sir Manuel. Mid-twenties. She brought him to see me in *The Letter* last autumn but I didn't talk to them; he was too tired to come round afterwards."

It was Dora who brought them back from gossip to grandeur. "In his day he was said to be the world's greatest flautist. I remember when he founded that school at Wellridge and Princess Margaret came down to open it."

"D'you know what its pupils call it? Windyridge." Sheila mimed the blowing of a woodwind, fingers dancing. Then, suddenly, the tears had started once more to her eyes. "Oh, to die like that!"

Who's Who is not a volume to be found in many private houses. Wexford had a copy because Sheila was in it. He took it down from the shelf, turned to the C's and read aloud:

"Camargue, Sir Manuel, Knight. Companion of Honor, Order of the British Empire, Chevalier of the Legion of Honor. British fluteplayer. Born Pamplona, Spain, 3 June, 1902, son of Aristide Camargue and Ana Parral. Educated privately with father, then at Barcelona Conservatoire. Studied under Louis Fleury.

"Professor of Flute, Madrid Conservatoire, 1924 to 1932. Fought on Republican side Spanish Civil War, escaped to England 1938. Married 1942 Kathleen Lister. One daughter. Naturalized British subject 1946. Concert flautist, has toured Europe, America, Australia, New Zealand and South Africa. Founded 1964 at Wellridge, Sussex, the Kathleen Camargue School of Music in memory of his wife, and in 1968 the Kathleen Camargue Youth Orchestra. Recreations apart from music: walking, reading, dogs. Address: Sterries, Ploughman's Lane, Kingsmarkham, Sussex."

"They say it's a dream of a house," said Sheila. "I wonder if she'll sell, that one daughter? Because if she does Andrew and I might really consider . . . Wouldn't you like me living just up the road, Pop?"

"He may have left it to your friend," said Wexford.

"So he may. Well, I do hope so. Poor Dinah, losing her first husband that she *adored* and then her second that never was. She deserves some compensation. I shall write her a letter of sympathy. No, I won't. I'll go and see her. I'll phone her first thing in the morning and I'll . . . ."

"I'd leave it a day or two if I were you," said her father. "First thing in the morning is going to be the inquest."

"*Inquest?*" Sheila uttered the word in the loaded, aghast tone of Lady Bracknell. "Inquest? But surely he died a perfectly natural death?"

Dora, conjuring intricately with three different shades of wool, looked up from her pattern. "Of course he didn't. Drowning, or whatever happened to him, freezing to death, you can't call that natural."

"I mean, he didn't do it on purpose and no one did it to him."

It was impossible for Wexford to keep from laughing at these ingenuous definitions of suicide and homicide. "In most cases of sudden death," he said, "and in all cases of violent death there must be an inquest. It goes without saying the verdict is going to be that it was an accident."

.   .   .

Misadventure.

This verdict, which can sound so grotesque when applied to the death of a baby in a cot or a patient under anesthetic, appropriately described Camargue's fate. An old man, ankle-deep in snow, had lost his foothold in the dark, slipping over, sliding into water to be trapped under a lid of ice. If he had not drowned he would within minutes have been dead from hypothermia. The snow had continued to fall, obliterating his footprints. And the frost, ten degrees of it, had silently sealed up the space into which the body had slipped. Only a glove—it was of thick black leather and it had fallen from his left hand—remained to point to where he lay, one curled finger rising up out of the drifts. Misadventure.

Wexford attended the inquest for no better reason than to keep warm, the police station central heating having unaccountably broken down the night before. The venue of the inquest (Kingsmarkham Magistrates' Court, Court Two, Upstairs) enjoyed a reputation for being kept in winter at a temperature of eighty degrees. To this it lived up. Having left his rubber boots just inside the door downstairs, he sat at the back of the court, basking in warmth, surreptitiously peeling off various disreputable layers, a khaki green plastic mack of muddy translucency, an aged black-and-gray herringbone-tweed overcoat, a stole-sized scarf of matted fawnish wool.

Apart from the *Kingsmarkham Courier* girl in one of the press seats, there were only two women present, and these two sat so far apart as to give the impression of choosing each to ostracize the other. One would be the daughter, he supposed, one the bride. Both were dressed darkly, shabbily and without distinction. But the woman in the front row had the eyes and profile of a Callas, her glossy black hair piled in the fashion of a Floating World geisha, while the other, seated a yard or two from him, was a little mouse, headscarfed, huddled, hands folded. Neither, as far as he could see, bore the remotest resemblance to the face on the record sleeve with its awareness and its spirituality. But when, as the verdict came, the geisha woman turned her head and her eyes, dark and brilliant, for a moment met his, he saw that she was far older than Sheila, perhaps ten years older. This, then, must be the daughter. And as the conviction came to him, the coroner turned his gaze upon her and said he would like to express his sympathy with Sir Manuel's daughter in her loss and a grief which was no less a personal one because it was shared by the tens of thousands who had loved, admired and been inspired by his music. He did not think he would be exceeding his duty were he to quote Samuel Johnson and say that it matters not how a man dies but how he has lived.

Presumably no one had told him of the dead man's intended remarriage. The little mouse got up and crept away. Now it was all over, the beauty with the black eyes got up too—to be enclosed immediately in a circle of men. This of course was chance, Wexford told himself, they were the escort who had brought her, her father's doctor, his servant, a friend or two. Yet he felt inescapably that this woman would always wherever she was be in a circle of men, watched, admired, desired. He got back into his coverings and ventured out into the bitter cold of Kingsmark-ham High Street.

Here the old snow lay heaped at the pavement edges in long, low mountain ranges and the new snow, gritty and sparkling, dusted it with fresh whiteness. A yellowish-leaden sky looked full of snow. It was only a step from the court to the police station, but a long enough step in this weather to get chilled to the bone.

On the forecourt, between a panda car and the chief constable's Rover, the heating engineer's van was still parked. Wexford went tentatively through the swing doors. Inside it was as cold as ever and Sergeant Camb, sitting behind his counter, warmed mittened hands on a mug of steaming tea. Burden, Wexford reflected, if he had any sense would have taken himself off somewhere warm for lunch. Very likely to the Carousel Café, or what used to be the Carousel before it was taken over by Mr. Haq and became the Pearl of Africa.

This was a title or sobriquet given (according to Mr. Haq) to Uganda, his native land. Mr. Haq claimed to serve authentic Ugandan cuisine, what he called "real" Ugandan food, but since no one knew what this was, whether he meant food consumed by the tribes before colonization or food introduced by Asian immigrants or food eaten today by westernized Ugandans, or what these would be anyway, it was difficult to query any dish. Fried potatoes and rice accompanied almost every-thing, but for all Wexford knew this might be a feature of Ugandan cooking. He rather liked the place; it fascinated him, especially the plastic jungle vegetation.

Today this hung and trembled in the steamy heat and seemed to sweat droplets on its leathery leaves. The windows had become opaque, entirely misted over with condensation. It was like a tropical oasis in the Arctic. Inspector Burden sat at a table eating Nubian chicken with rice Ruwenzori, anxiously keeping in view his new sheepskin jacket, a Christmas present from his wife, which Mr. Haq had hung up on the palm tree hatstand. He remarked darkly as Wexford walked in that anyone might make off with it, you never could tell these days.

"Round here they might cook it," said Wexford. He also ordered the chicken with the request that for once potatoes might not come with it. "I've just come from the inquest on Camargue."

"What on earth did you go to that for?"

"I hadn't anything much else on. I reckoned it would be warm too and it was."

"All right for some," Burden grumbled. "I could have found a job for you." Since their friendship had deepened, some of his old deference to his chief, though none of his respect, had departed. "Thieving and break-ins, we've never had so much of it. That kid old Atkinson let out on bail, he's done three more jobs in the meantime. And he's not seventeen yet, a real little villain." Sarcasm made his tone withering. "Or that's what I call him. The psychiatrist says he's a pathological kleptomaniac with personality-scarring caused by traumata broadly classifiable as paranoid." He snorted, was silent, then said on an altered note, "Look, do you think you were wise to do that?"

"Do what?"

"Go to that inquest. People will think . . . I mean, it's possible they might think . . ."

"People will think!" Wexford scoffed. "You sound like a dowager lecturing a debutante. What will they think?"

"I only meant they might think there was something fishy about the death. Some hanky-panky. I mean, they see you there and know who you are and they say to themselves, he wouldn't have been there if it had all been as straightforward as the coroner . . ."

He was saved from an outburst of Wexford's temper by an intervention from outside. Mr. Haq had glided up to beam upon them. He was small, smiling, very black yet very Caucasian, with a mouthful of startlingly white, madly uneven, large teeth.

"Everything to your liking, I hope my dear?" Mr. Haq called all his customers "my dear," irrespective of sex, perhaps supposing it to be a genderless term of extreme respect such as "excellency." "I see you are having the rice Ruwenzori." He bowed a little. "A flavorful and scrumptious recipe from the peoples who live in the Mountains of the Moon." Talking like a television commercial for junk food was habitual with him.

"Very nice, thank you," said Wexford.

"You are welcome, my dear." Mr. Haq smiled so broadly that it seemed some of his teeth must spill out. He moved off among the tables, ducking his head under the polythene fronds which trailed from polyethylene pots in polystyrene plant-holders.

"Are you going to have any pudding?"

"Shouldn't think so," said Wexford, and he read from the menu with gusto, "Cake Kampala or ice cream eau-de-Nil—does he mean the color or what it's made of? Anyway, there's enough ice about without eating it." He hesitated. "Mike, I don't see that it matters what people think in this instance. Camargue met his death by misadventure, there's no doubt about that. Surely, though interest in the man will endure for years, the manner of his death can only be a nine days' wonder. As a matter of fact, the coroner said something like that."

Burden ordered coffee from the small, shiny, damson-eyed boy, heir to Mr. Haq, who waited at their table. "I suppose I was thinking of Hicks."

"The manservant or whoever he was?"

"He found that glove and then he found the body. It wasn't really strange but it might look strange the way he found the dog outside his back door and took her back to Sterries and put her inside without checking to see where Camargue was."

"Hicks's reputation won't suffer from my presence in court," said Wexford. "I doubt if there was a soul there, bar the coroner, who recognized me." He chuckled. "Or if they did it'd only be as Stewardess Curtis's dad."

They went back to the police station. The afternoon wore away into an icy twilight, an evening of hard frost. The heating came on with a pop just as it was time to go home. Entering his living room. Wexford was greeted by a large, bronze-colored Alsatian, baring her teeth and swinging her tail. On the sofa, next to his daughter, sat the girl who had crept away from the inquest, Camargue's pale bride.

3

He had noticed the Volkswagen parked in the ruts of ice outside but had thought little of it. Sheila got up and introduced the visitor.

"Dinah, this is my father. Pop, I'd like you to meet Dinah Sternhold. She was engaged to Sir Manuel, you know."

It was immediately apparent to Wexford that she had not noticed him at the inquest. She held out her small hand and looked at him without a flicker of recognition. The dog had backed against her legs and now sat down heavily on her feet, glaring at Wexford in a sullen way.

"Do forgive me for bringing Nancy." She had a soft low unaffected voice. "But I daren't leave her alone, she howls all the time. My neighbors complained when I had to leave her this morning."

"She was Sir Manuel's dog," Sheila explained.

A master-leaver and a fugitive, Wexford reflected, eyeing the Alsatian who had abandoned Camargue to his fate. Or gone to fetch help? That, of course, was a possible explanation of the curious behavior of the dog in the night.

Dinah Sternhold said, "It's Manuel she howls for, you see. I can only hope she won't take too long to—to forget him. I hope she'll get over it."

Was she speaking of the dog or of herself? His answer could have applied to either. "She will. She's young."

"He often said he wanted me to have her if—if anything happened to him. I think he was afraid of her going to someone who might not be kind to her."

Presumably she meant the daughter. Wexford sought about in his mind for some suitable words of condolence, but finding none that sounded neither mawkish or pompous, he kept quiet. Sheila, anyway, could always be relied on to make conversation. While she was telling some rather inappropriate Alsatian anecdote, he studied Dinah Sternhold. Her little round sallow face was pinched with a kind of bewildered woe. One might almost believe she had loved the old man and not merely been in it for the money. But that was a little too much to swallow, distinguished and reputedly kind and charming as he had been. The facts were that he had been seventy-eight and she was certainly fifty years less than that.

Gold-digger, however, she was not. She appeared to have extorted little in the way of pre-marital largesse out of Camargue. Her brown tweed coat had seen better days, she wore no jewelry but an engagement ring, in which the ruby was small and the diamonds pinheads.

He wondered how long she intended to sit there, her hand grasping the dog's collar, her head bowed as if she were struggling to conquer tears or at least conceal them. But suddenly she jumped up.

"I must go." Her voice became intense, ragged, charged with a sincerity that was almost fierce. "It was so *kind* of you to come to me, Sheila. You don't know how grateful I am."

"No need," Sheila said lightly. "I wanted to come. It was kind of *you* to drive me home. I had a hire car, Pop, because I was scared to drive in the snow but Dinah wasn't a bit scared to bring me back in the snow and the dark."

They saw Dinah Sternhold out to her car. Ice was already forming on the windscreen. She pushed the dog on to the back seat and got to work competently on the windows with a de-icing spray. Wexford was rather surprised that he felt no compunction about letting her drive away, but her confidence seemed absolute, you could trust her somehow to look after herself and perhaps others too. Was it this quality about her that Camargue had needed and had loved? He closed the gate, rubbed his hands. Sheila, shivering, ran back into the house.

"Where's your mother?"

"Round at Syl's. She ought to be back any minute. Isn't Dinah nice? I felt so sorry for her, I went straight over to Forby as soon as the inquest was over. We talked and talked. I think maybe I did her a bit of good."

"Hmm," said Wexford.

The phone started to ring. Andrew, punctual to the minute. "Oh, darling," Wexford heard Sheila say, "do you remember my telling you about someone I know who was going to marry . . ." He began picking Alsatian hairs off the upholstery.

Father and daughter is not the perfect relationship. According to Freud, that distinction belongs to mother and son. But Wexford, looking back, could have said that he had been happy with his daughters and they with him, he had never actually quarreled with either of them, there had never been any sort of breach. And if Sheila was his favorite he hoped this was so close a secret that no one but himself, not even Dora, could know it.

Any father of daughters, even today, must look ahead when they are children and anticipate an outlay of money on their wedding celebrations. Wexford realized this and had begun saving for it out of his detective inspector's salary, but Sylvia had married so young as almost to catch him napping. For Sheila he had been determined to be well prepared, then gradually, with wonder and a kind of dismay, he had watched her rise out of that income bracket and society in which she had grown up, graduate into a sparkling, lavish jet set whose members had wedding receptions in country mansions or else the Dorchester.

For a long time it had looked as if she would not marry at all. Then Andrew Thorverton had appeared, a young businessman, immensely wealthy, it seemed to Wexford, with a house in Hampstead, a cottage in the country somewhere that his future father-in-law suspected was a sizable house, a boat and an amazing car of so esoteric a manufacture that Wexford had never before heard of it. Sheila, made old-fashioned and sentimental by love, announced she would be married from home and, almost in the same breath, that she and Andrew would be paying for the entertainment of two hundred people to luncheon in the banquet room of the Olive and Dove. Yes, she insisted, it must be so and Pop must lump it or else she'd go and get married in a register office and have lunch at the Pearl of Africa.

He was slightly humiliated. Somehow he felt she ought to cut garment according to cloth, and his cloth would cover a buffet table for fifty. That was absurd, of course. Andrew wouldn't even notice the few thousand it would cost, and the bride's father would give her away, make a speech and hang on to his savings. He heard her telling Andrew she would be coming up to spend the weekend with him, and then Dora walked in.

"She won't be supporting her friend at the cremation then?"

Sheila had put the phone down. She was sometimes a little flushed and breathless when she had been talking to Andrew. But it was not now of him that she spoke. "Dinah's not going to it. How could she bear it? Two days after what would have been their wedding day?"

"At least it's not the day itself," said Wexford.

"Frankly, I'm surprised Sir Manuel's daughter didn't fix it on the day itself. She's capable of it. There's going to be a memorial service at St. Peter's on Tuesday and everyone will be there. Solti is coming and probably Menuhin. Dinah says there are sure to be crowds, he was so much loved."

Wexford said, "Does she know if he left her much?"

Sheila delivered her reply slowly and with an actress's perfect timing.

"He has not left her anything. He has not left her a single penny." She sank to the floor, close up by the fire, and stretched out her long legs. "Her engagement ring and that dog, that's all she's got."

"How did that come about? Did you ask her?"

"Oh, Pop darling, of course I did. Wasn't I with her for hours and hours? I got the whole thing out of her."

"You're as insatiably inquisitive as your father!" cried Dora, revolted. "I thought you went to comfort the poor girl. I agree it's not like losing a young fiancé, but just the same . . ."

"Curiosity," quoted Wexford, "is one of the permanent and certain characteristics of a vigorous intellect." He chuckled. "The daughter gets it all, does she?"

"Sir Manuel saw his daughter a week before he died and that was the first time he'd seen her for nineteen years. There'd been a family quarrel. She was at the Royal Academy of Music but she left and went off with an American student. The first Camargue and his wife knew of it was a letter from San Francisco. Mrs. Camargue—he wasn't a Sir then—got ill and died but the daughter didn't come back. She didn't come back at all till last November. Doesn't it seem frightfully unfair that she gets everything?"

"Camargue should have made a new will."

"He was going to as soon as they were married. Marriage invalidates a will. Did you know that, Pop?"

He nodded.

"I can understand divorce would but I can't see why marriage." She turned her legs, toasting them.

"You'll get scorch marks," said Dora. "That won't look very nice on the beach in Bermuda."

Sheila took no notice. "And what's more, he was going to cut the daughter out altogether. Apparently, that one sight of her was enough."

Dora, won uneasily on the side of the gossips, said, "I wish you wouldn't keep calling her the daughter. Doesn't she have a name?"

"Natalie Arno. Mrs. Arno, she's a widow. The American student died some time during those nineteen years. Dinah was awfully reticent about her, but she did say Camargue intended to make a new will, and since he said this just after he'd seen Natalie I put two and two together. And there's another thing, Natalie only got in touch with her father after his engagement to Dinah was announced. The engagement was in the *Telegraph* on 10 December, and on the 12th he got a letter from Natalie telling him she was back and could she come and see him? She wanted a reconciliation. It was obvious she was scared stiff of the marriage and wanted to stop it."

"And your reticent friend told you all this?"

"She got it out of her, Dora. I can understand. She's a chip off the old block, as you so indignantly pointed out." He turned once more to Sheila. "Did she try to stop it?"

"Dinah wouldn't say. I think she hates discussing Natalie. She talked much more about Camargue. She really loved him. In a funny sort of daughterly, worshipping, protective sort of way, but she did love him. She likes to talk about how wonderful he was and how they met and all that. She's a teacher at the Kathleen Camargue School and he came over last Founder's Day and they met and they just loved each other, she said, from that moment."

The somewhat cynical expressions on the two middle-aged faces made her give an embarrassed laugh. She seemed to take her mother's warning to heart at last, for she got up and moved away from the fire to sit on the sofa where she scrutinized her smooth, pale golden legs. "At any rate, Pop darling, it's an ill wind, as you might say, because now the house is bound to be sold. I'd love to get a look at it, wouldn't you? Why wasn't I at school with Natalie?"

"You were born too late," said her father. "And there must be simpler ways of getting into Sterries."

There were.

"You?" said Burden first thing the next morning. "What do *you* want to go up there for? It's only a common-or-garden burglary, one of our everyday occurrences, I'm sorry to say. Martin can handle it."

Wexford hadn't taken his overcoat off. "I want to see the place. Don't you feel any curiosity to see the home of our former most distinguished citizen?"

Burden seemed more concerned with dignity and protocol. "It's beneath you *and* me, I should think." He sniffed. "And when you hear the details you'll feel the same. The facts are that a Mrs. Arno—she's the late Sir Manuel's daughter— phoned up about half an hour ago to say the house had been broken into during the night. There's a pane of glass been cut out of a window downstairs and a bit of a mess made and some silver taken. Cutlery, nothing special, and some money from Mrs. Arno's handbag. She thinks she saw the car the burglar used and she's got the registration number."

"I like these open-and-shut cases," said Wexford. "I find them restful."

The fingerprint man (Detective Constable Morgan) had already left for Sterries. Wexford's car only just managed to get up Ploughman's Lane, which was glacier-like in spite of gritting. He had been a determined burglar, Burden remarked, to get his car up and down there in the night.

The top of the hill presented an alpine scene, with dark-green and gold and gray conifers rising sturdily from the snow blanket. The house itself, shaped like a number of cuboid boxes pushed irregularly together and with a tower in the midst of them, looked not so much white as dun-colored beside the dazzling field of snow. A sharp wind had set the treble-clef weathervane spinning like a top against a sky that was now a clear cerulean blue.

Morgan's van was parked on the forecourt outside the front door, which was on the side of the house furthest from the lane. Some attempt had been made to keep this area free of snow. Wexford, getting out of the car, saw a solidly built man in jeans and anorak at work sweeping the path which seemed to lead to a much smaller house that stood in a dip in the grounds. He looked in the other direction, noting in a shallow tree-fringed basin the ornamental water newspapers had euphe-mistically called a lake. There Camargue had met his death. It was once more iced over and the ice laden with a fleecy coat of snow.

The front door had been opened by a woman of about forty in trousers and bulky sweater whom Wexford took to be Muriel Hicks. He and Burden stepped into the warmth and on to thick soft carpet. The vestibule with its cloaks cupboard was rather small but it opened, through an arch, into a hall which had been used to some extent as a picture gallery. The paintings almost made him whistle. If these were originals . . .

The dining-room was open, revealing pale wood paneling and dark red wood furnishing, and in the far corner Morgan could be seen at his task. A flight of stairs, with risers of mosaic tile and treads that seemed to be of oak, led upwards. However deferential and attentive Mrs. Hicks may have been towards Sir Manuel—and according to Sheila he had been adored by his servants—she had no courtesy to spare for policemen. That "she" was upstairs somewhere was the only introduction they got. Wexford went upstairs while Burden joined Morgan in the dining room.

The house had been built on various different levels of land so that the drawing room where he found himself was really another ground floor. It was a large, airy and gracious room, two sides of which were made entirely of glass. At the farther end of it steps led down into what must surely be the tower. Here the floor was covered by a pale yellow Chinese carpet on which stood two groups of silk-covered settees and chairs, one suite lemon, one very pale jade. There was some fine *famille jaune* porcelain of that marvelous yellow that is both tender and piercing, and suspended from the ceiling a chandelier of startlingly modern design that resembled a torrent of water poured from a tilted vase.

But there was no sign of human occupation. Wexford stepped down under the arch where staghorn ferns grew in troughs at ground level and a *Cissus antarctica* climbed the columns, and entered a music room. It was larger than had appeared from outside and it was dodecagonal. The floor was of very smooth, polished, pale gray slate on which lay three Kashmiri rugs. A Broadwood grand piano stood between him and the other arched entrance. On each of eight of the twelve sides of the room was a picture or bust in an alcove, Mozart and Beethoven, among the latter, among the former Cocteau's cartoon of Picasso and Stravinsky, Rothenstein's drawing of Parry, and a photograph of the Georgian manor house in which the music school was housed at Wellridge. But on one of the remaining sides Camargue had placed on a glass shelf a cast of Chopin's hands and on the last hung in a glass case a wind instrument of the side-blown type which looked to Wexford to be made of solid gold. Under it was the inscription: "Presented to Manuel Camargue by Aldo Cazzini, 1949." Was it a flute and could it be of gold? He lifted the lid of a case which lay on a low table and saw inside a similar instrument but made of humbler metal, perhaps silver.

He was resolving to go downstairs again and send Muriel Hicks to find Mrs. Arno, when he was aware of a movement in the air behind him and of a presence that was not wholly welcoming. He turned round. Natalie Arno stood framed in the embrasure of the further arch, watching him with an unfathomable expression in her eyes.

4

Wexford was the first to speak.

"Good morning, Mrs. Arno."

She was absolutely still, one hand up to her cheek, the other resting against one of the columns which supported the arch. She was silent.

He introduced himself and said pleasantly, "I hear you've had some sort of break-in. Is that right?"

Why did he feel so strongly that she was liberated by relief? Her face did not change and it was a second or two before she moved. Then, slowly, she came forward.

"It's good of you to come so quickly." Her voice was as unlike Dinah Stern-hold's as it was reasonably possible for one woman's voice to differ from another's. She had a faint American accent and in her tone there was an underlying hint of amusement. He was always to be aware of that in his dealings with her. "I'm afraid I may be making a fuss about nothing. He only took a few spoons." She made a comic grimace, pursing her lips as she drew out the long vowel sound. "Let's go into the drawing room and I'll tell you about it."

The cast of her countenance was that which one would immediately categorize as Spanish, full-fleshed yet strong, the nose straight if a fraction too long, the mouth full and flamboyantly curved, the eyes splendid, as near to midnight black as a white woman's eyes can ever be. Her black hair was strained tightly back from her face and knotted high on the back of her head, a style which most women's faces could scarcely take but which suited hers, exposing its fine bones. And her figure was no less arresting than her face. She was very slim but for a too-full bosom, and this was not at all disguised by her straight skirt and thin sweater. Such an appearance, the ideal of men's fantasies, gives a woman a slightly indecent look, particularly if she carries herself with a certain provocative air. Natalie Arno did not quite do this but when she moved as she now did, mounting the steps to the higher level, she walked very sinuously with a stressing of her narrow waist.

During his absence two people had come into the drawing room, a man and a woman. They were behaving in the rather aimless fashion of house guests who have perhaps just got up or at least just put in an appearance, and who are wondering where to find breakfast, newspapers and an occupation. It occurred to Wexford for the first time that it was rather odd, not to say presumptuous, of Natalie Arno to have taken possession of Sterries so immediately after her father's death, to have moved in and to have invited people to stay. Did his solicitors approve? Did they know?

"This is Chief Inspector Wexford who has come to catch our burglar," she said. "My friends, Mr. and Mrs. Zoffany."

The man was one of those who had been in the circle round her after the inquest. He seemed about forty. His fair hair was thick and wavy and he had a

Viking's fine golden beard, but his body had grown soft and podgy and a flap of belly hung over the belt of his too-tight and too-juvenile fawn cord jeans. His wife, in the kind of clothes which unmistakably mark the superannuated hippie, was as thin as he was stout. She was young still, younger probably than Camargue's daughter, but her face was worn and there were coarse, bright threads of gray in her dark curly hair.

Natalie Arno sat down in one of the jade armchairs. She sat with elegant slim legs crossed at the calves, her feet arched in their high-heeled shoes. Mrs. Zoffany, on the other hand, flopped on to the floor and sat cross-legged, tucking her long patchwork skirt around her knees. The costume she wore, and which like so many of her contemporaries she pathetically refused to relinquish, would date her more ruthlessly than might any perm or pair of stockings on another woman. Yet not so long ago it had been the badge of an élite who hoped to alter the world. Sitting there, she looked as if she might be at one of the pop concerts of her youth, waiting for the entertainment to begin. Her head was lifted expectantly, her eyes on Natalie's face.

"I'll tell you what there is to tell," Natalie began, "and I'm afraid that's not much. It must have been around five this morning I thought I heard the sound of glass breaking. I've been sleeping in Papa's room. Jane and Ivan are in one of the spare rooms in the other wing. You didn't hear anything, did you, Jane?"

Jane Zoffany shook her head vehemently. "I only wish I had. I might have been able to *help*."

"I didn't go down. To tell you the truth I was just a little scared." Natalie smiled deprecatingly. She didn't look as if she had ever been scared in her life. Wexford wondered why he had at first felt her presence as hostile. She was entirely charming. "But I did look out of the window. And just outside the window—on that side all the rooms are more or less on the ground floor, you know—there was a van parked. I put the light on and took a note of the registration number. I've got it here somewhere. What did I do with it?"

Jane Zoffany jumped up. "I'll look for it, shall I? You put it down somewhere in here. I remember, I was still in my dressing gown . . ." She began hunting about the room, her scarves and the fringe of her shawl catching on ornaments.

Natalie smiled, and in that smile Wexford thought he detected patronage. "I didn't quite know what to do," she said. "Papa didn't have a phone extension put in his room. Just as I was wondering I heard the van start up and move off. I felt brave enough to go down to the dining room then, and sure enough there was a pane gone from one of the casements."

"A pity you didn't phone us then. We might have got him."

"I know." She said it ruefully, amusedly, with a soft sigh of a laugh. "But there were only those half-dozen silver spoons missing and two five-pound notes out of my purse. I'd left my purse on the sideboard."

"But would *you* know exactly what was missing, Mrs. Arno?"

"Right. I wouldn't really. But Mrs. Hicks has been round with me this morning and she can't find anything else gone."

"It's rather curious, isn't it? This house seems to me full of very valuable objects. There's a Kandinsky downstairs and a Boudin, I think." He pointed. "And those are signed Hockney prints. That yellow porcelain . . ."

She looked surprised at his knowledge. "Yes, but . . ." Her cheeks had slightly flushed. "Would you think me very forward if I said I had a theory?"

"Not at all. I'd like to hear it."

"Well, first, I think he knew Papa used to sleep in that room and now poor Papa is gone he figured no one would be in there. And, secondly, I think he saw my light go on before he'd done any more than filch the spoons. He was just too scared to stop any longer. How does that sound?"

"Quite a possibility," said Wexford. Was it his imagination that she had expected a more enthusiastic or flattering response? Jane Zoffany came up with the van registration number on a piece of paper torn from an exercise book. Natalie Arno didn't thank her for her pains. She rose, tensing her shoulders and throwing back her head to show off that amazing shape. Her waist could easily have been spanned by a pair of hands.

"Do you want to see the rest of the house?" she said. "I'm sure he didn't come up to this level."

Wexford would have loved to, but for what reason? "We usually ask the householder to make a list of missing valuables in a case like this. It might be wise for me to go round with Mrs. Hicks . . ."

"Of course."

Throughout these exchanges Ivan Zoffany had not spoken. Wexford, without looking at him, had sensed a brooding concentration, the aggrieved attitude perhaps of a man not called on to participate in what might seem to be men's business. But now, as he turned his eyes in Zoffany's direction, he got a shock. The man was gazing at Natalie Arno, had probably been doing so for the past ten minutes, and his expression, hypnotic and fixed, was impenetrable. It might indicate contempt or envy or desire or simple hatred. Wexford was unable to analyze it but he felt a pang of pity for Zoffany's wife, for anyone who had to live with so much smoldering emotion.

Passing through the music room, Muriel Hicks took him first into the wing which had been private to Camargue. Here all was rather more austere than what he had so far seen. The bedroom, study-cum-sitting-room and bathroom were all carpeted in Camargue's favorite yellow—wasn't it in the Luscher Test that you were judged the best-adjusted if you gave your favorite colour as yellow?—but the furnishings were sparse and there were blinds at the windows instead of curtains. A dress of Natalie's lay on the bed.

Muriel Hicks had not so far spoken beyond asking him to follow her. She was not an attractive woman. She had the bright pink complexion that sometimes goes with red-gold hair and piglet features. Wexford who, by initially marrying one, had surrounded himself with handsome women, wondered at Camargue, who had a beautiful daughter yet had picked an ugly housekeeper and a nonentity for a second wife. Immediately he had thought that he regretted it with shame. For, turning round, he saw that Mrs. Hicks was crying. She was standing with her hand on an armchair, on the seat of which lay a folded rug, and the tears were rolling down her round, red cheeks.

She was one of the few people he had ever come across who did not apologize for crying. She wiped her face, scrubbing at her eyes. "I've lost the best employer," she said, "and the best friend anyone could have. And I've taken it hard, I can tell you."

"Yes, it was a sad business."

"If you'll look out of that window you'll see a house over to the left. That's ours. Really ours, I mean—he *gave* it to us. God knows what it's worth now. D'you know what he said? I'm not having you and Ted living in a tied cottage, he said. If you're good enough to come and work for me you deserve to have a house of your own to live in."

It was a largish Victorian cottage and it had its own narrow driveway out into Ploughman's Lane. Sheila wouldn't have wanted it, he supposed, its not going with Sterries would make no difference to her. He put up a show for Mrs. Hicks's benefit of scrutinizing the spot where Natalie Arno said the van had been.

"There weren't many like him," said Muriel Hicks, closing the door behind Wexford as they left. It was a fitting epitaph, perhaps the best and surely the simplest Camargue would have.

Along the corridor, back through the music room, across the drawing room, now deserted, and into the other wing. Here was a large room full of books, a study or a library, and three bedrooms, all with bathrooms *en suite*. Their doors were all open but in one of them, standing in front of a long glass and studying the effect of various ways of fastening the collar of a very old Persian lamb coat, was Jane Zoffany. She rushed, at the sight of Wexford, into a spate of apologies—very nearly saying sorry for existing at all—and scuttled from the room. Muriel Hicks's glassy stare followed her out.

"There's nothing missing from here," she said in a depressed tone. "Anyway, those people would have heard something." There was a chance, he thought, that she might lose another kind of control and break into a tirade against Camargue's daughter and her friends. But she didn't. She took him silently into the second room and the third.

Why had Natalie Arno chosen to occupy her father's bedroom, austere, utilitarian and moreover the room of a lately dead man and a parent, rather than one of these luxurious rooms with fur rugs on the carpets and duckdown duvets on the beds? Was it to be removed from the Zoffanys? But they were her friends whom she had presumably invited. To revel in the triumph of possessing the place and all that went with it at last? To appreciate this to the full by sleeping in the inner sanctum, the very holy of holies? It occurred to him that by so doing she must have caused great pain to Mrs. Hicks, and then he reminded himself that this sort of speculation was pointless, he wasn't investigating any crime more serious than petty larceny. And his true reason for being here was to make a preliminary survey for a possible buyer.

"Is anything much kept in that chest?" he asked Mrs. Hicks. It was a big teak affair with brass handles, standing in the passage.

"Only blankets."

"And that cupboard?"

She opened it. "There's nothing missing."

He went downstairs. Morgan and his van had gone. In the hall were Burden, Natalie Arno and the Zoffanys, the man who had been sweeping the path, and a woman in a dark brown fox fur who had evidently just arrived.

Everyone was dressed for the outdoors and for bitterly cold weather. It struck Wexford forcefully, as he descended the stairs towards them, that Natalie and her friends looked thoroughly disreputable compared with the other three. Burden was always well turned-out and in his new sheepskin he was more than that. The newcomer was smart, even elegant, creamy cashmere showing above the neckline of the fur, her hands in sleek gloves, and even Ted Hicks, in aran and anorak, had the look of a gentleman farmer. Beside them Natalie and the Zoffanys were a rag-bag crew, Zoffany's old overcoat as shabby as Wexford's own, his wife with layers of dipping skirts hanging out beneath the hem of the Persian lamb. Nothing could make Natalie less than striking. In a coat that appeared to be made from an old blanket and platform-soled boots so out of date and so worn that Wexford guessed she must have bought them in a secondhand shop, she looked raffish and down on her luck. They were hardly the kind of people, he said to himself with an inward chuckle, that one (or the neighbors) would expect to see issuing from a house in Ploughman's Lane.

That the woman in the fur was one of these neighbors Burden immediately explained. Mrs. Murray-Burgess. She had seen the police cars and then she had encountered Mr. Hicks in the lane. Yes, she lived next door, if next door it could be called when something like an acre separated Kingsfield House from Sterries, and she thought she might have some useful information.

They all trooped into the dining room where Hicks resumed his task of boarding up the broken window. Wexford asked Mrs. Murray-Burgess the nature of her information.

She had seen a man in the Sterries grounds. No, not last night, a few days before. In fact, she had mentioned it to Mrs. Hicks, not being acquainted with Mrs. Arno. She gave Natalie a brief glance that seemed to indicate her desire for a continuation of this state of affairs. No, she couldn't recall precisely when it had been. Last night she had happened to be awake at five-thirty—she always awoke early—and had seen the lights of a vehicle turning out from Sterries into the lane. Wexford nodded. Could she identify this man were she to see him again?

"I'm sure I could," said Mrs. Murray-Burgess emphatically. "And what's more, I *would*. All this sort of thing has got to be stopped before the country goes completely to the dogs. If I've got to get up in court and say that's the man!—well, I've got to and no two ways about it. It's time someone gave a lead."

Natalie's face was impassive but in the depths of her eyes Wexford saw a spark of laughter. Almost anyone else in her position would now have addressed this wealthy and majestic neighbor, thanking her perhaps for her concern and public spirit. Most people would have suggested a meeting on more social terms, on do-bring-your-husband-in-for-a-drink lines. Many would have spoken of the dead and have mentioned the coming memorial service. Natalie behaved exactly as if Mrs. Murray-Burgess were not there. She shook hands with Wexford, thanking him warmly while increasing the pressure of her fingers. Burden was as prettily thanked and given an alluring smile. They were ushered to the door, the Zoffanys following, everyone coming out into the crisp cold air and the bright sunlight. Mrs. Murray-Burgess, left stranded in the dining room with Ted Hicks, emerged in offended bewilderment a moment or two later.

Wexford, no doubt impressing everyone with his frown and preoccupied air, was observing the extent of the double glazing and making rough calculations as to the size of the grounds. Getting at last into their car, he remarked to Burden—a propos of what the inspector had no idea—that sometimes these cogitations still amazed the troubled midnight and the noon's repose.

5

The owner of the van was quickly traced through its registration number. He was a television engineer called Robert Clifford who said he had lent the van to a fellow-tenant of his in Finsbury Park, north London, a man of thirty-six called John Cooper. Cooper, who was unemployed, admitted the break-in after the spoons had been found in his possession. He said he had read in the papers about the death of Camargue and accounts of the arrangements at Sterries.

"It was an invite to do the place," he said impudently. "All that stuff about valuable paintings and china, and then that the housekeeper didn't sleep in the house. She didn't either, the first time I went."

When had that been?

"Tuesday night," said Cooper. He meant Tuesday the 29th, two days after Camargue's death. When he returned to break in. "I didn't know which was the old man's room," he said. "How would I? The papers don't give you a plan of the bloody place." He had parked the van outside that window simply because it seemed the most convenient spot and couldn't be seen from the road. "It gave me a shock when the light came on." He sounded aggrieved, as if he had been wantonly interrupted while about some legitimate task. His was a middle-class accent. Perhaps, like Burden's little villain, he was a pathological kleptomaniac with personality-scarring. Cooper appeared before the Kingsmarkham magistrates and was remanded in custody until the case could be heard at Myringham Crown Court.

Wexford was able to give Sheila a favorable report on Camargue's house, but she seemed to have lost interest in the place. (One's children had a way of behaving like this, he had noticed.) Andrew's house in Keats Grove was really very nice, and he did have the cottage in Dorset. If they lived in Sussex they would have to keep a flat in town as well. She couldn't go all the way back to Kingsmarkham after an evening performance, could she? The estate agents had found a buyer for her own flat in St. John's Wood and they were getting an amazing price for it. Had Mother been to hear her banns called for the second time? Mother had.

The day of the memorial service was bright and sunny. Alpine weather, Wexford called it, the frozen snow sparkling, melting a little in the sun, only to freeze glass-hard again when the sun went down. Returning from his visit to Sewingbury Comprehensive School—where there was an alarming incidence of glue-sniffing among fourteen-year-olds—he passed St. Peter's church as the mourners were leaving. The uniform men wear disguises them. Inside black overcoat and black Homburg might breathe equally Sir Manuel's accompanist or Sir Manuel's wine merchant. But he was pretty sure he had spotted James Galway, and he stood to gaze like any lion-hunting sightseer.

Sheila, making her escape with Dinah Sternhold to a hire car, was attracting as much attention as anyone—a warning, her father thought, of what they might expect in a fortnight's time. The Zoffanys were nowhere to be seen but Natalie Arno, holding the arm of an elderly wisp of a man, a man so frail-looking that it seemed wonderful the wind did not blow him about like a feather, was standing on the steps shaking hands with departing visitors. She wore a black coat and a large black hat, new clothes they appeared to be and suited to the occasion, and she stood erectly, her thin ankles pressed together. By the time Wexford was driven away by the cold, though several dozen people had shaken hands with her and passed on, four or five of the men as well as the elderly wisp remained with her. He smiled to himself, amused to see his prediction fulfilled.

By the end of the week Sheila had received confirmation from the estate agents that her flat was sold, or that negotiations to buy it had begun. This threw her into a dilemma. Should she sign the contract and then go merrily off on her Bermuda honeymoon, leaving the flat full of furniture? Or should she arrange to have the flat cleared and the furniture stored before she left? Persuaded by her prudent mother, she fixed on the Wednesday before her wedding for the removal and Wexford, who had the day off, promised to go with her to St. John's Wood.

"We could go to Bermuda too," said Dora to her husband.

"I know it was the custom for Victorian brides to take a friend with them on their honeymoon," said Wexford, "but surely even they didn't take their parents."

"Darling, I don't mean at the same time. I mean we could go to Bermuda later on. When you get your holiday. We can afford it now we aren't paying for this wedding."

"How about my new car? How about the new hall carpet? And I thought you'd decided life was insupportable without a freezer."

"We couldn't have all those things anyway."

"That's for sure," said Wexford.

A wonderful holiday or a new car? A thousand pounds' worth of sunshine and warmth took priority now, he reflected as he was driven over to Myringham and the crown court. The snow was still lying and the bright weather had given place to freezing fog. But would he still feel like this when it was sunny here and spring again? Then the freezer and the carpet would seem the wiser option.

John Cooper was found guilty of breaking into and entering Sterries and of stealing six silver spoons, and, since he had previous convictions, sent to prison for six months. Wexford was rather surprised to hear that one of these convictions, though long in the past, was for robbery with violence. Mrs. Murray-Burgess was in court and she flushed brick-red with satisfaction when the sentence was pronounced. Throughout the proceedings she had been eyeing the dark, rather handsome, slouching Cooper in the awed and fascinated way one looks at a bull or a caged tiger.

It occurred to Wexford to call in at Sterries on his way back and impart the news to Natalie Arno. He had promised to let her know the outcome. She would very likely be as delighted as her neighbor, and she could have her spoons back now.

A man who tried to be honest with himself, he wondered if this could be his sole motive for a visit to Ploughman's Lane. After all, it was a task Sergeant Martin or even Constable Loring could more properly have done. Was he, in common with those encircling men, attracted by Natalie? Could she have said of him too, like Cleopatra with her fishing rod, "Aha, you're caught"? Honestly he asked himself—and said an honest, almost unqualified no. She amused him, she intrigued him, he suspected she would be entertaining to watch at certain manipulating ploys, but he was not attracted. There remained with him a nagging little memory of how, in the music room at Sterries, before he had ever spoken to her, he had sensed her presence behind him as unpleasing. She was good to look at, she was undoubtedly clever, she was full of charm, yet wasn't there about her something snake-like? And although this image might dissolve when confronted by the real Natalie, out of her company he must think of her sinuous movements as reptilian and her marvelous eyes when cast down as hooded.

So in going to Sterries he knew he was in little danger. No one need tie him to the mast. He would simply be calling on Natalie Arno for an obligatory talk, perhaps a cup of tea, and the opportunity to watch a powerful personality at work with the weak. If the Zoffanys were still there, of course. He would soon know.

It was three o'clock on the afternoon of a dull day. Not a light showed in the Sterries windows. Still, many people preferred to sit in the dusk rather than anticipate the night too soon. He rang the bell. He rang and rang again, was pleased to find himself not particularly disappointed that there was no one at home.

After a moment's thought he walked down the path to Sterries Cottage. Ted Hicks answered his ring. Yes, Mrs. Arno was out. In fact, she had returned to London. Her friends had gone and then she had gone, leaving him and his wife to look after the house.

"Does she mean to come back?"

"I'm afraid I've no idea about that, sir. Mrs. Arno didn't say." Hicks spoke respectfully. Indeed, he had far more the air of an old fashioned servant than his wife. Yet again Wexford felt, as he had felt with Muriel Hicks, that at any moment the discreet speaker might break into abuse, either heaping insults on Natalie or dismissing her with contempt. But nothing like this happened. Hicks compressed his lips and stared blankly at Wexford, though without meeting his eyes. "Would you care to come in? I can give you Mrs. Arno's London address."

Why bother with it? He refused, thanked the man, asked almost as an afterthought if the house was to be sold.

"Very probably, sir." Hicks, stiff, soldierly almost, unbent a little. "This house will be. The wife and me, we couldn't stick it here now Sir Manuel's gone."

It seemed likely that Natalie had taken her leave of Kingsmarkham and the town would not see her again. Perhaps she meant to settle in London or even return to America. He said something on these lines to Sheila as he drove her up to London on the following morning. But she had lost interest in Sterries and its future and was preoccupied with the morning paper which was carrying a feature about her and the forthcoming wedding. On the whole she seemed pleased with it, a reaction that astonished Wexford and Dora. They had been appalled by the description of her as the "beautiful daughter of a country policeman" and the full-length photograph which showed her neither as Stewardess Curtis nor in one of her Royal Shakespeare Company roles, but reclining on a heap of cushions in little more than a pair of spangled stockings and a smallish fur.

"Dorset Stores It" was the slogan on the side of the removal van that had arrived early in Hamilton Terrace. Two men sat in its cab, glumly awaiting the appearance of the owner of the flat. Recognition of who that owner was mollified them, and on the way up in the lift the younger man asked Sheila if she would give him her

autograph for his wife, who hadn't missed a single instalment of *Runway* since the
serial began.

The other man looked very old. Wexford was thinking he was too old to be of
much use until he saw him lift Sheila's big bow-fronted chest of drawers and set it
like a light pack on his shoulders. The younger man smiled at Wexford's astonishment.

"Pity you haven't got a piano," he said. "He comes from the most famous
piano-lifting family in the country."

Wexford had never before supposed that talents of that kind ran in families or
even that one might enjoy a reputation for such a skill. He looked at the old man,
who seemed getting on for Camargue's age, with new respect.

"Where are you taking all this stuff?"

A list was consulted. "This piece and them chairs and that chest up to Keats
Grove and . . ."

"Yes, I mean what isn't going to Keats Grove."

"Down the warehouse. That's our warehouse down Thornton Heath, Croydon
way if you know it. The lady's not got so much she'll need more than one container." He named the rental Sheila would have to pay per week for the storage of
her tables and chairs.

"It's stacked up in this container, is it, and stored along with a hundred others?
Suppose you said you wanted it stored for a year and then you changed your mind
and wanted to get, say, one item out?"

"That'd be no problem, guv'nor. It's yours, isn't it? While you pay your rent
you can do what you like about it, leave it alone if that's what you want like or
inspect it once a week. Thanks very much lady." This last was addressed to Sheila,
who was dispensing cans of beer.

"Give us a hand, George," said the old man.

He had picked up Sheila's four-poster on his own, held it several inches off the
ground, then thought better of it. He and the man called George began dismantling
it.

"You'd be amazed," said George, "the things that go on. We're like a very old-
established firm and we've got stuff down the warehouse been stored since before
the First War . . ."

"The Great War," said the old man.

"O.K. then, the *Great* War. We've got stuff been stored since before 1914.
The party as stored it's dead and gone and the rent's like gone up ten, twenty times,
but the family wants it kept and they go on paying. Furniture that's been stored
twenty years, that's common, that's nothing out of the way. We got one lady, she
put her grand piano in store 1936 and she's dead now, but her daughter, she keeps
the rent up. She comes along every so often and we open up her container for her
and let her have a look her piano's O.K."

"See if you can shift that nut, George," said the old man.

By two they were finished. Wexford took Sheila out to lunch, to a little French restaurant in Blenheim Terrace, a far cry from Mr. Haq's. They shared a bottle of Domaine du Parc and as Wexford raised his glass and drank to her happiness he felt a rush of unaccustomed sentimentality. She was so very much his treasure. His heart swelled with pride when he saw people look at her, whisper together and then look again. For years now she had hardly been his, she had been something like public property, but after Saturday she would be Andrew's and lost to him forever. . . . Suddenly he let out a bark of laughter at these maudlin indulgences.

"What's funny, Pop darling?"

"I was thinking about those removal men," he lied.

He drove her up to Hampstead where she was staying the night and began the long haul back to Kingsmarkham. Not very experienced in London traffic, he had left Keats Grove at four and by the time he came to Waterloo Bridge found himself in the thick of the rush. It was after seven when he walked, cross and tired, into his house.

Dora came out to meet him in the hall. She kept her voice low. "Reg, that friend of Sheila's who was going to marry Manuel Camargue is here. Dinah Whatever-it-is."

"Didn't you tell her Sheila wouldn't be back tonight?"

Dora, though aware that she must move with the times, though aware that Sheila and Andrew had been more or less living together for the past year, nevertheless still made attempts to present to the world a picture of her daughter as an old-fashioned maiden bride. Her husband's accusing look—he disapproved of this kind of Mrs. Grundy-ish concealment—made her blush and say hastily:

"She doesn't want Sheila, she wants you. She's been here an hour, she insisted on waiting. She says . . ." Dora cast up her eyes. "She says she didn't know till this morning that you were a policeman!"

Wedding presents were still arriving. The house wasn't big enough for this sort of influx, and now the larger items were beginning to take over the hall. He nearly tripped over an object which, since it was swathed in corrugated cardboard and brown paper, might have been a plant stand, a lectern or a standard lamp, and cursing under his breath made his way into the living room.

This time the Alsatian had been left behind. Dinah Sternhold had been sitting by the hearth, gazing into the heart of the fire perhaps while preoccupied with her own thoughts. She jumped up when he came in and her round pale face grew pink.

"Oh, I'm so sorry to bother you, Mr. Wexford. Believe me, I wouldn't be here if I didn't think it was absolutely—well, absolutely vital. I've delayed so long and I've felt so bad and now I can't sleep with the worry . . . But it wasn't till this morning I found out you were a detective chief inspector."

"You read it in the paper," he said, smiling, " 'Beautiful daughter of a country policeman.' "

"Sheila never told me, you see. Why should she? I never told her my father's a bank manager."

Wexford sat down. "Then what you have to tell me is something serious, I suppose. Shall we have a drink? I'm a bit tired and you look as if you need Dutch courage."

On doctor's orders, he could allow himself nothing stronger than vermouth but she, to his surprise, asked for whisky. That she wasn't used to it he could tell by the way she shuddered as she took her first sip. She lifted to him those grayish-brown eyes that seemed full of soft light. He had thought that face plain but it was not, and for a moment he could intuit what Camargue had seen in her. If his looks had been spiritual and sensitive so, superlatively, were hers. The old musician and this young creature had shared, he sensed, an approach to life that was gentle, impulsive and joyous.

There was no joy now in her wan features. They seemed convulsed with doubt and perhaps with fear.

"I know I ought to tell someone about this," she began again. "As soon as—as Manuel was dead I knew I ought to tell someone. I thought of his solicitors but I imagined them listening to me and knowing I wasn't to—well, inherit, and thinking it was all sour grapes . . . It seemed so—so *wild* to go to the police. But this morning when I read that in the paper—you see, I know you, you're Sheila's father, you won't . . . I'm afraid I'm not being very articulate. Perhaps you understand what I mean?"

"I understand you've been feeling diffident about giving some sort of information but I'm mystified as to what it is."

"Oh, of course you are! The point is, I don't really believe it myself. I can't, it seems so—well, outlandish. But Manuel believed it, he was so sure, so I don't think I ought to keep it to myself and just let things go ahead, do you?"

"I think you'd better tell me straight away, Mrs. Sternhold. Just tell me what it is and then we'll have the explanations afterwards."

She set down her glass. She looked a little away from him, the firelight reddening the side of her face.

"Well, then. Manuel told me that Natalie Arno, or the woman who calls herself Natalie Arno, wasn't his daughter at all. He was absolutely convinced she was an impostor."

6

He said nothing and his face showed nothing of what he felt. She was looking at him now, the doubt intensified, her hands lifted and clasped hard together under her chin. In the firelight the ruby on her finger burned and twinkled.

"There," she said, "that's it. It was something to—to hesitate about, wasn't it? But I don't really believe it. Oh, I don't mean he wasn't marvelous for his age and his mind absolutely sound. I don't mean that. But his sight was poor and he'd worked himself into such an emotional state over seeing her, it was nineteen years, and perhaps she wasn't very kind and—oh, I don't know! When he said she wasn't his daughter, she was an impostor, and he'd leave her nothing in his will, I . . ."

Wexford interrupted her. "Why don't you tell me about it from the beginning?"

"Where is the beginning? From the time she, or whoever she is . . ."

"Tell me about it from the time of her return to this country in November."

Dora put her head round the door. He knew she had come to ask him if he was ready for his dinner but she retreated without a word. Dinah Sternhold said:

"I think I'm keeping you from your meal."

"It doesn't matter. Let's go back to November."

"I only know that it was in November she came back. She didn't get in touch with Manuel until the middle of December—12 December it was. She didn't say anything about our getting married, just could she come and see him and something about healing the breach. At first she wanted to come at Christmas but when Manuel wrote back that that would be fine and I should be there and my parents, she said no, the first time she wanted to see him alone. It sounds casual, putting it like that, Manuel writing back and inviting her, but in fact it wasn't a bit. Getting her first letter absolutely threw him. He was very—well, excited about seeing her and rather confused and it was almost as if he was afraid. I suggested he phone her —she gave a phone number—but he couldn't bring himself to that and it's true he was difficult on the phone if you didn't know him. His hearing was fine when he could *see* the speaker. Anyway, she suggested 10 January and we had the same excitement and nervousness all over again. I wasn't to be there or the Hickses, Muriel was to get the tea ready and leave him to make it and she was to get one of the spare rooms ready in case Natalie decided to stay.

"Well, two or three days before, it must have been about the 7th, a woman called Mrs. Zoffany phoned. Muriel took the call. Manuel was asleep. This Mrs. Zoffany said she was speaking on behalf of Natalie who couldn't come on the 10th because she had to go into hospital for a check-up and could she come on the 19th instead? Manuel got into a state when Muriel told him. I went over there in the evening and he was very depressed and nervous, saying Natalie didn't really want a reconciliation, whatever she may have intended at first, she was just trying to get out of seeing him. You can imagine. He went on about how he was going to die soon and at any rate that would be a blessing for me, not to be tied to an old man *et cetera*. All nonsense, of course, but natural, I think. He was *longing* to see her. It's a good thing I haven't got a jealous nature. Lots of women would have been jealous."

Perhaps they would. Jealousy knows nothing of age discrepancies, suitability. Camargue, thought Wexford, had chosen for his second wife a surrogate daughter, assuming his true daughter would never reappear. No wonder, when she did, that emotions had run high. He said only:

"I take it that it was on the 19th she came?"

"Yes. In the afternoon, about three. She came by train from Victoria and then in a taxi from the station. Manuel asked the Hickses not to interrupt them and Ted even took Nancy away for the afternoon. Muriel left tea prepared on the table in the drawing room and there was some cold duck and stuff for supper in the fridge."

"So that when she came Sir Manuel was quite alone?"

"Quite alone. What I'm going to tell you is what he told me the next day, the Sunday, when Ted drove him over to my house in the morning.

"He told me he intended to be rather cool and distant with her at first." Dinah Sternhold smiled a tender, reminiscent smile. "I didn't have much faith in that," she said. "I knew him, you see. I knew it wasn't in him not to be warm and kind. And in fact, when he went down and opened the front door to her he said he forgot all about that resolve of his and just took her in his arms and held her. He was ashamed of that afterwards, poor Manuel, he was sick with himself for giving way.

"Well, they went upstairs and sat down and talked. That is, Manuel talked. He said he suddenly found he had so much to say to her. He talked on and on about his life since she went away, her mother's death, his retirement because of the arthritis in his hands, how he had built that house. She answered him, he said, but a lot of things she said he couldn't hear. Maybe she spoke low, but my voice is low and he could always hear me. However . . ."

"She has an American accent," said Wexford.

"Perhaps that was it. The awful thing was, he said, that when he talked of the long time she'd been away he actually cried. I couldn't see it was important, but he was so ashamed of having cried. Still, he pulled himself together. He said they must have tea and he hoped she would stay the night and would she like to see over the house? He was always taking people over the house, I think it was something his generation did, and then . . ."

Wexford broke in, "All this time he believed her to be his daughter?"

"Oh, yes! He was in no doubt. The way he said he found out—well, it's so crazy . . . Anyway, he actually told her he was going to make a new will after his marriage, and although he intended to leave me the house and its contents, everything else was to go to her, including what remained of her mother's fortune. It was a lot of money, something in the region of a million, I think.

"He showed her the bedroom that was to be hers, though she did say at this point that she couldn't stay, and then they went back and into the music room. Oh, I don't suppose you've ever been in the house, have you?"

"As a matter of fact, I have," said Wexford.

She gave him a faintly puzzled glance. "Yes. Well, you'll know then that there are alcoves all round the music room and in one of the alcoves is a flute made of gold. It was given to Manuel by a sort of patron and fan of his, an American of

Italian origin called Aldo Cazzini, and it's a real instrument, it's perfectly *playable*, though in fact Manuel had never used it.

"He and Natalie went in there and Natalie took one look in the alcove and said, "You still have Cazzini's golden flute," and it was at this point, he said, that he knew. He knew for certain she wasn't Natalie."

Wexford said, "I don't follow you. Surely recognizing the flute would be confirmation of her identity rather than proof she was an impostor?"

"It was the way she pronounced it. It ought to be pronounced Catzini and this woman pronounced it Cassini. Or so he said. Now the real Natalie grew up speaking English, French and Spanish with equal ease. She learned German at school and when she was fifteen Manuel had her taught Italian because he intended her to be a musician and he thought some Italian essential for a musician. The real Natalie would never have mispronounced an Italian name. She would no more have done that, he said—these are his own words—than a Frenchman would pronounce Camargue to rhyme with Montague. So as soon as he heard her pronunciation of Cazzini he knew she couldn't be Natalie."

Wexford could almost have laughed. He shook his head in dismissal. "There must have been more to it."

"There was. He said the shock was terrible. He didn't say anything for a moment. He looked hard at her, he studied her, and then he could *see* she wasn't his daughter. Nineteen years is a long time but she couldn't have changed that much and in that way. Her features were different, the color of her eyes was different. He went back with her into the drawing room and then he said, "You are not my daughter, are you?""

"He actually asked her, did he?"

"He asked her and—you understand, Mr. Wexford, that I'm telling you what he said—I feel a traitor to him, doubting him, as if he were senile or mad—he wasn't, he was wonderful, but. . . ."

"He was old," said Wexford. A foolish, fond old man, fourscore years . . . "He was overwrought."

"Oh, yes, exactly! But the point is he said he asked her and she admitted it."

Wexford leaned forward, frowning a little, his eyes on Dinah Sternhold's flushed, intent face.

"Are you telling me this woman admitted to Sir Manuel that she wasn't Natalie Arno? Why didn't you say so before?"

"Because I don't believe it. I think that when he said she admitted she wasn't Natalie and seemed ashamed and embarrassed, I think he was—well, dreaming. You see, he told her to go. He was trembling, he was terribly distressed. It wasn't in him to shout at anyone or be violent, you understand, he just told her not to say any more but to go. He heard her close the front door and then he did something he absolutely never did. He had some brandy. He never touched spirits in the normal way, a glass of wine sometimes or a sherry, that was all. But he had some brandy to steady him, he said, and then he went to lie down because his heart was racing—and he fell asleep."

"It was next day when you saw him?"

She nodded. "Next day at about eleven. I think that while he was asleep he dreamt that bit about her admitting she wasn't Natalie. I told him so. I didn't humor him—ours wasn't that kind of relationship. I told him I thought he was mistaken. I told him all sorts of things that I believed and believe now—that eye color fades and features change and one can forget a language as one can forget anything else. He wouldn't have any of it. He was so sweet and good and a genius —but he was terribly impulsive and stubborn as well.

"Anyway, he started saying he was going to cut her out of his will. She was a fraud and an impostor who was attempting to get hold of a considerable property by false pretenses. She was to have nothing, therefore, and I was to have the lot. Perhaps you won't believe me if I say I did my best to dissuade him from that?"

Wexford slightly inclined his head. "Why not?"

"It would have been in my own interest to agree with him. However, I did try to dissuade him and he was sweet to me as he always was but he wouldn't listen. He wrote to her, telling her what he intended to do, and then he wrote to his solicitors, asking one of the partners to come up to Sterries on February 4th—that would have been two days after our wedding."

"Who are these solicitors?"

"Symonds, O'Brien and Ames," she said, "in the High Street here."

Kingsmarkham's principal firm of solicitors. They had recently moved their premises into the new Kingsbrook Precinct. It was often Wexford's lot to have dealings with them.

"He invited Mr. Ames to lunch with us," Dinah Sternhold said, "and afterwards he was to draw up a new will for Manuel. It must have been on the 22nd or the 23rd that he wrote to Natalie and on the 27th—he was drowned." Her voice shook a little.

Wexford waited. He said gently, "He had no intention of coming to us and he wasn't going to confide in his solicitor?"

She did not answer him directly. "I think I did right," she said. "I prevented that. I couldn't dissuade him from the decision to disinherit her but I did manage to stop him going to the police. I told him he would make a—well, a scandal, and he would have hated that. What I meant to do was this. Let him make a new will if he liked. Wills can be unmade and remade. I knew Natalie probably disliked me and was jealous but I thought I'd try to approach her myself a month or so after we were married, say, and arrange another meeting. I thought that somehow we'd all meet and it would come right. It would turn out to have been some misunderstanding like in a play, like in one of those old comedies of mistaken identity."

Wexford was silent. Then he said, "Would you like to tell me about it all over again, Mrs. Sternhold?"

"What I've just told?"

He nodded. "Please."

"But why?"

To test your veracity. He didn't say that aloud. If she were intelligent enough she would know without his saying, and her flush told him that she did.

Without digressions this time, she repeated her story. He listened concentratedly. When she had finished he said rather sharply:

"Did Sir Manuel tell anyone else about this?"

"Not so far as I know. Well, no, I'm sure he didn't." Her face was pale again and composed. She asked him, "What will you do?"

"I don't know."

"But you'll do something to find out. You'll prove she *is* Natalie Arno?"

Or that she is not? He didn't say it, and before he had framed an alternative reply she had jumped up and was taking her leave of him in that polite yet child-like way she had.

"It was very good and patient of you to listen to me, Mr. Wexford. I'm sure you understand why I had to come. Will you give my love to Sheila, please, and say I'll be thinking of her on Saturday? She did ask me to come but of course that wouldn't be possible. I'm afraid I've taken up a great deal of your time . . ."

He walked with her out to the Volkswagen, which she had parked round the corner of the street on an ice-free patch. She looked back once as she drove away and raised her hand to him. How many times, in telling her story, had she said she didn't believe it? He had often observed how people will say they are sure of something when they truly mean they are unsure, how a man will hotly declare that he doesn't believe a word of it when he believes only too easily. If Dinah Sternhold had not believed, would she have come to him at all?

He asked himself if he believed and if so what was he going to do about it?

Nothing till after the wedding . . .

7

The success or failure of a wedding, as Wexford remarked, is no augury of the marriage itself. This wedding might be said to have failed. In the first place, the thaw set in the evening before and by Saturday morning it was raining hard. All day long it rained tempestuously. The expected crowd of well-wishers come to see their favorite married, a youthful joyous crowd of confetti-hurlers, became in fact a huddle of pensioners under umbrellas, indifferently lingering on after the Over-Sixties meeting in St. Peter's Hall. But the press was there, made spiteful by rain and mud, awaiting opportunities. And these were many: a bridesmaid's diaphanous skirt blown almost over her head by a gust of wind, a small but dismaying accident when the bride's brother-in-law's car went into the back of a press photographer's car, and later the failure of the Olive and Dove management to provide luncheon places for some ten of the guests.

The Sunday papers made the most of it. Their pictures might have been left to speak for themselves, for the captions, snide or sneering, only added insult to injury. Dora wept.

"I suppose it's inevitable." Wexford, as far as he could recall it and with a touch of paraphrase, quoted Shelley to her. "They scatter their insults and their slanders without heed as to whether the poisoned shafts light on a heart made callous by many blows or one like yours composed of more penetrable stuff."

"And is yours made callous by many blows?"

"No, but Sheila's is."

He took the papers away from her and burned them, hoping none would have found their way into the Burdens' bungalow where they were going to lunch. And when they arrived just after noon, escorted from their car by Burden with a large colored golf umbrella, there was not a newspaper to be seen. Instead, on the coffee table, where the *Sunday Times* might have reposed, lay a book in a glossy jacket entitled *The Tichborne Swindle*.

In former days, during the lifetime of Burden's first wife and afterwards in his long widowerhood, no book apart from those strictly necessary for the children's school work was ever seen in that house. But when he remarried things changed. And it could not be altogether due to the fact that his wife's brother was a publisher, though this might have helped, that the inspector was becoming a reading man. It was even said, though Wexford refused to believe it, that Burden and Jenny read aloud to each other in the evenings, that they had got through Dickens and were currently embarking on the Waverley novels.

Wexford picked up the book. It had been, as he expected, published by Carlyon Brent, and was a reappraisal of the notorious nineteenth-century Tichborne case in which an Australian butcher attempted to gain possession of a great fortune by posing as heir to an English baronetcy. Shades of the tale he had been told by Dinah Sternhold . . . The coincidence of finding the book there decided him. For a little while before lunch he and Burden were alone together.

"Have you read this yet?"

"I'm about halfway through."

"Listen." He repeated the account he had been given baldly and without digressions. "There aren't really very many points of similarity," he said. "From what I remember of the Tichborne case the claimant didn't even look like the Tichborne heir. He was much bigger and fatter for one thing and obviously not of the same social class. Lady Tichborne was a hysterical woman who would have accepted practically anyone who said he was her son. You've almost got the reverse here. Natalie Arno looks very much like the young Natalie Camargue and, far from accepting her, Camargue seems to have rumbled her within half an hour."

" 'Rumbled' sounds as if you think there might be something in this tale."

"I'm not going to stomp up and down raving that I don't believe a word of it, if that's what you mean. I just don't know. But I'll tell you one thing. I expected you to have shouted you didn't believe it long before now."

Burden gave one of his thin, rather complacent little smiles. In his domestic circle he behaved, much as he had during his first marriage, as if nobody but he had ever quite discovered the heights of marital felicity. Today he was wearing a new suit of smooth matt cloth the color of a ginger nut. When happy he always seemed to grow thinner and he was very thin now. The smile was still on his mouth as he spoke. "It's a funny old business altogether, isn't it? But I wouldn't say I don't believe it. It's fertile ground for that sort of con trick, after all. A nineteen-year absence, an old man on his own with poor sight, an old man who has a great deal of money . . . By the way, how do you know this woman looks like the young Natalie?"

"Dinah Sternhold sent me this." Wexford handed him a snapshot. "Camargue was showing her a family photograph album, apparently, and he left it behind in her house."

The picture showed a dark, Spanish-looking girl, rather plump, full-faced and smiling. She was wearing a summer dress in the style known at the time when the photograph was taken as "the sack" on account of its shapelessness and lack of a defined waist. Her black hair was short and she had a fringe.

"That could be her. Why not?"

"A whitely wanton with a velvet brow," said Wexford, "and two pitchballs stuck in her face for eyes. Camargue said the eyes of the woman he saw were different from his daughter's and Dinah told him that eyes fade. I've never heard of eyes or anything else fading to black, have you?"

Burden refilled their glasses. "If Camargue's sight was poor I think you can simply discount that sort of thing. I mean, you can't work on the premise that she's not Natalie Camargue because she looks different or he thought she did. The pronouncing of that name wrong, that's something else again, that's really weird."

Wexford, hesitating for his figure's sake between potato crisps, peanuts or nothing at all, looked up in surprise. "You think so?"

The thin smile came again. "Oh, I know you reckon on me being a real philistine but I've got kids, remember. I've watched them getting an education if I've never had much myself. Now my Pat, she had a Frenchwoman teaching them French from when she was eleven, and when she speaks a French word she pronounces the R like the French, sort of rolls it in her throat. The point I'm making is, it happens naturally now, Pat couldn't pronounce a French word with an R in it any other way and *she never will*."

"Mm hmm." While pondering Wexford had absentmindedly sneaked two crisps. He held his hands firmly together in his lap. "There's always the possibility Camargue *heard* the name incorrectly because of defective hearing while it was, in fact, pronounced in the proper way. What I'm sure of is that Dinah is telling the truth. I tested her and she told the same story almost word for word the second time as she had the first, dates, times, everything."

"Pass over those crisp things, will you? I don't see what motive she'd have for inventing it, anyway. Even if Natalie were out of the way she wouldn't inherit."

"No. Incidentally, we must find out who would. Dinah could have had spite for a motive, you know. If Natalie is the real Natalie no one of course could hope to prove she is not, and no doubt she could very quickly prove she *is*, but an inquiry would look bad for her, the mud would stick. If there were publicity about it and there very likely would be, there would be some people who would always believe her to be an impostor and many others who would feel a doubt."

Burden nodded. "And there must inevitably be an inquiry now, don't you think?"

"Tomorrow I shall have to pass on what I know to Symonds, O'Brien and Ames," said Wexford, and he went on thoughtfully, "It would be deception under the '68 Theft Act. Section Fifteen, I believe." And he quoted with some small hesitations, "A person who by any deception dishonestly obtains property belonging to another, with the intention of permanently depriving the other of it, shall on conviction on indictment be liable to imprisonment for a term not exceeding ten years."

"No one's obtained anything yet. It'll take a bit of time for the will to be proved." Burden gave his friend and superior officer a dubious and somewhat wary look. "I don't want to speak out of turn and no offence meant," he said, "but this could be the kind of thing you get—well, you get obsessional about."

Wexford's indignant retort was cut off in mid-sentence by the entry of Jenny and Dora to announce lunch.

Kingsmarkham's principal firm of solicitors had moved their offices when the new Kingsbrook shopping precinct was built, deserting the medieval caverns they had occupied for fifty years for the top floor above the British Home Stores. Here all was light, space and purity of line. The offices had that rather disconcerting quality, to be constantly met with nowadays, of looking cold and feeling warm. It was much the same in the police station.

Wexford knew Kenneth Ames well by sight, though he couldn't recall ever having spoken to him before. He was a thin, spare man with a boyish face. That is, his face like his figure had kept its youthful contours, though it was by now seamed all over with fine lines as if a web had been laid upon the skin. He wore a pale gray suit that seemed too lightweight for the time of year. His manner was both chatty and distant, which gave the impression, perhaps a false one, that his mind was not on what he was saying or listening to.

This made repeating Dinah Sternhold's account a rather uneasy task. Mr. Ames sat with his elbows on the arms of an uncomfortable-looking metal chair and the tips of his fingers pressed together. He stared out of the window at St. Peter's spire. As the story progressed he pushed his lips and gradually his whole jaw forward until the lower part of his face grew muzzle-like. This doggy expression he held for a moment or two after Wexford had finished. Then he said:

"I don't think I'd place too much credence on all that, Mr. Wexford. I don't think I would. It sounds to me as if Sir Manuel rather got a bee in his belfry, you know, and this young lady, Mrs.—er, Steinhalt, is it?—Mrs. Steinhall maybe gilded the gingerbread." Mr. Ames paused and coughed slightly after delivering these confused metaphors. He studied his short clean fingernails with interest. "Once Sir Manuel was married he'd have had to make a new will. There was nothing out of the way in that. We have no reason to believe he meant to disinherit Mrs. Arno." The muzzle face returned as Mr. Ames glared at his fingernails and enclosed them suddenly in his fists as if they offended him. "In point of fact," he said briskly, "Sir Manuel invited me to lunch to discuss a new will and to meet his bride, Mrs.—er, Sternhill, but unfortunately his death intervened. You know, Mr. Wexford, if Sir Manuel had really believed he'd been visited by an impostor, don't you think he'd have said something to us? There was over a week between the visit and his death and during that week he wrote to me and phoned me. No, if this extraordinary tale were true I fancy he'd have said something to his solicitors."

"He seems to have said nothing to anyone except Mrs. Sternhold."

An elastic smile replaced the muzzle look. "Ah, yes. People like to make trouble. I can't imagine why. You may have noticed?"

"Yes," said Wexford. "By the way, in the event of Mrs. Arno not inheriting, who would?"

"Oh dear, oh dear, I don't think there's much risk of Mrs. Arno not inheriting, do you, really?"

Wexford shrugged. "Just the same, who would?"

"Sir Manuel had—has, I suppose I should say if one may use the present tense in connection with the dead—Sir Manuel has a niece in France, his dead sister's daughter. A Mademoiselle Thérèse Something. Latour? Lacroix? No doubt I can find the name for you if you really want it."

"As you say, there may be no chance of her inheriting. Am I to take it then that Symonds, O'Brien and Ames intend to do nothing about this story of Mrs. Sternhold's?"

"I don't follow you, Mr. Wexford." Mr. Ames was once more contemplating the church spire which was now veiled in fine driving rain.

"You intend to accept Mrs. Arno as Sir Manuel's heir without investigation?"

The solicitor turned round. "Good heavens, no, Mr. Wexford. What can have given you that idea?" He became almost animated, almost involved. "Naturally, in view of what you've told us we shall make the most thorough and exhaustive inquiries. No doubt, you will too?"

"Oh, yes."

"A certain pooling of our findings would be desirable, don't you agree? It's quite unthinkable that a considerable property such as Sir Manuel left could pass to an heir about whose provenance there might be the faintest doubt." Mr. Ames half closed his eyes. He seemed to gather himself together in order to drift once more into remoteness. "It's only," he said with an air of extreme preoccupation, "that it doesn't really do, you know, to place too much credence on these things."

As the receiver was lifted the deep baying of a dog was the first sound he heard. Then the soft gentle voice gave the Forby number.

"Mrs. Sternhold, do you happen to know if Sir Manuel had kept any samples of Mrs. Arno's handwriting from *before* she went away to America?"

"I don't know. I don't think so." Her tone sounded dubious, cautious, as if she regretted having told him so much. Perhaps she did, but it was too late now. "They'd be inside Sterries, anyway." She didn't add what Wexford was thinking, that if Camargue had kept them and if Natalie was an impostor, they would by now have been destroyed.

"Then perhaps you can help me in another way. I gather Sir Manuel had no relatives in this country. Who is there I can call on who knew Mrs. Arno when she was Natalie Camargue?"

Burden's Burberry was already hanging on the palm tree hatstand when Wexford walked into the Pearl of Africa. And Burden was already seated under the plastic fronds, about to start on his antipasto Ankole.

"I don't believe they have shrimps in Uganda," said Wexford, sitting down opposite him.

"Mr. Haq says they come out of Lake Victoria. What are you going to have?"

"Oh, God. Avocado with Victorian shrimps, I suppose, and maybe an omelette. Mike, I've been on to the California police through Interpol, asking them to give us whatever they can about the background of Natalie Arno, but if she's never been in trouble, and we've no reason to think she has, it won't be much. And I've had another talk with Dinah. The first—well, the only really—Mrs. Camargue had a sister who's still alive and in London. Ever heard of a composer called Philip Cory? He was an old pal of Camargue's. Either or both of them ought to be able to tell us if this is the real Natalie."

Burden said thoughtfully, "All this raises something else, doesn't it? Or, rather, what we've been told about Camargue's will does. And in that area it makes no difference whether Natalie is Natalie or someone else."

"What does it raise?"

"You know what I mean."

Wexford did. That Burden too had seen it scarcely surprised him. A year or two before the inspector had often seemed obtuse. But happiness makes so much difference to a person, Wexford thought. It doesn't just make them happy, it makes them more intelligent, more aware, more alert, while unhappiness deadens, dulls and stupefies. Burden had seen what he had seen because he was happy, and happiness was making a better policeman of him.

"Oh, I know what you mean. Perhaps it was rather too readily assumed that Camargue died a natural death."

"I wouldn't say that. It's just that then there was no reason to suspect foul play, nothing and no one suspicious seen in the neighborhood, no known enemies, no unusual bruising on the body. A highly distinguished but rather frail old man happened to go too near a lake on a cold night in deep snow."

"And if we had known what we know now? We can take it for granted that Natalie's aim—whether she is Camargue's daughter or an impostor—her aim in coming to her father was to secure his property or the major part of it for herself. She came to him and, whether he actually saw through her and denounced her or thought he saw through her and dreamed he denounced her, he at any rate apparently wrote to her and told her she was to be disinherited."

"She could either attempt to dissuade him," said Burden, "or take steps of another sort."

"Her loss wouldn't have been immediate. Camargue was getting married and had therefore to make a new will after his marriage. She might count on his not wishing to make a new will at once and then another after his marriage. She had two weeks in which to act."

"There's a point too that, whereas she might have dissuaded him from cutting her out, she couldn't have dissuaded him from leaving Sterries to Dinah. But there don't seem to have been any efforts at dissuasion, do there? Dinah doesn't know of any or she'd have told you, nor did Natalie come to Sterries again."

"Except perhaps," said Wexford, "on the night of Sunday, 27 January."

Burden's answer was checked by the arrival of Mr. Haq, bowing over the table.

"How are you doing, my dear?"

"Fine, thanks." Any less hearty reply would have summoned forth a stream of abject apology and the cook from the kitchen as well as causing very real pain to Mr. Haq.

"I can recommend the mousse Maherere."

Mr. Haq, if his advice was rejected, was capable of going off into an explanation of how this dish was composed of coffee beans freshly plucked in the plantations of

Toro and of cream from the milk of the taper-horned Sanga cattle. To prevent this, and though knowing its actual provenance to be Sainsbury's instant dessert, Burden ordered it. Wexford always had the excuse of his shaky and occasional diet. A bowl of pale brown froth appeared, served by Mr. Haq's own hands.

Quietly Wexford repeated his last remark.

"The night of 27 January?" echoed Burden. "The night of Camargue's death? If he was murdered, and I reckon we both think he was, if he was pushed into that water and left to drown, Natalie didn't do it."

"How d'you know that?"

"Well, in a funny sort of way," Burden said almost apologetically, "she told me so."

"It was while we were up at Sterries about that burglary. I was in the dining room talking to Hicks when Natalie and the Zoffany couple came downstairs. She may have known I was within earshot but I don't think she did. She and Mrs. Z. were talking and Natalie was saying she supposed she would have to get Sotheby's or someone to value Camargue's china for her. On the other hand, there had been that man she and Mrs. Z. had met that someone had said was an expert on Chinese porcelain and she'd like to get hold of his name and phone number. Zoffany said what man did she mean and Natalie said he wouldn't know, he hadn't been there, it had been at so-and-so's party *last Sunday evening.*"

"A bit too glib, wasn't it?"

"Glib or not, if Natalie was at a party there'll be at least a dozen people to say she was, as well as Mrs. Z. And if Camargue was murdered *we will never prove it.* If we'd guessed it at the time it would have been bad enough with snow lying everywhere, with snow falling to obliterate all possible evidence. No weapon but bare hands. Camargue cremated. We haven't a hope in hell of proving it."

"You're over-pessimistic," said Wexford, and he quoted softly, "If a man will begin with certainties, he shall end in doubts, but if he will be content to begin with doubts he shall end in certainties."

8

A shop that is not regularly open and manned seems to announce this fact to the world even when the "open" sign hangs on its door and an assistant can be seen pottering inside. An indefinable air of neglect, of lack of interest, of precarious existence and threatened permanent closure hangs over it. So it was with the Zodiac, nestling in deep Victoriana, tucked behind a neo-Gothic square, on the borders of Islington and Hackney.

Its window was stacked full of paperback science fiction, but some of the books had tumbled down, and those which lay with their covers exposed had their gaudy and bizarre designs veiled in dust. Above the shop was a single story—for this was a district of squat buildings and wide streets—and behind it a humping of rooms, shapelessly huddled and with odd little scraps of roof, gables protruding, seemingly superfluous doors and even a cowled chimney. Wexford pushed open the shop door and walked in. There was a sour, inky, musty smell, inseparable from second-hand books. These lined the shop like wallpaper, an asymmetrical pattern of red and green and yellow and black spines. They were all science fiction, *The Trillion Project, Nergal of Chaldea, Neuropodium, Course for Umbrial, The Triton Occultation*. He was replacing on the shelf a book whose cover bore a picture of what appeared to be a Boeing 747 coated in fish scales and with antennae, when Ivan Zoffany came in from a door at the back.

Recognition was not mutual. Zoffany showed intense surprise when Wexford said who he was, but it seemed like surprise alone and not fear.

"I'd like a few words with you."

"Right. It's a mystery to me what about but I'm easy. I may as well close up for lunch anyway."

It was ten past twelve. Could they hope to make any sort of living out of this place? Did they try? The "open" sign was turned round and Zoffany led Wexford into the room from which he had come. By a window which gave on to a paved yard and scrap of garden and where the light was best, Jane Zoffany, in antique gown, shawl and beads, sat sewing. She appeared to be turning up or letting down the hem of a skirt and Wexford, whose memory was highly retentive about this sort of thing, recognized it as the skirt Natalie had been wearing on the day they were summoned after the burglary.

"What can we do for you?"

Zoffany had the bluff, insincere manner of the man who has a great deal to hide. Experience had taught Wexford that what such a nature is hiding is far more often some emotional disturbance or failure of nerve than guilty knowledge. He could hardly have indulged in greater self-deception than when he had said he was easy. There was something in Zoffany's eyes and the droop of his mouth when he was not forcing it into a grin that spoke of frightful inner suffering. And it was more apparent here, on his home ground, than it had been at Sterries.

"How long have you known Mrs. Arno?"

Instinctively, Jane Zoffany glanced towards the ceiling. And at that moment a light footstep sounded overhead. Zoffany didn't look up.

"Oh, I'd say a couple of years, give or take a little."

"You knew her before she came to this country then?"

"Met her when my poor sister died. Mrs. Arno and my sister used to share a house in Los Angeles. Perhaps you didn't know that? Tina, my sister, she died the summer before last, and I had to go over and see to things. Grisly business but someone had to. There wasn't anyone else, barring my mother, and you can't expect an old lady of seventy—I say, what's all this in aid of?"

Wexford ignored the question as he usually ignored such questions until the time was ripe to answer them. "Your sister and Mrs. Arno shared a house?"

"Well, Tina had a flat in her house."

"A room actually, Ivan," said Jane Zoffany.

"A room in her house. Look, could you tell me why you want. . . ?"

"She must have been quite a young woman. What did she die of?"

"Cancer. She had cancer in her twenties while she was still married. Then she got divorced, but she didn't keep his name, she went back to her maiden name. She was thirty-nine if you want to know. The cancer came back suddenly, it was all over her, carcinomatosis, they called it. She was dead in three weeks from the onset."

Wexford thought he spoke callously and with a curious kind of resentment. There was also an impression that he talked for the sake of talking, perhaps to avoid an embarrassing matter.

"I hadn't seen her for sixteen or seventeen years," he said, "but when she went like that someone had to go over. I can't think what you want with all this."

It was on the tip of Wexford's tongue to retort that he had not asked for it. He said mildly, "When you arrived you met Mrs. Arno? Stayed in her house perhaps?"

Zoffany nodded, uneasy again.

"You got on well and became friends. After you came home you corresponded with her and when you heard she was coming back here and needed somewhere to live, you and your wife offered her the upstairs flat."

"That's quite correct," said Jane Zoffany. She gave a strange little skittish laugh. "I'd always admired her from afar, you see. Just to think of my own sister-in-law living in Manuel Camargue's own daughter's house! I used to worship him when I was young. And Natalie and I are very close now. It was a really good idea. I'm sure Natalie has been a true friend to me." She re-threaded her needle, holding the eye up against the yellowed and none-too-clean net curtain. "Please, why are you asking all these questions?"

"A suggestion has been made that Mrs. Arno is not in fact the late Sir Manuel Camargue's daughter but an impostor."

He was interested by the effect of these words on his hearers. One of them expected this statement and was not surprised by it, the other was either flabbergasted or was a superb actor. Ivan Zoffany seemed stricken dumb with astonishment. Then he asked Wexford to repeat what he had said.

"That is the most incredible nonsense," Zoffany said with a loaded pause between the words. "Who has suggested it? Who would put about a story like that? Now just you listen to me . . ." Wagging a finger, he began lecturing Wexford on the subject of Natalie Arno's virtues and misfortunes. "One of the most charming, delightful girls you could wish to meet, and as if she hasn't had enough to put up with . . ."

Wexford cut him short again. "It's her identity, not her charm, that's in dispute." He was intrigued by the behavior of Jane Zoffany, who was sitting hunched up, looking anywhere but at him, and who appeared to be very frightened indeed. She had stopped sewing because her hands would have shaken once she moved each out of the other's grasp.

He went back into the shop. Natalie Arno was standing by the counter on the top of which now lay an open magazine. She was looking at this and laughing with glee rather than amusement. When she saw Wexford she showed no surprise, but smiled, holding her head a little on one side.

"Good morning, Mr.—er, Wexford, isn't it? And how are you today?" It was an Americanism delivered with an American lilt and one that seemed to require no reply. "When you close the shop, Ivan," she said, "you should also remember to lock the door. All sorts of undesirables could come in."

Zoffany said with gallantry, but stammering a little, "That certainly doesn't include you, Natalie!"

"I'm not sure the chief inspector would agree with you." She gave Wexford a sidelong smile. She knew. Symonds, O'Brien and Ames had lost no time in telling her. Jane Zoffany was afraid but she was not. Her black eyes sparkled. Rather ostentatiously, she closed the magazine she had been looking at, revealing the cover which showed it to belong to the medium hard genre of pornography. Plainly, this was Zoffany's under-the-counter solace that she had lighted on. He flushed, seized it rather too quickly from under her hands and thrust it between some catalogues in a pile. Natalie's face became pensive and innocent. She put up her hands to her hair and her full breasts in the sweater rose with the movement, which seemed to have been made quite artlessly, simply to tuck in a tortoiseshell pin.

"Did you want to interrogate me, Mr. Wexford?"

"Not yet," he said. "At present I'll be content if you'll give me the name and address of the people whose party you and Mrs. Zoffany went to on the evening of 27 January."

She told him, without hesitation or surprise.

"Thank you, Mrs. Arno."

At the door of the room where Jane Zoffany was he paused, looked at him and giggled. "You can call me Mrs. X, if you like. Feel free."

A housekeeper in a dark dress that was very nearly a uniform admitted him to the house in a cul-de-sac off Kensington Church Street. She was a pretty, dark-haired woman in her thirties who doubtless looked on her job as a career and played her part so well that he felt she *was* playing, was acting with some skill the role of a deferential servant. In a way she reminded him of Ted Hicks.

"Mrs. Mountnessing hopes you won't mind going upstairs, Chief Inspector. Mrs. Mountnessing is taking her coffee after luncheon in the little sitting room."

It was a far cry from the house in De Beauvoir Square to which Natalie had sent him, a latter-day Bohemia where there had been Indian bedspreads draping the walls and a smell of marijuana for anyone who cared to sniff for it. Here the wall decorations were hunting prints, ascending parallel to the line of the staircase whose treads were carpeted in thick soft olive-green. The first-floor hall was wide, milk chocolate with white cornice and moldings, the same green carpet, a *Hortus siccus* in a copper trough on a console table, a couple of fat-seated, round-backed chairs upholstered in golden-brown velvet, a twinkling chandelier and a brown table lamp with a cream satin shade. There are several thousand such interiors in the Royal Borough of Kensington and Chelsea. A paneled door was pushed open and Wexford found himself in the presence of Natalie Arno's Aunt Gladys, Mrs. Rupert Mountnessing, the sister of Kathleen Camargue.

His first impression was of someone cruelly encaged and literally gasping for breath. It was a fleeting image. Mrs. Mountnessing was just a fat woman in a too-tight corset which compressed her body from thighs to chest into the shape of a sausage and thrust a shelf of bosom up to buttress her double chin. This constrained flesh was sheathed in biscuit-colored wool and upon the shelf rested three strands of pearls. Her face had become a cluster of pouches rather than a nest of wrinkles. It was thickly painted and surmounted by an intricate white-gold coiffure that was as smooth and stiff as a wig. The only area of Mrs. Mountnessing which kept some hint of youth was her legs. And these were still excellent: slender, smooth, not varicosed, the ankles slim, the tapering feet shod in classic court shoes of beige glacé kid. They reminded him of Natalie's legs, they were exactly like. Did that mean anything? Very little. There are only a few types of leg, after all. One never said "She has her aunt's legs" as one might say a woman had her father's nose or her grandmother's eyes.

The room was as beige and gold as it owner. On a low table was a coffee cup, coffee pot, sugar basin and cream jug in ivory china with a Greek key design on it in gold. Mrs. Mountnessing rose when he came in and held out a hand much beringed, the old woman's claw-like nails filed to points and painted dark red.

"Bring another cup, will you, Miranda?"

It was the voice of an elderly child, petulant, permanently aggrieved. Wexford thought that the voice and the puckered face told of a lifetime of hurts, real or imagined. Rupert Mountnessing was presumably dead and gone long ago, and Dinah Sternhold had told him there had been no children. Would Natalie, real or false, hope for an inheritance here? Almost the first words uttered by Mrs. Mountnessing told him that, if so, she hoped in vain.

"You said on the phone you wanted to talk to me about my niece. But I know nothing about my niece in recent years and I don't—I don't want to. I should have explained that to you, I realize that now. I shouldn't have let you come all this way when I've nothing at all to tell you." Her eyes blinked more often or more obviously than most people's. The effect was to give the impression she fought off tears. "Thank you, Miranda." She took the coffee cup and listened, subsiding back into her chair as he told her the reason for his visit.

"Anastasia," she said.

The Tichborne Claimant had been recalled, now the Tsar's youngest daughter. Wexford did not relish the reminder, for wasn't it a fact that Anastasia's grandmother, the one person who could positively have identified her, had refused ever to see the claimant, and that as a result of that refusal no positive identification had ever been made?

"We hope it won't come to that," he said. "You seem to be her nearest relative, Mrs. Mountnessing. Will you agree to see her in my presence and tell me if she is who she says she is?"

Her reaction, the look on her face, reminded him of certain people he had in the past asked to come and identify, not a living person, but a corpse in the mortuary. She put a hand up to each cheek. "Oh no, I couldn't do that. I'm sorry, but it's impossible. I couldn't ever see Natalie again."

He accepted it. She had forewarned him with her mention of Anastasia. If he insisted on her going with him the chances were she would make a positive identification simply to get the whole thing over as soon as possible. Briefly he wondered what it could have been that her niece, while still a young girl, had done to her, and then he joined her at the other end of the room where she stood contemplating a table that was used entirely as a stand for photographs in silver frames.

"That's my sister."

A dark woman with dark eyes, but nevertheless intensely English. Perhaps there was something of the woman he knew as Natalie Arno in the broad brow and pointed chin.

"She had cancer. She was only forty-five when she died. It was a terrible blow to my poor brother-in-law. He sold their house in Pomfret and built that one in Kingsmarkham and called it Sterries. Sterries is the name of the village in Derbyshire where my parents had their country place. Kathleen and Manuel first met there."

Camargue and his wife were together among the photographs on the table. Arm-in-arm, walking along some Mediterranean sea front; seated side by side on a low wall in an English garden; in a group with a tall woman so like Camargue that she had to be his sister, and with two small dark-haired smiling girls. A ray of sunlight, obliquely slanted at three on a winter's afternoon, fell upon the handsome mustached face of a man in the uniform of a colonel of the Grenadier Guards. Rupert Mountnessing, no doubt. A little bemused by so many faces, Wexford turned away.

"Did Sir Manuel go to the United States after your niece went to live there?"

"Not to see *her*. I think he went there on a tour—yes, I'm sure he did, though it must be ten or twelve years since he gave up playing. His arthritis crippled him, poor Manuel. We saw very little of each other in recent years, but I was fond of him, he was a sweet man. I would have gone to the memorial service but Miranda wouldn't let me. She didn't want me to risk bronchitis in that terrible cold."

Mrs. Mountnessing, it seemed, was willing to talk about any aspect of family life except her niece. She sat down again, blinking back non-existent tears, held ramrod stiff by her corset. Wexford persisted.

"He went on a tour. Did he make any private visits?"

"He may have done." She said it in the way people do when they dodge the direct affirmative but don't want to lie.

"But he didn't visit his daughter while he was there?"

"California's three thousand miles from the east coast," she said, "it's as far again as from here."

Wexford shook his head dismissively. "I don't understand that for nineteen years Sir Manuel never saw his daughter. It's not as if he was a poor man or a man who never traveled. If he had been a vindictive man, a man to bear a grudge—but everyone tells me how nice he was, how kind, how good. I might say I'd had golden opinions from all sorts of people. Yet for nineteen years he never made an effort to see his only child and allegedly all because she ran away from college and married someone he didn't know."

She said so quietly that Wexford hardly heard her, "It wasn't like that." Her voice gained a little strength but it was full of distress. "He wrote to her—oh, ever so many times. When my sister was very ill, was in fact dying, he wrote to her and asked her to come home. I don't know if she answered but she didn't come. My sister died and she didn't come. Manuel made a new will and wrote to her, telling her he was leaving her everything because it was right she should have his money and her mother's. She didn't answer and he gave up writing."

I wonder how you come to know that? he asked himself, looking at the crumpled profile, the chin that now trembled.

"I'm telling you all this," said Mrs. Mountnessing, "to make you understand that my niece is cruel, cruel, a cruel unfeeling girl and violent too. She even struck her mother once. Did you know that?" The note in her voice grew hysterical and Wexford, watching the blinking eyes, the fingers clasping and unclasping in her lap, wished he had not mentioned the estrangement. "She's a nymphomaniac too. Worse than that, it doesn't matter to her who the men are, her own relations, it's too horrible to talk about, it's too . . ."

He interrupted her gently. He got up to go. "Thank you for your help, Mrs. Mountnessing. I can't see a sign of any of these propensities in the woman I know."

Miranda showed him out. As he crossed to the head of the stairs he heard a very soft whimpering sound from the room he had left, the sound of an elderly child beginning to cry.

9

A birth certificate, a marriage certificate, an American driving license complete with immediately recognizable photograph taken three years before, a United States passport complete with immediately recognizable photograph taken the previous September, and perhaps most convincing of all, a letter to his daughter from Camargue, dated 1963, in which he informed her that he intended to make her his sole heir. All these documents had been readily submitted to Symonds, O'Brien and Ames, who invited Wexford along to their offices in the precinct over the British Home Stores to view them.

Kenneth Ames, distant and chatty as ever, said he had personally seen Mrs. Arno, interviewed her exhaustively and elicited from her a number of facts about the Camargue family and her own childhood which were currently being verified. Mrs. Arno had offered to take a blood test but since this could only prove that she was *not* Camargue's daughter, not that she was, and since no one seemed to know what Camargue's blood group had been, it was an impracticable idea. Mr. Ames said she seemed heartily amused by the whole business, a point of course in her favor. She had even produced samples of her handwriting from when she was at the Royal Academy of Music to be compared with her writing of the present day.

"Do you know what she said to him?" Wexford said afterwards, meeting Burden for a drink in the Olive and Dove. "She's got a nerve. 'It's a pity I didn't do anything criminal when I was a teenager,' she said. 'They'd have my fingerprints on record and that would solve everything.' "

Burden didn't smile. "If she's not Natalie Camargue, when could the change-over have taken place?"

"Provided we accept what Zoffany says, not recently. Say more than two years ago but after the death of Vernon Arno. According to Ames, he would seem to have died in a San Francisco hospital in 1971."

"He must have been young still." Burden echoed Wexford's words to Ivan Zoffany. "What did he die of?"

"Leukemia. No one's suggesting there was anything odd about his death, though there's a chance we'll know more when we hear from the California police. But, Mike, if there was substitution, if this is an assumed identity, it was assumed for some other reason. That is, it wasn't put on for the sake of inheriting from Camargue."

Burden gave a dubious nod. "It would mean the true Natalie was dead."

"She may be but there are other possibilities. The true Natalie may be incurably ill in some institution or have become insane or gone to live in some inaccessible place. And the impostor could be someone who needed an identity because keeping her own was dangerous, because, for instance, she was some kind of fugitive from justice. That Camargue was rich, that Camargue was old, that Natalie was to be his sole heir, all these facts might be *incidental*, might be a piece of luck for the impostor which she only later decided to take advantage of. The identity would have been taken on originally as a safety measure, even perhaps as the only possible lifeline, and I think it was taken on at a point where the minimum of deception would have been needed. Maybe at the time the move was made from San Francisco to Los Angeles or much later, at the time when Tina Zoffany died."

Burden, who seemed not to have been concentrating particularly on any of this, said suddenly, looking up from his drink and fixing Wexford with his steel-colored eyes:

"Why did she come to this country at all?"

"To make sure of the dibs," said Wexford.

"No." Burden shook his head. "No, that wasn't the reason. Impostor or real, she was in no doubt about what you call the dibs. She'd had that letter from Camargue, promising her her inheritance. She need do nothing but wait. There was no need to re-establish herself in his eyes, no need to placate him. If she'd felt there was she'd have tried it before. After all, he was getting on for eighty.

"And it's no good saying she came back because he was getting married again. No one knew he was getting married till 10 December, when his engagement was in the *Telegraph*. She came back to this country in November but she made no attempt to see Camargue until after she read about his engagement. She was here for three or four weeks before that. Doing what? Planning what?"

Admiration was not something Wexford had often felt for the inspector in the past. Sympathy, yes, affection and a definite need, for Burden had most encouragingly fulfilled the function of an Achates or a Boswell, if not quite a Watson. But admiration? Burden was showing unexpected deductive powers that were highly gratifying to witness, and Wexford wondered if they were the fruit of happiness or of reading aloud from great literature in the evenings.

"Go on," he said.

"So why did she come back? Because she was sentimental for her own home, her ain countree, as you might say?" As Scott might say, thought Wexford. Burden went on, "She's a bit young for those feelings. She's an American citizen, she was settled in California. If she is Natalie Camargue she'd lived there longer than here, she'd no relatives here but a father and an aunt she didn't get on with, and no friends unless you count those Zoffanys.

"If she's an impostor, coming back was a mad thing to do. Stay in America and when Camargue dies his solicitors will notify her of the death, and though she'll no doubt then have to come here and swear affidavits and that sort of thing, *no one will question who she is*. No one would have questioned it if she hadn't shown herself to Camargue."

"But she had to do that," Wexford objected. "Her whole purpose surely in going to see him was to persuade him not to remarry."

"She didn't know that purpose would even exist when she left the United States in November. And if she'd stayed where she was she might never have known of Camargue's remarriage until he eventually died. What would that announcement have merited in a California newspaper? The *Los Angeles Times*, for instance? A paragraph tucked away somewhere. 'Former world-famous British flautist . . .' "

"They say flutist over there."

"Flautist, flutist, what does it matter? Until we know *why* she came here I've got a feeling we're not going to get at the truth about this."

"The truth about who she is, d'you mean?"

"The truth about Camargue's death." And Burden said with a certain crushing triumph, "You're getting an obsession about who this woman is. I knew you would, I said so. What interests me far more is the murder of Camargue and who did it. Can't you see that in the context of the murder, who she is is an irrelevance?"

"No," said Wexford. "Who she is is everything."

The California police had nothing to tell Wexford about Natalie Arno. She was unknown to them, had never been in any trouble or associated with any trouble.

"The litigation in the Tichborne case," said Burden gloomily, "went on for three years and cost ninety thousand pounds. That was in 1874. Think what the equivalent of that would be today."

"We haven't had any litigation yet," said Wexford, "or spent a single penny. Look on the bright side. Think of the claimant getting a fourteen-year sentence for perjury."

In the meantime Kenneth Ames had interviewed two people who had known Camargue's daughter when she was an adolescent. Mavis Rolland had been at the Royal Academy of Music at the same time as Natalie Camargue and was now head of the music department at a girls' school on the South Coast. In her opinion there was no doubt that Natalie Arno was the former Natalie Camargue. She professed to find her not much changed except for her voice, which she would not have recognized. On the other hand, Mary Woodhouse, a living-in maid who had worked for the Camargue family while they were in Pomfret, said she would have known the voice anywhere. In Ames's presence Mrs. Woodhouse had talked to Natalie about Shaddough's Hall Farm where they had lived and Natalie had been able to recall events which Mrs. Woodhouse said no impostor could have known.

Wexford wondered why Natalie had not proffered as witnesses for her support her aunt and that old family friend, Philip Cory. It was possible, of course, that in the case of her aunt (if she really was Natalie Arno) the dislike was mutual and that, just as he had feared Mrs. Mountnessing would recognize her as her niece to avoid protracting an interview, so Natalie feared to meet her aunt lest animosity should make her refuse that recognition. But Cory she had certainly seen since she returned home, and Cory had so surely believed in her as to cling to her arm in the excess of emotion he had no doubt felt at his old friend's obsequies. Was there some reason she didn't want Cory brought into this?

In the early years of broadcasting Philip Cory had achieved some success by writing incidental music for radio. But this is not the kind of thing which makes a man's name. If Cory had done this at all it was on the strength of his light opera *Aimée*, based on the story of the Empress Josephine's cousin, the French Sultana. After its London season it had been enthusiastically taken up by amateur operatic societies, largely because it was comparatively easy to sing, had a huge cast, and the costumes required for it could double for *Entführung* or even *Aladdin*. This was particularly the case in Cory's own locality, where he was looked upon as something of a pet bard. Driving out to the environs of Myringham where the composer lived, Wexford noted in the villages at least three posters announcing that *Aimée* was to be performed again. It was likely then to be a disappointed man he was on his way to see. Local fame is gratifying only at the beginning of a career, and it could not have afforded much solace to Cory to see that his more frivolous work was to be staged by the Myfleet and District Operatic Society (tickets £1.20, licensed bar opens seventy-thirty) while his tone poem *April Fire* and his ballet music for the *Flowers of Evil* were forgotten.

Parents can of course (as Wexford knew personally) enjoy success vicariously. Philip Cory might be scarcely remembered outside village-hall audiences, but his son Blaise Cory was a celebrity as only a television personality can be. His twice-weekly show of soul-searching interviews, drumming up support for charities, and professing aid for almost anyone out of a job, a home or a marriage, vied for pride of place with *Runway* in the popularity ratings. The name was as much a household word as Frost or Parkinson; the bland, handsome, rather larger-than-life face instantly familiar.

"But he doesn't live here, does he?" said Burden, whose *bête noire* Blaise Cory was.

"Not as far as I know." Wexford tapped the driver on the shoulder. "Those are the gates up ahead, I think. On the left."

It had been necessary to keep an eye out for Moidore Lodge, which was in deep country, was three miles from the nearest village and, Cory had told Wexford on the phone, was invisible from the road. The pillars that supported the gates and on which sat a pair of stone wolves or possibly Alsatians—they very much resembled Nancy—were, however, unmistakable. The car turned in and, as the drive descended, entered an avenue of plane trees. And very strange and sinister they looked at this season, their trunks and limbs half covered in olive-green bark, half stripped to flesh color, so that they appeared, or would have appeared to the fanciful, like shivering forms whose nakedness was revealed through rags. At the end of this double row of trees Moidore Lodge, three floors tall, narrow, and painted a curious shade of pale pea-green, glared formidably at visitors.

To ring the front-door bell it was necessary to climb half a dozen steps, though at the top of them there was no covered porch, nothing but a thin railing on each side. The wind blew sharply off the downs. Wexford, accustomed of late, as he remarked to Burden, to moving among those in the habit of being waited on, expected to be let in by a man or a maid or at least a cleaning woman, and was surprised when the door was opened by Cory himself.

He was no bigger than the impression of him Wexford had gained from that glimpse outside St. Peter's, a little thin old man with copious white hair as silky as floss. Rather than appearing disappointed, he had a face that was both cheerful and peevish. He wore jeans and the kind of heavy navy-blue sweater that is called a guernsey, which gave him a look of youth, or the look perhaps of *a* youth who suffers from some terrible prematurely aging disease. Before speaking, he looked them up and down closely. Indeed, they had passed through the over-heated, dusty, amazingly untidy and untended hall and were in the overheated, dusty rubbish heap of a living room before he spoke.

"Do you know," he said, "you are the first policemen I've ever actually had in my house. In any house I've ever lived in. Not the first I've ever *spoken* to, of course. I've *spoken* to them to ask the way and so forth. No doubt, I've lived a sheltered life." Having done his best to make them feel like lepers or untouchables, Cory cracked his face into a nervous smile. "The idea was distinctly strange to me. I've had to take two tranquilizers. As a matter of fact, my son is coming. I expect you've heard of my son."

Burden's face was a mask of blankness. Wexford said, Who hadn't? and proceeded to enlighten Cory as to the purpose of their visit. The result of this was that the old man had to take another Valium. It took a further full ten minutes to convince him there was a serious doubt about Natalie Arno's identity.

"Oh dear," said Cory, "oh dear, oh dear, how dreadful. Little Natalie. And she was so kind and considerate to me at poor Manuel's memorial service. Who could possibly have imagined she wasn't Natalie at all?"

"Well, she may be," said Wexford. "We're hoping you can establish that one way or the other."

Looking at the distracted little man on whom tranquilizers seemed to have no effect, Wexford couldn't help doubting if the truth could be established through his agency. "You want me to come with you and ask her a lot of questions? How horribly embarrassing that will be." Cory actually ran his fingers through his fluffy hair. Then he froze, listening like, and looking for all the world like, an alerted rabbit. "A car!" he cried. "That will be Blaise. And none too soon. I must say, really, he knew what he was about when he insisted on being here to support me."

If the father was no larger than Wexford had anticipated, the son was much smaller. The screen is a great deceiver when it comes to height. Blaise Cory was a small, wide man with a big face and eyes that twinkled as merrily as those of Santa Claus or a friendly elf. He came expansively into the room, holding out both hands to Wexford.

"And how is Sheila? Away on her honeymoon? Isn't that marvelous?" Forewarned, astute, one who had to make it his business to know who was who, he had done his homework. "You know, she's awfully like you. I almost think I should have known if I hadn't known, if you see what I mean."

"They want me to go and look at poor Manuel's girl and tell them if she's really her," said Cory dolefully.

His son put up his eyebrows, made a soundless whistle. "You don't mean it? Is *that* what it's about?"

He seemed less surprised than his father or Mrs. Mountnessing had been. But perhaps that was only because he daily encountered more surprising things than they did.

"Do you also know her, Mr. Cory?" Wexford asked.

"Know her? We took our first violin lessons together. Well, that's an exaggeration. Let me say we, as tots, went to the same master."

"You didn't keep it up, Blaise," said Cory senior. "You were never a *concentrating* boy. Now little Natalie was very good. I remember little Natalie playing so beautifully to me when she was fifteen or sixteen, it was Bach's Chaconne from the D minor Partita and she . . ."

Blaise interrupted him. "My dear father, it is twelve-thirty, and though I seem to remember promising to take you out to lunch, a drink wouldn't come amiss. With the possible exception of Macbeth, you must be the world's worst host." He chuckled irrepressibly at his own joke. "Now surely you have something tucked away in one of these glory holes?"

Once more Cory put his hands through his hair. He began to trot about the room, opening cupboard doors and peering along cluttered shelves as if he were as much a stranger to the house as they were. "It's because I've no one to look after me," he said distractedly. "I asked Natalie—or whoever she is, you know—I asked her if she didn't want those Hickses and if she didn't, would they come and work for me? She was rather non-committal, said she'd ask them, but I haven't heard another word. How do *you* manage?"

Wexford was saved from replying by a triumphant shout from Blaise Cory, who had found a bottle of whisky and one of dry sherry. It was now impossible to refuse a drink especially as Blaise Cory, with ferocious twinkles, declared that he knew for a fact policemen did drink on duty. The glasses were dusty and fingermarked, not to be too closely scrutinized. Nothing now remained but to fix a time with Philip

Cory for visiting Natalie, and Wexford felt it would be wise, in spite of Burden's prejudice, to invite Blaise too.

"Ah, but I've already seen her. And frankly I wouldn't have the foggiest whether she was the late lamented Sir Manuel's daughter or not; I hadn't set eyes on her since we were teenagers. She said she was Natalie and that was good enough for me."

"You were also at the memorial service?"

"Oh, no, no, no. Those morbid affairs give me the shivers. I'm a *life* person, Mr. Wexford. No, I gave Natalie lunch. Oh, it must have been a good five or six weeks ago."

"May I ask why you did that, Mr. Cory?"

"Does one have to have a reason for taking attractive ladies out to lunch apart from the obvious one? No, I'm teasing you. It was actually Natalie who phoned me, recalled our former acquaintance and asked me if I could get a friend of hers a job, a man, she didn't say his name. I'm afraid it was all rather due to my program. I don't know if a busy man like you ever has a moment to watch it? A poor thing, but mine own. I do make rather bold claims on it—not, however, without foundation *and* results—to aid people in finding—well, niches for themselves, This chap was apparently some sort of musician. Fancied himself on the box, I daresay. Anyway, I couldn't hold out much hope but I asked her to have lunch with me. Now I come to think of it, it was January 17th. I remember because that was the dear old dad's birthday."

"I was seventy-four," said Cory senior in the tone of one intending to astonish nobody, as indeed he had.

"And when you met her that day you had no doubt she was the Natalie Camargue you had once known?"

"Now wait a minute. When it came to it, I didn't meet her that day. She canceled on account of some medical thing she had to have, a biopsy, I think she said. We made a fresh date for the following Tuesday. She kept that and I must say we had a delightful time, she was absolutely charming, full of fun. I was only sorry to have to say I hadn't anything cooking for this bloke of hers. But, you know, I couldn't actually tell you if she was *our* Natalie. I mean, it obviously never occurred to me." He let his eyes light on Burden as being closer to his own age than the others. "Would you recognize a lady you hadn't seen since you were nineteen?"

Burden responded with a cold smile which had no disconcerting effect on Blaise Cory.

"It's all rather thrilling, isn't it? Quite a tonic it must be for the dear old dad."

"No, it isn't," said the composer. "It's very upsetting indeed. I think I'll come back to London with you, Blaise, since I've got to be up there tomorrow. And I think I may stay awhile. I suppose you can put up with me for a couple of weeks?"

Blaise Cory put an arm round his father's shoulders and answered with merry affirmatives. Perhaps it was Wexford's imagination that the twinkle showed signs of

strain. The kind of coincidence that leads to one's coming across a hitherto unknown word three times in the same day or receiving a letter from an acquaintance
one has dreamed of the night before was no doubt responsible for the poster in the
window of the Kingsbrook Precinct travel agents. *Come to sunny California, land
of perpetual spring* . . . A picture of what might be Big Sur and next to it one of
what might be Hearst Castle. Wexford paused and looked at it and wondered what
the chief constable would say if he suggested being sent to the Golden West in
quest of Natalie Arno's antecedents. He could just imagine Colonel Griswold's
face.

Presently he turned away and went back to the police station. He had come
from Symonds, O'Brien and Ames. Their handwriting expert had examined the
writing of the eighteen-year-old Natalie Camargue and that of the thirty-seven-
year-old Natalie Arno and expressed his opinion that, allowing for normal changes
over a period of nearly two decades, the two samples had in all probability been
made by the same person. Wexford had suggested the samples also be examined by
an expert of police choosing. Without making any positive objection, Ames murmured that it would be unwise to spoil the ship with too many cooks.

Wexford thought he saw a better way.

"Mike," he said, putting his head round the door of Burden's office, "where
can we get hold of a violin?"

10

Burden's wife was something of a paragon. She was a history teacher, she was well
read in English literature, she was an excellent cook and dressmaker and now it
appeared she was musical too.

"You never told me Jenny played the violin," said Wexford.

"As a matter of fact," said Burden rather shyly, "she used to be with the Pilgrim
String Quartet." This was a local ensemble that enjoyed a little more than local
fame. "I expect we could borrow her Hills if we were very careful with it."

"Her *what*?"

"Her Hills. It's a well-known make of violin."

"If you say so, Stradivarius."

Burden brought the violin along in the morning. They were going to call for
Philip Cory at his son's home and drive him to De Beauvoir Place. It was a bright
sunny day, the first since the snow had gone.

Blaise Cory lived on Campden Hill, not far from Mrs. Mountnessing, and work
seemed to have claimed him, for his father was alone in the big penthouse flat.
Although he popped a Valium pill into his mouth as soon as he saw them, a night
in London had evidently done him good. He was sprightly, his cheeks pink, and
he had dressed himself in a dark suit with a thin red stripe, a pink shirt and a

burgundy silk tie, more as if he were going to a smart luncheon party than taking part in a criminal investigation.

In the car he was inclined to be talkative.

"I think I shall write to those Hickses personally. I've no reason to believe they're not well disposed towards me. I understand they like the country and the thing about Moidore Lodge is, it's in the real country. Charming as poor Manuel's place is, I always used to think there was something Metroland-ish about it. One might as well be living in Hampstead Garden Suburb. Do you know, I thought it would be quite an ordeal facing little Natalie today, but actually I feel rather excited at the prospect. London is such a stimulus, don't you find? It seems to tone up one's whole system. And if she isn't Natalie, there's nothing to be embarrassed about."

Wexford had no intention of going into the bookshop. The door to the upstairs flat was at the side of the building, a paneled door with a pane of glass in it, set under a porch with a steep tiled roof. As they walked up the path, Wexford leading and Burden bringing up the rear with the violin, the door opened, a woman came out and it immediately closed again. The woman was elderly and so tiny as to be almost a midget. She wore a black coat and a brightly colored knitted hat and gloves. Cory said:

"Good gracious me! It's Mrs. Woodhouse, isn't it?"

"That's right, sir, and you're Mr. Cory." She spoke with a Sussex burr. "How have you been keeping? Mustn't grumble, that's what I always say. I see Mr. Blaise on the telly last night, he's a real scream, just the same as ever. You living in London now, are you?"

"Oh dear, no," said Cory. "Down in the same old place." His eyes widened suddenly as if with inspiration. "I haven't anyone to look after me. I don't suppose . . ."

"I'm retired, sir, and never had so much to do. I don't have a moment for myself let alone other folks, so I'll say bye-bye now and nice to see you after all this time."

She scuttled off in the direction of De Beauvoir Square, looking at her watch like the White Rabbit as she went.

"Who was that?" said Burden.

"She used to work for poor Manuel and Kathleen when they lived at Shaddough's Hall Farm. I can't think what she's doing up here."

The door, though closed, had been left on the latch. Wexford pushed it open and they went up the steep staircase. Natalie had come out on to the landing and was waiting for them at the top. Wexford had thought about her so much, had indeed become so obsessive about her, that since last seeing her he had created an image of her in his mind that was seductive, sinister, Mata Hari-like, corrupt, guileful and serpentine. Before the reality this chimera showed itself briefly for the absurd delusion it was and then dissolved. For here, standing before them, was a charming and pretty woman to whom none of these pejorative expressions could possibly apply. Her black hair hung loose to her shoulders, held back by a velvet Alice band. She wore the skirt Jane Zoffany had been altering and with it a simple white shirt and dark blue cardigan. It was very near a school uniform and there was something of the schoolgirl about her as she brought her face down to Cory's and kissed him, saying with the slightest edge of reproach:

"It's good to see you, Uncle Philip. I only wish the circumstances were different."

Cory drew his face away. He said in a kind of sharp chirp, "One must do one's duty as a citizen."

She laughed at that and patted his shoulder. They all went into a small and unpretentious living room from which a kitchen opened. It was all a far cry from Sterries. The furnishings looked as if they had come down to the Zoffanys from defunct relatives who hadn't paid much for them when they were new. Nothing seemed to have been added by Natalie except a small shelf of paperbacks which could only be designated as non-Zoffany because none of them was science fiction.

There was an aroma of coffee and from the kitchen the sound, suggestive of some large hibernating creature snoring, that a percolator makes.

"Do sit down," said Natalie, "Make yourselves at home. Excuse me while I see to the coffee." She seemed totally carefree and gave no sign of having noticed what Burden had brought into the flat. There's no art, thought Wexford, to find the mind's construction in the face.

The coffee, when it came, was good. "The secret," said Natalie gaily, "is to put enough in." Uttering this cliché, she laughed. "I'm afraid the British don't do that."

She surely couldn't be enjoying herself like this if she was not Natalie, if there was any chance of her failing the test ahead of her. He glanced at Burden, whose eyes were on her, who seemed to be studying her appearance and was recalling perhaps newspaper photographs or actual glimpses of Camargue. Having taken a sip of his coffee into which he ladled three spoonfuls of sugar, Cory started at once on his questioning. He would have made a good quizmaster. Perhaps it was from him that Blaise had inherited his talents.

"You and your parents went to live at Shaddough's Hall Farm when you were five. Can you remember what I gave you for your sixth birthday?"

She didn't hesitate. "A kitten. It was a gray one, a British Blue."

"Your cat had been run over and I gave you that one to replace it."

"We called it Panther."

Cory had forgotten that. But Wexford could see that now he remembered and was shaken. He asked less confidently: "Where was the house?"

"On the Pomfret to Cheriton road. You'll have to do better than that, Uncle Philip. Anyone could have found out where Camargue lived."

For answer he threw a question at her in French. Wexford wasn't up to under-

standing it but he gave Cory full marks for ingenuity. There was more to this old
man than at first met the eye. She answered in fluent French and Cory addressed
her in what Wexford took to be Spanish. This was something he was sure Symonds,
O'Brien and Ames had not thought of. But what a sound test it was. Momentarily
he held his breath, for she was not answering, her face had that puzzled foolish
look people have when spoken to in a language they know less thoroughly than
they have claimed.

Cory repeated what he had said. Burden cleared his throat and moved a little
in his chair. Wexford held himself perfectly still, waiting, knowing that every
second which passed made it more and more likely that she had been discovered
and exposed. And then, as Cory was about to speak for the third time, she broke
into a flood of fast Spanish so that Cory himself was taken aback, uncomprehending
apparently, until she explained more slowly what it was that she had said.

Wexford drank his coffee and she, looking at him mischievously, refilled his
cup. On Burden she bestowed one of her sparkling smiles. Her long hair fell
forward, Cleopatra-like, in two heavy tresses to frame her face. It was a young face,
Wexford thought, even possibly too young for the age she professed to be. And
wasn't it also *too Spanish*? Natalie Camargue's mother had been English, typically
English, her father half-French. Would their daughter look quite so much like one
of Goya's women? None of the evidence, convincing though it was, was as yet
conclusive. Why shouldn't an impostor speak Spanish? If the substitution had taken
place in Los Angeles she might even be Mexican. Why not know about the kitten
and its name if she had been a friend of the true Natalie and had set out to absorb
her childhood history?

"What was the first instrument you learned to play?" Cory was asking.

"The recorder."

"How old were you when you began the violin?"

"Eight."

"Who was your first master?"

"I can't remember," she said.

"When you were fifteen you were living at Shaddough's Hall Farm and you
were on holiday from school. It was August. Your father had just come back from
a tour of—America, I think."

"Canada."

"I do believe you're right." Cory, having been determined almost from Wexford's first words on the subject to consider her an impostor, grew more and more
astonished as the interrogation went on. "You're right, it was. God bless my soul.
Do you remember my coming to dinner with your parents? I and my wife? Can
you remember that evening?"

"I think so. I hadn't seen you for about a year."

"Before dinner I asked you to play something for me and you did and . . ."

She didn't even allow him to finish.

"I played Bach's Chaconne from the D minor Partita."

Cory was stunned into silence. He stared at her and then turned on Wexford an affronted look.

"It was too difficult for me," she said lightly. "You clapped but I felt I'd made a mess of it." The expressions on the three men's faces afforded her an amused satisfaction. "That's proof enough, isn't it? Shall we all have a drink to celebrate my reinstatement?" She jumped up, took the tray and went into the kitchen, leaving the door open.

It was perhaps this open door and the sound of their hostess humming light-heartedly that stopped Cory from rounding on Wexford. Instead he raised his whiskery white eyebrows almost into his fluffy white hair and shook his head vigorously, a gesture that plainly said he felt he had been brought here on a wild-goose chase. If she wasn't Natalie, Wexford thought, there was no way she could have known about that piece of music. It was impossible to imagine circumstances in which the true Natalie would have spoken of such a thing to the false. If she had done so it would presuppose her having recounted every occasion on which she had played to a friend, listing every friend and every piece of music, since it could never have been foreseen that this particular piece would be inquired about. That Cory would ask this question, a question that had no doubt come into his mind because of his reference to the Bach Chaconne on the previous day, could only have been guessed at by those who had been present at the time, himself, Burden and Blaise.

So one could almost agree with her and acclaim her reinstated as Camargue's heir. She had passed the test no impostor could have passed. He looked at her wonderingly as she returned to the room, the contents of the tray now exchanged for a couple of bottles and an ice bucket. If she was, as she now seemed undoubtedly to be, Natalie Arno, how had Camargue possibly been deceived in the matter? This woman would never have mispronounced a word or a name in a foreign language known to her. And if Camargue had indeed accused her of doing so, it had been in her power to correct that misapprehension at once and to furnish him with absolute proof of who she was. For now Wexford had no doubt that if Camargue had asked her she would have recalled for him the minutest details of her infancy, of the family, of esoteric domestic customs which no one living but he and she could have known. But Camargue had been an old man, wandering in his wits as well as short-sighted and growing deaf. That tiresome woman Dinah Sternhold had wasted their time, repeating to him what was probably only one amongst several of a dotard's paranoid delusions.

Burden looked as if he was ready to leave. He had reached down to grasp once more the handle of the violin case.

"Would you play that piece of music for us now, Mrs. Arno?" Wexford said.

If she had noticed the violin, as she surely must have done, she had presumably supposed it the property of Cory and unconnected with herself, for with his question her manner changed. She had put the tray down and had been about to lift her hands from it, but her hands remained where they were and slightly stiffened. Her face was unaltered, but she was no longer quite in command of the situation and she was no longer amused.

"No, I don't think I would," she said.

"You've given up the violin?"

"No, I still play in an amateurish sort of way, but I'm out of practice."

"We'll make allowances, Mrs. Arno," said Wexford. "The inspector and I aren't competent to judge, anyway." Burden gave him a look implying that *he* might be. "If you'll play the violin so as to satisfy Mr. Cory I will myself be satisfied that Sir Manuel had—made a mistake."

She was silent. She sat still, looking down, considering. Then she put out her hand for the violin case and drew it towards her. But she seemed not quite to know how to open it, for she fumbled with the catch.

"Here, let me," said Burden.

She got up and looked at the tray she had brought in. "I forgot the glasses. Excuse me."

Burden lifted out the violin carefully, then the bow. The sight of it restored Cory's temper and he touched one of the strings lightly with his finger. From the kitchen came a sudden tinkle of breaking glass, an exclamation, then a sound of water running.

"You may as well put that instrument away again," said Wexford quietly.

She came in and her face was white. "I broke a glass." Wrapped round her left hand was a bunch of wet tissues, rapidly reddening, and as she scooped the sodden mass away, Wexford saw a long thin cut, bright red, across three fingertips.

11

It should have been the beginning, not the end. They should have been able to proceed with a prosecution for deception and an investigation of the murder of Sir Manuel Camargue. And Wexford, calling on Symonds, O'Brien and Ames with what he thought to be proof that Natalie Arno was not who she said she was, felt confident he had a case. She might speak French and Spanish, she might know the most abstruse details about the Camargues' family life, but she couldn't play the violin and that was the crux. She had not dared to refuse so she had deliberately cut her fingers on the tips where they must press the strings. Kenneth Ames listened to all this with a vagueness bordering on indifference which would have alarmed Wexford if he hadn't been used to the man's manner. He seemed reluctant to disclose the address of Mrs. Mary Woodhouse but finally did so when pressed.

She lived with her son and daughter-in-law, both of whom were out of work, in a council flat on the Pomfret housing estate. While Wexford talked to her, explaining gently but at some length what he suspected, she at first sat still and attentive, but when the purpose of his visit became clear to her, she pushed her brows together and stuck out her underlip and picked up the work on which she had been engaged before he arrived. This was some sort of bed cover, vast in size, of dead-white cotton crochet work. Mrs. Woodhouse's crochet hook flashed in and out as she expended her anger through her fingers.

"I don't know what you're talking about, I don't know what you mean." She repeated these sentences over and over whenever he paused for a reply. She was a small, sharp-featured old woman whose dark hair had faded to charcoal color. "I went to see Mrs. Arno because she asked me. Why shouldn't I? I've got a sister living in Hackney that's been a bit off-color. I've been stopping with her and what with Mrs. Arno living like only a stone's throw away, it's only natural I'd go and see her, isn't it? I've known her since she was a kiddy, it was me brought her up as much as her mother."

"How many times have you seen her, Mrs. Woodhouse?"

"I don't know what you mean. Hundreds of times, thousands of times. If you mean been to her place like this past week, just the twice. The time you saw me and two days previous. I'd like to know what you're getting at."

"Were some of those 'hundreds of times' last November and December, Mrs. Woodhouse? Did Mrs. Arno go and see you when she first arrived in this country?"

"I'll tell you when I first saw her. Two weeks back. When that solicitor, that Mr. Ames, come here and asked me the same sort of nonsense you're asking me. Only he knew when he was beaten." The crochet hook jerked faster and the ball of yarn bounced on Mary Woodhouse's lap. "Had I any doubt Mrs. Arno was Miss Natalie Camargue?" She put a wealth of scorn into her voice. "Of course I hadn't, not a shadow of doubt."

"I expect Mrs. Arno asked you a great many questions, didn't she? I expect she asked you to remind her of things in her childhood which had slipped her mind. The name of a gray kitten, for instance?"

"Panther," said Mrs. Woodhouse. "That was his name. Why shouldn't I tell her? She'd forgotten, she was only a kiddy. I don't know what you mean, asking me things like that. Of course I've got a good memory, I was famous in the family for my memory. Mr. Camargue—he was Mr. Camargue then—he used to say, Mary, you're just like an elephant, and people'd look at me, me being so little and thin, and he'd say, You never forget a thing."

"I expect you understand what conspiracy is, don't you, Mrs. Woodhouse? You understand what is meant by a conspiracy to defraud someone of what is theirs by right of law? I don't think you would want to be involved in something of that kind, would you? Something which could get you into very serious trouble?"

She repeated her formula fiercely, one hand clutching the crochet hook, the other the ball of yarn. "I don't know what you mean. I don't know what you're talking about."

Mavis Rolland, the music teacher, was next on his list to be seen. He had the phone in his hand, he was about to dial the school number and arrange an appointment with her when Kenneth Ames was announced.

It was as warm in Wexford's office as it was in the Kingsbrook Precinct, but Ames removed neither his black, waisted overcoat nor his black-and-gray check worsted scarf. He took the chair Wexford offered him and fixed his eyes on the northern aspect of St. Peter's spire just as he was in the habit of contemplating its southern elevation from his own window.

The purpose of his call, he said, was to inform the police that Symonds, O'Brien and Ames had decided to recognize Mrs. Natalie Kathleen Camargue Arno as Sir Manuel Camargue's rightful heir.

In fact, said Ames, it was only their regard for truth and their horror of the possibility of fraud that had led them to investigate in the first place what amounted to malicious slander.

"We were obliged to look into it, of course, though it never does to place too much credence on that kind of mischief-making."

"Camargue himself . . ." Wexford began.

"My dear chap, according to Mrs. Steinbeck, according to *her*. I'm afraid you've been a bit led up the garden. Lost your sense of proportion too, if I may say so. Come now. You surely can't have expected my client to play you a pretty tune on that fiddle when she'd got a nasty cut on her hand."

Wexford noted that Natalie Arno had become "my client." He was more surprised than he thought he could be by Ames's statement. He was shocked, and he sat in silence, digesting it, beginning to grasp its implications. Still staring skywards, Ames said chattily:

"There was never any real doubt, of course." He delivered one of his strange confused metaphors. "It was a case of making a mare's nest out of a molehill. But we do now have incontrovertible proof."

"Oh yes?" Wexford's eyebrows went up.

"My client was able to produce her dentist, chappie who used to see to the Camargue family's teeth. Man called Williams from London, Wigmore Street, in point of fact. He'd still got his records and—well, my client's jaw and Miss Natalie Camargue's are indisputably one and the same. She hasn't even lost a tooth."

Wexford made his appointment with Miss Rolland but was obliged to cancel it next day. For in the interim he had an unpleasant interview with the chief constable. Charles Griswold, with his uncanny resemblance to the late General de

Gaulle, as heavily built, grave and intense a man as Ames was slight, shallow and *distrait*, stormed in upon him on the following morning.

"Leave it, Reg, forget it. Let it be as if you had never heard the name Camargue."

"Because an impostor has seduced Ames into believing a pack of lies, sir?"

"*Seduced?*"

Wexford made an impatient gesture with his hand. "I was speaking metaphorically, of course. *She is not Natalie Arno.* My firm belief is that ever since she came here she's been employing a former servant of the Camargue family to instruct her in matters of family history. As for the dentist, did Symonds, O'Brien and Ames check on him? Did they go to him or did he come to them? If this is a conspiracy in which a considerable number of people are involved . . ."

"You know I haven't the least idea what you're talking about, don't you? All I'm saying is, if a reputable firm of solicitors such as Symonds, O'Brien and Ames will accept this woman and permit her to inherit a very significant property, we will accept her too. And we'll forget way-out notions of pushing old men into frozen lakes when we have not a shred of evidence that Camargue died anything but a natural death. Is that understood?"

"If you say so, it must be, sir."

"It must," said the chief constable.

Not the beginning but the end. Wexford had become obsessional about cases before, and the path these obsessions took had been blocked by just such obstacles and opposition. The feeling of frustration was a familiar one to him but it was none the less bitter for that. He stood by the window, cursing under his breath, gazing at the opaque pale sky. The weather had become raw and icy again, a white mist lifting only at midday and then hanging threateningly at tree height. Sheila was coming back today. He couldn't remember whether she was due in at ten in the morning or ten at night and he didn't want to know. That way he couldn't worry too precisely about what was happening to her aircraft in the fog, unable to land maybe, sent off to try Luton or Manchester, running short of fuel . . . He told himself sternly, reminded himself, that air transport was the safest of all forms of travel, and let his thoughts turn back to Natalie Arno. Or whoever. Was he never to know now? Even if it were only for the satisfaction of his own curiosity, was he never to know who she was and how she had done it? The switch from one identity to another, the impersonation, the murder . . .

After what Griswold had said, he dare not, for his very job's sake, risk another interview with Mary Woodhouse, keep his appointment with Mavis Rolland, attempt to break down the obduracy of Mrs. Mountnessing or set about exposing that fake dentist, Williams. What could he do?

The way home had necessarily to be via the Kingsbrook Precinct, for Dora had asked him to pick up a brace of pheasants ordered at the poulterers there. Proximity to the premises of Symonds, O'Brien and Ames angered him afresh, and he wished he might for a split moment become a delinquent teenager in order to daub appropriate graffiti on their brass plate. Turning from it, he found himself looking once more into the window of the travel agents.

A helpful young man spread a handful of brochures in front of him. What had been Dora's favorites? Bermuda, Mexico, anywhere warm in the United States. They had discussed it endlessly without coming to a decision, knowing this might be the only holiday of such magnitude they would ever have. The poster he had seen in the window had its twin and various highly colored siblings inside. He glanced up and it was the skyscraper-scape of San Francisco that met his eyes.

The fog had thickened while he was in there. It seemed to lay a cold wet finger on the skin of his face. He drove home very slowly, thinking once more about Sheila, but as he put his key into the front door lock the door was pulled open and there she was before him, browner than he had ever seen her, her hair bleached pale as ivory.

She put out her arms and hugged him. Dora and Andrew were in the living room.

"Heathrow's closed and we had to land at Gatwick," said Sheila, "so we thought we'd come and see you on our way. We've had such a fabulous time, Pop, I've been telling Mother, you just have to go."

Wexford laughed. "We are going to California," he said.

Part Two

12

The will, published in the *Kingsmarkham Courier*, as well as in the national press, showed Sir Manuel Camargue to have left the sum of £1,146,000 net. This modest fortune became Natalie Arno's a little more than two months after Camargue's death.

"I shouldn't call a million pounds modest," said Burden.

"It is when you consider all the people who will want their pickings," Wexford said. "All the conspirators. No wonder she's put the house up for sale."

She had moved into Sterries, but immediately put the house on the market, the asking price being £110,000. For some weeks Kingsmarkham's principal estate agents, Thacker, Prince and Co., displayed in their window colored photographs of its exterior, the music room, the drawing room and the garden, while less distinguishable shots of it appeared in the local press. But whether the house itself was too stark and simplistic in design for most people's taste or whether the price was too high, the fact was that it remained on sale throughout that period of the year when house-buying is at its peak.

"Funny to think that we know for sure she's no business to be there and no right to sell it and no right to what she gets for it," said Burden, "and there's not a damn thing we can do about it."

But Wexford merely remarked that summer had set in with its usual severity and that he was looking forward to going somewhere warm for his holiday.

The Wexfords were not seasoned travelers and this would be the farthest away from home either had ever been. Wexford felt this need not affect the preparations they must make, but Dora had reached a point just below the panic threshold. All day she had been packing and unpacking and repacking, confessing shamefacedly that she was a fool and then beginning to worry about the possibility of the house being broken into while they were away. It was useless for Wexford to point out that whether they were known to be in San Francisco or Southend would make little difference to a prospective burglar. He could only assure her that the police would keep an eye on the house. If they couldn't do that for him, whom could they do it for? Sylvia had promised to go into the house every other day in their absence and he set off that evening to give her a spare key.

Wexford's elder daughter and her husband had in the past year moved to a newer house in north Kingsmarkham, and it was only a slightly longer way round to return from their home to his own by taking Ploughman's Lane. To go and look at the house Camargue had built, and on the night before he set out to prove Natalie Arno's claim to it fraudulent, seemed a fitting act. He drove into Ploughman's Lane by way of the side road which skirted the grounds of Kingsfield House. But if Sterries had been almost invisible from the roadway in January and February, it was now entirely hidden. The screen of hornbeams, limes and planes that had been skeletons when last he was there were in full leaf and might have concealed an empty meadow rather than a house for all that could be seen of it.

It was still light at nearly nine. He was driving down the hill when he heard the sound of running feet behind him. In his rear mirror he saw a flying figure, a woman who was running down Ploughman's Lane as if pursued. It was Jane Zoffany.

There were no pursuers. Apart from her, the place was deserted, sylvan, silent, as such places mostly are even on summer nights. He pulled in to the curb and got out. She was enough in command of herself to swerve to avoid him but as she did so she saw who it was and immediately recognized him. She stopped and burst into tears, crying where she stood and pushing her knuckles into her eyes.

"Come and sit in the car," said Wexford.

She sat in the passenger seat and cried into her hands, into the thin gauzy scarf which she wore swathed round her neck over a red and yellow printed dress of Indian make. Wexford gave her his handkerchief. She cried some more and laid her head back against the headrest, gulping, the tears running down her face. She had no handbag, no coat or jacket, though the dress was sleeveless, and on her stockingless feet were Indian sandals with only a thong to attach them. Suddenly she began to speak, pausing only when sobs choked her voice.

"I thought she was wonderful. I thought she was the most wonderful, charming, gifted, *kind* person I'd ever met. And I thought she liked me, I thought she actually wanted my company. I never thought she'd really noticed my husband much, I mean except as my husband, that's all I thought he was to her, I thought it was *me* . . . And now he says . . . oh God, what am I going to do? Where shall I go? What's going to become of me?"

Wexford was nonplussed. He could make little sense of what she said but guessed she was spilling all this misery out on to him only because he was there. Anyone willing to listen would have served her purpose. He thought too, and not for the first time, that there was something unhinged about her. You could see disturbance in her eyes as much when they were dry as when they were swollen and wet with tears. She put her hand on his arm.

"I did everything for her, I bent over backwards to make her feel at home, I ran errands for her, I even mended her clothes. She took all that from me and all the time she and Ivan had been—when he went out to California they had a relationship!"

He neither winced nor smiled at the incongruous word, relic of the already outdated jargon of her youth. "Did she tell you that, Mrs. Zoffany?" he asked gently.

"He told me. Ivan told me." She wiped her face with the handkerchief. "We came down here on Wednesday to stay, we meant to stay till—oh, Sunday or Monday. The shop's a dead loss anyway, no one ever comes in, it makes no difference whether we're there or not. She invited us and we came. I know why she did now. She doesn't want him but she wants him in love with her, she wants him on a string." She shuddered and her voice broke again. "He told me this evening, just now, half an hour ago. He said he'd been in love with her for two years, ever since he first saw her. He was longing for her to come and live here so that they could be together and then when she did come she kept fobbing him off and telling him to wait and now . . ."

"Why did he tell you all this?" Wexford interrupted.

She gulped, put out a helpless hand. "He had to tell someone, he said, and there was no one but me. He overheard her talking to someone on the phone like he was her lover, telling him to come down once we'd gone but to be discreet. Ivan understood then. He's broken-hearted because she doesn't want him. He told his own wife that, that he doesn't know how he can go on living because another woman won't have him. I couldn't take it in at first, I couldn't believe it, then I started screaming. She came into our room and said what was the matter? I told her what he'd said and she said, 'I'm sorry, darling, but I didn't know you then.' She said that to *me*. 'I didn't know you then,' she said, 'and it wasn't anything important anyway. It only happened three or four times, it was just that we were both lonely.' As if that made it better!"

Wexford was silent. She was calmer now, though trembling. Soon she would begin regretting that she had poured out her heart to someone who was almost a stranger. She passed her hands over her face and dropped her shoulders with a long heavy sigh.

"Oh God. What am I going to do? Where shall I go? I can't stay with him, can I? When she said that to me I ran out of the house, I didn't even take my bag, I just ran and you were there and—oh God, I don't know what you must think of me talking to you like this. You must think I'm out of my head, crazy, mad. Ivan says I'm mad. 'If you're going to carry on like that,' he said, 'a psychiatric ward's the best place for you.' " She gave him a sideways look. "I've been in those places, that's why he said that. If only I had a friend I could go to but I've lost all my friends, in and out of hospital the way I've been. People don't want to know you any more when they think you've got something wrong with your mind. In my case it's only depression, it's a disease like any other, but they don't realize." She gave a little whimpering cry. "Natalie wasn't like that, she knew about my depression, she was *kind*. I thought she was, but all the time . . . I've lost my only friend as well as my husband!"

Her mouth worked unsteadily from crying, her eyes were red. She looked like a hunted gypsy, the graying bushy hair hanging in shaggy bundles against her cheeks. And it was plain from her expression and her fixed imploring eyes that, because of his profession and his manner and his having caught her the way he had, she expected him to do something for her. Wreak vengeance on Natalie Arno, restore an errant husband or at least provide some dignified shelter for the night.

She began to speak rapidly, almost feverishly. "I can't go back there, I can't face it. Ivan's going home, he said so, he said he'd go home tonight, but I can't be with him, I can't be alone with him, I couldn't bear it. I've got my sister in Wellridge but she won't want me, she's like the rest of them . . . There must be somewhere I could go, you must know somewhere, if you could only . . ."

There flashed into Wexford's mind the idea that he could take her home with him and get Dora to give her a bed for the night. The sheer nuisance this would be stopped him. They were going on holiday tomorrow, their flight went at one p.m., which meant leaving Kingsmarkham for Heathrow at ten. Suppose she refused to leave? Suppose Zoffany arrived? It just wasn't on.

She was still talking non-stop. "So If I could possibly be with you there are lots of things I'd like to tell you. I feel if I could only get them off my chest I'd be that much better and they'd help you, they're things you'd want to know."

"About Mrs. Arno?" he said sharply.

"Well, not exactly about her, about *me*. I need someone to listen and be sympathetic, that does you more good than all the therapy and pills in the world, I can tell you. I can't be alone, don't you understand?"

Later he was to castigate himself for not giving in to that first generous impulse. If he had done he might have known the true facts that night and, more important, a life might have been saved. But as much as the unwillingness to be involved and to create trouble for himself, a feeling of caution prevented him. He was a policeman, the woman was a little mad . . .

"The best thing will be for me to drive you back up the hill to Sterries, Mrs. Zoffany. Let me . . ."

"No!"

"You'll very probably find your husband is ready to leave and waiting for you. You and he would still be in time to catch the last train to Victoria. Mrs. Zoffany, you have to realize he'll get over this, it's something that will very likely lose its force now he's brought it into the open. Why not try to . . . ?"

"No!"

"Come, let me take you back."

For answer, she gathered up her skirts and draperies and half jumped, half tumbled out of the car. In some consternation, Wexford too got out to help her, but she had got to her feet and as he put out his arm she threw something at him, a crumpled ball. It was his handkerchief.

She stood for a little while a few yards from him, leaning against the high jasmine-hung wall of one of these sprawling gardens. She hung her head, her hands up to her chin, like a child who has been scolded. It was deep dusk now and growing cool. Suddenly she began to walk back the way she had come. She walked quite briskly up the hill, up over the crown of the hill, to be lost amid the soft, hanging, darkening green branches.

He waited a while, he hardly knew what for. A car passed him just as he started his own, going rather fast down the hill. It was a mustard-colored Opel, and although it was much too dark to see at all clearly, the woman at the wheel looked very much like Natalie Arno. It was a measure, of course, of how much she occupied his thoughts.

He drove home to Dora, who had packed for the last time and was watching Blaise Cory's program on the television.

13

Wexford was driving on the wrong side of the road. Or that was how he put it to himself. It wasn't as bad as he had expected; the San Diego Freeway had so many lanes and traffic moved at a slower pace than at home. What was alarming and didn't seem to get any better was that he couldn't judge the space he had on the right-hand side so that Dora exclaimed, "Oh, Reg, you were only about an inch from that car. I was sure you were going to scrape!"

The sky was a smooth hazy blue and it was very hot. Nine hours' flying had taken its toll of both of them. Stopped at the lights—traffic lights hung somewhere up in the sky here—Wexford glanced at his wife. She looked tired, she was bound to, but excited as well. For him it wasn't going to be much of a holiday, unless you agreed with those who say that a change is as good as a rest, and he was beginning to feel guilty about the amount of time he would have to spend apart from her. He had tried to explain that if it wasn't for this quest of his they wouldn't be coming here at all, and she had taken it with cheerful resignation. But did she understand quite what he meant? It was all very well her saying she was going to look up those long-lost friends of hers, the Newtons. Wexford thought he knew just how much they would do for a visitor, an invitation to dinner was what that would amount to.

He had just got used to the road, was even beginning to enjoy driving the little red automatic Chevette he had rented at the airport, when the palms of Santa Monica were before them and they were on Ocean Drive. He had promised Dora two days here, staying in luxury at the Miramar, before they set off for wherever his investigations might lead them.

Where was he going to begin? He had one meager piece of information to go on. Ames had given it to him back in February and it was Natalie Arno's address in Los Angeles. The magnitude of his task was suddenly apparent as, once they had checked in and Dora had lain down in their room to sleep, he stood under the eucalyptus trees, looking at the Pacific. Everything seemed so big, a bigger sea, a bigger beach, a vaster sky than he had ever seen before. And as their plane had come in to land he had looked down and been daunted by the size of the sprawling, glittering, metallic-looking city spread out there below them. The secret of Natalie Arno had appeared enormous in Kingsmarkham; here in Los Angeles it was surely capable of hiding itself and becoming forever lost in one of a hundred million crannies.

But one of these crannies he would explore in the morning. Tuscarora Avenue, where Natalie had lived for eight years after coming south from San Francisco, Tuscarora Avenue in a suburb called Opuntia. The fancy names suggested to Wexford that he might expect a certain slumminess, for at home Vale Road would be the site of residential elegance and Valhalla Grove of squalor.

The shops were still open. He walked up Wilshire Boulevard and bought himself a larger and more detailed street plan of Los Angeles than the car hire company had provided.

The next morning when he went out Dora was preparing to phone Rex and Nonie Newton. A year or two before she met Wexford Dora had been engaged to Rex Newton; a boy-and-girl affair it had been, they were both in their teens, and Rex had been supplanted by the young policeman. Married for thirty years now, Rex had retired early and emigrated with his American wife to California. Wexford hoped wistfully that they would be welcoming to Dora, that Nonie Newton would live up to the promises she had made in her last letter. But he could only hope for the best. By ten he was on his way to Opuntia.

The names had misled him. Everything here had an exotic name, the grand and tawdry alike. Opuntia wasn't shabby but paintbox bright with houses like Swiss chalets or miniature French chateaux set in garden plots as lush as jungles. He had previously only seen such flowers in florist's shops or the hothouses of public gardens, oleanders, bougainvilleas, the orange-and-blue bird-of-paradise flower, emblem of the City of the Angels. No wind stirred the fronds of the fan palms. The sky was blue, but white with smog at the horizon.

Tuscarora Avenue was packed so tightly with cars that two drivers could hardly pass each other. Wexford despaired of finding a niche for the Chevette up there, so he left it at the foot of the hill and walked. Though there were side streets called Mar Vista and Oceania Way, the sea wasn't visible, being blocked from view by huge apartment buildings which raised their penthouse tops out of a forest of palm and eucalyptus. 1121 Tuscarora, where Natalie Arno had lived, was a small squat house of pink stucco. It and its neighbors, a chocolate-colored mini-castle and a baby hacienda painted lemon, reminded Wexford of the confections on the sweets trolley at the Miramar the previous night. He hesitated for a moment, imagining Natalie there, the light and the primary colors suiting her better than the pallor and chill of Kingsmarkham, and then he went up to the door of the nearest neighbor, the chocolate-fudge-iced 1123.

A man in shorts and a T-shirt answered his ring. Wexford, who had no official standing in California, who had no right to be asking questions, had already decided to represent himself as on a quest for a lost relative. Though he had never before been to America, he knew enough of Americans to be pretty sure that this kind of thing, which might at home be received with suspicion, embarrassment and taciturnity, would here be greeted with warmth.

The householder, whose shirt campaigned in red printed letters for the Equal Rights Amendment, said he was called Leo Dobrowski and seemed to justify Wexford's belief. He asked him in, explained that his wife and children had gone to church, and within a few minutes Wexford found himself drinking coffee with Mr. Dobrowski on a patio hung with the Prussian-blue trumpets of morning glory.

But in pretending to a family connection with Tina Zoffany he had made a mistake. Leo Dobrowski knew all about Tina Zoffany and scarcely anything about Natalie Arno or any other occupants of 1121 Tuscarora. Hadn't Tina, in the two years she had lived next door, become Mrs. Dobrowski's closest friend? It was a pleasure, though a melancholy one, for Mr. Dobrowski at last to be able to talk about Tina to someone who *cared*. Her brother, he thought, had never cared, though he hoped he wasn't speaking out of turn in saying so. If Wexford was Tina's uncle, he would know what a sweet lovely person she had been and what a tragedy her early death was. Mrs. Dobrowski herself had been made sick by the shock of it.

If Wexford would care to wait until she came back from church he knew his wife had some lovely snapshots of Tina and could probably let him have some small keepsake of Tina's. Her brother had brought all her little odds and ends to them, wouldn't want the expense of sending them home, you could understand that.

"You sure picked the right place when you came to us," said Mr. Dobrowski. "I guess there's not another family on Tuscarora knew Tina like we did. You have ESP or something?"

After that Wexford could scarcely refuse to meet the church-going wife. He promised to come back an hour later. Mr. Dobrowski beamed his pleasure and the words on his T-shirt—"Equality of rights under the law shall not be denied or abridged by the United States or any state on account of sex"—expanded with his well-exercised muscles.

The occupants of 1125—this time Wexford was a cousin of Natalie's and no nonsense about it—were new to the district and so were those who lived further down the hill in a redwood-and-stucco version of Anne Hathaway's cottage. He went to 1121 itself and picked up from the man he spoke to his first piece of real information, that the house had not been bought but was rented from Mrs. Arno. Who was there in the neighborhood, Wexford asked him, who might have known Mrs. Arno when she lived here? Try 1122 on the opposite side, he was advised. In an ever-changing population, the people at 1122, the Romeros, had been in residence longest.

Natalie's cousin once more, he tried at 1122.

"You English?" said Mrs. Donna Romero, a woman who looked even more Spanish than Natalie and whose jet-black hair was wound on to pink plastic rollers.

Wexford nodded.

"Natalie's English. She went home to her folks in London. That's all I know. Right now she's somewhere in London, England."

"How long have you been living here?"

"I just love your accent," said Mrs. Romero. "How long have we been here? I guess it'd be four years, right? We came the summer Natalie went on that long vacation up the coast. Must've been the summer of '76. I guess I just thought the house was empty, no one living there, you know, you get a lot of that round here, and then one day my husband says to me, there's folks moved into 1121, and that was Natalie."

"But she'd lived there before?"

"Oh, sure she lived there before but we didn't, did we?" Donna Romero said this triumphantly as if she had somehow caught him out. "She had these roomers, you know? There was this guy she had, he was living here illegally. Well, I guess everyone knew it, but my husband being in the Police Department—well, he had to do what he had to do, you know?"

"You mean he had him deported?"

"That's what I mean."

Wexford decided he had better make himself scarce before an encounter threatened with the policeman husband. He contented himself with merely asking when this deportation had taken place. Not so long ago, said Mrs. Romero, maybe only last fall, as far as she could remember.

It was now noon and growing fiercely hot. Wexford reflected that whoever it was who had first described the climate of California as perpetual spring hadn't had much experience of an English April. He went back across the road.

The presence on the drive of 1123 of a four-year-old maneuvering a yellow and red truck and a six-year-old riding a blue bicycle told him Mrs. Dobrowski was back. She greeted him so enthusiastically and with such glistening if not quite tearful eyes that he felt a thrust of guilt when he thought of her conferring later with the man at 1121 and with Patrolman (Lieutenant? Captain?) Romero. But it was too late now to abandon the role of Tina's uncle. He was obliged to listen to a catalogue of Tina's virtues while Mrs. Dobrowski, small and earnest and wearing a T-shirt campaigning for the conservation of the sea otter, pressed Tina souvenirs on him, a brooch, a pair of antique nail scissors, and a curious object she said was a purse ashtray.

At last he succeeded in leading the conversation to Natalie by saying with perfect truth that he had seen her in London before he left. It was immediately clear that Mrs. Dobrowski hadn't approved of Natalie. Her way of life had not been what Mrs. Dobrowski was used to or expected from people in a nice neighborhood. Turning a little pink, she said she came from a family of Baptists, and when you had children you had standards to maintain. Clearly she felt that she had said enough on the subject and reverted to Tina, her prowess as what she called a stenographer, the sad fact of her childlessness, the swift onset of the disease which had killed her. Wexford made a second effort.

"I've often wondered how Tina came to live here."

"I guess Natalie needed the money after Rolf Ilbert moved out. Johnny was the one who told Tina Natalie had a room for rent."

Wexford made a guess. "Johnny was Natalie's—er, friend?"

Mrs. Dobrowski gave him a grim smile. "I've heard it called that. Johnny Fassbender was her lover."

The name sounded German but here might not be. When Wexford asked if he were a local man Mrs. Dobrowski said no, he was Swiss. She had often told Tina that one of them should report him to the authorities for living here without a residence permit, and eventually someone must have done so, for he was discovered and deported.

"That would have been last autumn," Wexford said.

"Oh, no. Whatever gave you that idea? It was all of three years ago. Tina was still alive."

There was evidently a mystery here, but not perhaps one of pressing importance. It was Natalie's identity he was primarily concerned with, not her friendships. But Mrs. Dobrowski seemed to feel that she had digressed too far for politeness and moved rapidly on to her visitor's precise relationship to Tina. Was he her true uncle or uncle only by marriage? Strangely, Tina had never mentioned him. But she had mentioned no one but the brother who came over when she died. She, Mrs. Dobrowski, would have liked Ivan to have stayed at her house while he was in Los Angeles but hadn't known how to broach this as she had hardly exchanged a word with Natalie all the years they had lived there. Wexford pricked up his ears at that. No, it was true, she had never set foot inside 1121 or seen Natalie closer than across the yard.

Wexford noted that what she called the yard was, by Kingsmarkham standards, a large garden, dense with oleanders, peach trees and tall cacti. In order not to offend Mrs. Dobrowski, he was obliged to carry off with him the brooch as a keepsake. Perhaps he could pass it on to the Zoffanys.

"It's been great meeting you," said Mrs. Dobrowski. "I guess I can see a kind of look of Tina about you now. Around the eyes." She gathered the four-year-old up in her arms and waved to Wexford from the porch. "Say hello to Ivan for me."

In the heat of the day he drove back to the Miramar and took Dora out to lunch in a seafood restaurant down by the boardwalk. He hardly knew how to tell her he was going to have to leave her alone for the afternoon as well. But he did tell her and she bore it well, only saying that she would make another attempt to phone the Newtons. In their room she dialed their number again while he consulted the directory, looking for Ilberts. There was no Rolf Ilbert in the Los Angeles phone book or in the slimmer Santa Monica directory, but in this latter he did find a Mrs. Davina Lee Ilbert at a place called Paloma Canyon.

Dora had got through. He heard her say delightedly, "Will you really come and pick me up? About four?" Considerably relieved, he touched her shoulder, got a wide smile from her, and then he ran out to the lift, free from guilt at least for the afternoon.

It was too far to walk, halfway to Malibu. He found Paloma Canyon without difficulty and encouraged the car up an impossibly steep slope. The road zigzagged as on some alpine mountainside, opening up at each turn bigger and better views of the Pacific. But otherwise he might have been in Ploughman's Lane. All super residential areas the world over are the same, he thought, paraphrasing Tolstoy, it is only the slums that differ from each other. Paloma Canyon was Ploughman's Lane with palms. And with a bluer sky, daisy lawns and an architecture Spanish rather than Tudor.

She wasn't the wife but the ex-wife of the man called Rolf Ilbert. No, she didn't mind him asking, she would be only too glad if there was anything she could do to get back at Natalie Arno. Would he mind coming around to the pool? They always spent their Sunday afternoons by the pool.

Wexford followed her along a path through a shrubbery of red and purple fuchsias taller than himself. She was a tall thin woman, very tanned and with bleached blond hair, and she wore a sky-blue terry-cloth robe and flat sandals. He wondered what it must be like to live in a climate where you took it for granted you spent every Sunday afternoon round the pool. It was extremely hot, too hot to be down there on the beach, he supposed.

The pool, turquoise blue and rectangular with a fountain playing at the far end, was in a patio formed by the balconied wings of the lemon-colored stucco house. Davina Lee Ilbert had evidently been lying in a rattan lounging chair, for there was a glass of something with ice in it and a pair of sunglasses on the table beside it. A girl of about sixteen in a bikini was sitting on the rim of the fountain and a boy a bit younger was swimming lengths. They both had dark curly hair and Wexford supposed they must resemble their father. The girl said "Hi" to him and slipped into the water.

"You care for iced tea?" Mrs. Ilbert asked him.

He had never tasted it but he accepted. While she was fetching it he sat down in one of the cane peacock chairs, looking over the parapet to the highway and the beaches below.

"You want to know where Rolf met her?" Davina Ilbert took off her robe and stretched out on the lounger, a woman of forty with a good if stringy figure who had the discretion to wear a one-piece swimsuit. "It was in San Francisco in '76. Her husband had died and she was staying with friends in San Rafael. The guy was a journalist or something and they all went into the city for this writers' conference that was going on, a cocktail party, I guess it was. Rolf was there."

"Your former husband is a writer?"

"Movie and TV scripts," she said. "You wouldn't have heard of him. Whoever heard of script writers? You have a serial called *Runway* on your TV?"

Wexford said nothing, nodded.

"Rolf's done some of that. You know the episodes set at Kennedy? That's his stuff. And he's made a mint from it, thank God." She made a lithe quick gesture at the balconies, the fountain, her own particular expanse of blue sky. "It's Natalie you want to know about, right? Rolf brought her back to L.A. and bought that house on Tuscarora for her."

The boy came out of the pool and shook himself like a dog. His sister said something to him and they both stared at Wexford, looking away when he met their eyes.

"He lived there with her?" he asked their mother.

"He kind of divided his time between me and her." She drank from the tall glass. "I was really dumb in those days, I trusted him. It took me five years to find out and when I did I flipped. I went over to Tuscarora and beat her up. No kidding."

Wexford said impassively, "That would have been in 1976?"

"Right. Spring of '76. Rolf came back and found her all bruised and with two black eyes and he got scared and took her on a trip up the coast to get away from me. It was summer, I don't suppose she minded. She was up there—two, three months? He'd go up and join her when he could but he never really lived with her again." She gave a sort of tough chuckle. "I'd thrown him out too. All he had was a hotel room in Marina del Rey."

The sun was moving round. Wexford shifted into the shade and the boy and girl walked slowly away into the house. A hummingbird, no larger than an insect, was hovering on the red velvet threshold of a trumpet flower. Wexford had never seen one before. He said:

"You said 'up the coast.' Do you know where?"

She shrugged. "They didn't tell me their plans. But it'd be somewhere north of San Simeon and south of Monterey, maybe around Big Sur. It could have been a motel, but Rolf was generous, he'd have rented a house for her." She changed her tone abruptly. "Is she in trouble? I mean, real trouble?"

"Not at the moment," said Wexford. "She's just inherited a very nice house and a million from her father."

"Dollars?"

"Pounds."

"Jesus, and they say cheating never pays."

"Mrs. Ilbert, forgive me, but you said your former husband and Mrs. Arno never lived together again after the summer of '76. Why was that? Did he simply get tired of her?"

She gave her dry bitter laugh. "*She* got tired of him. She met someone else. Rolf was still crazy about her. He told me so, he told me all about it."

Wexford recalled Jane Zoffany. Husbands seemed to make a practice of confiding in their wives their passion for Natalie Arno. "She met someone while she was away on this long holiday?"

"That's what Rolf told me. She met this guy and took him back to the house on Tuscarora—it was hers, you see, she could do what she wanted—and Rolf never saw her again."

He never saw her again?"

"That's what he said. She wouldn't see him or speak to him. I guess it was because he still hadn't divorced me and married her, but I don't know. Rolf went crazy. He found out this guy she was with was living here illegally and he got him deported."

Wexford nodded. "He was a Swiss called Fassbender."

"Oh, no. Where d'you get that from? I don't recall his name but it wasn't what you said. He was English. Rolf had him deported to England."

"Did *you* ever see her again?"

"Me? No, why would I?"

"Thank you, Mrs. Ilbert. You've been very frank and I'm grateful."

"You're welcome. I guess I still feel pretty hostile towards her for what she did to me and my kids. It wouldn't give me any grief to hear she'd lost that house and that million."

Wexford drove down the steep hill, noticing attached to a house wall something he hadn't seen on the way up. A printed notice that said "No Solicitors." He chuckled. He knew very well that this was an American equivalent of the "nice" suburb's injunction to hawkers or people delivering circulars, but it still made him laugh. He would have liked to prise it off the wall and take it home for Symonds, O'Brien and Ames.

Dora was out when he got back to the Miramar and there was a note for him telling him not to wait for dinner if she wasn't back by seven-thirty. Rex Newton, whom he had rather disliked in the days when they had been acquaintances, he now blessed. And tomorrow he would devote the whole day exclusively to Dora.

14

From the map it didn't look as if there was much in the way of habitation in the vicinity of Big Sur, and Wexford's idea that Natalie Arno's trail might therefore easily be followed was confirmed by an elderly lady in the hotel lobby. This was a Mrs. Lewis from Denver, Colorado, who had spent, it appeared, at least twenty holidays in California. There was hardly a house, hotel or restaurant, according to Mrs. Lewis, between San Simeon in the south and Carmel in the north. The coast was protected, Wexford concluded, it was conserved by whatever the American equivalent might be of the National Trust.

The Miramar's enormous lobby had carpet sculpture on the walls. Although it was probably the grandest hotel Wexford had ever stayed in, the bar was so dark as to imply raffishness or at least that it would be wiser not to see what one was drinking. In his case this was white wine, the pleasant, innocuous, rather weak chablis which must be produced here by the millions of gallons considering the number of people he had seen swilling it down. What had become of the whisky sours and dry martinis of his reading? He sat alone—Dora and Mrs. Lewis were swapping family snaps and anecdotes—reflecting that he should try to see Rolf Ilbert before he began the drive northwards. Ilbert was surely over Natalie by now and would have no objection to telling him the name of the place where she had stayed in the summer of 1976. Wexford finished his second glass of wine and walked down past the sculptured carpet palms to phone Davina Ilbert, but there was no reply.

In the morning, when he tried her number again, she told him her ex-husband was in London. He had been in London for two months, researching for a television series about American girls who had married into the English aristocracy. Wexford realized he would just have to trace Natalie on what he had. They drove off at lunchtime and stopped for the night at a motel in Santa Maria. It was on the tip of Wexford's tongue to grumble to Dora that there was nothing to do in Santa Maria, miles from the coast and with Route 101 passing through it. But then it occurred to him that a visitor might say exactly that about Kingsmarkham. Perhaps there was only ever something obvious to do in the center of cities or by the sea. Elsewhere there was ample to do if you lived there and nothing if you didn't. He would have occupation soon enough and then his guilt about Dora would come back.

Over dinner he confided his theory to her.

"If you look at the facts you'll see that there was a distinct change of personality in 1976. The woman who went away with Ilbert had a different character from the woman who came back to Los Angeles. Think about it for a minute. Camargue's daughter had led a very sheltered, cared-for sort of life, she'd never been out in the world on her own. First there was a secure home with her parents, then elopement with and marriage to Arno, and when Arno died, Ilbert. She was always under the protection of some man. But what of the woman who appears *after* the summer of '76? She lets off rooms in her house to bring in an income. She doesn't form long steady relationships but has casual love affairs—with the Swiss Fassbender, with the Englishman who was deported, with Zoffany. She can't sell the house Ilbert bought for her so she lets it out and comes to England. Not to creep under her father's wing as Natalie Camargue might have done, but to shift for herself in a place of her own."

"But surely it was a terrible risk to go to Natalie's own house and live there as Natalie? The neighbors would have known at once, and then there'd be her friends. . ."

"Good fences make good neighbors," said Wexford. "There's a lot of space between those houses, it's a shifting population, and if my idea is right Natalie Camargue was a shy, reserved sort of woman. Her neighbors never saw much of her. As to friends—if a friend of Natalie's phoned she had only to say Natalie was still away. If a friend comes to the house she has only to say that she herself is a friend who happens to be staying there for the time being. Mrs. Ilbert says Ilbert never saw her after she came back. Now if the real Natalie came back it's almost impossible Ilbert never saw her. Never was alone with her maybe, never touched her, but never saw her? No, it was the impostor who fobbed him off every time he called with excuses, with apologies, and at last with direct refusals, allegedly on the part of the real Natalie, ever to see him again."

"But, Reg, how could the impostor know so much about the real Natalie's past?"

He took her up quickly. "You spent most of last evening talking to Mrs. Lewis. How much do you know about her from, say, two hours' conversation?"

Dora giggled. "Well, she lives in a flat, not a house. She's a widow. She's got two sons and a daughter. One of the sons is a realtor, I don't know what that is."

"Estate agent."

"Estate agent, and the other's a vet. Her daughter's called Janette and she's married to a doctor and they've got twin girls and they live in a place called Bismarck. Mrs. Lewis has got a four-wheel drive Chevrolet for the mountain roads and a holiday house, a log cabin, in the Rockies and . . ."

"Enough! You found all that out in two hours and you're saying the new Natalie couldn't have formed a complete dossier of the old Natalie in—what? Five or six weeks? And when she came to England she had a second mentor in Mary Woodhouse."

"All right, perhaps she could have." Dora hesitated. He had had a feeling for some hours that she wanted to impart—or even break—something to him. "Darling," she said suddenly, "You won't mind, will you? I told Rex and Nonie we'd be staying at the Redwood Hotel in Carmel and it so happens, I mean, it's a complete coincidence, that they'll be staying with Nonie's daughter in Monterey at the same time. If we had lunch with them once or twice—or I did—well, you won't mind, will you?"

"I think it's a wonderful idea."

"Only you didn't used to like Rex, and I can't honestly say he's changed."

"It's such a stupid name," Wexford said unreasonably. "Stupid for a man, I mean. It's all right for a dog."

Dora couldn't help laughing. "Oh, come. It only just misses being the same as yours."

"A miss is as good as a mile. What d'you think of my theory then?"

"Well—what became of the old Natalie?"

"I think it's probable she murdered her."

The road came back to the sea again after San Luis Obispo. It was like Cornwall, Wexford thought, the Cornish coast gigantically magnified both in size and in extent. Each time you came to a bend in the road another bay opened before you, vaster, grander, more majestically beautiful than the last. At San Simeon Dora wanted to see Hearst Castle, so Wexford drove her up there and left her to take the guided tour. He went down on the beach where shade was provided by eucalyptus trees. Low down over the water he saw a pelican in ponderous yet graceful flight. The sun shone with an arrogant, assured permanence, fitting for the finest climate on earth.

There wasn't much to San Simeon, a car park, a restaurant, a few houses. And if Mrs. Lewis was to be believed, the population would be even sparser as he drove north. The Hearst Castle tour lasted a long time and they made no more progress that day, but as they set off next morning Wexford began to feel something like dismay. It was true that if you were used to living in densely peopled areas you might find the coast here sparsely populated, but it wasn't by any means *un*popu-lated. Little clusters of houses—you could hardly call them villages—with a motel or two, a store, a petrol station, a restaurant, occurred more often than he had been led to believe. And when they came to Big Sur and the road wandered inland through the redwood forest, there were habitations and places to stay almost in plenty.

They reached the Redwood Hotel at about eight that night. Simply driving through Carmel had been enough to lower Wexford's spirits. It looked a lively place, a considerable seaside resort, and it was full of hotels. Another phone call to Davina Ilbert elicited only that she had no idea of Ilbert's London address. Wexford realized that there was nothing for it but to try all the hotels in Carmel, armed with his photograph of Natalie.

All he derived from that was the discovery that Americans are more inclined to be helpful than English people, and if this is because they are a nation of salesmen just as the English are a nation of small shopkeepers, it does little to detract from the overall pleasant impression. Hotel receptionists exhorted him on his departure to have a good day, and then when he was still at it after sundown, to have a nice evening. By that time he had been inside every hotel, motel and lobby of apart-ments-for-rent in Carmel, Carmel Highlands, Carmel Woods and Carmel Point, and he had been inside them in vain.

Rex Newton and his American wife were sitting in the hotel bar with Dora when he got back. Newton's skin had gone very brown and his hair very white, but otherwise he was much the same. His wife, in Wexford's opinion, looked twenty years older than Dora, though she was in fact younger. It appeared that the New-tons were to dine with them, and Newton walked into the dining room with one arm round his wife's waist and the other round Dora's. Dora had given them to understand he was there on official police business—what else could she have said? —and Newton spent most of his time at the table holding forth on the American legal system, American police, the geography and geology of California and the rival merits of various hotels. His wife was a meek, quiet little woman. They were going to take Dora to Muir Woods, the redwood forest north of San Francisco, on the following day.

"If he knows so much," Wexford grumbled later, "he might have warned you there are more hotels up here than in the West End of London."

"I'm sorry, darling. I didn't ask him. He does rather talk the hind leg off a donkey, doesn't he?"

Wexford didn't know why he suddenly liked Rex Newton very much and felt even happier that Dora was having such a good time with him.

For his own part, he spent the next day and the next making excursions down the coast the way they had come, visiting every possible place to stay. In each he got the same response—or worse, that the motel had changed hands or changed management and that there were no records for 1976 available. He was learning that in California change is a very important aspect of life and that Californians, like the Athenians of old, are attracted by any new thing.

Nonie Newton was confined to bed in her daughter's house with a migraine. Wexford cut short his inquiries in Monterey to get back to Dora, who would have been deserted by her friends. The least he could do for her was take her on the beach for the afternoon. He asked himself if he hadn't mismanaged everything. The trip wasn't succeeding either as an investigation or as a holiday. Dora was out when he got back, there was no note for him, and he spent the rest of the day missing his wife and reproaching himself. Rex Newton brought her back at ten and, in spite of Nonie's illness, sat in the bar for half an hour, holding forth on the climate of California, seismology and the San Andreas Fault. Wexford couldn't wait for him to be gone to unburden his soul to Dora.

"You could always phone Sheila," she said when they were alone.

"Sure I could," he said. "I could phone Sylvia and talk to the kids. I could phone your sister and my nephew Howard and old Mike. It would cost a great deal of money and they'd all no doubt say hard cheese very kindly, but where would it get me?"

"To Ilbert," she said simply.

He looked at her.

"Rolf Ilbert. You said he does part of the script for *Runway*. He's in London. Even if he's not working on *Runway* now, even if she's never met him, Sheila's in a position to find out where he is, she could easily do it."

"So she could," he said slowly. "Why didn't I think of that?"

It was eleven o'clock on the Pacific coast but three in London, and he was lucky to find her in. Her voice sounded as if she were in the next room. He knew exactly what her voice in the next room would sound like because his hotel neighbors had had *Runway* on for the past half-hour.

"I don't know him, Pop darling, but I'm sure I can find him. Nothing easier. I'll shop around some likely agents. Where shall I ring you back?"

"Don't call us," said her father. "We'll call you. God knows where we'll be."

"How's Mother?"

"Carrying on alarmingly with her old flame."

He would have laughed as he said that if Dora had shown the least sign of laughing.

Because it wasn't his nature to wait about and do nothing he spent all the next day covering what remained of the Monterey Peninsula. Something in him wanted to say, forget it, make a holiday of the rest of it, but it was too late for that. Instead of relaxing, he would only have tormented himself with that constantly recurring question, where had she stayed? It was awkward phoning Sheila because of the time difference. All the lines were occupied when he tried at eight in the morning, midnight for her, and again twelve hours later, her noon. When at last he heard the ringing there was no answer. Next day, or the day after at the latest, they would have to start south and leave behind all the possible places where Natalie Arno might have changed her identity. They had only had a fortnight and eleven days of it were gone.

As he was making another attempt to phone Sheila from the hotel lobby, Rex Newton walked in with Dora. He sat down, drank a glass of chablis, and held forth on Californian vineyards, migraine, the feverfew diet and the gluten-free diet. After half an hour he went, kissing Dora—on the cheek but very near the mouth—and reminding her of a promise to spend their last night in America staying at the Newtons' house. And also their last day.

"I suppose I'm included in that," Wexford said in a rather nasty tone. Newton was still not quite out of earshot.

She was cool. "Of course, darling."

His investigation was over, failed, fruitless. He had rather hoped to have the last two days alone with his wife. But what a nerve he had and how he was punished for it!

"I'm hoist with my own petard, aren't I?" he said and went off to bed.

The Newtons were flying back that morning. It would be a long weary drive for Wexford. He and Dora set off at nine.

The first of the *Danaus* butterflies to float across the windscreen made them both gasp. Dora had seen one only once before, Wexford never. The Milkweed, the Great American Butterfly, the Monarch, is a rare visitor to the cold British Isles. They watched that one specimen drift out over the sea, seeming to lose itself in the blue meeting the blue, and then a cloud of its fellows were upon them, thick as autumnal leaves that strow the brooks in Vallombrosa. And like leaves too, scarlet leaves veined in black, they floated rather than flew across the span of California One, down from the cliffs of daisies, out to the ocean. The air was red with them. All the way down from Big Sur they came, wings of cinnabar velvet, butterflies in flocks like birds made of petals.

"The Spanish for butterfly is *mariposa*," said Dora. "Rex told me. Don't you think it's a beautiful name?"

Wexford said nothing. Even if he managed to get hold of Sheila now, even if she had an address or a phone number for him, would he have time to drive back perhaps a hundred miles along this route? Not when he had to be in Burbank or wherever those Newtons lived by nightfall. A red butterfly came to grief on his windscreen, smashed, fluttered, died.

They stopped for a late lunch not far north of San Luis Obispo. He tried in vain to get through to Sheila again and then Dora said she would try. She came back from the phone with a little smile on her lips. She looked young and tanned and happy, but she hadn't been able to reach Sheila. Wexford wondered why she should look like that if she hadn't been talking to anyone. The Newtons would have been back in their home for hours by now. He felt that worst kind of misery, that which afflicts us as the result entirely of our own folly.

The road that returned from inland to the coast wound down through yellow hills. Yuccas pushed their way up through the sun-bleached grass and the rounded mountains were crowned with olives. The hills folded and dipped and rose and parted to reveal more hills, all the same, all ocherish in color, until through the last dip the blue ocean appeared again. Dora was occupied with her map and guide book.

There was a little seaside town ahead. A sign by the roadside said: Santa Xavierita, height above sea level 50.2 meters, population 482. Dora said:

"According to the book there's a motel here called the Mariposa. Shall we try it?"

"What for?" said Wexford crossly. "Half an hour's kip? We have to be two hundred miles south of here by eight and it's five now."

"We don't have to. Our plane doesn't go till tomorrow night. We could stay at the Mariposa. I think we're meant to, it was a sign."

He nearly stopped the car. He chuckled. He had known her thirty-five years but he didn't know her yet. "You phoned Newton back there?" he said but in a very different tone from the one he would have used if he had asked that question ten minutes before. "You phoned Newton and said we couldn't make it?"

She said demurely, "I think Nonie was quite relieved really."

"I don't deserve it," said Wexford.

Santa Xavierita had a wide straggly street with a dozen side turnings at right angles to it, as many petrol stations, a monster market, a clutch of restaurants and among a dozen motels, the Mariposa. Wexford found himself being shown, not to a room, but to a little house rather like a bungalow at home in Ramsgate or Worthing. It stood in a garden, one of a score of green oases in this corner of Santa Xavierita, and up against its front door was a pink and white geranium as big as a tree.

He walked back between sprinklers playing on the grass to the hotel reception desk and phoned Sheila on a collect call. In London it was nine o'clock in the morning and pouring with rain. Sheila had got Ilbert's address. She had had it for two days and couldn't understand why her father hadn't phoned. Ilbert was staying at Durrant's Hotel in George Street by Spanish Place. Wexford wrote down the number. He looked round for someone to inform that he intended to make a call to London.

There was no sign of the little spry man called Sessamy who had checked them in. No doubt he was somewhere about, watering the geraniums and fuchsias and the heliotrope that smelt of cherries. Wexford went back to find Dora and tell her the news, such as it was. She was in the kitchen of their bungalow, arranging in a glass bowl, piling like an Arcimboldo still life, the fruit they had bought.

"Reg," she said, turning round, a nectarine in her hand, "Reg, Mrs. Sessamy who owns this place, she's English. And she says we're the first English people to stay here since—a Mrs. Arno in 1976."

15

"Tell me about it," Wexford said.

"I don't know anything about it. I don't know any more than I've told you. Your Natalie Arno stayed here in 1976. After we've eaten we're to go and have coffee with Mrs. Sessamy and she'll enlighten you."

"Will she now? And how did you account for my curiosity? What did you tell her about me?"

"The truth. The idea of you being a real English policeman almost made her cry. She was a G.I. bride, I think, she's about the right age. I honestly think she expects you to turn up in a blue uniform and say 'ere, 'ere, what's all this about? and she'd love it!"

He laughed. It was rare for him to praise his wife, almost unknown for him to call her by an endearment. That wasn't his way, she knew it and wouldn't have wanted it. It would have bracketed her with those he loved on the next level down. He put his hand on her arm.

"If something comes of all this," he said, "and one of us gets sent back here at the government's expense, can I come too?"

There was, of all things, a Lebanese restaurant in the main street of Santa Xavierita. They walked there and ate delicate scented versions of humous and kebab and honey cake. The sun had long gone, sunk almost with a fizzle into that blue sea, and now the moon was rising. The moonlight painted the little town white as with frost. It was no longer very warm. In the gardens, which showed as dark little havens of lushness in aridity, the sprinklers still rotated and sprayed.

Wexford marveled at his wife and, with hindsight, at his own ignorant presumption. Instead of allowing herself to be a passive encumbrance, she had made him absurdly jealous and had hoodwinked him properly. By some sixth sense or some gift of serendipity, she had done in an instant what had eluded him for nearly a fortnight—found Natalie Arno's hideout. And like Trollope's Archdeacon of his wife, he wondered at and admired the greatness of that lady's mind.

The Sessamys lived in a white-painted frame building, half their home and half the offices of the motel. Their living room was old-fashioned in an unfamiliar way, furnished with pieces from a thirties culture more overblown and Hollywood-

influenced than that which Wexford himself had known. On a settee, upholstered
in snow-white grainy plastic, a settee that rather resembled some monstrous dessert,
a cream-coated log perhaps, rolled in coconut, sat the fattest woman Wexford had
ever seen. He and Dora had come in by way of the open French windows, as she
had been instructed, and Mrs. Sessamy struggled to get to her feet. Like a great fish
floundering to raise itself over the rim of the keeper net, she went on struggling
until her guests were seated. Only then did she allow herself to subside again. She
gave a big noisy sigh.

"It's such a pleasure to see you! You don't know how I've been looking forward
to it ever since Mrs. Wexford here said who you was. A real bobby! I turned on the
waterworks, didn't I, Tom?"

Nearly forty years' domicile in the United States had not robbed her of a particle
of her old accent or given her a hint of new. She was a Londoner who still spoke
the cockney of Bow or Limehouse.

"Bethnal Green," she said as if Wexford had asked. "I've never been back. My
people all moved out to one of them new towns, Harlow. Been there, of course.
Like every other year mostly we go, don't we, Tom?"

Her husband made no reply. He was a little brown monkey of a man with a
face like a nut. He suggested they have a drink and displayed a selection of bottles
ranged behind a small bar. There was no sign of the promised coffee. When Dora
had apologetically refused bourbon, rye, chablis, Hawaiian cocktail, Perrier, grape
juice and gin, Mrs. Sessamy announced that they would have tea. Tom would
make it, the way she had taught him.

"It's such a pleasure to see you," she said again, sinking comfortably back into
white plastic. "The English who come here, mostly they stop up at the Ramada or
the Howard Johnson. But you picked the old Mariposa."

"Because of the butterflies," said Dora.

"Come again?"

"*Mariposa*—well, it means butterfly, doesn't it?"

"It does?" said Tom Sessamy, waiting for the kettle to boil. "You hear that,
Edie? How about that then?"

It seemed the policy of the Sessamys to question each other frequently but
never to answer. Mrs. Sessamy folded plump hands in her enormous lap. She was
wearing green trousers and a tent-like green and pink flowered smock. In her broad
moon face, in the grayish-fair hair, could still be seen traces of the pretty girl who
had married an American soldier and left Bethnal Green for ever.

"Mrs. Wexford said you wanted to know about that girl who lived here—well,
stopped here. Though she must have been here three months. We thought she'd
go on renting the chalet forever, didn't we, Tom? We thought we'd got a real
sinecure."

"I'd heard it was up around Big Sur she stayed," said Wexford.

"So it was at first. She couldn't stick it, not enough life for her, and it was too far to drive to Frisco. You can get up to San Luis in twenty minutes from here by car. She had her own car and he used to come up in a big Lincoln Continental."

"Ilbert?"

"That's right, that was the name. I will say for her she never pretended, she never called herself Mrs. Ilbert. Couldn't have cared less what people thought."

Tom Sessamy came in with the tea. Wexford, who, while in California, had drunk from a pot made with one teabag, had seen tea made by heating up liquid out of a bottle or by pouring warm water on to a powder, noted that Tom had been well taught by his wife.

"I never did fancy them bags," said Edith Sessamy. "You can get tea loose here if you try."

"Hafta go to the specialty shop over to San Luis," said Tom.

Mrs. Sessamy put cream and sugar into her cup. "What more d'you want to know about her?" she said to Wexford.

He showed her the photograph. "Is that her?"

She put on glasses with pink frames and rhinestone decoration. Mrs. Sessamy had become Californian in all ways but for her tea and her speech. "Yes," she said, "yes, I reckon that's her." Her voice was full of doubt.

"I guess that's her," said Tom. "It's kinda hard to say. She kinda wore her hair loose. She got this terrific tan and wore her hair loose. Right, Edie?"

Edith Sessamy didn't seem too pleased by her husband's enthusiastic description of Natalie Arno. She said rather sharply, "One man wasn't enough for her. She was two-timing that Ilbert the minute he was off to L.A. For instance, there used to be a young fella hung about here, kipped down on the beach, I reckon you'd have called him a beachcomber in olden times."

"Kinda hippie," said Tom.

"She carried on with him. I say he slept on the beach, that summer I reckoned he slept most nights in Natalie's chalet. Then there was an English chap, but it wasn't long before she left she met him, was it, Tom?"

"Played the guitar at the Maison Suisse over to San Luis."

"Why did she leave?" Wexford asked.

"Now that I can't tell you. We weren't here when she left. We were at home, we were in England."

"Visiting with her sister over to Harlow," said Tom.

"She was living here like she'd stay for the rest of her life when we left. That'd have been the end of July, I reckon. Tom's cousin from Ventura, she come up to run the place like she always does when we're off on our holidays. She kept in touch, I reckon we got a letter once a week. I remember her writing us about that woman who got drowned here, don't you, Tom? But she never mentioned that girl leaving. Why should she? There was guests coming and going all the time."

"You weren't curious yourselves?"

Edith Sessamy heaved up her huge shoulders and dropped them again. "So if we were? There wasn't much we could do about it, six thousand miles away. She wasn't going to tell Tom's cousin why she upped and went, was she? When we come back we heard that's what she'd done, a moonlight flit like. Ilbert come up the next day but the bird was flown. She went off in her car, Tom's cousin said, and she'd got a young chap with her, and she left that poor mug Ilbert to pay the bill."

Wexford woke up very early the next morning. The sun was perhaps the brightest and the clearest he had ever seen and the little town looked as if it had been washed clean in the night. Yet Edith Sessamy had told him that apart from a few showers the previous December they had had no rain for a year. He bathed and dressed and went out. Dora was still fast asleep. He walked down the narrow straight road bordered with fan palms, feather dusters on long tapering handles, that led to Santa Xavierita state beach.

The sky was an inverted pan of speckless blue enamel, the sea rippling blue silk. Along the silver sand a young man in yellow T-shirt and red shorts was jogging. Another, in swimming trunks, was doing gymnastic exercises, sit-ups, press-ups, toe-touching. There was no one in the water. In the middle of the beach was a chair raised up high on stilts for the use of the lifeguard who would sit on it and halloo through his trumpet at over-venturesome swimmers.

Wexford's thoughts reverted to the night before. There was a question he ought to have asked, that he had simply overlooked at the time, because of the crushing disappointment he had felt at the paucity of Edith Sessamy's information. Disappointment had made him fail to select from that mass of useless matter the one significant sentence. He recalled it now, picking it out as the expert might pick out the uncut diamond from a handful of gravel.

Two hours later, as early as he decently could, he was waiting in the motel's reception area by the counter. Ringing the bell summoned Tom Sessamy in shortie dressing gown which left exposed hairless white legs and long white feet in sandals of plaited straw.

"Hi, Reg, you wanna check out?"

"I wanted to ask you and your wife a few more questions first if you'll bear with me."

"Edie, are ya decent? Reg's here ta pick your brains."

Mrs. Sessamy was rather more decent than her husband in an all-enveloping pink kimono printed with birds of paradise. She sat on the white sofa drinking more strong black tea, and on her lap on a tray were fried eggs and fried bacon and hash browns and English muffins and grape jelly.

"It's been such a pleasure meeting you and Dora, I can't tell you." She had told him at least six times already, but the repetition was somehow warming and pleasant to hear. Wexford returned the compliment with a few words about how much they had enjoyed themselves.

"You wanna cup of Edie's tea?" said Tom.

Wexford accepted. "You said last night a woman was drowned here. While you were away. D'you know any more than that? Who she was? How it happened?"

"Not a thing. Only what I said, a woman was drowned. Well, it was a young woman, a girl really, I do know that, and I reckon I heard she was on holiday here from the East somewhere."

"You hafta talk to the cops over to San Luis," said Tom.

"Wait a minute, though—George Janveer was lifeguard here then, wasn't he, Tom? I reckon you could talk to George."

"Why don't I call George right now?" said Tom.

He was dissuaded from this by his wife, since it was only just after eight. They would phone George at nine. Wexford wasn't pressed for time, was he? No, he wasn't, not really, he had all day. He had a 200-mile drive ahead of him, of course, but that was nothing here. Edith Sessamy said she knew what he meant, it was nothing here.

He walked slowly back. At last a clear pattern was emerging from the confusion. The pieces fluttered and dropped into a design as the colored fragments do when you shake a kaleidoscope. Camargue too had been drowned, he thought.

Just after nine he went back and paid his bill. Tom said apologetically that he had phoned George Janveer's home and talked to Mrs. Janveer, who said George had gone to Grover City but she expected him back by eleven.

"Oughta've called him at eight like I said," said Tom.

Wexford and Dora put the cases in the car and went to explore what they hadn't yet seen of Santa Xavierita. Wouldn't it be best, Wexford asked himself, to head straight for San Luis Obispo and call on the police there and see what facts he could get out of them? But suppose he couldn't get any? Suppose, before they imparted anything to him, they required proof of who he was and what he was doing there? He could prove his identity, of course, and present them with bona fides but it would all take time and he hadn't much left. He had to be at Los Angeles international airport by six in time for their flight home at seven. Better wait for Janveer who would know as much as the police did and would almost certainly talk to him.

Mrs. Janveer was as thin as Edith Sessamy was fat. She was in her kitchen baking something she called devil's food and her overweight black labrador was sitting at her feet, hoping to lick out the bowl.

It was after eleven and her husband still hadn't come back from Grover City. Maybe he had met a friend and they had got drinking. Mrs. Janveer did not say this in a shrewish or condemnatory way or even as if there were anything to be defensive about. She said it with exactly the same tone, casual, indifferent, even slightly complacent, she would have used to say he had met the mayor or gone to a meeting of the Lions.

Wexford was driven to ask her if she remembered anything about the drowned woman. Mrs. Janveer put the tin of chocolate cake mixture into the oven. The dog's tail began to thump the floor. No, she couldn't say she remembered much about it at all, except the woman's first name had been Theresa, she recalled that because it was hers too, and after the drowning some of her relations had come out to Santa Xavierita, from Boston, she thought it was, and stayed at the Ramada Inn. She put the mixing bowl under the tap and her hand to the tap. The dog let out a piteous squeal. Mrs. Janveer shrugged, looking upset, and slapped the bowl down in front of the dog with a cross exclamation.

Wexford waited until half-past eleven. Janveer still hadn't come. "Considering what I know now," he said to Dora, "they're bound to send me back here. It's only time I need."

"It's a shame, darling, it's such bad luck."

He drove quickly out of the town, heading for the Pacific Highway.

16

The difference between California and Kingsmarkham was a matter of color as well as temperature. The one was blue and gold, the sun burning the grass to its own color; the other was gray and green, the lush green of foliage watered daily by those massy clouds. Wexford went to work, not yet used to seeing grass verges instead of daisy lawns, shivering a little because the temperature was precisely what Tom Sessamy had told him it could fall to in Santa Xavierita in December.

Burden was waiting for him in his office. He had on a lightweight silky suit in a shade of taupe and a beige silk shirt. No one could possibly have taken him for a policeman or even a policeman in disguise. Wexford, who had been considering telling him at once what he had found out in California, now decided not to and instead asked him to close the window.

"I opened it because it's such a muggy, stuffy sort of day," said Burden. "Not cold, are you?"

"Yes, I am. Very cold."

"Jet lag. Did you have a good time?"

Wexford grunted. He wished he had the nerve to start the central heating. It probably wouldn't start, though, not in July. For all he knew, the chief constable had to come over himself on 1 November and personally press a button on the boiler. "I don't suppose there've been any developments while I was away?" he said.

Burden sat down. "Well, yes, there have. That's what I'm doing in here. I thought I ought to tell you first thing. Jane Zoffany has disappeared."

Zoffany had not reported her missing until she had been gone a week. His story, said Burden, was that he and his wife had been staying at Sterries with their friend Natalie Arno, and on the evening of Friday, 27 June his wife had gone out alone for a walk and had never come back. Zoffany, when pressed, admitted that immediately prior to this he and his wife had quarreled over an affair he had had with another woman. She had said she was going to leave him, she could never live with him again, and had left the house. Zoffany himself had left soon after, taking the 10:05 p.m. train to Victoria. He believed his wife would have gone home by an earlier train.

However, when he got to De Beauvoir Place she wasn't there. Nor did she appear the next day. He concluded she had gone to her sister in Horsham. This had apparently happened once before after a quarrel. But Friday 4 July had been Jane Zoffany's birthday, her thirty-fifth, and a birthday card came for her from her sister. Zoffany then knew he had been wrong and he went to his local police station.

Where no one had shown much interest, Burden said. Why should they? That a young woman should temporarily leave her husband after a quarrel over his infidelity was hardly noteworthy. It happened all the time. And of course she wouldn't tell him where she had gone, that was the last thing she had wanted him to know. Burden only got to hear of it when Zoffany also reported his wife's disappearance to the Kingsmarkham police. He seemed genuinely worried. It would not be putting it too strongly to say he was distraught.

"Guilt," said Wexford, and as he pronounced the word he felt it himself. It was even possible he was the last person—the last but one—to have seen Jane Zoffany alive. And he had let her go. Because he was off on holiday, because he didn't want to inconvenience Dora or upset arrangements. Of course she hadn't taken refuge with her sister or some friend. She had had no handbag, no money. He had let her go, overwrought as she was, to walk away into the dusk of Ploughman's Lane—to go back to Sterries and Natalie Arno.

"I had a feeling we ought to take it a bit more seriously," Burden said. "I mean, I wasn't really alarmed but I couldn't help thinking about poor old Camargue. We've got our own ideas about what kind of a death that was, haven't we? I talked to Zoffany myself, I got him to give me the names of people she could possibly have gone to. There weren't many and we checked on them all."

"And what about Natalie? Have you talked to her?"

"I thought I'd leave that to you."

"We'll have to drag the lake," said Wexford, "and dig up the garden if necessary. But I'll talk to her first."

The effect of her inherited wealth was now displayed. A new hatchback Opel, mustard-colored, automatic transmission, stood on the gravel circle outside the front door. Looking at her, staring almost, Wexford remembered the skirt Jane Zoffany had mended, the old blanket coat. Natalie wore a dress of some thin clinging jersey material in bright egg-yellow with a tight bodice and full skirt. Around her small neat waist was tied a belt of yellow with red, blue and purple stripes. It was startling and effective and very fashionable. Her hair hung loose in a glossy black bell. There was a white gold watch on one wrist and a bracelet of woven white gold threads on the other. The mysterious lady from Boston, he thought, and he wondered how you felt when you knew your relatives, parents maybe, and your friends thought you were dead and grieved for you while in fact you were alive and living in the lap of luxury.

"But Mr. Wexford," she said with her faint accent—a New England accent? "But, Mr. Wexford, Jane never came back here that night." She smiled in a way a model does when her mouth and not her eyes are to show in the toothpaste ad. "Her things are still in the room she and Ivan used. Would you like to see?"

He nodded. He followed her down to the spare rooms. On the carved teak chest stood a Chinese bowl full of Peace roses. They went into the room where he had once before seen Jane Zoffany standing before the long mirror and fastening the collar of a Persian lamb coat. Her suitcase lay open on the top of a chest of drawers. There was a folded nightdress inside it, a pair of sandals placed heel to toe and a paperback edition of Daphne du Maurier's *Rebecca*. On the black-backed hairbrush on the dressing table and the box of talcum powder lay a fine scattering of dust.

"Has Mrs. Hicks left you?"

"In the spirit if not the flesh yet, Mr. Wexford. She and Ted are going to Uncle Philip." She added, as if in explanation to someone who could not be expected to know intimate family usage, "Philip Cory, that is. He was just crazy to have them and it's made him so happy. Meanwhile this place is rather neglected while they get ready to leave. They've sold their house and I think I've sold this one at last. Well, practically sold it. Contracts have been exchanged." She chatted on, straightening the lemon floral duvet, opening a window, for all the world as if he too were a prospective purchaser rather than a policeman investigating an ominous disappearance. "I'm having some of the furniture put in store and the rest will go to the flat I've bought in London. Then I'm thinking of going off on vacation somewhere."

He glanced into the adjoining bathroom. It had evidently been cleaned before Muriel Hicks withdrew her services. The yellow bath and basin were immaculate and fresh honey-colored towels hung on the rail. Without waiting for permission, he made his way into the next room, the one Natalie had rejected in favor of using Camargue's very private and personal territory.

There were no immediately obvious signs that this room had ever been occupied since Camargue's death. In fact, it seemed likely that the last people to have slept here were Dinah Sternhold's parents when they stayed with Camargue at Christmas. But Wexford, peering quickly, pinched from the frill that edged one of the green and blue flowered pillows, a hair. It was black but it was not from Natalie's head, being wavy and no more than three inches long.

This bathroom too lacked the pristine neatness and cleanliness of the other. A man no more than ordinarily observant might have noticed nothing, but Wexford was almost certain that one of the blue towels had been used. On the basin, under the cold tap, was a small patch of tide mark. He turned as Natalie came up softly behind him. She was not the kind of person one much fancied creeping up on one, and he thought, as he had done when he first met her, of a snake.

"That night," he said, "Mrs. Zoffany ran out of the house and then afterwards her husband left. How long afterwards?"

"Twenty minutes, twenty-five. Shall we say twenty-two and a half minutes, Mr. Wexford, to be on the safe side?"

He gave no sign that he had noticed the implicit mockery. "He walked to the station, did he?"

"I gave him a lift in my car."

Of course. Now he remembered that he had seen them. "And after that you never saw Mrs. Zoffany again?"

"Never." She looked innocently at Wexford, her black eyes very large and clear, the lashes lifted and motionless. "It's the most extraordinary thing I ever came across in my life."

Considering what he knew of her life, Wexford doubted this statement. "I should like your consent to our dragging the lake," he said.

"That's just a polite way of saying you're going to drag it anyway, isn't it?"

"Pretty well," he said. "It'll save time if you give your permission."

Out of the lake came a quantity of blanket weed, sour green and sour smelling; two car tires, a bicycle lamp, half a dozen cans and a broken wrought-iron gate as well as a lot of miscellaneous rubbish of the nuts and bolts and nails variety. They also found Sir Manuel Camargue's missing glove, but there was no trace of Jane Zoffany. Wexford wondered if he had chosen the lake as the first possible place to search because of the other drownings associated with Natalie Arno.

It was, of course, stretching a point to touch the garden at all. But the temptation to tell the men to dig up the flowerbed between the lake and the circular forecourt was very great. It was, after all, no more than three or four yards from the edge of the lake and the soil in it looked suspiciously freshly turned and the bedding plants as if they had been there no more than a day or two. Who would put out bedding plants in July? They dug. They dug to about three feet down and then even Wexford had to admit no body was buried there. Ted Hicks, who had been watching them for hours, now said that he had dug the bed over a week ago and planted out a dozen biennials. Asked why he hadn't said so before, he said he hadn't thought it his place to interfere. By then it was too late to do any more, nine on a typical English July evening, twilight, grayish, damp and cool.

Wexford's phone was ringing when he got in. The chief constable. Mrs. Arno had complained that he was digging up the grounds of her house without her permission and without a warrant.

"True," said Wexford, because it was and it seemed easier to confess than to get involved in the ramifications of explaining. A scalding lecture exploded at him from the mouthpiece. Once again he was overstepping the bounds of his duty and his rights, once again he was allowing an obsession to warp his judgment. And this time the obsession looked as if it were taking the form of a vindictive campaign against Mrs. Arno.

Had her voice on the phone achieved this? Or had she been to Griswold in person, in the yellow dress, holding him with her glowing black eyes, moving her long pretty hands in feigned distress? For the second time he promised to persecute Natalie Arno no more, in fact to act as if he had never heard her name.

What changed the chief constable's mind must have been the systematic searching of the Zodiac. Two neighbors of Ivan Zoffany went independently to the police, one to complain that Zoffany had been lighting bonfires in his garden by night, the other to state that she had actually seen Jane in the vicinity of De Beauvoir Place on the night of Sunday, 29 June.

The house and the shop were searched without result. Zoffany admitted to the bonfires, saying that he intended to move away and take up some other line of work, and it was his stock of science-fiction paperbacks he had been burning. Wexford applied for a warrant to search the inside of Sterries and secured one three days after the dragging of the lake.

17

The house was empty. Not only deserted by its owner but half-emptied of its furnishings. Wexford remembered that Natalie Arno had said she would be going away on holiday and also that she intended having some of the furniture put in store. Mrs. Murray-Burgess, that inveterate observer of unusual vehicles, told Burden when he called at Kingsfield House that she had seen a removal van turn out of the Sterries drive into Ploughman's Lane at about three on Tuesday afternoon. It was now Thursday, 17 July.

With Wexford and Burden were a couple of men, detective constables, called Archbold and Bennett. They were prepared not only to search but to dismantle parts of the house if need be. They began in the double garage, examining the cupboards at the end of it and the outhouse tacked on to its rear. Since Sterries Cottage was also empty and had been since the previous day, Wexford intended it to be searched as well. Archbold, who had had considerable practice at this sort of thing, picked the locks on both front doors.

The cottage was bare of furniture and carpets. Like most English houses, old or new, it was provided with inadequate cupboard space. Its walls were of brick but were not cavity walls, and at some recent period, perhaps when Sir Manuel and the Hickses had first come, the floors at ground level had been relaid with tiles on a concrete base. No possibility of hiding a body there and nowhere upstairs either. They turned their attention to the bigger house.

Here, at first, there seemed even less likelihood of being able safely to conceal the body of a full-grown woman. It was for no more than form's sake that they cleared out the cloaks cupboard inside the front door, the kitchen broom cupboard and the small room off the kitchen which housed the central-heating boiler and a stock of soap powders and other cleansers. From the first floor a great many pieces had gone, including the pale green settee and armchairs, the piano and all the furniture from Camargue's bedroom and sitting room. Everywhere there seemed to be blank spaces or marks of discoloration on the walls where this or that piece had stood. The Chinese vase of Peace roses, wilted now, had been stuck on the floor up against a window.

Bennett, tapping walls, discovered a hollow space between the right-hand side of the hanging cupboard and the outside wall in Camargue's bedroom. And outside there were signs that it had been the intention on someone's part to use this space as a cupboard for garden tools or perhaps to contain a dustbin, for an arch had been built into which to fit a door and this arch subsequently filled in with bricks of a slightly lighter color.

From the inside of the hanging cupboard Bennett set about unscrewing the panel at its right-hand end. Wexford wondered if he were getting squeamish in his old age. It was with something amounting to nausea that he stood there anticipating the body falling slowly forward as the panel came away, crumpling into Bennett's arms, the tall thin body of Jane Zoffany with a gauzy scarf and a red and yellow dress of Indian cotton for a winding sheet. Burden sat on the bed, rubbing away fastidiously at a small powder or plaster mark that had appeared on the hem of his light fawn trousers.

The last screw was out and the panel fell, Bennett catching it and resting it against the wall. There was nothing inside the cavity but a spider which swung across its webs. A little bright light and fresh air came in by way of a ventilator brick. Wexford let out his breath in a sigh. It was time to take a break for lunch.

Mr. Haq, all smiles and gratified to see Wexford back, remarked that he was happy to be living in a country where they paid policemen salaries on which they could afford to have holidays in California. With perfect sincerity, he said this made him feel more secure. Burden ordered for both of them, steak Soroti, an innocuous beef stew with carrots and onions. When Mr. Haq and his son were out of earshot he said he often suspected that the Pearl of Africa's cook hailed from Bradford. Wexford said nothing.

"It's no good," said Burden, "we aren't going to find anything in that place. You may as well resign yourself. You're too much of an optimist sometimes for your own good."

"D'you think I want the poor woman to be dead?" Wexford retorted. "Optimist, indeed." And he quoted rather crossly, "The optimist proclaims that we live in the best of all possible worlds. The pessimist fears this is true."

"You want Natalie Arno to be guilty of something and you don't much care what," said Burden. "Why should she murder her?"

"Because Jane Zoffany knew who she really is. Either that or she found out how the murder of Camargue was done and who did it. There's a conspiracy here, Mike, involving a number of conspirators and Jane Zoffany was one of them. But there's no more honor among conspirators than there is among thieves, and when she discovered how Natalie had betrayed her she saw no reason to be discreet any longer." He told Burden what had happened when he encountered Jane Zoffany in Ploughman's Lane on 27 June. "She had something to tell me, she would have told me then only I didn't realize, I didn't give her a word of encouragement. Instead she went back to Sterries and no doubt had the temerity to threaten Natalie. It was a silly thing to do. But she was a silly woman, hysterical and unstable."

The steak Soroti came. Wexford ate in silence. It was true enough that he wanted Natalie Arno to have done something, or rather that he now saw that charging her with something was almost within his grasp. Who would know where she had gone on holiday? Zoffany? Philip Cory? Would anyone know? They had the ice cream eau-ue-nil to follow but Wexford left half of his.

"Let's get back there," he said.

It had begun to rain. The white walls of Sterries were streaked with water. Under a lowering sky of gray and purple cloud the house had the shabby faded look which belongs particularly to English houses built to a design intended for the Mediterranean. There were lights on in the upper rooms.

Archbold and Bennett were working on the drawing room, Bennett having so thoroughly investigated the chimney as to clamber half-way up inside it. Should they take up the floor? Wexford said no, he didn't think so. No one could hope to conceal a body for long by burying it under the floor in a house which was about to change hands. Though, as Wexford now told himself, it wasn't necessarily or exclusively a body they were looking for. By six o'clock they were by no means finished but Wexford told them to leave the rest of the house till the next day. It was still raining, though slightly now, little more than a drizzle. Wexford made his way down the path between the conifers to check that they had closed and locked the door of Sterries Cottage.

In the wet gloom the Alsatian's face looking out of a ground-floor window and almost on a level with his own made him jump. It evoked strange ideas, that there had been a time shift and it was six months ago and Camargue still lived. Then again, from the way some kind of white cloth seemed to surround the dog's head . . .

"Now I know how Red Riding Hood felt," said Wexford to Dinah Sternhold.

She was wearing a white raincoat with its collar turned up and she had been standing behind the dog, surveying the empty room. A damp cotton scarf was tied under her chin. She smiled. The sadness that had seemed characteristic of her had left her face now. It seemed fuller, the cheeks pink with rain and perhaps with running.

"They've gone," she said, "and the door was open. It was a bit of a shock."

"They're working for Philip Cory now."

She shrugged. "Oh well, I suppose there was no reason they should bother to tell me. I'd got into the habit of bringing Nancy over every few weeks just for them to see her. Ted loves Nancy." She took her hand from the dog's collar and Nancy bounded up to Wexford as if they were old friends. "Sheila said you'd been to California."

"For our summer holiday."

"Not entirely, Mr. Wexford, was it? You went to find out if what Manuel thought was true. But you haven't found out, have you?"

He said nothing, and she went on quickly, perhaps thinking she had gone too far or been indiscreet. "I often think how strange it is she could get the solicitors to believe in her and Manuel's old friends to believe in her and the police and people who'd known the Camargues for years, yet Manuel, who wanted to believe, who was pretty well geared up to believe anything, saw her on that one occasion and didn't believe in her for more than half an hour." She shrugged her shoulders again and gave a short little laugh. Then she said politely as was her way, "I'm so sorry, I'm keeping you. Did you want to lock up?" She took hold of the dog again and walked her out into the rain. "Has she sold the house?" Her voice suddenly sounded thin and strained.

Wexford nodded. "So she says."

"I shall never come here again."

He watched her walk away down the narrow lane which led from the cottage to the road. Raindrops glistened on the Alsatian's fur. Water slid off the flat branches of the conifers and dripped on to the grass. Uncut for more than a week, it was already shaggy, giving the place an unkempt look. Wexford walked back to the car.

Burden was watching Dinah Sternhold shoving Nancy on to the rear seat of the Volkswagen. "It's a funny thing," he said. "Jenny's got a friend, a Frenchwoman, comes from Alsace. But you can't call her an Alsatian, can you? That word always means a dog."

"You couldn't call anyone a Dalmatian either," said Wexford.

Burden laughed. "Americans call Alsatians German Shepherds."

"We ought to. That's their proper name and I believe the Kennel Club have brought it in again. When they were brought here from Germany after the First World War there was a lot of anti-German feeling—hence we used the euphemism 'alsatian'. About as daft as refusing to play Beethoven and Bach at concerts because they were German."

"Jenny and I are going to German classes," said Burden rather awkwardly.

"What on earth for?"

"Jenny says education should go on all one's life."

Next morning it was heavy and sultry, the sun covered by a thick yellow mist. Sterries awaited them, full of secrets. Before he left news had come in for Wexford through Interpol that the woman who drowned in Santa Xavierita in July 1976 was Theresa or Tessa Lanchester, aged thirty, unmarried, a para-legal secretary from Boston, Massachusetts. The body had been recovered after having been in the sea some five days and identified a further four days later by Theresa Lanchester's aunt, her parents both being dead. Driving up to Sterries, Wexford thought about being sent back to California. He wouldn't mind a few days in Boston, come to that.

Archbold and Bennett got to work on the spare bedrooms but without positive result and after lunch they set about the study and the two bathrooms.

In the yellow bathroom they took up the honey-colored carpet, leaving exposed the white vinyl tiles beneath. It was obvious that none of these tiles had been disturbed since they were first laid. The carpet was replaced and then the same procedure gone through in the blue bathroom. Here there was a shower cabinet as well as a bath. Archbold unhooked and spread out the blue and green striped shower curtain. This was made of semi-transparent nylon with a narrow machine-made hem at the bottom. Archbold, who was young and had excellent sight, noticed that the machine stitches for most of the seam's length were pale blue but in the extreme right-hand corner, for about an inch, they were not blue but brown. He told Wexford.

Wexford, who had been sitting on a window-sill in the study, thinking, watching the cloud shadows move across the meadows, went into the blue bathroom and looked at the curtain and knelt down. And about a quarter of an inch from the floor, on the paneled side of the bath, which had been covered for nearly half an inch by the carpet pile, were two minute reddish-brown spots.

"Take up the floor tiles," said Wexford.

Would they find enough blood to make a test feasible? It appeared so after two of the tiles had been lifted and the edge of the one which had been alongside the bath paneling showed a thick dark encrustation.

18

"You might tell me where we're going."

"Why? You're a real ignoramus when it comes to London." Wexford spoke irritably. He was nervous because he might be wrong. The chief constable had said he was and had frowned and shaken his head and talked about infringements of rights and intrusions of privacy. If he was wrong he was going to look such a fool. He said to Burden, "If I said we were going to Thornton Heath, would that mean anything to you?"

Burden said nothing. He looked huffily out of the window. The car was passing through Croydon, through industrial complexes, estates of small red terraced houses, shopping centers, big spreadeagled roundabouts with many exits. Soon after Thornton Heath station Wexford's driver turned down a long bleak road that was bounded by a tall wire fence on one side and a row of sad thin poplars on the other. Thank God there were such neighbors about as Mrs. Murray-Burgess, thought Wexford. A woman endowed with a memory and a gimlet eye as well as a social conscience.

"An enormous removal van," she had said, "a real pantechnicon, and polluting what's left of our country air with clouds of the filthiest black diesel fumes. Of course I can tell you the name of the firm. I sat down and wrote to their managing director at once to complain. William Dorset and Company. I expect you've seen that slogan of theirs, 'Dorset Stores It,' it's on all their vans."

The company had branches in north and south London, in Brighton, Guildford, and in Kingsmarkham, which was no doubt why both Sheila and Natalie Arno had employed them. Kingsmarkham people moving house or storing furniture mostly did use Dorset's.

Here and there along the road was the occasional factory as well as the kind of long, low, virtually windowless building whose possible nature or use it is hard for the passerby to guess at. Perhaps all such buildings, Wexford thought as they turned into the entrance drive to one of them, served the same purpose as this one.

It was built of gray brick and roofed with red sheet iron. What windows it had were high up under the roof. In the concrete bays in front of the iron double doors stood two monster vans, dark red and lettered "Dorset Stores It" in yellow.

"They're expecting us," Wexford said. "I reckon that's the office over there, don't you?"

It was an annex built out on the far side. Someone came out before they reached the door. Wexford recognized him as the younger of the two men who had moved Sheila's furniture, the one whose wife had not missed a single episode of *Runway*. He looked at Wexford as if he thought he had seen him somewhere before but knew just the same that he was mistaken.

"Come in, will you, please? Mr. Rochford's here, our deputy managing director. He reckoned he ought to be here himself."

Wexford's heart did not exactly sink but it floundered a little. He would so much rather have been alone, without even Burden. Of course he could have stopped all these people coming with him, he had the power to do that, but he wouldn't. Besides, two witnesses would be better than one and four better than two. He followed the man who said his name was George Prince into the office. Rochford, a man of Prince's age and in the kind of suit which, while perfectly clean and respectable, looks as if it has been worn in the past for emergency manual labour and could be put to such use again if the need arose, sat in a small armchair with an unopened folder on his knees. He jumped up and the folder fell on the floor. Wexford shook hands with him and showed him the warrant.

Although he already knew the purpose of the visit, he turned white and looked nauseated.

"This is a serious matter," he said miserably, "a very serious matter."

"It is."

"I find it hard to believe. I imagine there's a chance you're wrong."

"A very good chance, sir."

"Because," said Rochford hopefully and extremely elliptically, "in summertime and after—well, I mean, there's been nothing of that sort, has there, George?"

Not yet, thought Wexford. "Perhaps we might terminate this suspense," he said, attempting a smile, "by going and having a look?"

"Oh yes, yes, by all means. This way, through here. Perhaps you'll lead the way, George. I hope you're wrong, Mr. Wexford, I only hope you're wrong."

The interior of the warehouse was cavernous and dim. The roof, supported by girders of red iron, was some thirty feet high. Up there sparrows flitted about and perched on these man-made branches. The sunlight was greenish, filtering through the tinted panes of high, metal-framed windows. George Prince pressed a switch and strip lighting came on, setting the sparrows in flight again. It was chilly inside the warehouse, though the outdoor temperature had that morning edged just into the seventies.

The place had the air of a soulless and shabby township erected on a grid plan. A town of caravans, placed symmetrically a yard or two apart and with streets crossing each other at right angles to give access to them. It might have been a camp for refugees or the rejected spill-over of some newly constituted state, or the idea of such a place in grim fiction or cinema, a settlement in a northern desert without a tree or a blade of grass. Wexford felt the fantasy and shook it off, for there were no people, no inhabitants of this container camp but himself and Burden and George Prince and Rochford padding softly up the broadest aisle.

Of these rectangular houses, these metal cuboids ranked in rows, iron red, factory green, camouflage khaki, the one they were making for stood at the end of the topmost lane to debouch from the main aisle. It stood up against the cream-washed wall under a window. Prince produced a key and was about to insert it into the lock on the container door when Rochford put out a hand to restrain him and asked to see the warrant again. Patiently, Wexford handed it to him. They stood there, waiting while he read it once more. Wexford had fancied for minutes now that he could smell something sweetish and fetid but this became marked the nearer he got to Rochford and it was only the stuff the man put on his hair or his underarms. Rochford said:

"Mrs. N. Arno, 27a De Beauvoir Place, London, N1. We didn't move it from there, did we, George? Somewhere in Sussex, didn't you say?"

"Kingsmarkham, sir. It was our Kingsmarkham branch done it."

"Ah, yes. And it was put into store indefinitely at the rate of £5.50 per week starting from 15 July?"

Wexford said gently, "Can we open up now, sir, please?"

"Oh, certainly, certainly. Get it over, eh?"

Get it over . . . George Prince unlocked the door and Wexford braced himself for the shock of the foul air that must escape. But there was nothing, only a curious staleness. The door swung silently open on oiled hinges. The place might be sinister and evocative of all manner of disagreeable things, but it was well-kept and well-run for all that.

The inside of the container presented a microcosm of Sterries, a drop of the essence of Sir Manuel Camargue. His desk was there and the austere furnishings from the bedroom and sitting room in his private wing, the record player too and the lyre-backed chairs from the music room and the piano. If you closed your eyes you could fancy hearing the first movement from the Flute and Harp Concerto. You could smell and hear Camargue and nothing else. Wexford turned away to face the furniture from the spare bedrooms, a green velvet ottoman in a holland cover, two embroidered footstools, sheathed in plastic, a pair of golden Afghan rugs rolled up in hessian, and under a bag full of quilts and cushions, the carved teak chest, banded now with two stout leather straps.

The four men looked at it. Burden humped the quilt bag off on to the ottoman and knelt down to undo the buckles on the straps. There was a rattly intake of breath from Rochford. The straps fell away and Burden tried the iron clasps. They were locked. He looked inquiringly at Prince who hesitated and then muttered something about having to go back to the office to check in his book where the keys were.

Wexford lost his temper. "You knew what we'd come for. Couldn't you have checked where the keys were before we came all the way down here? If they can't be found I'll have to have it broken open."

"Look here . . ." Rochford was almost choking. "Your warrant doesn't say anything about breaking. What's Mrs. Arno going to say when she finds her property's been damaged? I can't take the responsibility for that sort of . . ."

"Then you'd better find the keys."

Prince scratched his head. "I reckon she said they were in that desk. In one of the pigeonholes in that desk."

They opened the desk. It was entirely empty. Burden unrolled both rugs, emptied the quilt bag, pulled out the drawers of the bedside cabinet from Camargue's bedroom.

"You say you've got a note of where they are in some book of yours?" said Wexford.

"The note says they're in the desk," said Prince.

"Right. We break the chest open."

"They're down here," said Burden. He pulled out his hand from the cleft between the ottoman's arm and seat cushion and waved at them a pair of identical keys on a ring.

Wexford fitted one key into the lock on the right-hand side, turned it, and then unlocked the left-hand side. The clasps opened and he raised the lid. The chest seemed to be full of black heavy-duty polythene sheeting. He grasped a fold of it and pulled.

The heavy thing that was contained in this cold glossy slippery shroud lurched against the wooden wall and seemed to roll over. Wexford began to unwrap the black stuff and then a horrible thing happened. Slowly, languidly, as if it still retained life, a yellowish-white waxen arm and thin hand rose from the chest and loomed trembling over it. It hung in the air for a moment before it subsided. Wexford stepped back with a grunt. The icy thing had brushed his cheek with fingers of marble.

Rochford let out a cry and stumbled out of the container. There was a sound of retching. But George Prince was made of tougher stuff and he came nearer to the chest with awe. With Burden's help, Wexford lifted the body on to the floor and stripped away its covering. Its throat had been cut and the wound wadded with a bloody towel, but this had not kept blood off the yellow dress, which was splashed and stained with red all over like some bizarre map of islands.

Wexford looked into the face, knowing he had been wrong, feeling as much surprise as the others, and then he looked at Burden.

Burden shook his head, appalled and mystified, and together they turned slowly back to gaze into the black dead eyes of Natalie Arno.

19

"*Cui bono?*" said Kenneth Ames. "Who benefits?" He made a church steeple of his fingers and looked out at St. Peter's spire. "Well, my dear chap, the same lady who would have benefitted had you been right in your preposterous assumption that poor Mrs. Arno was not Mrs. Arno. Or to cut a tall story short, Sir Manuel's niece in France."

"You never did tell me her name," said Wexford.

He did not then. "It's an extraordinary thing. Poor Mrs. Arno simply followed in her father's footmarks. It's no more than a week ago she asked me if she should make a will and I naturally advised her to do so. But, as was true in the case of Sir Manuel, she died before a will was drawn up. She too had been going to get married, you know, but she changed her mind."

"No, I didn't know."

Ames made his doggy face. "So, as I say, the beneficiary will be this French lady, there being no other living relatives whatsoever. I've got her name somewhere." He hunted in a drawer full of folders. "Ah, yes. A Mademoiselle Thérèse Lerémy. Do you want her precise address?"

The transformation of Moidore Lodge was apparent long before the house was reached. The drive was swept, the signboard bearing the name of the house had been re-painted black and white, and Wexford could have sworn the bronze wolves (or Alsatians) had received a polish.

Blaise Cory's Porsche was parked up in front of the house and it was he, not Muriel Hicks, who opened the door. They send for him like other people might send for their solicitor, thought Wexford. He stepped into a hall from which all dust and clutter had been removed, which even seemed lighter and airier. Blaise confided, looking once or twice over his shoulder:

"Having these good people has made all the difference to the dear old dad. I do hope you're not here to do anything which might—well, in short, which might put a spanner in the works."

"I hardly think so, Mr. Cory. I have a question or two to ask Mrs. Hicks, that's all."

"Ah, that's what you people always say." He gave the short, breathy, fruity laugh with which, on his show, he was in the habit of receiving the more outrageous of the statements made by his interviewees. "I believe she's about the house, plying her highly useful equipment."

The sound of a vacuum cleaner immediately began overhead as if on cue, and Wexford would have chosen to go straight upstairs but he found himself instead ushered into Philip Cory's living room.

Ted Hicks was cleaning the huge Victorian French windows, the old man, once more attired in his boy's jeans and guernsey, watching him with fascinated approval. Hicks stopped work the moment Wexford came in and took up his semi-attention stance.

"Good morning, sir!"

"Welcome, Chief Inspector, welcome." Cory spread out his meager hands expansively. "A pleasure to see you, I'm sure. It's so delightful for me to have visitors and not be ashamed of the old place, not to mention being able to find things. Now, for instance, if you or Blaise were to require a drink I shouldn't have to poke about looking for bottles. Hicks here would bring them in a jiffy, wouldn't you, Hicks?"

"I certainly would, sir."

"So you have only to say the word."

It being not yet ten in the morning, Wexford was not inclined to utter any drink-summoning word but asked if he might have a talk in private with Mrs. Hicks.

"I saw in the newspaper about poor little Natalie," said Cory. "Blaise thought it would upset me. Blaise was always a very *sensitive* boy. But I said to him, how can I be upset when I don't know if she was Natalie or not?"

Wexford went upstairs, Hicks leading the way. Moidore Lodge was a very large house. Several rooms had been set aside to make a dwelling for the Hickses without noticeably depleting the Cory living space. Muriel Hicks, who had been cleaning Cory's own bedroom with its vast four-poster, came into her own rooms, drying her newly washed hands on a towel. She had put on weight since last he saw her and her pale red hair had grown longer and bushier. But her brusque and taciturn manner was unchanged.

"Mrs. Arno was going away on her holidays. She says to me to see to the moving when the men came next day. It wasn't convenient, we were leaving ourselves and I'd got things to do, but that was all the same to her, I daresay." Her husband flashed her an admonitory look, implying that respect should be accorded to *all* employers, or else perhaps that she must in no way hint at ill of the dead. Her pink face flushed rosily. "Well, she said that was the only day Dorset's could do it, so it was no use arguing. She'd had a chap there staying the weekend . . ."

"A *gentleman*," said Hicks.

"All right, Ted, a gentleman. I thought he'd gone by the Sunday, and maybe he had, but he was back the Monday afternoon."

"You saw him?"

"I *heard* him. I went in about six to check up with her what was going and what was staying, and I heard them talking upstairs. They heard me come in and they started talking French so I wouldn't understand, and she laughed and said in English, 'Oh, your funny Swiss accent!' By the time I got upstairs he'd hid himself."

"Did you hear his name, Mrs. Hicks?"

She shook her head. "Never heard his name and never saw him. She was a funny one, she didn't mind me knowing he was there and what he was to her like, but she never wanted me nor anyone to actually see him. I took it for granted they both went off on their holidays that same evening. She said she was going, she told me, and the car was gone."

"What happened next day?"

"The men came from Dorset's nine in the morning. I let them in and told them what to take and what not to. She'd left everything labeled. When they'd gone I had a good clear-up. There was a lot of blood about in the blue bathroom, but I never gave it a thought, reckoned one of them had cut theirselves." Wexford remembered the deliberate cutting of Natalie's fingertips in the bathroom in De Beauvoir Place and he almost shuddered. Muriel Hicks was more stolid about it than he. "I had a bit of a job getting it off the carpet," she said. "I saw in the paper they found her at Dorset's warehouse. Was she . . . ? I mean, was *it* in that chest?"

He nodded.

She said indifferently, "The men did say it was a dead weight."

Blaise Cory walked out to the car with him. It was warm today, the sky a serene blue, the leaves of the plane trees fluttering in a light frisky breeze. Blaise said suddenly and without his usual affected geniality:

"Do you know Mrs. Mountnessing, Camargue's sister-in-law?"

"I've seen her once."

"There was a bit of a scandal in the family. I was only seventeen or eighteen at the time and Natalie and I—well, it wasn't an affair or anything, we were like brother and sister. We were close, she used to tell me things. The general made a pass at her and the old girl caught them kissing."

"The general?" said Wexford.

Blaise made one of his terrible jokes. "Must have been caviar to him." He gave a yelp of laughter. "Sorry. I mean old Roo Mountnessing, General Mountnessing. Mrs. M. told her sister and made a great fuss, put all the blame on poor little Nat, called her incestuous and a lot of crap like that. As if everyone didn't know the old boy was a satyr. Camargue was away on a tour of Australia at the time or he'd have intervened. Mrs. Camargue and her sister tried to lock Nat up, keep her a sort of prisoner. She got out and hit her mother. She hit her in the chest, quite hard, I think. I suppose they had a sort of brawl over Natalie trying to get out of the house."

"And?"

"Well, when Mrs. Camargue got cancer Mrs. Mountnessing said it had been brought on by the blow. I've heard it said that can happen. The doctors said no but Mrs. M. wouldn't listen to that and she more or less got Camargue to believe it too. I've always thought that's why Natalie went off with Vernon Arno, she couldn't stand things at home."

"So that was the cause of the breach," said Wexford. "Camargue blamed her for her mother's death."

Blaise shook his head. "I don't think he did. He was just confused by Mrs. M. and crazy with grief over his wife dying. The dear old dad says Camargue tried over and over again to make things right between himself and Nat, wrote again and again, offered to go out there or pay her fare home. I suppose it wasn't so much him blaming her for her mother's death as her blaming herself. It was guilt kept her away."

Wexford looked down at the little stocky man.

"Did she tell you all this when you had lunch with her, Mr. Cory?"

"Good heavens, no. We didn't talk about that. I'm a *present* person, Chief Inspector, I live in the moment. And so did she. Curious," he said reflectively, "that rumor which went around back in the winter that she was some sort of impostor."

"Yes," said Wexford.

It was not a long drive from Moidore Lodge to the village on the borders of St. Leonard's Forest. It was called Bayeux Green, between Horsham and Wellridge, and the house Wexford was looking for bore the name Bayeux Villa. Well, it was not all that far from Hastings, there was another village nearby called Doomsday Green, and very likely the name had something to do with the tapestry.

He found the house without having to ask. It was in the center of the village, a narrow, detached, late nineteenth-century house, built of small pale gray bricks and with only a small railed-in area separating it from the pavement. The front door was newer and inserted in it was a picture in stained glass of a Norman soldier in chain mail. Wexford rang the bell and got no answer. He stepped to one side and looked in at the window. There was no sign of recent habitation. The occupants, at this time of the year, were very likely away on holiday. It seemed strange that they had made no arrangements for the care of their houseplants. Tradescantias, peperomias, a cissus that climbed to the ceiling on carefully spaced strings, a Joseph's coat, a variegated ivy, all hung down leaves that were limp and parched.

He walked around the house, looking in more windows, and he had a sensation of being watched, though he could see no one. The two little lawns looked as if they had not been cut for a month and there were weeds coming up in the rosebed. After he had rung the bell again he went to the nearest neighbor, a cottage separated from Bayeux Villa by a greengrocer's and a pair of garages.

It was a comfort to be himself once more, to have resumed his old standing. The woman looked at his warrant card.

"They went off on holiday—oh, it'd be three weeks ago. When I come to think of it, they must be due back today or tomorrow. They've got a caravan down in Devon, they always take three weeks."

"Don't they have friends to come in and keep an eye on the place?"

She said quickly, "Don't tell me it's been broken into."

He reassured her. "Nobody's watered the plants."

"But the sister's there. She said to me on the Saturday, my sister'll be staying while we're away."

This time he caught her off guard. He came up to the kitchen window and their eyes met. She had been on the watch for him too, creeping about the house, looking out for him. She was still wearing the red and yellow dress of Indian cotton, she had been shut up in there for three weeks, and it hung on her. Her face looked sullen, though not frightened. She opened the back door and let him in.

"Good morning, Mrs. Zoffany," he said. "It's a relief to find you well and unharmed."

"Who would harm me?"

"Suppose you tell me that. Suppose you tell me all about it."

She said nothing. He wondered what she had done all by herself in this house since 27 July. Not eaten much, that was obvious. Presumably, she had not been out. Nor even opened a window. It was insufferably hot and stuffy and a strong smell of sweat and general unwashedness emanated from Jane Zoffany as he followed her into the room full of dying plants. She sat down and looked at him in wary silence.

"If you won't tell me," he said, "shall I tell you? After you left me on that Friday evening you went back to Sterries and found the house empty. Mrs. Arno had driven your husband to the station. As a matter of fact, her car passed me as I was driving down the hill." She continued to eye him uneasily. Her eyes had more madness in them than when he had last seen her. "You took your handbag but you left your suitcase; didn't want to be lumbered with it, I daresay. There's a bus goes to Horsham from outside St. Peter's. You'd have had time to catch the last one, or else maybe you had a hire car."

She said stonily, "I haven't money for hire cars. I didn't know about the bus, but it came and I got on."

"When you got here you found your sister and her husband were leaving for their summer holiday the next day. No doubt they were glad to have someone here to keep an eye on the place while they were gone. Then a week later you got yourself a birthday card . . ."

"No." She shook her head vehemently. "I only posted it. My sister had bought a card for me and written in it and done the envelope and everything. She said, here, you'd better have this now, save the postage. I went out at night and posted it." She gave a watery vague smile. "I liked hiding, I enjoyed it."

He could understand that. The virtue for her would be twofold. To some extent she would lose her identity, that troubling self, she would have hidden here from herself as successfully as she had hidden from others. And there would be the satisfaction of becoming for a brief while important, of causing anxiety, for once of stimulating emotions.

"What I don't see," he said, "is how you managed when the police came here making inquiries."

She giggled. "That was funny. They took me for my sister."

"I see."

"They just took it for granted I was my sister and they kept on talking about Mrs. Zoffany. Did I have any idea where Mrs. Zoffany might be? When had I last seen her? I said no and I didn't know and they had to believe me. It was funny, it was a bit like . . ." She put her fingers over her mouth and looked at him over the top of them.

"I shall have to tell your husband where you are. He's been very worried about you."

"Has he? Has he *really*?"

Had she, during her semi-incarceration, watched television, heard a radio, seen a newspaper? Presumably not, since she had not mentioned Natalie's death. He wouldn't either. She was safe enough here, he thought, with the sister coming back. Zoffany himself would no doubt come down before that. Would they perhaps get her back into a mental hospital between them? He had no faith that the kind of treatment she might get would do her good. He wanted to tell her to have a bath, eat a meal, open the windows, but he knew she would take no advice, would hardly hear it.

"I thought you'd be very angry with me."

He treated that no more seriously than if the younger of his grandsons had said it to him. "You and I are going to have to have a talk, Mrs. Zoffany. When you've settled down at home again and I've got more time. Just at present I'm very busy and I have to go abroad again."

She nodded. She no longer looked sullen. He let himself out into Bayeux Green's little high street, and when he glanced back he saw her gaunt face at the window, the eyes following him. In spite of what he had said, he might never see her again, he might never need to, for in one of those flashes of illumination that he had despaired of ever coming in this case, he saw the truth. She had told him. In a little giggly confidence she had told him everything there still remained for him to know.

In the late afternoon he drove out to the home of the chief constable, Hightrees Farm, Millerton. Mrs. Griswold exemplified the reverse of the Victorian ideal for children; she was heard but not seen. Some said she had been bludgeoned into passivity for forty years with the colonel. Her footsteps could sometimes be heard overhead, her voice whispering into the telephone. Colonel Griswold himself opened the front door, something which Wexford always found disconcerting. It was plunging in at the deep end.

"I want to go to the South of France, sir."

"I daresay," said Griswold. "I shall have to settle for a cottage in north Wales myself."

In a neutral voice Wexford reminded him that he had already had his holiday. The chief constable said yes, he remembered, and Wexford had been somewhere very exotic, hadn't he? He had wondered once or twice how that sort of thing would go down with the public when the police started screaming for wage increases.

"I want to go to the South of France," Wexford said more firmly, "and I know it's irregular but I would like to take Mike Burden with me. It's a little place *inland*—" Griswold's lips seemed silently to be forming the syllables St. Tropez, "—and there's a woman there who will inherit Camargue's money and property. She's Camargue's niece and her name is Thérèse Lerémy."

"A French citizen?"

"Yes, sir, but . . ."

"I don't want you going about putting people's backs up, Reg. Particularly foreign backs. I mean, don't think you can go over there and arrest this woman on some of your thin suspicions and . . ."

But before Wexford had even begun to deny that this was his intention he knew from the moody truculent look which had replaced obduracy in Griswold's face that he was going to relent.

20

From the city of the angels to the bay of the angels. As soon as they got there the taxi driver took them along the Promenade des Anglais, though it was out of their way, but he said they had to see it, they couldn't come to Nice and just see the airport. While Wexford gazed out over the Baie des Anges, Burden spoke from his newly acquired store of culture. Jenny had a reproduction of a picture of this by a painter called Dufy, but it all looked a bit different now.

It was still only late morning. They had come on the early London to Paris flight and changed planes at Roissy-Charles de Gaulle. Now their drive took them through hills crowned with orange and olive trees. Saint-Jean-de-l'Éclaircie lay a few miles to the north of Grasse, near the river Loup. A bell began to chime noon as they passed through an ivy-hung archway in the walls into the ancient town. They drove past the ocher-stone cathedral into the Place aux Eaux Vives where a fountain was playing and where stood Picasso's statue "Woman with a Lamb," presented to the town by the artist (according to Wexford's guide book) when he lived and worked there for some months after the war. The guide book also said that there was a Fragonard in the cathedral, some incomparable Sèvres porcelain in the museum, the Fondation Yeuse, and a mile outside the town the well-preserved remains of a Roman amphitheater. The taxi driver said that if you went up into the cathedral belfry you could see Corsica on the horizon.

Wexford had engaged rooms for one night—on the advice of his travel agent in the Kingsbrook Precinct—at the Hotel de la Rose Blanche in the *place*. Its vestibule was cool and dim, stone-walled, stone-flagged, and with that indefinable atmosphere that is a combination of complacency and gleeful anticipation and which signifies that the food is going to be good. The chef's in his kitchen, all's right with the world.

Kenneth Ames had known nothing more about Mademoiselle Lerémy than her name, her address and her relationship to Camargue. It was also known that her parents were dead and she herself unmarried. Recalling the photograph of the two little girls shown him by Mrs. Mountnessing, Wexford concluded she must be near the age of Camargue's daughter. He looked her up in the phone book, dialed the number apprehensively because of his scanty French, but got no reply.

They lunched off seafood, bread that was nearly all crisp crust, and a bottle of Monbazillac. Wexford said in an abstracted sort of voice that he felt homesick already, the hors d'oeuvres reminded him of Mr. Haq and antipasto Ankole. He got no reply when he attempted once more to phone Thérèse Lerémy, so there seemed nothing for it but to explore the town.

It was too hot to climb the belfry. On 24 July Saint-Jean-de-l'Éclaircie was probably at its hottest. The square was deserted, the narrow steep alleys that threaded the perimeter just inside the walls held only the stray tourist, and the morning market which had filled the Place de la Croix had packed up and gone. They went into the cathedral of St. Jean Baptiste, dark, cool, baroque. A nun was walking in the aisle, eyes cast down, and an old man knelt at prayer. They looked with proper awe at Fragonard's "Les Pains et Les Poissons," a large hazy canvas of an elegant Christ and an adoring multitude, and then they returned to the bright white sunshine and hard black shadows of the *place*.

"I suppose she's out at work," said Wexford. "A single woman would be bound to work. It looks as if we'll have to hang things out a few hours."

"It's no hardship," said Burden. "I promised Jenny I wouldn't miss the museum."

Wexford shrugged. "O.K."

The collection was housed in a sienna-red stucco building with Fondation Yeuse lettered on a black marble plaque. Wexford had expected it to be deserted inside but in fact they met other tourists in the rooms and on the winding marble staircase. As well as the Sèvres, Burden had been instructed to look at some ancient jewelery discovered in the Condamine, and Wexford, hearing English spoken, asked for directions from the woman who had been speaking correctly but haltingly to an American visitor. She seemed to be a curator, for she wore on one of the lapels of her dark red, near-uniform dress an oval badge inscribed Fondation Yeuse. He forced himself not to stare—and then wondered how many thousands before him had forced themselves not to stare. The lower part of her face was pitted densely and deeply with the scars of what looked like smallpox but was almost certainly acne. In her careful stumbling English she instructed him where to find the jewelery. He and Burden went upstairs again where the American woman had arrived before them. The sun penetrating drawn Venetian blinds shone on her flawless ivory skin. She had hands like Natalie Arno's, long and slender, display stands for rings as heavy and roughly made as those on the linen under the glass.

"We may as well get on up there," said Wexford after they had bought a *flacon* of Grasse perfume for Dora and a glazed stoneware jar in a Picasso design for Jenny. "Get on up there and have a look at the place."

The two local taxis, which were to be found between the fountain and the Hotel de la Rose Blanche, were not much in demand at this hour. Their driver spoke no English but as soon as Wexford mentioned the Maison du Cirque he understood and nodded assent.

On the north-eastern side of the town, outside the walls, was an estate of depressing pale gray flats and brown wooden houses with scarlet switchback roofs. It was as bad as home. Worse? ventured Burden. But the estate was soon left behind and the road ran through lemon groves. The driver persisted in talking to them in fast, fluent, incomprehensible French. Wexford managed to pick out two facts from all this, one that Saint-Jean-de-l'Éclaircie held a lemon festival each February, and the other that on the far side of the hill was the amphitheater.

They came upon the house standing alone at a bend in the road. It was flat-fronted, unprepossessing but undoubtledly large. At every window were wooden shutters from which most of the paint had flaked away. Big gardens, neglected now, stretched distantly towards olive and citrus groves, separated from them by crumbling stone walls.

"Mariana in the moated grange," said Wexford. "We may as well go to the circus while we're waiting for her."

The driver took them back. The great circular plain which was the base of the amphitheater was strangely green as if watered by a hidden spring. The tiers of seating, still defined, still unmistakable, rose in their parallel arcs to the hillside, the pines, the crystalline blue of the sky. Wexford sat down where some prefect or consul might once have sat.

"I hope we're in time," he said. "I hope we can get to her before any real harm has been done. The woman has been dead nine days. He's been here, say, eight . . ."

"If he's here. The idea of him being here is all based on your ESP. We don't know if he's here and, come to that, we don't know who he is or what he looks like or what name he'll be using."

"It's not as bad as that," said Wexford. "He would naturally come here. This place, that girl, would draw him like magnets. He won't want to lose the money now, Mike."

"No, not after plotting for years to get it. How long d'you reckon we're going to be here?"

Wexford shrugged. The air was scented with the herbs that grew on the hillsides, sage and thyme and rosemary and bay, and the sun was still very warm. "However long it may be," he said enigmatically, "to me it would be too short." He looked at his watch. "Martin should have seen Williams by now and done a spot of checking up for me at Guy's Hospital."

"Guy's Hospital?"

"In the course of this case we haven't remembered as often as we should that Natalie Arno went into hospital a little while before Camargue died. She had a biopsy."

"Yes, what *is* that?"

"It means to look at living tissue. It usually describes the kind of examination that is done to determine whether certain cells are cancerous or not."

Once this subject would have been a highly emotive one for Burden, an area to be avoided by all his sensitive acquaintances. His first wife had died of cancer. But time and his second marriage had changed things. He responded not with pain but only with an edge of embarrassment to his voice.

"But she didn't have cancer."

"Oh, no."

He sat down in the tier below Wexford. "I'd like to tell you what I think happened, see if we agree." On the grass beside him the shadow of Wexford's head nodded. "Well, then. Tessa Lanchester went on holiday to that place in California, Santa—what was it?"

"Santa Xavierita."

"And while she was there she met a man who played the guitar or whatever in a restaurant in the local town. He was living in America illegally and was very likely up to a good many other illegal activities as well. He was a con man. He had already met Natalie Arno and found out from her who her father was and what her expectations were. He introduced Tessa to Natalie and the two women became friends.

"He persuaded Tessa not to go back home to Boston but to remain longer in Santa Xavierita learning all she could about Natalie's life and past. Then he took Natalie out swimming by night and drowned her and that same night left with Tessa for Los Angeles in Natalie's car with Natalie's luggage and the key to Natalie's house. From then on Tessa became Natalie. The changes Natalie's body had undergone after five days in the sea made a true identification impossible and, since Tessa was missing, the corpse was identified as that of Tessa.

"Tessa and her accomplice then set about their plan to inherit Camargue's property, though this was somewhat frustrated by Ilbert's intervening and the sub-sequent deportation. Tessa tried in vain to sell Natalie's house. I think at this time she rather cooled off the plan. Otherwise I don't know how to account for a delay of more than three years between making the plan and putting it into practice. I think she cooled off. She settled into her new identity, made new friends, and, as we know, had two further love affairs. Then one of these lovers, Ivan Zoffany, wrote from London in the autumn of 1979 to say he had heard from his sister-in-law who lived near Wellridge that Camargue was about to remarry. That alerted her and fetched her to England. There she was once more able to join forces with the man who had first put her up to the idea. They had the support and help of Zoffany and his wife. How am I doing so far?"

Wexford raised his eyebrows. "How did they get Williams and Mavis Rolland into this? Bribery?"

"Of course. It would have to be a heavy bribe. Williams's professional integrity presumably has a high price. I daresay Mrs. Woodhouse could be bought cheaply enough."

"I never took you for a snob before, Mike."

"It's not snobbery," said Burden hotly. "It's simply that the poorer you are the more easily you're tempted. Shall I go on?"

The shadow nodded.

"They hesitated a while before the confrontation. Tessa was naturally nervous about this very important encounter. Also she'd been ill and had to have hospital treatment. When she finally went down to Sterries she blundered, not in having failed to do her homework—she knew every fact about the Camargue household she could be expected to, she knew them like she knew her own family in Boston —but over the pronunciation of an Italian name. Spanish she knew—many Americans do—French she knew, but it never occurred to her she would have to pronounce Italian.

"The rest we know. Camargue told her she would be cut out of his will, so on the following Sunday she made a sound alibi for herself by going to a party with Jane Zoffany. *He* went down to Sterries, waited for Camargue in the garden and drowned him in the lake."

Wexford said nothing.

"Well?"

As befitted a person of authority sitting in the gallery of an amphitheater, Wexford turned down his thumbs. "The last bit's more or less right, the drowning bit." He got up. "Shall we go?"

Burden was still muttering that it had to be that way, that all else was impossible, when they arrived back at the Maison du Cirque. Ahead of them a bright green Citroën 2 CV had just turned into the drive.

The woman who got out of it, who came inquiringly towards them, was the curator of the Fondation Yeuse.

21

The sun shone cruelly on that pitted skin. She had done her best to hide it with heavy makeup, but there would never be any hiding it. And now as she approached these two strangers she put one hand up, half covering a cheek. Close to, she had a look of Camargue, all the less attractive traits of the Camargue physiognomy were in her face, too-high forehead, too-long nose, too-fleshy mouth, and added to them that acne-scarred skin. She was sallow and her hair was very dark. But she was one of those plain people whose smiles transform them. She smiled uncertainly at them, and the change of expression made her look kind and sweet-tempered.

Wexford introduced them. He explained that he had seen her earlier that day. Her surprise at being called upon by two English policemen seemed unfeigned. She was astonished but not apparently nervous.

"This is some matter concerning the *musée*—the museum?" she asked in her heavily accented English.

"No, mademoiselle," said Wexford. "I must confess I'd never heard of the Fondation Yeuse till this morning. You've worked there long?"

"Since I leave the university—that is, eighteen years. M. Raoul Yeuse, the Paris art dealer, he is, was, the brother of my father's sister. He has founded the museum, you understand? Excuse me, monsieur, I fear my English is very bad."

"It is we who should apologize for having no French. May we go into the house, Mademoiselle Lerémy? I have something to tell you."

Did she know already? The announcement of the discovery of the body at Dorset's would have scarcely appeared in the French newspapers until three days ago. And when it appeared would it have merited more than a paragraph on an inside page? A murder, in England, of an obscure woman? The dark eyes of Camargue's niece looked merely innocent and inquiring. She led them into a large high-ceilinged room and opened latticed glass doors on to a terrace. From the back of the Maison du Cirque you could see the green rim of the amphitheater and smell the scented hillsides. But the house itself was shabby and neglected and far too big. It had been built for a family and that family's servants in days when perhaps money came easily and went a long way.

Now that they were indoors and seated she had become rather pale. "This is not bad news, I hope, monsieur?" She looked from one to the other of them with a rising anxiety that Wexford thought he understood. He let Burden answer her.

"Serious news," said Burden. "But not personally distressing to you, Miss Lerémy. You hardly knew your cousin Natalie Camargue, did you?"

She shook her head. "She was married. I have not heard her husband's name. When last I am seeing her she is sixteen, I seventeen. It is many years . . ."

"I'm afraid she's dead. To put it bluntly, she was murdered and so was your uncle. We're here to investigate these crimes. It seems the same person killed them both. For gain. For money."

Both hands went up to her cheeks. She recoiled a little.

"But this is terrible!"

Wexford had decided not to tell her of the good fortune this terrible news would bring her. Kenneth Ames could do that. If what he thought was true she would be in need of consolation. He must now broach the subject of this belief of his. Strange that this time he could be so near hoping he was wrong . . .

Her distress seemed real. Her features were contorted into a frown of dismay, her tall curved forehead all wrinkles. "I am so sorry, this is so very bad."

"Mademoiselle Lerèmy . . ."

"When I am a little girl I see him many, many times, monsieur. I stay with them in Sussex. Natalie is, was, nice, I think, always laughing, always very gay, have much sense of *humeur*. The world has become a very bad place, monsieur, when such things as this happen." She paused, bit her lip. "Excuse me, I must not say 'sir' so much, is it not so? This I am learning to understand . . ." She hesitated and hazarded, "Lately? Recently?"

Her words brought him the thrill of knowing he was right—and sickened him too. Must he ask her? Burden was looking at him.

The telephone rang.

"Please excuse me," she said.

The phone was in the room where they were, up beside the windows. She picked up the receiver rather too fast and the effect on her of the voice of her caller was pitiful to see. She flushed deeply and it was somehow apparent that this was a flush of intense fearful pleasure as well as embarrassment.

She said softly, "Ah, Jean . . . We see each other again tonight? Of course it is all right, it is fine, very good." She made an effort, for their benefit or her caller's, to establish formality. "It will be a great pleasure to see you again."

He was here all right then, he was talking to her. But where was he? She had her back to them now. "When you have finished your work, yes. *Entends*, Jean, I will fetch—pick up—pick you up. Ten o'clock?" Suddenly she changed into rapid French. Wexford could not understand a word but he understood *her*. She had been speaking English to a French speaker so that her English hearers would know she had a boy friend, a lover. For all her scarred face, her plainness, her age, her obscure job in the backwater, she had a lover to tell the world about.

She put the phone down after a murmured word or two, a ripple of excited laughter. Wexford was on his feet, signaling with a nod to Burden.

"You do not wish to ask me questions concerning my uncle and my *cousine* Natalie, monsieur?"

"It is no longer necessary, mademoiselle."

The taxi driver had gone to sleep. Wexford woke him with a prod in his chest.

"La Rose Blanche, *s'il vous plaît.*"

The sun was going down. There were long violet shadows and the air was sweet and soft.

"He's a fast worker if ever there was one," said Burden.

"The material he is working on could hardly be more receptive and malleable."

"Pardon? Oh, yes, I see what you mean. Poor girl. It's a terrible handicap having all that pitting on her face, did you notice? D'you think he knew about that? Before he came here, I mean? The real Natalie might have known—you usually get that sort of acne in your teens—but Tessa Lanchester wouldn't have. Unless she picked it up when she was gathering all the rest of her info in Santa Xavierita."

"Mrs. Woodhouse might have known." said Wexford. "At any rate, he knew she was unmarried and an heiress and no doubt that she worked in the museum here. It was easy enough for him to scrape up an acquaintance."

"Bit more than an acquaintance," said Burden grimly.

"Let's hope it hasn't progressed far yet. Certainly his intention is to marry her."

"Presumably his intention was to marry that other woman, but at the last she wouldn't have him and for that he killed her." Burden seemed gratified to get from Wexford a nod of approval. "Once he'd done that he'd realized who the next heir was and come here as fast as he could. But there's something here doesn't make sense. In putting her body in that chest he seems to have meant to keep it concealed for months, possibly even years, but the paradox there is that until the body was found death wouldn't be presumed and Thérèse Lerèmy wouldn't get anything."

Wexford looked slyly at him. "Suppose he intended by some means or other to prove, as only he could, that it was Natalie Arno and not Tessa Lanchester who drowned at Santa Xavierita in 1976? If that were proved Thérèse would become the heir at once and in fact *would have been* the rightful possessor of Sterries and Camargue's money for the past six months."

"You really think that was it?"

"No, I don't. It would have been too bold and too risky and fraught with problems. I think this was what was in his mind. He didn't want the body found at once because if he then started courting Thérèse even someone as desperate as she might suspect he was after her money. But he wanted it found at some time in the not too distant future or his conquest of Thérèse would bring him no profit at all. What better than that the presence of a corpse in that warehouse should make itself apparent after, say, six months? And if it didn't he could always send the police an anonymous letter."

"That's true," said Burden. "And there was very little to connect him with it, after all. If you hadn't been to California we shouldn't have known of his existence."

Wexford laughed shortly. "Yes, there was some profit in it." They walked into the hotel. Outside Burden's room where they would have separated prior to dressing, or at least sprucing up, for dinner, Burden said, "Come in here a minute. I want to ask you something." Wexford sat on the bed. From the window you could see, not the square and the fountain but a mazy mosaic of little roofs against the backdrop of the city walls. "I'd like to know what we're going to charge those others with. I mean, Williams and Zoffany and Mary Woodhouse. Conspiracy, I suppose —but not conspiracy to murder?"

Wexford pondered. He smiled a little ruefully. "We're not going to charge them with anything."

"You mean their evidence will be more valuable as prosecution witnesses?"

"Not really. I shouldn't think any of them would be a scrap of use as witnesses of any kind. They didn't witness anything and they haven't done anything. They all seem to me to be perfectly blameless, apart from a spot—and I'd guess a very small spot—of adultery on the part of Zoffany." Wexford paused. "That reconstruction of the case you gave me while we were at the amphitheater, didn't it strike you there was something unreal about it?"

"Sort of illogical, d'you mean? Maybe, bits of it. Surely that's because they were so devious that there are aspects which aren't clear and never will be?"

Wexford shook his head. "Unreal. One can't equate it with what one knows of human nature. Take, for instance, their foresight and their patience. They kill Natalie in the summer of 1976 and Tessa impersonates her. Fair enough. Why not go straight to England, make sure Natalie is the beneficiary under Camargue's will and then kill Camargue?"

"I know there's a stumbling block. I said so."

"It's more than a stumbling block, Mike, it's a bloody great barrier across the path. Think what you—and I—believed they did. Went back to Los Angeles, ran the risk of being suspected by the neighbors, exposed by Ilbert—returned to and settled in what of all cities in the world was the most dangerous to them. And for what?"

"Surely she stayed there to sell the house?"

"Yet she never succeeded in selling it, did she? No, a delay of three-and-a-half years between the killing of Natalie and the killing of Camargue was too much for me to swallow. I can come up with just one feeble reason for it—that they were waiting for Camargue to die a natural death. But, as I say, that's a feeble reason. He might easily have lived another ten years." Wexford looked at his watch. "I'll leave you to your shaving and showering or whatever. A wash and brush-up will do me. Laquin won't be here before seven."

They met again in the bar where they each had a Stella Artois. Wexford said:

"Your suggestion is that Tessa came to England finally because, through Zoffany's sister-in-law, she heard that Camargue intended to marry again. Doesn't it seem a bit thin that Jane Zoffany's sister should come to know this merely because she lives in a village near the Kathleen Camargue School?"

"Not if she was set by the others to watch Camargue."

Wexford shrugged. "The others, yes. There would be five of them, our protagonist and her boy friend, the Zoffanys and Jane Zoffany's sister. Five conspirators working for the acquisition of Camargue's money. Right?"

"Yes, for a start," said Burden. "There were finally more like eight or nine."

"Mary Woodhouse to give Tessa some advanced coaching, Mavis Rolland to identify her as an old school chum, and Williams the dentist." Wexford gave a little shake of the head. "I've said I was amazed at their foresight and their patience, Mike, but that was nothing to the trouble they took. That staggered me. All these subsidiary conspirators were persuaded to lie, to cheat or to sell their professional integrity. Tessa studied old samples of Natalie's handwriting, had casts made of her jaw, took lessons to perfect her college French and Spanish—though she neglected to polish up her Italian—while one of the others made a survey of the lie of the land round Sterries and of Camargue's habits. Prior to this Zoffany's sister-in-law was sending a secret agent's regular dispatches out to Los Angeles. Oh, and let's not forget—Jane Zoffany was suborning her neighbors into providing a fake alibi. And all this machinery was set in motion and relentlessly kept in motion for the sake of acquiring a not very large house in an acre of ground and an *unknown sum of money* that, when the time came, would have to be split between eight people.

"I've kept thinking of that and I couldn't believe in it. I couldn't understand why those two had chosen Camargue as their prey. Why not pick on some tycoon? Why not some American oil millionaire? Why an old musician who wasn't and never had been in the tycoon class?"

Burden supplied a hesitant answer. "Because his daughter fell into their hands, one supposes. Anyway, there's no alternative. We know there was a conspiracy, we know there was an elaborate plan, and one surely simply comments that it's impossible fully to understand people's motivations."

"But isn't there an alternative? You said I was obsessed, Mike. I think more than anything I became obsessed by the complexity of this case, by the deviousness of the protagonist, by the subtlety of the web she had woven. It was only when I saw how wrong I'd been in these respects that things began to clear for me."

"I don't follow you."

Wexford drank his beer. He said rather slowly, "It was only then that I began to see that this case wasn't complicated, there was no deviousness, there was no plotting, no planning ahead, no conspiracy whatsoever, and that even the two murders happened so spontaneously as really to be unpremeditated." He rose suddenly, pushing back his chair. Commissaire Mario Laquin of the Compagnies Républicaines de Securité of Grasse had come in and was scanning the room. Wexford raised a hand. He said absently to Burden as the commissaire came towards their table, "The complexity was in our own minds, Mike. The case itself was simple and straightforward, and almost everything that took place was the result of accident or of chance."

.   .   .

It was a piece of luck for Wexford that Laquin had been transferred to Grasse from Marseilles some six months before, for they had once or twice worked on cases together and since then the two policemen and their wives had met when M. and Mme. Laquin were in London on holiday. It nevertheless came as something of a shock to be clasped in the commissaire's arms and kissed on both cheeks. Burden stood by, trying to give his dry smile but succeeding only in looking astonished.

Laquin spoke English that was almost flawless. "You pick some charming places to come for your investigations, my dear Reg. A little bird tells me you have already had two weeks in California. I should be so lucky. Last year when I was in pursuit of Honorat L'Eponge, where does he lead me to but Dusseldorf, I ask you!"

"Have a drink," said Wexford. "It's good to see you. I haven't a clue where this chap of ours is. Nor do I know what name he's going under while here."

"Or even what he looks like," said Burden for good measure. He seemed cheered by the presence of Laquin whom he had perhaps expected to speak with a Peter Sellers accent.

"I know what he looks like," said Wexford. "I've seen him."

Burden glanced at him in surprise. Wexford took no notice of him and ordered their drinks.

"You'll dine with us, of course?" he said to Laquin.

"It will be a pleasure. The food here is excellent."

Wexford grinned wryly. "Yes, it doesn't look as though we'll be here to enjoy it tomorrow. I reckon we're going to have to take him at the Maison du Cirque, in that wretched girl's house."

"Reg, she has known him no time at all, a mere week at most."

"Even so quickly can one catch the plague . . . You're right, of course."

"A blessing for her we're going to rid her of him, if you ask me," said Burden. "A couple of years and he'd have put her out of the way as well."

"She implied he was working here . . ."

"Since Britain came in the European Economic Community, Reg, there is no longer need for your countrymen to have work permits or to register. Therefore to trace his whereabouts would be a long and laborious business. And since we know that later on tonight he will be at the Maison du Cirque . . ."

"Sure, yes, I know. I'm being sentimental, Mario, I'm a fool." Wexford gave a grim little laugh. "But not such a fool as to warn her and have him hop off on the next plane into Switzerland."

After *bouillabaisse* and a fine *cassoulet* with brie to follow and a small Armagnac each, it was still only nine. Ten-thirty was the time fixed on by Wexford and Laquin for their visit to the house by the amphitheater. Laquin suggested they go to a place he knew on the other side of the Place aux Eaux Vives where there was sometimes flamenco dancing.

In the evening there was some modest floodlighting in the square. Apparently these were truly living waters and the fountain was fed by a natural spring. While they dined tiers of seating had been put for the music festival of Saint-Jean-de-l'Éclaircie, due to begin on the following day. A little warm breeze rustled through the plane and chestnut leaves above their heads.

The flamenco place was called La Mancha. As they passed down the stairs and into a kind of open, deeply sunken courtyard or cistern, a waiter told Laquin there would be no dancing tonight. The walls were made of yellow stone over which hung a deep purple bougainvillea. Instead of the dancers a thin girl in black came out and sang in the manner of Piaf. Laquin and Burden were drinking wine but Wexford took nothing. He felt bored and restless. Nine-thirty. They went up the stairs again and down an alley into the cobbled open space in front of the cathedral.

The moon had come up, a big golden moon flattened like a tangerine. Laquin had sat down at a table in a pavement café and was ordering coffee for all three men. From here you could see the city walls, part Roman, part medieval, their rough stones silvered by the light from that yellow moon.

Some teenagers went by. They were on their way, Laquin said, to the discotheque in the Place de la Croix. Wexford wondered if Camargue had ever, years ago, sat on this spot where they were. And that dead woman, when she was a child . . . ? It was getting on for ten. Somewhere in Saint-Jean she would be meeting him now in the little green Citroën. The yellow hatchback Opel was presumably left in the long-term car park at Heathrow. He felt a tautening of tension and at the same time relief when Laquin got to his feet and said in his colloquial way that they should be making tracks.

Up through the narrow winding defile once more, flattening themselves tolerantly against stone walls to let more boys and girls pass them. Wexford heard the music long before they emerged into the Place aux Eaux Vives. A Mozart serenade. The serenade from *Don Giovanni*, he thought it was, that should properly be played on a mandolin.

Round the last turn in the alley and out into the wide open square. A group of young girls, also no doubt on their way to the discotheque, were clustered around the highest tier of the festival seating. They clustered around a man who sat on the top, playing a guitar, and they did so in the yearning, worshipping fashion of muses or nymphs on the plinth of some statue of a celebrated musician. The man sat aloft, his tune changed now to a Latin American rhythm, not looking at the girls, looking across the square, his gaze roving as if he expected at any moment the person he waited for to come.

"That's him," said Wexford.

Laquin said, "Are you sure?"

"Absolutely. I've only seen him once before but I'd know him anywhere."

"I know him too," said Burden incredulously. "I've seen him before. I can't for the life of me think where, but I've seen him."

"Let's get it over."

The little green 2CV was turning into the *place* and the guitarist had seen it. He drew his hand across the strings with a flourish and jumped down from his perch, nearly knocking one of the girls over. He didn't look back at her, he made no apology, he was waving to the car.

And then he saw the three policemen, recognizing them immediately for what they were. His arm fell to his side. He was a tall thin man in his late thirties, very dark with black curly hair. Wexford steadfastly refused to look over his shoulder to see her running from the car. He said:

"John Fassbender, it is my duty to warn you that anything you say will be taken down and may be used in evidence . . ."

22

They were in the Pearl of Africa, having what Wexford called a celebration lunch. No one could possibly feel much in the way of pity for Fassbender, so why not celebrate his arrest? Burden said it ought to be called an elucidation lunch because there were still a lot of things he didn't understand and wanted explained. Outside it was pouring with rain again. Wexford asked Mr. Haq for a bottle of wine, *good* moselle or a riesling, none of your living waters from Lake Victoria. They had got into sybaritic habits during their day in France. Mr. Haq bustled off to what he called his cellar through the fronds of polyethylene Spanish moss.

"Did you mean what you said about there having been no conspiracy?"

"Of course I did," Wexford said, "and if we'd had a moment after that I'd have told you something else, something I realized before we ever went to France. The woman we knew as Natalie Arno, the woman Fassbender murdered, was never Tessa Lanchester. Tessa Lanchester was drowned in Santa Xavierita in 1976 and we've no reason to believe either Natalie or Fassbender even met her. The woman who came to London in November of last year came solely because Fassbender was in London. She was in love with Fassbender and since he had twice been deported from the United States he could hardly return there."

"How could he have been deported twice?" asked Burden.

"I wondered that until the possibility of dual nationality occurred to me and then everything about Fassbender became simple. I'd been asking myself if she had two boyfriends, an Englishman and a Swiss. There was a good deal of confusion in people's minds over him. He was Swiss. He was English. He spoke French. He spoke French with a Swiss accent. He was deported to London. He was deported to Geneva. Well, I'll come back to him in a minute. Suffice it to say that it was after he had been deported a second time that she followed him to London."

He stopped. Mr. Haq, beaming, teeth flashing and spilling, was bringing the wine, a quite respectable-looking white medoc. He poured Wexford a trial half-glassful. Wexford sipped it, looking serious. He had sometimes said, though, that he would rather damage his liver than upset Mr. Haq by sending back a bottle. Anyway, the only fault with this wine was that it was at a temperature of around twenty-five degrees Celsius.

"Excellent," he said to Mr. Haq's gratification, and just stopped himself from adding, "Nice and warm." He continued to Burden as Mr. Haq trotted off, "She had a brief affair with Zoffany during Fassbender's first absence. I imagine this was due to nothing more than loneliness and that she put it out of her head once Zoffany had departed. But he kept up a correspondence with her and when she needed a home in London he offered her a flat. Didn't I tell you it was simple and straightforward?

"Once there, she saw that Zoffany was in love with her and hoped to take up their relationship (to use Jane Zoffany's word) where it had ended a year and a half before. She wasn't having that, she didn't care for Zoffany at all in that way. But it made things awkward. If she had Fassbender to live with her there, would Zoffany be made so jealous and angry as to throw her out? She couldn't live with Fassbender, he was living in one room. The wisest thing obviously was to keep Fassbender discreetly in the background until such time as he got a job and made some money and they could afford to snap their fingers at Zoffany and live together. We know that Fassbender was in need of work and that she tried to get him a job through Blaise Cory. The point I'm making is that Zoffany never knew of Fassbender's existence until he overheard Natalie talking on the phone to him *last month*.

"I suspect, though I don't know for certain, that there was no urgency on her part to approach Camargue. Probably she gave very little thought to Camargue. It was the announcement of his engagement that brought her to get in touch with him—perhaps reminded her of his existence. But there was no complex planning about that approach, no care taken with the handwriting or the style of the letter, no vetting of it by, say, Mrs. Woodhouse . . ."

Young Haq came with their starter of prawns Pakwach. This was a shocking pink confection into which Burden manfully plunged his spoon before saying, "There must have been. It may be that the identity of the woman we found in that chest will never be known, but we know very well she was an impostor and a fraudulent claimant."

"Her identity is known," said Wexford. "She was Natalie Arno, Natalie Camargue, Camargue's only child."

Pouring more wine for them, Mr. Haq burst into a flowery laudation of various offerings among the entrées. There was caneton Kioga, wild duck breasts marinated in a succulent sauce of wine, cream and basil, or T-bone Toro, tender steaks *flambés*. Burden's expression was incredulous, faintly dismayed. Fortunately, his snapped "Bring us some of that damned duck," was lost on Mr. Haq, who responded only to Wexford's gentler request for two portions of caneton.

"I don't understand you," Burden said coldly when Mr. Haq had gone. "Are you saying that the woman Camargue refused to recognize, the woman who deliberately cut her hand to avoid having to play the violin, whose antecedents you went rooting out all over America—that woman was Camargue's daughter all the time? We were wrong. Ames was right, Williams and Mavis Rolland and Mary Woodhouse and Philip Cory were right, but we were wrong. Camargue was wrong. Camargue was a senile half-blind old man who happened to make a mistake. Is that it?"

"I didn't say that," said Wexford. "I only said that Natalie Arno was Natalie Arno. Camargue made no mistake, though it would be true to say he misunderstood." He sighed. "We were such fools, Mike—you, me, Ames, Dinah Sternhold. Not one of us saw the simple truth, that though the woman who visited Camargue was not his daughter, she was not his daughter, if I may so put it, for just one day."

"You see," he went on, "an illusion was created, as if by a clever trick. Only it was a trick we played upon ourselves. We were the conjurers and we held the mirrors. Dinah Sternhold told me Camargue said the woman who went to see him wasn't his daughter. I jumped to the conclusion—you did, Dinah did, we all did—that therefore the woman *we* knew as Natalie Arno wasn't his daughter. It never occurred to us he could be right and yet she might still be his daughter. It never occurred to us that the woman he saw might not be the woman who claimed to be his heir and lived in his house and inherited his money."

"It wasn't Natalie who went there that day but it was Natalie before and always Natalie after that?" Burden made the face people do when they realize they have been conned by a stratagem unworthy of their caliber. "Is that what you're saying?"

"Of course it is." Wexford grinned and gave a rueful shake of the head. "I may as well say here and now that Natalie wasn't the arch-villainess I took her for. She was cruel and devious and spiteful only in my imagination. Mind you, I'm not saying she was an angel of light. She may not have killed her father or plotted his death, but she connived at it afterwards and she had no scruples about taking an inheritance thus gained. Nor did she have any scruples about appropriating other women's husbands either on a temporary or a permanent basis. She was no paragon of virtue but she was no Messalina either. Why did I ever think she was? Largely, I'm ashamed to say, because Dinah Sternhold told me so.

"Now Dinah Sternhold is a very nice girl. If she blackened Natalie's character to me before I'd even met her, I'm sure it was unconscious. The thing with Dinah, you see, is that odd though it undoubtedly seems, she was genuinely in love with that old man. He was old enough to be her grandfather but she was as much in love with him as if he'd been fifty years younger. Have you ever noticed that it's only those who suffer most painfully from jealousy that say, 'I haven't a jealous nature'? Dinah said that to me. She was deeply jealous of Natalie and perhaps with justification. For in marrying her, wasn't Camargue looking to replace his lost daughter? How then must she have felt when that lost daughter turned up? Dinah was jealous and in her jealousy, all unconsciously, without malice, she painted Natalie as a scheming adventuress and so angled the tale of the visit to Camargue to make her appear at once as a fraudulent claimant."

"I'd like to hear your version of that visit."

Wexford nodded. The duck had arrived, modestly veiled in a thick brown sauce. Wexford took a sip of his wine instead of a long draught, having decided with some soul-searching that it would hardly do to send for a second bottle. He sampled the duck, which wasn't too bad, and said after a few moments:

"The first appointment Natalie made with her father she couldn't keep. In the meantime something very disquieting had happened to her. She discovered a growth in one of her breasts."

"How d'you know that?"

"A minute scar where the biopsy was done showed at the post-mortem," said Wexford. "Natalie went to her doctor and was sent to Guy's Hospital, the appointment being on the day she had arranged to go down to Sterries. She didn't want to talk to her father on the phone—I think we can call that a perfectly natural shrinking in the circumstances—so she got Jane Zoffany to do it. Shall I say here that Natalie was a congenital slave-owner and Jane Zoffany a born slave?

"Well, Jane made the call and a new date for the 19th. Natalie went to the hospital where they were unable to tell her whether the growth was malignant or not. She must come into their Hedley Atkins Unit in New Cross for a biopsy under anaesthetic.

"Now we're all of us afraid of cancer but Natalie maybe had more reason than most of us. She had seen her young husband die of leukemia, a form of cancer, her friend Tina too, but most traumatic for her, her mother had died of it and died, it had been implied, through her daughter's actions. Moreover, at the time she had only been a few years older than Natalie then was. Small wonder if she was terrified.

"Then—due no doubt to some aberration on the part of the Post Office—the letter telling her she was to go into the Hedley Atkins Unit on 17 January didn't arrive till the morning before. This meant she couldn't go to Kingsmarkham on the 19th. I imagine she was past caring. All that mattered to her now was that she shouldn't have cancer, shouldn't have her beautiful figure spoilt, shouldn't live in dread of a recurrence or an early death. Jane Zoffany could deal with her father for her, phone or write or send a telegram."

From staring down at his empty plate, Burden now lifted his eyes and sat bolt upright. "It was Jane Zoffany who came down here that day?"

Wexford nodded. "Who else?"

"She too is thin and dark and about the right age . . . But why? Why pose as Natalie? For whatever possible purpose?"

"It wasn't deliberate," Wexford said a shade testily. "Haven't I said scarcely anything in this case was deliberate, planned or premeditated? It was just typical silly muddled Jane Zoffany behavior. And what months it took me to guess it! I suppose I had an inkling of the truth, that wet day in the garden at Sterries, when Dinah said how strange it was Natalie could get the solicitors and Camargue's old friends to believe in her, yet Camargue who wanted to believe, who was longing to believe, saw her *on that one occasion* and didn't believe in her for more than half an hour. And when Jane Zoffany said how the police had taken her for her own sister and then stuck her hand up over her mouth—I knew then, I didn't need to be told any more."

"But she did tell you more?"

"Sure. When I talked to her last night. She filled in the gaps."

"Why did she go down to Sterries at all?" asked Burden.

"Two reasons. She wanted to see the old man for herself—she'd been an admirer of his—and she didn't want his feelings hurt. She knew that if she phoned and told him Natalie had yet again to keep a hospital appointment he'd think she was making excuses not to see him and he'd be bitterly hurt. For nineteen years his daughter had stayed away from him and now that she had come back and they were on the brink of a reunion, he was to be fobbed off with a phone call—and a second phone call at that. So she decided to go down and see him herself. But not, of course, with any idea of posing as Natalie, nothing of that sort entered her head. It's just that she's a rather silly, muddled creature who isn't always quite mentally stable."

"You mean," said Burden, "that she came down here simply because it seemed kinder and more polite to call in person? She came to explain why Natalie couldn't come and—well, sort of assure him of Natalie's affection for him? Something like that?"

"Something very much like that. And also to get a look at the man who had been acclaimed the world's greatest flautist." Wexford caught Mr. Haq's eye for their coffee. "Now Camargue," he said, "was the first person to cast a doubt on Natalie's identity, it was Camargue who started all this, yet it was Camargue himself who took Jane Zoffany for his daughter because it was *his daughter that he expected to see.*

"He had waited for nineteen years—eventually without much hope. Hope had reawakened in the past five weeks and he was keyed up to a pitch of very high tension. He opened the door to her and put his arms round her and kissed her before she could speak. Did she try to tell him then that he had made a mistake? He was deaf. He was carried away with emotion. She has told me she was so confused and aghast that she played along with him while trying to decide what to do. She says she was embarrassed, she was afraid to disillusion him.

"She humored him by speaking of the Cazzini gold flute—which Natalie had possibly mentioned to her but which was in any case clearly labeled—and having no knowledge of Italian, she mispronounced the name. We know what happened then. Camargue accused her of imposture. But it was no dream of Camargue's, no senile fantasy, that his visitor confessed. Jane Zoffany freely admitted what she had been longing to admit for the past half-hour—but it did her no good. Camargue was convinced by then this was a deception plotted to secure Natalie's inheritance and he turned her out of the house.

"And that, Mike, was all this so-called imposture ever amounted to, half an hour's misunderstanding between a well-meaning neurotic and a 'foolish, fond old man.' "

While Burden experimented yet again with ice cream eau-de-Nil, Wexford contented himself with coffee.

"Natalie," he said, "came out of hospital on January 20th and she was so elated that the biopsy had shown the growth to be benign that instead of being angry she was simply amused by Jane's activities. As I've said, she had a very lively sense of fun. I think it must have tickled her to imagine the pair of them at cross-purposes, the wretched Jane Zoffany confessing and the irate Camargue throwing her out. What did it matter, anyway? She hadn't got cancer, she was fit and well and on top of the world and she could easily put that nonsense with her father right again. Let her only see if she could get a job out of Blaise Cory for her Johnny and then she'd see her father and patch things up.

"Before she could get around to that Camargue had written to her, informing her she should inherit nothing under the new will he intended to make."

"Which led her," said Burden, "to plan on killing him first."

"No, no, I've told you. There was no planning. Even after that letter I'm sure Natalie was confident she could make things smooth with her father. Perhaps she even thought, as Dinah says *she* did, that this could best be effected after the marriage. Natalie was not too concerned. She was amused. The mistake she made was in telling Fassbender. Probably for the first time Fassbender realized just how potentially wealthy a woman his girl friend actually was."

"Why do you say for the first time?"

"If he'd known it before," Wexford retorted, "why hadn't he married her while they were both in California? That would have been a way of ensuring he didn't get deported. She was an American citizen. In those days, no doubt, she would have been willing enough to marry him, so if they didn't it must have been because he couldn't see there was anything in it for him. But now he did. Now he could see there was a very pleasant little sinecure here for the rest of their lives if only she wasn't so carefree and idle as to cast it all away.

"That Sunday Natalie went to a party with Jane Zoffany. She went because she liked parties, she liked enjoying herself, her whole life had been blithely dedicated to enjoying herself. There was no question of establishing an alibi. Nor, I'm sure, did she know Fassbender had taken himself off down to Kingsmarkham to spy out the land and have a look at the house and the affluence Natalie was apparently so indifferent to. It was on the impulse of the moment, in a sudden frenzy of— literally—taking things at the flood, that he seized Camargue and forced him into the water under the ice."

For a moment they were both silent. Then Burden said:

"He told her what he'd done?"

A curious look came into Wexford's face. "I suppose so. At any rate, she knew. By the time of the inquest she knew. How much she cared I don't know. She hadn't seen her father for nineteen years, but still he was her father. She didn't care enough to shop Fassbender, that's for sure. Indeed, you might say she cared so little that she was prepared to take considerable risks to *defend* Fassbender. No doubt, she liked what she got out of it. Life had been a bit precarious in the past four years, hadn't it? Once rid of Ilbert, it was a hand-to-mouth affair, and one imagines that while she was in De Beauvoir Place she was living solely on the rent from her house in Los Angeles. But now she had Sterries and the money and everything was fine. I'd like to think it was his murdering her father that began the process of going off Fassbender for Natalie, but we've no evidence of that."

"What I don't understand is, since she *was* Natalie Arno, why did she play around half pretending she wasn't? It was a hell of a risk she was taking. She might have lost everything."

"There wasn't any risk," said Wexford. "There wasn't the slightest risk. If she wasn't Natalie there might be many ways of apparently proving she was. But since she was Natalie it could never possibly be proved that she was not."

"But why? Why do it?"

Burden had never had much sense of humor. And lately, perhaps since his marriage, Wexford thought, this limited faculty had become quiescent. "For fun, Mike," he said, "for fun. Don't you think she got enormous fun out of it? After all, by that time she believed there was no question of our associating Camargue's death with foul play. What harm could she do herself or Fassbender by just ever so slightly hinting she might be the impostor Dinah Sternhold said she was? And it must have been fun, I can see that. It must have been hilarious dumbfounding us by answering Cory's questions and then really giving me hope by nicking her fingers with a bit of glass.

"I said we were fools. I reckon I was an arch-fool. Did I really believe an impostor would have had her instructor with her on the very morning she knew we were coming? Did I really believe in such an enormous coincidence as Mary Woodhouse leaving that flat by chance the moment we entered it? What fun Natalie must have got out of asking her old nanny or whatever she was to come round for a cup of coffee and then shooing her out when our car stopped outside. Oh, yes, it was all great fun, and as soon as it had gone far enough she had only to call in her dentist and prove beyond the shadow of a doubt who she was. For Williams is genuinely her dentist, a blameless person of integrity who happens to keep all his records and happens to have been in practice a long time." Wexford caught Mr. Haq's eye. "D'you want any more coffee?"

"Don't think so," said Burden.

"I may as well get the bill then." Mr. Haq glided over through the jungle. "Once," Wexford said, "she had proved herself Natalie Arno to the satisfaction of Symonds, O'Brien and Ames, everything was plain sailing. The first thing to do was sell Sterries, because it wouldn't do to have Fassbender show his face much around Kingsmarkham. But I think she was already beginning to go off Fassbender. Perhaps she saw that though he hadn't been prepared to marry her in America, even for the reward of legal residence there, he was anxious to do so now she was rich. Perhaps, after all, she simply decided there was no point in marrying. She hadn't done much of it, had she? Once only and she'd been a widow for nine years. And what would be the point of marrying when she now had plenty of money of her own and was happily independent? Still, this sort of speculation is useless. Suffice it to say that she had intended to marry Fassbender but she changed her mind. They quarreled about it on the very eve of their going away on holiday together, and in his rage at being balked of possession of the money he had killed for, had been to prison for, he attacked her and cut her throat.

"The body he put into that chest, which he locked, knowing it would be removed by Dorset's on the following day. Then off he went in the yellow Opel to Heathrow to use one of the two air tickets they had bought for their holiday in the South of France."

Wexford paid the bill. It was modest, as always. By rights he ought, months ago, to have run Mr. Haq in for offences under the Trade Descriptions Act. He would never do that now. They walked out into the High Street where the sun had unaccountably begun to shine. The pavements were drying up, the heavy gray clouds rushing at a great rate away to the horizon. At too great a rate away to the horizon. At too great a rate, though, for more than temporary disappearance.

The Kingsbrook tumbled under the old stone bridge like a river in winter spate. Burden leaned over the parapet. "You knew Fassbender when we came upon him in that place in France," he said. "I've been meaning to ask you how you did. You hadn't seen him in America, had you?"

"Of course I hadn't. He wasn't in America while I was. He'd been back here for over a year by then."

"Then where had you seen him?"

"Here. Back at the very start of this case. Back in January just after Camargue died. He was at Sterries too, Mike. Can't you remember?"

"You saw him too," Wexford went on. "You said when we spotted him, 'I've seen him somewhere before.' "

Burden made a gesture of dismissal. "Yes, I know I did. But I was mistaken. I couldn't have seen him, I was mixing him up with someone else. One wouldn't forget that name."

Instead of replying, Wexford said, "Fassbender's father was a Swiss who lived here without ever becoming naturalized. I don't know what his mother was or is, it hardly matters. John Fassbender was born here and has dual nationality, Swiss and British, not at all an uncommon thing. Ilbert had him deported to this country in 1976 but of course there was nothing to stop him going back into America again on his Swiss passport. When Romero shopped him three years later he was sent back to Switzerland but he soon returned here. Presumably, he liked it better here. Maybe he just preferred the inside of our prisons—he'd seen enough of them."

"He's got a record, has he?"

Wexford laughed. "Don't happen to have your German dictionary on you, do you?"

"Of course I don't carry dictionaries about with me."

"Pity. I don't know why we've walked all the way up here. We'd better take shelter, it's going to rain again heavens hard."

He hustled Burden down the steps into the Kingsbrook Precinct. A large drop of rain splashed against the brass plate of Symonds, O'Brien and Ames, a score more against the travel agency's windows, blurring the poster that still invited customers to sunny California.

"In here," said Wexford and pushed open the door of the bookshop. The dictionaries section was down at the back on the left-hand side. Wexford took down a tome in a green-and-yellow jacket. "I want you to look up a word. It won't be much use to you in your studies, I'm afraid, but if you want to know where you saw Fassbender before you'll have to find out what his name means."

Burden put the book down on the counter and started on the Fs. He looked up. "Spelled Fassbinder, a barrel maker, a maker of casks . . ."

"Well?"

"A cooper . . ." He hesitated, then said slowly, "John Cooper, thirty-six, Selden Road, Finsbury Park. He broke into Sterries the night after the inquest on Camargue."

Wexford took the dictionary away from him and replaced it on the shelf. "His father called himself Cooper during the war—Fassbender wasn't generally acceptable then, on the lines of Beethoven and German shepherds, one supposes. Fassbender held his British passport in the name of Cooper and his Swiss as Fassbender.

"That burglary was the only bit of planning he and Natalie did and that was done on the spur of the moment. It was a desperate measure taken in what they saw as a desperate situation. What alerted Natalie, of course, was Mrs. Murray-Burgess telling Muriel Hicks she'd seen a suspicious-looking character in the Sterries grounds and that without a doubt she'd know him again. The only thing was, she couldn't quite remember which night. Natalie and Fassbender knew which night, of course. They knew it was the night Camargue drowned. So they faked up a burglary. Natalie slept in her late father's room, not to keep away from the amorous marauding Zoffany, still less to wound the feelings of Muriel Hicks, but to be in a room where she could credibly have heard breaking glass and seen the van's number.

"She had to have seen that to facilitate our rapidly getting our hands on Fassbender. Then Mrs. Murray-Burgess could do her worst—it was a burglar she had seen and not a killer. In the event, he served four months. He came out in June, with two months' remission for good conduct."

"I only saw him once," said Burden. "I saw him down the station here when we charged him."

"With nicking six silver spoons," said Wexford. "Come on, the rain's stopped."

They went outside. Once more a bright sun had appeared, turning the puddles into blinding mirrors.

Burden said doubtfully, "It was a bit of a long shot, wasn't it? I mean, weren't they—well, over-reacting? They were supposing in the first place that Mrs. Murray-Burgess would come to us and secondly that if she did we'd connect the presence of a man in the Sterries garden on an unspecified night with an old man's accidental death."

"There was more to it than that," said Wexford with a grin. "She'd seen me, you see."

"Seen you? What d'you mean?"

"At the inquest. You said at the time people would think things and you were right. Someone must have told Natalie who I was, and that was enough. I only went there because our heating had broken down, I was looking for somewhere to get warm, but she didn't know that. She thought I was there because at that early stage we suspected foul play."

Burden started to laugh.

"Come," said Wexford, "let us shut up the box and the puppets, for our play is played out."

And in the uncertain sunshine they walked up the street to the police station.

Ed McBain

SADIE WHEN SHE DIED

Although the roster at the 87th Precinct has the standard number of detectives, purists would not classify the 87th Precinct novels Evan Hunter (1926–) writes under the Ed McBain pseudonym as traditional detective fiction. Hunter agrees. He once told an interviewer, "I write police procedure and not detective novels because they are more true to life. Private detectives don't solve crimes. They spend their time spying on husbands and wives. And no single policeman solves a case alone. I don't like intricate clockwork capers, because most criminals just don't work that way. Most criminals aren't masterminds. They are usually caught by a lot of supposedly dumb cops working out of a filthy station house."

In the McBain novels and stories, the station house is the hero, rather than any particular men who work there. The staff has remained fairly steady since the first of the series was publised in 1956: Steve Carella and Meyer Meyer (both of whom tend to get starring roles), Andy Parker (the bad apple), Desk Sergeant Dave Murchison, Bert Kling (the kid), and others. And although the series has been running for more than a quarter of a century, no one has aged noticeably. Early on, Hunter froze their ages. "If I hadn't done that," he says, "I'd now have a precinct of doddering old men."

Hunter has said that he begins all the Ed McBain novels by making up a pithy title (Give the Boys a Great Big Hand, Long Time No See, etc.) and then writes a plot to go with it. "Sadie When She Died" must have been a title he especially liked; after the short story was published, he used it for a full-length novel.

Sadie When She Died

"**I**'M VERY GLAD she's dead," the man said.

He wore a homburg, muffler, overcoat and gloves. He stood near the night table, a tall man with a narrow face, and a well-groomed gray mustache that matched the graying hair at his temples. His eyes were clear and blue and distinctly free of pain or grief.

Detective Steve Carella wasn't sure he had heard the man correctly. "Sir," Carella said, "I'm sure I don't have to tell you—"

"That's right," the man said, "you don't have to tell me. It happens I'm a criminal lawyer and am well aware of my rights. My wife was no good, and I'm delighted someone killed her."

Carella opened his pad. This was not what a bereaved husband was supposed to say when his wife lay disemboweled on the bedroom floor in a pool of her own blood.

"Your name is Gerald Fletcher."

"That's correct."

"Your wife's name, Mr. Fletcher?"

"Sarah. Sarah Fletcher."

"Want to tell me what happened?"

"I got home about fifteen minutes ago. I called to my wife from the front door, and got no answer. I came into the bedroom and found her dead on the floor. I immediately called the police."

"Was the room in this condition when you came in?"

"It was."

"Touch anything?"

"Nothing. I haven't moved from this spot since I placed the call."

"Anybody in here when you came in?"

"Not a soul. Except my wife, of course."

"Is that your suitcase in the entrance hallway?"

"It is. I was on the Coast for three days. An associate of mine needed advice on a brief he was preparing. What's your name?"

"Carella. Detective Steve Carella."

"I'll remember that."

While the police photographer was doing his macabre little jig around the body to make sure the lady looked good in the rushes, or as good as any lady can look in her condition, a laboratory assistant named Marshall Davies was in the kitchen of the apartment, waiting for the medical examiner to pronounce the lady dead, at which time Davies would go into the bedroom and with delicate care remove the knife protruding from the blood and slime of the lady, in an attempt to salvage some good latent prints from the handle of the murder weapon.

Davies was a new technician, but an observant one, and he noticed that the kitchen window was wide open, not exactly usual on a December night when the temperature outside hovered at twelve degrees. Leaning over the sink, he further noticed that the window opened onto a fire escape on the rear of the building. He could not resist speculating that perhaps someone had climbed up the fire escape and then into the kitchen.

Since there was a big muddy footprint in the kitchen sink, another one on the floor near the sink, and several others fading as they traveled across the waxed kitchen floor to the living room, Davies surmised that he was onto something hot. Wasn't it possible that an intruder *had* climbed over the windowsill, into the sink and walked across the room, bearing the switchblade knife that had later been pulled viciously across the lady's abdomen from left to right? If the M.E. ever got through with the damn body, the boys of the 87th would be halfway home, thanks to Marshall Davies. He felt pretty good.

The three points of the triangle were Detective-Lieutenant Byrnes, and Detectives Meyer Meyer and Steve Carella. Fletcher sat in a chair, still wearing homburg, muffler, overcoat and gloves as if he expected to be called outdoors at any moment. The interrogation was being conducted in a windowless cubicle labeled Interrogation Room.

The cops standing in their loose triangle around Gerald Fletcher were amazed but not too terribly amused by his brutal frankness.

"I hated her guts," he said.

"Mr. Fletcher," Lieutenant Byrnes said, "I *still* feel I must warn you that a woman has been murdered—"

"Yes. My dear, wonderful wife," Fletcher said sarcastically.

". . . which is a serious crime. . . ." Byrnes felt tongue-tied in Fletcher's presence. Bullet-headed, hair turning from iron-gray to ice-white, blue-eyed, built like a compact linebacker, Byrnes looked to his colleagues for support. Both Meyer and Carella were watching their shoelaces.

"You have warned me repeatedly," Fletcher said, "I can't imagine why. My wife is dead—someone killed her—but it was not I."

"Well, it's nice to have your assurance of that, Mr. Fletcher, but this alone doesn't necessarily still our doubts," Carella said, hearing the words and wondering where the hell they were coming from. He was, he realized, trying to impress Fletcher. He continued, "How do we know it *wasn't* you who stabbed her?"

"To begin with," Fletcher said, "there were signs of forcible entry in the kitchen and hasty departure in the bedroom, witness the wide-open window in the aforementioned room and the shattered window in the latter. The drawers in the dining-room sideboard were open—"

"You're very observant," Meyer said suddenly. "Did you notice all this in the four minutes it took you to enter the apartment and call the police?

"It is my *job* to be observant," Fletcher said. "But to answer your question, no. I noticed all this *after* I had spoken to Detective Carella here."

Wearily, Byrnes dismissed Fletcher, who then left the room.

"What do you think?" Byrnes said

"I think he did it," Carella said.

"Even with all those signs of a burglary?"

"*Especially* with those signs. He could have come home, found his wife stabbed —but not fatally—and finished her off by yanking the knife across her belly. Fletcher had four minutes, when all he needed was maybe four seconds."

"It's possible," Meyer said.

"Or maybe I just don't like the guy," Carella said.

"Let's see what the lab comes up with," Byrnes said.

The laboratory came up with good fingerprints on the kitchen window sash and on the silver drawer of the dining-room sideboard. There were good prints on some of the pieces of silver scattered on the floor near the smashed bedroom window. Most important, there were good prints on the handle of the switchblade knife. The prints matched; they had all been left by the same person.

Gerald Fletcher graciously allowed the police to take *his* fingerprints, which were then compared with those Marshall Davies had sent over from the police laboratory. The fingerprints on the window sash, the drawer, the silverware and the knife did not match Gerald Fletcher's.

Which didn't mean a damn thing if he had been wearing his gloves when he'd finished her off.

On Monday morning, in the second-floor rear apartment of 721 Silvermine Oval, a chalked outline on the bedroom floor was the only evidence that a woman had lain there in death the night before. Carella sidestepped the outline and looked out the shattered window at the narrow alleyway below. There was a distance of perhaps twelve feet between this building and the one across from it.

Conceivably, the intruder could have leaped across the shaftway, but this would have required premeditation and calculation. The more probable likelihood was that the intruder had fallen to the pavement below.

"That's quite a long drop," Detective Bert Kling said, peering over Carella's shoulder.

"How far do you figure?" Carella asked.

"Thirty feet. At least."

"Got to break a leg taking a fall like that. You think he went through the window head first?"

"How else?"

"He might have broken the glass out first, then gone through," Carella suggested.

"If he was about to go to all that trouble, why didn't he just *open* the damn thing?"

"Well, let's take a look," Carella said.

They examined the latch and the sash. Kling grabbed both handles on the window frame and pulled up on them. "Stuck."

"Probably painted shut," Carella said.

"Maybe he *did* try to open it. Maybe he smashed it only when he realized it was stuck."

"Yeah," Carella said. "And in a big hurry, too. Fletcher was opening the front door, maybe already in the apartment by then."

"The guy probably had a bag or something with him, to put the loot in. He must have taken a wild swing with the bag when he realized the window was stuck, and maybe some of the stuff fell out, which would explain the silverware on the floor. Then he probably climbed through the hole and dropped down feet first. In fact, what he could've done, Steve, was drop the bag down first, and *then* he climbed out and hung from the sill before he jumped, to make it a shorter distance."

"I don't know if he had all that much time, Bert. He must have heard that front door opening, and Fletcher coming in and calling to his wife. Otherwise, he'd have taken his good, sweet time and gone out the kitchen window and down the fire escape, the way he'd come in."

Kling nodded reflectively.

"Let's take a look at that alley," Carella said.

In the alleyway outside, Carella and King studied the concrete pavement, and then looked up at the shattered second-floor window of the Fletcher apartment.

"Where do you suppose he'd have landed?" Kling said.

"Right about where we're standing." Carella looked at the ground. "I don't know, Bert. A guy drops twenty feet to a concrete pavement, doesn't break anything, gets up, dusts himself off, and runs the fifty-yard dash, right?" Carella shook his head. "My guess is he stayed right where he was to catch his breath, giving Fletcher time to look out the window, which would be the natural thing to do, but which Fletcher didn't."

"He was anxious to call the police."

"I still think he did it."

"Steve, be reasonable. If a guy's fingerprints are on the handle of a knife, and the knife is still in the victim—"

"*And* if the victim's husband realizes what a sweet setup he's stumbled into, wife lying on the floor with a knife in her, place broken into and burglarized, why *not* finish the job and hope the burglar will be blamed?

"Sure," Kling said. "Prove it."

"I can't," Carella said. "Not until we catch the burglar."

While Carella and Kling went through the tedious routine of retracing the burglar's footsteps, Marshall Davies called the 87th Precinct and got Detective Meyer.

"I think I've got some fairly interesting information about the suspect," Davies said. "He left latent fingerprints all over the apartment and footprints in the kitchen. A very good one in the sink, when he climbed through the window, and some middling-fair ones tracking across the kitchen floor to the dining room. I got some excellent pictures and some good blowups of the heel."

"Good," Meyer said.

"But more important," Davies went on, "I got a good walking picture from the footprints on the floor. If a man is walking slowly, the distance between his footprints is usually about twenty-seven inches. Forty for running, thirty-five for fast walking. These were thirty-two inches. So we have a man's usual gait, moving quickly, but not in a desperate hurry, with the walking line normal and not broken."

"What does that mean?"

"Well, a walking line should normally run along the inner edge of a man's heelprints. Incidentally, the size and type of shoe and angle of the foot clearly indicate that this *was* a man."

"OK, fine," Meyer said. He did not thus far consider Davies' information valuable nor even terribly important.

"Anyway, none of this is valuable nor even terribly important," Davies said, "until we consider the rest of the data. The bedroom window was smashed, and the Homicide men were speculating that the suspect had jumped through the window into the alley below. I went down to get some meaningful pictures, and got some picture of where he must have landed—on both feet, incidentally—and I got another walking picture and direction line. He moved toward the basement door and into the basement. But the important thing is that our man is injured, and I think badly."

"How do you know?" Meyer asked.

"The walking picture downstairs is entirely different from the one in the kitchen. When he got downstairs he was leaning heavily on the left leg and dragging the right. I would suggest that whoever's handling the case put out a physician's bulletin. If this guy hasn't got a broken leg, I'll eat the pictures I took."

.   .   .

A girl in a green coat was waiting in the apartment lobby when Carella and King came back in, still retracing footsteps, or trying to. The girl said, "Excuse me, are you the detectives?"

"Yes," Carella said.

"The super told me you were in the building," the girl said. "You're investigating the Fletcher murder, aren't you?" She was quite softspoken.

"How can we help you, miss?" Carella asked.

"I saw somebody in the basement last night, with blood on his clothes."

Carella glanced at King and immediately said, "What time was this?"

"About a quarter to eleven," the girl said.

"What were you doing in the basement?"

The girl sounded surprised. "That's where the washing machines are. I'm sorry, my name is Selma Bernstein. I live here in the building."

"Tell us what happened, will you?" Carella said.

"I was sitting by the machine, watching the clothes tumble, which is simply *fascinating*, you know, when the door leading to the back yard opened—the door to the alley. This man came down the stairs, and I don't even think he saw me. He went straight for the stairs at the other end, the ones that go up into the street. I never saw him before last night."

"Can you describe him?" Carella asked.

"Sure. He was about twenty-one or twenty-two, your height and weight, well, maybe a little shorter, five ten or eleven, brown hair."

Kling was already writing. The man was white, wore dark trousers, high-topped sneakers, and a poplin jacket with blood on the right sleeve and on the front. He carried a small red bag, "like one of those bags the airlines give you."

Selma didn't know if he had any scars. "He went by in pretty much of a hurry, considering he was dragging his right leg. I think he was hurt pretty badly."

What they had in mind, of course, was identification from a mug shot, but the I.S. reported that none of the fingerprints in their file matched the ones found in the apartment. So the detectives figured it was going to be a tough one, and they sent out a bulletin to all of the city's doctors just to prove it.

Just to prove that cops can be as wrong as anyone else, it turned out to be a nice easy one after all.

The call came from a physician in Riverhead at 4:37 that afternoon, just as Carella was ready to go home.

"This is Dr. Mendelsohn," he said. "I have your bulletin here, and I want to report treating a man early this morning who fits your description—a Ralph Corwin of 894 Woodside in Riverhead. He had a bad ankle sprain."

"Thank you, Dr. Mendelsohn," Carella said.

Carella pulled the Riverhead directory from the top drawer of his desk and quickly flipped to the C's. He did not expect to find a listing for Ralph Corwin. A man would have to be a rank amateur to burglarize an apartment without wearing gloves, then stab a woman to death, and give his name when seeking treatment for an injury sustained in escaping from the murder apartment.

Ralph Corwin was apparently a rank amateur. His name was in the phone book, and he'd given the doctor his correct address.

Carella and Kling kicked in the door without warning, fanning into the room, guns drawn. The man on the bed was wearing only undershorts. His right ankle was taped.

"Are you Ralph Corwin?" Carella asked.

"Yes," the man said. His face was drawn, the eyes in pain.

"Get dressed, Corwin. We want to ask you some questions."

"There's nothing to ask," he said and turned his head into the pillow. "I killed her."

Ralph Corwin made his confession in the presence of two detectives of the 87th, a police stenographer, an assistant district attorney, and a lawyer appointed by the Legal Aid Society.

Corwin was the burglar. He'd entered 721 Silvermine Oval on Sunday night, December 12, down the steps from the street where the garbage cans were. He went through the basement, up the steps at the other end, into the back yard, and climbed the fire escape, all at about ten o'clock in the evening. Corwin entered the Fletcher apartment because it was the first one he saw without lights. He figured there was nobody home. The kitchen window was open a tiny crack; Corwin squeezed his fingers under the bottom and opened it all the way. He was pretty desperate at the time because he was a junkie in need of cash. He swore that he'd never done anything like this before.

The man from the D.A.'s office was conducting the Q. and A. and asked Corwin if he hadn't been afraid of fingerprints, not wearing gloves. Corwin figured that was done only in the movies, and anyway, he said, he didn't own gloves.

Corwin used a tiny flashlight to guide him as he stepped into the sink and down to the door. He made his way to the dining room, emptied the drawer of silverware into his airline bag. Then he looked for the bedroom, scouting for watches and rings, whatever he could take in the way of jewelry. "I'm not a pro," he said. "I was just hung up real bad and needed some bread to tide me over."

Now came the important part. The D.A.'s assistant asked Corwin what happened in the bedroom.

A. There was a lady in bed. This was only like close to ten-thirty, you don't expect nobody to be asleep so early.

Q. But there was a woman in bed.

A. Yeah. She turned on the light the minute I stepped in the room.

Q. What did you do?

A. I had a knife in my pocket. I pulled it out to scare her. It was almost comical. She looks at me and says, "What are you doing here?

Q. Did you say anything to her?

A. I told her to keep quiet, that I wasn't going to hurt her. But she got out of bed and I saw she was reaching for the phone. That's got to be crazy, right? A guy is standing there in your bedroom with a knife in his hand, so she reaches for the phone.

Q. What did you do?

A. I grabbed her hand before she could get it. I pulled her off the bed, away from the phone, you know? And I told her again that nobody was going to hurt her, that I was getting out of there right away, to just please calm down.

Q. What happened next?

A. She started to scream. I told her to stop. I was beginning to panic. I mean she was really yelling.

Q. Did she stop?

A. No.

Q. What did you do?

A. I stabbed her.

Q. Where did you stab her?

A. I don't know. It was a reflex. She was yelling, I was afraid the whole building would come down. I just . . . I just stuck the knife in her. I was very scared. I stabbed her in the belly. Someplace in the belly.

Q. How many times did you stab her?

A. Once. She . . . She backed away from me. I'll never forget the look on her face. And she . . . fell on the floor.

Q. Would you look at this photograph, please?

A. Oh, no. . . .

Q. Is that the woman you stabbed?

A. Oh, no . . . I didn't think . . . Oh, no!

A moment after he stabbed Sarah Fletcher, Corwin heard the door opening and someone coming in. The man yelled, "Sarah, it's me, I'm home." Corwin ran past Sarah's body on the floor, and tried to open the window, but it was stuck. He smashed it with his airline bag, threw the bag out first to save the swag because, no matter what, he knew he'd need another fix, and he climbed through the broken window, cutting his hand on a piece of glass. He hung from the sill, and finally let go, droppig to the ground. He tried to get up, and fell down again. His ankle was killing him, his hand bleeding. He stayed in the alley nearly fifteen minutes, then finally escaped via the route Selma Bernstein had described to Carella and Kling.

He took the subway to Riverhead and got to Dr. Mendelsohn at about nine in the morning. He read of Sarah Fletcher's murder in the newspaper on the way back from the doctor.

On Tuesday, December 14, which was the first of Carella's two days off that week, he received a call at home from Gerald Fletcher. Fletcher told the puzzled Carella that he'd gotten his number from a friend in the D.A.'s office, complimented Carella and the boys of the 87th on their snappy detective work, and invited Carella to lunch at the Golden Lion at one o'clock. Carella wasn't happy about interrupting his Christmas shopping, but this was an unusual opportunity, and he accepted.

Most policemen in the city for which Carella worked did not eat very often in restaurants like the Golden Lion. Carella had never been inside. A look at the menu posted on the window outside would have frightened him out of six month's pay. The place was a faithful replica of the dining room of an English coach house, circa 1627: huge oaken beams, immaculate white cloths, heavy silver.

Gerald Fletcher's table was in a secluded corner of the restaurant. He rose as Carella approached, extending his hand, and said, "Glad you could make it. Sit down, won't you?"

Carella shook Fletcher's hand, and then sat. He felt extremely uncomfortable, but he couldn't tell whether his discomfort was caused by the room or by the man with whom he was dining.

"Would you care for a drink?" Fletcher asked.

"Well, are you having one?" Carella asked.

"Yes, I am."

"I'll have a Scotch and soda," Carella said. He was not used to drinking at lunch.

Fletcher signaled for the waiter and ordered the drinks, making his another whiskey sour. When the drinks came, Fletcher raised his glass. "Here's to a conviction," he said.

Carella lifted his own glass. "I don't expect there'll be any trouble," he said. "It looks airtight to me."

Both men drank. Fletcher dabbed his lips with a napkin and said, "You never can tell these days. I hope you're right, though." He sipped at the drink. "I must admit I feel a certain amount of sympathy for him."

"Do you?"

"Yes. If he's an addict, he's automatically entitled to pity. And when one considers that the woman he murdered was nothing but a—"

"Mr. Fletcher . . ."

"Gerry, please. And I know: it isn't very kind of me to malign the dead. I'm afraid you didn't know my wife, though, Mr. Carella. May I call you Steve?"

"Sure."

"My enmity might be a bit more understandable if you had. Still, I shall take your advice. She's dead, and no longer capable of hurting me, so why be bitter. Shall we order, Steve?"

Fletcher suggested that Carella try either the trout *au meunière* or the beef and kidney pie, both of which were excellent. Carella ordered prime ribs, medium rare, and a mug of beer.

As the men ate and talked, something began happening, or at least Carella *thought* something was happening; he might never be quite sure. The conversation with Fletcher seemed on the surface to be routine chatter, but rushing through this inane, polite discussion was an undercurrent that caused excitement, fear, and apprehension. As they spoke, Carella knew with renewed certainty that Gerald Fletcher had killed his wife. Without ever being told so, he knew it. *This* was why Fletcher had called this morning; *this* was why Fletcher had invited him to lunch; *this* was why he prattled on endlessly while every contradictory move of his body signaled on an almost extrasensory level that he *knew* Carella suspected him of murder, and was here to *tell* Carella (*without* telling him) that, "Yes, you stupid cop, I killed my wife. However much the evidence may point to another man, however many confessions you get, I killed her and I'm glad I killed her. And there isn't a damn thing you can do about it."

Ralph Corwin was being held before trial in the city's oldest prison, known to law enforcers and lawbreakers alike as Calcutta. Neither Corwin's lawyer nor the district attorney's office felt that allowing Carella to talk to the prisoner would be harmful to the case.

Corwin was expecting him. "What did you want to see me about?"

"I wanted to ask you some questions."

"My lawyer says I'm not supposed to add anything to what I already said. I don't even *like* that guy."

"Why didn't you ask for another lawyer? Ask one of the officers here to call the Legal Aid Society. Or simply tell him. I'm sure he'd have no objection to dropping out."

Corwin shrugged. "I don't want to hurt his feelings. He's a little cockroach, but what the hell."

"You've got a lot at stake here, Corwin.

"But I killed her, so what does it matter *who* the lawyer is? You got it all in black and white."

"You feel like answering some questions?" Carella said.

"I feel like dropping dead, is what I feel like. Cold turkey's never good, and it's worse when you can't yell."

"If you'd rather I came back another time . . ."

"No, no, go ahead. What do you want to know?"

"I want to know exactly how you stabbed Sarah Fletcher."

"How do you *think* you stab somebody? You stick a knife in her, that's how."

"Where?"

"In the belly."

"Left-hand side of the body?"

"Yeah. I guess so."

"Where was the knife when she fell?"

"I don't know what you mean."

"Was the knife on the *right*-hand side of her body or the *left*?"

"I don't know. That was when I heard the front door opening and all I could think of was getting out of there."

"When you stabbed her, did she *twist* away from you?"

"No, she backed away, straight back, as if she couldn't believe what I done, and . . . and just wanted to get *away* from me."

"And then she fell?"

"Yes. She . . . her knees sort of gave way and she grabbed for her belly, and her hands sort of—it was terrible—they just . . . they were grabbing *air*, you know? And she fell."

"In what position?"

"On her side."

"*Which* side?"

"I could still see the knife, so it must've been the opposite side. The side opposite from where I stabbed her."

"One last question, Ralph. Was she dead when you went through that window?"

"I don't know. She was bleeding and . . . she was very quiet. I . . . guess she was dead. I don't know. I guess so."

Among Sarah Fletcher's personal effects that were considered of interest to the police before they arrested Ralph Corwin was an address book found in the dead woman's handbag on the bedroom dresser. In the Thursday afternoon stillness of the squad room, Carella examined the book.

There was nothing terribly fascinating about the alphabetical listings. Sarah Fletcher had possessed a good handwriting, and most of the listings were obviously married couples (Chuck and Nancy Benton, Harold and Marie Spander, and so on), some were girlfriends, local merchants, hairdresser, dentist, doctors, restaurants in town or across the river. A thoroughly uninspiring address book—until Carella came to a page at the end of the book, with the printed word MEMORANDA at its top.

Under the word, there were five names, addresses and telephone numbers written in Sarah's meticulous hand. They were all men's names, obviously entered at different times because some were in pencil and others in ink. The parenthetical initials following each entry were all noted in felt marking pens of various colors:

Andrew Hart, 1120 Hall Avenue, 622-8400 (PB&G) (TG)
Michael Thornton, 371 South Linder, 881-9371 (TS)
Lou Kantor, 434 North 16 Street, FR 7-2346 (TPC) (TG)
Sal Decotto, 831 Grover Avenue, FR 5-3287 (F) (TG)
Richard Fenner, 110 Henderson, 593-6648 (QR) (TG)

If there was one thing Carella loved, it was a code. He loved a code almost as much as he loved German measles. He flipped through the phone book and the address for Andrew Hart matched the one in Sarah's handwriting. He found an address for Michael Thornton. It, too, was identical to the one in her book. He kept turning pages in the directory, checking names and addresses. He verified all five.

At a little past eight the next morning, Carella got going on them. He called Andrew Hart at the number listed in Sarah's address book. Hart answered, and was not happy. "I'm in the middle of shaving," he said. "I've got to leave for the office in a little while. What's this about?"

"We're investigating a homicide, Mr. Hart."

"A *what?* A homicide? Who's been killed?"

"A woman named Sarah Fletcher."

"I don't know anyone named Sarah Fletcher," he said.

"She seems to have known you, Mr. Hart."

"Sarah *who?* Fletcher, did you say?" Hart's annoyance increased.

"That's right."

"I don't know anybody by that name. Who says she knew me? I never heard of her in my life."

"Your name's in her address book."

"*My* name? That's impossible."

Nevertheless, Hart agreed to see Carella and Meyer Meyer at the offices of Hart and Widderman, 480 Reed Street, sixth floor, at ten o'clock that morning.

At ten, Meyer and Carella parked the car and went into the building at 480 Reed, and up the elevator to the sixth floor. Hart and Widderman manufactured watchbands. A huge advertising display near the receptionist's desk in the lobby proudly proclaimed "H&W Beat the Band!" and then backed the slogan with more discreet copy that explained how Hart and Widderman had solved the difficult engineering problems of the expansion watch bracelet.

"Mr. Hart, please," Carella said.

"Who's calling?" the receptionist asked. She sounded as if she were chewing gum, even though she was not.

"Detectives Carella and Meyer."

"Just a minute, please," she said, and lifted her phone, pushing a button in the base. "Mr. Hart," she said, "there are some cops here to see you." She listened for a moment and then said, "Yes, sir." She replaced the receiver on its cradle, gestured toward the inside corridor with a nod of her golden tresses, said, "Go right in, please. Door at the end of the hall," and then went back to her magazine.

The gray skies had apparently infected Andrew Hart. "You didn't have to broadcast to the world that the police department was here," he said immediately.

"We merely announced ourselves," Carella said.

"Well, okay, now you're here," Hart said, "let's get it over with." He was a big man in his middle fifties, with iron-gray hair and black-trimmed eyeglasses. "I told you I don't know Sarah Fletcher and I don't."

"Here's her book, Mr. Hart," Carella said. "That's your name, isn't it?"

"Yeah," Hart said, and shook his head. "But how it got there is beyond me."

"Is it possible she's someone you met at a party, someone you exchanged numbers with?"

"No."

"Are you married, Mr. Hart?"

"No."

"We've got a picture of Mrs. Fletcher. I wonder—"

"Don't go showing me any pictures of a corpse," Hart said.

"This was taken when she was still very much alive, Mr. Hart."

Meyer handed Carella a manila envelope. He opened the flap and removed from the envelope a framed picture of Sarah Fletcher which he handed to Hart. Hart looked at the photograph, and then immediately looked up at Carella.

"What is this?" he said. He looked at the photograph again, shook his head, and said, "Somebody killed her, huh?"

"Yes, somebody did," Carella answered. "Did you know her?"

"I knew her."

"I thought you said you didn't."

"I didn't know Sarah Fletcher, if that's who you think she was. But I knew *this* broad, all right."

"Who'd *you* think she was?" Meyer asked.

"Just who she told me she was. Sadie Collins. She introduced herself as Sadie Collins, and that's who I knew her as. Sadie Collins."

"Where was this, Mr. Hart? Where'd you meet her?"

"A singles bar. The city's full of them."

"Would you remember when?"

"At least a year ago."

"Ever go out with her?"

"I used to see her once or twice a week."

"When did you stop seeing her?"

"Last summer."

"Did you know she was married?"

"Who, Sadie? You're kidding."

"She never told you she was married?"

"Never."

Meyer asked, "When you were going out, where'd you pick her up? At her apartment?"

"No. She used to come to my place."

"Where'd you call her when you wanted to reach her?"

"I didn't. She used to call me."

"Where'd you go, Mr. Hart? When you went out?"

"We didn't go out too much."

"What *did* you do?"

"She used to come to my place. The truth is, we never went out. She didn't want to go out much."

"Didn't you think that was strange?"

"No," Hart shrugged. "I figured she liked to stay home."

"Why'd you stop seeing her, Mr. Hart?"

"I met somebody else. A nice girl. I'm very serious about her."

"Was there something wrong with Sadie?"

"No, no. She was a beautiful woman, beautiful."

"Then why would you be ashamed—"

"Ashamed? Who said anything about being ashamed?"

"I gathered you wouldn't want your girlfriend—"

"Listen, what *is* this? I stopped seeing Sadie six months ago. I wouldn't even talk to her on the phone after that. If the crazy babe got herself killed—"

"Crazy?"

Hart suddenly wiped his hand over his face, wet his lips, and walked behind his desk. "I don't think I have anything more to say to you gentlemen."

"What did you mean by crazy?" Carella asked.

"Good day, gentlemen," Hart said.

Carella went to see Lieutenant Byrnes. In the lieutenant's corner office, Byrnes and Carella sat down over coffee. Byrnes frowned at Carella's request.

"Oh, come on, Pete!" Carella said. "If Fletcher *did* it—"

"That's only *your* allegation. Suppose he *didn't* do it, and suppose *you* do something to screw up the D.A.'s case?"

"Like what?"

"I don't know like what. The way things are going these days, if you spit on the sidewalk, that's enough to get a case thrown out of court."

"Fletcher hated his wife," Carella said calmly.

"Lot of men hate their wives. Half the men in this city hate their wives."

"But her little fling gives Fletcher good reason for . . . Look, Pete, he had a motive; he had the opportunity, a golden one, in fact; and he had the means—another man's knife sticking in Sarah's belly. What more do you want?"

"Proof. There's a funny little system we've got here—it requires proof before we can arrest a man and charge him with murder."

"Right. And all I'm asking is the opportunity to *try* for it."

"Sure, by putting a tail on Fletcher. Suppose he sues the city?"

"Yes or no, Pete? I want permission to conduct a round-the-clock surveillance of Gerald Fletcher, starting Sunday morning. Yes or no?"

"I must be out of my mind," Byrnes said, and sighed.

Michael Thornton lived in an apartment building several blocks from the Quarter, close enough to absorb some of its artistic flavor, distant enough to escape its high rents. A blond man in his apartment, Paul Wendling, told Kling and Meyer that Mike was in his jewelry shop.

In the shop, Thornton was wearing a blue work smock, but the contours of the garment did nothing to hide his powerful build. His eyes were blue, his hair black. A small scar showed white in the thick eyebrow over his left eye.

"We understand you're working," Meyer said. "Sorry to break in on you this way."

"That's okay," Thornton said. "What's up?"

"You know a woman named Sarah Fletcher?"

"No," Thornton said.

"You know a woman named Sadie Collins?"

Thornton hesitated. "Yes," he said.

"What was your relationship with her?" Kling asked.

Thornton shrugged. "Why? Is she in trouble?"

"When's the last time you saw her?"

"You didn't answer my question," Thornton said.

"Well, you didn't answer ours either," Meyer said, and smiled. "What was your relationship with her, and when did you see her last?"

"I met her in July, in a joint called *The Saloon*, right around the corner. It's a bar, but they also serve sandwiches and soup. It gets a big crowd on weekends, singles, a couple of odd ones for spice—but not a gay bar. I saw her last August, a brief, hot thing, and then good-bye."

"Did you realize she was married?" Kling said.

"No. Is she?"

"Yes," Meyer said. Neither of the detectives had yet informed Thornton that the lady in question was now unfortunately deceased. They were saving that for last, like dessert.

"Gee, I didn't know she was married." Thornton seemed truly surprised. "Otherwise, nothing would've happened."

"What *did* happen?"

"I bought her a few drinks and then I took her home with me. Later, I put her in a cab."

"When did you see her next?"

"The following day. It was goofy. She called me in the morning, she said she was on her way downtown. I was still in bed. I said, 'So come on down, baby.' And she did. *Believe* me, she did."

"Did you see her again after that?" Kling asked.

"Two or three times a week."

"Where'd you go?"

"To my pad on South Lindner."

"Never went anyplace but there?"

"Never."

"Why'd you quit seeing her?"

"I went out of town for awhile. When I got back, I just didn't hear from her again. She never gave me her number, and she wasn't in the directory, so I couldn't reach her."

"What do you make of this?" Kling asked, handing Thornton the address book.

Thornton studied it and said, "Yeah, what about it? She wrote this down the night we met—we were in bed, and she asked my address."

"Did she write those initials at the same time, the ones in parentheses under your phone number?"

"I didn't actually see the page itself. I only saw her writing in the book."

"Got any idea what the initials mean?"

"None at all." Suddenly he looked thoughtful. "She *was* kind of special, I have to admit it." He grinned. "She'll call again, I'm sure of it."

"I wouldn't count on it." Meyer said. "She's dead."

His face did not crumble or express grief or shock. The only thing it expressed was sudden anger. "The stupid . . ." Thornton said. "That's all she ever was, a stupid, crazy . . ."

On Sunday morning, Carella was ready to become a surveillant, but Gerald Fletcher was nowhere in sight. A call to his apartment from a nearby phone booth revealed that he was not in his digs. He parked in front of Fletcher's apartment building until 5:00 p.m. when he was relieved by Detective Arthur Brown. Carella went home to read his son's latest note to Santa Claus, had dinner with his family, and was settling down in the living room with a novel he had bought a week ago and not yet cracked when the telephone rang.

"Hello?" Carella said into the mouthpiece.

"Hello, Steve? This is Gerry. Gerry Fletcher."

Carella almost dropped the receiver. "How are you?"

"Fine, thanks. I was away for the weekend, just got back a little while ago, in fact. Frankly I find this apartment depressing as hell. I was wondering if you'd like to join me for a drink."

"Well," Carella said. "It's Sunday night, and it"s late . . . "

"Nonsense, it's only eight o'clock. We'll do a little old-fashioned pub crawling."

It suddenly occured to Carella that Gerald Fletcher had already had a few drinks before placing his call. It further occurred to him that if played this *too* cozily, Fletcher might rescind his generous offer.

"Okay. I'll see you at eight-thirty, provided I can square it with my wife."

"Good," Fletcher said. "See you."

Paddy's Bar & Grill was on the Stem, adjacent to the city's theater district. Carella and Fletcher got there at about nine o'clock while the place was still relatively quiet. The action began a little later, Fletcher explained.

Fletcher lifted his glass in a silent toast. "What kind of person would you say comes to a place like this?"

"I would say we've got a nice lower-middle-class clientele bent on making contact with members of the opposite sex."

"What would you say if I told you the blonde in the clinging jersey is a working prostitute?"

Carella looked at the woman. "I don't think I'd believe you. She's a bit old for the young competition, and she's not *selling* anything. She's waiting for one of those two or three older guys to make their move. Hookers don't wait, Gerry. *Is* she a working prostitute?"

"I haven't the faintest idea," Fletcher said. "I was merely trying to indicate that appearances can sometimes be misleading. Drink up, there are a few more places I'd like to show you."

He knew Fletcher well enough by now to realize that the man was trying to tell him something. At lunch last Tuesday, Fletcher had transmitted a message and a challenge: *I killed my wife, what can you do about it?* Tonight, in a similar manner, he was attempting to indicate something else, but Carella could not fathom exactly what.

Fanny's was only twenty blocks away from Paddy's Bar and Grill, but as far removed from it as the moon. Whereas the first bar seemed to cater to a quiet crowd peacefully pursuing its romantic inclinations, Fanny's was noisy and raucous, jammed to the rafters with men and women of all ages, wearing plastic hippie gear purchased in head shops up and down Jackson Avenue.

Fletcher lifted his glass. "I hope you don't mind if I drink myself into a stupor," he said. "Merely pour me into the car at the end of the night." Fletcher drank. "I don't usually consume this much alcohol, but I'm very troubled about that boy."

"What boy?" Carella asked.

"Ralph Corwin," Fletcher said. "I understand he's having some difficulty with his lawyer and, well, I'd like to help him somehow."

"*Help* him?"

"Yes. Do you think the D.A.'s office would consider it strange if I suggested a good defense lawyer for the boy?"

"I think they might consider it passing strange, yes."

"Do I detect a note of sarcasm in your voice?"

"Not at all."

Fletcher squired Carella from Fanny's to, in geographical order, The Purple Chairs and Quigley's Rest. Each place was rougher, in its way, than the last. The Purple Chairs catered to a brazenly gay crowd, and Quigley's Rest was a dive, where Fletcher's liquor caught up with him, and the evening ended suddenly in a brawl. Carella was shaken by the experience, and still couldn't piece out Fletcher's reasons.

Carella received a further shock when he continued to pursue Sarah Fletcher's address book. Lou Kantor was simply the third name in a now wearying list of Sarah's bedmates, until she turned out to be a tough and striking woman. She confirmed Carella's suspicion's immediately.

"I only knew her a short while," she said. "I met her in September, I believe. Saw her three or four times after that."

"Where'd you meet her?"

"In a bar called The Purple Chairs. That's right," she added quickly. "That's what I am."

"Nobody asked," Carella said. "What about Sadie Collins?"

"Spell it out, Officer, I'm not going to help you. I don't like being hassled."

"Nobody's hassling you, Miss Kantor. You practice your religion and I'll practice mine. We're here to talk about a dead woman."

"Then talk about her, spit it out. What do you want to know? Was she straight? Everybody's straight until they're *not* straight anymore, isn't that right? She was willing to learn. I taught her."

"Did you know she was married?"

"She told me. So what? Broke down in tears one night, and spent the rest of the night crying. I knew she was married."

"What'd she say about her husband?"

"Nothing that surprised me. She said he had another woman. Said he ran off to see her every weekend, told little Sadie he had out-of-town business. *Every* weekend, can you imagine that?"

"What do you make of this?" Carella said, and handed her Sarah's address book opened to the MEMORANDA page.

"I don't know any of these people," Lou said.

"The initials under your name," Carella said. "TPC and then TG. Got any ideas?"

"Well, the TPC is obvious, isn't it? I met her at The Purple Chairs. What else could it mean?"

Carella suddenly felt very stupid. "Of course. What else could it mean?" He took back the book. "I'm finished," he said. "Thank you very much."

"I miss her," Lou said suddenly. "She was a wild one."

Cracking a code is like learning to roller-skate; once you know how to do it, it's easy. With a little help from Gerald Fletcher, who had provided a guided tour the night before, and a lot of help from Lou Kantor, who had generously provided the key, Carella was able to crack the code wide open—well, almost. Last night, he'd gone with Fletcher to Paddy's Bar and Grill, or PB&G under Andrew Hart's name; Fanny's, F under Sal Decotto; The Purple Chairs, Lou Kantor's TPC; and Quigley's Rest, QR for Richard Fenner on the list. Probably because of the fight, he hadn't taken Carella to The Saloon, TS under Michael Thornton's name—the place where Thornton had admitted first meeting Sarah.

Except, what the hell did TG mean, under all the names but Thornton's?

By Carella's own modest estimate, he had been in more bars in the past twenty-four hours than he had in the past twenty-four years. He decided, nevertheless, to hit The Saloon that night.

The Saloon was just that. A cigarette-scarred bar behind which ran a mottled, flaking mirror; wooden booths with patched, fake leather seat cushions; bowls of pretzels and potato chips; jukebox gurgling; steamy bodies.

"They come in here," the bartender said, "at all hours of the night. Take yourself. You're here to meet a girl, am I right?"

"There was someone I was hoping to see. A girl named Sadie Collins. Do you know her?"

"Yeah. She used to come in a lot, but I ain't seen her in months. What do you want to fool around with her for?"

"Why? What's the matter with her?"

"You want to know something?" the bartender said. "I thought she was a hooker at first. Aggressive. You know what that word means? Aggressive? She used to come dressed down to here and up to there, ready for action, selling everything she had, you understand? She'd come in here, pick out a guy she wanted, and go after him like the world was gonna end at midnight. And always the same type. Big guys. You wouldn't stand a chance with her, not that you ain't big, don't misunderstand me. But Sadie liked them gigantic, and mean. You know something?"

"What?"

"I'm glad she don't come in here anymore. There was something about her—
like she was compulsive. You know what that word means, compulsive?"

Tuesday afternoon, Arthur Brown handed in his surveillance report on Gerald
Fletcher. Much of it was not at all illuminating. From 4:55 p.m. to 8:45 p.m.
Fletcher had driven home, and then to 812 North Crane and parked. The report
did become somewhat illuminating when, at 8:46 p.m., Fletcher emerged from
the building with a redheaded woman wearing a black fur coat over a green dress.
They went to Rudolph's restaurant, ate, and drove back to 812 Crane, arrived at
10:35 p.m. and went inside. Arthur brown had checked the lobby mailboxes, which
showed eight apartments on the eleventh floor, which was where the elevator
indicator had stopped. Brown went outside to wait again, and Fletcher emerged
alone at 11:40 p.m., and drove home. Detective O'Brien relieved Detective Brown
at 12:15 a.m.

Byrnes said, "This woman could be important."

"That's just what I think," Brown answered.

Carella had not yet spoken to either Sal Decotto or Richard Fenner, the two
remaining people listed in Sarah's book, but saw no reason to pursue that trial any
further. If the place listings in her book had been chronological, she'd gone from
bad to worse in her search for partners.

Why? To give it back to her husband in spades? Carella tossed Sarah's little
black book into the manila folder bearing the various reports on the case, and
turned his attention to the information Artie Brown had brought in last night. The
redheaded woman's presence might be important, but Carella was still puzzling
over Fletcher's behavior. Sarah's blatant infidelity provided Fletcher with a strong
motive, so why take Carella to his wife's unhappy haunts, why *show* Carella that
he had good and sufficient reason to kill her? Furthermore, why the offer to get a
good defense attorney for the boy who had already been indicted for the slaying?

Sometimes Carella wondered who was doing what to whom.

At five o'clock that evening, Carella relieved Detective Hal Willis outside
Fletcher's office building downtown, and then followed Fletcher to a department
store in midtown Isola. Carella was wearing a false mustache stuck to his upper lip,
a wig with longer hair than his own and of a different color, and a pair of sunglasses.

In the department store, he tracked Fletcher to the Intimate Apparel department. Carella walked into the next aisle, pausing to look at women's robes and
kimonos, keeping one eye on Fletcher, who was in conversation with the lingerie
salesgirl.

"May I help you, sir?" a voice said, and Carella turned to find a stocky woman at his elbow, with gray hair, black-rimmed spectacles, wearing Army shoes and a black dress. Her suspicious smile accused him of being a junkie shoplifter or worse.

"Thank you, no," Carella said. "I'm just looking."

Fletcher made his selections from the gossamer undergarments which the sales-girl had spread out on the counter, pointing first to one garment, then to another. The salesgirl wrote up the order and Fletcher reached into his wallet to give her either cash or a credit card; it was difficult to tell from an aisle away. He chatted with the girl a moment longer, and then walked off toward the elevator bank.

"Are you *sure* I can't assist you?" the woman in the Army shoes said, and Carella answered, "I'm positive," and moved swiftly toward the lingerie counter. Fletcher had left the counter without a package in his arms, which meant he was *sending* his purchases. The salesgirl was gathering up Fletcher's selections and looked up when Carella reached the counter.

"Yes, sir," she said. "May I help you?"

Carella opened his wallet and produced his shield. "Police officer," he said. "I'm interested in the order you just wrote up."

The girl was perhaps nineteen years old, a college girl working in the store during the Christmas rush. Speechlessly, she studied the shield, eyes bugging.

"Are these items being sent?" Carella asked.

"Yes, *sir*," the girl said. Here eyes were still wide. She wet her lips and stood up a little straighter, prepared to be a perfect witness.

"Can you tell me where?" Carella asked.

"Yes, *sir*," she said, and turned the sales slip toward him. "He wanted them wrapped separately, but they're all going to the same address. Miss Arlene Orton, 812 North Crane Street, right here in the city, and I'd guess it's a swell—"

"Thank you very much," Carella said.

It felt like Christmas already.

The man who picked the lock on Arlene Orton's front door, ten minutes after she left her apartment on Wednesday morning, was better at it than any burglar in the city, and he happened to work for the Police Department. It took the technician longer to set up his equipment, but the telephone was the easiest of his jobs. The tap would become operative when the telephone company supplied the police with a list of so-called bridging points that located the pairs and cables for Arlene Orton's phone. The monitoring equipment would be hooked into these and whenever a call went out of or came into the apartment, a recorder would automatically tape both ends of the conversation. In addition, whenever a call was made from the apartment, a dial indicator would ink out a series of dots that signified the number being called.

The technician placed his bug in the bookcase on the opposite side of the room. The bug was a small FM transmitter with a battery-powered mike that needed to be changed every twenty-four hours. The technician would have preferred running his own wires, but he dared not ask the building superintendent for an empty closet or workroom in which to hide his listener. A blabbermouth superintendent can kill an investigation more quickly than a squad of gangland goons.

In the rear of a panel truck parked at the curb some twelve feet south of the entrance to 812 Crane, Steve Carella sat behind the recording equipment that was locked into the frequency of the bug. He sat hopefully, with a tuna sandwich and a bottle of beer, prepared to hear and record any sounds that emanated from Arlene's apartment.

At the bridging point seven blocks away and thirty minutes later, Arthur Brown sat behind equipment that was hooked into the telephone mike, and waited for Arlene Orton's phone to ring. He was in radio contact with Carella.

The first call came at 12:17 p.m. The equipment tripped in automatically and the spools of tape began recording the conversation, while Brown simultaneously monitored it through his headphone.

"Hello?"

"Hello, Arlene?

"Yes, who's this?"

"Nan."

"Nan? You sound so different. Do you have a cold or something?"

"Every year at this time. Just before the holidays. Arlene, I'm terribly rushed, I'll make this short. Do you know Beth's dress size?"

The conversation went on in that vein, and Arlene Orton spoke to three more girlfriends in succession. She then called the local supermarket to order the week's groceries. She had a fine voice, deep and forceful, punctuated every so often (when she was talking to her girlfriends) with a delightful giggle.

At 4:00 p.m., the telephone in Arlene's apartment rang again.

"Hello?"

"Arlene, this is Gerry."

"Hello, darling."

"I'm leaving here a little early. I thought I'd come right over."

"Good."

"I'll be there in, oh, half an hour, forty minutes."

"Hurry."

Brown radioed Carella at once. Carella thanked him, and sat back to wait.

On Thursday morning, two days before Christmas, Carella sat at his desk in the squad room and looked over the transcripts of the five reels from the night before. The conversation on that reel had at one point changed abruptly in tone and content. Carella thought he knew why, but he wanted to confirm his suspicion:

FLETCHER: I meant after the *holidays,* not the trial.

MISS ORTON: I may be able to get away, I'm not sure. I'll have to check with my shrink.

FLETCHER: What's he got to do with it?

MISS ORTON: Well, I have to pay whether I'm there or not, you know.

FLETCHER: Is he taking a vacation?

MISS ORTON: I'll ask him.

FLETCHER: Yes, ask him. Because I'd really like to get away.

MISS ORTON: Ummm. When do you think the case (inaudible).

FLETCHER: In March sometime. No sooner than that. He's got a new lawyer, you know.

MISS ORTON: What does that mean, a new lawyer?

FLETCHER: Nothing. He'll be convicted anyway.

MISS ORTON: (Inaudible).

FLETCHER: Because the trial's going to take a lot out of me.

MISS ORTON: How soon after the trial . . .

FLETCHER: I don't know.

MISS ORTON: She's dead, Gerry, I don't see . . .

FLETCHER: Yes, but . . .

MISS ORTON: I don't see why we have to wait, do you?

FLETCHER: Have you read this?

MISS ORTON: No, not yet. Gerry. I think we ought to set a date now. A provisional date, depending on when the trial is. Gerry?

FLETCHER: Mmmm?

MISS ORTON: Do you think it'll be a terribly long, drawn-out trial?

FLETCHER: What?

MISS ORTON: Gerry?

FLETCHER: Yes?

MISS ORTON: Where are you?

FLETCHER: I was just looking over some of these books.

MISS ORTON: Do you think you can tear yourself away?

FLETCHER: Forgive me, darling.

MISS ORTON: If the trial starts in March, and we planned on April for it . . .

FLETCHER: Unless they come up with something unexpected, of course.

MISS ORTON: Like what?

FLETCHER: Oh, I don't know. They've got some pretty sharp people investigating this case.

MISS ORTON: What's there to investigate?

FLETCHER: There's always the possibility he didn't do it.

MISS ORTON: (Inaudible) a signed confession?

FLETCHER: One of the cops thinks I killed her.

MISS ORTON: You're not serious. Who?

FLETCHER: A detective named Carella. He probably knows about us by now. He's a very thorough cop. I have a great deal of admiration for him. I wonder if he realizes that.

MISS ORTON: Where'd he even get such an idea?

FLETCHER: Well, I told him I hated her.

MISS ORTON: What? Gerry, why the hell did you do that?

FLETCHER: He'd have found out anyway. He probably knows by now that Sarah was sleeping around with half the men in this city. And he probably knows I knew it, too.

MISS ORTON: Who cares what he found out? Corwin's already confessed.

FLETCHER: I can understand his reasoning. I'm just not sure he can understand mine.

MISS ORTON: Some reasoning. If you were going to kill her, you'd have done it ages ago, when she refused to sign the separation papers. So let him investigate, who cares? Wishing your wife dead isn't the same thing as killing her. Tell that to Detective Copolla.

FLETCHER: Carella. (Laughs).

MISS ORTON: What's so funny?

FLETCHER: I'll tell him, darling.

According to the technician who had wired the Orton apartment, the living-room bug was in the bookcase on the wall opposite the bar. Carella was interested in the tape from the time Fletcher had asked Arlene about a book—"Have you read this?"—and then seemed preoccupied. It was Carella's guess that Fletcher had discovered the bookcase bug. What interested Carella more, however, was what Fletcher had said *after* he knew the place was wired. Certain of an audience now, Fletcher had:

1. Suggested the possibility that Corwin was not guilty.
2. Flatly stated that a cop named Carella suspected him.
3. Expressed admiration for Carella, while wondering if Carella was aware of it.
4. Speculated that Carella had already doped out the purpose of the bar-crawling last Sunday night, was cognizant of Sarah's promiscuity, and knew Fletcher was aware of it.
5. Made a little joke about "telling" Carella.

Carella felt as eerie as he had when lunching with Fletcher and later when drinking with him. Now he'd spoken, through the bug, directly to Carella. But what was he trying to say? And why?

Carella wanted very much to hear what Fletcher would say when he *didn't* know he was being overheard. He asked Lieutenant Byrnes for permission to request a court order to put a bug in Fletcher's automobile. Byrnes granted permission, and the court issued the order.

Fletcher made a date with Arlene Orton to go to The Chandeliers across the river, and the bug was installed in Fletcher's 1972 car. If Fletcher left the city, the effective range of the transmitter on the open road would be about a quarter of a mile. The listener-pursuer had his work cut out for him.

By ten minutes to ten that night, Carella was drowsy and discouraged. On the way out to The Chandeliers, Fletcher and Arlene had not once mentioned Sarah or the plans for their impending marriage. Carella was anxious to put them both to bed and get home to his family. When they finally came out of the restaurant and began walking toward Fletcher's automobile, Carella actually uttered an audible, "At *last*," and started his car.

They proceeded east on Route 701, heading for the bridge, and said nothing. Carella thought at first something was wrong with the equipment, then finally Arlene spoke and Carella knew just what had happened. The pair had argued in the restaurant, and Arlene had been smoldering until this moment when she could no longer contain her anger.

"Maybe you don't want to marry me at all," she shouted.

"That's ridiculous," Fletcher said.

"Then why won't you set a date?"

"I have set a date."

"You haven't set a date. All you've done is say after the trial. *When*, after the trial? Maybe this whole damn thing has been a stall. Maybe you *never* planned to marry me."

"You know that isn't true, Arlene."

"How do I know there really *were* separation papers?"

"There were. I told you there were."

"Then why wouldn't she sign them?"

"Because she loved me."

"If she loved you, then why did she do those horrible things?"

"To make me pay, I think."

"Is that why she showed you her little black book?"

"Yes, to make me pay."

"No. Because she was a slut."

"I guess. I guess that's what she became."

"Putting the little TG in her book every time she told you about a new one. *Told Gerry*, and marked a little TG in her book."

"Yes, to make me pay."

"A slut. You should have gone after her with detectives. Gotten pictures, threatened her, forced her to sign—"

"No, I couldn't have done that. It would have ruined me, Arl."

"Your precious career."

"Yes, my precious career."

They both fell silent again. They were approaching the bridge now. Carella tried to stay close behind them, but on occasion the distance between the two cars lengthened and he lost some words in the conversation.

"She wouldn't sign the papers and I (   ) adultery because (   ) have come out."

"And I thought (   )."

"I did everything I possibly could."

"Yes, Gerry, but now she's dead. So what's your excuse now?"

"I'm suspected of having *killed* her, damn it!"

Fletcher was making a left turn, off the highway. Carella stepped on the accelerator, not wanting to lose voice contact now.

"What difference does that make?" Arlene asked.

"None at all, I'm sure," Fletcher said. "I'm sure you wouldn't mind at all being married to a convicted murderer."

"What are you talking about?"

"I'm talking about the possibility . . . Never mind."

"Let me hear it."

"All right, Arlene. I'm talking about the possibility of someone accusing me of the murder. And of my having to stand trial for it."

"That's the most paranoid—"

"It's not paranoid."

"Then what is it? They've caught the murderer, they—"

"I'm only saying suppose. How could we get married if I killed her, if someone says I killed her?"

"No one has said that, Gerry."

"Well, *if* someone should."

Silence. Carella was dangerously close to Fletcher's car now, and risking discovery. Carella held his breath and stayed glued to the car ahead.

"Gerry, I don't understand this," Arlene said, her voice low.

"Someone could make a good case for it."

"Why would anyone do that? They know that Corwin—"

"They could say I came into the apartment and . . . They could say she was still alive when I came into the apartment. They could say the knife was still in her and I . . . I came in and found her that way and . . . finished her off."

"Why would you do that?"

"To end it."

"You wouldn't kill anyone, Gerry."

"No."

"Then why are you even suggesting such a terrible thing?"

"If she wanted it . . . If someone accused me . . . If someone said I'd done it . . . that I'd finished the job, pulled the knife across her belly, they could claim she *asked* me to do it."

"What are you saying, Gerry?"

"I'm trying to explain that Sarah might have—"

"Gerry. I don't think I want to know."

"I'm only trying to tell you—"

"No, I don't want to know. Please. Gerry, you're frightening me."

"*Listen* to me, damn it! I'm trying to explain what *might* have happened. Is that so hard to accept? That she might have *asked* me to kill her?"

"Gerry, please, I—"

"I *wanted* to call the hospital, I was *ready* to call the hospital, don't you think I could *see* she wasn't fatally stabbed?"

"Gerry, please."

"She begged me to kill her, Arlene, she begged me to end it for her, she . . . Damn it, can't *either* of you understand that? I tried to show him, I took him to all the places, I thought he was a man who'd understand. Is it that difficult?"

"Oh, my God, *did* you kill her? *Did* you kill Sarah?"

"No. Not Sarah. Only the woman she'd become, the slut I'd forced her to become. She was Sadie, you see, when I killed her—when she died."

"Oh, my God," Arlene said, and Carella nodded in weary acceptance.

Carella felt neither elated nor triumphant. As he followed Fletcher's car into the curb in front of Arlene's building, he experienced only a familiar nagging sense of repetition and despair. Fletcher was coming out of his car now, walking around to the curb side, opening the door for Arlene, who took his hand and stepped onto the sidewalk, weeping. Carella intercepted them before they reached the front door of the building. Quietly, he charged Fletcher with the murder of his wife, and made the arrest without resistance.

Fletcher did not seem at all surprised.

So it was finished, or at least Carella thought it was.

In the silence of his living room, the telephone rang at a quarter past one. He caught the phone on the third ring.

"Hello?"

"Steve," Lieutenant Byrnes said, "I just got a call from Calcutta. Ralph Corwin hanged himself in his cell, just after midnight. Must have done it while we were still taking Fletcher's confession in the squad room."

Carella was silent.

"Steve?" Byrnes said.

"Yeah, Pete."

"Nothing," Byrnes said, and hung up.

Carella stood with the dead phone in his hands for several seconds and then replaced it on the hook. He looked into the living room, where the lights of the tree glowed warmly, and thought of a despairing junkie in a prison cell, who had taken his own life without ever having known he had not taken the life of another.

It was Christmas day.

Sometimes, none of it made any sense at all.

Acknowledgments

Grateful acknowledgment is made to the following for permission to reprint previously published material:

Don Congdon Associates, Inc.: "Yesterday I Lived!" by Ray Bradbury. Copyright 1944 by Ray Bradbury. Copyright renewed 1972 by Ray Bradbury. Reprinted by permission of Don Congdon Associates, Inc.

Dodd, Mead & Company, Inc., and A. P. Watt Ltd.: "The Invisible Man" from *The Innocence of Father Brown* by G. K. Chesterton. Copyright 1911 by Dodd, Mead & Company, Inc. Copyright renewed 1938 by Frances B. Chesterton. Reprinted by permission of Dodd, Mead & Company, Inc., and A. P. Watt Ltd. Also reprinted by permission of *Dodd, Mead & Company, Inc.,* "The Girl in the Train" from *The Golden Ball and Other Stories* by Agatha Christie. Copyright 1924, 1926, 1929, 1934, © 1971 by Christie Copyrights Trust.

John Farquharson Ltd.: "Sadie When She Died" by Ed McBain. Copyright © 1972 by Evan Hunter. Reprinted by permission of John Farquharson Ltd.

Harper & Row, Publishers, Inc., and David Higham Associates Ltd.: "The Queen's Square" from *Lord Peter: A Collection of All the Lord Peter Wimsey Stories* by Dorothy L. Sayers. Copyright 1933 by Dorothy Leigh Sayers Fleming. Renewed 1961 by Lloyds Bank Ltd., Executors. Reprinted by permission of Harper & Row, Publishers, Inc., and David Higham Associates Ltd.

Lillian Hellman: "A Man Called Spade," "They Can Only Hang You Once," and "Too Many Have Lived" by Dashiell Hammett. Copyright 1932 by American Mercury, Inc. Copyright renewed 1960 by Dashiell Hammett, as author. Reprinted by permission of Lillian Hellman.

Houghton Mifflin Company: "Trouble Is My Business" from *The Simple Art of Murder* by Raymond Chandler. Copyright 1950 by Raymond Chandler. Copyright renewed 1978 by Helga Greene. Reprinted by permission of Houghton Mifflin Company.

Hutchinson Publishing Group Ltd.: *Death Notes* by Ruth Rendell. Copyright © 1981 by Kingsmarkham Enterprises Ltd. Reprinted by permission of Hutchinson Publishing Group Ltd.

International Creative Management, Inc.: "The Murder of Santa Claus" by P. D. James. Copyright © 1983, 1984 by P. D. James. Reprinted by permission of International Creative Management, Inc.

Alfred A. Knopf, Inc.: *The Chill* by Ross Macdonald. Copyright © 1963 by Ross Macdonald. Reprinted by permission of Alfred A. Knopf, Inc.

Random House, Inc.: "Hand Upon the Waters" from *Knight's Gambit* by William Faulkner. Copyright 1939 by the Curtis Publishing Co.; "Never Shake a Family Tree" from *The Curious Facts Preceding My Execution and Other Fictions* by Donald E. Westlake. Copyright © 1961 by Donald E. Westlake. Reprinted by permission of Random House, Inc.

Scott Meredith Literary Agency, Inc.: "The Adventure of Abraham Lincoln's Clue" by Ellery Queen. Copyright © 1963 by Frederic Dannay and Manfred B. Lee. Reprinted by permission of the authors' estates, and the agents for the estates, Scott Meredith Literary Agency, Inc., 845 Third Avenue, New York, N. Y. 10022.

Charles Scribner's Sons, and William Heinemann Ltd.: "The Murder on the Lotus Pond" from *Judge Dee at Work* by Robert van Gulik. Copyright © 1967 by Robert van Gulik. Reprinted by permission of Charles Scribner's Sons, and William Heinemann Ltd.

Viking Penguin Inc.: "See No Evil" ["The Squirt and the Monkey"] from *Triple Jeopardy* by Rex Stout. Copyright 1951 by Rex Stout. Copyright renewed 1979 by Pola Stout, Barbara Stout, and Rebecca Bradbury. Reprinted by permission of Viking Penguin, Inc.

Walker & Company, and A. P. Watt Ltd.: "The Hunchback Cat" from *Fen Country* by Edmund Crispin. Copyright © 1980 by Edmund Crispin. Reprinted by permission of Walker & Company, A. P. Watt Ltd., and Mrs. Ann Montgomery.